flashback

DAN SIMMONS

flashback

Quercus

First published in Great Britain in 2011 by

Quercus
21 Bloomsbury Square
London
WC1A 2NS

A CIP catalogue record for this book is available
from the British Library

ISBN 978 0 85738 124 8 (HB)
ISBN 978 0 85738 346 4 (TPB)

Printed and bound in Great Britain by Clays Ltd, St Ives plc

10 9 8 7 6 5 4 3 2 1

This book is for

TOM AND JANE GLENN,

who are the real future

We find a little of everything in our memory; it is a sort of pharmacy, a sort of chemical laboratory, in which our groping hand may come to rest now on a sedative drug, now on a dangerous poison.

—Marcel Proust, from "The Captive,"
Remembrance of Things Past, translated by
C. K. Scott Moncrieff, Terence
Kilmartin, and Andreas Mayor

1.00

Japanese Green Zone Above Denver — Friday, Sept. 10

Y**OU'RE PROBABLY** wondering why I asked you to come here today, Mr. Bottom," said Hiroshi Nakamura.

"No," said Nick. "I know why you brought me here."

Nakamura blinked. "You do?"

"Yeah," said Nick. He thought, *Fuck it. In for a penny, in for a pound. Nakamura wants to hire a detective. Show him you're a detective.* "You want me to find the person or persons who killed your son, Keigo."

Nakamura blinked again but said nothing. It was as if hearing his son's name spoken aloud had frozen him in place.

The old billionaire did glance to where his squat but massive security chief, Hideki Sato, was leaning against a step-*tansu* near the open *shoji* that looked out on the courtyard garden. If Sato gave his employer any response by movement, wink, or facial expression, Nick sure as hell couldn't see it. Come to think of it, he didn't remember having seen Sato *blink* during the ride up to the main house in the golf cart or during the introductions here in Nakamura's office. The security chief's eyes were obsidian marbles.

Finally Nakamura said, "Your deduction is correct,

3

Mr. Bottom. And, as Sherlock Holmes would say, an *elementary* deduction since you were the homicide detective in charge of my son's case when I was still in Japan and you and I have never met nor had any other contact."

Nick waited.

After the glance in Sato's direction, Nakamura had returned his gaze to the single sheet of interactive e-vellum in his hand, but now his gray eyes looked up and bored into Nick.

"Do you think you *can* find my son's killer or killers, Mr. Bottom?"

"I'm certain I can," lied Nick. What the old billionaire was really asking him, he knew, was *Can you turn back the clock and keep my only son from being killed and make everything all right again?*

Nick would have said *I'm certain I can* to that question as well. He would have said anything he had to say to get the money this man could pay him. Enough money for Nick to return to Dara for years to come. Perhaps a lifetime to come.

Nakamura squinted slightly. Nick knew that one didn't become a hundred-times-over billionaire in Japan, or one of only nine regional Federal Advisors in America, by being a fool.

"What makes you think that you can be successful *now*, Mr. Bottom, when you failed six years ago, at a time when you were a real homicide detective with the full resources of the Denver Police Department behind you?"

"There were four hundred homicide cases pending then, Mr. Nakamura. We had fifteen homicide detectives working them all, with new cases coming in every day. This time I'll have just this one case to concentrate on and to solve. No distractions."

Nakamura's gray gaze, as unblinking as Sato's darker stare and already chilly, grew noticeably chillier. "Are you saying, former detective sergeant Bottom, that you did not give my son's murder the attention it deserved six years ago, despite the... ah...high profile of it and direction to give it priority from the governor of Colorado and from the president of the United States herself?"

Nick felt the flashback itch crawling in him like a centipede. He wanted to get out of this room and pull the warm wool cover of *then, not-now, her, not-this* over himself like a blanket.

"I'm saying that the DPD didn't give *any* of its murder cases the manpower or attention they deserved six years ago," said Nick. "Including your son's case. Hell, it could have been the president's kid murdered in Denver and the Major Crimes Unit couldn't have solved it then." He looked Nakamura straight in the eye, betting everything on this absurd tactic of honesty.

"Or solve it now," he added. "It's fifty times worse today."

The billionaire's office had not a single chair to sit in, not even one for Mr. Nakamura, and Nick Bottom and Hiroshi Nakamura stood facing each other across the narrow, chest-high expanse of the rich man's slim, perfectly bare mahogany stand-up desk. Sato's casual posture over at the *tansu* didn't obscure the facts—at least to Nick Bottom's eye—that the security chief was fully alert, would have been dangerous even if he weren't armed, and had the indefinable lethality of an ex-soldier or cop or member of some other profession that had trained him to kill other men.

"It is, of course, your expertise after many years on the Denver Police Department, and your invaluable insights into the investigation, that are the prime reason we are considering you for this investigation," Mr. Nakamura said smoothly.

Nick took a breath. He'd had enough of playing by Nakamura's script.

"No, sir," he said. "Those *aren't* the reasons you're considering hiring me. If you hire me to investigate your son's murder, it's because I'm the only person still alive who—under flashback—can see every page of the files that were lost in the cyberattack that wiped out the DPD's entire archives five years ago."

Nick thought to himself—*And it's also because I'm the only person who can, under the flash, relive every conversation with the witnesses and suspects and other detectives involved. Under flashback, I can reread the Murder Book that was lost with the files.*

"If you hire me, Mr. Nakamura," Nick continued aloud, "it

will be because I'm the only person in the world who can go back almost six years to *see* and *hear* and *witness* everything again in a murder case that's grown as cold as the bones of your son buried in your family Catholic cemetery in Hiroshima."

Mr. Nakamura drew in a quick, shocked breath and then there was no sound at all in the room. Outside, the tiny waterfall tinkled softly into the tiny pond in the tiny gravel-raked courtyard.

Having played almost all of his cards, Nick shifted his weight, folded his arms, and looked around while he waited.

Advisor Hiroshi Nakamura's office in his private home here in the Japanese Green Zone above Denver, although recently constructed, looked as if it might be a thousand years old. And still in Japan.

The sliding doors and windows were *shoji* and the heavier ones *fusuma* and all opened out into a small courtyard with its small but exquisitely formal Japanese garden. In the room, a single opaque *shoji* window allowed natural light into a tiny altar alcove where bamboo shadows moved over a vase holding cut plants and twigs of the autumn season, the vase itself perfectly positioned on the lacquered floor. The few pieces of furniture in the room were placed to show the Nipponese love of asymmetry and were of wood so dark that each ancient piece seemed to swallow light. The polished cedar floors and fresh *tatami* mats, in contrast, seemed to emanate their own warm light. A sensuous, fresh dried-grass smell rose from the *tatami*. Nick Bottom had had enough contact with the Japanese in his previous job as a Denver homicide detective to know that Mr. Nakamura's compound, his house, his garden, this office, and the *ikebana* and few modest but precious artifacts on display here were all perfect expressions of *wabi* (simple quietude) and *sabi* (elegant simplicity and the celebration of the impermanent).

And Nick didn't give the slightest shit.

He needed this job to get money. He needed the money to buy more flashback. He needed the flashback to get back to Dara.

Since he'd had to leave his shoes back in the entry *genkan* where Sato had left his, Nick Bottom's prevalent emotion at the moment was simple regret that he'd grabbed this particular black sock this morning—the one on his left foot with a hole big enough to allow his big toe to poke through. He covertly scrunched his foot up, trying to worm the big toe back in the hole and out of sight, but that took two feet to do right and would be too obvious. Sato was paying attention to the squirming as it was. Nick curled the big toe up as much as he could.

"What kind of vehicle do you drive, Mr. Bottom?" asked Nakamura.

Nick almost laughed. He was ready to be dismissed and physically thrown out by Sato for his *gai-jin*'s impertinent mention of Nakamura's all-hallowed son Keigo's cold bones, but he hadn't expected a question about his car. Besides, Nakamura had almost certainly watched him drive up on one of the fifty thousand or so surveillance cameras that had been tracking him as he approached the compound.

He cleared his throat and said, "Ah...I drive a twenty-year-old GoMotors gelding."

The billionaire turned his head only slightly and barked Japanese syllables at Sato. Without straightening and with the slightest of smiles, the security chief shot back an even deeper and faster cascade of guttural Japanese to his boss. Nakamura nodded, evidently satisfied.

"Is your...ah...gelding a reliable vehicle, Mr. Bottom?"

Nick shook his head.

"The lithium-ion batteries are ancient, Mr. Nakamura, and with the way Bolivia feels about us these days, it doesn't look like they're going to be replaced any time soon. So, after a good twelve-hour charge, the piece of shi...the car...can go about forty miles at thirty-eight miles per hour or thirty-eight miles at forty miles per hour. We'll both just have to hope that there won't be any *Bullitt*-style high-speed chases in this investigation."

Mr. Nakamura showed no hint of a smile. Or of recognition. Didn't they watch great old movies in Hiroshima?

"We can supply you with a vehicle from the delegation for

the duration of your investigation, Mr. Bottom. Perhaps a Lexus or Infiniti sedan."

This time Nick couldn't stop himself from laughing. "One of your hydrogen skateboards? No, sir. That won't work. First of all, it'd just be stripped down to its carbon-fiber shell in any of the places I'll be parking in Denver. Secondly—as your director of security can explain to you—I need a car that blends in just in case I have to tail someone during the investigation. Low profile, we private investigators call it."

Mr. Nakamura made a deep, rumbling sound in his throat as if he were preparing to spit. Nick had heard this noise from Japanese men before when he'd been a cop. It seemed to express surprise and perhaps a little displeasure, although he'd heard it from the Nipponese men even when they were seeing something beautiful, like a garden view, for the first time. It was, Nick thought, probably as untranslatable as so many other things lost between this century's newly eager Nipponese and infinitely weary Americans.

"Very well, then, Mr. Bottom," Nakamura said at last. "Should we choose you for this investigation, you will need a vehicle with a greater range when the investigation takes you to Santa Fe, Nuevo Mexico. But we can discuss the details later."

Santa Fe, thought Nick. *Aww, God damn it. Not Santa Fe. Anywhere but Santa Fe.* Just the name of the town made the deep scar tissue across and inside his belly muscles hurt. But he also heard another voice in his head, a movie voice, one of hundreds that lived there—*Forget it, Jake. It's Chinatown.*

"All right," Nick said aloud. "We'll discuss the car thing and a Santa Fe trip later. *If* you hire me."

Nakamura was again looking at the single sheet of e-vellum in his hand.

"And you're currently living in a former Baby Gap in the former Cherry Creek Mall, is that correct, Mr. Bottom?"

Jesus Christ, thought Nick Bottom. With his entire future probably depending upon the outcome of this interview, and with ten thousand questions Mr. Nakamura could have asked him that he could have answered while retaining at least a shred of the few tatters that still remained of his dignity, it had to be *You're currently living in a former Baby Gap in the former Cherry Creek Mall?*

Yes, sir, Mr. Nakamura, sir, Nick was tempted to say, *currently living in one-sixth of a former Baby Gap in the former Cherry Creek Mall in a shitty section of a shitty city in one forty-fourth of the former United States of America, that's me, the former Nick Bottom. While you live up here with the other Japs on top of the mountain, surrounded by three rings of security that fucking Osama bin Laden's fucking* ghost *couldn't get through.*

Nick said, "The Cherry Creek Mall Condos it's called now. I guess the space my cubie's part of used to be a Baby Gap."

Of the three men, two were expensively dressed in the thin-lapelled, sleek-trousered, black-suited, crisp-white-shirted, white-pocket-squared, skinny-black-tied 1960s JFK look retrieved from more than seventy-five years earlier. Even Mr. Nakamura, in his late sixties, wouldn't have been able to remember that historical era, so why, Nick wondered, had the style gurus in Japan brought this style back for the tenth time? The dead-Kennedys style looked good on slim, elegant Mr. Nakamura, and Sato was dressed almost as beautifully as his boss, although his black suit probably cost a thousand or two new bucks less than Nakamura's. But the security chief's suit would have required more tailoring. Nakamura was lean and fit despite his years, while Sato was built like the proverbial brick shithouse, if that phrase even applied to men. And if the Japanese had ever *had* brick shithouses.

Standing there, feeling the cool air of the breeze from the garden flowing across his curled-up bare big toe and realizing that he was by far the tallest man in the room but also the only one whose posture included his now-habitual slump, Nick wished that he'd at least pressed his shirt. He'd meant to but had never found the time the past week since the call for this interview came. So now he stood there in a wrinkled shirt under a wrinkled, twelve-year-old suit jacket—no matching trousers, just the least rumpled and least stained of his chinos— all of it probably producing a combined effect that made him

9

look as if he'd slept not only *in* the clothes but *on* them. Nick had discovered only that morning in his cubie that he'd put on too much weight the last year or two to allow him to button these old trousers, or the suit jacket, or his shirt collar. He hoped that his too-wide-for-style belt might be hiding the opened trouser tops and the knot of his tie might be hiding the unbuttonable shirt collar, but the damned tie itself was three times wider than the ties on the two Japanese men. And it didn't help Nick's self-confidence when he considered that his tie, a gift from Dara, had probably cost one hundredth of what Nakamura had spent on his.

To hell with it. It was Nick's only remaining tie.

Born in the next-to-last decade of the previous century, Nick Bottom was old enough to remember a tune from a child's educational program that had been on TV then, and now the irritating singsong lyrics returned from childhood to rattle through his aching, flashback-hungry head — *One of these things is not like the others, one of these things just doesn't belong . . .*

To hell with it, thought Nick again and for a panicked second he was afraid he'd spoken aloud. It was becoming harder and harder for him to focus on anything in this miserable, increasingly unreal non-flashback world.

And then, because Mr. Nakamura seemed very comfortable with the stretching silence and Sato actively amused by it while Nick Bottom wasn't at all comfortable with it, he added, "Of course, it's been quite a few years since the Cherry Creek Mall was a mall or there were any stores there. BIAHTF."

Nick pronounced the old acronym "buy-ought-if" the way everyone did and always had, but Nakamura's expression remained blank or passively challenging or politely curious or perhaps a combination of all three. One thing was certain to Nick: the Nipponese executive wasn't going to make any part of this interview easy.

Sato, who would have spent time on the street here in the States, didn't bother to translate it to his boss.

"Before It All Hit The Fan," Nick explained. He didn't add that the more commonly used "die-ought-if" stood for

"Day It All Hit The Fan." He was certain that Nakamura knew both expressions. The man had been in Colorado as a federally appointed four-state Advisor for five months now. And he had undoubtedly heard all the American colloquialisms, even if only from his murdered son, years before.

"Ah," said Mr. Nakamura and again looked down at the sheet of e-vellum in his hand. Images, videos, and columns of text flicked onto the single, paper-flexible page and scrolled or disappeared at the slightest shift of Nakamura's manicured fingertips. Nick noticed that the older man's fingers were blunt and strong, a workingman's hands—although he doubted if Mr. Nakamura had ever used them for any physical labor that wasn't part of some recreation he'd chosen. Yachting perhaps. Or polo. Or mountain climbing. All three of which had been mentioned in Hiroshi Nakamura's gowiki-bio.

"And how long were you a member of the Denver Police Department, Mr. Bottom?" continued Mr. Nakamura. It seemed to Nick that the damned interview was running in reverse.

"I was a detective for nine years," said Nick. "I was on the force for a total of seventeen years." He was tempted to list some of his citations, but resisted. Nakamura had it all on his vellum database.

"A detective in both the Major Crimes Unit and then the Robbery-Homicide division?" read Nakamura, adding the question mark only out of politeness.

"Yes," said Nick while thinking *Let's get to it, God damn it.*

"And you were dismissed from the detectives' bureau five years ago for reasons of…?" Nakamura had quit reading as if the reasons weren't right there on the page and already well known to the billionaire. The question mark this time came only from Nakamura's politely raised left eyebrow.

Asshole, thought Nick, secretly relieved that they'd finally reached the hard part of the interview. "My wife was killed in an automobile accident five years ago," said Nick with no emotion, knowing that Nakamura and his security chief knew more about his life than he did. "I had some trouble…coping."

Nakamura waited but it was Nick's turn not to make this

part of the interview easy. *You know why you're going to hire me for this job, jerkwad. Let's get to it. Yes or no.*

Finally Mr. Nakamura said softly, "So your dismissal from the Denver Police Department, after a nine-month probationary period, was for flashback abuse."

"Yes." Nick realized that he was smiling at the two men for the first time.

"And this addiction, Mr. Bottom, was also the reason for the failure of your personal private-detective agency two years after you were...ah...after you left the police force?"

"No," lied Nick. "Not really. It's just a hard time for any small business. The country's in its twenty-third year of our Jobless Recovery, you know."

The old joke didn't seem to register on either of the Japanese men. Sato's easy, leaning stance somehow reminded Nick of Jack Palance as the gunfighter in *Shane*, despite the total difference in the two men's body form. Eyes never blinking. Waiting. Watching. Hoping that Nick will make his move so Sato–Palance can gun him down. As if Nick might still be armed after the multiple levels of security around this compound, after having his car CMRI'd and left half a mile down the hill, after having the 9mm Glock that he'd brought along—it would have seemed absurd, even to Sato, for him to have been traveling through the city without some weapon—confiscated.

Sato watched with the deadly, totally focused anticipation of a professional bodyguard. Or Jack Palance–in-*Shane* killer.

Instead of pursuing the flashback question, Mr. Nakamura suddenly said, "Bottom. This is an unusual last name in America, yes?"

"Yes, sir," said Nick, getting used to the almost random jump of questions. "The funny part is that the original family name was English, Badham, but some guy behind a desk at Ellis Island misheard it. Just like the scene where mute little Michael Corleone gets renamed in *Godfather Two*."

Mr. Nakamura, more and more obviously not an old-movie fan, just gave Nick that perfectly blank and inscrutable Japanese stare again.

Nick sighed audibly. He was getting tired of trying to make conversation. He said flatly, "Bottom's an unusual name, but it's been our name the hundred and fifty years or so my family's been in the States." *Even if my son won't use it,* he thought.

As if reading Nick's mind, Nakamura said, "Your wife is deceased but I understand you have a sixteen-year-old son, named…" The billionaire hesitated, lowering his gaze to the vellum again so that Nick could see the perfection of the razor-cut salt-and-pepper hair. "Val. Is Val short for something, Mr. Bottom?"

"No," said Nick. "It's just Val. There was an old actor whom my wife and I liked and…anyway, it's just Val. I sent him away to L.A. a few years ago to live with his grandfather—my father-in-law—a retired UCLA professor. Better educational opportunities out there. But Val's fifteen years old, Mr. Nakamura, not…"

Nick stopped. Val's birthday had been on September 2, eight days ago. He'd forgotten it. Nakamura was right; his son *was* sixteen now. God *damn* it. He cleared his suddenly constricted throat and continued, "Anyway, yes, correct, I have one child. A son named Val. He lives with his maternal grandfather in Los Angeles."

"And you are still a flashback addict, Mr. Bottom," said Hiroshi Nakamura. This time there was no question mark, either in the billionaire's flat voice or expression.

Here it is.

"No, Mr. Nakamura, I am not," Nick said firmly. "I *was.* The department had every right to fire me. In the year after Dara was killed, I was a total mess. And, yes, I was still using too much of the drug when my investigations agency went under a year or so after I left the…after I was fired from the force."

Sato lounged. Mr. Nakamura's posture was still rigid and his face remained expressionless as he waited for more.

"But I've beaten the serious addiction part," continued Nick. He raised his hands and spread his fingers. He was determined not to beg (he still had his ace in the hole, the reason they *had* to hire him) but for some stupid reason it was important to him that they trust him. "Look, Mr. Nakamura, you must *know* that it's estimated that about eighty-five percent of Americans use flashback these days, but not all of us are addicts the way I was…briefly. A lot of us use the stuff occasionally…recreationally…socially…the way people drink wine here or *sake* in Japan."

"Are you seriously suggesting, Mr. Bottom, that flashback can be used *socially?*"

Nick took a breath. The Japanese government had brought back the death penalty for anyone dealing, using, or even possessing flash, for God's sake. They feared it the way the Muslims did. Except that in the New Global Caliphate, conviction of using or possessing flashback by *sharia* tribunals meant immediate beheading broadcast around the world on one of the twenty-four-hour Al Jazeera channels that televised only such stonings, beheadings, and other Islamic punishments. The channel was busy—and watched—day and night throughout the Caliphate in what was left of the Mideast, Europe, and in American cities with clusters of *hajji* Caliphate fans. Nick knew that a lot of non-Muslims in Denver watched it for the fun of it. Nick watched on especially bad nights.

"No," Nick said at last. "I'm not saying it's a social drug. I just mean that, used in moderation, flashback isn't more harmful than…say…television."

Nakamura's gray eyes continued to bore.

"So, Mr. Bottom, you are not addicted to flashback the way you were in the years immediately following your wife's tragic death? And if you were hired by me to investigate my son's death, you would not be distracted from the investigation by the need to use the drug recreationally?"

"That's correct, Mr. Nakamura."

"Have you used the drug recently, Mr. Bottom?"

Nick hesitated only a second. "No. Absolutely not. I've had no urge or need to."

Sato reached into his inside suit pocket and removed a cell

phone that was a featureless chip of polished ebony smaller than Nick's National Identity and Credit Card. Sato set the phone on the polished surface of the top step of the *tansu*.

Instantly, five of the dark-wood surfaces in the austere room became display screens. In ultimate HD, but not full 3D, the view was clearer than looking out perfectly transparent windows.

Nick and the two Japanese men were looking at multiple hidden-camera views of a furtive flashback addict sitting in his car on a side street not four miles from here, the images recorded less than forty-five minutes ago.

Oh, God damn it, thought Nick.

The multiple videos began to roll.

1.01

Japanese Green Zone Above Denver — Friday, Sept. 10

NICK'S FIRST RESPONSE was professional, a product of his years on Vice and Major Crimes stakeouts — *This took five cameras, at least two of them in stealth-daylight MUAVs. Two with very long, stabilized lenses. One handheld impossibly close.*

It was him, on the screens, of course. Him in his clapped-out gelding, windows down because the day was already hot in the September morning sun, the vehicle parked under an over-hanging tree in a cul-de-sac in an abandoned development of new multimillion-dollar homes less than four miles down the hill from the Japanese Green Zone and about a mile off the Evergreen–Genesis exit from I-70. Nick had taken triple pre-cautions to be sure he hadn't been followed — although why would his prospective employer follow him *before* the hiring interview? No matter. He *liked* being paranoid. It had served him well during his years on the force. He'd even gotten out of the gelding and scanned the sky and overgrown shrubs and weeds growing out of the abandoned structures with his old IR, motion-sensor, and stealth-seeking binoculars. Nothing.

Now Nick watched himself settle back in the driver's seat

and remove from his rumpled suit coat pocket the only vial of flashback he'd brought along that morning.

He and the two Japanese men continued watching as the Nick on the screens closed his eyes, squeezed the vial and inhaled deeply, tossed the vial out the driver's-side window, and settled back farther into the headrest, his eyes rolling up within seconds as they always did with flashers, his mouth open a bit—just as it was open now.

Since he'd come up the hill from Denver early and still had almost thirty minutes to kill before reaching the Colorado State Police roadblocks around the Green Zone—the first of three concentric circles of security he knew he'd be going through—it had been only a ten-minute vial. *Ten measly bucks to relive ten easy fucks* the street sources liked to say.

Seeing himself from five angles, three of them close up, was no different from watching the thousands of flashers nodding on street corners: Nick's eyelids were lowered but not completely closed with just the bottom third of the rolled-up irises visible as they flicked back and forth in tune with the active REM. Nick's body and face twitched on the five displays as emotions and reactions almost, not quite, found their way to the right muscles. The closest camera picked up the silver trail of drool from the left corner of the twitching, spastic mouth, zoomed in on the jaw working numbly as the flasher tried to talk while deep in the throes of his relived memory-experience. No words emerged fully formed, just the usual flasher's idiot gabble-mumble. There was good audio pickup and Nick could now hear the soft rustle of the morning's breeze in the cottonwood branches above his car. He'd been oblivious to it fifty minutes earlier.

"You've made your point," he said after a couple of minutes to the two Japanese men, who seemed rapt in their attention to the five displays. "Are you going to make us watch all ten minutes of this crap?"

They were. Or, rather, Mr. Nakamura was. So the three men stood watching for the full ten minutes as Nick Bottom on the screens, as rumpled and sweaty as he was here in real life, drooled and twitched while the black dilated iris-dots on the hard-boiled eggs of his not-quite-lidded eyes flitted back and forth like two buzzing flies. Nick forced himself not to look down or away.

Why this is Hell. Nor am I out of it. It was one of the few non-movie quotes that he'd picked up from his English-major wife. Nick couldn't have cited the precise source of the quote if his life depended on it, but he guessed it had something to do with Faustus and the Devil. Like her father, Dara had spoken and read German and several other languages besides English. And both father and daughter had seemed to know all the plays and novels and good movies in all those languages as well. Nick had a master's degree in legal forensics—mildly unusual for a cop, even a homicide detective—but he'd always felt like an education impostor around Dara and her father.

He'd been flashing in the car on his honeymoon with Dara at the Hana Maui Hotel those eighteen years ago, and he was glad now that he hadn't included any of their actual lovemaking in the quick flash—choosing instead to relive just their swimming in the infinity pool looking out on the Pacific where the moon was rising, to relive their rush to shower and dress quickly in their *hale* because they were late for their dinner reservation, and finally to reexperience their walking up to the dining *lanai* between sputtering torches and their talking to each other as the stars came out in the dark skies above them. The air had been scented with tropical flowers and the clean salt-smell from the sea. Nick had avoided flashing on the sex because the last thing he needed in this interview was a moist semen stain on his trousers, but now he was simply glad that his video-recorded idiot's face wouldn't be showing the uncoordinated spastic echoes of his orgasms from eighteen years earlier.

The endless video finally closed with the Nick Bottom–on-screen coming up and out of his twitchy trance, shaking his head, running his hands through his hair, tugging his tie tighter, checking himself in the rearview mirror, starting the car with a scraping, dying-electric-motor hum, and driving off. The five cameras, even the aerial ones, did not follow. Four of the five displays in the room went back to being antique dark wood. The final display had zoomed to the time stamp and frozen.

Hiroshi Nakamura and Hideki Sato held their silence but shifted their gazes.

After an absurd minute of this, Nick said, "All right, so I'm still a flashback addict. I go under the flash all the time — at least six or eight hours a day, about the same amount of time Americans used to spend sucking on the glass tit of TV — so what? You'll still hire me for this job, Mr. Nakamura. And you'll pay for my flashback so that I can go back almost six years to reanimate your son's murder investigation."

Sato hadn't removed his chip-phone from the top of the antique *tansu*, and now all five display surfaces lit up with different photographs of twenty-year-old Keigo Nakamura.

Nick hardly gave the images a glance. He'd seen plenty of pictures of Keigo both alive and dead during the investigation six years ago and hadn't been impressed. The billionaire's son had a weak chin, slanty brown eyes, stupid spiked hair, and that pouty, surly, sneaky look that Nick had seen on too many young Asians here in the States. Nick had learned to hate that expression on the faces of young rich-shit Japanese tourists on their slumming-in-America expeditions. The only photos of Keigo Nakamura that had interested him at all had been the crime-scene and autopsy photos showing a huge smile — but one created by the ragged knife slash across the boy's neck that revealed the white glisten of cervical vertebrae. The unknown assailant had almost severed Keigo's head from his body when he'd cut the young heir's throat.

"If you're going to hire me, it's precisely because of flashback," Nick said softly. "Why don't we quit fucking around and either get to it or call it a day? I have things to do today, other people to see."

That last sentence was the biggest lie Nick had told.

Nakamura's and Sato's faces remained totally impassive, seemingly uninterested, as if Nick Bottom had already left the room.

Nakamura shook his head. Nick saw the man's age now in the subtle but growing pouches under the eyes, the lines of wrinkles flowing back from the corners of the eyes. "You are mistaken to think that you are indispensable, Mr. Bottom. We have hard copies of all the police reports both before and after the cyberattack, both before and after you were removed from my son's case. Mr. Sato has a complete dossier of everything the Denver Police Department had."

Nick laughed. For the first time he saw anger in the aging billionaire Advisor's eyes. He was glad to see it.

"You know better than that, Mr. Nakamura," he said. "That 'everything' the department shared with you, both before and after I was heading up the investigation, constituted less than ten percent of what we kept in digital form. Paper's too fucking expensive to print out tons of redundant crap, even for pushy Japanese billionaires with pull from the White House. Sato never even saw the Murder Book . . . did you, Hideki-san?"

The security chief's expression did not change at the taunt and familiarity, but his already cold eyes turned to black ice. There was no hint of amusement there now.

"So you need me if there's going to be a new investigation," said Nick. "For the last time, I suggest we cut the bullshit and get on with it. How much will you pay me for this job?"

Nakamura stared in silence for another moment and then said softly, "If you succeed in finding my son's killers, Mr. Bottom, I am prepared to pay you fifteen thousand dollars. Plus expenses."

"Fifteen thousand new bucks or old dollars?" asked Nick in only slightly choked tones.

"Old dollars," said Nakamura. "And expenses."

Nick folded his arms as if he were thinking, but the movement was actually an attempt to catch his balance. He suddenly felt faint.

Fifteen thousand old dollars was the equivalent of a little more than twenty-two *million* new bucks.

Nick had about $160,000 in new bucks in his NICC balance now and owed several million to his former friends and to bookies and flashback dealers and various loan sharks.

$60,000,000 bucks. Mother of Christ. Nick planted his feet wider so he wouldn't sway.

Still playing out his noir tough-guy string, he managed to put some energy in his voice. "All right, I want the fifteen thousand old dollars transferred to my card at once. No strings attached...'no strings' means no restrictions or tricks or evasions, Mr. Nakamura. Hire me and transfer the money. Now. Or call your golf cart guy to take me back to my car."

This time it was the billionaire's turn to laugh.

"Do you think us fools, Mr. Bottom? If we transferred the full payment to you now, you would flee at your first opportunity and spend it all on buying flashback for your own purposes."

Of course I would, thought Nick. *I'll be alive again. And rich enough to spend the rest of Dara's and my life together—several times over.*

Still dizzy, Nick said, "What do you suggest, then? Half now? Half when I catch the guy?" Seventy-five hundred old dollars was enough to keep him under the flash for years.

Nakamura said, "I will transfer a suitable amount for expenses to your NIC Card and increase it as is needed. These are *expenses*, mind you. In new dollars. The fifteen thousand old dollars will be transferred to your private account only after my son's killer is identified and the information has been verified by Mr. Sato."

"After you've killed the guy I finger, you mean," said Nick.

Mr. Nakamura ignored this. After a moment he said, "Our holistic contract has been transferred to your phone, Mr. Bottom. You can study it at your leisure. Your virtual signature will activate the contract and Mr. Sato will then transfer the money for initial expenses to your NICC. In the meantime, will you be so kind as to give Mr. Sato a ride back to Denver?"

"Why the hell should I do that?" said Nick.

"You will not see me again until this investigation is finished, Mr. Bottom, but you will be seeing much of Mr. Sato. He will be my full-time liaison with you for this investigation. Today I wish him to experience your vehicle and see your residence."

"*Experience my vehicle?*" laughed Nick. "See my residence? What on earth for?"

"Mr. Sato has never seen a Baby Gap store," said Hiroshi Nakamura. "It would amuse him to do so. This concludes our business, Mr. Bottom. Good day."

The billionaire bowed almost infinitesimally, the bow all but invisible in its shallow curtness.

Nick Bottom did not bow. He turned on his heel and walked back toward the *genkan* entranceway and shoe-storage area, feeling the soft *tatami* under his exposed big toe every step of the way.

Hideki Sato followed close behind him without making any noise at all.

2.00

Los Angeles — Friday, Sept. 10

VAL RECLINED in a *V* where rusted steel met pigeon-shit-stained concrete under a crumbling overpass high over an abandoned stretch of the 101 not far from what was left of Union Station. Val loved this place not only for its relative coolness, as in lower temperature here in the shade, but also for its *coolness*. He liked to think that the steel-trussed and concrete ledges such as the one he and the guys were resting on now were the buttresses of some abandoned Gothic cathedral and he was the hunchback up here with the gargoyles. Charles Laughton, maybe. Val's love of old movies was, he thought, probably the only thing he'd gotten from his old man before the bastard abandoned him.

The other guys in his little flashgang were coming out of flash now, their twitches and droolings changing to yawns, stretches, and shouts.

"All *right!*" screamed Coyne. He was as close to a leader as this raggedy-ass band of mewly white kids had ever managed.

"Fuckin' A all right!" echoed Gene D. The tall, acned boy was absentmindedly rubbing his crotch as he came fully up and out from under, evidently trying to finish after the flash what he'd failed to achieve during the actual rape.

"Do her again, Ben!" cried Sully. His tats not only ran up and down the more muscled sixteen-year-old's arms but turned his face into a Maori war mask.

Monk, Toohey, the Cruncher, and Dinjin twitched up and out of their repeated thirty-minute flashes and remained silent except for their yawns, belches, and farts. These four were all a year or two younger than Val and the other three older boys (but the Cruncher—Calvin—was by far the tallest and heaviest and stupidest of the eight). None of their attempts at sex had lasted even a minute before their premature whateveryoucallems, so Val wondered—*What have these morons been flashing on for the other twenty-nine minutes?* The stripping-her-naked part? The running-away part? Or did they just flash on their Magic Moment thirty times in a row, like a disc with a stuck Blu-ray beam?

The group had been flashing and reflashing on the rape of a spanic virgin girl a little more than an hour earlier. The plan—Coyne's plan, mostly—had been to snatch one of the cute little fourth-grade spanic girls on her way to school and gang-bust her cherry. "One of those sweet little virgins with just an ant trail of hair above her gash," as Coyne had so artfully put it. "Something we can flash on and get off on for weeks."

But they hadn't nabbed a sweet little fourth-grader. All those sweet little spanic girls were being driven to school by armed dads and older brothers, rumbling down the surface streets in their hybrid low-riders with the virgins peering out through the gunslit windows of the backseats. In the end, they'd just grabbed Hand Job Maria, the retarded ninth-grader who went to their own high school. HJM might have technically been a virgin—there had been some blood when Coyne had gone first—but the sight of her naked, the rolls of fat hanging down over her cheap underpants, her pasty white lump of a face with the vacant eyes staring up, her tits large but already old-looking, stretchmarked, and drooping—had excited Val in a sick-making way, but had also made him say he'd be lookout during the actual rape.

He'd flashed when the others did here under the high over-pass, but only a ten-minute return to his fourth-birthday party back in Denver. Val tended to go back to that party the way he'd read about schizophrenics repeatedly burning their arms with cigarettes in order to remind themselves they were still alive.

The seven reanimated boys lit cigarettes and sprawled out on the exposed girders. They liked the girders, but no one wanted to lie on the narrow bands of steel sixty feet above the empty highway while twitching under flash. All of them wore holed jeans, black combat boots, and faded interactive T-shirts of the sort that almost all middle-class high school kids wore to their classes: images front and back of chillsweet dudes like Che and Fidel, Hitler and Himmler, Mao Somebody and Charles Manson, Mohammed al Aruf and Osama bin Laden—all of whom they knew almost nothing about. Coyne had interactive and voice-responsive faded images—which could go holo and respond in real dialogue when spoken to—of Dylan Klebold and Eric Harris on the front and back of his T-shirt. Val and the others really didn't know anything about Klebold and Harris, either, other than they were chillsweet killers about the age of the guys in this pathetic little flashgang who'd tried to off their entire school back when that was a new idea sometime in the last century when dinosaurs and Republicans still walked the earth.

Val, like the other guys lounging and smoking here high above the highway, had often thought about and talked of killing everyone in his school. The problem, of course, was that schools weren't soft targets anymore. Klebold and Harris had had it easy (and word was that they'd screwed the pooch even so, their propane-tank bombs not even going off). Today the halls of Val's high school near the Dodger Stadium Detention Center had almost as many armed guards as students in the halls, the local militias protected the kids stupid enough still to be going to and from school, and even the damned teachers were required to pack heat and take regular target practice at the LAPD's firing range in the old Coca-Cola bottling plant off Central Ave.

Coyne stood up, unzipped, and took a leak out into space, the arc of urine falling six stories to the weed-spotted highway pavement far below. This started an epidemic of pissing. Monk, Toohey, the Cruncher, and Dinjin were the first to follow their leader, then Sully and Gene D. and finally Val. He didn't *have* to piss, but long flashback sessions often created that urge and he didn't want the other guys to know that he'd gone under for only a few minutes while they'd all been reflashing on their rape fun for an hour or more. Val unzipped and joined the piss brigade.

"Hey, stop!" Coyne shouted before the younger boys and Val were finished.

A roar echoed down the concrete canyon of the 101. It was hard to stop urinating once you started, but Val managed. Suddenly a dozen or so Harleys roared under them, the exposed tats and muscles of their male riders visible outside the black leather, the long black or gray hair streaming behind them.

"They're burning real fucking *gasoline!*" screamed Gene D.

The riders passed under them without looking up, despite the fact that the boys were plainly visible with their little peckers hanging out over the void. The roaring Harleys were doing about eighty miles per hour.

"Shit, I wish we were down the road a mile or so," breathed Sully.

They all knew what he meant. A little less than a mile ahead, with no exits in between, a twelve-foot chunk of the 101 had fallen away during the Big One, creating a twelve-foot gap dropping down sixty feet or so to darkness and concrete blocks studded with rebar stakes and twisted, rusted metal of old wrecks and, the boys had heard, scores of skeletons of other bikers. Some Harley-borne chillsweet had wedged a wide slab of concrete as a sort of ramp years ago and these bikers would have to hit that ramp at high speed, no more than three abreast, to jump that gap and go on their way to the first opening in the exit barricades out where the 101 met what was left of the Pasadena Freeway. Val had seen the stretch on both sides of this break in the raised highway and there were streaks of dried blood and torn rubber and sculpted rubble piles of chrome and steel on the west side of that ramp-jump gap. But the 101 curved just a little north here beyond Alameda and they couldn't see the jump point from this overpass.

The boys avidly watched the bikes recede, the Harleys already narrowing their formation and jostling for position, the huge, hairy leader with his red tats injected with real blood leading and accelerating away around the curve, and as the roar of power and fuck-you-death defiance grew and echoed around them, Val felt himself grow physically excited in a way he hadn't when the others had been banging poor Hand Job Maria.

Coyne caught his eye and smiled a bit, cigarette dangling from his thin lower lip, and Val knew that the older boy was also getting a hard-on. At times like this Val felt a little gay.

He spat loudly over the edge to hide his blush and embarrassment and zipped up, turning his back on the others. The roar of Harley engines grew, peaked, and diminished to the west.

Coyne reached under his T-shirt in back and pulled something from the waistband of his jeans.

"Holy shit!" shouted little Dinjin. "A gun."

It was indeed. All seven boys gathered around Coyne where he squatted at the edge of the pigeon-splattered ledge.

"M-nine Beretta nine millimeter," whispered Coyne to the huddled circle of heads above him. "Safety's here…" He pushed a little lever backward and forward. Val guessed that the red dot meant "safety off."

"Magazine release is here…" Coyne pushed a little button on the stock behind the trigger guard. The clip or magazine or whatever the hell it should be called slid out and Coyne caught it in his free hand. "Holds fifteen rounds. Can fire one in the chamber with the magazine out."

"Can I hold it? Can I? Can I?" breathed Sully. "Please. I'll just, you know, whatchamacallit, dry-fire it."

"Is that like dry-humping a girl?" asked Monk.

"Shaddup," said Val, Coyne, Sully, and Gene D. together. They didn't like it when a junior member spoke out of turn.

Coyne held the magazineless semiauto up and pointed the muzzle at Sully. "I'll give it to you if you know how to handle it. Can it shoot now?"

"Naww," laughed Sully. "The clip's..."

"Magazine," said Coyne.

"Right, yeah. The magazine's out. I can see the bullets packed in the...magazine. Gun's safe."

Val could see the bullets, too, or at least the top one in the magazine: brass-wrapped, lead-nosed, notched at the top as if cut with a penknife. It made him feel weird, stirred him the same way the roar of the Harley-Davidson motorcycles had.

"You're a moron," Coyne said to Sully. "Coulda killed yourself or me or any of these other rat-twats panting here." Coyne racked the slide back on the old gun and a bullet that had been in the chamber arced up and out. The leader caught that round, slug, cartridge, bullet—whatever you should call it—in his free hand.

"There was one in the pipe," Coyne said softly. "You would have blown your own dick off. Or killed one of us."

Sully grinned and blinked rapidly, admonished but obviously still so eager to hold the weapon that he forgot to act pissed at being rebuked.

The fuckhead probably would *have shot one of us*, thought Val.

Coyne moved the butterfly safety so the red dot was covered up, pulled the trigger so that the slide slammed forward again, and handed the semiautomatic pistol to Sully, his oldest friend and first disciple. The other guys crowded closer to Sully as Coyne and Val stepped back three paces.

Val had turned to look out at the city.

To his southeast was downtown with what was left of its towers, including the stump of the U.S. Bank Tower—what old farts like his grandfather still called the Library Tower—and the vertical rubble of the Aon Center. Most of the other remaining towers were largely abandoned and wearing their black anti-terrorist condoms.

But Val wasn't looking at old buildings.

He saw Los Angeles, as everyone did now, as sections of

owned and protected turf, almost as if the different areas he could see were pulsing in different colors. To his south and east was spanic turf, mostly *reconquista*. Straight south across the empty canyons of downtown were strongholds of nigger and chink turf with even more *reconquista* areas surrounding them. Behind Val, to the north, were serious chink, dink, and slope neighborhoods but all slowly giving way to the *reconquista* expansion, while farther west and north, especially up in the hills, the anglos had turned Mulholland Drive into a private road and protected the high ground not only with gates but with militia and electric fences. The Jap Green Zone was way west off the 405, up in the hills where the Getty Center museum used to be and surrounded by moats, electrified fences, security patrols, and MUAV kill zones. There were a hundred other less important—but rabidly defended—turfs in L.A. these days, and every goddamned one of them, Val knew, had its own checkpoints, roadblocks, and killing zones.

The rich-shit areas of Beverly Hills, Bel Air, Pacific Palisades, and parts of Santa Monica were where the real nighttime fun was these days, but Val's grandfather didn't have a car Val could steal, so he didn't try to go there. The gang wouldn't get into those gated and security-guarded richshit communities anyway. Coyne's pathetic little flashgang was on foot, so the Pacific Ocean was as unreachable as the moon.

"Want to hold it?" Coyne asked Val.

Coyne had been going around the circle holding out the Beretta semiautomatic like a priest offering the Communion wafer and now it was Val's turn.

Val took the pistol. He was surprised at how heavy it felt—even with the magazine out and still in Coyne's hand—and the crosshatched butt or handle or whatever you called it felt cool in Val's sweaty hand. Acting as if he knew what the fuck he was doing, Val racked the slide back and looked into the empty chamber.

"Sweet, isn't it?" asked Coyne. The other six boys hovered behind Coyne like the eager acolytes they were.

"Yeah, sweet," said Val and aimed the pistol at the distant stub of the U.S. Bank Tower. "Bang," he said softly.

Coyne laughed so the other six behind him giggled like idiots.

Val was thinking of who he might shoot if Coyne gave him the gun and the loaded magazine. His grandfather, of course, but what the fuck had Leonard ever done to Val other than hover over him like some surrogate parent? One of his teachers, maybe, on the way to or from school, but the only one he hated was Ms. Daggis, the English teacher in ninth grade who'd made him read his fucking essay in front of the whole class. That had been the last time Val had written anything worth a damn in school. He liked to write stuff and he'd simply forgotten himself that one time.

No…wait.

If he had this gun, Val realized, he could find a way back to Denver and shoot his old man in the belly. He couldn't fly there, Val knew. Shit, they stripped passengers stark naked these days, MRI'd them right there at the airport, and had fifty sensor-thingees sniff their orifices to make sure they hadn't packed Semtex up their wazoos. Plus, only the Japs and richest Americans—like Coyne's old lady—could travel by air.

No, he'd have to hitchhike, somehow get through a thousand miles or more of bandit country, staying away from the militia and fed-controlled Interstates, avoiding the walled city of Las Vegas, take those surface-street highways that the gypsy truckers knew about, and show up in Denver after his six years of exile and find his old man and…

Val realized that Coyne's hand was open and extended. He wanted the pistol back.

Val handed it to him and the leader slapped in the magazine with a practiced movement and then ratcheted the slide back and let it slap back into place. Theoretically there was a bullet in the spout now and thirteen—or was it fourteen?—more waiting in the magazine.

"This is the tool," said Coyne.

"This is the tool, fool," echoed Sully. The six others giggled. Val waited.

"This is the tool," repeated Coyne. "What we got to do now is make the real deal happen."

"The real deal," echoed Sully.

"Shut up, shithead," said Coyne.

"Shut up, shithead," said Sully and shut up with a goofy grin.

"We waste some people with this," said Coyne, turning his gray-eyed gaze on each of them in turn, "and we can flash on it for years. And it's got to be someone special."

"Mr. Amherst?" said Gene D. Amherst was the principal of their high school.

"Fuck Mr. Amherst," said Coyne. The six boys—everyone but Val, who was still thinking about wasting his old man—were so attentive that their mouths were hanging open. "For full flash value, we got to waste someone *important*. Someone no one expects to get offed. Someone who'll get our faces and names on all the twenty-four-seven news feeds, even while they can't catch us."

"A movie star?" breathed Gene D. The boy with the serious acne was getting into it.

Coyne shook his head.

"There's nothing in the 'verse like flashing after wasting somebody," said the older boy. Coyne was only a month away from his seventeenth birthday and mandatory induction into the army. Val faced the same abyss eleven months from now.

"But it's gotta be somebody special," said Coyne. He looked from face to face. Now even Val was interested.

"Who?" said the Cruncher.

"A Jap," said Coyne.

The other boys exploded into laughter.

"Zap a Jap!" cried Sully. "Clip a Nip!"

Val shook his head. "Their security's too good. Their fucking cars are armored. They've got ninja bodyguards and Secret Service guys and MUAVs up the ass. And their Green Zone is...I mean we couldn't...you can't get to them, Coyne."

"I can," said Coyne. "There are fourteen rounds in this Beretta. I can get my hands on three more semiautos just like it and I can get us close enough to a real live Jap Advisor that even

Dinjin couldn't miss. The flashback on it will be gold. Who's with me?"

Six of the seven other boys exploded in noise and high-fives and loud affirmation. Val just continued looking at Coyne's gray and slightly mad eyes for a long minute.

Then Val nodded slowly.

The junior flashgang moved off the overpass ledge and into the overgrown trees and weeds toward the wilderness of the Old Plaza and El Pueblo de Los Angeles Park with its graffiti-desecrated church. There were flash and gun dealers waiting there.

1.02

Denver — Friday, Sept. 10

SATO COULDN'T FIT in the car seat or get the damned seat belt harness on.

Nick had done the entire three-tier security thing in reverse with Sato in tow: Mr. Nakamura's personal security *ninjas* or whatever they were handing him off to the Nipponese Compound security people, the Japanese turning him over to the Colorado state troopers and the DS agents — the State Department's Office of Diplomatic Security charged with protecting foreign diplomats — who gave Nick back his Glock 9 in its clip-on holster. And then Nick got in the gelding and was ready to leave, except for the fact that Sato wouldn't fit.

"Sorry, power seat, but hasn't worked for a while," mumbled Nick as Sato's mass filled all the space between the seat back and the dashboard. "Been meaning to fix that stuck harness as well." The seat belt harness extended about twenty inches, which barely reached Sato's shoulder, and would not extend farther.

"Do you have airbag?" asked the security chief.

"Ahh...," said Nick and then remembered that the car had

been CMRI'd on its way in. Sato must know that all the ancient hybrid's airbags were missing. Nick had sold them years ago.

Sato fiddled with the unmoving power seat controls for a minute and then, just as Nick got out to come around to add his own useless fiddling, Sato planted his feet on the floorboards, gave out a sumo-wrestler's grunt-growl, and straightened his legs.

The stalled power seat screeched back as far as it could go, the bearings almost tearing off their railings, until the back of the half-reclined seat was almost touching the rear seat.

Sato gave another weight lifter's grunt and pulled down on the stuck shoulder harness with all his might.

Something in the mechanism tore and three yards of seat belt hung loose. Still half reclined, two feet farther back than the driver, Sato clicked the harness into the buckle.

Nick came back around and drove off. He would have rolled up the windows to shut out the DS agents' laughter, but it was already far too hot in the little car and the air-conditioning wasn't working with the batteries this low.

The low batteries were a problem.

Nick had popped his phone back in the dashboard slot and its nav function told him that the distance to the Cherry Creek Mall by the shortest route—reversing the way he'd come via Speer Boulevard, to 6, to I-70, and then the Evergreen exit to the Green Zone—was 29.81 miles. The DS guys had charged the gelding with their garage's high-speed 240-volt charger, but the phone and car readouts both said that the old batteries only had enough charge to travel 24.35 miles, even factoring in the downhill stretch on I-70 dropping out of the foothills.

The last thing that Nick Bottom wanted on this particular Friday was to be stuck with Mr. Hideki Sato somewhere on Speer Boulevard—probably in *reconquista* territory south of downtown—five miles from their destination.

Fuck it, thought Nick, not for the first time that morning. *No guts, no glory.*

The gelding hummed, hissed, and rattled its way out of the Green Zone toward I-70.

Sato's position, lying almost flat in the broken and fully

reclined passenger seat and so far back that it seemed that Nick was a chauffeur up front and Sato the passenger in the rear seat, looked absurd, but the hefty security chief didn't seem bothered by it. Sato folded his callused hands over his belly and looked up and out at the trees and sky.

Glancing at the sky, Nick said, "Mr. Sato, how did you get the video of me using the flashback on that cul-de-sac? Some of the shots looked to be from a handheld camera from about ten feet away."

"They were," said the security chief.

Nick tried to accelerate down the ramp onto the Interstate, but the gelding wasn't in the mood to accelerate — even heading downhill. At least there wasn't much traffic to merge into coming east on I-70. At one time, a time Nick could still remember clearly, a family could get on I-70 and drive 1,034 miles without ever leaving the Interstate except to pump gas — merging with I-15 about 500 miles from Denver in the Utah high desert and mountain country and staying on it the rest of the way to L.A. — ending up at the Pacific Ocean at the Santa Monica Pier.

Now an adventurous driver could get in his car and drive 98 miles west from Denver on I-70 to where state and federal protection ended at Vail. Beyond Vail, there be dragons.

"How did you get one of your people to within ten feet of my car with a camera?" asked Nick.

"Stealth suit," said Sato. The short but absurdly solid man seemed totally relaxed.

Nick stopped himself from replying. Stealth suits were the stuff of agencies like the former CIA, long since disbanded, and of sci-fi action movies. How could the expense of a stealth suit possibly be justified just to follow Nicholas Bottom to an interview? Even if they'd badly wanted the footage to embarrass him as they did during the interview — why a stealth suit? And how'd they get the operative *in* the stealth suit so close to Nick's car before Nick had zonked out under the flash — driving a stealth *car?* This was James Bond crap from the last century. Ridiculous.

Sato was almost certainly joking. But Nick, who still had a cop's ability to pick up most of the subtle physical and auditory signals that someone was lying (with some inner-city types the signal was simple—the perp's lips were moving), just couldn't get any reading on Sato. Except for the security chief's occasional and deliberate flashes of contempt, disdain, and amusement toward Nick, there was nothing. Beneath that Japanese layer of what Occidentals like Nick thought of as Asian inscrutability, Security Chief Sato wore another—probably professional—mask.

"The aerial video," persisted Nick. "All MUAVs?"

"Not all miniature," Sato said softly. "And one was a satellite feed."

Nick laughed out loud. Sato didn't join in the laugh or crack a smile.

Using full-size UAVs and tasking a recon satellite, even one of the Nakamura Group's corporate sats, to watch me snort some flashback? He mentally laughed again at the thought.

Sato continued lying there like a tipped-over Buddha, his fingers interlaced over his broad but heavily muscled belly.

Nick braked lightly on the 6 percent I-70 grade down the mountain toward Denver, slowing the crawling car to an even more glacial pace, hoping against hope that the regenerative braking would add enough juice to the dying li-ion batteries to get him home. Even other old clunkers honked and roared past. The hydrogen vehicles in the far-left VIP lane were blurs.

He changed the subject in an attempt to keep Sato talking.

"How did you translate 'gelding' to your boss?"

"As a male horse whose testicles have been removed. This is correct, yes?"

"Yes," said Nick. "But don't you have geldings—old hybrids with the gasoline engines removed—in Japan?"

"Not legal in Japan," said Sato. "Cars in Japan are inspected every year and must meet all modern standards. Few automobiles there are more than three years old. Hydrogen-powered vehicles are—how do you say it?—the norm in Japan."

Vehicres.

Still braking, watching his meters while trying to keep both his batteries and the conversation alive, Nick said, "Mr. Nakamura doesn't seem to like old movies."

Sato made that deep noise in his throat and chest. Nick had no idea how to interpret that. Different topic needed.

"You know," said Nick, "this liaison idea isn't going to work."

"Riaison?" repeated Sato.

Nick didn't smirk but he wondered if he'd brought up this conversation strand just to get Sato to mispronounce the word.

"The idea Mr. Nakamura brought up of you following me everywhere, reporting on everything I see and hear, being part of the investigation with me. It won't work."

"Why not, Mr. Bottom?"

"You know damn well why not," snapped Nick. He was approaching the bottom of the hill, emerging onto the high, mostly flat prairie that stretched east past Denver some eight hundred miles or so to the Mississippi River, and he'd have to decide in a few minutes whether to continue a little north and then due east on I-70 to the Mousetrap and a short stretch of I-25 south to Speer Boulevard, with no stops, or angle right to go back on Highway 6 to Speer the way he'd come. The 6 route was a little shorter, I-70 perhaps a little easier on the dying batteries.

"My witnesses and suspects won't talk with a Jap listening," continued Nick. "Sorry, Japanese person. You know what I mean."

Sato growled something that might mean assent.

Nick turned to look back and around and down at the security chief. "You weren't one of Nakamura's assistants or security people who dealt with the Denver PD six years ago when Keigo was murdered. I would have remembered you."

Sato said nothing.

At the last second, Nick took the Highway 6 exit. Shorter was better. Or it had damned well better be.

All the charge meters were reading flashing amber or red but Nick knew that the gelding, like him, had a few more miles hidden in it somewhere.

"So why didn't you come to the States with Mr. Nakamura when his son was killed?" demanded Nick. "It seems to me that as head of Nakamura's security detail, you would have been front and center in asking questions of the cops here. But your name's not even in the files."

Again Sato remained silent. He seemed to be almost asleep, his eyelids almost—but not quite—closed.

Nick looked back at him again. He suddenly understood. "You were on Keigo's security detail," he said softly.

"I *was* Keigo Nakamura's security detail," said Sato. "His life was in my hands the entire time he was here making his film about Americans and flashback addiction."

Nick rubbed his chin and cheek, feeling the stubble there from his hasty shave that morning. "Jesus."

The gelding hummed and rattled along for a few minutes. The regenerative braking had helped some, even though it didn't really show the added charge on the crappy gauges. Nick thought they might make it back to the Cherry Creek Mall Condos garage after all.

"Your name wasn't in the files," Nick said at last. "I'm certain of that even without checking under flashback. That means that you didn't come forward. Nor did Nakamura ever mention it during the investigation. You had vital evidence about the murder of Keigo Nakamura, but you and your boss kept it secret from the Denver PD and all of us."

"I do not know who murdered Keigo Nakamura," Sato said in low tones. "We were . . . briefly separated. When I found him, he was dead. I had nothing to offer the police. There was little reason to remain in the United States."

Nick barked a cop's laugh. "The man who found the body flees the country . . . nothing to offer the police. Cute. I guess the main question is, how are you still working for Hiroshi Nakamura after his son was killed while under your protection?"

It was a brutal thing to say and for a minute Nick's shoulder blades itched as he imagined the massive security chief firing his pistol through the back of Nick's driver's seat. Instead, there was only a slight intake of breath and Sato said, "Yes, that is an important question."

Nick had another revelation. He blinked as if flashbulbs had gone off in front of him. "You already *did* an investigation—you and your security guys—didn't you, Sato? What—five and a half years ago?"

"Yes."

"And even with all your technology and MUAVs and satellites and shit, you still couldn't find out who killed your boss's son."

"No, we could not."

"How long did your investigation run, Sato?"

"Eighteen months."

"How many operatives on the job for those eighteen months?"

"Twenty-seven."

"Holy shit," said Nick. "All that money and manpower. You couldn't find Keigo's murderer and you never told us—the Denver cops or the FBI—that you were carrying out your own investigation."

"No," confirmed Sato. His voice seemed to be coming from very far away.

"All that money and manpower and technology," repeated Nick, "and you couldn't find out who cut the boy's throat. But your boss expects me to find the killer with nothing but shoe leather and some flashback."

"Yes."

"What happens to you if this last try fails?" asked Nick. Somehow he knew the answer as soon as he asked the question, even if he couldn't remember the correct word at that moment.

"I commit *seppuku*," Sato said softly, neither his voice nor expression changing. "Just as I offered—but was denied permission to do—the first two times I failed my master. This time, permission has been granted ahead of time."

"Jesus Christ," whispered Nick.

His phone in the diskey slot buzzed a terrorist alert at the same instant he heard a distant THUMP through his open driver's-side window and he saw a plume of black smoke to the north and east of them. Black Homeland Security helicopters were clearly visible, circling like carrion crows two miles or so north.

Nick verbally queried his phone but the phone had no data yet.

He looked in the rearview mirror and saw Sato touch his left ear. The earphone had been so tiny that Nick had missed it earlier.

"What is it?" asked Nick. "What's going on?"

"A bombing. A car bomb, evidently. At the interchange of I-Seventy, I-Twenty-five, and Highway Thirty-six that you call the Mousetrap. Segments of two of the overpassing highways have collapsed. Several dozen vehicles are in the debris of the collapsed roadways. There seems to be no radiological, chemical, or bacteriological contamination detected."

"Christ. I almost went that way. We'd be there now. Do they know who did it?"

Sato shrugged.

Nick interpreted the shrug not as *I don't know* nor as *It's not on the Net yet* but as *Does it matter?*

And did it?

Hajji, AB, *reconquista*, flashgangs, anarchist syndicate, spanic militias, anglo militias, Black Muslims, Nuevo cartels, local cartels, Posse Comitatus, draft dodgers, aggrieved veterans, New Caliphate infiltrators...it didn't matter, Nick realized. Knowing *which* terrorists had blown the Mousetrap to bits wouldn't really help you avoid the *next* terrorist with a gun or IED or van full of fertilizer with a fuse.

But Nick was still irritated that Sato's phone was picking up secure data faster than Nick's not-quite-legal, grandfathered-in tap on the police tactical net.

He slowed at the Highway 6 overpass above I-25. Due north, beyond the huge black-oil-dipped wavy oval of the Mile High DHSDC, just west of the A-T-wrapped stubs of what was left of Denver's high-rise buildings downtown, beyond the bulks of Six Flags Over the Jews and Coors Field, black smoke continued to rise. The Homeland Security choppers continued to buzz and flit and circle the smoke like vultures, while the lesser carrion birds of news choppers circled much farther out, not yet allowed close enough to bring the scene to waiting viewers.

Nick crossed I-25 and turned right onto Speer Boulevard.

"So if I fail in this investigation—a case you couldn't solve five years ago in eighteen months of trying at a time when the witnesses' memories and clues were fresh," he said over his shoulder to Sato, "a case you couldn't solve with twenty-seven operatives working for you, more tech than the FBI has, and Nakamura's budget of billions of dollars behind you—you're going to disembowel yourself?"

The security chief nodded and closed his eyes.

1.03

Cherry Creek—Friday, Sept. 10

THE GELDING ROLLED up the last ramp to the third and top floor of the Cherry Creek Mall Condos' parking garage and died thirty feet short of the charging stations. Nick left it where it was, knowing that Mack or one of the boys would push it the rest of the way. The charging station in the Japanese Green Zone had taken fewer than forty minutes; here, with the mall's old charging equipment, it would be twelve hours even for the partial charge. Nick didn't care.

Sato had gotten through the two security checkpoints by handing over his NICC—the thin card was black rather than the usual diplomat's or visiting alien's green—and there'd been no problem. But Nick was looking forward to the last checkpoint at the armory check-room. If Sato thought his diplomatic status was going to allow him to carry a gun into the Cherry Creek Mall Condos interior, the security chief was in for a rude shock. The president of the United States couldn't get a weapon into this complex if she hid it in her bra.

They were in the security airlock and Gunny G., the senior weapons expert and top security man for the mall, was behind the gun-check counter. Probably one of the guys at the security checkpoints had phoned him. An ex-marine, Gunny G. was of that indeterminate age beyond sixty but still fit and dangerous, and his square, tanned face under the crew cut seemed held together by old scars.

Nick handed over his Glock 9 and waited.

The former shopping mall didn't have the Green Zone's CMRI or layers of security, but the X-ray machine and ancient explosives-gunpowder sniffer in the entrance airlock had done their work. Nick could see the images of Sato and him glowing on Gunny's screen to the left of the counter opening. Sato had some sort of oversized handgun in a shoulder holster in his left armpit, a small one in a belt holster around the curve of his left hip, a strap-on holster with a tiny semiautomatic on his right ankle, and a nasty-looking throwing knife on the belt above his right hip.

Before Gunny G. could growl his demands, Sato said, "Listen to this, please." *Risten. Prease.*

The security chief passed across his NICC and when Gunny G. scanned it, he put his earbud and e-glasses on to access the encrypted information there. The former marine's expression did not change, but when he handed Sato's identity card back, he growled, "Go on in, Mr. Sato." There was no attempt to disarm Sato.

Nick's jaw actually dropped in surprise. He'd heard that expression for decades, but had never seen anyone's jaw literally drop—much less experienced it himself.

The inner doors and gate opened and Sato stood to one side and made an "After you" gesture with his massive arm.

Nick led the way to his cubie. This section of town was obviously going through one of its daily brownouts and although generators kept the security doors, parking-area charging bays, security cameras, cubie doors, outside autoguns, and other essential equipment running, the lights were out above the second-floor mezzanine and the once-fancy skylight panels that ran the length of the ceiling were so caked with dust and grime that the light inside had paled to a sick, sad yellow. Most of the common-space ventilator fans were also out and since people propped their cubie doors open during the brownouts, the air

Dan Simmons

was thick with the funk of several thousand people and their dirty bedding and cooking smells and cubie garbage.

Nick paused at the railing twenty feet above the old fountain that used to splash in front of the Saks Fifth Avenue store. The space was still home to some of the pricier windowless cubies in the complex, although it wasn't overly inviting now, with its leaking trash bags heaped head-high outside the steel-shuttered entrance. He looked down at where the wild goose sculpture used to be.

The large, trapezoidal marble-sided fountain had long since been drained and filled in with soil so that some of the Saks-cubie residents could attempt to grow vegetables there, but a few steel cables still dropped from the high ceiling and one bronze goose remained. Originally, Nick remembered from the times he'd shopped here as a kid and young man, the sculpture had boasted a series of wild geese coming down in single file for a landing on the water—with the lowest goose, legs stiffly outstretched, seeming to throw up jets of spray to either side where its webbed feet contacted the surface of the water. How many geese had there been? Nick wondered. Six? Eight? More?

It would take flashback to find out and he wasn't going to waste the drug on that. But now this one goose remained about ten feet above the makeshift garden, its broad bronze wings outstretched, its legs just beginning to deploy like stiff, web-footed landing gear.

Nick didn't know why he paused here with Sato in tow… only that he always paused a second to stare at that lone remaining goose.

He shook his head angrily and led the way to the former Baby Gap and his home.

The residents of the other five cubies in the old commercial space were all home behind their partial walls and blankets since they were also on the dole and had nowhere to go during the long days. The old woman in the cubie next to Nick's was snoring. The couple in the cubie opposite were screaming at each other, their two-year-old kid joining in and bringing the melded screams perilously close to the death frequency. The old soldier's

44

cubie was silent as always—Nick always waited for the stench that would tell everyone that the old man had finally hanged or shot himself in there—but the other two cubies had their TVs on and blaring. The Baby Gap acoustical ceiling had been twelve feet high; the thin cubie walls went up only eight feet.

Nick opened the door and let Sato enter his tiny space, his rage at this invasion of his privacy growing. But Mr. Nakamura had insisted that the security chief visit Nick's home, and Nick would get the initial credit transfer only after the visit was complete.

Nick saw that he'd failed to make his bed that morning. The irony was that it had been an absurd little point of pride between Dara and him that he'd always made his bed, even before he met Dara, and if she hadn't gotten to it on the mornings when they were both rushed to get to work, he would.

The unmade bed was all the more obvious since it took up almost a third of the space in Nick's cubie.

Nick didn't suggest that Sato sit down since a) he hadn't invited him here and b) the only place to sit other than the unmade bed was the chair at the little desk on which Nick opened his phone's virtual keyboard and that chair probably wasn't sturdy enough to hold Sato. It was barely sturdy enough to hold Nick Bottom.

But the security chief showed no interest in sitting down. Crossing to the wall opposite Nick's bed and the seventy-inch flatscreen display there, Sato activated the TV and passed his card through the set's diskey slot.

Instantly three rows of faces, eighteen in all, appeared on the screen.

"You recognize these men and women?" asked Sato.

"Most of them. Some of them." They'd all been familiar to Nick once, witnesses and suspects in Keigo Nakamura's murder files, but flashback had the ironic side effect of dulling actual memory.

As if in response to this unspoken fact, Sato said, "Mr. Nakamura assumes that you will want to spend some hours reviewing their files and earlier interviews via the drug flashback before you begin your actual investigation. My strong recommendation is that you do such a flashback review for only one or two of these people at a time, so that the real-world investigation may begin and proceed as soon as possible. How many hours will you need for the flashback?"

Nick shrugged. "That homicide investigation took up four months of my life. If I were to review all of it under flashback, look back at all these people's files and interviews, I'd be ready to start around Christmas."

"That is, of course, totally unacceptable."

"All right. When do you and Mr. Nakamura think I should be starting the foot leather part of the new investigation? A month from now? Two weeks?"

"Early tomorrow morning," said Sato. "You are an expert at triggering flashback experiences. Choose critical memories to relive this afternoon and this evening, get a good night's sleep, and I shall join you as you begin the reopened investigation in the morning."

Nick opened his mouth to protest, then shut it. It didn't matter. All that mattered was the transfer of funds to his card.

Sato nodded for that card, passed it through his own phone's diskey, and handed it back.

"You have the first month's expenses now," said Sato. "Including money for flashback purchase, of course, but also for transportation — you will need a new car, as Mr. Nakamura pointed out — and other incidentals. Obviously all expenditures will be tracked in real time from our end."

Nick only nodded. But as Sato moved toward the door, Nick said, "Three of those eighteen are dead, you know."

"Yes."

"But you still want me to review them under flash and keep them as a focus of the investigation?"

"Yes."

Nick shrugged again. "I'll walk you out."

The phrase sounded archaic even to Nick's middle-aged ears. And he didn't give a damn whether the security chief had trouble finding his way out of the mall. He only wanted to make sure he was really gone.

Surprisingly, Sato didn't walk to any of the airlock exits. He crossed to the north mezzanine and the administrative corridor near the old Ralph Lauren store. Gunny G. and the black-armored security sergeant named Marx were there to meet him. The four men went through a door and up a flight of steps—the elevators weren't working in the brownout—and out onto the roof. Nick knew this roof access; he had its entry code memorized and a hundred feet of Perlon-3 climbing rope, carabiners, and a rappel-harness in his cubie closet in case he ever had to leave the building quickly via the roof.

Now he squinted in the hazy light. Smoke was still rising many miles to the northwest.

The helicopter that came in to fetch Sato was one of the new silent ones that looked more like a dragonfly than any of the Homeland Security, police, and other choppers that Nick had known. The only noise as it touched down—Nick couldn't have told anyone that the old mall had an infrared-marked heliport space on its roof—was the scrabble of gravel blowing across the grimy skylights and decommissioned solar panels.

Sato clambered in without saying a word to anyone and the Nakamura aircraft lifted off and flew due west.

On the way down the steps, Gunny G. said, "Some company you're keeping these days, Nick."

Nick grunted.

NICK DIDN'T HAVE TO leave the mall to get to his flashback dealer. Gary met him in the part of the subbasement that used to be the mall's boiler room.

"Holy shit," said the maintenance man when he saw the balance on Nick's NICC. "How much of this you want to spend on the flash?"

"All of it," said Nick. He handed the card to Gary and watched as the other man swiped it in his illicit, illegal, but quite effective black-market diskey.

"It's going to take me some time to get that many vials together."

"Ten minutes," said Nick, who knew where Gary kept his supplies. "One minute more and I'll do this buy on the street."

"Easy, easy," said Gary, making patting motions with his gnarled hands. "I'll get it all up to you at your cubie in ten minutes. But they gonna be a lotta unhappy flashers in the building tonight."

"Fuck 'em," said Nick. "But don't deliver to my cubie. I'll meet you here in ten minutes."

"You the buyer."

"You're damned right," said Nick.

———

GARY WAS BACK IN the boiler room in eight minutes and so was Nick. He'd dumped his card and phone in his cubie and showered and changed clothes and passed his old police bug detector over himself—just in case Sato had put a tracker on him—and come down to the basement carrying only his old olive-canvas messenger bag slung over one shoulder.

Even with the high number of twenty-hour vials Nick had specified, there were *a lot* of flashback vials coming out of Gary's duffel. Nick stuffed them into his messenger bag, wrapping them quickly in the towels he'd packed to keep them from rattling.

When Gary was gone, Nick went through the seldom-used door down into the pipe conduits and crawlspaces beneath the boiler room. There was a deeper crawlspace here going to the older pipes, most out of use now, that ran to and from the mall from the outside, and this access panel was locked with a number keypad for which no one working in the mall probably still had the code. Nick tapped in the seven-digit code. He knew this not from his time living at the mall but from a case ten years ago when he and other detectives had searched this whole maze of Cherry Creek underground heating and sewage pipes for a serial killer who'd specialized in children.

Clicking the access panel shut behind him, Nick pulled a tiny flashlight from his messenger bag and moved in a crouching run fifty yards or so, avoiding the rusty and corroded pipes that all but filled the space. Whatever was in there now—and dripping and oozing from those pipes—was bad enough to keep the street people out of this particular stretch of the underground maze. It was hard to breathe there.

Nick reached the first junction of tunnels and turned left. The tunnel here was just as small and just as foul-smelling. Nick counted twenty paces and stopped where several smaller pipes ran dripping into the concrete wall. An old inspection panel there looked corroded shut but it slid screechingly upward when Nick pulled.

The watertight plastic bag was there where he'd put it years ago and where he'd checked on it from time to time since. Nick removed the .32 semiautomatic pistol from its nest of oily rags and dropped it into his messenger bag. The weapon had been a throw-down belonging to Detective K. T. Lincoln, his last partner. Nick kept the wad of old bills in its own freezer bag but removed the cheap, traceless Walmart immigrant phone and tested it. The long-duration batteries were still good. The thing still got a signal down here.

Squatting in the steaming reek of the tunnel, Nick tapped in a number.

"Mothman here," said the Pakistani-accented voice.

"Moth, this is Dr. B. I need you to pick me up at the storm sewer opening under the old bridge over Cherry Creek in about five minutes."

There followed only the briefest of pauses. For more than a dozen years, Mohammed "Mothman" al Mahdi had been one of Detective Nicholas Bottom's best street informants. And "Dr. B." had been Mothman's highest-paying cop. Nick had often checked on Mothman's presence in the years since he was booted off the force, usually bringing a gift when he visited the cabbie. More to the point, Mothman was still afraid of Nick Bottom—both physically and because Nick knew enough about the Moth's past that he could drop a dime on him at any time.

"Be there in five, Dr. B."

———

IN THE MOVIES, STORM drains were always the size of the ones in L.A. You could drive a truck in those drains. They *had* driven an entire motorized regiment of Jeeps and trucks into those drains in the midtwentieth-century movie *Them* that Nick and Dara had liked. But storm drains in Denver were slimy, narrow affairs, and Nick was crawling on his belly and elbows by the time he kicked out the rusted rebar drain cover and dropped the four feet to the abandoned walkway under the old Cherry Creek bridge.

Mothman's bumblebee pedicab, imported from Calcutta when that city went to all electric cabs, was waiting just under the shadow of the bridge. Nick slid into the backseat.

"Grossven's cave," directed Nick.

Mothman nodded and pedaled. Nick sat back deeper on the soiled cushions, making sure his face was out of sight.

Mickey Grossven's flashcave was less than two miles along the river to the south. The condos here had burned in the original *reconquista* fighting and never been torn down or repaired. Nick slapped five dollars in old bucks cash into the Mothman's hand—it was two months' income for the illegal immigrant—and said, "You haven't seen me or heard from me. If anyone tracks me, I'll come hunting for *you*, Mohammed."

"Trust me, Dr. B."

Nick was already gone, ducking from the pedicab to the hole in the basement wall. Down a urine-reeking corridor, then up two flights of stairs, then to a halt in a corridor that led nowhere. A blank brick wall and burned debris ahead.

Nick stood there until the night-vision and infrared cameras could get a good look at him.

The wall slid open and Nick entered a windowless warehouse space half the size of a city block. The only light came from chemical glowsticks set into mounds of melted wax on the floor. There were hundreds of low cots in the dark room, perhaps a thousand, with a twitching form on each cot. Bottles hung above each cot and IV drips ran to each form.

Grossven and his huge bouncer met him in the entry area.

"Detective Bottom?" said Grossven. "We don't have a problem here, do we?"

Nick shook his head. "Not 'Detective' any longer, Mickey. I just need a cot and an IV."

Grossven showed his almost toothless grin and gestured to the huge, dark space. "Cots is what we got. Cots and time. All the time in the world. How much time you want, Detective?"

"Six hundred hours' worth."

Grossven had no eyebrows so he showed his surprise with his eyes only. "It's a good start. Cash or charge today, Detective?"

Nick gave him a fifty-dollar bill.

"Lawrence," said Grossven and the gigantic bouncer in dragonscale body armor led Nick to a cot in an uncrowded corner and expertly got the IV going. Nick set his bag under the cot, sliding the .32 into his pocket but knowing that his money and flashback vials would be safe here. It was what the hibernation caves were for. Mickey wouldn't have stayed alive for a month if he'd allowed his customers to be robbed, and he'd been in the cave business for more than a decade.

More than twenty hours under the flash at a time, Nick knew, led to kidney and bowel problems. No breaks from the flash also led to psychotic episodes when the mind, finally wakened, couldn't sort one reality from another.

Nick didn't give a damn about the psychotic problems—he already knew which reality he'd chosen—but he would accept the four-hour interruptions to walk a bit on the indoor track upstairs so his muscles wouldn't atrophy and to use the restroom and eat some energy bars. Once every week or two, he'd use the group showers next door. Maybe.

Six hundred hours with Dara wasn't enough—it wasn't even a full month—but it would be a start.

Lying back on his cot, the IV feed loose enough that it wouldn't get in the way in case he needed to reach for his pistol, Nick lifted the first twenty-hour vial, visualized his memory trigger point, broke the seal, and inhaled deeply.

3.00

Echo Park, Los Angeles—
Saturday, Sept. 11

PROFESSOR EMERITUS George Leonard Fox, PhD, moved slowly into the park, taking care not to trip, not to fall, not to break his increasingly brittle bones. It made him smile. *It's come to this*, he thought. *It's why old people hobble. To protect their brittle bones. And there now, with the grace or curse of God, am I.*

He realized he was being petulant and banished the childish emotion in return for increased vigilance as he slowly worked his way—but not hobbling, not yet, not quite—across the broken paving stones into the park. At age seventy-four Dr. George Leonard Fox had not yet begun using a cane or walking stick and he'd be damned if he'd hurt himself today so that he had to start using one. Broken flashback vials crunched underfoot but Leonard ignored the sound.

It was early, just after 7 a.m., and the air in Echo Park was relatively cool, the skies above a clear blue, the remaining tables and benches in the park damp with dew. During the weekday and weekend nights, countless gangs stabbed and shot each other for—for what? wondered Leonard. For possession of the park turf for a few hours? For status? For the fun of it?

For a man who had spent almost his entire lifetime struggling to understand things, Leonard realized that as he approached death from old age, should he be so lucky, he understood less and less.

But he understood that during the mornings on Saturdays and Sundays, the park belonged to old men such as himself.

Leonard raised his eyes from the treacherous sidewalk and saw that his friend Emilio Gabriel Fernández y Figueroa had staked out their favorite concrete chess table and was already setting up the chess pieces he'd brought.

"*Buenos días, mi amigo*," said Leonard as he approached the table.

"Good morning, Leonard," said Emilio with a smile.

The two spoke in Spanish or English on alternate Saturdays and Leonard had forgotten that it had been Spanish the previous week. How could he have forgotten? He'd had to struggle to remember the word "impoverishment"—*empobrecimiento* had been what Emilio had finally provided—so was he now showing the memory-loss effects of Alzheimer's as well as trouble with balance and fear for his brittle bones?

Leonard smiled and tapped Emilio's closed left fist. It was a black piece. Emilio got to be white again. He won the tap about three times out of four and always preferred to be white and to go first. Emilio sat on the concrete bench—the chessboard was already set up properly for him to be white from that side—and Leonard carefully took his place across from him. They used no chess clocks in their friendly games.

Emilio opened with his inevitable conservative pawn move. Leonard answered the opening with the same pawn move with which he always responded. The game moved into its predictable early stages and the men could relax and talk while they played.

"How goes your novel, Leonard?" Emilio asked the question as he was lighting a cigarette. Emilio Gabriel Fernández y Figueroa—the old man insisted that his grandfather had stolen the full family name from a character in a John Wayne movie— smoked a pack of cigarettes a day. Yet Emilio had been born in 1948, a full decade before Leonard, and was approaching his eighty-fourth birthday with no apparent worries about brittle bones, lung cancer, or anything else.

By his own admission, Emilio had lived a mostly charmed life. Coming as an illegal immigrant to California as a young man in the late 1960s, he'd made enough money as a translator and sometimes accountant to return to Mexico, get married, and then earn his master's degree and PhD at the Universidad Nacional Autónoma de México in Mexico City. He then taught Spanish literature there and at IPN, the Instituto Politécnico Nacional, for years until—at about the time of his retirement—two of his sons and three of his grandsons were killed in battles between the drug cartels and Mexican federal police.

When the cartel-federal battles reached the level of real civil war and more than twenty-three million Mexicans, cartels included, flowed north into the United States within a period of less than seven months, five of Emilio's surviving sons and eight of his grandsons joined the tsunami as leaders in the emerging *reconquista* effort separating the nascent Nuevo Mexico from much of the chaotic, cartel-controlled old Mexico. Professor Emilio Gabriel Fernández y Figueroa came north with his sons and grandsons and great-grandsons and most of his granddaughters and their families, returning to the United States—what was left of it—where he'd earned his original stake for his education and where he'd visited so many times as a respected academic.

Leonard had met Dr. Fernández y Figueroa in September of 2001, at a very high-profile literary conference at Yale. Both scholars had been presented to the conference as experts on the novels of Gabriel Gárcia Márquez, the Argentine fabulist Jorge Luis Borges, the Chilean poet Pablo Neruda, and the Cuban novelist Alejo Carpentier. It took less than an hour of panel discussion for Dr. George Leonard Fox to retreat on each of these fronts, deferring to the expertise of Professor Emilio Gabriel Fernández y Figueroa.

On the third day of that conference, aircraft hijacked by al Qaeda jihadists had flown into New York's World Trade Center, the Pentagon, and a field in Pennsylvania, and it had been the ensuing private conversations between Leonard and Emilio that had set the basis for their friendship in Los Angeles that endured more than three decades later.

Leonard sighed and said, "My novel is stuck, Emilio. My idea was for it to be a *War and Peace* overview of the last forty years, but I can't get beyond September 2008. I simply don't understand that first financial crisis."

Emilio smiled, exhaled smoke, and moved his bishop aggressively.

"Perhaps Proust should be your model, Leonard, and not Tolstoy."

Leonard blocked the bishop's line of attack by moving one of his pawns a single square. The pawn was protected by his knight.

After his initially conservative moves, Emilio would become overly aggressive through the use of a combination of his bishops and rooks, almost always at the expense of his other pieces. Leonard preferred his knights and a solid defense.

"No, Emilio, even if I had a magical madeleine, telling my own life interweaved with the events of the last decade would illuminate almost nothing. I wasn't on this planet. I was on university campuses."

Leonard *had* noticed a turning point when the nation and world started heading for hell... or at least his part of it. He had been teaching in both the classics and English departments at the University of Colorado in Boulder in the 1990s when the university—under a sort of blackmail from the instructor in question—appointed a fake scholar, fake Native American, fake professor (but true hater) named Ward Churchill to be head of their newly created Ethnic Studies Department. It had been a surrender to absolute political correctness—a term already inextricably intertwined with the term "university"—and a surrender to a type of rabid mediocrity. When he had returned from the Yale conference after 9-11 to find that this Ward Churchill had written an essay comparing the victims in the World Trade Center and Pentagon to "little Eichmanns," it hadn't surprised Professor George Leonard Fox. His students—the few English majors and even fewer classics majors—seemed to move apologetically through the hallways at CU, clinging to the walls, while Churchill's Ethnic Studies students—tattooed, multiply pierced, their fists commonly raised in anger—would stride like Gestapo.

"No," said Leonard again, "I don't have even a Proustian ghost of a life to write about. I wanted to document the era we've both lived through as broadly and brilliantly as Tolstoy documented his. I just don't *know* anything, *understand* anything...not war, not peace, not finances, not economics, not politics. Nothing."

Emilio chuckled, coughed, and moved a rook five squares forward to support both his bishops in an attempted pincers move.

"Tolstoy once said that *War and Peace* was not meant to be a novel at all."

"Well," said Leonard, bringing his other knight into play, "then I've equaled Tolstoy. My mess of pages isn't a novel either."

Emilio's bishop, protected by his rook, captured one of Leonard's pawns.

"Check," said Emilio.

Leonard calmly moved the knight he'd had in waiting, protecting his king and threatening Emilio's bishop. It was a... Leonard blushed at even thinking the term...Mexican standoff.

"You could skip writing the novel and just write an equivalent to Tolstoy's epilogue to *War and Peace*," said Emilio. "You know—themes such as the fact that forces in history act beyond human reason, that none of us are free but consciousness creates in each of us the illusion of freedom and free will, that since free will is an illusion, history must find its true laws, and that even personality depends upon time, space, emotion, and causality."

"That would be a treatise," said Leonard, watching Emilio bring his other rook into play through traffic. "Not a novel."

"No one reads novels anymore anyway, Leonard."

"I know," said Leonard, taking out Emilio's first protective rook with his own bishop. "Check."

Emilio frowned. It was too late to castle and he'd been profligate with the movement of his pawns and power pieces, leaving the royal hearth relatively unprotected. He abandoned his attack for a moment and swung his bishop back into a protective position.

"Check," Leonard said again after he'd taken the bishop with his own bishop.

Emilio grunted and finally used his torpid knight to take Leonard's bishop—Leonard had been prepared for the swap since Emilio depended more on his bishops—and now all pretense of formal defensive and offensive positions on the board melted away in a chaos of oddly placed pieces. Their games, so formal at the outset, almost always degraded into amateur play this way.

"It's an age of treatises at least," said Emilio Gabriel Fernández y Figueroa.

"It's an age of *Zeitstil*," Leonard said sharply.

Emilio knew the context of the phrase—"the style of the times"—and they'd discussed it more than once. The German intellectual Ernst Jünger had used that phrase in his *Kaukasische Aufzeichnungnen* secret notebooks during Hitler's reign. Leonard despised the memory of Jünger—at least the World War II Jünger rather than the more outspoken Cold War Jünger—because the German had, as Leonard had, decided it was enough to secretly despise and ridicule Hitler rather than openly oppose tyranny. *Zeitstil*—"the style of the times"—was Jünger's way of describing the use of euphemism and double-talk by those in power to wreck the very language that those in power had usurped. Jünger had seen it in 1930s and '40s Germany; Leonard had watched it during his lifetime in America. Neither had acted.

"*LTI*," whispered Emilio. It stood for *Lingua tertii imperii*— Jünger's code phrase, borrowed from Victor Klemperer, for "Language of the Third Empire" and a bitter scholarly pun. "It has always been with us."

Leonard shook his head. His knights were advancing against Emilio's scattered defenses now.

"Not always. Not like this."

"So your new *War and Peace* would have neither real war nor real peace in it, my friend. Only the confusion of our era and its language."

"Yes," said Leonard. Emilio had attempted defense by rook and now Leonard's bishop swept across the board to take that rook.

"*Solitudinem faciunt, pacem appellant,*" said Emilio.

"Yes," Leonard said again. The first time he'd heard that quote from Tacitus—"They make a desert and call it peace"—he'd been a freshman in college and the four words had struck him in the forehead like a fist. They still did.

"Check," said Leonard. "Checkmate."

"Ah, yes, very nice, very nice," muttered Emilio. He stubbed out his cigarette and lit a new one, leaning back and crossing his arms. "Something is bothering you, my friend. Your grandson?"

Leonard took three slow breaths and began rearranging the pieces for a new game before answering.

"Yes. Val's missed school all this week—I get the autocalls from the high school—and he comes in during the wee hours, sleeps late, and won't talk to me. He's not the boy he used to be."

"Perhaps he is becoming the man he is going to be," Emilio said softly.

"I hope not," said Leonard. "This is a dark phase for him. He's angry, resentful at everything—especially me—and, I think, using a lot of flashback."

"You've found the vials?"

"No. I just have a strong feeling he's doing the drug with his friends."

The two old men had discussed flashback many times. How could they not? Emilio insisted that he had never tried it; he preferred memory to a false, chemical reliving of things. Besides, he said, when a man is in his eighties, he cannot give up time from real living for so many minutes of "reliving." Leonard had admitted that he'd used flashback a few times, years before, but didn't like how it made him feel. Nor, he admitted, were there any people or times so important to him that he would pay so much money to relive his time with them. "One of the benefits—or drawbacks, perhaps—of being married four times," he'd said to Emilio.

Now Leonard expected to hear something philosophical from his older Mexican friend, perhaps consoling, but instead Emilio said, "A local spanic girl, Maria Hernandez, was raped yesterday while on her way to school. She had a—doubtful—reputation, but her father and brothers and the local *reconquista* militia have vowed to kill the boys who did it."

"The boys?" asked Leonard. His voice was so hollow that it seemed to echo in his own ears.

"A gang of eight or nine anglo boys," said Emilio. "Almost certainly one of these flashgangs we hear about every day now. They did it so they could *re*do it over and over."

Leonard licked his lips. "If you're thinking Val...no, not possible. Not Val. As angry and troubled as he is...no, not Val. Not rape. Never."

Emilio peered at his fellow academic and chess partner with sad eyes. "The girl—Maria—knew one of the boys who raped her. An anglo student from her school who likes to call himself Billy the Kid. A certain William Coyne."

Professor Emeritus George Leonard Fox thought that he might be physically ill. He'd met very few of Val's friends over the five years since Nick had sent his grandson to live with him, but the always smiling, respectful, courteous, and, somehow, Leonard knew from forty years of teaching, Eddie Haskell–devious Billy Coyne had been one who'd been to the house often.

"I think I have to get Val out of this city," said Leonard. Emilio had moved his white pawn forward, starting the second game, but Leonard wasn't focusing on it.

"*Sí*, it might be a good idea, my friend. Do you have the money for the airfare?"

Leonard laughed bitterly. "With fares now going for more than a million new bucks per ticket for a Los Angeles–to-Denver flight? Hardly."

"His father, perhaps? He was able to pay the boy's fare here five years ago."

Leonard shook his head. "Nick used almost all of my daughter's life-insurance money to buy that ticket."

"But he was a policeman…"

"*Was*," said Leonard. "He's nothing more than a flashback addict now. I used to have Val phone him monthly, but now Val doesn't want to speak to his father and Nick doesn't return my calls when I leave a message. I think he's forgotten that he has a son."

"Are there other relatives?"

Lost in thought, Leonard shook his head again. "You know about *my* family, Emilio. Four marriages over all those years but only three daughters. Dara dead in that Denver car accident. Kathryn married that French Muslim and moved to Paris more than twenty years ago—she's lost in dhimmitude there. Under the veil, as they say. I haven't heard from her at all in fifteen years. Eloise calls me from New Orleans three times a year—always to borrow money. She and her husband are both flash addicts. Neither has a job. The three ex-wives I loved are dead; the one I learned to hate—and who always hated me—is alive and rich and wouldn't take a phone call from me, much less my grandson from another wife."

"So," said Emilio, "the father."

"Yes. The father. Val says that he hates his father—when he says anything at all about him—but it would still be for the best, I think. And it would only be for eleven months until Val goes into the army. This city is getting too dangerous for the boy."

Emilio was looking at Leonard with a mournful expression. "It may soon be too dangerous for you as well, my friend. You should both go. Soon. Very soon."

Leonard blinked out of his reverie, all thoughts of chess gone. "What are you telling me, Emilio? What do you know?"

The older man sighed, raised his ivory-handled cane from where it was propped against their table, and leaned his weight on it. "The forces of La Raza and *reconquista* are very restless. There may be an effort to seize all power in Los Angeles soon."

Leonard laughed out of sheer surprise. The two rarely discussed politics per se. "Seize power?" he said too loudly. "Don't the spanics already run everything in L.A. except a few neighborhoods? Isn't it already a *law* that the mayor must be spanic?"

"Spanic, yes. But not true *reconquista*, Leonard. Not governing all of Los Angeles as a province of Nuevo Mexico. This is...coming."

Leonard could only stare. Finally he said, "That would mean civil war in the streets."

"Yes."

"How much...how much time do we have?"

Emilio leaned more heavily on his cane, his doleful expression becoming even sadder. Leonard was reminded of his Cervantes and the Knight of the Woeful Countenance.

"If you and your grandson can go, you should go...soon," whispered Emilio. He took a business card and a beautiful fountain pen from his pocket and wrote something on the card in Spanish and handed it across the table. Leonard could see that the card showed only Emilio's name and an address about two miles east of Echo Park—he'd never asked Emilio where he lived—and a brief handwritten sentence telling anyone who read the note to allow this man to pass, that he was a friend, and to convey him to the address on the card. The signature was *Emilio Gabriel Fernández y Figueroa.*

"But how?" asked Leonard, folding the card carefully and setting it in his billfold. "How?"

"There are the convoys, both the eighteen-wheeler truck convoys that sometimes carry paying passengers and the groups of motorists who band together."

"I don't own a car." Leonard was feeling the kind of vertigo that he'd always thought must assail a man just before a stroke or massive coronary. The heat of the September sun was suddenly too much to bear.

"I know."

"The checkpoints and roadblocks..."

"Come see me at that address when you are certain that the two of you are leaving," Emilio said in Castilian Spanish. "Something may be arranged."

Leonard set his hands flat on the concrete chess table and stared at the liver spots and raised veins, at the knuckles swollen with arthritis. Were these *his* hands? How could they be?

"Do you remember what the Roman legionnaire Flaminius Rufus said about the City of the Immortals in Borges's story 'The Immortal'?" Emilio asked, speaking in English again.

"Flaminius Rufus? I...no. I mean, yes, I remember the story, but I don't...no."

"Borges had his legionnaire say that the city is 'so horrible that its mere existence...contaminates the past and the future and in some way even jeopardizes the stars.'"

Leonard stared at the older man. He had no idea what Emilio was talking about.

"That is how the Nuevo Mexico *reconquista* warriors view the remaining gringo and Asian parts of Los Angeles, my friend," said Emilio. "There will be much blood shed. And soon. And if your grandson had anything to do with the rape of Maria Hernandez, he will not live long enough even to see the shedding of this blood throughout the City of Angels. Get out if you can, Leonard. Take your grandson. *Go.*"

1.04

Denver — Saturday, Sept. 11

"Y OU GOING TO sit out there drinking beer and looking at the stars all night or come in to bed?"

Dara's voice drifts out through the screen door to the tiny veranda where Nick sits looking up through the gaps in the old Siberian elms toward the tiny patch of visible late-summer sky. The night is rich with insect sounds, TV and stereo noises from the surrounding houses, and the occasional scream of sirens from distant Colfax Avenue.

"Third choice," says Nick. "You come out and sit on my lap while I teach you some of the constellations."

"I'm too fat to sit on anyone's lap," says Dara but she comes out through the squeaky screen door.

She is fat...for Dara...late in her eighth month of pregnancy and showing it. She's carrying another can of Coors but hands it to Nick. She's been very careful during her pregnancy.

Nick pats his lap but she kisses him on the forehead and sits in the old metal lawn chair next to him. She looks up and says softly, "I don't see many stars, much less any constellations."

"You have to let your eyes adapt to the dark awhile, kiddo."

"Not very dark here with all the city lights, is it? Wouldn't you like to live in the country—the mountains somewhere—where the stars are clear and so you could buy that astronomical telescope you've been ogling in your catalogue?"

"We'd go nuts in the country," says Nick, pulling the tab off the cold beer and setting the tab next to him on the chair rather than dropping it in the dark. He's proud of how neat their little backyard and veranda are. "Besides, city cops have to live in the city. It's the law." He sips and says, "But yes, I'd love to have a telescope and the dark skies of some high valley, say up by Estes Park. There's always the glow from the Front Range, but surrounding peaks or high foothills to the east could block out a lot of that."

"Maybe Santa Claus will remember you want a telescope," Dara says. She's still looking at the sky. A police helicopter is tacking back and forth over the rooftops.

Nick shakes his head adamantly. "No. Too expensive. There are a hundred things we can use that amount of money for that are more important...*if* I get the overtime this fall to earn the money."

"You will," Dara says sadly. He knows she hates it when he works weekends and late nights, even though the union-earned overtime pay is so important to them. But *this* weekend—it's Friday night—*this* weekend Nick is free and will spend it with her.

Wishing his former self would quit looking at the goddamned stars and would turn his head to look again at Dara in the soft light coming out through the kitchen windows and screen door—even while knowing to the second when *the former-Nick will do that— Nick realized why he so often chose this particular weekend when Dara was so pregnant to revisit whenever he had a forty-eight-hour vial. There will be sex, of sorts (and very sweet in its preconjugal heavy-petting way), but that was not the reason. It was just the simplicity of their time together that particular weekend, only weeks before Val was born and things changed so much, and the fact that every summer night during this relived time, Nick will go to sleep with his head resting on Dara's swollen breasts.*

"You would have been happier as an astronomer, Nicholas." Dara's voice is sleepy, relaxed. It stirs Nick as it always has.

"You mean *you'd* be happier if I were an astronomer rather than a cop." He sips his beer and looks for Aldebaran. A slight breeze stirs the leaves of their elms and the larger leaves of their neighbor's linden trees. Their not-yet-brittle sound is part of the late-summer night.

"Well," says Dara, "if you were an astronomer, we'd be living on a mountaintop somewhere, maybe in Hawaii, and far away from all this." Nick turns...

Exactly when Nick knew he would.

...and looks at his wife and sets his large hand on her much-larger abdomen.

"I don't think you'd want to be living on top of a volcano in Hawaii when your due date gets here, kiddo, with the closest hospital and obstetrician two miles lower and an island away."

Nick regrets the words as soon as he's said them. Dara's concern about the pregnancy, after the three miscarriages, is matched or exceeded only by his own worrying.

It'll be all right, thought the Nick floating both inside and above this moment. He faintly sensed—or imagined he sensed—his other flashback-selves thinking much the same thing at the same instant, although usually the flashback "viewer" could not register the presence of himself on previous visits. Certainly he couldn't overhear his other flashback-self's thoughts the way he could feel and share the then-Nick's thoughts and emotions.

"I'm a good cop, Dara," says Nick, embarrassed by what he said about the hospital and obstetrician, but defensive all the same. "A really good cop."

Dara puts her small hand atop his large one on her belly. "You probably would have been a good astronomer, my Nicholas. A *really* good astronomer. But the stars are objects of beauty which inspire wonder..."

"Like you, sweetums," jokes Nick, trying to derail her from what he's sure she's going to say.

"...which inspire wonder," repeats Dara firmly, not wanting to joke around. "While the objects of *your* profession—the perps, the addicts, the witnesses, too many of the other cops, even some of the victims and lawyers and jurists—just inspire disgust and cynicism and despair. You should have realized when you got out of college that you're too sensitive to be a cop, Nick. You enjoy surface parts of it—the irony mixed with adrenaline, I think, and some of the other cops, and being a good cop yourself—but underneath, it all eats at you like battery acid. It always will."

Nick removes his hand and sips his beer. The helicopter has been joined by a second one and the two move across the area north of the botanic gardens in a searchlight grid pattern. The searchlights change from looking like two blind men's white canes thrashing in the dark to an inverted, mini-version of searchlights in World War II Berlin or London. All that's lacking, Nick thinks, is a B-17 or Heinkel bomber caught in the converging beams. The searchlights and aircraft's navigation lights occlude the stars and the noise from the two choppers echoes from the brick homes and trees all down their street and along the alley lined with tiny, sagging, century-old garages from the 1920s.

Nick resents the machines' intrusion. Besides taking the entire weekend off, he's had the almost unheard-of Friday afternoon off and spent it—

—And shared it with the older Nick hovering, hearing, feeling, experiencing

—mowing the yard in the heat and clipping hedges and the drooping branches of his neighbor's untended trees and fixing the hinges of the ancient garage's doors and puttering around the house near Dara. She's also had the rare Friday off—she works as an executive assistant in the assistant district attorney's office—and she's spent the day catching up on house stuff and baby-preparation stuff while Nick mows, fixes, mends, and generally gets in her way. He's wearing his oldest, most comfortable chinos and short-sleeved denim shirt and the sneakers pollocked with white paint from their recent painting of what will be the baby's room and Dara's wearing a light blue maternity top and old capri pants, both so passed down that she'd never go out the front door with them on.

66

But several times that afternoon she's come out the back door carrying a glass of cold lemonade and—once, surprisingly, perfectly—fresh-baked chocolate chip cookies for her sweaty husband.

It's the only afternoon or evening in weeks that Nick hasn't carried a pistol in a holster on his left hip.

Nick Bottom loves their home and neighborhood and, he knows, so does Dara. This part of the city southwest of the Denver Botanic Gardens and south of Cheesman Park consists of a mixture of tall, brick, Denver-square homes mixed with small brick bungalows like the one Nick and Dara had just barely been able to purchase four years earlier thanks to the police credit union.

The neighborhood is also relatively safe thanks to cops, since even though the area had been tipping over to gangs and crime after the first waves of the recession a decade earlier, some of the biggest foreclosed-on homes turning into crack houses and warrens for illegal immigrants from the Mideast, older cops and detectives on the DPD had begun moving into the area in the second decade of the new century. That had brought more cops with their young families, and more stability. Even in the modern era—Dara's pregnancy year is being called the Year of Clear Vision by the new administration in Washington—an era in which almost every civilian carries a handgun, the presence of scores of cops and their families has had a calming effect on this neighborhood.

And since cops and their families have always had the bad habit—shared in a mirror-image way by the Mafia—of hanging out in their spare time almost exclusively with other cops and their families, it's added a real sense of community to the neighborhood for Nick. This last May there were more than sixty people at Nick and Dara's annual Memorial Day cookout and backyard croquet tournament. A patrolman named Jerry Connors, whom Nick has known for years and who shares Nick's and Dara's love of old movies, had digitally projected movies onto a sheet on the side of his garage on Saturday nights and half the off-duty precinct can be found there on lawn chairs in Jerry's backyard, drinking beer and waiting for the goofs and continuity errors—like the kid extra in the background in a Mount Rushmore cafeteria scene from Hitchcock's *North by Northwest* who sticks his fingers in both ears *before* Eva Marie Saint reaches for the semiauto in her purse to shoot Cary Grant—that Jerry loves to tell everyone about before the movies begin.

And Jerry also asks the pertinent philosophical questions for the cops and other neighbors in their lawn chairs to ponder during each film, such as—*Are James Mason and his number-one spy guy, Martin Landau, gay and hot for each other, or what? I mean, listen to Landau-as-Leonard's little speech about his woman's intuition and Mason saying "Why, Leonard, I do believe you're jealous"*...

Nick hopes their neighborhood will be a good place for their son or daughter to grow up. (He and Dara sometimes think that they're the only expectant parents in the city—maybe in the state or nation—who've repeatedly turned down the ultrasound, gene-scan, and other modern ways of knowing their kid's gender before birth.)

"Aren't you going to tell me your story?" says Dara.

Nick has to blink his way up and out of his I-love-my-house-and-neighborhood reverie. How many beers has he had this afternoon and evening anyway?

Not enough to dull your passion later tonight, thought the watching Nick.

"What story?" asks Nick in the real time of the summer Friday night from sixteen years and one month earlier.

"The story about your uncle Wally buying you that little telescope in Chicago and how it was the most precious thing you ever owned."

Nick snaps a glance at Dara, but she's smiling, not mocking, and now she takes his free hand in hers again. He shifts the beer to his left hand.

"Well...it was...," he says lamely. "The most precious thing I owned, I mean. For years."

"I know," Dara is whispering. "Tell me the part about how you tried to see the stars from the tenement landing in Chicago."

"It wasn't a tenement, kiddo." Nick sips the rest of his beer and vows to make it his last one for the evening. "Uncle Wally's apartment in Chicago was just a...you know...apartment in a neighborhood that had gone from Irish to Polish to mostly black."

"But you'd been visiting your uncle for two weeks...," prompts Dara.

Nick smiles. "I'd been visiting my uncle for two weeks—he was a cookie salesman, formerly an A and P manager, and my old man sent me to Chicago for two weeks every summer. I loved it."

"So you'd been visiting your uncle for two weeks," repeats Dara, smiling.

Nick makes a fist and hits her lightly on the knee. Then he takes her hand back. "So I'd been visiting for almost all of my two weeks and we used to go walking on Madison Street in the evening, a few blocks from his little third-floor apartment, and every time we'd walk past what I thought was this camera and electronics store—it was really a pawnshop—I'd ask to stop so we could admire this little telescope in the window. Not a real astronomical telescope, you understand, just the little kind that the captain of a ship would have used centuries ago, with tiny black tripod legs..."

"So on your last night in Chicago," Dara prompts again.

"Hey! You going to let me tell this or what?"

She sets her head against his shoulder.

"So on my last night in Chicago—it turned out to be the last time I ever saw my uncle, the only member of my family I knew outside my old man and mother, because Wally died of a massive coronary two months after I went back to Denver that summer—anyway, my last night in Chicago, after Wally and I had washed and dried the dishes—he was a bachelor, you know—and I was in the dining room packing my clothes into my little bag on the daybed where I slept, Wally called me out to the landing and..."

"Voilà!" says Dara, sounding truly happy.

"Voilà. The telescope. I couldn't believe it. It was the

coolest thing that anyone'd ever bought me, and it wasn't even close to my birthday or Christmas or anything. So we set it up on its little tripod legs on a chair propped on top of a garbage can there on the rear third-floor landing and I tried to find some stars or planets to look at, I was nuts about space at that age…"

"Which was?" asks Dara, her voice muffled against his arm.

"Age? About nine, I guess. Anyway, the city lights blocked out most of the stars, but we found one bright one shining through the murk. I later figured out it was Sirius. And Jupiter, too. It was bright that night."

"Way back in the nineteen-nineties," murmurs Dara. "Who knew they had modern stuff like telescopes way back then?"

"You're just jealous," says Nick. It's a running joke between them. Dara is a decade younger, born in the 1990s. Nick enjoys reminding her of all the neat things she missed in that decade. *Like Ronald Reagan's swan song? Bill Clinton's blow job?* she'd ask innocently. But they both sometimes find it odd that he was already sneaking peeks at porn on the Internet in the year she was born.

"I love the Uncle Wally telescope story," says Dara, rubbing her forehead against his shoulder as a cat would. Nick suspects that she has another headache.

"And I love…," begins Nick.

"Me?"

"The Friday Night Creature Feature on TCM," finishes Nick, standing and pulling her next to him. "And it's gonna start streaming in three minutes."

She laughs but sets her entire body against him, her hand soft against his left hip where his holster and gun usually sit. The helicopters have gone, their noise replaced by more distant and less urgent sirens and sounds.

Nick tosses the beer can in the recyclable bin by the door and sets both arms around her, pulling her tight to his chest. The top of her head doesn't even come up to his chin. Her late-pregnancy-full breasts feel strange against him after so many thousands of hugs in the past two years. Nick realizes, not for the first or thousandth time, how young she is. And how lucky he is.

"Do me one favor," whispers Dara.

You'll like this favor, thought Nick from where he floated, feeling his wife against him but also paying attention to the ambient sounds and movements he hadn't consciously noted that night sixteen years and one month earlier. The sudden breeze that moved the high branches of those miserable Siberian elms, just waiting to dump their countless leaves in the yard for raking and bagging in a month or two. The Bakers' TV blaring too loudly again from two houses away. The cat moving like a four-legged tightrope walker along the high fence back by the alley . . .

"I want you to . . ."

". . . get up, Bottom-san. Get up *now*. Wake up, damn you."

Somehow Dara is no longer hugging Nick but lifting him off the ground, shaking him fiercely. Nick can feel the bulk of her pregnancy against him as she shakes him.

Someone jammed a needle into his thigh.

"Hey, watch it, kiddo!" shouted Nick, pulling away from Dara in shock.

Dara lifted him higher, shook him harder. No.

Nick reached for his gun. It wasn't there.

Someone tore the IV needle out of his arm. Another needle was jammed into the same thigh as before. Nick felt the ice-water-in-the-veins shock of T4B2T counterflash throughout his body and he screamed.

"Mickey! Lawrence!"

Mickey was nowhere to be seen in the glowstick gloom. Lawrence the bouncer was down, his massive, armored body out cold and facedown and filling the narrow aisle between cots.

Dara against him, hugging him in the summer night . . .

Nick fought to slide back into flashback reality but the pain in his arm and thigh and the T4B2T in his veins kept him up, out, and away from her. He cried out again.

"Shut up," said Sato. The security chief was carrying him over his shoulder through the darkened warehouse as easily as Nick used to carry his son to bed when Val was a toddler. A few flashers came up and out of their fugue to peer angrily at the intrusion—being left alone and undisturbed was what flashcaves were *about*—but most slept and twitched on, oblivious.

Where was Mickey? Didn't he and Lawrence the bouncer keep a shotgun handy for just this sort of invasion?

Nick's arms and legs were tingling painfully from the T4B2T, fizzing inside like limbs that had fallen asleep for hours, so Nick couldn't use them yet—couldn't kick, couldn't even make a fist.

The September night air was chilly and there was a light drizzle. Nick realized that it was dark outside as Sato carried him down the alley, out of the alley to a side street with cars parked along the rain-filled gutter. Was it the same night? How long had he been under?

Sato beeped open the front passenger-side door of an old Honda electric, dumped Nick into the front seat, and then quickly handcuffed Nick's right hand, running the short cuff chain through a naked steel bolt in the overhead door frame before he clicked the left cuff tight.

The pain scouring through his awakening arms and hands made Nick feel like he was being crucified. He screamed again just as Sato slammed the door shut and walked around to the driver's side.

Nick shouted and Sato ignored him as he drove the Honda up Speer Boulevard in a cold rain that was coming down more heavily by the minute. The streets were almost empty. Even the thousands of homeless along the sunken Cherry Creek riverside walking paths and bikepaths were huddled in their shanties and boxes under the street-level overpasses. A dull lightening of the sky in the east told Nick that it was almost dawn. How long had he been under? Just the flash of that Friday afternoon with Dara back in the Year of Clear Vision and into that evening and night. No more than eight hours. *Damn.*

Nick shut up when Sato turned west on Colfax.

The Jap couldn't...he can't be...he wouldn't...

The Jap was. Crossing over I-25, Sato turned south on Federal Boulevard and then east onto West 23rd Street, then south onto Bryant—a narrow, barricaded street running along the bluff's edge above I-25 with ABSOLUTELY NO UNAUTHORIZED ADMITTANCE signs to either side and above.

"No!" cried Nick but Sato ignored him, stopping just long enough to show his ID to the automatic station and then to drive through the CMRI-torus tunnel. Nick felt his atoms being shifted into a different spin dimension—twice now in twenty-four hours—and wondered if this amount of exposure was unhealthy.

Far below and to their left, I-25 disappeared. To prevent conventional explosives damage, regular traffic was routed off I-25 two miles in either direction and had to bounce through what Californians called surface streets through the railyard district. VIP cars had single north- and southbound lanes in blastproof tubes two hundred feet under the surface.

He almost laughed then at his own concern, given the black-dipped edifice that was filling the windshield. The next checkpoint had the slanted one-way spikes rising from the empty access street's pavement, so once beyond that point there was literally no turning back.

"No," Nick said again, dully.

"Yes," said Sato. But he stopped the car.

The huge structure blotting out the cloudy sunrise in front of them had once been called Invesco Field at Mile High.

This "new" football stadium, opened in 2001, had replaced the old Mile High Stadium that had hosted football, soccer, and baseball games since 1948. The wavy top edge of the stadium had caused execs in Invesco, some long-defunct company that had seized naming rights for the new stadium in 2001, to sneeringly call the new home to the now equally defunct Denver Broncos "the Diaphragm." The place was built to hold more than 76,000 football fans and around 50,000 doped-out screamers for the rock concerts that used to be staged there. On August 28, 2008, Invesco Field at Mile High—a clumsy name that no one except announcers under strict orders had used even then—had reached an apotheosis of sorts when more than 84,000 people had crowded in (and a billion or so more had been present via early high-def TV) to listen to candidate

Barack Obama give his nomination acceptance speech as the last act to the spectacle that had been the 2008 Democratic Convention held nearby at the so-called Pepsi Center here in Denver.

Now Invesco, Pepsi, the Broncos, the NFL, public sporting events, and that iteration of the Democratic Party were all defunct, and so, of course, was the man nominated to the chant of Hope and Change that night more than twenty-eight years earlier.

No one who'd gone to those football games or attended the nominee's media bacchanalia of an acceptance speech in those naïve days would recognize Mile High Stadium today. The stadium, now the Department of Homeland Security Detention Center, looked as if it had been dipped in a hundred thousand gallons of 10W40-weight oil. This black foil-fabric, Nick knew, stretched across the top of the formerly roofless stadium, turning the 1.7 million square feet of space—rooms, corridors, ramps, steps, room for more than 76,000 seats, and hundreds of boxes and skyboxes—into a dimly lighted pit on even the brightest of days. The north entrance to the detention center was a concrete-lipped and steel-doored black cloaca large enough for two trucks to pass in opposite directions.

There was no light coming from the 150-foot-tall structure this dark morning.

No, that wasn't quite true; over the black oval entrance to the DHSDC was a giant blue demon-horse, red veins standing out on its belly, its hooves of razor-sharp steel, its demonic eyes firing two laser beams from its distorted horse-demon face. The beams cut through the moving fog—or perhaps low wisps of clouds—and whipped back and forth until they converged on the Honda, then on Nick Bottom, and stopped.

"Tell me everything you know about the horse, Bottom-san," Sato commanded softly.

The horse!? thought Nick, his thoughts scampering back and forth like rats trapped in a box. *Who cares about the fucking horse?* He rattled the short chain of his handcuffs against the doorframe D-bolt.

But then Nick heard his own voice answering in dulled, stupid tones.

"Originally the stadium horse was Bucky the Bronco. Bucky was twenty-seven feet tall and was cast and enlarged from an original mold of Roy Rogers's horse, Trigger, when Trigger was rearing up on his hind legs. Roy Rogers was a TV and movie cowboy around the middle of the last century. Roy allowed them to make the cast from his mold of Trigger before this version of the stadium was built only if the city and stadium owners promised that they wouldn't name the new horse 'Trigger.' The people voted, I think it was in the nineteen-seventies, and named this bigger Trigger 'Bucky the Bronco.'"

Why the goddamned hell am I telling Sato all this crap? wondered Nick. *I didn't even know I knew all this garbage...* He tried to clamp his jaws shut to stop the flow of stupid trivia but found that he literally couldn't keep his mouth shut.

"But that's not Bucky the Bronco," Nick droned on, straining to use his handcuffed left hand to point to the blue demon-stallion above the entrance to the detention center. "That insane blue horse was a sculpture that a New Mexico artist named Luis Jiménez—he wasn't much of an artist, mostly a guy who did fiberglass shells for spanic low-riders—made under commission to the Denver International Airport about forty years ago. The only reason this Jiménez won the bid was that the tens of millions of dollars set aside to buy art for the new airport had been turned into one big grab bag for minorities—spanics, blacks, Indians, you name it. Everybody but the Asians in Colorado. I guess they didn't qualify as minorities. Too smart. Anyway, the mayor at the time was black and his wife headed the committee that handed out all the art projects and all that counted was that the winners were minorities, not real artists, certainly not *good* artists."

Nick turned his face away from Sato and banged his forehead against the passenger-side window. The red laser spots moved with him—now on his forearms, now on his chest.

"Please continue, Bottom-san," said Sato. "Tell me *everything* you know about this horse."

75

Nick tried to drown out the sound of his own voice by squeezing his forearms against his ears, but he could hear himself through bone conduction.

"This blue stallion is thirty-two feet tall, bigger than the original Bucky the Bronco. The people who live in the dead artist's little town in Nuevo Mexico think the horse is accursed. It fell on the sculptor in his studio and killed him before he'd finished it. It was installed at DIA in 2008 and the contract stipulated that it had to be kept there for ten years, but as soon as that contract was up, the airport and city got rid of it. It shook up people arriving in Denver for the first time and all of us locals hated it. Homeland Security replaced Bucky the Bronco with this mad, haunted stallion and moved him to this entrance when they moved into Mile High about twelve years ago. The lasers serve a security function. But they're going to blind me if one of these fucking beams gets me in the retina."

"Is that all you know about the blue horse?" asked Sato.

"Yes!" screamed Nick. He shook his head wildly and strained more against the cuffs. Broad blood spatters joined the laser spots across the chest of his sweatshirt. "You fuck, you *fuck!* That second needle in my thigh was Pfizer TruTel, wasn't it?"

"Of course," said Sato. "If I gave you another chance at the investigation, Bottom-san, would you betray us again and abandon the investigation to go back under flashback at your earliest opportunity?"

"Yeah, of course I would," said Nick. "You betcha, Mr. Moto."

"Would you kill me if you got the chance, Bottom-san?"

"Yes, yes, absolutely," screamed Nick. "Oh, you *fuck.*"

"Do you honestly believe there is a chance that you can solve the mystery of Keigo Nakamura's murder, Bottom-san?"

"Not a chance in hell," Nick heard himself answer.

The security chief's black gaze looked appraisingly at Nick, and Nick stared back. Finally he managed, "Why are you taking me to the DHSDC?"

Everyone in Colorado knew that a lot of people went into

the black-oil cake of Mile High detention center, but almost no one came out.

Sato's voice was as flat as ever. "Bottom-san, you betrayed one of the nine Federal Advisors to the United States of America. You violated your word and your contract. Perhaps you planned to assassinate Hiroshi Nakamura."

"What?!?" screamed Nick, jerking at his restraints again until blood from his wrists spattered the windshield and dashboard.

Sato shrugged. "They will find the truth after sufficient interrogation."

Nick could feel his eyes straining in their sockets, like the mad, blue stallion's. Two wide red dots continued to move across his spattered chest like the bloody fingers of a blind lover. "You're as crazy as that fucking horse, Sato. You want to disappear me into Homeland Security hell here so you can declare the reopened investigation a failure. *Then* your boss will give you permission to commit *seppuku*."

Sato said nothing.

You can't get away with this, Nick started to shout like some minor character in a cheap TV series but with the help of Pfizer TruTel it came out, "And you *will* get away with it. Nakamura'll believe you and you'll get to kill yourself to atone for your failure and I'll rot here in the dark for fucking ever."

Sato looked at him another long minute, then nodded to himself and held up his NICC. Both lasers from the blue stallion's eyes flicked to the card, then one went back to Nick while the other continued to read the card.

Sato turned the Honda around on the wet street and drove back through the CMRI tunnel and down the lanes through the empty, littered gravel and wet stone wasteland where the parking lot and old neighborhood used to be around Mile High Stadium.

"I think, Bottom-san," said Hideki Sato, "that we should visit the scene of the crime."

2.01

The 10 and La Cienega, Los Angeles— Saturday, Sept. 11

BILLY COYNE AND Val were leading the other boys up the lashed-bamboo scaffolding to the Saturday Open Air Market on the collapsed section of the 10 when suddenly from the slab above and from the city below there came the unmistakable sound of hundreds of AK-47s firing into the air, amplified cries from *muezzin* calling out to the faithful from scores of L.A.'s minarets, church bells in the city ringing, and shouts from the Open Air Market they were heading for, as well as from the shaded surface streets below, of *"Allahu akbar! Allahu akbar!"*

All of the boys froze in their climbing, thinking that it was a *hajji* attack or suicide bomber.

Then Val realized that this was Los Angeles celebrating the events of that old holiday called 9-11, September 11, 2001, the date—as Val had been taught in school—of the beginning of successful resistance to the old imperialist American hegemony and a turning point in the creation of the New Caliphate and other hopeful signs of the New World Order. He knew that the Christian churches were ringing their bells in their annual attempt to join in the celebrations of *hajji*s at scores of Los

Angeles's mosques and to show their solidarity, understanding, and forgiveness.

Behind the climbing boys, in the direction of L.A.'s downtown, someone was sending red and orange rockets to crash and explode against the glass sides of the old city towers in an effort to enhance the citywide celebration. All eight boys climbed off the scaffolding onto the I-10 slab and watched the downtown show for a moment. Toohey, Cruncher, and Dinjin were cheering until they noticed that the older guys in the group weren't. Then they shut up, but still pumped their fists whenever a new rocket exploded against the side of a stumpy skyscraper.

As they turned back toward the market stalls, Val was reminded why there'd been so much shooting from the slab; a majority of the so-called gypsy vendors here were *hajji*—or at least of Mideastern descent—and most of the high-end stuff they were selling came into the country with the *hajji*s during their flights back from their homes in Pakistan or Indonesia or the Euro-Caliphates or that mother of all Caliphate nations, the Greater Islamic Republic, which curved across the former countries of the Mideast—Lebanon, Israel, Egypt, Saudi Arabia, Tunisia, Sudan—like a scimitar's blade. Unlike all the other kids he knew, Val had enjoyed geography in school and sometimes brought up maps on his phone's virtual screen so he could study them. They changed so quickly.

He also liked learning about history, but he blamed that on his grandfather. Leonard just gabbled on about it so much that some of it *had* to rub off on Val when he was younger.

Val did wonder how—at a time when even domestic flights within what was left of the U.S.A. cost millions of new bucks—these towelheads could afford to fly across the oceans so frequently. *Probably 'cause of the profit on the chillshit crap they're selling right here in front of you, stupid,* thought Val.

He had to admit that most of it was good chillshit crap.

The double line of market stalls ran about a hundred yards and the long space between the brightly canopied tables was already filled with early shoppers. Coyne nudged Val and nodded in each direction and Val understood that the older boy was pointing out the two pairs of LAPD cops in full black body armor at each end of the market and the mini-drones buzzing and hovering overhead. The cops' blunt, black automatic weapons reminded Val of why they were there.

But first they followed Toohey and Monk and the other younger boys to some of the fun stalls.

A few of the tables had women behind them and most of them wore just hijabs, although others, sitting behind the bearded men at the tables, were in full burkas. Val noticed the bright blue eyes of one young woman in a burka and could swear that she was Cindy from his Wednesday Social Responsibility class. He'd watched her eyes in class often enough.

"Chillshit stuff!" cried Sully. "Double chillshit stuff!"

The boys were clustered around the interactive-T-shirt tables. This was serious clothing, most of it costing $500,000 new bucks and up, but Coyne always seemed to have money on his card, so everyone in the gang looked.

An old, black-bearded *hajji* was holding up one of the longer and more expensive black T-shirts. The 3D image of Jeffrey Dahmer (an old serial killer who'd been having quite a resurgence of public and scholarly interest since the HBO series starring Gillie Gibson had started streaming) ran full length down the back of the black T-shirt. The cannibal (the real Dahmer, not the actor) was in the act of fucking one of the empty eye sockets in the skull of one of his victims. As Gene D. approached the offered shirt, Dahmer stopped his frenzied motion and, still holding the skull against his crotch, looked back over his shoulder at Gene D., Dahmer's head seeming to emerge from the black cloth like a face rising out of a lake of oil, while the AI in the fabric said in a voice from hell, "You...yeah, you, the kid with the pimples in the red shirt...I got an eyehole free here. You want to join me?"

Gene D. jumped backward and the seven other boys and twenty or thirty nearby shoppers roared with laughter. The old women in burkas chuckled and turned away modestly while lifting their veils higher. The *hajji* holding the shirt showed missing teeth through the black barbed wire of his beard.

"This is the one I'm interested in," said Coyne and pointed to a T-shirt in the back. One of the *hajji*'s teenaged assistants, a kid no older than Val with wispy attempts at a beard and wearing a coolshit *hajji* hat and bandolier over his vest and khaki shirt, held up the shirt Coyne wanted to see.

There was just a speck in the center of this T-shirt. But the speck grew larger—became a shirtless man walking toward the viewer—and pretty soon you could see the rapidly approaching man's face. Vladimir Putin.

"Oh, chillshit sweet," hummed Sully.

"Shut up, Sully," said Coyne.

Putin continued walking toward Coyne until just Czar Vladimir's powerful bare upper body and muscled arms and head filled the back of the shirt. Then just Putin's face. Then just Putin's narrowed eyes.

"God, he must be about a hundred and fifty years old," said Monk, his voice hushed in the presence of the world's longest-reigning strongman. And "strongman," with Putin, could be interpreted literally as well.

"Just eighty," said Val without thinking about it. "He was born in nineteen fifty-two...six years before my grandfather."

"Shut up," said Coyne. "Listen."

Turning its head to squint more directly at Coyne, the Putin image said, *"Moio sudno na vozdušnoy poduške polno ugrey."* Each syllable crooked like a bullet.

Coyne laughed wildly.

Val's head snapped around. Does Coyne really understand that Russian shit? Was Billy the C's mother Russian? Val couldn't remember.

"What's it mean, Coyne, huh?" asked Monk. "What'd he say?"

Coyne waved the question away. To the Putin eyes, he said, "Vladimir Vladimirovich, *skol'ko eto stoit? Footbalka?*"

Putin's head and powerful shoulders suddenly came up and out of the shirt. Val jerked back a step. In some weird way, this was scarier than the Dahmer cannibal.

"Eight hundred thousand bucks," said Putin in thickly

accented English, smiling thinly at Coyne while shooting glances at the other boys. Toohey, Cruncher, Dinjin, Sully, Monk, and Gene D. stepped back with Val.

"New bucks," added Putin. Then smiling even more thinly, he asked Coyne, "Are you trying to hang noodle soup on my ears, *droog?*"

"*Nyet*," said Coyne with another manic laugh. "*Davajte perejdjom na 'ty*,' Vladimir Vladimirovich."

"*Poshjoi ty!*" snapped the Putin AI, laughing nastily.

Risking a brush-off from Coyne, Val said, "What's that mean?"

"It means *Fuck you*," said Coyne. His laughter was strangely like the Putin AI's.

"What did you say to him?"

"It doesn't matter." Coyne turned to the bearded *hajji*. "I'll take the Putin shirt."

The *hajji* scanned Coyne's NICC and looked at the boy with something like respect. The teenager with the bandolier folded the T-shirt and was getting out a paper bag to put it in.

"No, I'll wear it," said Coyne. Unbuttoning the blue flannel shirt he was wearing and tossing it toward the trash, the tall boy tugged on the new black T-shirt. Val noticed the 9mm Beretta tucked into the back of Coyne's jeans, but he wasn't sure if anyone else did. Coyne didn't seem to care.

"Some *krutoj paren'*," said the Putin face that now filled the front of the shirt.

"What's that mean?" whined Monk.

"*Tough guy*," answered Coyne. Pulling the fabric of the shirt up a bit so he could look down at the face, Coyne said to Putin, "You're *kljovyj blin*, old dude. *Real* coolshit. And a real *shishka*. Now shut up while we finish our shopping."

The gang of eight guys spread out so as not to be so conspicuous. Also, they were interested in different things.

Toohey, Cruncher, Dinjin, and Sully went off to see the new games pirated in from Japan, Russia, Consolidated Korea, India, and the other high-tech countries. Gene D., still blushing fiercely at being called pimply by the Dahmer AI, stalked off by himself. Monk followed Coyne when the leader walked down the row of stalls to browse expensive—nothing under a million bucks—new VR and other optics. Alone, Val slumped along the stalls, ignoring the cries from the vendors and the shoves from the crowd—not worrying that his pocket might be picked since he had no cash today anyway and had left his NICC at home.

One long table presided over by two *hajji* Afghans wearing Taliban government clothing was heaped high with fatigue jackets, combat boots, and cheap body armor from American soldiers. Dinjin and the other younger kids, who still liked to wear such crap, loved to say that this surplus stuff was all taken from dead U.S. soldiers in China and South America—and usually there was at least one blasted and bloodstained piece of dragonarmor to support such a theory—but Val was old enough to know that most of it was just stolen from the U.S. Army fighting as mercenaries for Japan and India during the long and corrupt logistics trip to the shifting front lines.

For a guy now sixteen and staring at conscription just eleven months and a few days away, Val wasn't in the least tempted to wear castoff U.S. Army or marine clothing. He'd get his real boots and uniform and fatigues and subdural bar code soon enough.

Billy Coyne's older brother, Brad, had his parents buy him out of the draft. Then Brad had gone on to join the Aryan Brotherhood and ended up in a sort of uniform anyway. Plus a lot more efficient body armor and with cooler guns than the poorly equipped U.S. soldiers were using to fight warlords and Hugonistas. (It was Brad's story that made Coyne even more respected and accepted as a leader of this pathetic little white-boy flashgang, Val knew.)

When Val had told his grandfather about Brad—at least the part about Brad and Billy's folks buying his way out of the draft—and then asked whether his grandfather could do that for him, Leonard had just stared at him as if he'd gone insane.

Sometimes Val felt sorry that he'd first thought of killing his grandfather when Coyne showed him the Beretta. After all,

Val knew that the old man didn't *mean* to be a total asshole. He was just trained that way as an academic.

Val had just come to an expensive table where different types of roll-up and fold-up and other flexible and micro-thin 3D-high-def displays were being shown off. Since this table was also being run by *hajji* "importers"—Val had long since realized that the Open Air Market was the safest place in Los Angeles to be today since there was zero chance of a suicide bomber setting his vest and himself or herself off here—they had the displays tuned to the inevitable English-language Al Jazeera stoning and beheading death channels, but they were also showing various 9-11 ceremonies around the country and around the world.

Several of the feeds were from the relatively new Shahid al-Haram Mosque which had been built on the so-called Ground Zero or World Trade Center site in New York. Val thought that the mosque was beautiful, a sort of taller, more elegant and jet-black Taj Mahal. Right now New York's mayor, the U.S. vice president, and New York's chief imam were taking turns saying hopeful things near the hole where that stupid World Trade Center had once risen and then the 9-11 Memorial and a new Freedom Tower had been attempted before both had been destroyed in turn.

It made sense to Val that the site should be the place for North America's largest mosque to rise. No one's going to attack a mosque. (Although the Greater Islamic Republic, which was Shi'ite, Leonard had explained to Val, might do so, since the Shahid al-Haram Mosque was Sunni.) Leonard had also explained to Val that *Shahid al-Haram* meant something like *Martyrs of the Holy Place*, which evidently had irritated some old-think right-wingers and die-hard American hegemonists.

But some weeks ago, Val had come into the tiny TV room in their basement apartment to find his grandfather watching some show praising the Shahid al-Haram Mosque—and two hundred other huge, new mosques currently being built or just completed in the United States (not counting the Republic of Texas, of course, which was *not* part of the U.S. and was *not* mosque-friendly)—and damned if old Leonard wasn't blubbering silently. What the fuck was *that* about?

His grandfather had been embarrassed, telling the shocked and equally embarrassed Val that he only had a head cold, but it had started Val thinking—*What if Leonard goes Alzheimer's on me? What do I do then?*

But a day later, over a rare shared microwave-zapped dinner, Leonard had gone all teachy and preachy on Val, trying to tell him all about what it had been like on the real 9-11, and all about himself—he'd been teaching The Etymology of John Keats's Ass or some such crap at the University of Colorado in Boulder and had been between wives and raising Val's three-year-old mom at the time, going to school and joining other instructors in the faculty lounge as they watched the aftermath of the martyrs' planes crashing into the Pentagon and the World Trade Center and...

Val had cut him off. Who gave the slightest sparrowfart about such ancient history? What was he, Val, supposed to do next—get all emotionally worked up about Stonewall Jackson getting killed at Gettysburg? It was all old and done and *dead*, man.

Stonewall Jackson died before the Battle of Gettysburg was Leonard's pedantic response.

Well, had been Val's withering riposte, this right-wing anti-Caliphate crap died before Leonard had gotten senile. Like all American kids, Val had studied the Q'uran since kindergarten and Islam was the Religion of Peace—any dickshit knew that. Why would Leonard get all blubbery about the beautiful Mosque of the Martyrs of the Holy Place in New York? *What did he want?* demanded Val. For them to move warmonger Greg Dubbya Bush's bones to New York and build a crypt for them there?

"George W. Bush" had been Leonard's sad response.

Then Val had gone out to be with the flashgang all that night and the next morning and the conversation was never picked up again.

But now, looking at the New York mayor and vice president

slobbering all over the scowling, bearded New York chief imam on the TV images, Val felt uneasy for reasons he couldn't quite put his finger on. Maybe it had to do with all the *hajji*s here at the open market ripping everyone off. Or maybe it was as stupid as all those American boots and uniforms being piled up and sold as if they really *had* just been stripped off dead American soldiers on some unpronounceable Chinese battlefield.

Val shook his head to chase away stupid thoughts and sidled over to the gun table—the reason they'd come here this morning—to watch from a distance as Coyne tried to make his purchase.

Coyne was the oldest and tallest and darkest of the eight of them—his attempt to grow a beard wasn't completely successful, but at least he'd achieved some good, dark stubble—and although he couldn't tamper with his NICC, he had a separate military-exemption card, originally Brad's and then fucked around with by Brad's AB buddies, that said he *was* over eighteen. Obviously, if Coyne scored with the guns he wanted, he'd have to pay cash...but he seemed to have the cash.

The *hajji* in charge of the gun table had shooed Toohey and the other boys away—the cop and DHS mini-drones were buzzing and hovering just a few hundred feet overhead—and now the bearded Iranian glowered suspiciously at Coyne. But the military-exemption card seemed to pass his scanner's inspection. When the scowling *hajji* demanded Coyne's NICC, Coyne smiled, shrugged, and said he hadn't brought it—just his army-out card and a lot of cash. He was a hunter, you see, and wanted to stock up on some new weapons before deer season was over in Idaho.

That last line was such Coyne-ish bullshit that Val had to turn his face away at the nearby table where he was pretending to inspect some VRI glasses from Brazil. It was either turn away or laugh.

The *hajji* wasn't laughing, Val could see in the mirror provided for those trying on the glasses, but neither did he appear to be buying Coyne's bullshit. Still, the bearded men in the stall didn't chase Coyne away from the table. They were letting him inspect the guns.

Coyne had been able to buy two more guns for the gang at the Old Plaza but the weapons were crap: a .38 revolver that went back to Raymond Chandler days—Val did love to read, despite himself—and a new, plastic, folding frame-grip Indonesian pistol that fired toy biodegradable .228 cartridges, the whole thing designed to sneak aboard an airliner sometime in the happy *hajji* past. Gene D. was carrying the .38 belly gun—it had a two-inch barrel—and Monk had been placated with the Indonesian toy.

Coyne hadn't yet told the gang where or how they were supposed to do this endlessly flashable hit on an important Jap, but he was insisting that they all needed weapons and that he needed at least one serious auto-flechette mini-gun. To Val, he'd whispered that he'd give him the 9mm Beretta, which pleased Val. He'd liked the heft and feel of the gun in his hand and he was still having images of shooting his old man in the belly with one of those big dum-dummed bullets.

Coyne was lifting and checking the balance of a modern black, blocky OAO Izhmash flechette-spewer. It seemed to be what the flashgang leader wanted and he'd started dickering with the *hajji* when the glowering carpet-bumper, with a quick glance at the mini-drones overhead and the four LAPD black knights now walking the length of the stalls, suddenly and angrily waved Coyne away from the table.

Coyne shrugged and slouched away. But he was grinning when Val caught up to him at the games table.

"The nasty old fudge-packer slipped me this, Val." Coyne showed him a tiny green card with the address of a street Val knew to be under another condemned slab and a pencil-scribbled *2400* on the card. "Midnight market," whispered Coyne. "Tomorrow night. Towelhead'll sell me three of those beautiful OAO fuckers—more if I have the money—and by Monday we'll be set. You sure you don't want a mini-gun?"

Val shook his head. "I like the Beretta."

Coyne grinned and punched him on the arm just as the other guys showed up.

"Hey, B.C., saw you get chased away by the *hajji* stud,"

shouted Cruncher. "When we gonna hear about when we get to zip the Nip, zap the...*ooof!*"

This last noise was as the air went out of the big, slobby boy after Coyne had punched him—not at all in a friendly way—deep in the gut. Coyne hit him again and Cruncher went down like a bag of laundry. As the other boys stepped back, Coyne flicked a fast finger up at the drones.

One of the LAPD black-armored wraiths swiveled at the sound of Cruncher hitting the pavement and spoke into his helmet mike. The three other cops also then swiveled Coyne's way, their movements smooth and oily as those of robots in a sci-fi movie, and visors snicked down as the cops magnified the scene.

Grinning broadly, Coyne showed empty palms in the cops' direction and then offered his hand to help Cruncher up. Val started laughing stupidly as if it were all just play and a few of the smarter guys in the gang followed suit. Cruncher got up, scowling, his lower lip thrust out like a sulking four-year-old's, and Coyne led the way to the nearest down-ladder, his arm around the fat boy. Just a bunch of dumbshit homies on their early-morning adventure out to the grown-ups' market.

THREE BLOCKS AWAY AND in the musty-smelling darkness under an angled, low-hanging, block-long tumbled slab of the 10 and safely out of sight or mike-range of any interested thing aerial or on foot, Coyne hit Cruncher again, this time full in the mouth.

Val heard teeth snap off and watched coldly as the heavy, stupid fat boy went down again.

"You stupid *fuck*," snarled Coyne, standing astride the fallen Cruncher. "You *fucking* stupid cunt-stupid *fuck*. Do you think this is a fucking *game?* Don't you know that you can get us all *killed?* Dropped in the ass-fucking Dodger Stadium DHSDC *hole* for the rest of our fucking lives? Do you want to be manpussy for spanic and nigger humpbugger killers for the rest of your fucking life?"

Coyne twirled, fists still clenched and face still distorted into a snarling mask, to face the others—to face everyone, Val knew, except Val—and screamed, "Do *you,* you pansyassed motherfuckers? You want to get yourself picked up by DHS and tortured or just offed, *fucking do it!* But don't do it to me, goddamn you, or I'll do it to you first, you *fuckheads!*"

Suddenly the Beretta was in Coyne's right hand. Thinking about it later, Val still couldn't see him reaching back for it, making the motion toward it. One second Coyne's hand was a fist and in the next second—the black muzzle-circle of death was moving, aiming at all of them one after the other.

Everybody except Val was babbling an apology, was swearing he wouldn't fuck up, was saying he'd never say anything where anyone could hear it. Even Cruncher was spewing apologies along with shards of his broken teeth and gobbets of blood from his pulped lips.

Everyone was talking except Val.

Coyne aimed the Beretta—*Val's* Beretta it was supposed to be—straight at Val's face. "Do *you* understand, shitstain? Are *you* going to keep your mouth shut?"

Hurt, Val could only blink and nod. He felt a strange sensation with the gun aimed at him—a crawling around his scrotum, as if his testicles wanted to crawl back up inside his body, and a sudden urge to hide behind someone, anyone, even himself.

Val heard himself say, "You haven't told us how and where we can kill a Jap yet."

Coyne smiled, slid the gun under his now attentive and grimly smiling Putin shirt, and nodded in return. He gestured everyone into a crouching circle. Even Cruncher struggled to his knees to join.

"Not *a* Jap," whispered Coyne. "*The* Jap. Daichi Omura himself. The California Advisor."

Some of the boys whistled. Cruncher tried to but just winced and touched his ruined lips and broken teeth with tentative fingers.

"Shut up," Coyne said. Everyone shut up.

"This Friday evening, they're having a big city thing rededicating the Disney Performing Arts Center down on

Grand Avenue in the city center. The spanic mayor and
everyone'll be there, but no one but the top guys and us knows
that Advisor Omura's showing up, coming down from the Green
Zone and Getty Castle in a motorcade. I know right when he'll
arrive—to the second—and where the armored limo will pull
up and which side Omura will get out of the car on and where
the bodyguards will be."

"But how could...," squeaked Dinjin and was slapped into
silence by Toohey or one of the others.

Val, still blushing with anger and embarrassment, understood. Coyne had so much money because his divorced mother
worked for the city—worked as liaison for the Advisor's office
and the city. Worked in the transportation department.

"And we'll be there waiting," said Coyne. Looking from
face to face.

Gene D. was shaking his head. "I've seen that sorta thing
on TV, B.C. And no disrespect or nothing, but...I mean...
like...we ain't going to get within ten blocks of that Performing Arts place and whatever's goin' on inside. Especially if the
Advisor's going to be there. It'd be like a pope visiting and..."

"They killed a pope not long ago," interrupted Coyne.

Gene D. nodded, shook his head, found his strand again.
"No, I mean...you know...there's going to be state troopers
and whatchamacallims...the federal guys..."

"Homeland," said a sullen Sully.

"Yeah, but no," said Gene D., "that's not who I mean.
Those other federal guys..."

"The State Department Office of Security," said Coyne,
showing everyone how patient he was being.

"Yeah. And not only them but the Jap protection guys as
well...," said Gene D. and sort of wound down. It was a pretty
impressive showing by a not very impressive kid, thought Val.

When Val spoke, he was amazed how normal—even
solid—his voice sounded, given that he'd almost pissed himself a minute or so earlier when Coyne had pointed the Beretta
at him.

"What Gene D.'s saying," said Val, "is that we couldn't get

close, and even if we did get close, we couldn't kill Omura without getting gunned down by his security, and even if we did somehow get close and kill the Advisor and not get killed ourselves, we'd never get away. The whole city would go apeshit. They'd have our faces on every sat channel before we got half a block away...which we wouldn't get anyway."

Val heard how lame that finish had been, but he left it that way and crossed his arms.

Coyne smiled. "You're absolutely right, my man. Except for one thing. Sewers. I know the sewers and how to get there and where to wait and which one to shoot from and which ones to get away in."

Toohey made a scrunchy face. "Forget it, man. I ain't crawling through shit to kill no one."

Coyne rolled his eyes. "Not shit-sewers, stupid. Storm sewers. Rain runoff sewers. The city's riddled with them."

Val again remembered the 1954 movie *Them* about the giant ants and the finale where FBI guy James Arness and his sidekick, whatshisname, chased down the ants in the storm sewers that ran into the usually dry Los Angeles River with army Jeeps and big trucks roaring down the echoing underground corridors. Val's old man had loved that movie for some stupid reason—probably because Val's mother also loved it—and when Val was little, he'd loved watching the idiot black-and-white flatfilm with both his parents, the little room in the little house smelling of popcorn and the sprung old couch crowded...

He came up out of it—the memory had been almost as compelling as a flash, but only because he *had* flashed on those experiences so many times with the drug—and said, "No, Coyne. No. It's not like the city and Jap security people don't also know about those sewers. When someone like the Advisor goes somewhere public, I've read where they weld the sewer openings closed for a mile or so around..." Val could see Coyne grinning but he went ahead anyway. "Not just the round manhole-type sewer-sewers that Toohey was talking about, but storm sewer openings, too. Weld them shut or seal them up somehow."

The grin stayed on Coyne's smug face so Val shut up. He realized that his arms were still crossed. He wasn't buying any of Coyne's bullshit. And he hadn't liked having the muzzle of a loaded gun aimed at him. He wasn't going to forget that.

As if sensing Val's hostility, the flashgang's leader set his hand on Val's shoulder. His voice was soft, reasonable. "You're absolutely right, Valerino. City security and State Department Security and DHS security and Omura's own ninja guys will all make sure that all windows in nearby buildings will be sealed against snipers, all rooftops checked, all unauthorized vehicles hauled away, and all sewers—those carrying Toohey's shit and those for storms—will be sealed up..."

Coyne waited several beats like the son of a movie actor he was, his gaze moving from face to face—even to Cruncher's ruined face—and then he said, "But this storm sewer opening outside the Disney Pavilion is *already sealed up*. Has been for years and years. All the computer files say it's a permanent weld-job, but it ain't. It's an old rusty iron door made out of panels with a steel grate inside. We can cut through the grate ahead of time. And..."

Coyne looked around the faces again, drawing it out.

"...and *I've got the fucking key for the iron panels.*"

Six of the seven other boys started babbling and jostling one another.

"They'll never see us," said Coyne. "We'll shoot the Jap VIP from the sewer opening, just cut him down like a weed, and be gone before his security can turn around. We lock the iron panels behind us. By the time they get down into the sewers, we're a mile away through the whatchamacallit—labyrinth—of those old storm sewers, already out on the streets and blending with the crowds. I even know where to dump the guns on the way so they'll never be found."

The babbling and jostling stopped and all eight boys just looked at one another. Even Cruncher quit mopping his bleeding mouth.

"Holy shit," Val whispered at last. "It might work. Holy shit."

"We'll flash on this for years," said Coyne.

"Holy shit," repeated Val.

"Holy shit and amen," Coyne said, blessing everyone with his fingers like he was the new pope who'd taken over for the dead one.

"*Yurodivy!*" said the thinly smiling, smirking, full-face T-shirt image of Vladimir Vladimirovich Putin. "You are all... *holy fools.*"

1.05

LoDo, Denver — Saturday, Sept. 11

SATO DIDN'T TAKE the handcuffs off as he drove north to 20th Street and then east above I-25 again and down into the part of Denver called LoDo. Nick's wrists were already torn and bloody; the jouncing of the heavy—obviously armored—turd-brown Honda electric tore more flesh off his wrists and made Nick grind his molars rather than cry out again.

He'd wanted to kill Sato before this. Now he vowed to torture the Jap before he killed him.

LoDo was the cute name developers back in the 1980s—or maybe the '70s—gave to the old Lower Downtown warehouse district of Denver that squatted between the real downtown and the South Platte River. In the 1800s the area had been the site for whorehouses, saloons, saddleries, warehouses, and more saloons. By the middle of the 1900s even the saloons and whorehouses had gone out of business, leaving one saddle-seller, a few working warehouses, a lot of empty warehouses, and hundreds upon hundreds of winos, drug addicts, and street people. In the last decades of the twentieth century, urban renewal—and the city revitalizing itself toward the river—had chased the winos and addicts out to be replaced by upscale eateries and even more upscale condos with brick walls and exposed rafters. By the time the classic-looking Coors Field ballpark opened in 1995, LoDo was in full resurgence. It didn't begin its decline until after It All Hit The Fan, but by the Year of Clear Vision, LoDo was well on its way to its current state of boasting mostly whorehouses, a few saloons, abandoned condos haunted by flashback and other addicts, whorehouses, and more whorehouses.

Keigo Nakamura had died in a room on the third floor of a three-story building on Wazee Street, a long dark street with two-story whorehouses, saloons, and warehouses on one side and three-story warehouses, saloons, and whorehouses on the other side.

It was full light—or at least as light as it was going to get on this chilly, rainy September morning—when Sato parked the Honda at the curb outside the three-story building that looked exactly like all the other three-story buildings on the south side of Wazee Street. As the security chief came around to unlock the cuffs, Nick considered jumping Sato…then rejected the idea. He was too worn out by the night of flashing, the injections of T4B2T and TruTel, and from the sheer adrenaline of terror.

It would have to be another time.

Sato unlocked the cuffs and, seizing both of Nick's bleeding wrists in one gigantic hand, pulled an aerosol can from his suit pocket.

Mace! thought Nick and squeezed his eyes shut.

Sato sprayed something cold onto Nick's lacerated wrists. For a few seconds the pain was so terrible that Nick gasped loudly despite himself. Then…nothing. No pain at all. When Sato released his grip, Nick flexed his fingers. Everything worked fine and despite all the blood on his sweatshirt and the dash and windshield, the lacerations were superficial.

Sato grabbed Nick under the arm, lifted him out of the car, and plopped him down on the curb, steering him toward the old building. Shapes—sleeping flash addicts or winos, Nick assumed—stirred and stood in the dark entrance under the overhang.

Two men stepped out of the shadows but they weren't winos or addicts. They were well-dressed young Japanese men. Sato nodded to them and one of the athletic-looking young men unlocked the double lock on the door.

"Coming to the crime scene six years after the crime," said Nick, his voice shaking slightly from the cold and from the roil of fury inside him. "You think seeing this empty building after all this time is going to tell me anything?"

Sato's only reply was to switch on the lights.

Nick had been to this crime-scene building numerous times five years and eleven months ago, even though he hadn't been the responding homicide detective first on the scene, and he remembered the totally trashed mess of a site it was: three large rooms filled with couches and chairs and screens and a small kitchen on the first floor, furniture turned over everywhere, flashback vials crushed underfoot, lamps broken in the stampede of the witnesses to get out before the cops arrived that night, even wads of dirty clothing and the occasional used condom in corners.

No longer.

The furniture had been repaired and returned, the lamps were back in place and working, and although every surface was cluttered with dishes and glasses—a huge buffet had been set out down here on the first floor that night as a movie wrap party for Keigo's Japanese assistants, the interview subjects, and others involved in his documentary film—all three rooms and the kitchen were now clean and in a fairly orderly early-party-stage clutter again.

"I don't get it," said Nick.

Sato handed him a pair of stylish wrap-around tactical glasses.

Even before activating them, Nick noticed how tremendously light they were. The DPD tactical glasses had always seemed to weigh a pound or more and gave their users headaches after ten minutes. Not these glasses. They were as light as regular sunglasses and, being wrap-around, filled his entire field of vision. The DPD glasses had always been an island of virtual sight with a vertigo-inducing reality seeping in all around.

Nick touched the icon on the glasses' stem and just barely caught himself from exclaiming aloud. He took a few steps to confirm what he now saw.

All three party rooms and the kitchen were suddenly filled with people frozen in mid-stride, mid-conversation, mid-munch, mid-laugh, mid-flirt, and mid-flashback-inhalation. Real faces, real bodies. Real people.

He'd expected the figures to be there—it was what tac-glasses did—but he hadn't expected this level of reality. The DPD and American military tactical glasses he'd used generated little more than wire-frame stick people with cartoonish and barely recognizable faces floating above the armature bodies like Halloween masks on a stick.

These were *real* people. The quality of 3D digital rendering was on the level of virtual movies or TV series being streamed these days, including the popular *Casablanca* series starring Humphrey Bogart, Claude Rains, Ingrid Bergman, and such constant new guest stars as nineteen-year-old Lauren Bacall. And after a while on that series, Nick knew from his late-night viewings, it didn't seem at all strange to have other guest stars from different eras such as Tom Cruise, Leonardo DiCaprio, Kathleen Turner, Galen Watts, Byron Bezukhov, Sheba Tits, or even all-virt stars such as Natasha Lyubof or Tadanobu Takeshi on the show. They were all equally real.

As real as the people suddenly filling this space and the adjoining rooms.

He took the tac-glasses off and paced through the rooms that circled the central open staircase. Sato followed. The rooms were now empty of anyone but Sato and him. He put the glasses back on and felt the inevitable jolt of vertigo as more than two hundred people reappeared.

Walking closer and inspecting the face of the first witness and interview subject he'd recognized, the former Israeli poet Danny Oz—pores were visible on the haggard man's face and Nick could see the burst capillaries in Oz's eyes and nose—he said, "This must have cost Mr. Nakamura a fucking fortune."

Sato didn't find that comment worth responding to.

"All three floors virtualized like this?" asked Nick, moving around the room looking closely at the unblinking men and women. He paused to stare down the low bodice of a young blond woman he didn't recognize, perhaps one of the hookers hired for the party.

"Of course," said Sato.

Nick looked up at the security chief. Sato didn't appear any more or less three-dimensional, solid, or real than the other men and women and transvestites and gender-benders in the crowded room. Just broader and thicker than anyone else. Also, Sato was no longer the only Jap in the room. Besides two very young men and a young woman whom Nick recognized as being part of Keigo Nakamura's video and sound crew, there were three well-dressed bodyguards, also wearing tactical glasses.

Why would they be wearing tac-glasses? wondered Nick but set the question aside for now. His head hurt.

At first, out of practice with tactical and having never practiced with this *quality* of tactical, Nick made the rookie's mistake of stepping around and squeezing *between* the human forms in the crowded room. Then he shook his head ruefully and began walking *through* them to get where he was headed. The solid-looking three-dimensional digital maquettes didn't object.

In one corner, a stocky, handsome, sandy-haired former Google exec wearing saffron robes was explaining the karmic glories of Total Immersion to five or six rapt young people. Nick remembered the guy—Derek Somebody. He'd been on Sato's Top 18 list of witness-suspects yesterday morning...but Nick hadn't been paying much attention then. He remembered now that he'd had to drive up to Boulder to interview the Buddhist-robed jerkwad at the Naropa Institute there six years ago. Derek Somebody was a total flash addict whose goal was to relive every second of his forty-six years of life in a total-immersion flashback tank. The goal was *satori* via flashback.

"The murder floor is like this, too?" Nick asked while trying to remember the name of one of the more spaced-out men here standing in the small kitchen area and holding a glass filled with amber liquid that obviously had just come from a solid, real-world bottle of expensive-looking Scotch.

"Yes."

"Jesus," said Nick, remembering the crime-scene and autopsy photos. "Wait, has Mr. Nakamura seen all this?"

"Of course," Sato said in tones that couldn't get any flatter. "Many times."

"You did this for your private investigation," said Nick. He realized how dull-witted he sounded...no, *was*...but didn't feel apologetic about that. He had damned good reason to feel a little slow this morning.

Sato nodded ever so slightly. The big security chief was following Nick around the large living area and smaller kitchen space. He showed no hesitation at walking through people.

"In that suit," said Nick, talking just to shake the cobwebs out of his head, "you remind me of Goldfinger's guy...Oddjob."

Sato showed no sign of recognition and Nick mentally kicked himself for trying to make conversation. The rule of cop life—hell, of *life*—was that you don't try to converse with your own armpit or asshole, so don't try with ambulatory surrogates of same.

Nick sighed and said mostly to himself—"Still, if Mr. Nakamura keeps seeing all this and visiting his son's freshly murdered corpse upstairs, it must be..."

Nick froze. He turned slowly to stare at Sato and said, "Why, you miserable motherfucker."

One of Sato's dark eyebrows rose a few millimeters in query. Otherwise, the big man showed no expression.

"You sure in hell didn't get all this detail from witness statements or memory," said Nick.

"Perhaps some witnesses volunteered to submit to flashback before describing details?" suggested Sato. *Detairs.*

"My ass," said Nick.

Sato folded his hands over his crotch in the ancient posture of funeral directors, military men at ease during a dressing-down, and security men trying to disappear into the wallpaper or drapes behind them.

"My ass," repeated Nick for no other reason than he liked the sound of it. "You were here. You were on all three floors that night. You know how to observe better than any so-called witness there that night. You went under flashback—probably for weeks of sessions—to see and record all this incredible detail so you could give it to the VR programmers. *You* did."

Sato said nothing.

"It is illegal for all Japanese nationals to own, sell, possess, or use flashback, either in Japan or when traveling abroad," said Nick. "And, if convicted of the offense, the only punishment a judge may impose under Japanese law is death by lethal injection."

Sato stood there calmly.

"You motherfucker," repeated Nick, also just because he liked the sound of it. And because it was overdue. But he also hesitated in his newfound advantage. Why on earth would Sato give Nick such life-and-death leverage over him?

The answer was—he wouldn't.

Nick walked quickly from room to room, passing through frozen forms without hesitating. *This is simultaneous.* In all three rooms and the kitchen, what one could see of the other rooms was occurring at the same instant. Even if Sato had gone under the flash, he couldn't have recalled what was occurring simultaneously in different rooms here on the first floor, much less what might have been happening on the second and third floors.

Not for the first time this miserable morning, Nick Bottom felt like throwing up.

Sato nodded as if reading Nick's thoughts (again) and handed Nick two blue-glowing earbuds.

Nick set them in place with a sick dread at what would come next. And it did.

Sato pressed an icon on his phone's diskey and all the digitally re-created three-dimensional people around him and in the adjoining room came to life. Just the ambient roar of party noise made Nick reflexively throw his hands over his ears. With the tiny earbuds set deep, that obviously didn't help much.

Nick stood there motionless for a moment and watched the totally natural movement of people and endured the roar. Then he crossed quickly to the couch and leaned down between a far-too-handsome-to-be-natural young blond man who was, in turn, leaning forward to talk intimately with a far-too-beautiful-to-be-real young blond woman.

"I find the cocaine-three, brandy, flash, and fucking go really, really well together when you're, like, there doing it all," the male was whispering, "but you don't, like, get the buzz when you go back to it under the flash again."

"My experience also, like, you know, I mean, totally," said the female blonde while leaning literally into and through Nick to afford her blond interlocutor a better view of her breasts.

"Shit," whispered Nick as he stood upright, walked from room to room while watching and listening to more than two hundred people partying, and then stopped and stared at Sato. "It was all recorded at the time. Hidden cameras upstairs, too?"

The security chief gestured to the stairway and Nick led the way. A fourth Japanese security man in tac-glasses stood in front of a locked door on the landing. Nick stepped aside as Sato reached through the seemingly solid man to unlock the locked-in-the-real-world door with a real-world key.

The second-floor door was also locked and when Sato opened it, the door swung through a fifth young security man. Nick was taking off his glasses from time to time to make sure that none of these new security guards was real.

The second floor was just as Nick remembered it from his visits to the crime scene, except that it had been empty and totally trashed then. Now it was merely messy and very, very crowded.

Eight bedrooms ran off the central waiting area on this floor and all of the bedrooms were occupied. None of the doors here was locked. Nick chose a room at random and walked in.

A short, skinny felon whom Nick instantly recognized as Delroy Nigger Brown was in bed having sex with three white girls. None of the girls, Nick knew from his memory of the files at the time, was older than fifteen, and two of them had died of natural causes—if one considers being knifed by one's pimp or overdosing on heroin-plus-flash "natural causes"—within four months of Keigo's murder. Nick also knew that the pimp and drug supplier, Delroy N., should still be serving time at Coors Field...but not for the death of either of these particular girls. With another surge of nausea, Nick realized that if he was forced to go ahead with this investigation, he'd have to visit Delroy N. as one of the witnesses who were the last to see Keigo alive.

The felon had been Keigo's prime supplier of flashback and other drugs while the rich boy had been in Denver.

Nick confirmed that all the bedrooms were occupied and that many of the men in the other rooms were not as punctilious about not having sex with other males around as Delroy N. was. The energetic combinations in the eight rooms combined accounted for another forty or so party guests and with the twenty-some hookers and guests waiting in the center area, the total number of invited partiers, party crashers, caterers, prostitutes, and security guards seemed about right.

Not yet counting the two bodies upstairs.

By the time he'd looked in on all eight bedrooms—and wished he'd skipped at least three of them—Nick realized that the noise and motion had continued for more than ten minutes.

This had taken an astounding amount of supercomputer time to generate. These ten minutes alone created for the tacglasses must have equaled the cost of a comparable amount of time in a high-budget Hollywood all-digital movie.

"How long is the play loop?" Nick asked.

"One hour, twenty-nine minutes," said Sato.

"And it'll end when the bodies are discovered and everyone stampedes?"

"Plus seven minutes after young Mr. Nakamura's body—and the lady's—are discovered, yes."

Nick's jaw sagged. "You didn't have cameras up..."

"No."

It had been a stupid question and idea. If there had been cameras on the third floor, in Master Keigo's bedroom, there'd be no mystery.

Unless a certain security chief had destroyed the recordings. Right now, Hideki Sato was former homicide detective Nicholas Bottom's number-one suspect.

In front of the locked door that led to the staircase to the third floor was the digital Exhibit A in any prosecution of Sato for murder.

The broad-shouldered Japanese man wearing tactical glasses and standing with his hands folded over his crotch as he guarded the door might have been Sato's twin brother, even allowing for some age difference.

Through his headache and nausea, Nick racked his ravaged memory. "Takahishi Satoh," he said softly. "With an 'h.' Any relation to you, Hideki-san?"

"No."

"I remember him now. He was a little taller than you, but he could have been your double."

"Yes."

"He was in charge of security, is what he told us."

"Not quite, Bottom-san. He told you that his title was commander of security and that he was in charge of the five security men on Keigo Nakamura's U.S. security detail. This was true."

"But he didn't tell us that he took orders from *you*. That *you* were the real security chief."

"None of you asked Satoh-san if he had a superior...other than Mr. Nakamura Senior, I mean," said Sato.

"So when witnesses like Oz and the others described the big sumo-wrestler security chief with Keigo, it could have been you or could have been your pal here. They said 'Mr. Satoh.' Just too fucking cute for words, Hideki-san."

Sato said nothing.

"You realize, of course," spat Nick, "that this opens you up to charges of obstructing justice and lying under oath."

"I never lied under oath, Bottom-san."

"No, you didn't, because we didn't know you fucking *existed*," Nick said, turning from the projection of Satoh in his glasses to look at Sato wearing *his* glasses.

"Still…," began Sato. *Stirr*. "…if you examine the testimony of the five security men you and your officers interviewed six years ago, you will find that none of them lied to you."

"They damned well lied by omission," shouted Nick. He ran his hands through his hair. Shouting hurt his head. "They *obstructed justice!*"

Sato unlocked the door and opened it but Nick wasn't ready to go upstairs yet.

"Was this fake security chief's name even Satoh?"

"Of course it was."

"How long did it take you to find a look-alike security guy with a name that sounded just like yours, Hideki-san?"

Sato stood there holding the door open and waiting.

"Were you ever by Keigo's side in public during the months you were guarding him here?" asked Nick.

"A few times. Very rarely."

"Where'd you watch this party from, Hideki-san? From inside a van parked outside somewhere? A van full of screens? From a helicopter? From orbit?"

Sato waited.

Nick was not finished on the second floor yet. Or perhaps he just wasn't ready to see what was waiting for him upstairs.

"Where are the cameras?" he demanded.

Sato released the doorknob and took his phone out of his suit pocket. A laser pointer stabbed at least nine locations in the ceiling and walls and light fixtures.

"And at least four cameras in each bedroom and bathroom," said Sato. "There were a total of sixty-six cameras on this floor. Two hundred and thirty in the building."

Nick walked over to one of the walls.

"Show me again."

The laser dot winked on again.

"The lens is tiny or invisible," said Nick. "But, of course, you removed all the cameras after the murder."

"Of course," said Sato. "But you are looking at the wall through your glasses, so you see it as it was the night of the murder. The video pickups are…ah…very discreet."

Nick laughed at this, although whether it was the idea of two hundred and thirty video cameras in a flashcave-cum-drugpad-cum-whorehouse being discreet or just at how stupid he was this morning, he couldn't tell and didn't care.

He swung back to the real Sato and his digital Doppelgänger and said, "All right. Let's go upstairs."

Sato turned off the noise and movement of the party behind him as they climbed up the wide, steep staircase.

———

THE FOUR ROOMS ON the third floor had not been tidied up as had the first two floors of the building. They were still as they had looked on the night of the murder almost six years earlier. Nick and Sato both removed their tactical glasses before coming through the door at the top of the stairs and they kept them off as Nick led the way.

They emerged into a formal foyer with an open door to the small kitchen leading off this west end to their left—the DPD investigators had found the kitchen serviceable but almost unused, the fridge holding only a few bottles of beer and champagne—and on the south wall to their right, another high-tech door that opened onto a staircase to the rooftop.

One glance showed Nick that the kitchen looked untouched, but the foyer itself was still littered with the inevitable paper and plastic needle-cover detritus of the EMTs. Why they'd attempted resuscitation on an obvious corpse—other than the fact that the corpse and its father were worth billions of dollars—Nick had no idea. But they had, and some of the mess had spilled out of the bedroom through the living room and into this foyer. The expensive tiles in the foyer and frame of the wide door to the double stairway—there was no elevator, so all the furniture, kitchen appliances, and other large stuff on this floor had been carried up these stairs—were streaked and cracked where the paramedics' and then the coroner office's gurneys and equipment had left tracks and gouges. Some slob had stubbed out a cigarette on the tiles.

The foyer narrowed into a short hallway festooned with

expensive art. The wide glass-paned doors in the hall led left to the library and straight ahead into the living area and through there into the bedroom.

"Does Bottom-san wish to see any room before we go into the bedroom?" asked Sato.

"Anyone murdered in any of the rooms besides the bedroom?"

"No."

"Then let's start with the bedroom," said Nick.

Sato removed his shoes and left them in the tiled foyer. Nick left his shoes on. He was a cop... *had* been a cop, at least... not a guest for some fucking Tea Ceremony. Besides, Keigo Nakamura was beyond being offended by some *gai-jin* barbarian keeping his shoes on in his personal living space. (But Nick was counting on it offending the hell out of Hideki Sato.)

Nick saw that the living room was as large and littered as it had been six years ago. The double bedroom doors were wide open. The trail of paramedic debris seemed to lead *to* it rather than away from it.

The tac-glasses still in his hand, Nick walked in.

The expansive bedroom still stank of dried blood and brain matter. *After all these years?* thought Nick. *Not likely.*

But it did.

Instead of carpet, the floor was covered with rectangles of *tatami*. Nick had learned when he was a cop that the Japanese still tended to express the size of their rooms in units of the three-by-six-foot mats. A bedroom or tea room, Nick recalled, was often a four-and-a-half-mat room. All sorts of rules applied as to how the mats could meet—never in a grid pattern, he remembered, and there was some rule that in any layout there should never be a point where the corners of three or four mats touch. This bedroom was huge—maybe a thirty-mat room. Only these *tatami* didn't smell sweetly of dried grass like the floor of Mr. Nakamura's office.

The first patch of blood that caught the eye was on the big bed where the crumpled sheets had a dried splatter but the pillows and headboard and a bit of wall showed a head-sized red blotch. This was where the hooker had died. The larger patch of dried blood was on the floor, surrounded by discarded syringe covers and more paper and plastic paramedic detritus. This dried puddle covered all of one *tatami* and had blobbed over onto two adjacent ones.

Nick glanced into the master bedroom's large bathroom, checked the four windows, and then came over to stand next to the stained *tatami*.

"Would you move, please, Bottom-san?"

Sato had his glasses on and now Nick donned his and looked down. He was standing calf deep in Keigo Nakamura's naked loins. Nick stepped aside but couldn't resist grinning. He'd done that on purpose.

Keigo's corpse was naked. The young woman's corpse on the bed was dressed in jeans and a black bra. Keigo's throat had been slashed almost all the way through. The young woman— her name was Keli Bracque, Nick remembered—had been shot once in the middle of the forehead. Taking care not to step on or in Keigo again, Nick leaned closer to study Keli's wound. The .22-caliber round had left a tiny, clean, blue-rimmed hole in her pale forehead but had done its usual damage rattling around in her skull. Twenty-two's were still one of the weapons of choice for professional assassins, and several of Nick's DPD investigators had thought this suggested a professional hit.

Nick took two steps back and looked down. *If her hit was by a cool professional, then why this messy, rage-driven, amateur-looking job on Keigo? Sending a message? But a message to whom? Mr. Nakamura, obviously. Or maybe all the violence expended in Keigo's near-decapitation was merely a ruse to throw off investigators from how dispassionate and professional this hit actually was.*

There was a red paperback copy of a twentieth-century novel titled *Shōgun* open on the bedside table only inches from Keli Bracque's hand.

"These images are better than the death-scene photos I had," Nick said to Sato. "Who took them?"

"I did. Before the authorities arrived."

"Better and better," laughed Nick. "Not only leaving the scene of a crime, but concealing evidence...the video-camera recordings, these photos, the fact of your very existence as Keigo's head of security. You'll serve time for sure when an American court is through with you, Hideki-san."

Nick knew that he was repeating himself but he enjoyed hearing the charges again. Sato showed no more response than he had the first time.

"You're sure there are no animated tac images this time?" asked Nick.

"As I said, we had no cameras on the third floor, Bottom-san," Sato said.

"Yeah," said Nick, letting the sarcasm drip. He walked back to the bed, stepping on and through Keigo's head this time. If Sato was squeamish, fuck him.

Nick rubbed both of his temples as he looked at the dead girl's face and tried to remember her dossier. She was young—nineteen—and blond. And American. And tall. Almost a foot taller than Keigo at his diminutive five-foot-one height. All the Jap males seemed to have a thing about tall American blondes.

But, as was true of much of the food that Keigo Nakamura had eaten at home while he was in the States, Ms. Keli Bracque had been brought over from Japan. The orphan daughter of two American missionaries there, the girl had more or less been raised by the entertainment-and-relaxation branch of Naka-mura Heavy Industries. In the old days, Nick knew, Japanese businesses had sent their execs on sex holidays to Bangkok... not to the Patpong sex district that men from other nations flocked to, but to a more rigidly monitored sex district catering only to the Japanese. Even then, the HIV problem had gotten serious enough there that the big Japanese corporations had given up on Thailand and raised their own hookers. The dos-sier on Keli Bracque that Nakamura's firm had finally—reluctantly—surrendered hadn't said it outright, but odds were great that Keli had been sexually satisfying top execs there since she was a pre-teenager.

Or, thought Nick as he studied her dead face, *maybe not*.

Maybe this one had been saved for the boss's son. Or the boss *and* his son.

"She's half-dressed; he's still naked," he said aloud.

"Yes," said Sato.

Nick waited for the derision that such a statement of the obvious by a trained detective deserved, something along the lines of *No shit, Sherlock,* but Sato let the single flat syllable suffice.

"My point," Nick said finally, "is that Keigo and Ms. Bracque were up here alone for—what?—thirty-nine minutes? Forty?"

"Thirty-six minutes and twenty seconds before Mr. Satoh broke down the door after young Mr. Nakamura did not respond to his page," said Sato.

"Long enough to have sex," said Nick. He knew that "broke down the door" hadn't been quite accurate since the door at the head of the stairs could have resisted any number of battering rams. Security man Satoh had carried a tiny but powerful shaped charge, no larger than a kneaded eraser, for just such entry emergencies. But that was irrelevant.

"But," continued Nick, rubbing his stubbled cheek and looking through his glasses at the two dead bodies, "both autopsies showed that they hadn't had sex, even though that was the reason Keigo said he wanted the privacy up here during the party. Hell, I don't think Keli was getting dressed after some messing around between the two. I don't think she ever got *un*dressed, except to take her blouse and boots off."

"Perhaps young Mr. Nakamura and the young lady were chatting," said Sato.

Nick snorted. "Are NakamuraCo living sex toys famous for their conversational abilities?"

"Yes," said Sato. "Like the *geisha,* all Nakamura employees in the recreational division are trained to please by intelligent conversation, the playing of musical instruments, by knowing the proper technique of preparation and pouring in the Tea Ceremony...a wide range of abilities beyond mere...gratification of physical pleasure."

Nick was barely listening to the security chief. He pointed to the open paperback. "I think Ms. Bracque was reading her book when the killer entered the room. She only just had time to set it facedown, marking her place, when the assailant shot her."

Sato waited.

"Whoever it was, she wasn't alarmed by his or her sudden arrival," mused Nick. This was old ground for him, but he was rediscovering it as he went. It had been years since he'd mulled over the details of this murder. "You don't take time to mark your place in a book when someone who frightens you suddenly looms up in your bedroom."

"Bottom-san, you are saying that Miss Bracque knew her killer."

Nick was too lost in thought even to nod. Taking off his tactical glasses, he walked to the window nearest to the bed, nearest to the blood on the *tatami* and headboard, and touched the glass that wasn't quite glass. Sealed. Bulletproof. Blastproof for all but the most intense blasts. When Nick had read the specs six years earlier, he'd had the image of a major bombing event where the building here on Wazee was rubble but the windows remained, hanging in air like transparent Druid stones.

Since they couldn't be opened, the third-floor rooms were constantly refreshed by the whisper of forced air from ventilators. Tiny ventilators. A tiny ninja-assassin mouse might get in through those ventilators if it weren't for all the layers of active filters and screens. Nick held his hand close. The air was moving so the central system was still active.

"So Keigo and his hired girlfriend weren't up here screwing," Nick said to himself. "Maybe Keigo was just waiting for someone."

"Waiting for whom?" Sato asked in low tones.

Without putting on his glasses to look at the victims a last time—but carefully steering wide of the bloodstained *tatami* and the invisible corpse of Keigo on the floor—Nick said, "Let's go up on the roof."

In the foyer, Nick paused to study the door to the stairway

to the roof. Except for little black boxes at both top corners and one on the side where a card-swiper would be, it looked like any other metal door. But Nick knew that the damned thing cost more than he earned in ten years. It not only checked retina and fingerprints—how many movies had Nick seen where the good guy or bad guy just brought along someone's hand or eyeball to defeat those simple security checks?—but scraped and sniffed the person's DNA, measured his brainwaves, and performed about a dozen other acts of identification that would only work with a living, breathing person. Six years ago this coming October, all that technology had been keyed on Keigo Nakamura's retina, prints, DNA, brainwaves, and all the rest.

Now it seemed to be keyed on Hideki Sato. At least the heavy door clicked open after Sato had leaned close to one of the black boxes, scraped his thumb against it, and made his other contacts and magical passes. At the top of the stairway, he did the same thing with the magic door there.

Nick asked the same question he'd asked six years ago. "How do the maids and janitors get in and out of this apartment?"

There had been no answer from anyone six years ago and Sato did not answer now.

1.06

Wazee Street, Denver—
Saturday, Sept. 11

IT WAS RAINING harder but the clouds and fog had lifted. To the east rose the shrouded towers of downtown Denver; to the west the condo towers clustered along the river; to the south the large masses of the Pepsi Center and Mile High DHS Detention Center; to the north more low buildings and the two-hundred-foot-tall spike that anchored a pedestrian over-pass connecting LoDo to the river region over train tracks. West of everything, just visible through the low clouds, were the foothills. The high peaks were absent this morning.

There was nothing special about the rooftop of Keigo Nakamura's three-story building here on Wazee Street. A patio/garden area was delineated by a slightly raised wooden floor and vined latticework on two sides to give some privacy to the hot tub. On that October night six years ago, Nick knew, the hot tub had been burbling and preheated to the proper temperature—but unused by the victims, the coroners stated—but this mid-September morning it was cold and covered by a mildewing yellow tarp. The garden part of the rooftop was represented by several long planters lining the edge of the patio area and made of the same light wood, but no one had been gardening up here in recent years. There were a few weeds still growing and the desiccated skeletons of nobler plants.

Sato grunted as he leaned over to tie his polished black shoes.

Nick struggled to remember the security details of this unprepossessing rooftop. He recalled that there were multiple-wavelength invisible sensor-beams and waveguides extending ten feet high around the full perimeter...yes, there were the poles at the corners holding the projectors and equipment... and pressure sensors everywhere on the tarpaper and gravel rooftop except for the raised wooden patio area.

"Someone could have pole-vaulted in from the neighboring rooftops," Nick muttered. Sato ignored him.

Yes, someone could have pole-vaulted in, but unless they'd landed on the wooden patio, the pressure sensors would have recorded their landing. And none did.

But the doors...

"The doors were open...what?" said Nick, expecting an answer this time. "Two and a half minutes?"

"Two minutes and twenty-one seconds," said Sato.

Nick nodded. He remembered joking with his partner, then detective sergeant (now lieutenant) K. T. Lincoln, that he could kill a dozen Keigo Nakamuras in two minutes and twenty-one seconds.

"Speak for yourself" had been K.T.'s response. "I could kill a *hundred* fucking Keigos in two minutes and twenty-one seconds."

Nick remembered thinking that she probably could. K.T. was half-black, a bit more than half-lesbian, a fiercely secular converted Jew who had worn black in civilian life ever since the death of Israel, a beautiful woman in her own scowling way, and probably the best and most honest cop he'd ever worked with. And for some reason she hated Japs.

Now standing in the rain and looking at the unused patio and rooftop, Nick said, "I think I've solved the murder."

Sato leaned on the hot tub and cocked his head to show he was listening.

"There was all that newsblog blather about a locked-room mystery," continued Nick, "but the goddamned room wasn't even locked when the murders happened. Keigo unlocked the lower door, climbed the stairs, unlocked the upper door, and came out here. Wherever you were—a van, command post RV, a goddamned blimp—the remote door alarms showed you he'd opened them and you must have phoned Keigo to check that everything was all right."

Sato grunted. But this time Nick needed more than that.

"*Did* you phone him? Or contact him some other way?" he demanded.

"How do you say it," growled Sato, "when you interrupt static on an open line without speaking?"

"Breaking squelch," said Nick. At least that's the way he and a lot of former-military Denver cops had said it. Breaking squelch—just clicking to interrupt the carrier static—was as old as radios. When he'd been a patrolman, the guys out in their patrol cars had an entire code of breaking squelch—ways to tell each other things that no one wanted the dispatcher to hear or record.

Sato grunted again.

"So you broke squelch and Keigo broke squelch back and you knew he was okay when the doors opened," said Nick. "One interrogative break and two back?"

"Two interrogative and three back, Bottom-san."

"How many times did you do that before he quit answering because he was dead?"

"Twice."

"How long before he quit answering was the second query and answer... how long before you had Satoh break the door down and check on him?"

"One minute, twelve seconds."

Nick rubbed his chin again, hearing the scrape of whiskers.

"You said you had solved the murder," said Sato.

"Oh, yeah. Keigo didn't have sex with the girl because he *was* waiting for someone. Someone to arrive on the roof."

"Without tripping the perimeter and pressure sensors?"

"Exactly. The person arrived by helicopter and just stepped out onto the patio boards here. No sensors there."

"This was a busy night on Wazee Street, Bottom-san. Many people coming to and leaving this party alone. You think that they would not have noticed a helicopter hovering above the building?" *Hericopter.*

"Not if it was a stealth 'copter with that whisper technology that your dragonfly chopper had when you got picked up yesterday. What do you call those machines?"

"*Sasayaki-tonbo,*" said Sato.

"And what does that mean?"

"Whisper-dragonfly."

"Okay," said Nick. "So you'd been holding back, running the security from the background before that night, letting your cutely named Satoh-san appear to be running the show—just for purposes of later interviews should things go south, which they did—but that night you told Keigo that you wanted to meet him at one-thirty a.m...."

"One twenty-five it would have to be," said Sato.

Nick ignored him. "So Keigo kills some time with his sex toy, who doesn't even bother to get undressed for the heir apparent, and then comes up on the roof to meet you. You step out of the whisper-dragonfly, which probably goes up to hover until you are done with what you have to do, Keigo unlocks the door to lead you back down into his apartment, and the second you enter the room you shoot the girl in the forehead and then use a big knife on a very surprised Keigo."

Sato seemed to be considering the explanation. "How did I get back out to the roof, Bottom-san? Only young Mr. Nakamura could open the doors."

Nick laughed at that. "I don't know how you got *out.* Maybe you had an override code on those goddamned doors..."

"Then I would not have required arranging a meeting with young Mr. Nakamura to open them, would I, Bottom-san? I could have surprised him at any time."

"Whatever," snapped Nick. "Maybe you just propped the doors open with two of those rocks in the dead planter there.

115

But you had plenty of time to kill both of them and then be air-lifted off the roof again—without the whisper-dragonfly tripping any of the alarms up here."

Sato nodded as if convinced. "And my motive?"

"How the fuck should I know what your motive was?" Nick laughed again. "Sibling rivalry. Something that happened in Japan that we'll never find out about. Maybe you were sweet on little Miss Keli Bracque…"

"Sweet on her," repeated Sato, "so I shot her in the head."

"Yeah," said Nick. "Exactly."

"And then murdered young Mr. Nakamura out of some sort of jealousy."

Nick held up his hands. "I said I don't *know* the motive. I just know you had the opportunity and the access to weapons and the technology to get you in and out of Keigo's apartment."

"The technology being the *Sasayaki-tonbo*," said Sato.

"Yeah."

"You should really look into whether there were any *Sasayaki-tonbo* in America six years ago," said the security chief. "Or in Japan yet, for that matter."

Nick said nothing. After another minute of looking at the depressing rooftop and depressing low clouds, he said, "Let's go down and get out of the fucking rain."

———

LATER, NICK DIDN'T KNOW why he hadn't just left the damn building. His work there was done. There was nothing else to be discovered by gawking at the six-year-cold crime scene. He *should* have just left. Everything would have been different if he'd just left.

But he didn't.

They came out into the third-floor foyer and once again Nick imagined that he could smell the faded stench of spilled blood and brains from the bedroom two rooms away. Sato turned left toward the exit, but instead of waiting for Sato to unlock the door to the stairway down, Nick turned right in the foyer and then left through the hall doorway into the large room that looked out onto Wazee Street.

This was the library in Keigo Nakamura's permanent residence during the months he'd spent in the United States before being murdered, and it was the kind of space that young readers could only dream about. The floorboards were Brazilian cherry, the built-in bookcases on three walls were mahogany, the molding was handcrafted, the carpets were Persian, the long tables with their built-in magazine shelves and giant dictionaries atop them looked like they'd come out of Columbus's map room, and the two tiers of elegant wooden blinds on each of the eight tall windows were also cherry. The huge mahogany desk in front of the windows was regal and solid enough to have served some American president in the Oval Office and the piano on its raised dais was a Steinway. Club chairs scattered around the room and the long couch were of a leather so dark and soft that they looked to have come from some eighteenth-century British club.

Nick looked at the two thousand three hundred and nine books on the shelves. He knew there were precisely two thousand three hundred and nine books on those shelves because he'd had his people look through each and every one of them. The only clues they'd uncovered were three almost-century-old Polaroid snapshots of a naked young man asleep on a couch. The photos had been tucked into a hundred-and-fifty-year-old third volume of *The History of the Decline and Fall of the Roman Empire*. Since the naked young man in the photos — his face was averted — was sporting a semi-erection, some of Nick's sharper detectives had deduced some sort of connection with the title of the book. Others had decided that Keigo Nakamura, known both in Japan and the States as a ladies' man, had been secretly gay and probably killed by one of his young gay lovers.

In the end, neither the DPD's forensic people nor the FBI's experts had been able to track down either the photographer or his young subject, but Nick had found the interior designer who'd worked for Keigo Nakamura and the designer had confirmed that he'd bought all the library books by the yard at various California and Colorado estate auctions. And the books had been chosen primarily for the quality of their leather bindings, the interior designer had said.

As far as Nick's and the FBI's best analysts could tell, Keigo Nakamura had never cracked a single book on any of these shelves or tables and the naked young man in the Polaroid's story belonged to some other mystery.

The paperback that Keli Bracque had been reading on the day she was killed—*Shōgun*—hadn't come from the library.

Nick unhooked and parted the center set of wooden shutters and looked down at the rain falling on Wazee Street. He set his fingers against the cool glass, trying to fight the strange—almost forgotten—energies rising in him like a sudden spur of hunger.

He was actually beginning to be interested in solving this goddamned murder case. *Why?* Keigo Nakamura meant less than nothing to him. The arrogant rich kid had probably deserved to be murdered. His little movie documentary about flashback addiction in the United States wouldn't have been of interest to the Japanese or Americans.

But it was interesting enough to someone that they murdered him because of it, thought Nick. Keigo's phone and video camera and the camera's last three fingernail-drives with all the recent interviews on them had been missing. Was there something in those interviews that had doomed Keigo Nakamura?

Personally, Nick liked Hideki Sato as the new prime suspect. It would certainly explain why Sato had gone to such lengths to hide his very existence in the original investigations. As for motive—who would ever know? Keigo Nakamura had made at least one enemy willing and able to cut his throat. Sato would certainly have been capable of that.

And Nick also liked his little speech about the helicopter, the whisper-dragonfly. What had Sato called the silent chopper in Japanese? *Sasayaki-tonbo.* Nick loved the elegance, the sweet-solution quotient, of a DA explaining to a jury that Chief of Security Hideki Sato had stepped out of a *Sasayaki-tonbo* to kill his master's son.

The only problem with the *Sasayaki-tonbo* part of the theory was that Keigo Nakamura wasn't the only resident of Wazee Street six years ago who had a hot tub bubbling away on the roof. Both the FBI and the plodding DPD led by Detective Sergeant Nick Bottom had found a certain James Oliver Jackson, who'd been *in* his rooftop Jacuzzi—along with four young female friends—during the time of the Keigo party and murder. Mr. Jackson's hot tub was across the street and three buildings east and although that building was only two stories tall and had no view of Keigo's patio area due to the doorway superstructure and patio fence on the Nakamura building, Jackson and his giggling guests stated that they certainly would have noticed a helicopter hovering over a building so close. James Oliver Jackson's seat in the hot tub—Nick had checked—did have a perfect view of the airspace over the taller three-story Nakamura building, and Jackson and the co-eds had stated that there'd been a lot of uplight from the street that night, what with all the cars coming and going from Keigo's party.

But one man, dressed in black, coming down one of those long rappel ropes from a black and silent stealth helicopter? wondered Nick. He had to smile when he imagined any district attorney presenting this James Bond/killer-ninja story to a jury.

He smiled again when he tried to picture the bull-chested mass of Hideki Sato, all dressed up in his ninja-suit and mask, rappelling down a two-hundred-foot-long rope in the night. It had damned well better be a sturdy helicopter.

"Bottom-san, do we await something?" asked Sato from his place just inside the library's door.

Nick ignored him and ran his finger along the slightly fogged glass of the blastproof, bombproof, bulletproof window. He took the tactical glasses from his pocket and put them on. "You said you have the digital recordings for seven minutes after your Mr. Satoh broke down the door and rushed in to find Keigo's body. Show me those minutes, please."

"There were no cameras on this third floor…," began Sato.

"I know that. I don't want to be *in* the re-creation like down below. I just want to *see* it. Like any video. But I'm interested in

a view from an external camera, one as close to this view" —
Nick tapped the glass — "as possible."

"One minute, please," said Sato and tapped at his phone's
diskey.

Everything shifted again. Suddenly it was night and there
was confusion on the dark street three floors below. The viewpoint wasn't perfect — the camera must be up under the third-
floor eaves on the outside of the building — and the effect it
created in Nick's inner ear was that he had instantly swooped
up higher and to his right. The exterior cameras were in night-
vision mode and things glowed greenly, turning passing headlights into blurred and streaking white-green blobs. Faces of
people fleeing the party before the cops arrived were quite visible although the audio pickup would have to be filtered and
cleaned up to pull individual voices from the distant babble.

Nick saw an older, bald Naropa Institute savant he recognized, looking cold in his thin cotton robe and rope sandals,
running to a waiting van. Four or five of his acolytes, including
the sandy-haired Derek Somebody, whom, Nick knew, Keigo
had interviewed the day before his death, hurried to keep up.

Derek Dean, thought Nick. *The guy's name was Derek Dean.
Shit, I wonder if my passport's still good. I'll need it if I go up to
Boulder to reinterview him.*

Sirens were wailing down Wazee Street now and the rush
of people leaving the party became an undignified scramble.

*There's the ex-Israeli poet, Danny Oz, heading for a car with
Delroy Nigger Brown. What on earth were* those *two doing together
that night?*

Remembering that Delroy was the major street vendor for
drugs in this LoDo area, Nick figured that might answer his
question. Patrol cars were arriving from opposite directions now
and Nick recognized the white-blob faces of several patrolmen
whose semi-intelligible reports were the first to be read in the
giant pile that would become the K. Nakamura Murder Book.
Nick had seen almost everything he'd wanted to see, but he
kept the glasses on as the first ambulance arrived and EMTs
boiled out of it in a totally unnecessary rush.

"Do I get my gun back?" asked Nick as he kept watching.

"Ah, so sorry," said Sato. "The weapon you brought to the flashback cave is no longer available. But you have several at your shopping mall home, I trust."

"What about the cash I had at Mickey's?"

"So sorry," repeated Sato. "The money there was left with the proprietor to cover any damages or medical bills for his bouncer."

"Did you at least keep the flashback vials I bought?" asked Nick, feeling his anger beginning to burn again. If Sato did his Mr. Moto routine with that *So sorry* one more time, Nick thought he might go for the man's throat.

"No," said Sato. "The illegal drugs were also left behind."

"Well, I'm going to need some of those *illegal drugs* if I'm going to do the research for the interviews I wanted to do later today," snapped Nick.

"Whom do you think you will interview today, Bottom-san?"

"Oz, the writer, for sure," said Nick. "But I want to prepare for the Boulder fruit fly, Derek Dean, and drop in to see my old friend Delroy at Coors Field. That's three hours there, plus another two or three hours to flash on the reports themselves…"

"Four thirty-minute vials will be made available to you today," said Sato. "And, of course, this complete video and digital reconstruction is being downloaded to your phone site as we speak."

Swallowing his anger, Nick was reaching up to pluck off the glasses when he froze in place.

"Stop the recording!" he shouted. "Back it up…no, forward a little…back again…there! Stop!"

Sato put his glasses back on. "What is it, Bottom-san?"

Another patrol car had arrived as well as the unmarked GoMo Volta carrying the two plainclothes detectives on duty that night—Kendle and Sturgis. Cars that had been parked along the curb were driving up on the broad sidewalk to get past the growing cluster of emergency vehicles before they were hemmed in for good. Some people were just running away down the sidewalks to escape before the interviewing and ID'ing of witnesses began.

But Nick was looking at none of this.

Nick's attention was focused on a small white twin-blob of a forehead and forearm appearing over the top of a parked car half a block to the east.

The lower part of this person's face was hidden by the forearm and car roof, the person's hair hidden by darkness, the rest of the form simply not visible.

Dara, thought Nick and felt literally dizzy for a second.

What the hell was his wife doing there that night? This wasn't possible.

"Sato... forward a bit. Freeze. A little more now. Freeze again. Back..."

"Do you see someone, Bottom-san?"

Nick Bottom thought of his master's degree work and heard some long-forgotten professor's voice explaining that five million years and more of evolution had honed a *Homo sapiens* ability to distinguish a human face, however camouflaged or disguised, from its surroundings. The greatest enemy of man had always been man, said the professor, and the human mind was able to see another human face in even the most visually cluttered and ill-lit surroundings with more accuracy than one would think possible. The first thing a human infant can make out is his mother's face—more specifically, his mother's eyes and smile.

Nick saw no eyes or smile on this distant shape, only the white blur of a forehead, the white oblong of a forearm coming out of a dark coat to rest on the roof of a car, but he was certain it was his wife.

Dara?

Nausea and confusion rose in him. His first impulse was to rush Sato, take the big man down through the sheer kinetic energy of his assault, get his pistol, and hold the muzzle against the security chief's head until he admitted what he'd done here and told Nick why.

Why would *they fake this fuzzy image of Dara and insert it in the video?*

To get Nick sucked into the investigation. To get him personally involved. To set him up somehow?

"Run it forward again... please," said Nick.

The forehead bobbed down and out of sight. Was there a second person in the shadows with Dara or just refugees from the party moving past her in a hurry? The dark forms moved out of sight east along the sidewalk. Nick wasn't even able to make out the form of a woman. His headache had returned and now joined with the sense of vertigo from the glasses to increase his nausea. Could he enhance that first frozen image? Probably, but the recording already looked to be at the end of its pixel-enhancement range for such a distant, dark shot. He could try with these glasses and phone interfaced with his own 3D-high-def displays at home.

He tugged off the glasses and slid them in his pocket. "Nothing. I thought I saw someone... but it wasn't anyone. I'm tired. I need some rest and to get into the flashback of the interviews and documents."

"You can take the Honda electric back to your lodging," said Sato as he led the way out of the library to the foyer.

"So you can show off again by swooping away in your damned *Sasayaki-tonbo?*"

Sato shook his massive head. "I was thinking of calling for a taxi."

"I don't want your goddamned Honda electric, Hideki-san."

"Mr. Nakamura thought it might be more reliable than your current vehicle for your..."

"I said *I didn't want your fucking Honda!*" shouted Nick. His head was pounding with pain and the shouting made it worse. "Give me a ride home if you want, but I'll use my own car."

"As you wish," said Sato and waved Nick ahead of him through the door. The two men clattered down the wide stairway. Sato got them through the lower door and they crossed the cold, empty living area without speaking.

Outside, Sato handed the physical key for the outside door to one of the two Japanese men waiting. It was still raining.

Before getting into the passenger side of the Honda, Nick looked east down the street as if Dara might still be standing there.

What are you bastards up to? he wondered as he felt the car bob to Sato's weight. Nick ran both palms across the roof of the car and rubbed the cold water into his face before sliding into the passenger seat. Every part of Nick that could hurt did hurt, including his heart.

Neither man spoke during the fifteen-minute ride to Cherry Creek.

As Nick was getting out of the car at the shopping mall condos, Sato said softly, "Bottom-san, please to understand, if you call me 'motherfucker' again, I shall be forced to kill you."

3.01

Los Angeles: Sunday, Sept. 12— Friday, Sept. 17

SUNDAY

PROFESSOR EMERITUS George Leonard Fox sat in his tiny, cluttered, closet-sized excuse for an office, writing diary entries into a leather-bound blank book he'd owned for decades but had never written in until now.

How strange it was to be writing in longhand again! It reminded Leonard of the year he'd spent working on his dissertation—*Negative Capability in the Minor Poetry of John Keats*—with him scribbling madly on yellow legal pads into the wee hours of the morning and then waking to the sound of Sonja typing up his pages for review. Leonard tried to remember the approximate year... 1981. Reagan was the new president and he and Sonja and all the other graduate students and faculty were making fun of the man. Leonard had been twenty-three and Sonja nine years older and already, since he'd just begun a serious affair with a twenty-year-old undergraduate named Cheryl, destined to become Leonard's ex-first wife. Or perhaps, he thought, that should be "first ex-wife."

At any rate, the divorce he'd asked for had come through

four months after his dissertation was successfully defended and his first PhD obtained. Sonja had resented that typing under false pretenses, as she put it. But somehow she'd forgiven him and the two had remained friends until her death in 1997.

Professor Emeritus George Leonard Fox couldn't say the same about his other three wives. They were all still alive (although he'd recently heard that Nubia was all but lost to Alzheimer's), but none of them had forgiven him for the marriages or his hypothetical offenses. Wait... perhaps Nubia had if she no longer even remembered who he was. Leonard stopped writing in his diary and imagined, with some irony, hunting her up at whatever overcrowded government repository for dementia victims she was stored in and reintroducing himself.

He shook his head. Sometimes he wondered if he was showing early signs of Alzheimer's himself. (Although, he realized, at age seventy-four, the signs wouldn't be all that early, would they?)

Val hadn't come home the previous night. The boy had finally shown up as Leonard was finishing a late breakfast. His only response to his grandfather's "Good morning" had been an irritated grunt. Then Val had gone straight to bed and slept most of the Sunday away.

Whatever was going on in the sixteen-year-old's life, Leonard knew, was not going to be shared with his grandfather or any other adult. Leonard hated that aspect of his grandson's personality. The sulky, pouty, rebellious, noncommunicative teenager pose was such a terribly tiresome cliché. If Leonard hadn't seen the other side of the personality of his daughter's only child — Val's sensitivity (which he worked so hard to hide from his peers), his addiction to reading, his reluctance (at least as a younger child) to hurt other people — the aging ex-professor would have been sorely tempted to wash his hands of the boy and send him home, somehow, to his father.

Val's father. Several times in recent weeks, Leonard had come close to phoning Nick Bottom. But each time he'd held off. The first reason for doing so was the simple fact of nonlocal calls having become so difficult and expensive again, after decades of cheap instant contact with anyone anywhere. Leonard remembered from his childhood when one of his parents would say to the other, "It's a *long-distance call*," as if that involved paying for a call to the moon.

The other reasons for Leonard's hesitation were less obvious and petty: the fact that Nick Bottom had shown less and less interest in his son over the past five years; and finally the fact that Bottom was almost certainly still a serious flashback addict which, to Leonard, meant the person met the clinical description of malignant narcissist.

But still, he wrote in his diary, as the storm clouds continued to build over the Los Angeles basin, Leonard knew that he would have to do *something*.

He paused and flexed his aching right hand. Writing by hand, he realized now, aggravated his arthritis more than typing on a virtual keyboard. But speaking of clichés! "Storm clouds building"! Sonja would have chastised him in her strongest Swedish for that one.

But with heavier clouds of smoke filling parts of the sky over Los Angeles every day—first in the *reconquista* neighborhoods to the east and southeast, then in the Asian sections farther south and west and around UCLA, yesterday in the rich people's walled and gated and patrolled enclaves to the west and up in the hills toward Mulholland Drive—it certainly *looked* as if storm clouds were building and growing darker by the day.

Leonard resumed his diary entry. He'd decided to visit Emilio at the address the older man had given him—no phone or e-mail number, just the address—before the next weekend if Val's aberrant behavior continued and if the growing sense of imminent Armageddon in the city persisted. As risky and expensive as buying passenger fare into one of the truck convoys to Denver might seem, it was beginning to feel like a more prudent course than remaining in Los Angeles.

MONDAY

Leonard started the day with simple relief that Val went off to school. Later, Leonard phoned the district's autocheck line and confirmed that his grandson was actually there.

He'd tried to talk to Val over the boy's rushed breakfast—chugging a bottle of UltraCoke and grabbing a food bar—and Val's only response had been "If you're so worried about where I spend my time, you should have done a kid-finder implant on me."

If Val had been his own son, Leonard would have. But he'd come to him from Denver when Val was almost eleven years old—and in shock and mourning after the sudden death of his mother and the new addiction of his father—and it seemed too late to Leonard to take the boy to the LAPD for a tracker implant.

Leonard spent too much of Monday trying to run various errands, including stocking up on nonperishable food they could take with them if they did indeed decide to make a run for it the following weekend. As he rode his bicycle around his neighborhood and Chinatown, he was struck again by how impossible it was to get much done—or at least done efficiently—in this brave new world he lived in.

Flashback, he thought, was the greatest culprit. Leonard foolishly went to his bank, a real bank, to attempt a non-ATM transaction, and of course there were no human tellers available. One of his bank's main TV advertising points was that there would always be a minimum of two human tellers on duty during the bank's four half-days when they were open to the public, but Mondays—one of those half-days—was endemic with flashback absenteeism. Leonard knew he should have known better than to try to bank with a person on a Monday.

The supermarket was also a trial. It took Leonard almost fifteen minutes in line to get into the store through the various CMRI portals, sniffer credit checks, and DNA-recognition booths. Once inside, the only nonshoppers in sight were the beetle-armored security people with their ebony helmets, reflective visors, and clunky automatic weapons. Leonard had seen enough versions of this future in the movies so popular during his middle-aged years that he should have been used to it before it actually arrived, but now, even after almost two decades of growing security presence, it still bothered him.

The absence of clerks meant that when Leonard noticed that the fresh produce section was filled with rotting vegetables due to brownouts and negligence, his only option was to phone an automated national number. Somewhere in that echoing, horribly lighted building poxed with black security camera bubbles, he suspected, was a human, living, breathing store manager. But that manager certainly wanted nothing to do with his patrons. And Leonard seriously doubted if the Los Angeles chain was still owned by anyone named Ralph.

He had to bike many blocks out of his way coming home from his day's errands because of the constant chirping of his phone's terrorist-incident alarms. Tibetan suicide bombers had detonated themselves in Chinatown; Aryan Brotherhood California separatists were engaging in a shootout with LAPD and Homeland Security tactical units near Echo Park.

Val did not come home that night until almost 3 a.m.

TUESDAY

Leonard spent much of his day sitting in his study and sorting listlessly through the untidy stacks and piles of printouts of the various drafts of his huge failed and abandoned novel. Occasionally he would jot a note in his diary, usually questioning how a professor emeritus of English literature and classics could write so badly.

His goal, as he'd told Emilio and only a few others, had been to tell the story of the first third of this new century. But he realized, as he read pages and chapters of his abandoned work at random, all he'd done in his many drafts was to show his own ignorance. His characters were invariably *victims* of the social forces that had changed America and the world so much in the last twenty-five years, and their actions—such as they were (most of the drafts was just talk)—showed their own lack of understanding of those forces and their own impotence in the face of such change. In other words, his characters' perceptions were as dulled and buffered by the illusions and comforts of forty years of campus life as Professor George Leonard Fox's had been.

Leonard dropped pages as he read and had to smile. As he'd told Emilio, he'd attempted the ultimate authorial God-view of Leo Tolstoy and failed. In the end, he would have been happy to have achieved the minor godview of...say...Herman Wouk.

Leonard had read Wouk's two magnum opuses, *The Winds of War* and *War and Remembrance*, in the 1970s and had, along with all the other students and faculty he knew, dismissed them completely as middlebrow historical romances. Clumsy attempts to tell the story of the lead-up to World War II and the Holocaust, and the events themselves, in two huge volumes following scattered members of an American naval family—including the son's Jewish wife, Natalie, who was shipped to Auschwitz with her Jewish intellectual uncle and her small child. "Wouk chewed more than he bit off," he'd said wittily—not citing the real source—in an undergraduate course at Yale where the books had come up in some tangential discussion.

But Leonard now realized that Wouk—largely forgotten a third of the way through this following century—had *known* things about the world. The popular novels were rich with carefully observed detail, whether that applied to the clumsy machinery of a 1940s-era submarine or the more efficient bureaucratic machinery of the Holocaust. And Wouk wrote his forgotten masterpieces as if the salvation of his soul depended upon telling the tale of the Holocaust.

All Leonard's various drafts of a novel had done was record his passive characters' confusion—so perfectly matching his own—at why the world was changing for the worse around them.

Leonard tossed the stacks of manuscript into a large box and closed the top.

When *had* he realized that things in the United States of America were going in the wrong direction... not the wrong direction of a thousand intellectual crying-wolf outcries, the fashionable cries of Marx, Marcuse, Gramsci, Alinsky, and others... but *really* going to hell in a handbasket?

Recently, for reasons he couldn't trace, he'd been remembering the early days of the Obama administration. Leonard had been married to his last wife, Nubia, then—certainly the least stressful of his four marriages. And although they were living in Colorado at the time, Leonard teaching at CU Boulder and Nubia heading up the African-American Womyn's Studies Department at DU in Denver, she had insisted on returning to her hometown of Chicago to be there on the night Obama was elected in 2008. Nubia had been so certain that her candidate would win that she'd booked the flight to Chicago for both of them in August, the day after Obama was nominated at the Democratic Convention in Denver. Nubia had been a delegate at that convention.

They'd stayed at her mother's house. Nubia's three brothers and two sisters and all their spouses and kids were there to watch the returns and even before Obama reached the magic number of delegates, everyone had walked over to Grant Park for the final announcement and celebration.

Leonard remembered the cheering and the tears on Nubia's—and his own—cheeks. Leonard had been ten years old when police attacked protesters in the park not too far from where Obama was acknowledging his victory that night, too young to pay much attention to the turbulent 1960s. *This* night, with the hundreds of thousands of people streaming into Grant Park and the cheering and weeping and hugging of strangers when the huge TV displays showed CNN announcing Obama reaching the critical delegate number, seemed to be both the past and future of Chicago and America.

Things had been dark, but they had all reached the Promised Land together.

That feeling had faded faster for Leonard than it had for Nubia over the next few years, which was one reason the marriage had ended earlier than it might otherwise have.

It was not that Leonard, an intellectual and proud member and even leader of his faculty tribe then in his early, healthy fifties, had suddenly turned into a closet Republican. No, during all of those years of violent change, Leonard had remained a believer—in hope, in change, in the important role the federal government needed to play in everything from enforcing climate-change regulations to taking control of health care and a thousand other facets of American life.

But over that decade and the next, as the recession seemed to be ending and then slid back into something far worse and seemingly never-ending, as the foreign wars ended in defeat and retreat, and as the government and its many entitlement programs bet wrong on the future and went broke—Leonard began to doubt.

Doubt whether those social decisions toward ever-increasing government deficit spending in the midst of Round One of the great global recession had been the wise thing to do.

Doubt whether America's eventual retreat from the rising success of radical Islam's influence around the world was the wisest course.

Doubt whether the United States of America *should* have claimed its new and more humble role in the second decade of the twenty-first century as "just one nation among many." Despite Professor George Leonard Fox's deeply entrenched intellectual skepticism about anything even remotely bordering on vulgar patriotism, *hadn't* there been something unique about America... other than its oft-alluded-to offenses of racism, sexism, imperialism, and rampant capitalism?

As the second decade of the century ground on and ground so many people around the world down through bankruptcy, failure, and compromise with violent aggressors, Leonard began to wonder—and even express his questions to Nubia—whether there hadn't truly been something *exceptional* to the old view and power of the United States after all.

"I guess I shouldn't have expected anything more from someone born in the fucking nineteen-fifties," Nubia had said shortly before she'd left him. "You'll *always* live in the fucking nineteen-fifties, along with Senator George McCarthy and the House Un-American Activities Committee."

He hadn't corrected her on Joseph McCarthy's first name. Nubia had been twenty-one years younger than Leonard. And beautiful. He missed her to this day.

But he'd thought her accusation unfair. He'd explained to her once that he didn't have a very clear memory of the Communist witch hunts of the early 1950s since he'd been born in 1958. Leonard couldn't even tell her about the love-peace-drugs-rock-music '60s since he'd only been twelve years old when *that* decade ended.

He confessed that the actual world around his childhood had seemed... what? A more *ordered* time. A saner time. A safer time. Even a cleaner time, he realized.

But, he argued, as all progressive liberal Democrats and intellectuals argued to themselves about the time he'd married Nubia (he just turning fifty years old and the head of his English Department, his beautiful bride not quite thirty and struggling for power in her department), the nation would have been different for Obama if the right-wingers hadn't left them with an economy that was crumbling and a foreign policy that was failing everywhere. (Except, when Leonard continued being honest with himself, he didn't *really* remember exploding economies or disastrously failing foreign policies during his thirties and forties.)

Sometime around 2011 or 2012, before Nubia left him and he'd left Colorado to come teach at UCLA, Leonard had asked various professors of economics at CU what was going on with the recession that would not end and the continuing financial, real estate, fiscal, and other crises. (Leonard had never had the slightest interest in economics... refused to treat it as a real discipline for study, much less a science. But who else could he turn to at such times?)

Five or six of the top economists on the faculty had tried to explain the convulsions then just beginning in earnest in arcane — but hopeful — terms. Leonard had tried to follow the explanations and succeeded to some extent. But he'd remained unconvinced.

Then, by chance, at a party at a fellow classics professor's home in the foothills above Boulder, Leonard had found himself having a drink with an ancient retired professor of economics who listened to Leonard's question, then pulled a small laptop out of his briefcase. (Phones and computers were separate things in those days, as hard as that was to imagine.)

The wrinkled old prof, already three sheets to the wind from the Scotch whiskey he'd been drinking all evening, punched up a chart and showed it to Leonard. Later, he'd e-mailed it to the English lit professor so Leonard still had a hard copy of it around somewhere.

The old chart showed a continued 8 percent debt-growth scenario—starting in 2010—with the debt shown as percentage of GDP and based on different predictions of growth, ranging from –1 percent to a healthy (but never-achieved) +4 percent.

At that never-achieved 4 percent of growth, the national debt would have equaled the Gross Domestic Product—i.e., equaled 1.0 when debt was divided by GDP—by 2015. But of course, the economy hadn't performed that well, and the actual ratio of debt to GDP had been closer to 1.2.

The old economist's debt-growth scenario had shown that by 2035, even if the economy had grown 4 percent a year, the debt-to-GDP ratio would be 2.2. In truth, Leonard knew, the ratio was now more than 5.0 to 1.

The chart had ended with a prediction of debt to GDP being as low as 3.2 in 2045—if the country had actually grown that much—and as bad as 18.0 in 2045 at the –1 percent growth rate.

The United States would never reach that dismal 18-times-debt-to-gross-product ratio, Leonard knew. America had gone bankrupt years ago.

"Three other economists and I worked that chart up four years ago," slurred the drunken old Libertarian. (Or so Leonard now suspected with some alarm.) "That's just the goddamned debt outgrowing the goddamned GDP, just as it did in Japan, and now the dragon is here and devouring us. Understand?"

"No," said Leonard. Although part of him did, even then.

"Here," said the old economist and pulled up another chart.

It showed the risks of growing entitlement spending and had bar graphs demonstrating how mandatory entitlement spending—Social Security, Medicare, Medicaid, and all the hundreds of other federal programs—would exceed total government revenues sometime between 2030 and 2040.

The chart had been wrong, Leonard knew. In reality, mandated entitlement spending had exceeded total government revenues before 2022, about the time the nation was officially declared bankrupt.

"That was based on projected mandatory entitlement *before* Obama and the Democrats rammed through their stimulus bills and all the rest of their entitlements," growled the old prof. "Notice that somewhere in the early twenty-thirties, our mandatory spending on entitlement programs will exceed our national GDP. By twenty-fifty, the damned *interest* on money borrowed to pay for entitlement programs—the old, smaller entitlement programs—will be greater than the GDP."

"That's ridiculous," Leonard remembered saying. "That can't happen."

"It can't?" said the old economist, breathing Scotch fumes into Leonard's face.

"Certainly not. The president and Congress would never let it come to that."

The old man across from him was trying to focus his gaze. "I know you. I've read about you. You're hot shit in English lit. Well, tell me, Mr. E-Lit Hot Shit, where's this country going to get the *money* to pay for these programs?"

"The economy will come back," said Leonard.

"That's what they said three years ago. And every single Wall Street recovery's been as legless as a quadriplegic Iraq veteran. And the economy—never the same as Wall Street, you understand—is worse. Isn't it? *Isn't* it? Small businesses being taxed and bullied out of existence. Unemployment rising again. Hell, there's a permanent unemployed class in this country again for the first time since the nineteen-thirties. Inflation returning with a vengeance, making everyone poorer by the day. Shoppers aren't spending. Buyers aren't buying. Banks aren't lending. And China, who still holds most of our paper, coming apart at the seams. *Their* economy—their miracle eight-percent-growth-a-year economy—turned out to be a bigger sham and bubble than ours. Their 'eight percent growth' was a bunch of old Communists determining their economic growth by fiat ahead of time—and paying for it out of government funds—like a retail store operator counting his inventory as profit."

Leonard hadn't understood that at all. But he was following the news on what was happening to and in and around China. It was frightening.

"The president has a lot of smart people around him," Leonard said, standing and getting ready to move away from the retired old fool.

"It's too fucking late for smart people," slurred the economist, his gaze going out of focus again. He looked at his empty Scotch glass and scowled as if he'd been robbed. "The smart people are the ones who've fucked up this country and the world for our grandkids, Mr. Hot Shit English Lit. Remember that."

And, for some reason, Leonard had.

WEDNESDAY

Val didn't come home on Tuesday night nor on Wednesday morning. A little after noon, Leonard called the LAPD to report a missing child.

After forty-five minutes dealing with voice-mail and holding (for some reason the LAPD played some sort of Turkish-sounding music in the background while people waited on hold; it sounded to Leonard like the wailing of crime victims), he finally got through to a police sergeant, waited another ten minutes while his call was transferred to Missing Persons, and then he was prompted for the facts. As soon as Leonard gave his grandson's age as "sixteen" he heard the interest go out of the policeman on the other end. The final advice was — Wait a week. Call the parents of your grandson's friends — ask them if the boy is there. If your grandson doesn't come home by then, call us again.

Leonard had wanted to call the parents of Val's friends, but the only boy in that group whose name he'd known was William Coyne. There were no Coynes in the ever-dwindling online phone book.

Hadn't the boy, William, in that one time they'd met where the young Coyne was obviously shining Leonard on, said something almost condescending about his mother working for the Japanese Advisor? Or for the city in some liaison capacity with Omura's staff?

Leonard had his phone search through all the online city official and Getty Castle directories but there was no Coyne listed anywhere. Wait…hadn't Val said something last year about his friend Billy the C's parents getting divorced? It had been part of a contemptuous spiel that Val had launched at Leonard about *everyone Val knew being from broken homes*. If she was divorced and back to her maiden name, what might it be in the Advisor's staff directory?

Leonard had no clue. He gave up that avenue of search.

Finally, in early afternoon, Leonard left a note for Val to phone him if he came home before his grandfather returned and spent the afternoon on his bike, searching the downtown as far south as the 10, as far west as the roadblocks at Highland Avenue that kept him out of Beverly Hills, as far east as the *reconquista* checkpoints along Ramona, and north to Glendale.

Everywhere there were convoys of armored military vehicles — National Guard, Homeland Security, and even some regular Army. The smoke in the south was very thick. Los Angeles radio and local Internet news reported nothing out of the ordinary.

In the end, returning to their still-empty and dark basement apartment around 7 p.m., Leonard was beside himself with anger and concern.

Perhaps it was just the sight and diesel-stink of all the military vehicles he'd seen and madly pedaled out of the way of that day, but Leonard wondered if this increased belligerence and erratic behavior from Val were a result of him turning sixteen and having to face the draft now in less than a year. It was the last real *discussion* that Leonard and his grandson had really had, that afternoon of the boy's lonely birthday "party." Leonard was sure that Nick's failure to call his son must have hurt Val deeply, but there was no discussion of that. Val's questions that evening centered on the draft, possible ways to avoid it (there were essentially none for a healthy, white young American male who'd registered, as Val had, when the forms showed up on his phone screen), and about the various wars that American soldiers were fighting for India and Japan.

On that last query, Leonard had been less than helpful — he really had trouble understanding the NSEACPS hegemony, much less its war goals in China and elsewhere, and could only explain that sending the troops to fight for the financially more stable India and Nippon was one of America's few sources of hard currency.

"Mr. Hartley at school says there was an *old* Southeast Asia Co-Prosperity Sphere almost a hundred years ago," Val had said, "and that it had something to do with that big war fought then, but I didn't quite understand the connection."

The connection is irony, Leonard had thought, but he'd explained about the militarist Japanese Empire and its fancy name for its short rule over major parts of China, Malaysia, what was then called Indochina, and the Philippines and other islands of the South Pacific. He gave a quick explanation of how the Japanese during their rapid imperial expansion had touted their brutal military occupations as a throwing off of white imperial domination — which it certainly was — but only in exchange for a Japanese version of Hitler's Master Race form of imperial conquest. "They were very close to adding Australia to their so-called co-prosperity sphere and would have done it if it hadn't been for the Battle of Midway," said Leonard but stopped when he saw the birthday boy's eyes glazing over. Val was a reader, but he didn't enjoy history the way his grandfather thought he should. As was true of most American high school students in this era of politicized curricular "relevance," Val had never been made to place ... say ... the Civil War within a hundred years of its actual dates.

Was Val running away because of the draft? Tens of thousands of pre-seventeen-year-old American kids did, Leonard knew.

But he still had almost eleven months. Certainly Val wasn't so frightened of the draft and of fighting overseas that he'd act so recklessly *now*.

As if commenting on Leonard's thoughts, the twenty-four-hour TV news channel he had babbling in the background—there were more than sixty on this basic sat subscription, one catering to almost every political stance imaginable—announced that "United Nations forces" had, after "fierce fighting with local rebels loyal to Chinese warlord Lǔ fěi Zhōngzhèng," taken the key city of Langzhong. Leonard had no idea where Langzhong was nor did he ask his phone to find out. None of it mattered. He had a sudden flash of a kid born twenty years or so earlier than he'd been, before World War II, which Val thought of only as "that big war fought a hundred years or so ago," moving pins on giant wall maps as battles raged and American and Allied forces moved closer to Berlin or Tokyo.

The "United Nations forces" always cited in the news reports about fighting in China these days simply meant American forces. India, Japan, and the Group of Five so dominated the expanded Security Council that the UN did their bidding without so much as a threat of a veto. When the fighting dealt with the Balkans, Africa, or the Caribbean, Leonard knew, "UN forces" meant the Russians, who were trying as hard as the Americans to earn some hard currency by hiring out their military.

Leonard sighed and shifted the small phone from one hand to the other. He realized that he was doing the Academic's Shuffle—shifting his thought from real-world worries and fears, not to mention the need for rapid decision making, to vague historical musings and abstractions. It was almost 10:30 p.m. He would have to call Val's father in Denver. He had no other choice. The boy might be injured or kidnapped or dead...lying in a ditch somewhere in one of the taped-off and unrepaired earthquake zones near the old freeways. It was precisely the kind of place where flashgangs such as Val's loved to hang out.

Leonard realized that this moment was the first time he'd admitted to himself that Val was almost certainly running with a flashgang.

Sighing again, he lifted the phone to punch Nick Bottom's number.

Val stomped in smelling of gasoline and something sharper, more astringent—gunpowder? Cordite?

The boy didn't even look at his grandfather but went straight to his room. Deathcult Rock started blasting through the locked door.

Leonard marched angrily to that door and raised his fist to bang on it. Then he paused. What was he going to say to the boy that hadn't been said? What ultimatum was he going to give that he hadn't already given?

Leonard went back to his study and sat in the weak cone of light from the single desk lamp.

Tomorrow he'd go see Emilio. In the meantime, he could only hope that Val and his buddies would be caught in the act for some small crime they were committing. That way, if it were a first offense and since Val was a juvenile, the LAPD would implant a tracker in Val, and Leonard wouldn't have to pay for it or the tracker software.

Leonard was ashamed of what he was thinking and wishing for. But he still wished it.

THURSDAY

After Val left for school in the morning, Leonard went to find Emilio. He carried his life's savings in cash in a canvas messenger bag slung over his shoulder.

Leonard rode his bicycle southeast from Echo Park past

the Dodger Stadium Detention Center and under the Pasadena Freeway to where Sunset became Cesar Chavez Avenue. As the neighborhoods deteriorated, Leonard was certain that some-one would rob him for the bicycle and end up with the more than a million new dollars in his messenger bag. The older Pro-fessor George Leonard Fox got, the more he was certain that the only real god was Bitch Irony.

No one robbed him during his cycling east.

By midmorning he was at the old Union Station, a land-mark he loved—Leonard and his daughter Dara had once spent a weekend just watching old movies, most of them set in the 1930s to the 1950s, with major scenes shot in Union Station—and then south under the abandoned stretch of the 101. It was a hot day for September and Leonard was sweating through his white shirt by the time he reached his first road-block where Santa Fe Avenue ran into East 4th Street.

East 4th was barricaded. On both sides of the street hung the large green-white-red tricolors of Nuevo Mexico. Unlike the former United States of Mexico flag designed in 1968, the eagle in the center of these flags was not wrestling with a snake and was facing forward. It wore a crown. Emilio had once explained that this flag was based on the 1821 flag of the First Mexican Empire, but the new eagle was so stylized that it reminded Leonard more of the FDR-era National Recovery Act eagle or—more ominously—of the stylized Nazi eagle.

He didn't have time now to study the flags. Men armed with automatic weapons came out from behind the permanent barricades.

"*¿Qué quieres, viejo?*"

Professor George Leonard Fox didn't appreciate the "old man" but he presented the card Emilio had given him and answered in a voice he managed to keep from quavering, "*Exijo que me lleven a la casa de Gabriel Fernández y Figueroa.*"

Perhaps he shouldn't have used the verb "demand," but it was too late now. One of the spanics started to laugh but his comrade holding the small card showed it to him and the laugh-ter died.

"¿Por qué quieres ver a Don Fernández y Figueroa, gringo viejo?"

Leonard was tired of the smirks and insults. "Just take me there," he said in English. "Don Fernández y Figueroa is expecting me."

Five of the armed men conferred rapidly. Then the one with the card gestured Leonard toward a black Volkswagen G-wagen parked behind a barricade. "Come."

———

EMILIO LIVED IN A huge old home just east of Evergreen Cemetery.

Actually, Leonard realized as his escort led him through layers of roadblocks and sentries, it was far more an armed compound than a home. Military vehicles with the crowned-eagle Nuevo Mexico flag painted on the sides filled the streets for blocks around. Across the street, the wall and fence surrounding the huge Evergreen Cemetery had been knocked down and Leonard could see scores more wheeled and tracked vehicles parked on the faded grass. In front of Emilio's address, rows of large, black SUVs filled the street at roadblock angles. The compound's walls were topped with embedded broken glass and multiple rolls of razor wire.

His guide was stopped half a dozen times inside the compound's walls and in the house itself and each time the card was presented. Twice Leonard was frisked—aggressively, embarrassingly, thoroughly. It would have been absurdly easy for them to appropriate his bag of money, but other than a quick search through the rubber-banded stacks of bills, no one paid attention to his paltry life's savings.

On all sides of the tiled foyer hallway clustered groups of men in various rooms. They were smoking, arguing, bent over maps, gesturing. Everyone seemed to be talking on cell phones even as they argued and gestured. His escort led him up two flights of stairs and down a broad hallway. Two men in civilian clothes but carrying automatic weapons stood guard outside the open doorway of a library. Again the card was presented by his guide. Leonard was frisked a third and final time and they opened the door wider and allowed him to enter. Again the searchers looked at his messenger bag full of bank notes and said nothing.

The room was impressive. Bookcases filled with leather-bound old tomes rose twelve feet on three sides of the library. The fourth wall was windows and through it Leonard could see and hear black helicopters landing in a paved area of several acres within the walls of the compound. Emilio Gabriel Fernández y Figueroa was sitting behind a broad desk. Opposite him was a bald man in his early fifties and Leonard could see at once that the two men were related. Both stood as he approached.

"Leonard," said his Saturday-morning Echo Park chess partner of the past four years.

"Don Fernández y Figueroa," said Leonard, bowing slightly in respect.

"No, no," said the older man. "Emilio. I am Emilio. Allow me to introduce my son Eduardo. Eduardo, this is my chess and conversation partner of whom I have spoken with such respect, Professor Emeritus Dr. George Leonard Fox."

Eduardo bowed his bald head. His voice was very soft. *"Es un verdadero placer conocerlo, señor."*

"The pleasure is mine," said Leonard.

Saying to Emilio, "I will see to the dispositions, Father," Eduardo bowed toward Leonard again and left the room, shutting the tall door behind him.

Leonard felt his heart pounding. All these years he'd known that Emilio's sons and grandsons must be important in the *reconquista* movement in California and Los Angeles, but now he realized that it was *Emilio* who was in charge. Why had this important—and dangerous—man wasted so many slow Saturday mornings with a retired classics/English lit professor?

Leonard had never noticed bodyguards in Echo Park on those mornings, but now he realized that they must have been there.

"You have decided to leave Los Angeles, my friend?" said Emilio, waving Leonard to the empty chair and taking his own seat behind the broad, empty desk. Outside the window, more helicopters were landing and taking off.

"Yes."

"*Bueno*," said Emilio. "It is a good time for such a move." The older man hesitated a second, cleared his throat, and continued. "In two days—early Saturday morning, before dawn—the state of California will attempt to assassinate me here. They will use a Great White predator drone and will destroy this entire compound, hoping to kill me, my family, and everyone here."

"Good God…"

"*Sí*," said Emilio. "God *is* good. He allowed us to gain this valuable intelligence. My family and I shall not be here when the missiles strike. The forces of the *reconquista* are ready to respond. Within a week, all of the City of Angels will be under new leadership."

Leonard had no idea what to say to this so he set the heavy messenger bag on the desk.

"One million three hundred thousand in new dollars," he said in a strangely strangled voice. "My entire life's savings. I kept only a small bit for expenses during the trip."

Emilio did not look in the bag. He nodded courteously. "It is less than the usual price for two people being transported from here to Denver…you still wish to go to Denver, my friend?"

"Yes."

"It is less than the usual price, but the convoy leader owes me a favor," continued Emilio. The old man smiled, showing nicotine-stained teeth. "Also, our *reconquista* men and vehicles are providing security for this convoy. The convoy leader would not wish to alienate us over a few dollars one way or the other."

"When does the convoy leave?" asked Leonard. He felt hollow, almost buoyant, as if he'd downed several strong drinks. This dialogue belonged in a movie, not in Professor George Leonard Fox's life.

"Midnight Friday," said Emilio. "Mere hours before the scheduled attack on my home. There will be twenty-three eighteen-wheelers in this convoy, some private vehicles, and, of course, our security vehicles. You and your grandson will ride in one of the large trucks. In the extended cab, of course."

"Where do I go to find the convoy?" Leonard's worry was that the rendezvous point would be too deep in East Los Angeles for Val and him to get there on bicycle or foot. Or at least get there alive.

"The old railyards off North Mission Road, just above where the One-oh-One runs into the Ten," said Emilio. "You can get there easily by taking West Sunset past North Alameda to North Mission Road. There should be no roadblocks or checkpoints until you get to the railyards themselves. I have a letter of transit drafted and signed for you."

Letter of transit, thought Leonard. He'd never heard that phrase outside of the movie *Casablanca*. Now Don Emilio Gabriel Fernández y Figueroa was reaching into his desk and drawing out and handing to him such a document. Emilio's bold signature took up most of the width of the page.

The two men stood and Leonard used both his hands to shake Emilio's liver-spotted, heavily veined, but still powerful hand. "Thank you, my good friend," said Leonard. He was terrified and exhilarated and close to weeping.

Emilio called to him before he got to the door. "Your grandson...he will go with you?"

"He'll go," Leonard said grimly.

"Good. I doubt if we shall see each other again...at least in this life. Go with God, my dear friend."

"And you," said Leonard. "Good luck, Emilio."

Outside in the hallway, his former guide and Emilio's son Eduardo were waiting with three armed men.

———

VAL CAME HOME EARLY that evening, in time for dinner. As they ate their microwaved meal, Leonard told his grandson of the plan to leave at midnight of the next day. He did not phrase it as an option for the boy.

"I'm told the convoy will take about ten days to get to Denver," finished Leonard. "You'll see your father in a week and a half."

Val looked at him calmly, almost appraisingly. Whatever

objection he was going to raise, Leonard had the answer. If necessary, he would take Eduardo Emilio Fernández y Figueroa up on his offer to have two *reconquista* fighters come to Leonard's home and carry Val to the midnight rendezvous point.

But surprisingly—amazingly—Val said, "Midnight Friday? A convoy to Denver? That's a great idea, Leonard. What do we take with us?"

"Just what we can get in two small duffel bags," replied his astonished grandfather. "And that includes our own food for the trip."

"Great," said Val. "I'll go pack the few clothes I want to take. And a couple of books, I guess. Nothing else."

Leonard still couldn't believe it was going to be this simple. "You don't have to go to school tomorrow," he said. "And we can't let anyone know we're leaving, Val. Someone might try to stop us."

"Yeah," said the sixteen-year-old, his eyes slightly unfocused as if he were thinking about something else. "But no, I'll go to school. I need to clean a few things out of my locker. But I'll be home by nine tomorrow."

"No later than nine!" said Leonard. He was afraid of what the boy might be doing with his friends on that final evening.

"No later than nine, Grandpa. I promise."

Leonard could only blink. When was the last time that Val had called him Grandpa? He couldn't recall.

FRIDAY

Leonard spent the day sick with worry. The two duffels, packed full of food bars, canteens, fresh fruit, and a few clothes and books, sat near the kitchen door as if to mock the old man.

He'd started to phone Nick Bottom to tell him that they were coming and then put it off. He'd wait until they were actually on the road.

I don't believe this was his actual thought. He'd believe it when they crossed the California line into Nevada.

Val came home a few minutes after eight o'clock. The

boy's clothes were filthy with mud and there was blood on his forehead and shirt. His eyes were wide.

"Leonard, give me your phone!"

"What? What's wrong? What happened?"

"Give me your fucking phone!"

Leonard handed the phone to the crazed boy, wondering whom he was going to call and with what news. But Val smashed the phone under the heel of his heavy boot—once, twice, as many times as it took for the components to spill out. The boy grabbed the chip and ran out the door.

Leonard was too surprised to chase after him.

Val was back in three minutes. "I tossed it onto the back of a truck headed west," he panted.

"Val, sit down. You're bleeding."

The boy shook his head. "Not my blood, Grandpa. Turn on the TV."

The Los Angeles News Channel was in the middle of a special bulletin.

"...of a terrorist attack at the rededication of the Disney Center for the Performing Arts earlier this evening. Shots were fired at Advisor Daichi Omura, but the Advisor was not injured. We repeat, Advisor Omura was not injured during the terrorist attack, although two of his bodyguards were killed along with at least five of the terrorists. We have video now of..."

Leonard could no longer hear the announcer's words. Or, rather, he could no longer make sense of them.

There on the screen were the dead faces of several of the terrorists. They were all boys. Their faces were blood-streaked, their dead eyes open and staring. The camera paused on the last dead face.

It was the face of young William Coyne.

Leonard turned in horror toward his grandson. "What have you *done?*"

Val had both duffels and was shoving one against his grandfather's chest. "We gotta go, Leonard. *Now.*"

"No, we have to call the authorities...straighten this out..."

Val shook him with a strength that Leonard never would

have imagined in the boy. "There's nothing to straighten out, old man. If they catch me, they'll kill me. Do you understand? We have to *go!*"

"The rendezvous at the railyard's not until midnight...," mumbled Leonard. His extremities were tingling and he felt dizzy. He realized that he was in shock.

"It doesn't matter," gasped Val as he splashed water from the kitchen sink onto his face, wiping the blood away with the small towel hanging on the washing machine. "We'll hide there until it's time. But we have to *go...*now!"

"The lights...," said Leonard as Val dragged him out the back door.

Val said nothing as he tugged his grandfather to the bicycles and the old man and the boy began pedaling madly down the unlit alley.

1.07

Six Flags Over the Jews — Monday, Sept. 13

THERE WAS A MAN cruicified above the iron gates of the Denver Country Club but it didn't slow Nick down in his Monday-morning commute up Speer Boulevard to Six Flags Over the Jews. The phone news had no identity on the crucified man and there was no announcement yet on the reason for his crucifixion. Traffic moved briskly and Nick had to flog the gelding to keep up, getting only the briefest glimpse to his left of various emergency vehicles around the entrance and cops on ladders. The once-expensive and -exclusive country club hadn't been a country club for some years now and the golf course and tennis courts were covered with several hundred windowless blue tents of the sort the UN liked to bring in to Third World countries after tsunamis or plague. No one that Nick knew was aware of the purpose for these tents here at the club — or, for that matter, which country or corporation owned the country club these days — and no one seemed to care, including Nick.

He'd used all the flashback Sato had given him and slept all Sunday afternoon and Sunday night. This sort of full-systems crash happened often with heavy flashback users; the drug's effect seemed like sleep, down to the rapid eye movements, but it wasn't sleep. At least not the kind of deep sleep the human brain required. So once every couple of weeks, flashback users crashed and slept for twenty-four hours or more.

Except for a headache that felt like the world's worst hangover, Nick had to admit that he felt more refreshed.

The problem was that nothing around him—not Speer Boulevard with its overhanging trees, not the thrumming traffic in the two peasant lanes or the skateboard-low humming hydrogen-car traffic in the VIP lane, not the hundreds of make-shift shacks along the trickling course of Cherry Creek sunken between the bikepaths fifteen feet below the level of the street—seemed real. This had been the case for at least five years now but it seemed worse this month. The flashback hours with Dara were real; this nonsense interlude with Sato or impro-vising bad lines with the bit players in this poorly written, poorly lit, poorly acted play was certainly *not* real.

But what was confusing Nick Bottom now was his multiple use of flashback. He'd used it to review the interview with Danny Oz almost six years ago. He'd used it, as he had every day for the past five and a half years, to spend time with his dead wife.

But he'd also used hours of the drug to try to find out where Dara might have been on the night that Keigo Nakamura was killed.

He'd been out on a stakeout on Santa Fe Drive that night, down on the edge of the *reconquista* no-man's-land there, sitting in the backseat of an unmarked patrol car as the two detectives up front watched the home of a local warlord who, they knew, was moving guns and drugs into the city. As a Major Crimes day-shift detective, Nick Bottom had had no business in the backseat of that particular unmarked car on that particular stakeout on that particular night, but in that first year after his promotion he'd had the stupid idea that he could do his white-collar downtown detective work while still staying fully in touch with the mean streets and their denizens, both crook and cop.

He couldn't. It had been a stupid idea.

The two detectives sitting in the front seat that night—

Cummings, the detective third grade with seven years in as a patrol officer but less than a year's experience as detective, and Coleman, a twenty-five-year veteran in the DPD and nine years a detective first grade (the same grade as Nick)—had let him know that night that he was as useless and unwelcome as the proverbial tit on an equally proverbial boar.

Nick had been there anyway, shivering in the chill—they'd shut off the batteries to conserve power—and breathing in the well-known stakeout smell of sweat and old-car vinyl and coffee breath and the occasional silent but deadly fart from the front seat. God help him, he'd loved it the years he worked the street.

The flashback reliving of that hour had reminded Nick that he'd phoned Dara a little before midnight. He'd meant to phone earlier, but he'd been out at a corner all-night bodega getting coffee for Coleman and Cummings then. As it was, she didn't pick up. It had surprised Nick, but it hadn't worried him. When he was working on the street, she always left her phone on. That afternoon—he remembered this only through the flashback reliving of the hour around midnight—he'd told her he'd be working late, but he hadn't told her that he'd be on the street. She often turned her phone off when she knew he was safe doing office work at Central Division.

That night, Nick now remembered, he'd gotten about three hours' sleep on the couch at DPD CD and had been wakened when the call came in from the division commander, turning the Keigo murder case over to him and his partner, K. T. Lincoln. The word was that the responding detectives didn't have boots high enough for this sort of politically charged case. Nick was still a department golden boy then; K. T. Lincoln brought some nice racial, gender, and sexual-orientation balance to the whole thing. (The commander admitted that he would have assigned a Japanese detective to the case, if they'd had a Jap with a gold shield, which they didn't. In fact, the commander confessed, the entire Denver Police Department had only one officer of Japanese descent, and she was a rookie patrol officer taking her lumps and learning over in the Five Corners area. Nick Bottom and K. T. Lincoln would have to do.)

Nick had used a fifteen-minute vial of flashback reliving his call to Dara that morning. She'd been strangely unexcited about his news, even though closing the case could have meant a huge boost in his career. As assistant to a Denver ADA, she knew about such things. She sounded tired, even drugged. When Nick mentioned that he'd tried to call her around midnight the night before, there'd been a pause—more noticeable to the second-Nick reliving the moment via flashback than to the caffeine-jazzed real-time Nick that morning—and she'd said she'd taken a pill and turned off the phone and gone to bed early.

The three seconds' worth of video image of Dara's face across the street from Keigo's apartment that night haunted Nick more than anything had since she'd died. He'd down-loaded the video file into his phone and watched it a dozen times, using his wall-wide HD3D display in his cubie for the clearest image, and sometimes he was certain it was Dara; other times he was even more certain that it wasn't—that it was a woman who didn't even really *look* like Dara.

He'd also done three more fifteen-minute flashes of the phone conversation with her on the morning he'd told her about the Keigo murder, then flashed and reflashed an hour of the first time he'd seen her that next evening.

Did she seem false that evening? Did she seem to be hiding something from him?

Was he losing his mind?

Had he lost it long ago?

———

WHAT EVERYONE NOW CALLED Six Flags Over the Jews was just to the left of the overpass where Speer Boulevard met I-25. Across the highway on the hill to the southwest of the sprawling complex loomed the Mile High Homeland Security Detention Center.

Nick had been vaguely curious why they called the amusement-park-turned-refugee-center Six Flags, since the company that ran the other Six Flags amusement parks only owned this one for about ten years right at the beginning of the century.

For more than a century before that and for some years after the brief Six Flags era, the park had been called Elitch Gardens.

There were no gardens in sight now as Nick turned into the huge, empty parking area and followed concrete blast shields toward the first of several security checkpoints.

Nick knew about the old Elitch Gardens because of his grandfather. Nick's father, who'd died when Nick was fifteen, had been a state patrol officer. Nick's earliest memory of his old man was of his pistol, a large Smith & Wesson revolver. Nick's father hadn't died in a shootout (like Nick, he'd never fired his weapon in the line of duty), but in an accident on I-25 not two miles from where Nick's wife, Dara, and her boss, Assistant District Attorney Harvey Cohen, had died. Nick's father had pulled over to help a stranded motorist and a drunken sixteen-year-old driver had swerved onto the shoulder and killed him.

Nick's grandfather had been a bus driver in the city and his great-grandfather had been a motorman on the old trolleys that connected Denver and its suburbs and nearby towns before cars forced them out. From Grandpa Nicholas, Nick had heard lovely tales of the old Elitch Gardens, whose motto for decades was *Not to See Elitch's Is Not to See Denver.*

First opened in 1890, the original Elitch Gardens had been miles away from the downtown to the west, out at 38th Avenue and Tennyson Street in a suburb that was more like a separate village. That first Elitch Gardens, while growing, had kept its trees, extensive flower gardens, and shaded picnic areas where guests could eat lunches they'd packed for themselves. For forty years or so it had a zoo and for a century it boasted the Theater at the Gardens, first offering summer-stock performances and then, later in the twentieth century, visiting movie and TV stars. By the 1930s, Elitch's had added the Trocadero Ballroom for dancing and visiting jazz groups and big bands and Nick's grandfather had mentioned listening to *An Evening at the Troc* weekly national radio broadcast. Sometime in the 1950s the owners had added a Kiddieland with its little open-wheel race cars, two-seat rocket planes, and real floating "motorboats," and although big amusement parks had catered almost exclusively to adults up until then, Elitch's Kiddieland was a huge hit.

In 1994, Elitch's had moved to its present location near the downtown and two years later had been purchased by the corporation that operated other Six Flags parks across America. The new owners abandoned grass and gardens for cement and concrete, Kiddieland and slow sky rides for ever more inverted-high-g screaming rides, and entrance prices that required a bank loan for a family. When Six Flags sold it sometime around 2006, the new company, although restoring the name Elitch Gardens, finished the job of destroying the last vestige of gardens and enjoyment for anyone other than the seriously adrenaline-addicted.

Nick knew all this detail because his grandfather and mother both had used Elitch's as a metaphor for America in the last part of the twentieth century and early part of the twenty-first—abandoning shade and gardens and grace and affordable family fun for overpriced sun-glaring terror at six g's inverted.

Well, thought Nick as he parked the car and walked toward the checkpoint across the cracked, heaving, and weed-strewn parking pavement, America had got all the terror it could ever have hoped for.

THE SECURITY PEOPLE AT the entrance checkpoint were ex-DPD and remembered Nick and treated him well, and the magical black card that Nakamura had recently sent to him via Sato settled all other issues. One of the guards phoned ahead to alert Danny Oz to be ready for a visitor and even led Nick through the thick maze of hovels, tents, abandoned amusement park rides, and open-air kiosks.

"It looks like they have everything right in here," said Nick, just to make conversation.

"Oh, yeah," said the guard, a retired patrolman named Charlie Duquane, "the camp's pretty self-sufficient. They have their own doctors and dentists and psychiatrists and a decent medical clinic. They've even got six synagogues."

"What's the resident count?"

"Around twenty-six thousand," said Charlie. "Give or take a couple a hundred."

The resident count six years ago had been a little over thirty-two thousand. Nick knew that many of the Israeli refugees were older and cancer was rampant in all the camps. Almost none were released into the general population.

He met with the poet in an otherwise empty mess tent under the rusting steel coils and pillars of some upside-down high-speed scream ride.

The hand behind the handshake was listless, clammy, bony, and weak. Nick had just seen Danny Oz in his flashback preparation and in the 3D crime-scene re-creation back at Keigo Nakamura's LoDo apartment complex and there was no doubt that the man had aged horribly in the past six years. Oz had been thin and graying and vaguely tubercular-looking six years ago in a properly poetic way, his hair already turned mostly gray in his early fifties, but there had been a coiled-spring energy to the thin figure then and the eyes had been as animated as the poet's conversation. Now he was an animated corpse: skin and eyes a jaundiced yellow; gray hair as yellowed as the teeth of the heavy smoker; laugh lines and somewhat attractive scholarly wrinkles transformed to grooves and furrows in skin pulled far too tight over an eagerly emerging skull.

Nick knew that Danny Oz had come out of what the Jews called the Second Holocaust with some sort of radiation-induced cancer (all eleven of the bombs had been made very dirty indeed by the True Believers who'd built them), but he couldn't remember what kind of cancer it was.

It didn't matter. Whatever it was, it was slowly killing the poet.

"It's a pleasure to see you again, Detective Bottom. Did you ever catch young Mr. Nakamura's killer?"

"No 'Detective' before my name any longer, Mr. Oz," said Nick. "They fired me from the force more than five and a half years ago. And no, they're no closer to getting Keigo Nakamura's killer than they were six years ago."

Danny Oz drew deeply from his cigarette—Nick belatedly realized that it was cannabis, possibly for the cancer pain—and squinted through exhaled smoke. "If you're not with the police any longer, to what do I owe the pleasure of this visit, *Mr.* Bottom?"

Nick explained that he'd been hired by the victim's father while he noticed that, even allowing for the joint and the possibility that they'd wakened Oz for this visit, the poet's eyes were too unfocused, set in a stare above and beyond Nick's right shoulder. Nick recognized that kind of thousand-yard stare from those mornings when he decided to shave. Danny Oz was using a lot more flashback than he'd been on six years ago.

"So do we go through the same questions as six years ago or come up with new ones?" asked Danny Oz.

"Have you thought of anything else that might be of help, Mr. Oz?"

"Danny. And no, I haven't. You and your fellow investigators are still going on the assumption that it was something that came up during his video interviews that got Keigo Nakamura killed?"

"There aren't any 'fellow investigators,'" said Nick with a ghost of a smile. "And I don't have anything as elegant or advanced as a theory. Just going over old ground, I'm afraid."

"Well, it's still a pleasure to talk to a character from *A Midsummer Night's Dream*," said Oz. "And I've often thought of what you told me."

"What's that?"

"That you didn't *know* that you were a character in Shakespeare's play until your wife told you."

Nick did grin now. "You have a damned good memory, Mr. . . . Danny." *Unless you flashed on our last meeting, too. But why would you waste money and drug for that? To keep your story straight?* "But Dara wasn't my wife yet when she broke the news of the other Nick Bottom to me. We were dating . . . sort of. She was an undergraduate and I was already a cop, going back to school to get hours toward my master's degree."

"How did you take the news? Of your ears and possible sexual intimacy with the Queen of the Fairies, I mean."

"I dealt with it," said Nick. "It was the other Nick Bottom's vision—or what he said was a dream-vision he'd awakened from—that Dara was interested in. She thought that I had just such a joyous awakening…an epiphany, she called it…in my future. That first night on our date, she recited almost the entire passage from the play from memory. I was very impressed."

Danny Oz smiled, drew deeply from the joint, and stubbed it out in a coffee can lid he was using as an ashtray. He lit another cigarette—a regular one this time, which seemed to please him more—and squinted through the smoke as he recited:

"When my cue comes, call me and I will answer. My next is 'Most fair Pyramus.' Heigh-ho! Peter Quince? Flute the bellows-mender? Snout, the tinker? Starveling? God's my life! Stolen hence, and left me asleep! I have had a most rare vision. I have had a dream, past the wit of man to say what dream it was. Man is but an ass if he go about to expound this dream. Methought I was—there is no man can tell what. Methought I was—and methought I had—but man is but a patched fool if he will offer to say what methought I had. The eye of man hath not heard, the ear of man hath not seen, man's hand is not able to taste, his tongue to conceive, or his heart to report, what my dream was. I will get Peter Quince to write a ballad of this dream: it shall be called Bottom's Dream, because it hath no bottom; and I will sing it in the latter end of a play, before the Duke. Peradventure, to make it the more gracious, I shall sing it at her death."

Nick felt something like a hot electric shock run through his system. He'd never heard those words spoken aloud by anyone but Dara. "As I said, you've got one hell of a memory, Mr. Oz," he said.

The older man shrugged and drew deeply on his cigarette, as if the smoke were holding back his pain. "Poets. We remember things. That's part of what makes us poets."

"My wife had one of your books," said Nick and was immediately and painfully sorry he'd brought it up. "One of your books of poetry, I mean. In English. She showed it to me after I interviewed you six years ago."

Less than three months before she died.

Danny Oz smiled slightly, waiting.

Realizing that he had to say something about the poems, Nick said, "I don't really understand modern poems."

Now Oz's smile was real, showing the large, nicotine-stained teeth. "I'm afraid my verse never attained modernity, Detective... I mean, Mr. Bottom. I wrote in the epic form, old in Homer's day."

Nick showed his palms in surrender.

"Did you and your wife," began Oz, "on your first date, I mean, get into what Shakespeare's Bottom was talking about in that passage?"

The Santa Fe knife wounds deep in Nick Bottom's deeper belly muscles were hurting as if they were new, shooting threads of fire deeper into him. Why the goddamn hell had he brought up Dara and that fucking passage from the play? Oz wouldn't even know that Dara was dead. Nick's belly clenched in anticipation of what the dying poet might say next. He hurried to fill the silence before Oz could speak.

"Yeah, sort of. My wife was the English major. We both thought it was weird that Bottom waking from his dream had his senses all mixed up. You know—the eye hath not heard, the ear hath not seen, the hand is not able to taste—all that stuff. We decided Bottom's dream had messed up his senses, like that real disease of the nerves... whatchamacallit."

"Synesthesia," said Danny Oz, tipping ashes into the coffee can lid. Another brief flick of what could have been a wry, self-mocking smile. "I only know the word because it's the same one used in writing where a metaphor uses terms from one kind of sense impression to describe another, like... oh... a 'loud color.' Yes, that was very strange and Shakespeare uses synesthesia again later in the play when the actors in the play-within-a-play ask Theseus, the Duke of Athens, whether he'd prefer to 'hear' a bergamask dance or 'see' an epilogue."

"I don't really understand any of that literary stuff," said

Nick. He wondered if he should just abort the interview and stand up and walk away.

Oz persisted. His pain-filled eyes seemed to catch a new gleam of interest as he squinted through the smoke. "But it is very queer, to use an old word that's coming back into proper usage. Bottom says at the end of his dream-epiphany speech that after his friend Peter Quince turns the revelation in his, Bottom's, dream into a ballad, 'I shall sing it at her death.' But whose death? Who is the 'she' who will be dying?"

The knife twisted in Nick Bottom's bowels. He spoke through gritted teeth. "Whatshername. The character who dies in the play the Bottom guy is putting on in front of the Duke."

Danny Oz shook his head. "Thisbe? No, I think not. Nor is he speaking of the death of Titania, the fairy queen that Bottom may have slept with. The woman at whose death he'll be singing this all-important ballad is a total mystery...something above or outside the play. It's like a clue to a Shakespearean mystery that no one has noticed."

Ask me if I give a fucking shit, Nick thought fiercely. Surely the older man could see Nick's pain even through his own smugness and smoke. But the thousand-yard stare seemed more focused on Nick and at ease than at any time before. Nick was very aware of the 9mm semiautomatic pistol on his hip. If he shot Danny Oz in the head today, both he and the poet would feel better.

Oz said, "As enjoyable as literary criticism connected to your name is, Mr. Bottom, I imagine you want to ask me a few questions."

"Just a few," said Nick, realizing that his hand was already on the butt of the pistol under his loose shirt. It took an effort to relax his grip and bring the sweaty hand back up to the table. "Mostly I just wanted to see if you remembered anything else about the interview with Keigo Nakamura."

Oz shook his head. "Totally banal...both the questions and my answers, I mean. Young Mr. Nakamura was interested in us...in me...in all of the Israeli refugees here, only in terms of our flashback use."

"And you told him that you did use flashback," said Nick.

Oz nodded. "One thing I was curious about six years ago but was too nervous to ask about, Mr. Bottom. You questioned all of us who'd been interviewed by Keigo Nakamura in his last days with a focus on what questions he'd asked in the interviews. Why didn't you just view the video he shot? Or were you testing our memory for some reason? Or our honesty?"

"The camera and memory chips were stolen when Keigo Nakamura was murdered that night," said Nick. "Other than some scribbled prep notes and the memory of some of his assistants, we had no idea what questions he asked you and the others in the final four days of interviews."

"Ah," said Oz. "That makes sense. You know, one thing that Keigo Nakamura asked me that I don't believe I remembered in the police interviews years ago...it just came to me recently...he asked me if I would use F-two."

"F-two?" said Nick, shocked. "Did he act as if he thought it was real?"

"That's the strange thing, Mr. Bottom," said Oz. "He did."

F-two, Flashback-two, had been a rumor for more than a decade now. It was supposed to be an improvement on the drug flashback where one could not only relive one's actual past, but live fantasy alternatives to one's past reality. Those who kept insisting that the drug would appear on the streets any day now, and who had insisted this for almost fifteen years, said that F-two was a mixture of regular flashback and a complex hallucinogenic drug that keyed on endorphins, so the F-two fantasies would always be pleasurable, never nightmares. One would never feel pain in an F-two dream.

F-two believers compared the mythical drug to splicing an existing film—or editing video with special digital effects—so that the memories currently available to be relived through all one's senses via flashback would be a sort of raw material for happy dreams with all of the sight, smell, taste, and touch of flashback, but directed by one's fantasies. Until Nick had realized that F-two really was a myth, that it had never appeared on the street anywhere in the world, he'd imagined using it himself so that he could not only relive his *past* with Dara but live a new, imagination-structured *future* with her.

"What'd you tell Keigo when he asked?" said Nick.

"I said that I didn't believe there ever was going to be a drug like F-two," said Oz, inhaling deeply as he smoked, holding the smoke in, and exhaling almost regretfully. "And I told him that if there were such a drug in the future, I almost certainly wouldn't use it, since I produced enough fantasies in my own mind. I told him that I used flashback to remember a single memory...over and over." The poet's cigarette was mostly ash now. "You might say that I'm obsessive."

"Do you still use flashback?" asked Nick. He knew the answer, but he was curious if Oz would admit to it.

The poet laughed. "Oh, yes, Mr. Bottom. More than ever. I spend at least eight hours a day under the flash these days. I'll probably be flashing when this prostate cancer finally kills me."

Where do you get all the fucking money for the drugs? was Nick's thought. But instead of asking that, he nodded and said, "In the interview six years ago, I don't believe you told me what you were flashing on. You said that Keigo hadn't asked you... although I would have thought that this would have been his focus with all flashback users."

"He didn't ask me," said Oz. "Which was decidedly odd. But then it was odd that he chose me to interview at all."

"Why's that?"

"Because, as you know, Keigo Nakamura was making a video documentary about *Americans'* use of flashback. His entire theme and central metaphor were about the decline of a once-great culture that had turned its face away from the future and sunken into obsession with its own past—with three hundred and forty million individual pasts. But I'm not an American, Mr. Bottom. I'm Israeli. Or was."

This question of why Keigo had chosen to talk to Oz hadn't come up in the interview and Nick didn't know if it was important or not. But it was definitely odd.

"So what do you flash on, Mr. Oz?"

The poet lit a new cigarette from the butt of the last and

ground the dying one out. "I lost all of my extended family in the attack, Mr. Bottom. Both my parents were still alive. Two brothers and two sisters. All married. All with families. My young second wife and our young boy and girl—David was six, Rebecca eight. My ex-wife, Leah, with whom I was on good terms, and our twenty-one-year-old son Lev. All gone in twenty minutes of nuclear fire or murdered later by the Arab invaders in their cheap Russian-made radiation suits."

"So you flash to spend time with them all," Nick said wearily. He was supposed to go to Boulder later this afternoon for the interview with Derek Dean at Naropa, but right now he didn't have the energy to drive that far, much less do another interview.

"Never," said Danny Oz.

Nick sat up and raised an eyebrow.

Oz smiled with almost infinite sadness and flicked ashes. "I've never once used the drug to go back to my family."

"What then? What *do* you flash on, Mr. Oz?" Nick should have added an *If you don't mind me asking* or some such polite phrase, but he'd forgotten that he was no longer a cop. That forgetting hadn't happened for a while.

"The day of the attack," said Danny Oz. "I replay the day my country died over and over and over. Every day of my life. Every time I go under the flash."

Nick must have shown his skepticism.

Oz nodded as if he agreed with the skepticism and said, "I was with an archaeologist friend at a site in southern Israel called Tel Be'er Sheva. It was believed to be the remains of the biblical town Be'er Sheva or Beersheba."

Nick had never heard of it, but then he hadn't read anything from the Bible for thirty years or more and knew very little about the geography. There was no longer any reason to know the geography of that dead zone.

"Tel Be'er Sheva was just north of the Havat MaShash Experimental Agricultural Farm," said Oz.

Nick had certainly heard of *that*. Havat MaShash Experimental Agricultural Farm, everyone had learned after the destruction of Israel, had been the cover location for an underground Israeli biowar lab where the aerosol drug now called flashback had been developed and mass-produced. Evidently forms of the original drug had been a neurological experiment to be used for interrogations. It had escaped the Havat MaShash lab and was being sold in Europe and elsewhere in the Mideast months before the destruction of Israel.

Nick mentioned this coincidence of geography.

The poet Danny Oz shook his head. "I don't think there was any biolab there, Mr. Bottom. I'd spent years with my archaeologist friends in that region. I had other friends who worked on and who helped administrate the real Havat MaShash Agricultural Farm. There was no secret underground installation. They just worked on agricultural stuff—the closest they probably ever came to a secret drug were the chemicals they used in improving pesticides so they wouldn't harm the environment."

Nick shrugged. Let Oz deny it if he wanted to. After the bombs fell, *everyone* knew that flashback had originated at the Havat MaShash biological warfare lab. Some felt that the nuclear attack had been, at least in part, a punishment for letting that drug escape, be copied, and sold.

Nick didn't care one way or the other.

"What was a poet doing at an archaeological site?" he asked. Nick felt in his sport coat pocket for the small notebook he'd carried all his years as a detective, but it wasn't there.

"I was writing a series of poems about time overlapping, the past and present coexisting, and the power of certain places which allow us to see that conjunction."

"Sounds like sci-fi."

Danny Oz nodded, squinted through the smoke, and flicked ashes. "Yes, it does. At any rate, I was at Tel Be'er Sheva for a few days with Toby Herzog, grandson of the Tel Aviv University archaeologist who first excavated the site, and his team. They'd found a new system of cisterns, deeper and more extensive even than the huge cisterns discovered decades ago. The site was famous for its water—deep wells and ancient cisterns riddled the deep rock—and the area had been inhabited since the Chalcolithic period, around 4000 BCE. 'Be'er' means 'well.' The town is mentioned many times in the Tanakh, often as a sort of ritual way of describing the extent of Israel in those days, such as being from 'Be'er Sheva to Dan.'"

"So being underground at the dig saved your life," Nick said impatiently.

Oz smiled and lit a new cigarette. "Precisely, Mr. Bottom. Have you ever wondered how ancient builders got light into their caves and deep diggings? Say at Ellora or Ajanta temple-caves in India?"

No, thought Nick. He said, "Torches?"

"Often, yes. But sometimes they did as we did at Tel Be'er Sheva—the generator Toby Herzog had brought was on the fritz—so his grad students aligned a series of large mirrors to reflect the sunlight down into the recesses of the cave, a new mirror at every twisting or turning. That's how I saw the end of the world, Mr. Bottom. Nine times reflected on a four-by-six-foot mirror."

Nick said nothing. Somewhere in a tent or hovel nearby an old man was either chanting or crying out in pain.

Oz smiled. "Speaking of mirrors, many are covered here today. My more Orthodox cousins are sitting shiva for their just-deceased rabbi—colon cancer—and I believe it's time for *seudat havra'ah*, the meal of consolation. Would you like a hard-boiled egg, Nick Bottom?"

Nick shook his head. "So you told Keigo in the interview that you flashed only on your memories of looking at explosions in a mirror?"

"*Nuclear* explosions," corrected Oz. "Eleven of them—they were all visible from Tel Be'er Sheva. And, no, I didn't tell young Mr. Nakamura this because, as I said earlier, he never asked. He was more interested in asking about how extensive flashback usage was in the camp, how we purchased it, why the authorities allowed it, and so forth."

Nick thought it was probably time to leave. This crazy old poet had nothing of interest to tell him.

"Have you ever seen nuclear explosions, Mr. Bottom?"

"Only on TV, Mr. Oz."

The poet exhaled more smoke, as if it could hide him. "We knew Iran and Syria had nukes, of course, but I'm certain that Mossad and Israeli leadership didn't know that the embryonic Caliphate had moved on to crude Teller-Ulum thermonuclear warheads. Too heavy to put on a missile or plane, but—as we all know now—they didn't require missiles or planes to deliver what they'd brought us." Perhaps sensing Nick's impatience, Oz hurried on. "But the actual explosions are incredibly beautiful. Flame, of course, and the iconic mushroom cloud, but also an incredible spectrum of colors and hues and layers: blue, gold, violet, a dozen shades of green, and white—those multiple expanding rings of white. There was no doubt that day that we were witnessing the power of Creation itself."

"I'm surprised it didn't create an earthquake and bury all of you," said Nick.

Oz smiled and inhaled smoke. "Oh, it did. It *did*. It took us nine days to dig our way out of the collapsed Tel Be'er Sheva cisterns and that premature entombment saved our lives. We were only a few hours on the surface when a U.S. military helicopter found us and flew us out to an aircraft carrier—those of us who'd survived the cave-in. I spend all of my waking, non-flashback time trying to capture the beauty of those explosions, Mr. Bottom."

Stone crazy, thought Nick. *Well, why shouldn't he be?* He said, "Through your poetry." It was not a question.

"No, Mr. Bottom. I haven't written a real poem since the day of the attack. I taught myself to paint and my cubie here is filled with canvases showing the light of the pleroma unleashed by the archons and their Demiurge that day. Would you like to see the paintings?"

Nick glanced at his watch. "Sorry, Mr. Oz. I don't have the time. Just one or two more questions and I'll be going. You were at Keigo Nakamura's party on the night he was killed."

"Is that the question, Mr. Bottom?"

"Yes."

"You asked me that six years ago and I'm sure you know the answer. Yes, I was there."

"Did you talk to Keigo Nakamura that evening?"

"You asked me that as well. No, I never saw the filmmaker during the party. He was upstairs—where he was murdered— and I was on the first floor all evening."

"You didn't have any…ah…trouble getting to the party?"

Oz lit a new cigarette. "No. It was a short walk. But that's not what you mean, is it?"

"No," said Nick. "I mean, you're a resident of the refugee camp here. You're not allowed to travel. How'd you just happen to walk over to Keigo Nakamura's party?"

"I was invited," said Oz, inhaling deeply on the new cigarette. "We're allowed to wander a little bit, Mr. Bottom. No one's worried. All of us refugee Jews have implants. Not the juvenile-offender kind, but the deep-bone variety."

"Oh," said Nick.

Oz shook his head. "The poison it releases wouldn't kill us, Mr. Bottom. Just make us increasingly more ill until we return to the camp for the antidote."

"Oh," Nick said again. Then he asked, "The night of the murder, you left the party with Delroy Nigger Brown. Why?"

Oz exhaled smoke in a cough that might have been meant as a laugh. "Delroy supplied me with my flashback, Dete… *Mr*. Bottom. The guards here sell it to us, but they add fifty percent to the price. When I could, I bought it from Delroy Brown. He lives in an old Victorian house on the hill just west of the Interstate."

Nick rubbed his cheek and realized that he'd forgotten to shave that morning. Oz's reason made sense but it was still odd that Keigo Nakamura would have interviewed both Brown and Oz during the same last days of his life. Unless Brown had led Keigo to Oz. It probably didn't really matter.

"I never understood why the U.S. government didn't just let you Jewish refugees integrate into society here," Nick said. "I mean, there are twenty-five million or so Mexicans here now and that group sure as hell doesn't reflect the education and training of you ex-Israelis."

"Ah," said Danny Oz. "You are too kind, Mr. Bottom. But the U.S. government couldn't just turn us loose and let us live with family members here in America. There were more than three hundred thousand Israeli survivors that came here, you remember. And with your economy and the Jobless Recovery now in its twenty-third year..."

"Still...," began Nick.

Oz's voice was suddenly sharp. Angry. "The U.S. government was and is terrified of angering the Global Caliphate, Mr. Bottom. The Caliphate is waiting to exterminate us, and what's laughingly called the U.S. government is terrified of angering them. Grow up."

Nick blinked as if slapped.

"You're one of those who pretend as if the Caliphate and partitioned Europe don't exist, aren't you?" demanded Danny Oz. "One of those who ignore the fact that Islam is the fastest-growing religion in what's left of your United States."

"I don't ignore anything," Nick said stiffly. In truth, he did ignore the Caliphate and all foreign problems. What the hell did it matter to him? Dara had had some half sister disappeared into dhimmitude in France or Belgium or one of the other partitioned countries where *sharia* law predominated, but what the hell was that to him? Dara had never met the woman.

Oz smiled again. "Isn't it interesting that they killed six million of us again, Mr. Bottom?"

Nick stared at the poet.

"It seems to be the magic number, doesn't it?" said Oz. "The population of Israel at the time of the attack was somewhere around eight and a quarter million people, but more than two million of those were Israeli Arabs or non-Jewish immigrants. About a million of those Arab Israelis died with the target population, but it was still six million Jews who either died in the attacks, from the radiation shortly after—they were very dirty bombs, weren't they, Mr. Bottom?—or from the invading

Arab armies. Some four hundred thousand Jews incinerated in Tel Aviv–Jaffa. Three hundred thousand burned to ash in Haifa. Two hundred and fifty thousand in Rishon LeZiyyon. And so on. Jerusalem wasn't bombed, of course, since that city—intact— was the reason for the attacks, both nuclear and military. Those six hundred thousand–some Jews were taken prisoner by the radiation-suited armies and just never seen again, although there are reports of a large canyon in the Sinai filled with corpses. What I'll never understand was why the Samson Option wasn't executed."

"What's that?" said Nick.

"I was a liberal, you understand, Mr. Bottom. I spent a good portion of my adult life protesting the policies of the state of Israel, marching for peace, writing for peace, and trying to identify with the poor, downtrodden Palestinian people—Gaza was more than decimated, by the way, with eighty percent fatalities when the fallout from the bomb that took out Beersheva—just two hundred thousand incinerated Jews— drifted to the north and east. But I wonder daily about the absence of the Samson Option I'd heard about my entire life… the rumored policy of the Israeli government, if attacked by weapons of mass destruction or if a successful invasion of the state of Israel was imminent, to use its own nukes to take out the capitals of every Arab and Islamic nation within reach. And Israel's reach in those days, Mr. Bottom, was longer than one might think. Decades and decades ago, but after the first Israeli bombs were secretly built, a general named Moshe Dayan was quoted as saying '*Israel must be like a mad dog, too dangerous to bother.*' But in the end, you see, we weren't. We weren't at all."

"No," said Nick. "You weren't."

He got up to go.

"I'll see you to the gate," said Danny Oz as he lit a new cigarette.

They walked out of the tent to find that storm clouds had come in from over the mountains. The rusted steel skeleton of the two-hundred-foot-tall Tower of Doom loomed over them. A rafting ride called Disaster Canyon had been all but dismantled for building materials behind them. From some tent or hovel or abandoned ride came that Jewish-sounding chanting or cry of grief again.

Nearing the gate, Danny Oz said, "Please give my best to your wife, Dara, Mr. Bottom."

Nick whirled. "What?"

"Oh, didn't I mention it? I met her six years ago. A delightful woman. Please give her my warmest regards."

The 9mm Glock was in Nick's hand in an instant, the muzzle pressed against Danny Oz's temple as Nick slammed into the frail poet, shoving him up against a metal stanchion, Nick's forearm tight and heavy across Oz's throat. "What the fuck are you talking about? Where did you meet her? How?"

The pistol had gotten the old poet's attention, but Nick could see something like eagerness in the man's eyes. He *wanted* Nick to pull the trigger. That was fine with Nick.

"I...met her...I...can't talk...with your...forearm..."

Nick let up the pressure on his forearm slightly and increased the pressure on the muzzle of the Glock. The circle of steel had broken the parchment-brittle skin on the dying man's forehead.

"Talk," said Nick.

"I met Mrs. Bottom on the day that Keigo Nakamura interviewed me," said Oz. "She was here about an hour and I introduced myself and..."

"My wife was here with Keigo Nakamura?" Nick thumbed the hammer back.

"No, no...at least I don't believe so. She and a man were standing back with the crowd but apart from it slightly, watching the interview—which was done quite publicly, you understand, so the old merry-go-round would be in the background of the shot."

"Who was the man with her?"

"I have no idea."

"What did he look like?"

"Short, heavy, early middle age, almost bald. He carried a beat-up old briefcase and had a mustache and wore old-fashioned glasses. The kind without the rims."

Nick knew who that was—Harvey Cohen, the assistant district attorney for whom Dara had worked as executive assistant. But why the *hell* were those two here at Six Flags Over the Jews on the day that Keigo Nakamura interviewed Oz?

"Did you see the woman you thought was my wife talking to Keigo or his people?"

"No," said Oz.

"What did she say to you when you introduced yourself?"

"Just how interesting the interview had been, how nice the day was for October…small talk. But when she said that her name was Dara Fox-Bottom, we discussed *A Midsummer Night's Dream*. She said that her husband was a detective for the Denver Police Department."

"Why the *fuck* didn't you mention meeting her when I interviewed you six years ago?" demanded Nick, pressing the muzzle of the Glock even deeper into Oz's bleeding forehead.

"It didn't seem appropriate then," gasped Oz, still having trouble breathing even though Nick had let up most of the pressure from his forearm. "There was that woman detective with you when you interviewed me…I mean, I didn't think there was anything *wrong* about your wife being here during a workday with that short, balding gentleman, but since I was a suspect in Keigo Nakamura's murder, I thought it best then not to mention it."

"Why mention her now, then?" demanded Nick. His finger was on the trigger, not the trigger guard.

"Because of our conversation today…about Bottom's dream," said Oz. "Shoot me if you're going to shoot me, Mr. Bottom. But otherwise *let me go*."

A minute later, Nick did. There was nothing else to find out. It was starting to rain when Nick turned his back on the dying Jew and on all the other dying Jews and left the camp.

Out in the parking lot next to Nick's gelding, Hideki Sato was waiting. Nick ignored the security man and got in his car, slammed the door shut, and thumbed the ignition.

Nothing. The gauges showed a flat charge. The car was totally dead, even though the batteries should have given him another dozen miles or so today.

"Fuck," screamed Nick Bottom. "Fuck! Fuck! Fuck!"

He was out of the car and clicking off the safety of the Glock. Sato stepped back behind his own vehicle.

Nick put five shots through the hood into the batteries and long-emasculated engine, six shots through the windshield, and four more shots into the front tires and hood again. "Fuck! Fuck! Fuck! Fuck!"

He kept squeezing the trigger but the hammer fell on an empty chamber.

Four guards came running from the entrance gate, their visors down and automatic weapons raised. Sato held up his badge and waved them away. Nick turned the Glock toward Sato but the slide was back, magazine empty.

Sato was looking at Nick's gelding. The car was emitting some sort of murdered-battery ticking from under the hood and there came a dying hiss from the deflating tires.

"I have always wanted to do that to a car," said Sato. He turned to Nick. "Having a bad day, are we?"

1.08

The People's Republic of Boulder—
Monday, Sept. 13

THE MOTIONLESS LINE of giant wind turbines ran along the entire visible span of the Continental Divide, from Wyoming in the north to beyond Pikes Peak a hundred and sixty miles south. The abandoned turbine-towers looked to Nick Bottom like nothing so much as a dilapidated, unpainted picket fence with each rusted picket post rising almost four hundred feet into the Colorado sky. A picket fence or—perhaps—a cage.

Growing up, Nick had loved looking at the high peaks and the snowcapped skyline of these peaks but in the past decades he'd learned to avoid looking west. Some scientist had estimated that the "greening" of the nation's power system with wind turbines killed more than four billion migrating and night-flying birds a year. Nick always imagined huge heaps of bird carcasses at the base of these flaked and rusting turbines... back when they still worked.

The turbines had never generated enough power to earn their maintenance and upkeep, and the visible network of power cables laid across the snowfields and hard-rock face of the high peaks reminded Nick of the varicose veins on the mottled legs of a dying old man. The former EU had abandoned most of its

uneconomical wind turbines just as the U.S., under its vision-
ary new administrations, was pouring the last of its fortune
into "green" technologies. The People's Republic of Boulder
now bought its actual power from one of the standardized-for-
manufacture HTGC (high-temperature gas-cooled) reactors on
the plains west of Cheyenne, Wyoming, but the city-republic's
official stance was that it still relied only on "green" power.

Nick wouldn't have gone to the People's Republic this
afternoon to keep his appointment with Keigo interview subject Derek Dean if he'd had a choice. Given that choice, Nick
would have gone back to his Cherry Creek cubie and spent
hours flashing on conversations with Dara around the time of
the first Oz interview six years ago. Perhaps he'd missed something she'd said at the time that would explain...

He didn't have a choice.

Sato was driving and insisting on keeping the appointment. More than that, Sato had Nick's next stash of flash in the
backseat of the car and wasn't going to release it to Nick until
after the goddamned useless interview.

So Nick sat dumbly, not conversing with Sato, numbed by
what Danny Oz had said about Dara being there during the
Keigo interview, and stared at the approaching white metal
cage bars of the once-proud Continental Divide.

The line of cars at the customs entrance for those heading
northwest along Highway 36 to the People's Republic was at
least forty-five minutes long.

"You have your physical passport, Bottom-san?" asked Sato.

Nick nodded.

Sato swung the armored Honda into the empty far-left diplomatic lane, produced two black NIC Cards and their old hard-
copy passports that the PRoB still demanded, and they were
waved through the rest of the inspection gates in half a minute.

———

EVERYONE IN COLORADO ENJOYED a love-hate, love-love, or pure
hate-hate relationship with what was now the People's Republic
of Boulder. Nick's father had held strong opinions on the place.

According to the grumblings of Nick's state patrolman dad, in the 1960s the town of Boulder and its university had been one of the national loci for drugs, sex, outdoor sports, and total rejection of authority (assuming one's parents kept paying one's tuition and bills). Nick's father liked to tell his son that these midcontinent refugees from the Summer of Love grew up, grew old—still with their graying ponytails, which Nick's dad had called dork knobs—and passed laws.

Two decades before Nick was born, the salt-and-pepper-dork-knobbed Boulder city council passed draconian laws on the city's growth, thus almost immediately doubling, then tripling, then quadrupling housing prices and driving any true middle class out of the city. Within fifteen years, according to State Trooper Bottom, Boulder was a comfortable and self-satisfied mixture of dork-knobbed trust-fund babies and louse-infected street people.

During the 1980s the city again deliberated deeply and—with the support of the anti-Reagan, anti-defense populace—passed resolutions declaring Boulder a "nuclear-free zone." The upshot of that effort, Nick's father had explained, was that in all the decades since then, not a single nuclear-powered air-craft carrier or submarine had tied up in Boulder.

In the 1990s, the same city council—the men's long dork knobs and the women's short, severe Phys Ed–instructor hair-cuts grew grayer but the faces remained largely the same according to Nick's father—labored for months before decid-ing that there would and could be no more "pets" in Boulder, Colorado. Dogs and cats were to be entrusted to human "guard-ians." The changes in licensing paperwork alone cost a fortune. In *old* dollars.

Also in the 1990s, about the time that Nick Bottom was in third grade, the investigation of the murder of a six-year-old child named JonBenét Ramsey in her home on Christmas Day was so botched by the police, district attorney, and other author-ities that almost every city official who came in contact with the case lost his or her job. Nick's father had been fascinated with the almost total ineptitude of the JonBenét Ramsey investigation. It showed, he'd later told his teenage son, that this Boulder metro area of almost two hundred thousand people definitely had not been ready for prime time. When the case was accidentally solved by an independent investigator more than twenty-five years later—after almost all the principals, family members, and suspects were dead—the answer to the mystery was as clear and obvious as it had been on the day the body was found.

Nick was sorry that his father hadn't lived long enough to hear the solution. He thought that his old man would have appreciated the irony.

Into the twenty-first century, the Boulder city council could never restrain itself from taking sides on issues that had nothing to do with a medium-sized city: coming out in support of Nicaraguan Marxist rebels, officially opposing wars in Iraq, Afghanistan, and elsewhere, refusing to support state laws restricting marijuana and other drug use, harboring illegal Mexican immigrants as political refugees (although there was no place in the city for low-paid immigrants to live, so after the very public "harboring" they were always quietly ejected from the city limits), and finally going on record to say that the city of Boulder would not "collaborate" with any Republican president of the United States.

Of course, Nick knew that his father's view of Boulder—even before it had declared itself an independent republic shortly after Texas did—wasn't fair. Despite the graying dork knobs (who were mostly dead now anyway), Boulder had once been a thriving science center. The University of Colorado at Boulder, CU, had boasted an excellent science department and was one of the few universities in the world where students actually controlled orbital satellites. (That disappeared when America's predominance in spaceflight and satellite technology was surpassed by the Japanese, Russians, Chinese, Indians, Saudis, the New Caliphate, and Brazilians.) A beautiful 1960 modernist glass-and-sandstone structure designed by I. M. Pei up near the Flatirons—the only building allowed in the greenbelt—had been built to house NCAR, the National Center for Atmospheric Research, pronounced "En-car."

The revelations of hoaxes and totally false data sets in Anthropogenic Global Warming studies, confessed to by scores of scientists only after hundreds of billions of dollars and euros had gone down that rat hole, followed by more scandals that led to the collapse of the Global Carbon Trading Networks and that collapse's contribution to the Day It All Hit The Fan, had finally resulted in NCAR's budget being reduced by 85 percent. Their new headquarters in Omaha, Nebraska, were much more modest.

And there had been the National Bureau of Standards in Boulder, which for decades had brought scientists with international reputations to the city. Both the NCAR building high in the greenbelt and the Bureau of Standards complex of buildings were now leased by the Naropa Institute and its Rinpoche School of Disembodied Transpersonal Wisdom.

The Old Man missed the best of it, thought Nick as they approached the city near the foothills. For it had been since die-ought-if, the Day It All Hit The Fan, that the People's Republic of Boulder had truly come into its own.

———

THE FENCES AND MINEFIELDS and armed patrols and custom gates ran along the highest ridge three miles to the southeast of Boulder. As one descended into the valley beyond that last high ridge, the beauty of the city and its surroundings became more obvious. The hardwoods in the city were beginning to change color and the foothills along the giant sandstone slabs called the Flatirons were thick with green pines. The high peaks and damned wind turbines disappeared as one dropped lower toward the town. The air was cleaner and more clear than it had been in a hundred and fifty years.

No automobiles or powered vehicles of any sort were allowed in Boulder. Even the police cars and fire engines depended on bicycle power. Sato was directed to one of the underground parking garages that ran for two miles along the east-west line of Table Mesa Road. Parking was expensive since each slot was in its own bombproof cradle (and this after having to pass through two CMRI portals on the way in). From the garage, one could proceed into Boulder on foot, but since the metro area of about two hundred thousand people was almost twenty-eight square miles in size, most visitors opted for renting a city-owned Segway or—much cheaper—a bicycle, human-pulled rickshaw, pedal-yourself pedicab, or bicycle-pulled rickshaw. (Every time Nick visited the People's Republic, he thought of how his old man would have enjoyed the irony of the city that couldn't stand the thought of dogs and cats being degraded as "pets" having a transportation system based on human beings, mostly immigrants housed in city barracks, pulling rickshaws.)

Sato and Nick opted for a double-wide rickshaw pulled by two Malaysian men on bikes.

The ride was about three miles and Nick tried to relax as the rickshaw jolted up Table Mesa to Broadway, Broadway to Baseline, and Baseline west a half mile or so toward Chautauqua Park.

The Boulder Chautauqua had been there since 1898. Based on the idea of the original Chautauqua, in western New York, and part of the burgeoning Chautauqua Movement in the 1890s, it had been founded in Boulder by Texans who wanted a place with cottages, a dining hall, and a barn for lectures and musical events where they could escape the Texas summer heat. When Mark Twain lost his fortune through bad investments in a typesetting machine and took to the lecture circuit again just before he turned sixty, the circuit was mostly through Chautauquas around the nation. Many summer Chautauquas were mere tent cities, but a few such as the one in Boulder boasted permanent residences and large buildings for the educational, religious, and cultural lectures and courses.

This Chautauqua was perched on a grassy shelf above Boulder that backed against the greenbelt and a web of hiking trails. Nick had come up to Boulder with his parents when he was a little kid to hike those trails. It was still a popular hiking area for Boulderites, although occasional sniper attacks and a resurgence in the mountain lion population had somewhat reduced the number of hikers.

Much farther to their right, beyond Canyon Road at the edge of this residential district, rose the high minaret of Masjid Ahl al-Hadeeth Mosque. Boulder's prohibition on any structure taller than five stories was more than sixty years old, but the city council had waived that restriction for the Masjid Ahl al-Hadeeth and its minaret was three times the old legal building height. Local Muslims and the New Caliphate had shown their appreciation with major financial contributions to the city and by demanding that Boulder evict any and all Jews currently living within the city limits. The city council was taking the request under advisement (and Nick had seen the online *Boulder Daily Camera* blog editorials arguing that there were very few Jews in Boulder anyway, so little would be lost in honoring the Muslim request). Boulder had already allowed an exemption for all Boulder Muslims—their population was now up to around 15 percent of the total with more immigration welcomed by the city—not to be tried under Colorado laws but only under *sharia* should they be accused of a crime.

Sato interrupted Nick's broodings by saying, "It's a good thing that our Advisor diplomatic status allows us to keep our weapons."

Nick grunted.

"You did not bring an extra magazine, did you, Bottom-san," Sato said softly.

"My daddy taught me that if fifteen isn't enough, another fifteen or thirty won't help," Nick said tersely.

Sato nodded. "Indeed. But those Government Motors geldings are hard to kill. Well, you should not need your weapon here in Boulder. It is the most peaceful city in Colorado, is it not?"

"One of them," said Nick. *Except for the huge rise in honor killings and of gays and lesbians having walls dropped on them.*

Besides the occasional rickshaw or pedicab, the streets were filled with spandexed and heavily helmeted cyclists on featherlight bikes that cost a million new bucks or more. There were also joggers and runners everywhere—hundreds and thousands of joggers and runners, many in sweaty spandex but some almost nude and others totally nude.

"The People's Republic seems to be a very healthy place," Sato said. "Not modest, but healthy."

"Oh, yes," said Nick. "Have you ever heard the expression 'Body Nazi'? Lots and lots of Body Nazis in the People's Republic."

Sato snorted what could have been a laugh. "'Body Nazi,'" he repeated. "No, I have not heard that term before, but I believe it appropriate nonetheless."

Joggers passed the rickshaw on the left and right, their fists and lean forearms pumping, their distracted gazes fixed on some distant but reachable goal of physical immortality.

With the foothills of Flagstaff Mountain looming, the rickshaw cyclists turned left into the broad-lawned and leafy expanse of the Chautauqua grounds. The huge auditorium higher on the hill loomed over the Arts and Crafts dining hall and other structures.

After Sato had paid off the two pedalers, Nick said, "What do you know about this place? Not Chautauqua, but the Naropa Institute that rents it most of the year?"

The big security chief shrugged. "Only what the telephone told me, Bottom-san. The university was founded in nineteen seventy-four by the exiled Tibetan tulku Chögyam Trungpa Rinpoche. The name Naropa comes from an eleventh-century Buddhist sage from India. The university was officially accredited sometime in the late nineteen-eighties but unlike most religious universities in your country, it hasn't really distanced itself from its larger Buddhist organization—Shambhala International, I believe."

"Are you Buddhist, Sato?" Nick asked.

Sato stared until Nick got tired of seeing himself in the security chief's sunglasses. Finally the big man spoke. "This way to the administration building, I believe. We'll have to hurry or be late for our interview with Mr. Dean."

"*Our* interview?" demanded Nick.

"I have interest in hearing what this gentleman has to say," said Sato. "As chief investigator, you may, of course, ask all the questions, Bottom-san."

"Fuck you," said Nick. But he stayed away from the word *motherfucker*.

They hurried.

———

NICK HAD HEARD THAT the big wood-framed Chautauqua Auditorium, despite being little more than an oversized barn, had — for almost a century and a half — earned performing artists' praise for its outstanding acoustics. When Nick had come here with his parents as a kid to watch and hear such twentieth-century marvels as Bobby McFerrin, the Chautauqua people had finally patched the roof — previous generations of audiences had been able to look up and see the moon and stars through the cracks and missing shingles — but one could still see the leaves of the trees and sky through gaps in the ancient wooden sidewalls. Now Naropa had rebuilt the walls so there was no view through them any longer.

The stage of the auditorium remained but the rest of the space had been altered for winter institute use, the ancient, rock-hard folding seats taken out and scores of low platforms set up to level the floor. On each platform were dozens of comfortable beds and each bed was ringed by a fortune's worth of monitoring devices showing pulse, blood pressure, EEG, and the various spikes and sine waves of sleep. Men and women — it was sometimes hard to tell which because of the shaved heads — wearing saffron robes monitored the monitors. Nick guessed that the room held at least a thousand beds.

Nick instantly saw the place for what it was — an infinitely cleaner version of Mickey Grossven's flashcave: a place where flashers who wanted to go long under the flash had someone to guard them and their belongings and make sure they didn't stay under so long that their muscles atrophied or their digestive systems shut down from receiving only IV fluids. And where Mickey's cave had a staff-to-sleeping-flasher ratio of about one to three hundred, the Naropa Institute must have had at least one hovering "expert" to each four bodies under the flash.

Their escort had just left them so Nick was free to say to Sato,

"This is where Naropa has made its real fortune the last decade or so. Somebody on the Naropa board of directors decided that the Buddhist goal of 'being present in the moment' included having to relive that moment...*all* moments. The Naropa students here and at NCAR and the former Bureau of Standards building—I think there are about fifteen thousand such students who've come to Boulder and Naropa—are doing what they call 'interior work.'"

"Based on Vajrayana teachings on finding and applying internal esoteric energies," whispered Sato.

"Yeah, whatever," said Nick. "It maxes out on the BQ meter."

"BQ meter, Bottom-san?"

"Bullshit Quotient."

"Ah, so."

"The Naropa Institute's also into your Japanese Tea Ceremony, *faux*-Christian labyrinth stuff, *ikebana*, healing crystals, out-of-body experiences, Druid ritual, and Wikkan ceremonies...that's witchcraft to you, Sato-san."

"Ikebana and the Tea Ceremony are worthy forms of meditation," the huge security chief said softly. "But not, perhaps, in the hands of these charlatans."

One of the saffron-robed medics came up a ramp to where Nick and Sato waited by the door. The man looked to be American but had the shaved head of all the teachers and students here. He put his hands together, bowed low, and said, "*Namaste.*"

Since no one in the group was from India, Nick replied with "How ya doin'?"

The monk or teacher or medic or whatever he was showed no irritation, but neither did he identify himself. "You are here to meet with Mr. Dean?"

"We are," said Nick, flashing his Advisor's black card badge. "Is he awake yet?"

"Oh, yes," said the monk. "It has been more than three hours since his awakening from the Previous Reality. Mr. Dean has done his exercises, enjoyed his meal, and spent an hour with one of our transpersonal counselors reviewing his most recent Previous Reality experience."

"So where is he?" asked Nick.

"In the contemplation garden to the rear of this building," said the monk. "Would you wish me to escort you?"

"No, we'll find him," said Nick. "I'll just look for a bald guy in an orange bathrobe."

"*Namaste*," said the bowing monk, hands together again.

"Later, reincarnator," said Nick.

NICK AND SATO REVIEWED notes as they walked out to the garden. It had rained a little in Denver before they left Six Flags, then let up during the drive up to the People's Republic, but now more gray clouds were moving in low just yards above the sharp tops of the five sandstone Flatirons. But the day remained comfortably warm. Nick took off his sports coat and draped it over his shoulder.

Derek Dean had been a young millionaire exec in the last days of the Google empire. He'd lived in a world high above the messy post–Day It All Hit The Fan world that almost everyone else wallowed and struggled in. Dean had spent most of his adult life in New York penthouses, Malibu beach houses, armored limos, and private executive jets while having his own private bodyguards make sure that he was not disturbed. After his company's last tech investment googled down the drain, Dean's diversified investments and connections only made him richer.

Then, seven years ago, at the age of forty-five, Dean found religion. As far as Nick and the other Denver detectives could tell, Derek Dean had no connections with Keigo Nakamura or Keigo's daddy before the video interview a day before Keigo's murder. But Dean had been the only Total Immersion Naropa student that Keigo had chosen to interview on camera. He'd only been in Total Immersion a year at that point, but according to the interview with Dean that Nick had flashed on the night before, the exec was a true believer.

One had to be a true believer to pay for the Naropa Total Immersion soul-therapy. Flashback was cheap—a dollar for every minute to be relived—but the Naropa people insisted on using a more potent and sacred version of flashback that they called *stotra*.

Nick knew that there was no such thing as a more potent version of flashback. Flashback was flashback. Always and everywhere. It couldn't be attenuated and still work and it couldn't be improved upon. It was what it was.

But where street flash sold for $15 for a fifteen-minute flash, the same amount at Naropa cost $375.

So Derek Dean was under the flash for eighteen hours a day at $25 a minute. Beyond that, he was paying hundreds of thousands of dollars for the medical monitoring, for the special diet, and for the "spiritual counseling."

And these were old dollars.

"Even a fortune of hundreds of millions would disappear quickly in such a quest for enlightenment," Sato said softly as they approached the garden. It was a hedge maze, but the hedges were only four feet tall so the chances of becoming lost in the maze were low.

"And our friend is only seven years into the process of reliving his entire life," said Nick. "He has thirty-eight years more to go under the Naropa version of the flash before he catches up to where he started the year before Keigo interviewed him."

"Does he then have to relive the decades spent reliving?" asked Sato.

Nick glanced quickly, but the security chief's expression was as stern and unchanging as ever. "That's a good question," said Nick. "Shall we ask him?"

"No," said Sato. "As you might put it, Bottom-san, neither of us gives the slightest shit as to what the answer might be."

Nick grinned despite himself and they entered the maze.

———

THE CHANGE IN DEREK Dean was shocking. Nick had seen the man just hours ago while flashbacking the interview, but six years of Total Immersion had taken their toll. Dean had been slightly stocky six years earlier but very energetic, quick, and fit: the kind of country club tennis player who can give the resident pro a decent game. Now Dean had lost at least forty pounds. The once-strong and -florid face, almost always graced with a CEO's confident smile during Nick's first interview, was now gaunt and expressionless save for the vague, confused stare that Nick associated with Down syndrome children. Dean's arms emerging from the loose saffron robe were skeletal stems with flaccid vestiges of muscles hanging loose beneath the bones. The formerly sturdy hands were now an old man's extension of quivering and twitching sticks in lieu of fingers. Perhaps most disturbing to Nick were Dean's fingernails, which were three inches long, curved, and piss-yellow.

Dean was sitting on a low bench between the hedge and gravel path, his haunted gaze firmly fixed on the rear door of the auditorium.

Nick sat down on the bench opposite and introduced himself. He did not introduce Sato or offer to shake hands.

"It's almost time for me to go back…into…under…back," mumbled Derek Dean in a brittle husk of a voice. "Almost time."

"Do you remember me, Mr. Dean?" demanded Nick, sharpening his voice to get the man's attention.

The unfocused gaze moved across Nick's face. "Yes. Detective Bottom…they told me…Detective Bottom come to see me again. But it's almost time to go, you see…to go back…you see."

"We'll keep it short," said Nick, not disabusing the former exec of his mistake regarding Nick's detective status. If Dean's believing that he was still a cop would move the interview along, then so be it. Nick had identified himself only by name.

Dean had been a shaven-head acolyte six years ago, but Nick had seen photos of the exec with a full head of short, sandy-colored hair. His skin had looked tanned and healthy. Now Dean's shaven skull was fishbelly white and pocked with small sores.

"Do you remember our earlier interview, Mr. Dean?" asked Nick, resisting the urge to snap his fingers to get the man's attention.

The limpid but hungry gaze tore itself away from the auditorium door and tried to focus on Nick. "Yes, several weeks ago...yes, Detective. About that Japanese boy who just died. Yes. But you see, since then, Mrs. Howe has said I can work on the Alamo mural in the art room during recess. Did you know that Davy Crockett died at the Alamo?"

Sato made a grumbling interrogative noise.

Nick said, "Is Mrs. Howe your teacher, Derek?"

Dean beamed. He'd lost several teeth in the last six years, despite the fortune he paid for constant medical and dental care here at Naropa. "Yes, Mrs. Howe is my teacher."

"What grade are you in, Derek?"

"I'm in third grade. Just beginning third grade. And Mrs. Howe said that Calvert and Juan and Judy and I can work on the Alamo mural in the art room during recess. We have enough crayons."

"Can you remember what I asked you about the murder of Keigo Nakamura, Derek? Do you remember the questions I asked you last time?"

Dean frowned and for a moment seemed to be on the verge of tears. "That was *weeks and weeks* ago you were here, Detective Bottom. I've been *so* busy since."

"I can see that," Nick said.

"If you're going to shed yourself of karma, you have to visit every moment it accumulated," said Dean in a stronger, older voice. "Total Immersion is the only possible way to achieve full, mindful awareness in a soul-transformative way, Detective. My spiritual counselors help me reintegrate everything with insight."

The man sounded like a student reciting something in a foreign language from rote.

"Mr. Dean, did you kill Keigo Nakamura?" said Nick.

"What...*kill*...a human person?" said Dean, his emaciated fingers going to his cracked lips and sunken cheeks. "*Did* I, Detective? Do you know? It would help if one of us knew for sure. Did I?"

"Why were you at Keigo Nakamura's party the night of the murder, Derek?"

"Was I there? Was I *really* there, Detective? Reality is a relative term, you know. Davy Crockett and Jim Bowie might be dead…or maybe they're still alive somewhere on a contiguous plane."

"Why were you at Keigo Nakamura's party the night he was murdered, Derek? Take your time to remember."

Dean frowned theatrically and set his bony fist under his chin to show that he was thinking hard. After a minute he looked up and showed that gapped, childish smile again. "I was invited! I went because I was invited! And my teacher said that I could go and came with me."

"Your teacher Mrs. Howe?" asked Nick.

Dean shook his head pendulously and for too long, like a drunk or an annoying child. "No, no, my teacher here at the institute. Shantarakshita Padmasambhava. We called him Art. Art had founded the Yogachara-Madhyamika and was a Great Soul and a great blessing to the institute."

"Is Art still here? At the Naropa Institute, I mean."

Dean looked around apprehensively. His hungry gaze returned to the rear door to the auditorium. "Is Shantarakshita Padmasambhava still here at the institute? Yes, of course he is."

Nick glanced at Sato, who was making a note in his phone.

"Did you…," began Nick.

"Shantarakshita Padmasambhava died some years ago," Dean continued happily, "but he's still here. Yes. This afternoon at recess, Mrs. Howe will let me work on the Alamo mural with Judy and Calvert and…and…and I forget who else. I'm sorry. I try to remember, I try so hard, but I forget."

The former Google exec began to weep. Snot ran down his cleanly shaven upper lip.

"Juan," said Nick. "Mrs. Howe said that you could do the mural with Judy and Calvert and Juan."

Dean beamed and wiped the mucus away with the back of his hand. "Thank you, Detective Bottom." The fifty-two-year-old giggled. "Bottom is a funny name. Do they call you Ass Boy at school, Detective?"

"Never more than once," said Nick. He went over to the

other bench, sat next to Dean, and grasped the man firmly by the shoulder. It was like grabbing pure, brittle bone. Nick knew that if he squeezed hard he would hear snapping sounds. "Mr. Dean, did you kill Keigo Nakamura or do you know who did?"

Dean raised his right hand to fondle Nick's bare wrist. "I love you, Detective Bottom."

Sorry that he hadn't brought a second magazine of 9mm rounds, Nick nodded and said, "I love you, too, Derek. Did you kill Keigo Nakamura or do you know who did?"

"No, Detective, I don't think so. But I *will* know!"

"When?"

Dean licked his lips and made a show of counting on his fingers. "I'm seven now...almost seven and a half. That only leaves...a lot of years...before I come back to when Keigo talked to me and died the next day. I'm sorry, Detective." He began to weep again.

"Jesus Christ," breathed Nick.

"A great teacher," said Dean, brightening but not wiping away his tears or snot this time. "But not able to lead us on the true path to *satori* as quickly or surely as...say...Bodhidharma would." He turned to look at Sato. The security chief was still using his stylus to write in his phone. "You're Keigo's friend Takahishi Satoh, aren't you? I remember you from the day we recorded the interview."

Sato grunted.

Dean suddenly jumped to his feet. His expression radiated pure joy through his tears. Two monks had come out of the auditorium's rear door and were headed for the garden maze and Derek Dean.

Nick and Sato also stood. Nick said, "Do we need any more of this?"

Sato shook his head.

They watched as the two monks, each grasping an elbow, led Derek Dean back into the auditorium toward the waiting bed and IV drip. Dean turned once to wave good-bye, waving his entire forearm, palm flat toward them, the way a seven-year-old would.

Nick and Sato walked down the hill and around the dining hall to where several rickshaws and pedicabs waited, their owners squatting nearby or lounging on their backs in the grass. Across the acres of the Chautauqua Green, sunlight gleamed on circles of saffron robes and bald heads in earnest conversation or silent meditation.

"Grab us a double-wide cab," said Nick. "I'll check something in the admin building here and be back in a second."

Nick ran uphill under the elms, but instead of going straight to the administration building, he reentered the auditorium and jogged down steps, checking beds as he went. The monks were just preparing to administer the intravenous flashback to Derek Dean when Nick leaned in between them and the skeleton in saffron.

"Sir," the tall male monk said softly, "you must not interfere with…"

"Shut up," said Nick. He grabbed Derek Dean by his saffron robe front with both hands and lifted him closer until their faces were inches apart. Nick could smell death in the older man's breath and pouring from his pores.

"Can you hear me, Dean?" He shook the man. The rattling sound was not imaginary; it was Derek Dean's loose teeth clacking together. "Can you hear me?"

The former exec nodded. His eyes were very wide.

"Did you meet my wife — Dara — either when Keigo was interviewing you or later, perhaps at the party?"

"Wife…," Dean repeated.

"Focus, you worthless sonofabitch." One of the monks reached to intervene but Nick shook him away as one would a child. "Have you ever seen this woman?"

Nick was holding up his phone with Dara's photo filling the entire screen.

"No. I don't think so." It was a whisper.

"Be sure," hissed Nick, holding the photo closer. "If I find out you're lying to me, I swear to Christ I'll come back here and kill you."

Derek Dean's gaze sharpened, focused on the photograph.

"No, Detective, I have never seen that woman. But I would enjoy fucking her, if I did see her...which I haven't. I don't think."

"I must protest," cried one of the hovering monks. "We shall call security. We shall..."

"Go to hell," said Nick. He dropped Dean back onto the crisp-sheeted bed, tucked his phone away, and left the auditorium.

It took less than a minute at the adjoining administrative building to get the information on Dean's former teacher from a rather attractive bald young woman at the main desk. Evidently she hadn't yet been alerted that Nick had just threatened to kill one of their paying Total Immersion students. Yes, she confirmed, Shantarakshita Padmasambhava had indeed been one of the outstanding teachers at the Naropa Institute. Eighty-four years old when he had accepted Mr. Derek Dean as an applicant for the Path of Total Immersion, the beloved Sensei Shantarakshita Padmasambhava had shuffled off this mortal coil three years ago. His ashes had been scattered from the top of Flagstaff Mountain looming above the Chautauqua campus.

Nick thanked the young woman with the shapely skull and healthy, tanned scalp and—for some reason he couldn't explain even to himself—asked for her phone number. She showed a wide, white, sincere, perfect smile and put her palms together and said, *"Namaste."*

———

THEY WAITED UNTIL THEY were out of the pedicab, in Sato's car, out of Boulder, through and beyond the exit customs checkpoints, and over the ridge to where the People's Republic was no longer in the rearview mirror before talking about things.

"Well, Sato-san," said Nick, "did we just buy the biggest load of pure, unfiltered, overacted bullshit in the history of total bullshit answers, or is suspect Mr. Derek Dean well and truly too nuts to keep on our list of suspects?"

"If he is not too crazy now, Bottom-san," said Sato, "he certainly will be by the time he enters...what do you call it here...sixth grade."

Nick grunted. He hadn't told the security chief about his final, brief interaction with Dean back at the totally immersed asshole's auditorium bed.

"There is always the question of motive," added Sato. "Mr. Dean appears to have had none."

"No one we have on our suspect list appears to have had one," said Nick, settling back in the car seat and closing his eyes. He had a headache that was pounding spikes of pain deeper with every beat of his heart.

"Someone had a motive," Sato said sharply. "But I fail to see it with Mr. Dean. Our own investigations showed absolutely no cross-referencing between Dean and Keigo or Mr. Nakamura."

"Dean was a corporate bigwig in the last days of a world empire of a corporation," said Nick without opening his eyes. "Professional competition? Trade jealousies? Google made a lot of enemies before it was broken up and flushed."

"No," said Sato. "There is no record of any interactions—hostile or otherwise—between Mr. Dean when he was a relatively minor corporate officer and any of Mr. Nakamura's interests. Should there have been some sort of corporate animosity, it is very unlikely that it would have extended as far down as Mr. Dean's level. He was a player but, in all senses of the word, a very, very minor player."

"Maybe he just took a dislike to Keigo when the boy interviewed him," said Nick. Sato's armored Honda had good shocks, but every bump on the worn, potholed, and poorly maintained highway sent more hard-driven nails of pain into his skull.

"Disliked him enough on first sight to kill him?" said Sato.

Nick shrugged. "It happens. I know the feeling myself. But in this case, perhaps Derek Dean did it for precisely the same reason that these roving flashgangs do—to give him something powerful, almost climactic and orgasmic, to flash on during his fucking Total Immersion therapy."

"To flash on in forty-four years plus as many years added on due to the six hours a day out of flashback...," began Sato.

"Eleven years extra," said Nick. "He spends eighteen

hours a day under the flash, six out…more or less. So, if he keeps with the chronological real-time flashing the way he's going now, it would be fifty-five years until the murder would roll around again. He'd be ninety-seven years old."

Sato grunted. "The odds then are low that there will be an orgasm involved if Mr. Dean makes it to that age. But Bottom-san, let us consider the possibility that Mr. Dean is flashing on the murder every day and that all that 'Mrs. Howe is letting us do the Alamo mural' was pure misdirection. The Naropa Total Immersion program would then serve as a wonderful alibi for a murderer who has to hide from the world."

"Good point," said Nick. "But although Derek might have been capable of faking the overdosing flashbacker's idiocy, he wasn't faking the physical decline. He was a dead man walking." He opened his eyes and took the pain the light added, grateful that the low clouds hid the full hammerstroke of the sun.

"Shall we go straight to Coors Field?" asked Sato. He sounded eager.

"This afternoon?" said Nick. "No way. Take me home, please. You have the flashback vials for my preparation for the next interviews, don't you?"

"In my briefcase," said Sato. "But it is still relatively early. We could…"

"No, the light has to be better than this for Coors Field. It's supposed to be clear weather tomorrow. We'll wait until early afternoon when the slant of light will be right."

"Why must the light be better, Bottom-san?"

"There's no artificial light in the ballpark during the day," said Nick.

"Yes?"

"The light should be to your best advantage," said Nick. "Since you're going to have to be my sniper-second."

"Me? The detention center provides professional snipers."

"For officers of the law and lawyers there by court order it does," said Nick. "You and I have no more official business there than a family member."

"Certainly the official status of the Advisor's office...," began Sato.

"Will allow me to provide my own sniper-second," said Nick. "That's you. How good are you with a long gun?"

Sato said nothing.

"Well, it doesn't really matter," said Nick.

"How can this be the case, Bottom-san?"

"There are thirty-some thousand rapists, thieves, thugs, and murderers in Coors Field," said Nick. "If even half a dozen or so come after me at once — or if they pull me behind a girder or into one of their hovels and out of sight — you're not going to be able to stop them in time. The sniper-second is really there to put the captured visitor out of his misery before the fiends and felons start having too much creative fun."

"Ah, so," said Sato. He did not seem overly horrified or displeased by the news.

Sato's phone told them through the car speakers that a major IED blast had gone off at the Pecos Street and Highway 36 interchange and that all traffic was being diverted south on Federal Boulevard for the detour. Nick could see the smoke and dust rising ahead, just as it had from the Mousetrap explosion a few days — a few years — earlier.

———

DARA, WHO IS READING in bed, closes her book and says, "Nick, how is the investigation going?"

He closes his car magazine but keeps his finger in place for a bookmark. "In circles, kiddo. None of it makes any sense."

"Well, it's early days, as the British used to say."

"Yeah."

He expects her to go back to her reading — Thomas Hardy — but she keeps the book shut and looks at him. "There's no danger for you in this investigation, is there, Nick?"

Surprised, he looks her straight in the eyes and says, "None at all. Why should there be?"

"It's political, Nick. I hate anything involving politics,

much less with the son of a famous Japanese industrialist or whatever the hell he is."

"Nakamura's people are cooperating," says Nick. "What danger could there be for a police officer?"

Dara rolls her eyes. "There's always *some* danger, damn you. Don't treat me as if I just fell off the turnip truck or just married a newbie patrolman without knowing the lay of the land."

Nick shakes his head and grins. "I like that verb."

"What verb?"

"Lay. As in, to be laid, to get laid."

The hovering Nick is surprised. Do they make love this night? He's never flashed on this time before—had had trouble even finding an entry point for the thirty-minute flash—and has no idea whether they ended the evening with sex. He'd only barely remembered the conversation.

It's Dara's turn to shake her head. She's not amused and not distracted. "They're not going to send you back to Santa Fe, are they?"

The torn abdominal muscles of six-years-ago Nick Bottom flinch and tighten at that question even as the gut of the now-Nick also tightens in fear.

"No," he says seriously, looking into her eyes again. "There's no chance of that, Dara."

"You said there was a suspect or potential witness or something down there..."

"Not so important that Captain Sheers or the department's going to risk one or both of their chief investigating detectives," interrupts Nick. "New Mexico's more hostile territory than three years ago when...than three years ago. We'll phone the Santa Fe sheriff's office and have him or her get what we need."

Dara is looking dubious. She's set Thomas Hardy on the bedside table.

"I swear, kiddo," says Nick. "I'm not going back to Santa Fe. I'd resign first."

"Good," says Dara, smiling for the first time. "Because I think I'd shoot you first."

He tosses his car magazine aside and puts his arm around her.

Fifteen minutes later, coming up and out of the flash, Nick wonders how he ever could have forgotten the lovemaking of that evening.

———

IT WASN'T QUITE 10 p.m. when Nick came up out of that flash. He had no intention of using the vials he'd received from Sato to flash on Delroy Brown or any other suspect's interview. He was planning the next six or eight hours in terms of finding every conversation he could with Dara on what she was doing for ADA Harvey Cohen, hunting for any clue as to why they might have been at Six Flags Over the Jews the day of Keigo's interview with Danny Oz.

Nick knew that he couldn't restrict this investigation — his *real* investigation now — to flashback sessions. He'd have to go interview Dara and Cohen's former boss, District Attorney Mannie Ortega, and probably have to ask his old partner K. T. Lincoln for help in getting access to files.

The thought of seeing K.T. again — of having to ask her for help — made Nick's insides hurt.

And, he realized, he'd have to get rid of Sato so that he could interview DA Ortega, K.T., and others. He had to know more about the auto accident that had killed his wife. He had to know more about what she and fat, balding Harvey Cohen were doing *before* that accident.

The phone chirped.

Without identifying himself, Hideki Sato asked, "What do you think about the Santa Fe trip, Bottom-san? Tomorrow after Coors Field or later in the week?"

Nick waited until his insides unclenched a bit before answering. "Whenever Mr. Nakamura's plane or helicopter is ready."

"Plane?" said Sato. "Helicopter? There is no plane or helicopter."

"Bullshit," said Nick. The fear was rising in him like a terrible tide, making his arms and legs feel weak. "I saw you fly

194

away from the roof of my building here in one, remember? That silent, stealthy *Sasayaki-tonbo* whisper-dragonfly or whatever you called it. And Keigo took one of his daddy's corporate choppers down there six years ago."

"The skies between here and Santa Fe were not so dangerous six years ago," said Sato. "Mr. Nakamura has no aircraft tasked for this trip. The company's insurance carriers would not allow it."

"Then how the hell are we supposed to get there?" shouted Nick. He hadn't meant to shout.

"Two vehicles. Armored and weaponized. Four extra security people."

"Blow me," said Nick.

"I shall set the trip for Wednesday," said Sato.

Not trusting his voice, Nick broke the connection. His hands were trembling too much to prepare the flashback vial or to concentrate on the entry point.

Padding over to his dresser, Nick poured three fingers of cheap Scotch and drank it down in two gulps.

When the trembling in his fingers abated some, Nick prepared a half-hour vial. He'd go back to a favorite time with Dara to clear his mind before doing more searching through the time after Keigo's death and before hers.

2.02

Disney Concert Hall at Performing Arts Center — Friday, Sept. 17

THEY WERE ALL scared shitless. Everyone except Billy Coyne, that is. And Val had long since decided that Billy the C was as crazy as a shithouse rat.

Val had gotten that old-timer's phrase — "crazy as a shithouse rat" — from the Old Man, who, he'd once told Val, had got it from *his* Old Man.

And Billy Coyne was as crazy as a shithouse rat.

Coyne continued to give orders all that last week, but he reserved most of his real conversation for the Vladimir Putin AI in his T-shirt. And *that* conversation was mostly in Russian.

The seven boys had spent the week following Coyne's orders and preparing everything in the sewer. They'd spent a day and a half in the darkness cutting through the rusted old rebar of the steel grate on the inside, but just in a few places to allow them to get at the steel panels covering the storm sewer opening. They left the majority of the inner grate intact to keep their pursuers from sliding in and following them. Then they'd spent another day filing through the soldered welding joining the two steel panels that covered the opening to the storm sewer.

Everything depended upon Billy Coyne's information—supposedly from his mother—being correct about exactly where the Advisor's limo would be dropping him off. The storm sewer opening was on the north side of 2nd Street on the south side of the Walt Disney Concert Hall. When they dared to peek out on Thursday night after their many hours of soft sawing and filing and more sawing, they were looking away from the weird Disney Concert Hall building itself. Coyne insisted that the streets would be shut off except for official traffic and that Advisor Omura's armored limo would come south down Grand Avenue, turn right onto the short block of 2nd Street, and stop just beyond the corner. The photographers, TV guys, and press were supposed to be cordoned off in the median between 2nd Street and an equally narrow lane called General Thaddeus Kosciuszko Way so all their lenses would be aiming north toward the concert hall and the steps that Omura, the mayor, and their security people and entourages would be climbing to enter the hall.

The eight members of the flashgang would have only two or three seconds to fling open the storm sewer doors and to open fire.

But they would be able to see out the closed steel panels. When the city workers welded the doors shut years ago, they'd left narrow horizontal slits near the bottom to handle the usual amount of runoff from heavy rains that built up there on 2nd Street. The gaps were too small to use as gunslits, but the boys could peer out of them until they saw Omura step out of his limo.

In the wee hours of the morning, with Sully standing guard on 2nd Street to let them know when it was clear of security guards, they'd rehearsed throwing the metal drain-cover doors open wide and crowding into the six feet or so of space to fire their weapons. The limo letting Advisor Omura out on this north side would be stopped less than twelve feet away. All the boys would be wearing ski masks, just like real terrorists. Coyne had bought Palestinian keffiyeh scarves for everybody, but Val definitely thought that this was a bridge too far. Too cute.

After they all blazed away, semiautos and flechette guns, the plan then was to run like hell. A curve in the sewer path just twenty feet from the opening would give them cover, although Coyne warned them to stay away from the walls. Ricochets would travel far down there. The inner grate would keep the cops or security people from sliding in to chase them and all the nearby manhole covers and storm sewer entrances were firmly welded shut. The cops wouldn't know which direction to hunt for them. The first exit from the sewers was more than a mile east of where they planned to do the shooting, but Coyne's plan was for them to run almost half a mile north and then west through the ever-twisting maze before coming up and out near Cigna Hospital. They'd hacksawed and cut that storm sewer door open as well. There was a Dumpster for biohazard materials next to the storm sewer behind that hospital—Coyne had carefully cut through the padlock chain so that the cut shouldn't be noticed—and all their guns would be tossed there. They'd wear gloves during the shooting.

The I-10 Open Air Market *hajji* who'd sold them the weapons kept no records.

"We'll all be in our own homes watching the replay on CNN before the cops and Jap security guys pull their thumbs out of their asses," said Coyne.

"What if some of us get wounded or killed?" asked Val. "Then it's just a matter of time before the cops and FBI find the names of the rest of us in the flashgang."

Coyne had scowled furiously at Val. "*Nobody's* gonna get wounded or killed, *ty mudak*."

Val's phone later told him that the Russian meant, roughly, "you asshole."

The leering face of Vladimir Putin also scowled at Val but seemed to be speaking to Coyne. "*Eto trus, yavlyaet—sya slabym zvenom v tsepochke, malen kii Koi n. Vy dolzhny ubit yego.*"

Val hadn't used his phone to translate that. He got the general idea and knew that the Putin T-shirt would love to see him dead.

Coyne had come over and put his arm around Val, gesturing the others closer until it had turned into a goddamned group hug. "Nobody's gonna get wounded or dead, Val my droogy pal," Coyne said confidently. "This is a lark. We're gonna flash on this for the rest of our lives."

"As long as the rest of our lives isn't counted in minutes," muttered Val.

Coyne had laughed and punched Val in the upper arm. "No guts, no glory. You wanna be like the rest of the walking dead up there in the world?"

"No," said Val after a few seconds of thought. "I don't."

***

VAL SPENT THE WEEK trying to figure out what to do. He was neither an idiot—as Dinjin, Toohey, Cruncher, Sully, Monk, and Gene D. increasingly seemed to be—or crazy as a shithouse rat, which he was all but sure Billy Coyne was. Shooting at a Nipponese Federal Advisor these days was as serious (and probably more serious) than shooting at the president of the United States. The FBI and Homeland Security would become involved *immediately* and Val had no doubt that the nine Advisors' security people had their own investigative resources around the whole country.

Even the hardcores like Aryan Brotherhood and al Qaeda–America knew better than to try to kill a Japanese Advisor.

Val knew that something was behind Coyne's certainty—nuts or not—and he poked around on the Internet with his phone computer for three days before he found it on a city-Advisor liaison bulletin board site: Ms. Galina Kschessinska—formerly Mrs. Galina Coyne, according to archived bulletins going back six years—a much-lauded executive assistant in charge of liaison between the City of Los Angeles Transportation Department and the office of Federal Advisor Daichi Omura for the past nine years, was taking early retirement so that she could return to Moscow to be with her extended family. Friday, September 17, was her last day and she planned to leave for Moscow on Saturday the eighteenth. Ms. Kschessinska would be taking her sixteen-year-old son with her. Plans for a return to the U.S. were indefinite. "I just want to see my family—get reacquainted," Ms. Kschessinska told the Transportation Department's bulletin reporter, "and then, of course, we'll be coming back so my son can fulfill his Selective Service obligation."

Val almost giggled as he read this. Billy Coyne was as crazy as a shithouse rat, all right, but not quite as self-destructive-crazy as Val had thought. Mommy and little Billy wouldn't be coming back from Russia.

Billy's mother must have tried to buy her second son's way out of the draft the way she'd bought his older brother, Brad's, freedom, but evidently that hadn't worked this time. Coyne had bragged to Val many a time that Brad was already in Russia and rising quickly in the mafia there. And neither Coyne nor his mother had any intention of Billy getting drafted into the United States Army and dying fighting for India or Japan in rural China.

So old Coyne had a built-in, mommy-driven getaway waiting the morning after his gang's kamikaze attack on Advisor Omura. Val wondered if Coyne would even show up at the Friday-evening assassination attempt.

He thought he probably would. As much fun as sending his seven *compadres* off to almost certain death—or at least future captivity—might seem to shithouse rat Billy the C, taking part in it and then getting away scot-free (Russia had no extradition treaty with the United States) must appeal to him more. Coyne was a sociopath *and* a flash addict and Val thought that the allure of Billy the C's flashing on Omura's murder—probably as incentive to even bigger and better escapades in Mother Russia—must be compelling.

So Coyne will probably be there Friday night, thought Val. *But will I?*

For four days of that workweek leading up to what he was already thinking of as the Friday Night Massacre, *But will I?* was the operative question for Val.

That had been his central question, in a slightly different form, for some months now. Val Bottom... or Val Fox, as he preferred to be known in his run-down, chaotic Los Angeles high school…had been depressed enough to consider suicide.

To be or not to be, that is the question.

Except that some late literary guy named Harold Bloom, whom Val had looked up on his own due to his interest in *Hamlet*, said that the "To be or not to be…" soliloquy wasn't debating suicide after all. That fact would be a big surprise to Mr. Herrendet, his junior English teacher, who taught *Hamlet* but obviously had never really *read* it.

Up to now, Val's thoughts of self-destruction had been fairly unserious because all the *means* to it available to him — jumping off high places, hanging, stealing enough sleeping pills to do it, stealing a car or motorcycle and putting it into an overpass column at ninety miles per hour — had been so off-putting that his consciousness shied away from any planning involving such solutions to his melancholy.

But now he had the 9mm Beretta.

Coyne had given him the gun on Monday, after the leader had purchased his own OAO Izhmash flechette-spewer at the midnight market. It was the kind of modern automatic weapon that the grinning *hajji*s called a synagogue sweeper, and Coyne was delighted with it despite the fact that being caught with it meant a no-plea-bargain minimum hard eight years in Dodger Stadium.

That night Val had downloaded and printed out a step-by-step "How to Love and Care for Your 9mm Beretta" and had purchased the proper oil, found the correct sort of clean rags and cleaning rods, and spent his free time cleaning, inspecting, and learning about the semiautomatic. He'd removed the magazine, checked to make sure there was no round in the chamber, and set the muzzle against his forehead.

Another online piece of advice (he did not download this one), titled "Suicide Is Your Unalienable Right: How to Do It," told Val that even a large-caliber bullet like a 9mm was not always guaranteed to penetrate the thick bone of the skull. Even the slightest deflection, said the helpful article, turned a suicide bullet into a ticket for years of being a drooling vegetable.

The only certainty, went the online advice, was to set the pistol's muzzle against the soft palate in the roof of your mouth. That was guaranteed to put a bullet into your brain, ending all pain and doubt.

Val tried it but the heavy taste of gun oil and the bulk of the blocky 9mm pistol's squarish barrel filling his mouth made him retch until he vomited. The act also felt faggy as hell.

What other options?

Suicide by cop, of course. Just get in front of the mob of demented children at the storm sewer opening on Friday night and take a few rounds for the flashgang.

But would that guarantee a quick and relatively painful death? Probably, but not definitely.

When he was eight or nine, Val had watched an old movie from the last century called *The Great Northfield Minnesota Raid* with the Old Man, who loved old cowboy movies. In the movie, a really slimy Jesse James and his brother Frank, joined by a bunch of other brother-outlaws, including Cole Younger and his brother, tried to knock over an "easy bank" in Northfield, Minnesota. Evidently Northfield didn't like having its easy bank robbed since—in the movie, at least—every man, boy, and dog in the little town grabbed a shotgun or rifle and shot the outlaws to bits.

Cole Younger, already hit five times in Northfield, was shot several more times during a gunfight in a swamp, including in the hand, the chest, and the head. He survived to be captured and tried and sent off to the Minnesota State Penitentiary at Stillwater, but he'd suffered eleven serious gunshot wounds during the process.

Val, who'd been interested enough to find some library books on the subject, remembered that the total take from Northfield's bank was $26.70.

Of course, those were old dollars and probably worth something, but even so...

Val tried to imagine Advisor Omura's security guys shooting him eight, nine, eleven times and him still surviving. Being shot must hurt like hell. Cole Younger had been tossed into the back of a wagon along with his more severely wounded pals and, even though he was bleeding almost to death from his eleven wounds, had joked with his captors, and when they got to the town of Madelia, Cole managed to stand up, take off his muddy and bloody hat, and bow to some ladies passing by.

Learning this kind of coolshit stuff about the world and history was the reason that Val kept reading.

But could he be as coolshit gutsy as Cole Younger with eleven bullet holes in him? Val doubted it. He wanted to blubber like a girl when Leonard brought him to the black-market dentist in the basement tenement near Echo Park. How would he deal with a piece of lead traveling faster than the speed of sound slamming into his body, tearing up internal organs and arteries?

What other ways out were there?

He could open up on Coyne and the others before they assassinated Omura. Would that make him a hero to the city? Would the Advisor and mayor pardon him? Would he get a parade?

But killing all seven of the flashgang punks without getting shot himself seemed like a long shot to Val, even if he could bring himself to do it. He'd try for Coyne first, but all of those acned geeks were armed now. Val tried to imagine getting hit by a cloud of flechettes from Billy's OAO Izhmash. Those things were three inches long and barbed. Jesus. The thought made Val want to throw up again.

Also, Val didn't want to be pardoned. He definitely didn't want to be a hero. He'd rather go the soft palate route than be the centerpiece in a parade.

What *did* he want?

To die rather than to keep on living in this fucked-up city and world...maybe. Probably.

The only thing that appealed to Val more than dying right now was somehow getting back to Denver and shooting the Old Man. That bastard had abandoned him after Val's mother died—had abandoned him and forgotten about him, Val knew this for a certainty—and almost nothing would be sweeter than seeing Nick Bottom's face in the few seconds before Val pulled the trigger of his Beretta.

And then, on Thursday—right when Val was sure that the only choice he really had was to shoot himself in the head later that night, just hoping that his skull wasn't thick enough to deflect the slug—dear old Leonard had changed everything by telling him about the truck ride to Denver that his grandpa's rich old spanic friend had arranged for them.

He'd almost broken down in tears right then but was glad he didn't. Leonard would never have understood such tears of gratitude not only because he wouldn't have to die that night, but that he'd get to see and kill his father.

Coyne had his magical getaway to Russia with his old lady the morning after the assassination of Omura. Now Val Fox had something coolshit better—his own midnight getaway with black-market truckers.

But what about the plan to kill Omura? Now Val could just shuck it off, not show up at the rendezvous Friday evening, stay out of sight until Coyne had to go on without him.

Or he could go watch—it would be something to flash on for years, no matter how it turned out—and never have to fire a shot himself. Or to *get* shot himself.

Val went to sleep smiling that Thursday night, but not before he used a twenty-minute vial of flashback.

———

HE IS FOUR YEARS old. Today is Val's birthday and he's four years old now. He can imagine how the four candles on the angel food cake with chocolate frosting will look because now he can count to four. He is four years old and his mommy is still alive and he doesn't hate his daddy and his daddy doesn't hate him and it's his birthday.

Mommy and Val and Val's four-year-old best friend Samuel from two houses down the street and Samuel's grandmother— his playmate lives with only his grandmother for some reason— are all in the kitchen of the house where, less than seven years later, people in black will come to drink coffee and eat cake and other food after his mother's funeral. But the now-Val shuts that memory of the then-future out of his mind as he surrenders himself to the flashback moment—slowly, deliberately, deliciously—as if lowering himself into a bathtub filled with very, very hot water.

Val is in the tall wooden chair that his mommy bought at the unpainted furniture place and decorated with painted flowers and animals just for him after he'd outgrown his high chair. Even though he's a grown-up four today, he loves the tall chair that allows him to look across the table almost eye to eye with his daddy.

When his daddy is there. Which he's not for this birthday dinner. Not yet.

He'd heard his mommy on the phone earlier: "But you *promised*, Nick. No, we can't delay it any longer... Val's sleepy after his long day and Samuel will have to go home soon. Yes, you'd *better* try. He's depending on you today and so am I."

She is smiling when she comes back to the kitchen table, but Val feels his four-year-old self sense the tension in his mother. Her smile is too wide, her eyes a little red.

"Why don't you open a couple of your presents while we wait for Daddy?" his mother says.

"Oh, what a good idea!" says Samuel's grandmother. It's strange to see an old woman clap her hands in excitement as if she were a little girl.

Val watches his stubby fingers open his wrapped presents. A toy boat from Samuel, although his playmate is as surprised as Val at what was in the wrapped package. A pop-up picture book of skyscrapers from Samuel's mother. Little Val can't read most of the words in the book but sixteen-year-old Val peering out of Little Val's eyes can.

"Let's have your cake now and open presents from Mommy and Daddy after you blow out your candles," says his mommy.

Val's and Samuel's eyes grow wide after Samuel's grandmother turns out the kitchen lights. There's enough September evening light coming through the mostly closed blinds to keep it from being totally scary, but Val feels his younger self's heart pounding with excitement and anticipation.

"Happy birthday to you, happy birthday to you…" His mommy and Samuel's grandmother are both singing. The candlelight is magical.

Val blows out the candles, getting some help from his mommy on the last one, and he points to each candle as he counts. "One…two…three…FOUR!"

Everyone applauds. His mommy turns the lights back on and there standing in the kitchen in his gray suit and red tie is Daddy.

Val raises his arms and his daddy sweeps him up into the air. "Happy birthday, big guy," Daddy says and hands him a clumsily wrapped package. Whatever's inside is soft. "Go ahead, open it," says his daddy.

It's a baseball mitt. Kid-size but real. Val tugs it on his left hand, his daddy helping him get it right, and then buries his face in the cupped and oiled palm of the mitt, smelling the leather.

His mommy hugs him and Daddy at the same time while his daddy is still holding him high against his chest and for a moment Val is almost squashed as everyone hugs everyone, but he keeps the sweet-smelling leather glove over his face — because for some reason he doesn't understand he's crying like a little baby — and Samuel is shouting something and…

———

VAL CAME UP OUT of the twenty-minute flash to the sound of sirens, helicopters, and gunshots somewhere in the neighborhood. The air coming in through his bedroom screen smelled of garbage.

You are such a total pussy, he told himself. *Sixteen years old and flashing on crap like this. You are a total pussy.*

Still, he wished he'd used a thirty-minute vial.

Val rolled over in bed and reached behind his old dresser to the hiding place behind the loose board in the wainscoting.

He removed the two items there and rolled onto his back.

The leather mitt — darker and tattered, the leather laces

replaced and rewoven a dozen times and the webbing torn—smelled almost the same. The leather had a deeper, more knowledgeable smell now. He held the glove, too small to get his hand fully into, over his face.

Total pussy, he told himself. This was one of the reasons he kept his bedroom door locked. And, truth be told, he felt the same guilt with these two talismans as he did when he downloaded porn from a stroke site. But different... different.

He set the old mitt next to him on the pillow.

The other object was an old blue phone. His mother's. He'd taken it and hidden it away the day after her funeral and although his old man had eventually gotten around to searching for the thing, he hadn't searched very hard.

The phone was useless as a phone since its phone and access functions had been cancelled by the Old Man and shut off by Verizon shortly after his mother's death. But there were invaluable things still on it.

Val tapped an earbud into his right ear and thumbed the controls. His mother had used the voice-memo function for three years before the accident that killed her and he knew his favorite dates by heart. One of them from September six years ago was a list of possible gifts for him... for Val's tenth birthday. There were similar notes from that last Christmas just two weeks before the accident.

But the voice memos didn't have to relate to Val to be wonderful. The notes to herself could be about dental appointments or school conferences... it didn't matter. Just the sound of her voice allowed him to fall asleep on these nights when he couldn't sleep. Usually she sounded busy, distracted, rushed at work, sometimes even annoyed, but still... the sound of his mother's voice touched something in the core of him.

There was a text section to the phone, of course, and large files there the last seven months of her life, but they were encrypted and after a few lazy attempts to break the cipher, Val left those text files alone. It might be a diary she'd been keeping, but whatever it was, his mother had wanted to keep it private. If his parents' marriage was in trouble or if it were some other grown-up angst that she'd used an encryption file to keep anyone from overhearing, Val thought it was none of his business.

He just wanted to hear her voice.

You are such *a pussy, Val Bottom. Less than a year away from getting drafted into the army or marines, and here you are . . .*

Val ignored that voice and listened to his mother's, his cheek and nose against the flattened baseball mitt.

Even with tomorrow and the Omura thing hanging over him like a black-garbed ghost, the soft voice and the leather smell cleared his mind and allowed him to fall asleep within ten minutes.

His last waking thought was *I have to pack these two things at the bottom of my duffel tomorrow where Leonard won't find them . . .*

————

"YOU MOTHERFUCKER!"

"Motherfucker yourself, Coyne," said Val. "And fuck you too."

Val was ten minutes late for their rendezvous at the Cigna Hospital entrance to the storm sewers. He almost hadn't come at all but—in the end—knew that he'd always doubt his own courage if he didn't show up.

"We were just leaving without you, Bottom-wipe," snarled Coyne. The leader was wearing a leather jacket open to show a squinting, scowling Putin. Coyne already had his ski mask on, although the balaclava was rolled up high on his head.

"Did you bring your gun, Bottom-wipe?" asked Gene D. with a high, almost hysterical-sounding giggle.

Val slapped the taller boy across his cheek with a flick of two fingers.

"Hey!" screamed Gene D.

Coyne laughed. "*I* get to call Bottom-wipe here Bottom-wipe. Nobody else does. Zip up your fly, pimple-head."

Gene D. looked down and the other boys laughed too loudly. Everyone sounded like they were wound too tight.

"Got your flashlight?" asked Coyne. He was carrying the

bulky OAO Izhmash right here in the open behind the hospital medical-waste Dumpster. It was twilight, but not really dark yet. Anyone driving into the parking lot could see it.

Val held his flashlight up.

"Let's go," said Coyne.

Dinjin banged the storm sewer cover open and one by one they slid down into the dank and dark passageway. Coyne led the way as they walked the half mile or so to the downtown through the labyrinth of twists and turns they'd memorized rather than marked. No one spoke as their flashlight beams danced across the moldy, heavily tagged concrete walls. Once in the tunnels near the Cigna entrance, flashback vials crunched underfoot and the floor of the tunnel—dusty and dry—showed a litter of toilet paper, old mattresses, and used condoms that the boys fastidiously avoided.

Val was amazed that all eight of them had shown up. Did the younger kids like Toohey, Cruncher, Monk, and Dinjin have any sense of what they were getting into?

Did the older kids—Sully, Gene D., even Coyne?

Did he himself have a clue? wondered Val. If he did, why was he here?

They reached the Performing Arts Center outlet sooner than Val wanted.

"Turn off your flashlights," hissed Coyne. "Pull your ski masks down."

"It's another ten minutes before…," began Sully.

"Shut up and do it," said Coyne.

The boys pulled their balaclavas down. Val hated the smell and feel of wet wool against his face. At first it seemed like absolute darkness—Val could see nothing at all and a sudden panic made his bowels go watery—but then the light through the rain slits in the closed metal panels filtered in and their eyes began to adapt, at least to the point where they could see one another's dark shapes standing there. Val sensed someone next to him—Monk?—and felt the other boy's arms and body trembling hard with terror or anxiety.

Coyne shoved and pulled until all eight of them were piled

in as close to the rebar grating and steel panels as they could get. By straining their heads and necks forward through the grate, they could get a glimpse outside through the six tiny slits. The youngest boys took turns at their two slits.

When Val peeped through he thought his heart was going to race itself to death. There were already people and automobiles out there, although the prime parking spot just ten or twelve feet from the storm sewer was still open and empty. The sound of voices, traffic, shouts from the reporters and photographers, and a general crowd buzz seemed to be all around them despite the barriers of concrete and steel. All the other times they'd been here, all the hours they'd spent cutting away parts of the rebar grating and making sure the key Coyne had would actually unlock the swinging cover panels, 2nd Street had been empty and the bit of late-night traffic on Grand Avenue had sounded far away.

Now it was all *here*.

What the hell had they been thinking? Val knew that it had been a boy's fantasy up to this point—playing pirates in a cave with real guns—but this was *real*.

"Coyne," Val whispered. "We can't…"

Coyne hit Val in the face with his closed fist. Val went down heavily, the Beretta still in his belt. He felt the strange, squarish muzzle of the OAO Izhmash flechette-spewer pressing painfully into his cheek. "Shut the fuck *UP*, asshole," hissed Coyne. "Or I fucking swear I'll do you here, now, rather than later."

Flechette guns, Val knew, made little noise, not much more than a whooshing sound. Coyne might risk the noise to… no, Val realized with a sickening lurch of absolute certainty, Coyne *was going to risk being heard by killing Val right here and now*. With that flood of certainty came the twin realization that Coyne had always planned to kill Val here, this night. Maybe Coyne planned to kill all of the flashgang members before the shooting was over.

Val's Beretta was in his waistband, under his hooded sweatshirt and flannel shirt, and before he could fumble it out in the darkness, he heard Coyne ratchet back something on the flechette sprayer—a safety, most probably. The next sound he heard would have to be his last...

"He's here!" shouted Monk. "The limo's here."

"What?" whispered back Coyne. "Too early. Another three minutes..." Their leader had obviously been watching his expensive watch.

"He's getting out!" shouted Gene D. There was no attempt to stay silent now.

The padlock was unlocked, the chain off, and now six of the boys stumbled over themselves reaching for the four-foot-long pieces of rebar they'd propped against the wall under the sewer opening. These short metal poles were the way they'd practiced swinging the steel panels open in the early hours of the morning, with Monk or Dinjin outside and ready to run forward and push the doors back in place.

"It's him!" screeched Sully at one of the slits. "Omura!"

"Shut up! Shut up!" whispered Coyne, but it was too late to control things now. Events were creating themselves.

At least the OAO Izhmash wasn't aimed at his head any longer. Val took a breath and began crawling away, slithering on his back toward the darker areas yards away from the opening.

The boys had practiced pushing the panels open smoothly, working together, but now they were banging and prodding almost at random, rebar against flat steel. The panels screeched, scraped, began to open. Light from streetlamps, car headlights, TV lights, and photography flashes flooded into their tunnel and almost blinded eight pairs of eyes that had adapted themselves to near-total darkness.

"Shoot! Shoot! Shoot!" Cruncher was shouting, fumbling to pull back the hammer on his heavy .357 Magnum.

"No, wait, wait, wait!" shouted Coyne.

What does he have planned? Val wondered dumbly. Whatever it was, he couldn't wait around to find out. He stumbled to his feet and ran toward the curve in the sewer tunnel.

"Fucker!" screamed Coyne and fired the flechette sweeper at him.

The other boys took that as an order to open fire. The sound of six weapons firing at once was absolutely deafening in the echoing cement and concrete vault. Gene D. didn't even have the right-side panel fully open yet, and sparks leaped off the steel. The rest of the boys shoved and jostled to fire through the four feet or so of open space between the partially opened shutters.

Val had ducked around the abutment in the turning tunnel just as Coyne had fired and fifty or more barbed flechettes sparked against the walls and continued ricocheting down the long passageway. If Val hadn't made the turn just when he had, he'd be dead. If he'd continued running, the barbs would have shredded him in full flight and he'd be dead.

Then Coyne was shouting with the others and obviously firing out through the gap in the shutters, pushing other boys in front of him even as he did so. Val knew this because—even though he knew it was the most stupid thing he could do—he *had* to see what was going on and he'd peeked around the barb-gouged corner.

Someone, probably Omura's security, was firing back. Val saw Toohey's shaven head explode in a red and gray mist and the slim boy's body tumbled against Cruncher and went down. Dinjin screamed something and then he was hit and his body went down like a sack of potatoes. There was none of the dramatic flying backward that Val had seen in a million movies, just a deadly, final, sickening *drop* when a boy was hit.

"Keep shooting! Keep shooting!" screamed Coyne in a weird falsetto. Even as he backed away from the opening, he was lowering his flechette sweeper toward the huddled backs of his screaming, shooting friends.

Fuck this. Val turned and ran as hard as he could. It took bouncing off a cement wall at the first branching of the tunnel to make him realize that he'd dropped and forgotten his flashlight. He'd been running blind in the darkness. He had to turn left along a narrow side tunnel at the next branching, but he'd never even *find* the branching in this darkness. He was screwed.

He'd picked himself up and was shaking his head when

there came a flash brighter than the sun and then a sound louder and more terrible than anything Val Fox had ever heard. A blast wave picked him up and threw him fifteen feet down the main corridor. He was only vaguely aware of losing skin on his knees and elbows as he hit and slid on cement, his jeans and sweatshirt ripping.

Flame billowed and blossomed around the first turn in the tunnel behind him. Val glimpsed a scarecrow silhouette throwing itself aside right where Val had hidden a few seconds earlier, and then the second shock wave hit him and rolled him another ten feet down the black corridor.

He could see now.

Val pulled the ski mask off and tugged the Beretta from his waistband. The pistol was under the wool as he ran. The storm drain was illuminated red and orange by unseen flames, Val's shadow leaping ahead of him as he ran for his life, ducking rebar hanging down here and there, listening to the chaos still exploding thirty yards behind.

Somebody from outside must have fired an RPG or something. Or something. There was no way that any of the boys still in that first section of the drain could be alive after that.

Men's shouts. More shots. Security people or cops or military were *inside the drain with him.* Their clever idea of keeping them out by leaving the interior grate rebar in place hadn't worked for thirty seconds. Someone had just blown the shit out of the steel panels, rebar grate, boys' bodies, everything.

And now they were inside.

Val was running so hard and panting so loudly that he almost tore right past the narrow defile extending to the left of the main drain passage. He skidded, sneaker soles screeching, and doubled back and in.

The flames were receding behind him, and this narrow passage—barely wide enough for his shoulders—was dark.

To get to the higher drain and eventual exit, he had to find the narrow, round opening above him with the metal rungs. But he'd never see it in this blackness.

More shouts. Men were running past his side passage now,

shooting ahead of themselves down the tunnel. They had machine guns.

Of course *they have machine guns, dipshit.*

The best Val could do to find his vertical pipeline was to keep jumping every few paces, dragging his free left hand along the roof. He was still carrying his ski mask and Beretta in his right hand. The odds of missing the small aperture were great, but he was goddamned if he was going to slow down.

Problem was, he'd checked out this sewer drain and it dead-ended about thirty yards beyond the vertical access he needed.

More shouts behind him. Footsteps on cement. Lots of men running. A voice echoed down his passage, although he couldn't tell what the man was screaming.

They're all dead. Coyne, Monk, Gene D., Sully, Toohey, Cruncher, Dinjin. All dead.

The fingers of his left hand flicked against nothingness.

Val skidded to a stop, stepped back, jumped and swung his left arm vertically, guessed where the rungs must be, and leaped blindly.

His left hand caught a rung but his weight almost pulled his shoulder out of its socket. He dropped the Beretta and mask, caught both of them against his rising thigh, grabbed them clumsily in the darkness, and used that hand to find the next rung, fighting not to drop the gun again even as three fingers on his right hand gripped the rung.

He was climbing, his feet found rungs, and he was up. Val heaved himself onto the dry concrete of the higher passage that headed east and he could feel his breath puffing dust up against his face.

Bleeding, hurting—although he was fairly sure that none of the barbed flechettes had caught him—Val struggled to his feet and began staggering down the corridor with his left hand sliding against the south wall of the tunnel. Thank God it only went one way from the vertical standpipe he'd come up. If he'd had to choose directions in this total darkness, he would have been lost for sure.

Val was less than a hundred feet down the tunnel when he heard a slipping, sliding noise behind and to his right.

Rat?

Even before the thought was complete, he was blinded by a flashlight beam directly in his eyes.

Cops! Would they allow him to surrender or just gun him down? If the other guys had hit Advisor Omura with their wild firing, Val thought he knew the answer to that question.

He still started to raise his hands in surrender when Billy Coyne's voice from behind the circle of blinding light said, "I always knew you were a total pussy, Val."

Incredibly, absurdly, Val's terrified but not panicked mind flashed on the old James Bond and Bourne and Kurtz movies that he and the Old Man used to watch. "*The villains' ultimate undoing,*" the Old Man said from the couch, the popcorn between them, "*talk, talk, talk. They always explain, and keep talking rather than just shooting the hero and getting it over with.*"

"I'm gonna flash on this tomorrow when I'm flying to Moscow with my mother—in first class, asshole," said Coyne, his voice still high and weird and adrenaline-driven as it had been back at the gunslits, "and I'm gonna get off thinking about how a hundred barbed flechettes just tore your fucking wimp body to…"

Val fired the Beretta through the bunched-up ski mask that concealed it.

Coyne said, "Ugh," and dropped the flashlight, which hit on its metal side and did not shatter. The beam of light rolled in a slow circle.

Val threw himself to the right, trying to stay out of the beam of light. It was too fast, but it crossed him and kept going.

Val dropped to one knee, braced his right arm, and aimed the pistol low.

The flashlight beam came to a stop on Coyne on his knees, using the big OAO Izhmash as a sort of crutch to keep himself upright. Coyne was staring at his own chest where, just above and to the right of Vladimir Putin's pale brow, a small red circle was beginning to blotch wider and spread.

215

Coyne looked up with a stupid, smirking grin. "You shot me." He sounded almost amused. He began struggling with the bulky flechette sweeper.

Val didn't think that Coyne had the strength to lift and aim the thing, but he didn't care to wait and see if he was wrong. He shot Coyne again, in the throat this time.

Coyne's head snapped back as his neck exploded, then the boy fell forward into the circle of the flashlight beam. The sound of his teeth snapping off as he hit the cement face-first, jaw wide open, would stay with Val always.

More shouts from behind and below.

Val was panting as if he'd run a hundred-yard dash. He felt a queer numbness spreading through him and doubted if he could walk now, much less run the distance he had to. He grabbed the flashlight and had started to turn away when a voice from Coyne's corpse said, "*Vy rasstrelyali nas, vy ublyudok!*"

Val whirled and crouched, Beretta extended. Coyne lay still on his face. The pool of blood continued widening.

Approaching warily, Val set his sneaker to Coyne's right shoulder and rolled him over.

Coyne's eyes were wide and sightless, his mouth with the shattered front teeth opened wide. The throat below the bloodied jaw was shredded. The second shot had almost decapitated the boy.

Vladimir Putin sneered up at Val, the thin-lipped little mouth snarling, "*Ty ubil nas, svoloch. Vy proklyatye fucking parshivo…*"

Knowing he was wasting a bullet and not caring, Val shot Vladimir Putin directly between his beady little eyes.

The AI stopped talking.

Voices from just beneath the standpipe now. Perhaps they hadn't seen the vertical access. Val prayed they hadn't. He had a few seconds to get around the first bend.

Flashlight in his left hand and Beretta in his right, Val ran. And ran.

1.09

Denver and Coors Field — Tuesday, Sept. 14

N**O ONE IN** the Denver Police Department when Nick was there ever blurred female detective K. T. Lincoln's initials to sound like the soft, feminine "Katie." At least not to her face. When talking to Detective Lincoln on a first-name basis, it was always "K...T" with a certain pause of respect, if not outright fear, separating the hard-edged consonants. It was rumored that no one, not even the captain or commissioner or those in Human Resources who handled her paperwork, had a clue as to what the K or T stood for. Behind her back, of course, there were plenty of foul and sexist variations. She tended to scare men and — as Nick had quickly discovered when he was her partner — the more insecure the men, the more quickly they frightened.

Detective First Grade K. T. Lincoln had never scared Nick Bottom, but it was probably because the two had worked together so well.

But now, seeing the scowl on her face as she came striding toward the booth near the back of the Denver Diner where Nick sat waiting, he felt some of that insecurity and fear. The absolute certainty that this hard-featured, frizzy-haired, six-foot-two scowling woman of color was packing a 9mm Glock on her hip never helped ameliorate that particular stab of anxiety.

"I've got some coffee coming for you," said Nick as she slid into the booth opposite him. They used to catch breakfast here often after a night shift at Denver Center. Dara had never minded, nor had K.T.'s partner.

It had been almost five and a half years since Nick had seen or talked to K.T. She'd been promoted to lieutenant and made squad commander since then...a position that Nick himself might be filling if it hadn't been for his flashback addiction. And his total screwing of the proverbial pooch on every front.

"I don't want any coffee," K.T. said coldly. "And the answer to what you're going to ask me is no. Now, is there anything else, Mr. Bottom? I have an early meeting with Delvecchio's Emergency Service Unit guys. I need to shove off."

That mutt Delvecchio is running ESU now? thought Nick. He said, "What are you saying no to, K.T.? I haven't asked anything of you yet. What did you *think* I was going to ask?"

"I won't be your sniper-second at Coors Field this afternoon," the lieutenant said. Although Nick had never once come on to K. T. Lincoln, he'd always seen her as an attractive woman despite her size, rugged features, and short wild hair. Nick had once told Dara that he was able to imagine K.T. being descended from Abraham Lincoln—if the former president had mated with a beautiful black woman with K.T.'s café-au-lait complexion and chicory-bitter personality. Like President Lincoln (despite the inevitable rumors by second-rate history writers desperately seeking a new angle on the most-written-about president in U.S. history), K. T. Lincoln preferred women in matters of romance.

But it was her deeply recessed, dark, and strangely Lincolnesque—and only sometimes sympathetic—brown eyes that were the main similarity between the sainted president and the scowling and silent squad commander.

"How'd you know I was going into Coors?" asked Nick.

"You've gotta be shitting me," said K.T. "Everybody in the department's been watching you make an asshole of yourself working for Nakamura. You think you're going to get special permission from the governor on down to see Oz, Dean, Delroy Nigger Brown, and the rest of these chumps—everything being greased from the Advisor's office—and not have us know what you're doing? Come back to Planet Earth, Bottom."

"What happened to 'Nick'?" asked Nick.

"He died at the bottom of a flashback addict's sniffer vial," snapped K.T.

Stung, Nick said, "I have a sniper-second for Coors."

"One of Nakamura's thugs," she said. "Good. You don't need me, then. If there won't be anything else…" She started scooting out of the booth.

The waitress accidentally blocked K.T.'s exit for a moment, bringing both their coffees and Nick's big breakfast of eggs, bacon, and hash browns. Nick said hurriedly, "It's about Dara."

The lieutenant paused. Then sat down.

"What's about Dara?" asked K.T. sharply when the waitress had refilled their coffees and left.

"Danny Oz, the Israeli poet who was one of the last people interviewed by Keigo Nakamura…"

"I remember who Oz was," said K.T.

"…told me yesterday that he met Dara and an unidentified fat, balding guy who must've been ADA Harvey Cohen on the day that Keigo interviewed him. I need to know why she was there, K.T."

K.T. lifted her coffee cup with both hands and sipped slowly, obviously just as a way to find time to think. "Oz never mentioned your wife in any of the other five investigations into Keigo's murder," she said softly.

"Five?" said Nick. "Five? I just knew about our department's joint investigation with the Feebies and then the Japs themselves, Nakamura Senior, doing it again a couple of years later."

"There've been three more since," said K.T. while she looked down at her coffee. "DHS three years ago, then our office again after the governor put a rocket up Peña Junior's ass. Then, a year and a half ago, the Feebies again with the CIA or some damned spook group looking into the nasty corners where the feds usually can't go."

"So my investigation makes six in six years," murmured Nick.

"Your investigation makes five and one one-hundredth," snapped K.T. For a fleeting instant there was a rare expression on her face, as if she wished she hadn't said what she'd said.

But Nick just nodded. "Why has Nakamura hired me after all that firepower has come up empty? But the truth is, I don't care why…I just want to find out why Dara and Harvey Cohen were there in Six Flags that September day. There's also a chance that she was at the party in LoDo the night Keigo was murdered there."

K.T. looked up. "At Keigo's digs? No chance, Nick. All the investigations have combed that party list and the video recordings a thousand times. Hell, Nakamura's people even re-created the whole thing in a three-D simulation. No sign of Dara."

"Simulations come out of a computer," growled Nick. "Computers depend on what goes into them. And on one of the outside videos I caught a glimpse of…someone…who could've been Dara, across the street about half a block away. Right when everyone was hightailing it out of the building before the cops got there."

K.T. shook her head. "The FBI and the other tech investigations enhanced all those outdoor night videos. No matches with anyone of interest."

"Well," said Nick, setting words in place like sliding bullets into a revolver, "maybe my dead wife wasn't of interest to them. But she's of interest to *me*. I need to find out why she was at Six Flags that day and maybe at the party that night and to do that, I need your help, K.T."

The lieutenant leaned back and away from him. "Jesus, Nick. You've been watching or reading too many goddamned private-eye stories where the defrocked ex-cop still has a pal on the force that does all the heavy lifting for him, despite the fact that it'd cost a real cop in the real world her gold shield. Well, I'm not your pal anymore, Nick Bottom, and I wouldn't do it if I were."

"You were Dara's pal," Nick said flatly, his hands clasped together and his forefingers pointing at K.T.'s chest like a pistol. "Or you acted like you were back then."

"Fuck you, Bottom."

"And fuck you, Lincoln. You're not worried about losing your gold shield. You're worried about losing your next promotion. But what's next to get promoted to, K.T.? Commissioner? Mayor? Queen of Colorado?"

Nick had chosen a booth near the back of the diner, near the restrooms and away from the windows and early-morning crowd, but people were still turning to stare over the backs of their booths.

Nick leaned closer and whispered, "I need your help, K.T."

The lieutenant's expression had not changed except perhaps for a slight narrowing of her eyes. "What you need, Nick, is a shave, a haircut, to get your teeth cleaned, and to lose about twenty-five pounds. A new suit and a tie might help as well."

Nick felt the wince inside but did not show it. "I need your help, K.T. I need to know why Dara was at Six Flags. And if she was near Keigo's apartment that night."

"She never said anything to you about Cohen or the district attorney looking into anything having to do with Keigo Nakamura?"

"Nothing that I remember. I'm going through those days one at a time with flashback and everything she says or doesn't say seems suspicious to me now. I need to talk to the district attorney then, Ortega."

"Mannie Ortega?" K.T. chuckled and took a piece of bacon from Nick's plate. "Good luck in seeing the mayor to ask questions about something he probably didn't even know about six years ago. The word downtown is that Ortega sees being mayor of Denver as a temporary stepping-stone. He has national aspirations."

"Well, fuck him and his national aspirations," hissed Nick. "I just need to know what Harvey Cohen was working on that might have put him and Dara in Six Flags Over the Jews that day."

"Maybe you can get away with pulling your Advisor strings once to get in to see Ortega," said K.T., "but your...investigation...doesn't have a damned thing to do with who killed Keigo Nakamura anymore, does it?"

"I don't know," Nick said truthfully. "I just know that right now I don't give a shit about who killed that kid unless it has something to do with Dara. And maybe even Dara's…accident."

K.T.'s strong eyebrows shot up. "Her accident? You're not suggesting that the car crash that killed her and Harvey Cohen was more than an accident?"

Nick shrugged and looked down at his cooling and congealing breakfast.

"Nick, the state patrol, sheriff's office, and DA's office all shared their investigation notes with you five and a half years ago. I know they did. Traffic was moving fast when Cohen's car started to exit I-Twenty-five to East Fifty-eighth Avenue—Harvey always drove too fast around the city. The old couple in the Buick gelding in front of them stopped suddenly. No reason…someone just slowed in front of them and they slammed on the brakes, the way old drivers do so often. Harvey couldn't stop in time or get out of their way, neither could the driver of the eighteen-wheeler behind them, and all three vehicles went into the barrier. The old couple and the trucker also died in the fire. For God's sake, where is there anything but an accident in that, Nick?"

He looked at her through bloodshot eyes. "Did you ever hear of a swoop-and-squat, K.T.?"

The lieutenant snorted. "Sure I have. One of the oldest auto insurance scams on record. But I've never heard of the braking car in front of the targeted auto being an old anglo couple with not a single moving violation to the driver's name, nor the squat car being an eighteen-wheeler. Nor have I heard of swoop-and-squat scamsters volunteering to die in a fire. You have to do better than that, Nick."

"Where the hell were they coming from, K.T.?"

"Who?"

"Harvey and Dara. Where were they coming from when this 'accident' happened?"

"Lunch, I think the report said." K.T. suddenly sounded tired.

"They'd been out of the office for more than three hours by then," snarled Nick. "Long goddamned lunch. And where the hell were they going? The DA's office at the time just said they were going to take a deposition of someone in Globeville — no other details. Who the hell goes to Globeville to get a deposition?"

"I guess ADAs and their assistants do when the person being deposed lives in Globeville," said K.T. "Why didn't you bring these questions up at the time?"

"They didn't seem important at the time," said Nick. "Nothing seemed important at the time."

K.T. looked down at her strong fingers where they were splayed on the tabletop. "You'll have to see Ortega and the current district attorney for all that information," she said very softly. "What do you want *me* to do?"

"First, get me everything that the state highway patrol, sheriff's office, and DA's office didn't show me almost six years ago," said Nick. "And everything from the coroner's office that I didn't see."

She stared at him for a long moment. Finally, she said, "Nick, do you really want to see the accident-site photos of Dara's crumpled and burned body?"

"Yes," said Nick, returning her stare with some ferocity. "I do. Also Harvey's body, the old couple's, and the truck driver's. And I need to see everything the department had on everyone involved in that crash. I want to know everything there is to know about that trucker and the old farts."

"Is that all?"

"No," said Nick. "I need you to poke around and see if any branch of the department or the FBI or anyone else was looking into anything about Keigo Nakamura before he was murdered...anything that might have brought the DA's office in and sent Dara and Harvey Cohen to Six Flags that day in September."

"That won't be easy," said K.T.

"You're squad commander, Lieutenant Lincoln," said Nick. "When you and I were detectives second grade, we considered that position second only to God's."

"Yeah?" said K.T., looking at him. "Well, it's not."

She started scooting out of the booth again. "You have the same phone number?"

"Yeah," said Nick but hesitated. "But if you could report to me personally—in private like this—it might be a better idea. Hard copies of the info rather than digital."

K.T. paused and cocked her head. "Getting a little paranoid, are we?"

"Even paranoids have enemies, K.T.," said Nick. "If the FBI and CIA kept coming back to this investigation of Keigo's murder, odds are strong that they suspect some sort of conspiracy against Nakamura and his holdings by those cabals of corporations they have there."

K.T. was standing next to the booth now, but she leaned over and lowered her voice. "That would be a dangerous area to poke around in, Nick. For you or for me. Since the Day It All Hit The Fan, Japan's gone almost feudal again. You know that. Those clusters of companies—*keiretsu* they call them—are like fiefdoms. You've heard of the resurgence of the *keiretsu* in Japan, haven't you?"

"Sure," said Nick.

"Then you need to remember that the prime minister and members of the National Diet are nobodies. Heads of these corporate-alliance *keiretsu* like Hiroshi Nakamura, who also head up their own family monopolies called *zaibatsu* that have made such a comeback, all want to be *Shogun* of the new Southeast Asia Co-Prosperity Sphere that the Japs are carving out of China and the rest of Asia. Being an Advisor to America the way Nakamura is means that he's one of the top players in that feudal nightmare that these Nipponese samurai-businessmen call a culture. Assassination has always been fair game between these *keiretsu* and *zaibatsu*. You really don't want to get involved in their wars, Nick."

He looked up at her. They were so close that he could smell the subtle fragrance that she'd worn when they were partners working out of the 16th Street house. "I have to get involved in it, K.T. If there's the slightest chance that Dara was involved, I have to be, too."

K. T. Lincoln straightened up and seemed to be looking at the blank wall behind the booth. But she didn't leave. After a few seconds, she said, "Do you know why I'm part of the tiny five percent of Americans who've never once tried flashback, Nick?"

"You're Amish?"

His former partner didn't smile. "No, it's because I already have too many important dead that I'd spend most of my time visiting in the haze of that motherfucking drug. I read in a report that you saw that Google punk Derek Dean yesterday. So you know how sick this habit of going to live that false life with the dead is, Nick. Every hour under the flash is an hour lost from your real life forever."

Nick looked at her without blinking. When he did speak, his voice was firm, emotionless. "*What* real life, K.T.?"

She closed her eyes for a second, then turned to leave but paused, speaking over her shoulder. "Be careful at Coors Field this afternoon. The department has info that this Hideki Sato you chose as your sniper-second is one of these *zaibatsu* assassins we were talking about."

"Good," said Nick. "Then he should be able to shoot straight. Call me as soon as you have something and we'll meet again."

Lieutenant Lincoln walked out of the diner with the same confident, aggressive strides she'd used to enter.

———

NO VISITOR WENT INTO Coors Field armed, so Nick spent more than a half hour donning the Kevlar-Plus armor that went under his street clothes and up and over his neck and head like an overlappingly scaled and lightweight metal-ballistic-cloth balaclava. Nick's face was exposed, so an inmate could always shoot him there—and there were guns as well as shivs, cleavers, spears, spikes, saps, and full-scale combat knives in the prison called Coors Field—but the K-Plus would turn away most blades and other cutting edges and, with luck, allow his sniper-second to step in.

But a long blade in the eye socket, struck in with lightning speed and an inmate's Body Nazi–exercised and honed muscle, would serve as well as any bullet. These hard cases in Coors Field were the fittest and strongest men in the state of Colorado.

"Only men here?" asked Sato. Warden Bill Polansky and head guard and chief of the sniper squad Paul Campos were there watching Nick armor up. Polansky was the kind of quiet but solid midlevel administrator who, if he were in public education, would either be superintendent by the time he was forty-five or ready to blow his brains out.

Campos—with his head of silver, short-cropped curls and deep-water tan—was a man who'd blow any other man's brains out before his own. And he'd do the job not happily but with absolute efficiency.

"Only men," said Warden Polansky. "We have no indoor cells here except the emergency isolation holding cells under the stands. Women are housed in the nearby ex–Pepsi Center."

"I used to watch the Nuggets and Avalanche play there," Campos said. "And I heard Bruce Springsteen there once. Are you familiar with the rifle, Mr. Sato?"

Sato grunted and nodded.

Busy fitting the body armor over his genitals, Nick looked at the unloaded rifle that Sato was hefting. It was a basic M40A6 bolt-action sniper rifle of the sort the U.S. Marines still used. Nick could see that it had a five-round detachable box magazine. The range in Coors Field was relatively short—about one hundred eighty meters maximum—so it made sense that the prison snipers used the lighter 7.62 × 51mm former NATO cartridges rather than heavy, armor-piercing .50-caliber models.

Campos tapped the scope. "A modified Schmidt and Bender 3–12 × 50 Police Marksman II L with illuminated reticle. Daytime scope. You'll probably be shooting into shadow under the second deck—that's where D. Nigger Brown lives—but this will gather enough light to give you a clear shot, even if it gets cloudy." Campos paused. "Have you used this particular weapon before, sir?"

"Yes, I have," said Sato. He set the long gun down on its bipod on the table.

"We don't want anyone dead," Warden Polansky said tiredly just as Nick was pulling the K-Plus balaclava over his head. "Colorado abolished the death penalty years ago and never got around to reinstating it. So every prisoner you shoot creates a lot of paperwork for all of us. Actually, there's more paperwork if a prisoner dies than if the visitor is killed."

Sato nodded. Nick stared out through the eyeholes of his new headgear. His ears were covered but microphone pickups conveyed both external sounds and kept him in radio touch with Sato and others in the old press box. There was a 3D mini-cam and dual pickup microphones on the headpiece, so Sato and the others could monitor everything he was seeing and hearing…unless one of the inmates cut his head off and stashed it somewhere.

Nick started pulling on his outer clothes. The K-Plus gloves would be the last thing he put on.

Warden Polansky came over to Nick, turned on the cameras and mikes, stepped back, and folded his arms. He was scowling. "We want to accommodate Advisor Nakamura, Mr. Bottom, but is interrogating this particular prisoner really worth all this hassle?"

"Probably not," said Nick. Fully dressed, he flexed his arms and fingers and moved his head around. He felt as if someone had sheathed him in metal-and-plastic shrinkwrap. The sweat was already pooling up under the K-Plus armor. "Let's go," he said.

NICK CAME OUT THROUGH the door in the centerfield wall and began the long walk across the playing field. Delroy Brown's hovel was on the first level behind home plate, halfway up. Being a mere drug dealer in for a mere three-year fall, Brown wouldn't warrant such a prime location, but he'd been in often and for more serious offenses and he had friends here.

Nick didn't look over his shoulder but he knew Sato was up there behind the reflective, bulletproof glass of what used to be the second-level outfield VIP restaurant. Now it was a sniper's roost.

In the early days of Coors Field's use as an outdoor prison, the entire playing field was kept free for exercise purposes. Now outfield and infield—both grassless—were filled with blanket tents, cardboard and scrap-tin shacks, and junk-heap hovels. Those who lived down here were the newbies and nobodies, since their cobbled-together cubies suffered the full force of the weather. Coors Field had never had a roof, retractable or otherwise. The black prisoners had pride of place, owning all the covered area behind home plate and spreading to beyond both the first- and third-base-side dugouts. Whites owned the covered left-field areas on both the first and second tiers. Spanics had both tiers of right field and an uncovered part of the centerfield stands once called the Rockpile. It was still called the Rockpile by its inhabitants.

The expensive enclosed luxury boxes were now windowless hovels for the VIP prisoners—they paid the guards and warden a fortune for them—and the third-tier seats were a melange of shacks and tents for eccentrics and aging prisoners who just wanted to be left the fuck alone.

There was a sort of trail from the centerfield-wall door through the hovels to home plate and Nick kept to it. Sullen eyes glared out from under tents and cardboard shacks, but no one came close to him here. The understood shooting zone for visitors was six feet.

It was a long walk and the K-Plus armor made Nick's body heat build up until he almost felt faint.

He knew the drill: if one or more inmates attack you with edged weapons, roll up in a ball, cover your face with your K-Plus hands, and let your sniper-second handle things while the inmates stab away at you. Then, when the attackers are all down, get up and run like hell for the nearest exit.

Only the nearest exit was now some four hundred feet away across the entire infield and outfield.

Nick paused about where home plate used to be and peered up into the stands. The backstop and net were right where they used to be before this felon-inhabited state began parking its captured felons here. The reality of the place surprised him since he was so used to seeing the digital version in the Rockies games he followed during the summer. Most people had thought that the death of public gatherings would be the death of professional sports, but televised 3D digital-virtual games, in all sports, were more popular than the original live versions. One reason was probably the better players: the new Colorado Rockies team boasted such players as Dante Bichette, Larry Walker, Andrés Galarraga, and Vinny Castilla, who had all played for the team more than forty years earlier. The only rule now in major league baseball was that the virtual player on the roster must have played with that team sometime in the past (and could only be digitally resurrected to play on one team), thus the joyous return of the Brooklyn Dodgers with Sandy Koufax, Don Drysdale, Jackie Robinson, Duke Snider, Pee Wee Reese, Gil Hodges, and the rest. Those Dodgers faced a New York Yankees lineup that included Derek Jeter, Mickey Mantle, Roger Maris (tuned to his best year), Lou Gehrig, Dwight Gooden, and Babe Ruth.

There was endless bitching about the fairness and accuracy of the virtual MLB players and teams, but baseball fans loved the resurrection era. Few would go back to the steroid-riddled players of the last, scandal-ridden decades of the live game.

Nick, like the Old Man before him, loved boxing and often watched *Friday Night Fights*, where a young Cassius Clay could be found fighting Rocky Marciano or Jack Johnson...

"Bottom-san, are you paying attention?" whispered Sato's voice in Nick's ear. "Man approaching from your right."

Nick whirled.

The man coming out of the tent-and-shack village toward him was tall, thin, white-haired, black, and old. The old man wore baggy khaki shorts, sandals, and a spotless white shirt. He walked slowly but almost regally, stopping about seven feet away from Nick and opening his hands to show that they were empty.

"Welcome, sir, to our modest world of Coors Field, *sans* baseball, *sans* fans, *sans* hot dogs and Cracker Jack, *sans* Coors beer, *sans* everything but incarcerated felons, myself included, sir." The old man bowed slightly but very gracefully. His voice was rich, full, deep, mesmerizing, in the way those of some Shakespearean actors and old-time sports announcers used to be.

Nick nodded slightly but looked around, his gaze flicking everywhere, wondering if this was the setup for some trap. *Move on*, his brain told him. *Move on, idiot.*

"My name is Soul Dad," said the old man. "Soul with a 'u.' May I inquire as to your name, sir?"

Move on. Move on. Nothing good could come from Nick's giving his name to some senile old felon.

"My name is Nick Bottom." Nick heard his own voice as if from a distance. Something about his early-morning conversation with K. T. Lincoln had distracted him at a time when he couldn't afford to be distracted. It was as if all this—the hovels and felons and sunlight and ravaged old ballpark, even the crazy old man with the amazing voice—was part of some flashback session and Nick was hovering above it all.

Hovering will get you killed, asshole.

Soul Dad chuckled in the same resonant, rich tones. "Well, Mr. Nick Bottom, you left your ass's ears at home today, sir."

Nick glanced at the old man and moved slightly to his right, keeping the same distance between them but putting the old man between him and anyone with a gun in the stands straight ahead or to the immediate right, without blocking Sato's shot.

When Nick didn't reply, Soul Dad said, "I've always thought that when the awakening Nick Bottom in *A Midsummer Night's Dream* says, '*It shall be called Bottom's Dream, because it hath no bottom; and I will sing it in the latter end of a play, before the Duke. Peradventure, to make it the more gracious, I shall sing it at her death,*' the 'her' he's talking about is Juliet from *Romeo and Juliet*. Shakespeare wrote the two about the same time, you see, Mr. Bottom...perhaps *at* the same time, although that would have been very unusual for the Bard...and I believe he allowed one reality to bleed over into another in Nick Bottom's line there, just as flashback users often let one of their realities seep into another. Sometimes until they can't tell the difference."

Nick could only blink. It was odd that the Israeli poet Danny Oz had also brought up the question of who the "her" was in the "sing it at her death" part of that quotation.

Knowing he was wasting time and making himself more of a target, Nick said, "You seem to know quite a bit about Shakespeare, Mr. Soul Dad."

The old man threw his head back and laughed deeply and delightedly. His teeth were large and white and only one was missing on the upper right side, despite his age. Something about the laugh made Nick think that the old man was Jamaican, although he had none of the accent. Whether he was laughing at being called Mr. Soul Dad or because of the Shakespeare compliment, Nick had no clue.

"I lived for more than forty years in a small railroad-yard shack in Buffalo, New York, with a sterno-addicted philosophy professor of great learning, Mr. Bottom," said Soul Dad. "Some things rub off."

Nick knew it was stupid to ask a question and drag things out with this old man, but sometimes one had to be stupid. "Soul Dad," he said softly, "what are you in here for?"

Again that full-throated laugh. "I am in here for living under an overpass in winter and fouling the view of the Platte River for people paying much money to live in a tall glass tower along the river park," said Soul Dad. "What, may I ask in return, are *you* here for, Mr. Bottom? Or, rather, whom are you searching for here?"

"Delroy...Brown."

Soul Dad showed his strong teeth again in a broad grin. "How gallant of you to leave out the n-word, Mr. Bottom. And I agree with you on the choice. Of all the things I have seen and suffered in my eighty-nine years of life, my people's return to the never-really-abandoned n-word of our centuries of servitude is the greatest self-inflicted folly."

Soul Dad turned and pointed to a hovel halfway up the first tier behind home plate, where, of course, all the seats had long since been torn out. "Mr. Delroy Nigger Brown is there, sir, and expecting you."

"Thank you," Nick said absurdly and started to step forward.

Blocking the gesture from the sight of those behind him, Soul Dad held up a hand with one finger raised. "They plan to kill you," the old man said very softly.

Nick paused.

"Not Mr. Brown, whom you seek, but a certain Bad Nigger Ajax. You know the man?"

"I know the man," Nick said just as softly. He'd been the arresting officer and his testimony had sent Ajax away more than ten years before for repeatedly sodomizing a six-year-old girl. The girl had died of internal hemorrhaging.

"It will be like this," said Soul Dad in the same quick, soft, reverberant whisper. "Mr. Brown will invite you into his tent-hovel. You will wisely decline. Mr. Brown will say, 'Let us step up here where it is private.' Ten steps up, Mr. Ajax will pop up from behind another tent and shoot you in the face. His friends—or, rather, his fearful acolytes, since Mr. Ajax has no friends here—will block the view of your sniper with their bodies while Mr. Ajax escapes into the crowds toward left field. The pistol will not be found."

Nick stared at the old man. Eighty-nine years old. Soul Dad—whatever his original name was—had been born in the early days of World War II.

Before Nick could speak, even inanely to say "Thank you" again—although he had no idea if the old man was telling the truth or setting him up for some other form of assassination—Soul Dad put his hands together, bowed, turned, and walked away down what once was the third-base line.

Nick took two steps back while surveying the maze of tents and shacks filling the entire first tier behind home plate. "Did you hear that?" he whispered.

"We heard it," came Sato's voice in his ear. "I am looking at a photo of Ajax right now."

Nick licked his dry and chapped lips. "Any suggestions on what I should do?"

"Mr. Campos suggests that you should come back through the centerfield fence, Bottom-san. He says to jog and weave. Ajax's pistol is probably of small caliber."

Sweat was running into Nick's eyes but he resisted the urge to wipe it away. "I'm going to go up and find Delroy. Can you react fast enough to take Ajax out when and if he pops up?"

"It will be in deep shadow up there." Sato's voice was calm in Nick's ear. "He will expose himself for only a second. And I have something to confess to you, Bottom-san."

"What?"

"All American black men look pretty much the same to me, Bottom-san."

Nick laughed despite himself. "Bad Nigger Ajax weighs around three hundred pounds," he said, covering his mouth with his hand so no one in the stands could read his lips. *How many pitchers have done that here with their mitts?* he wondered.

"I confess, Bottom-san, that all three-hundred-pound American blacks look the same to me. So sorry."

"Well," said Nick behind his hand, "shoot the one aiming a gun at me. If you can."

"Warden Polansky will not appreciate the paperwork," Sato said with no hint of emotion. Nick had no idea if the big security chief was joking. And he didn't care.

———

NICK WENT UP THE dirt ramp into the stands. Men outside their tents shrank away from him—or, rather, from the killing circle that moved with him. He felt their gazes on his back as he climbed the steps. The center railing that had been there in baseball days had long since been torn out.

Halfway up the first section, he paused near the tent that Soul Dad had pointed out. "Delroy Nigger Brown!" he shouted. His only satisfaction was that his voice still sounded strong, no quaver. Less satisfying was the sudden urge to piss down his own leg through the K-Plus armor. "Delroy Nigger Brown! Come out!"

"Who wants me?" came a familiar weaselly voice from inside the tent.

"Come out here and I'll tell you," said Nick, lowering his own voice a little but still using his never-take-no-for-an-answer cop tones. "*Now*."

"You all come on inside the tent where it be quiet," whined Delroy. "Nothin' in here to be, you know, afraid of, cop-man."

"Out here, *now*," repeated Nick. Each syllable was flat, hard, and imperative.

Delroy Nigger Brown came wriggling out of the low tent-shack. He was dressed as Soul Dad had been, in shorts, shirt, and flip-flops, but everything on Brown was as filthy as Soul Dad's had been immaculate. When he came closer and stood straight, he still barely came up to Nick's shoulder.

"I ain't done nothing, man," complained Delroy. "I only be in here for eight months for selling a li'l flashback is all what it is. And that be 'staken identity."

Nick had to smile despite his continued urge to run. "Nobody gets sent to Coors Field for selling flash, Delroy," he barked. "You were hauling coke, X-H, heroin, flashback, and Terror up from New Mexico with you. And selling it to kids. I just have a couple of questions for you...not about any of the drugs or guns or other crap you got caught with."

"Not about none of that what my, you know, lawyer wouldn' let me, you know what I'm sayin' to you, talk about?"

"Right," said Nick, not even sure what the sniveling dealer had said.

"All right," said Delroy, brightening suddenly as if Nick were a friend or customer visiting. "Why don't we, you know, go up there a bit where no one can, you know what I'm tellin' you, listen and where it be a little, you know what I'm sayin', out of the sun and like that?"

"All right," Nick heard himself say. He grabbed Delroy's upper left arm in a grip so tight that the little dealer let out a yelp.

One step up together, Delroy squirming to get free.

Two steps up. Three. Four.

There was the sudden stink of fresh urine. Nick realized that Delroy had pissed himself. The little weasel hadn't planned to be next to Nick when the gunfire started.

Five steps. Six. Eight.

"No!" screamed Delroy and tried to pull out of Nick's grip. He couldn't.

There were blurs of movement all around. Men dodging, diving, shoving forward, pushing back, coming out of tents and leaping into tents.

The crack of the rifle shot echoed through Coors Field, sounding very much like the crack of a baseball on a wooden bat connecting for a home run. Nick saw the explosion of blood, brains, and skull fragments three rows up and fifteen feet to his right, exactly where Soul Dad had said Ajax would be shooting from.

Doesn't mean that there aren't three more waiting, Nick's brain shouted at him as he dragged a soggy and sagging Delroy up the old seat levels toward the fallen shooter. Men were running wildly now, knocking down hovels and other men to get away from the killing zone that encircled Nick.

In the movies, someone always kneels next to a gunshot victim and puts three fingers against the fallen man or woman's neck to see if there's a pulse. Nick had never had to do that—after a while, you could tell at a glance when the person was dead. Of course, it helped—as in Bad Nigger Ajax's case here—when a third of the man's head had been blown away and his brains were spread across dirty concrete like so much spilled oatmeal.

Nick was after the gun and he found it—a .22-caliber target pistol with a long barrel. Giving no thought whatsoever to fingerprints, he picked it up, jammed the narrow muzzle deep into the soft skin under Delroy Nigger Brown's sagging jaw, and pulled the little man with him back down the steps. Nick didn't look back once at Ajax's sprawled and spavined corpse.

Men were still fleeing on both sides, toward the outfield

walls or the third-base-side dugout or the first-base-side dugout, as Nick pulled Delroy along with him across the open field. Tents were being knocked down and hovels were flying apart in the frenzied exodus. Nick now held the pistol high enough that everyone could see it. Any movement even partially toward him and the gun moved to cover it. There wasn't much movement.

It reminded Nick of that scene that he and Val and Dara had always enjoyed where Charlton Heston as Moses parted the Red Sea. Pre-CGI special effects, but cool nonetheless.

You're too cool nonetheless, Nick's cop brain warned him. *Odds are good that there are still people out here waiting to kill you.*

It couldn't be helped. Nick didn't have permission to take Delroy Nigger Brown out of Coors Field — that would require a court order and two hearings with Delroy's public defender present, probably three months' time, only to have the request denied — and he needed information now.

About where the grass of centerfield would have begun, Nick kicked the drug dealer's legs out from under him. Delroy fell to his knees. Nick set the muzzle against the little man's forehead. He could see lice moving in what was left of Delroy's thinning hair.

"I won't ask any question twice," barked Nick.

"Nossir. Yessir. Oh shit and fuck. But nossir," quavered Delroy.

"What did Keigo Nakamura ask you about when he interviewed you six years ago and what did you tell him?"

"*What?*" shouted the kneeling man. "*Who? When?*"

"You heard me," said Nick, digging the small muzzle deep enough into Delroy's temple that it broke the skin.

"Oh, the Jap? That Jap with the camera and the, you know what I'm sayin', sexy snatch assistant? *That* motherfuckin' Jap?"

"That motherfuckin' Jap."

"Whattya want? I mean, you know what I mean…"

"What did he *ask* you?" repeated Nick, pressing the muzzle tighter. Blood began to flow. "What did you *tell* him?"

"The motherfuckin' Jap wanted to know where I got the,

you know, the motherfuckin' flashback that I, you know what I'm tellin' you, sold," whined Delroy.

"What'd you tell him?"

"You know, man — told him the motherfuckin' truth. No reason not to, know what I'm sayin'?"

Nick dug the muzzle deeper. "Tell *me* the truth or there'll be two men named Nigger in this yard minus their brains. I swear to God, Delroy."

"*I'm tellin', I'm tellin', I'm motherfuckin' tellin',*" screamed Delroy, raising his shaking hands but keeping them away from the pistol. "What was, like, you know, the question?"

"Where'd you get the flashback?"

"Where I got all my good drugs then, man. This be six motherfuckin' years ago. Got all my good shit, 'cludin' the flashback, from Don Khozh-Ahmed Noukhaev at his big motherfuckin' hacienda down in Santa Fe. He's the, you know what I'm sayin', head of the Bratva fucking Russian motherfuckin' mafia down there."

Damn, thought Nick. All roads always lead to Santa Fe. He'd have to go through with the trip Sato had planned for tomorrow.

"What else did you tell Keigo Nakamura during that interview?"

"Just about the motherfuckin' flashback, man. He wasn't even interested in the heroin or coke or nothin', you know what I'm sayin'? Just wanted to know all about the flash — how I get it from fuckin' Don Khozh-Ahmed Noukhaev, how we drive it back with the motherfuckin' pass to get past the motherfuckin' *reconquistas,* that sort of shit."

"What else?" demanded Nick, moving the pistol's muzzle to Delroy's soft eye socket.

The dealer squealed. "*Nothing* else. Jap didn't wanna talk about anything else. Look at the motherfuckin' videos if you don't believe me."

"Why'd you leave the party with Danny Oz the night Keigo was killed?"

"*What?* With *who?*"

"You heard me."

"You mean that Jew-boy over to Six Flags?"

"Yeah."

"Why do you *think* I left with him, man? Somebody just got his ass murdered at that party, you know what I'm tellin' you? Time to go, Joe. We had to get out of there and whatshisname, the Jew, the wizard of Oz or what the fuck, wanted some product. We went to my house up on the motherfuckin' hill. I didn't bring no vials to the party."

"Which product, Delroy?"

"Flashback. That Jew never bought nothing else."

Nick held out his phone with Dara's photo filling the screen. "Look at this picture..."

"Nice white snatch...," began Delroy.

Nick dug the muzzle of the .22 target pistol deep enough behind the dealer's left eye that he could have popped the eyeball out with a twist of his wrist. Delroy screamed. Nick let up some of the pressure. The barrel and muzzle were wet with blood trickling down from Delroy's forehead.

"What the *fuck*, man? You want me to look without no motherfuckin' eye?"

"Where have you seen her before? And when? Be specific or you'll lose more than an eye, I swear to God."

Delroy waved his right hand in a placating way and leaned closer to the screen, squinting. "I ain't never seen her, man. Nowhere. No time."

"Look again."

"I don't have to fuckin' look again. I don't know her, never sold to her, never paid her for nothin', never fuckin' seen her, you hear what I'm tellin' you?"

Nick slipped the phone away. "I hear what you're telling me." He hit the little man just hard enough with the barrel to drop him to the dirt.

Nick walked quickly toward the centerfield wall. He refused to run, to keep the last of his dignity, although the back of his head waited for a bullet to strike it and his shoulders scrunched up despite his best efforts to keep them from doing so. The K-Plus might deflect the body shot, but the blow to the back of his head would kill him even if it didn't penetrate the Kevlar balaclava.

"Warden Polansky will not be happy with us," whispered Sato's voice in his ear. "But by great good coincidence, Bottom-san, your video and audio pickups seem to have failed the last two minutes or so."

"Okay," said Nick, not caring. "Tell Polansky and Campos that they have to get Soul Dad out of the yard...right away. Everyone saw him talking to me before you took out Ajax."

The centerfield fence and door were less than fifty feet away now. How many outfielders had rushed at that flaking green wall while chasing a fly ball? How many relief pitchers had come through that door and walked toward the mound with their hearts pounding and body jagging with adrenaline the way Nick's was now?

Only the top of the centerfield wall then hadn't been covered with rolls of razor wire as it was now.

Chief sniper Campos's voice buzzed in his ear. "We don't need to get Soul Dad out, Mr. Bottom. He's almost worshipped here at Coors Field. A lot of the blacks think he's hundreds of years old and some kind of wizard. Even the whites and spanics leave him alone. No one will harm him."

"But...," began Nick.

"Trust me," continued Campos. "Soul Dad is in no danger. I don't know why he warned you, but he must have had his reasons. And he was right about Bad Nigger Ajax having no friends here. Lots of toadies and butt-boys, but they hated Ajax even more than the others who were terrified of him. Soul Dad's all right."

Nick shrugged. He would have jogged the last fifteen feet or so to the high wall and door, but his legs were weak with the retreat of adrenaline.

He could hear someone on the other side loosening the heavy latch. Someone opening it with the rusty hinges screeching like a dying man's scream. Except Bad Nigger Ajax hadn't had time to scream.

Then Nick was through. Then he was out.

1.10

Raton Pass and New Mexico—
Wednesday, Sept. 15

WHEN SATO CALLED him sometime after 6 a.m. and told him to be on the roof of the Cherry Creek Mall Condos by 7 a.m. to wait for a pickup by the *Sasayaki-tonbo* dragonfly 'copter, Nick felt a shameful rush of relief so profound that it almost affected his bowels. He'd not known before this that he was such a coward.

He didn't care. Flying to Santa Fe—despite the Naka-mura Corporation's worries about shoulder-launched or other kinds of missiles—had to be a hell of a lot safer than trying to drive.

There were no clouds visible from the roof of the former mall. Sixty-some miles to the south, Pikes Peak caught the low, sharp morning sunlight. The dragonfly 'copter came in from the west, circled, and set down lightly. Nick tossed his duffel in the open back door and ignored Sato's offered hand as he clambered up and in by himself.

The oversized bag was heavy. Besides the Glock 9 he had holstered on his belt, the duffel held full police body dragon armor that he'd bought on the black market after losing his job (much more serious stuff than yesterday's K-Plus undies), a

240

sheathed KA-BAR fighting knife, an M4A1 assault rifle that
had belonged to the Old Man, an M209 grenade launcher that
Nick had bought to attach to the old M4A1, a box of M406 HE
grenades in their egg crates, a Negev-Galil flechette sweeper,
and a compact Springfield Armory EMP 1911-A1 9mm semiautomatic pistol. Nick had also brought an S&W Model 625 .45-
caliber revolver that he'd used to good effect in DPD shooting
competitions—firing six shots, reloading with a moon clip or
other speedloader, and firing six more in just over three seconds—
and, finally, boxes of appropriate ammunition for everything
that required ammunition.

"Be careful with the duffel," he said to Sato as he took his
fold-down webbed seat against the aft bulkhead and dragged
the heavy bag under it.

"Ah, you brought your toys along, Bottom-san?" said Sato.
There was almost no engine or rotor noise, but as the dragonfly
'copter rose, leveled off, and headed south, the roar of air
through the open doors was loud enough that Sato handed Nick
a set of earphones and shouted the number of the private channel they should use.

They were flying steadily at about three thousand feet of
altitude. Nick looked out the open door as the southern suburbs of Denver melded into the northern suburbs of Castle
Rock.

It was cooler this morning, the first really cool morning of
this September, and the sunlight fell on buildings and cars that
seemed clean and normal, a product of a sane world. Even the
abandoned, rusting windmills running along the Continental
Divide to their right looked pretty and clean in this rich morning light. The high peaks themselves, save for the looming
Pikes Peak, seemed to be receding westward as the dragonfly
continued to fly due south above I-25.

Nick almost grinned. He knew he should be ashamed of
the relief that he'd felt since Sato's call about the dragonfly, but
there was far more relief in him than guilt. He just really hadn't
wanted to make that all-day drive to Santa Fe in the treacherous daylight.

"What made you change your mind?" he asked Sato over their private intercom.

"Change mind about what, Bottom-san?" The security chief looked sleepy this morning. Either that or he'd been meditating in the square of sunlight falling on their seats and the rear bulkhead.

"About flying to Santa Fe rather than driving."

Sato shook his head in that awkward, Oddjobby way. "Ah, no. We take the *Sasayaki-tonbo* only as far as Raton Pass and the state line. From there we take two trucks into New Mexico the rest of the way to Santa Fe. Getting to the vehicles was faster this way."

Nick managed to limit his reaction to a nod. He turned his face away from Sato and concentrated on watching the abandoned ranches and subdivisions between cities and the little-used highway passing beneath them. They'd passed over Colorado Springs, and the Pikes Peak massif, already with some snow on its broad summit eleven thousand feet higher than the helicopter, was falling behind to their right.

———

"NICK, WHY DON'T WE try that new drug, F-two?" asks Dara.

They're lying together in their bedroom on a sunny Saturday in January just ten days before Dara is to die. They've just made love in that slow, undramatic, but wonderful way that sometimes happens to married couples who've found the next level of intimacy.

For nearly six years, Nick has avoided flashing on these last months before Dara's death, even the nicest memories, since the sense of impending doom overwhelms the pleasure of being with his beloved. But he's made an exception this time because the half-remembered conversation from that January Saturday from five and a half years ago may be relevant to his new investigation.

Val is ten years old and away at a birthday party under Laura McGilvrey's supervision all this long, slow afternoon.

"Seriously," says Dara, stretching out naked against him.

"You won't try regular flashback with me, but why don't we try this Flash-two everyone's talking about? I hear it only allows happy thoughts."

Nick grunts. He's given up smoking but at this particular postcoital-glow moment he's very aware of a hidden pack on the shelf in the closet just a few paces away. "Flash-two isn't real," he says. "It's an urban myth. Sorry to break it to you, kid."

"Well, heck and spit," says Dara. "I assumed that this was just the official line but that you'd really busted F-two users and had vials and vials of the stuff in your evidence room."

"Nope," says Nick and draws his finger up the curve of her bare side. He enjoys watching the goose bumps break out. "Pure nonsense. No such drug. But why the hell would you want to use it if it were real? We've never even tried regular flashback."

"Because you wouldn't let us if I wanted to," fake-pouted his young wife. This was an old joke, her wanting to use various illicit substances, this oh-so-daring child bride of his who thinks that an extra glass of wine with dinner is a sin.

He takes her head in his large hands and shakes it gently. "What's bothering you? Something is."

She rolls over and props herself on her elbows so she can look at him. "I so wish we could talk, Nick. We can't *talk*."

Knowing that it's the worst possible thing to do in this sort of marital conversation, Nick still has to laugh.

Dara moves a few inches farther away from him and pulls up a pillow to hide her lovely breasts.

"Sorry," says Nick. And he is. He knows he's hurt her feelings. And he's sad that she's covering herself in front of him. "It's just that we talk all the *time*, kiddo."

"When you're home."

"And when *you're* home," he retorts. "You've been coming home late and traveling weekends as much or more than I have." And again he's sorry he said anything.

"Our jobs...," she whispers.

Hovering above the conversation, listening in on his own thoughts from *then* as well as to his and Dara's dialogue from that day more than five years ago, Nick is close to deciding that his hunch was wrong...she hadn't said anything pertinent that day.

"I thought we liked our jobs," Nick-then says. *Idiot. Dolt*, thinks Nick-now.

"We do. I did. But they keep us from talking about...well, work things."

The then-Nick thinks he understands. There's a lot about the Keigo Nakamura investigation that he hasn't been free to talk to Dara about since she works for District Attorney Mannie Ortega. The then-Nick thinks that she resents his silence.

"I'm sorry, Dara. There are just things that I haven't been able to talk about and..."

Amazingly, she balls her hand into a fist and hits him on his chest. It isn't a joke-punch; she strikes hard enough to make a red mark.

"You idiot," she says and he's even more startled to see tears in her eyes. "Does it ever occur to you that there are things about *my* job that *I* can't talk to *you* about but would like to? *Need* to?"

He's smart enough—for a change—*not* to admit this, but in truth this possibility hasn't really occurred to Nick. Since Dara is head researcher for one of the assistant district attorneys, old Harvey Cohen, with whom Nick has never been that impressed, he can't imagine much in her work life that she couldn't talk to Nick about if she wanted to. As far as he knows, the DA's office, much less Harvey, doesn't have any cases pending that Nick has been involved in or would have to go to court to testify about.

"It's not *right*," says Dara, putting her flushed face into the pillow. "But I guess it doesn't matter...it's almost over...just a few more days, maybe a week, Mannie says..."

"Mannie Ortega?" says Nick. He's never liked the ambitious, shrewd, but not very bright DA. "What the hell has he got to do with anything?"

"Nothing, nothing, nothing," says Dara and rolls over on her side, facing away from him now and still hugging the pillow to her chest.

But her lovely back and lovely backside are bare, and Nick presses himself against them, putting his left arm around her, his forearm encountering only pillow. "I'm sorry I've been so busy…"

She reaches back over her head and touches the top of his head with her fingers. "It's stupid. Forget everything I said, Nick. I'll explain… when I can. Soon."

He kisses her neck.

And, he realizes floating above the conversation at the end of this fifteen-minute flash, he almost *had* forgotten the entire conversation. He still didn't understand what she'd been talking and crying about. Something at work—*her* work—obviously had been bothering her for some time.

"Shall we take that nap we came in for an hour ago?" whispers Dara, turning back toward him. Her breath is sweet from tears.

"Sure, let's take a short snooze," says Nick. "I'll lock the door in case Val gets home from the birthday party before we wake up."

THE SUMMIT OF RATON Pass was only 7,834 feet, but Major Malcolm's headquarters was in a military trailer set a few hundred feet higher on a low peak just to the west of Interstate 25.

The major obviously knew that Sato was coming and that he represented the Advisor, so Malcolm treated Nakamura's security chief with that minimum of obviously irritated you're-wasting-my-time-but-I-have-to-do-this respect that military officers are so good at projecting. Sato had introduced Nick only by name—no explanation of his presence—and Major Malcolm's nod had been totally dismissive.

There'd been a time when Nick would have been insulted by that attitude, but now he found it convenient. He wanted to think his own thoughts and *not* be involved.

Also, he was tired. He'd done flashback most of the night, getting less than an hour's sleep. Not a smart strategy for a day when he knew he might need all his survival skills—whatever he had left—but he didn't have time enough *not* to have spent the hours under the flash.

They were in the trailer and the major was gesturing toward one screen on a wall of screens, pointing at what seemed to be tiny dust puffs swirling against a textured and three-dimensional tan-and-brown wall.

"These dust fountains," said Major Malcolm, stabbing his blunt finger into the 3D images, "are what's left of the Republic of Texas's Third Armored Division, retreating toward their initial staging area in Dalhart and Dumas. These..."

His hand disappeared into the raised images as he touched the screen where darker, broader smudges rose. "This black wall here is actually more than a thousand smoke plumes between Wagon Mound and Las Vegas, a lot of them near the old Fort Union National Monument...and beneath those plumes are hundreds of burning tanks, APCs, and other armored elements, mostly Texan. The battle lasted ten days and some of our historians are already saying that it was the largest tank fight since the Battle of Kursk in late summer of nineteen forty-three."

"Who won?" asked Nick.

Major Malcolm looked at him as if he'd farted. "Strategically speaking, the Russians, because they stopped the German Blitzkrieg," said the major. "Although the Soviets lost more than six thousand tanks and assault guns against the Germans' seven hundred or so in the whole battle, the Wehrmacht had to retreat. They'd lost the initiative on the Eastern Front and it was the last strategic offensive Hitler managed to mount in the east."

Sato cleared his throat. "I believe what my colleague is asking, Major, is who won *this* particular battle—the Mexicans or Texans?"

"Oh," said Malcolm, not visibly embarrassed. "The spanics and cartels beat the R-oh-T's back with significant losses for the Texans. That's what I meant when I used the word 'retreating.'"

Colorado's southern border, effectively the southern border of the United States, was protected by National Guardsmen, but their commander and this unit at Raton Pass were regular Army. The real regular Army was too valuable serving as mercenaries to the Japanese and others—one of America's few sources of hard currency—to waste on mere American security issues. Nick made an informed guess that Major Malcolm had taught military history at West Point or somewhere before he'd been ordered here to watch the weekend-warrior doofuses who were watching the border.

None of it mattered.

"Are these satellite or drone images?" Sato was asking.

"Satellite," said Major Malcolm. "We buy time on the Indian and civilian sats. The Nuevo Mexican forces knock down our drones."

"The *reconquistas* control all airspace south of here?" said Sato.

Malcolm shrugged. "Technically speaking, the Texans have controlled the airspace the last year or so...they even use piloted aircraft. But in the last three months, the Nuevo forces have brought in Iron Dome and Magic Wand mobile antimissile solid THEL laser batteries. It's given the *reconquistas* multiple-point defenses against Texan Republic IRBMs, but it's also cleared the air of anything that flies...including our drones."

"But the *reconquistas* have not put up their own aircraft?" asked Sato, his massive forearms folded in front of him.

Malcolm shook his head. "The Texans have airborne versions of the old Israeli Nautilus Skyguard that can take down anything in eastern New Mexico airspace from two hundred miles behind the Republic of Texas border. Trust me, Mr. Sato...*no one* owns the air down there."

Sato shot a glance at Nick, but Nick had no idea what the security chief might be trying to tell him. That it would have been a bad idea to try to fly to Santa Fe? Nick looked at the multiple screens, all filled with smudged plumes that meant moving armored divisions or burning vehicles and men. *It's sure in hell not a good idea to try to* drive *through that,* he thought.

"The air corridors from L.A. to Santa Fe are still open, aren't they?" asked Nick.

Major Malcolm squinted at Sato as if to say *Who is this guy?*
"Those narrow air corridors to the west from Santa Fe are
open," admitted Malcolm. "Too many millionaires, movie pro-
ducers, and actors who need access via private plane to their
second homes in Santa Fe to close those routes."

Nick sighed softly. *If Nakamura had been willing to spend a
little money to fly us to L.A. and from there direct to Santa Fe in
some transponder-friendly movie producer's plane, we could avoid
all this crap.*

"Sir, with all that fighting along the I-Twenty-five corridor," Sato was saying to the major, "would you suggest we take
Highway Sixty-four to Taos and down?"

Nick knew Highway 64. He'd driven it in a police convoy
the last time he'd gone to Santa Fe, more than ten years ago. It
had been a nightmare then—bandits in the hills, dropped
bridges, roving paramilitary units of every nasty persuasion—
but at least the Duchess of Taos, a great-granddaughter of some
socialist fiction-writer who'd lived there since the 1960s, sent
patrols out forty miles or so, almost half the distance between
Taos and Raton, to keep things a little sane. From Taos it was
only a couple of hours along the Low Road to Santa Fe.

"Actually," said Major Malcolm, "I can't recommend to
you or the Advisor that you go either way now."

When Sato said nothing, the major put his hand back into
one of the screens. "The only civilian traffic that's tried to get
to Santa Fe in the past two weeks was a twelve-truck convoy—
Coca-Cola and Home Depot teaming up—with three military-
vehicle outriders for protection. We lost touch with them shortly
after they passed our barricades, they never got to Santa Fe,
and we think this is them right...*here.*"

Nick leaned forward the better to see the orange-and-black
smudge under Malcolm's pointing finger. About halfway between
the tiny towns of Springer and Wagon Mound, which looked to
be about twenty miles apart on the high plains along I-25.

"We have to go, sir," said Sato. "Would you recommend
the I-Twenty-five route or the canyon road to Taos?"

Malcolm dropped his arm and shrugged. "To be honest,

I-Twenty-five may be the slightly better bet this week. Gallagos's cannibals have extended their raiding circle from the old Philmont Boy Scout camp near Cimarron along the canyon highway. The Duchess's cavalry hasn't been clearing the last thirty miles of Highway Sixty-four of obstacles and bandits the way she usually has them do…some say she's died. Maybe in all the confusion after the battle, the Interstate Twenty-five route gives you a slightly better chance of going undetected. There's a chance of that. Maybe. Small chance."

Sato nodded, shook hands with the major, and led Nick out of the trailer and down the hill to where the two tan, modified Toyota Land Cruisers they'd be driving into New Mexico sat by the side of the road. Tanks were parked in the turnouts near the summit of the pass and Nick could see National Guard artillery units along the ridgeline to the north and south. The dragonfly 'copter had already departed.

The four ninjas working for Sato were waiting by the vehicles. When Sato had introduced the four young men to Nick—"Joe," "Willy," "Toby," and "Bill"—all Nick could say in response to their nods was "Uh-huh." It reminded him of when he was a child before the turn of the century and would call for tech help on his computer or software and the heavily accented voice from somewhere in India would say "My name is Joe." Uh-huh.

The four had been in faded jeans and cheap noninteractive T-shirts when Nick had met them, but in the short period he and Sato had been in Major Malcolm's trailer, they'd changed into their body armor. This was a serious transformation. No black ninja slippers and clothing and balaclavas for these four boys. Their hideously expensive post-dragon body armor—seemingly as thin as silk covered with overlapping scales—was based on samurai armor from the eighth or tenth century A.D. or some such time. Each man's armor was different, but each included studded shoulder pads, a sort of skirt, a helmet, studded gloves, and shin guards.

"Whoa," said Nick, staring. "As my son would say, those are totally coolshit."

"*Hai*," grunted Joe. He was the only one of the four wearing his helmet and it was an impressive piece of work, complete with elaborately carved horns or small-hockey-stick-shaped prongs that clicked up from their inset place along the curve of the otherwise modern Kevlar-9 impact-armored headpiece.

Nick pointed to the helmet extensions. "Joe, do you mind me asking what the superhero antelope prongs there are about?"

"Clan symbols," Joe grunted fiercely. But some of the ferocity was offset by the young mercenary's sudden grin and by the fact that he was chewing gum. "Nakamura clan," he added with no grin.

Nick looked at the other three helmets held under the men's left arms as they waited by the open doors of the Land Cruisers. All had the same elaborately painted, click-up Nakamura-clan-symbol goalpost horns. So, Nick realized, Sato's men weren't just *ronin*, masterless mercenaries—they were some sort of ninja-samurai *bushi* not just in the employ of Hiroshi Nakamura but almost certainly fanatically loyal to the Nakamura family corporation.

"What are these things called?" asked Nick, pointing to but not quite touching Joe's dangling shoulder pads. They *looked* heavy, but Nick realized that they were made of the same superlight Kevlar-9 woven material as the rest of the body armor.

"*Sendan-no-ita, kyubi-no-ita*," said Joe.

Nick thought that this was a long name for a relatively small shoulder pad. "And why the extra layer of red K-nine on the left arm and not the right?"

Toby answered. He was the shortest and slimmest of the four young fighters, but his voice was almost absurdly deep. "The extra left-arm armor is called *kote*, Bottom-san. It can be held up quickly to deflect a sword thrust or bullet. It's only on the left arm because the right arm must be free to allow the samurai to fire a bow."

"Or a nine-K-forty-six Igla shoulder-launched surface-to-air missile," added Bill as he tapped a cylindrical case strung over his shoulder.

Sato came around the closer Land Cruiser. The security chief was in his own samurai armor—all red, pure blood red, including the helmet and metallic mask. Although the mask was pushed back on his head and not yet in place, Nick could see that it had some sort of pale, whiskery fibers protruding from it like white whiskers. An actual samurai sword— sheathed—was in the stocky man's belt.

Nick had no urge whatsoever to laugh.

"Tsugi no fourtsu desu ka yaban to jōdan owa~tsu ta no?" Sato barked at his four fighters.

The four young men bowed at once. And they bowed low.

"Hai! Junbi ga deki te, bosu ni id shi masu," said Joe.

Sato turned toward Nick, who thought the security chief looked infinitely more at home in the samurai armor than he had in his usual black or gray suits and ties. "Joe will be riding with us, the other three in the second truck. You had best get into your body armor, Bottom-san."

———

THEIR TWO VEHICLES WERE made to look like Toyota Land Cruisers, but once Nick saw the scale with men standing next to them, he realized that both SUVs—a quaint term from Nick's childhood and young-adult years—were about twice the size of even the largest vehicle from the venerable line of what he and Dara had called Land Crushers. He'd also noticed that the "Land Cruisers" had no windows of any sort—not even windshields. Every part of the rugged, dull-matte-painted surface was the same desert-tan mix of steel, Kevlar-9, and various alloys.

In truth, Sato explained after Nick had struggled into his definitely-not-samurai-looking cop armor, these vehicles were the Japanese military's blend of the most effectively armored-up civilian trucks they had along with the twenty-year-old but constantly refined U.S. Army's Oshkosh B'Gosh M-ATV, which stood, Sato explained, for "Mine-Resistant Ambush-Protected All-Terrain Vehicle."

This Land Cruiser's belly was four feet off the ground and

V-shaped to deflect IED blasts from beneath. In an age where every granny lady on the block paid extra to have her Chevrolet up-armored so she could get to the supermarket without being blown away, this M-ATV was still exceptional.

The huge Michelin tires were not only centrally inflatable from the cabin and two-hundred-mile run-flats, but were woven of metallic mesh. The four wheels were connected to TAK-7 military independent suspensions that would transmit only the slightest of bumps if the big vehicle decided to run over a platoon of enemy soldiers. Instead of batteries or an internal-combustion engine demanding gasoline or diesel, the two trucks were moved by two Caterpillar C10, inline-8, 700-horsepower, 1,880-pound-feet of torque turbines powered by "radioactive elements" in the vehicle's armored core of cores. In other words, Sato explained, the two Land Cruiser–Oshkoshes could drive twice around the world without stopping to refuel.

"Decent mileage" was Nick's response. Joe was helping him to strap in and the restraints included not only five-point metal-mesh harnesses but a series of restraint clips that attached him permanently to his sarcophagus of a passenger seat. Enmeshed in his body armor as well as the deep tub of the crash seat and harnesses, Nick suddenly wished he'd taken time to pee.

As if reading his mind, the red-samurai-armored figure behind the wheel said, "There's a relief tube there in the door that you can attach for urinary purposes, Bottom-san. The urine will be stored in a receptacle—up to three gallons—there in the door until we stop to empty it."

"Three gallons," said Nick. "Great."

There were no windows or windshields visible from the outside of the Land Cruiser, but there was the perfect illusion from the *inside* of two large windshields in front of Sato and Nick. It was 3DHD, the image gathered from a multitude of external micro-cams, and the data and smaller images superimposed on the "windshield" at the driver's command furthered the illusion by looking like a regular heads-up display.

Joe was trying to put an oxygen mask on Nick.

"I don't need that."

"You do," came Sato's voice in his earphones. "If the vehicle is hit by a shell or IED blast, there will be no oxygen in the compartment."

Nick assumed that this was because of fire-quenching elements such as CO_2 or some sort of firefighting foam and let it go. The oxygen mask had a microphone embedded in it and the surrounding helmet of the sarcophagus-seat had the earphones pressed against his head. Sato showed him the floor switch that Nick could click once with his foot to put him on a private comm line with Sato, twice to include Joe, and three times to tie into the radio band between the two vehicles and all six men.

"What else should I do here from the passenger seat?" asked Nick. He was all but encircled by high-tech consoles, LCD panels, switches, and levers.

"Absolutely nothing," said Sato. "Touch nothing, Bottom-san."

"Great," said Nick, wondering if he should use the relief tube yet. He decided to wait until Sato and Joe were busy with something else.

Nick couldn't shift in his concave cradle of a seat to look back at Joe as the third man got busy behind him, but the dash monitor showed an interior view so Nick could watch the mercenary tuck himself into his own seat.

The rest of the Land Cruiser wasn't exactly showroom stock. The rear seat and cargo areas were empty except for lockers everywhere on the bulkheads and Joe's elaborate chair. To Nick's surprise, that chair now rose through the roof of the truck with Joe clutching what looked to be an M260 7.62mm machine gun.

Nick looked at an exterior view and saw the black bubble up there enlarge and the barrel of the machine gun extend through the glass or plastic and lock in place. The vertical pillar of the seat assembly hummed behind Nick and he could see the barrel turning slowly as Joe and the gun barrel pivoted in a full circle. It reminded Nick of the top-gunner in the B-17 movies—*Twelve O'Clock High, The Memphis Belle*—that he and Val had loved to watch.

Then it struck him: the barrel had gone *through* the black glass or plastic or Plexiglas.

"Osmotic glass?" asked Nick. When Sato didn't answer, Nick clicked the intercom floor button once and repeated the question.

"*Hai,*" grunted Sato. He seemed to be going through a checklist on his phone screen. "Semipermeable bulletproof plastic. A ten-centimeter patch on the top weapons dome. It molds in around the weapon."

Nick laughed out loud. "That plastic alone is more expensive than any air tickets from Denver to L.A. and then on to Santa Fe would be. These damned vehicles...they must cost Nakamura *thousands* of times what he's paying me for this investigation."

"Of course," came Sato's flat voice on Nick's earphones.

"Then why even bring me along?" demanded Nick. "'Touch nothing, Bottom-san.' I'm just a fucking passenger."

"Not at all, Bottom-san. It is you who will be interrogating Don Khozh-Ahmed Noukhaev when we get to his compound in Santa Fe."

"Why me?" Nick's voice was bitter and he was glad he was on the private comm circuit with Sato. "I'm just being hauled along on this trip like so much dirty laundry."

"Did you interview Don Khozh-Ahmed Noukhaev six years ago?" asked Sato.

"No, you know I didn't. He was out of the country."

"And the same was true for three of the four other attempts to interview him. There was a brief FBI interview with the Don—via satellite hookup—two years ago, but the special agents asked poor questions. Yours will be the first true interview with the man...the man who was one of the last to be interviewed on camera by Keigo Nakamura and who might have had serious motives for not wanting that interview seen by anyone else."

"So you think that Khozh-Ahmed Noukhaev is the prime

suspect?" asked Nick, trying and failing to turn his head far enough to look directly at Sato.

"He is the most important person in the investigation yet to be interviewed by a competent investigator, Bottom-san."

Nick almost laughed again. He felt like anything and everything but a "competent investigator" at that moment.

Sato touched buttons and a high whine seemed to be buzzing in Nick's skull.

"What's that? The turbines?"

"No, the large gyroscopes," said Sato. "Coming up to speed."

"What the hell do we need gyroscopes for?"

"They help right the vehicle, along with hydraulic jacks, should the Land Cruiser be knocked off its wheels."

This time, Nick *did* laugh.

"There is something funny, Bottom-san?"

"Yeah, there's something funny. A minute ago, when Joe went up through the roof, I thought I was in a World War Two B-seventeen movie—you know, *Twelve O'Clock High* or something. Now I realize I'm caught in the middle of *Mad Max* or *Road Warrior*."

"These are also American movies about World War Two?" asked Sato as he pushed more buttons. The huge turbos fired up and added to the din in Nick's aching skull. Joe's turret-gun contraption whirred behind him.

"No," said Nick, reminding himself not to shout into the microphone. "They were twentieth-century movies—Australian, I think—about a shitty future where everything had gone to hell and men killed men in their weird cars on the lawless highway."

"Ahhh," grunted Sato. "Skiffy."

"What?"

"American skiffy."

"What's that?" asked Nick as Sato checked on comm with the Land Cruiser carrying Willy, Toby, and Bill. "Skiffy? What is that?"

"You know," said Sato, shifting the heavy vehicle into gear.

Nick could hear the Oshkosh M-ATV's heavy transmission grinding beneath him. "Skiffy."

"Spell it," said Nick.

"S-c-i-hyphen-f-i," said Sato, taking the lead in front of the second Land Cruiser and guiding them past a tank and toward the gap a military crane had opened for them in the wall of concrete barriers across the highway. "Skiffy."

Nick laughed harder than before.

"You're absolutely right, Hideki-san," he said at last, wondering how he was going to wipe away the snot under his oxygen mask. "This whole thing is skiffy and getting skiffier by the moment."

They rolled out of Colorado and the United States and downhill into New Mexico.

3.02

***

Las Vegas, Nevada, and Beyond— Wednesday, Sept. 22

FROM PROFESSOR EMERITUS GEORGE LEONARD FOX'S PRIVATE JOURNAL

Five days of travel. Five days. These last five days seem more eventful to me, more lived, *than my last five years. And when I say* "lived," *I mean more filled with* life *defined in the rich, overflowing-with-consciously-realized-experience mode exemplified by only a few of my favorite literary characters such as, say, Alys, the Wife of Bath. So perhaps I've* lived *more in the last five days than I have in my last fifteen years. Or in my last fifty years.*

Or perhaps I've never lived this fully before.

One reason I can write this with such cautious joy is that so far no one in our party has been harmed. By "party" I'm not sure if I'm talking about just Val and me, or Val and me and our drivers Julio and Perdita Romano, or Val, me, Julio, Perdita, and the hundreds of others in this truck convoy. In my joy and terror at being alive this week, I have become large. I contain multitudes.

It's hard to believe that only two nights ago I was witnessing with my own aged eyes the spectacle that is Las Vegas—Las Vegas and all the joyfully riotous caravan encampments circled and sprawled across the torchlit desert beyond the wall that protects Las Vegas, Nevada, from the violent twenty-first-century cemetery that surrounds this last holdout of a twentieth-century city (but which so far does not intrude upon and which so far has not prevailed over Las Vegas's own bright, improbable, tenuous, and surreal reality).

The high, transparent wall with its complement of beacons, lasers, banners, and warning lights began just to the south of where the 215 bypass used to come into Interstate 15. The wall continued beyond 215 up the west side of the city and out almost to Henderson to the east. McCarran Airport was deep inside the walled and protected part of the city, of course, as were all the great casinos.

From our encampment on a low rise southwest of the city, we were able to see the tower of the Stratosphere far to the north (with its roller coaster and other rides at the top still running) all the way to the Luxor near the south wall, the glass pyramid's laser spotlight visibly stabbing into space during the day as well as night. But it was at night that Las Vegas was in its true element: the lights and searchlights and lasers of what had been the MGM Grand and the Mandalay Bay and the Excalibur and Paris and New York–New York. Some came complete with their somehow touching miniatures, the Statue of Liberty and the scaled-down Eiffel Tower. We could also see the curve of the Bellagio and not-quite-topless towers of Bally's, Harrah's, the Imperial Palace, Treasure Island, the Google Grand, and the Mirage towering over the low, midcentury clusters of Caesars Palace and the downtown Sahara, Riviera, and the old Circus Circus.

Just east of the airport were the lighted white domes of the Taj Mahal — 120 percent scale of the original — but only the lower domes there were casinos and hotels; the main dome was the India-built reactor that cooled and lighted Las Vegas now that Hoover Dam was only a memory.

Since almost all of the small towns that once defied Nevada's heat and dryness are abandoned now — the Mesquites and Tonopahs and Elys and Elkos and Battle Mountains and Pahrumps and Searchlights, everything up to the size of Reno and Carson City that had their own reactors but still had lost more than 80 percent of their populations — I could only imagine how brilliant Las Vegas must look from space when the terminator of night has been drawn across this part of the American West.

Beside the flickering, blazing lights inside the walled city itself— the very translucent walls, inhabited as they are now by hotel rooms and casinos of their own, glowing golden at night—there were myriad more lights encamped out on the desert: huge trucks by the thousands, their rig lights flashing, and in their lighted circles the giant campfires with wood hauled a thousand miles and more for just that purpose.

It struck me three nights ago while watching the celebrations outside the city walls of Las Vegas—the rodeos and fairs, the traveling circuses with their lighted Ferris wheels and roller coasters and rocket whips, the hundreds of taverns, pubs, and bars driven in or opened under a tent, the motorcycle and motocross races roaring past canvas whorehouses in dusty tent cities that were constantly tearing themselves down and rebuilding, an eternal Midway set without the walls of a city that is in itself a Midway for the millions of millionaires that somehow still inhabit the bankrupt Earth (my grandson Val tells me the names of the machines, the millionaires' red-and-green-blinking, landing-light-blazing Learjets and Gulfstreams and Hawker Siddeleys and Falcons and Cessna Citation Excels and Challengers and supersonic Sukhoi Putin-Sokolis landing every few seconds at McCarran)—that Las Vegas, both inside the wall and out, was America's single greatest exception to our new No Clusterfuck Rule of don't-gather-in-crowds.

For Julio and Perdita Romano and the thousands of other truckers and their passengers celebrating out there on the cracked hardpan beyond the glowing Vegas walls, there was no fear of suicide bombers in their midst. The truckers—some of them Canadians southbound to Old Mexico, others Mexicans from south of the old border hauling their loads northbound to Canada, many of them American drivers headed north, south, east, west, or a combination of these—had come too far and worked too hard to get here to this day or two of rest and fun, the twenty-first century's highway equivalent of America's early-nineteenth-century Rendezvous for free trappers and Indians and the buyers of their beaver pelts, to ruin it with suicide bombings and political murders.

Such insanity was reserved for the rest of the world.

THE 417 PETERBILT SLEEPER *that Julio and Perdita own and operate is an incredible machine. The front of the cab with its two massive, upholstered UltraRide seats with the bank of controls facing the driver is their space. Val and I are allowed to ride on two comfortable jump seats behind and a little higher than the UltraRide seats. Behind our jump seats is a wide and comfortable bed for the Romanos—always perfectly made in the daytime and rarely used by both of them since one is usually driving—and above and behind that, separated by an accordion door, is a smaller bunk space up under the transparent air dam.*

When Val and I are tucked in there and chatting in privacy before falling asleep—both Julio and Perdita tend to drive together far into the night before one or the other crawls into the bunk below— we can look up at a sky of undimmed stars. If we sit up in our comfortable cot-bed, we can look down and forward over the roof and hood of the Peterbilt at the highway rushing at us through the night.

For the first two days after our escape, Val said almost nothing, but now he is talking, making eye contact, and otherwise coming alive again. To be honest, this new Val—however shaken he has been by recent events that he's still not willing to talk about in detail—is more like the interesting and intelligent boy who came to live with me more than five years ago. I had grown weary of the newer, sullen, uncommunicative teenager who seemed always on the brink of some inner violence.

Our last night in Los Angeles was a nightmare.

I was on the verge of either going out to search for Val or calling the police or his father—not sure whether to report him as missing or turn him in as a possible criminal—when Val rushed in and smashed my phone and we both watched the faces of his dead flashgang friends on the TV. There was no doubt that Val himself was in some sort of shock—he was paler than paper—but rather than it being a debilitating shock of the sort that would have made me or most people I know dysfunctional, this shock seemed to have turned the sixteen-year-old into a cold, robotic, but hugely efficient version of his father.

We did not have to hide in the railyards. Julio and Perdita Romano and their truck were already there with dozens of others and when I showed the Romanos the written letter of transit from Don Emilio Gabriel Fernández y Figueroa they allowed us to hide in the sleeping cab of their Peterbilt as police helicopters circled overhead and as Los Angeles burned behind us.

It was only the next day that I realized how profoundly lucky Val and I had been. The Romanos had already been paid. The little money I had left I was carrying in cash in my bag. Had the Romanos and other truckers not been honorable people, they could have left us behind that terrible Friday night or killed us on their way out of town, dumped our bodies, and no one in the world would have been the wiser.

As it was, because of the attempted assassination of Advisor Omura and the opening of the battle between reconquista *forces and the city, there were highway patrol roadblocks before the 15 began its long climb toward Victorville. Julio Romano risked everything they had—not only their expensive truck but their very freedom—by taking Val and me and our luggage to the side of their Peterbilt and showing each of us where to hide in secret compartments set into the fuel tanks on opposite sides of the truck.*

Even there, a touch of a switch might have released the liquefied natural gas which the trucks used as fuel into the hiding spaces and we would have been one less thing for the Romanos to worry about. Just something frozen and dead to dump in the desert. No threat to them and no loss of prepaid revenue.

But they were honorable people. After having the convoy papers provided by Emilio inspected and being passed through the highway patrol roadblocks, Julio and Perdita released us from the tiny spaces in the fuel tanks and led us back to the high seats in the Peterbilt cab and we rolled on with the convoy toward Barstow and the desert.

When either Julio or Perdita crawled into the rest area to watch their satellite TV, they allowed Val and me to watch with them. What we saw there was Los Angeles burning behind us.

The fighting was more terrible than either side—the state of California or the Nuevo Mexico reconquista *cartels with their armies and gangs—could possibly have predicted. These were no mere riots. The police were not a factor and concentrated on staying out of the line of fire. Governor Lohan promised more National Guard troops to reinforce those being overrun throughout the city, but few commentators thought that this would do much good. When the governor threatened to petition the president to send in federal troops, Julio just laughed. This had been an all but empty threat for years; our federal troops were fighting in China and elsewhere for foreign masters.*

But while the city and state forces had seriously underestimated the power of the reconquista *forces—they seemed totally surprised by the amount of armor and artillery brought north from Old Mexico (some of which I'd seen parked under camouflage nets in the huge cemetery across from Emilio's compound)—at the same time, Emilio's and his spanic allies' forces were obviously being surprised by blacks rising up in South Central, by Asians fighting in the western suburbs, by the mercenaries hired by the wealthy in Beverly Hills, Bel Air, the Mulholland highlands, and elsewhere, and by a score of other fighting cadres aligned with neither the state of California nor the forces of Nuevo Mexico. Because of this, the simple* reconquista-versus–California *National Guard battle over the future of Los Angeles almost immediately turned into a twenty-sided brawl. Los Angeles was becoming a purely Hobbesian state . . . every man pitted against every other man.*

When I mentioned this to Julio and Perdita, they understood and agreed immediately. They'd both read Thomas Hobbes's Leviathan. *So much for my lifelong assumptions about truck drivers and their levels of education.*

And speaking of education, Val is receiving an interesting one on this truckers' convoy.

After his first night and day of being almost catatonic—and I'll write more about that later—I saw Val begin to pay serious attention to his surroundings and the people in them.

During our two nights camped with scores of other eighteen-wheelers' convoys in the desert outside the walled-off but still beckoning lights of Las Vegas, I noticed Val's avid—almost hungry—interest in what the men and women around the campfires had to say. Poor Val . . . by law and by Department of Education fiat, he's had to celebrate "diversity" (for diversity's sake alone) almost every hour in school since his first day in kindergarten in Denver almost a dozen years ago. But he'd never really experienced *diversity until this convoy. Val has grown up in two cities, Denver and Los Angeles, where neighborhoods are racial, ethnic, linguistic, and (more and more) religious fiefdoms, each sparring and warring for a larger share of some theoretical cake in an endless zero-sum game of politics, gangs, and outright warfare.*

But during these five days and nights he's seen and listened to "Gauge" Devereaux, a black man from the South who says openly that the return to the epithet "nigger" is a statement of failure by his race and the nation at large. Devereaux has been driving his big rig for thirty-eight years and has no plans to stop now just because the cities he delivers to have become separated by wider and wider tracts of chaos.

Val's listened to the fireside stories of Henry Big Horse Begay, a Navajo who—with his wife, Laurette—has been driving his rig for twenty-six years and who defies any bureaucrat or army or roadside bandit to stop him. Henry laughs openly—his one missing top tooth making the others seem all the whiter—at the irony that the white men who put his people on reservations are having their Manifest Destiny rolled back like a cheap carpet, but I'm convinced that there is absolutely no malice in the man. He's simply a student of history.

—It happens to every race and group and nation, *Henry Big Horse Begay says, still laughing.* The days of greatness roll in like some great, undeserved tide, are smugly celebrated by the lucky peoples—even as mine once did—as if they had earned it, which they had not, and then the tide ebbs and the nations and tribes and peoples find themselves standing there dumb and dumbfounded on the dry and garbage-strewn beach.

Strange to hear an ocean metaphor from a man who grew up in the deserts of Arizona.

Val listens to others like Julio and Perdita, who grew up in the teeming eastern cities but who had found happiness only on the open highways—or what is left of them—and to spanics such as the Valdezes, who were born in Mexico but who have driven American Interstates since the 1980s and who refuse allegiance to any clan or gang or nation that defines itself at the expense of outsiders. And then there are the Ellises, Jan and Bob and their three kids—the children being "cab schooled," as Jan likes to say. They're from the South, they're evangelicals, but they're also witty, clever, soft-spoken, open-minded (they say they consider proselytizing an intrusion on others and don't flaunt their faith), and the three kids—according to Val, who spent a long afternoon with them—know more geography, history, astronomy, literature, and basic science than any of Val's fellow high school juniors.

I sensed that Val was most interested in Cooper Jakes (called Old Jakes Brakes by the other truckers for some impenetrable reason)—an ancient philosopher more ancient and wise than I, easily in his 80s if not 90s, but also as thin, tough, resilient, and seemingly immortal as gristle. Cooper Jakes's silhouette makes up in white beard what he lacks in body fat, and, in the tradition of all great prophets, his prodigious eyebrows are jet black. Those brows can, in an instant, become as cocked and intimidating as two aimed pistol muzzles. When he is angry, Cooper Jakes reminds me of Ahab.

But most of the time, Cooper is in a relaxed and humorous (however sardonic, especially on such subjects as politics and religion) mood. The old man has been driving large rigs (he says) since he was seventeen years old. He's never had a wife, family, or home (he says) and has never wanted one. His cab has been his ark—his words—through all the "floods of shit" that have been dropped on America by a pissed-off God in his lifetime.

Val can't seem to get enough of the old reprobate's barbed but almost iambic commentaries. I watch Val's gleaming eyes across the campfire and think of young Prince Hal in Eastcheap's Boar's-Head Tavern at the rhetorical feet of Falstaff. (I was one of those scholars who infinitely preferred Falstaff—a source of wit not only in himself but in others and a potential Aristotle/Socrates tutor of the true humanities to the young prince in training—to the wordy killing-machine-cum-lying-politician that Henry V became in Shakespeare's work, however moving the much-trotted-out "band of brothers" St. Crispin's Day speech may be.)

But I digress.

Val actually said something to me yesterday in a tone devoid of the contempt, guardedness, and sarcasm that have ruled all his speech in my presence for the last four years or so.

—I could be a trucker, Grandpa.

I said nothing at the time but I came close to weeping to hear those few unguarded words slip out. (Including, I admit, the childish "Grandpa" that I've missed so very much.) Val has not spoken of being or becoming anything—other than his unconscious but continuous attempt at becoming a black-hole source of disillusionment so unrelenting as to approach pure nihilism—since he was twelve years old.

Before I become too sentimental, I need to remind myself here that it is likely that my grandson killed someone last week. Or at least tried *to kill someone.*

He seemed almost in shock that last Friday night in Los Angeles when he saw the photograph of his dead friend William Coyne on the 3DHD screen. The only thing I could get out of him about the attack on Advisor Omura in the first forty-eight hours of our flight was his repeated statement—I was with those idiot fuckers, but I didn't shoot at Omura, Leonard. I swear it.

But Val never said clearly that he hadn't shot someone, *and the few times I brought up the Coyne boy's name, Val's violent reaction—his gaze dropping, his head snapping to look in another direction, his entire body stiffening—suggested to me that* some-thing *had happened between the two adolescents on that last night in Los Angeles.*

Whatever the source of the trauma in L.A., Val dealt with it by sleeping most of the time we weren't stopped for rest during those first few days or nights. Because of the way he slept—twitching, shaking— I thought he might be using flashback, but a cursory search of his duffel bag while he slept didn't turn up any vials of the drug.

It did turn up a black pistol which I considered confiscating but decided to leave in his duffel. We might need it before this trip is over.

WHEN VAL WAS AWAKE *during the daylight hours on the third through fifth days of our exile, I listened in as he quizzed Julio and Perdita on the security details of our convoy.*

It seems that our convoy consists of twenty-three eighteen-wheelers, some of which are armed with mini-guns and other serious weapons, while we're also accompanied by four combat vehicles and a small recon-attack helicopter. The combat vehicles—I forget the details about their armament and such, but Val visibly devoured every caliber and horsepower and armor fact with great interest— are manned by mercenaries from a security company called TrekSec and paid for by these independent truckers or their firms.

Perdita showed us on their satellite nav system that another such convoy, made up of seventeen vehicles, is traveling about fifteen miles ahead of us and a much larger one is about twenty-four miles behind us on I-15. They keep in touch with one another.

According to Julio, the main problem on the Las Vegas–to- Mesquite-and-beyond-to–St. George stretch of I-15 is bandits, although the reconquista *still make their occasional foray into the southern reaches of Nevada. Nuevo Mexico's cartels' repeated fail- ures at adding Las Vegas to their territory is, according to Julio, forc- ing the* reconquista *military forays to be less and less frequent. He added that the increasingly effective anglo guerrilla raids around Kingman and Flagstaff have pretty effectively tied down the N.M. occupation forces over the past year or two.*

Our immediate problem, Julio and Perdita showed us, lies just beyond the embattled and mostly abandoned town of Mesquite ahead where I-15 crosses from Nevada to Arizona and from the Pacific Time Zone into the Mountain Time Zone: the twenty-nine miles of Interstate that make their tiny cut across the northwest corner of Ari- zona and then into Utah and north have been wonderfully scenic and composed mostly of elevated highway, but bandits and warring U.S. and N.M. forces have dropped most of those bridges and elevated sec- tions over the past decade.

Because of the Mormon Range and other mountains that run north and south along the state border like a sheer wall, the convoys will take an entire day picking their way along rubble-strewn make- shift surface roads—just ruts through the tumbled boulders and slabs of the former highway—along the Virgin River into Utah. Julio showed us satellite images of the winding canyon road where the trucks will be vulnerable to any bandit on the clifftops who wants to roll rocks down on us.

—Can't we just go around? *asked Val.* Take a detour to the north?

Perdita showed us how there are no roads except desert tracks and dry gullies along the forty miles or so north of Mesquite to the tiny, abandoned towns of Carp and Elgin along the misnamed Meadow Valley Wash dry river, then almost a two-hundred-mile detour on old state roads 93 and 319 into Utah on their battered Highway 56.

—The twenty-nine miles in Arizona called the Diagonal of Death by truckers is slow and dangerous, *said Julio.* But it's still faster than any of the half-assed detours. We're still truckers. We need to get products to their destination *on time.*

So tonight we're sleeping in a defensive circle off the highway just short of the abandoned town of Bunkerville. The name is appropriate, since a few military bunkers remain here.

A mile to the east, the mountains rise up like some terrible obstacle in one of the J.R.R. Tolkien–inspired movies. The opening for the Virgin River and the former I-15 looks like a dark and open maw—waiting.

We'll be moving at first light. Perdita assured us that with the recon helicopter and our convoy's firepower, there shouldn't be a serious confrontation—just ten hours of bumping and jolting along in the truck's lowest gears.

Val said to me tonight—

—This is like those old World War Two B-seventeen movies the Old Man and I used to watch. These convoys are like those packs of bombers huddled together for protection against German fighter planes.

It was the first time in several years that I'd heard Val mention his father without overt hostility.

———

THE COOKING FIRES WERE *doused by 9 p.m. tonight and there was no frivolity around the campfires. The mood was somber. There was no bluster. Everyone knows that tomorrow will be one of the most dangerous parts of the voyage but there's almost no talk of it. Plans and preparations have been made.*

I'm terrified about tomorrow's slow, exposed twenty-nine-mile gauntlet, but Val seems quietly excited…almost enthusiastic. The immortality of youth, I suppose.

Later tonight, when everyone had turned in, I talked to him after I saw him shutting off the little cell phone he'd brought along and removing the earbud.

I'd noticed the old phone our second night out and challenged Val about it—he had, after all, insisted that I throw away my phone because it might be tracked by authorities chasing him—and he'd explained how it had been his mother's, and how all of the phone and GPS chips had long since been removed. Reluctantly, he told me that he listened to the daily diary function on it just to hear his mother's voice.

This fact made my chest ache.

Val was willing to say more. I'm fairly certain that his good mood and talkativeness were a direct result of the marijuana joint that he'd joined Julio and Henry Big Horse Begay and Gauge Devereaux and Cooper Jakes in smoking just an hour earlier around the last campfire of the evening. It had been my impression that Val had been using a lot of flashback over the past few years and perhaps some stronger drugs such as cocaine from time to time—I wasn't sure about the latter— but had never got in the habit of smoking pot with his friends.

So now, in our high cots under the clear Kevlarglas air dam with the stars bright above us—the surprisingly effective acoustic curtain drawn between our cots and the Romanos' bed below—Val gave me a very un-Val-like loopy smile and showed me the phone.

—It was my mom's, your…you know. So like I said, it doesn't have any of the trackable, traceable chips left in it—I pulled them out myself five years ago—but it's got her daily voice reminders and a lot of text diary that I'd like to read but can't.

I nodded but felt uneasy. This conversation was as thin and fragile as a stray strand of cobweb. The slightest wrong word or tone from me would, I knew, sever it or simply blow it away. I heard myself say softly…

—Are you sure you *want* to hear her voice and private thoughts, Val? Sometimes grown-ups say things in private that they wouldn't necessarily want to have shared with…

Val grunted and shook his head and I knew that if it weren't for the friendly effects of the potent grass that Joe Valdez and his wife, Juanita, had brought up from Old Mexico, I'd be looking at Val's angry back. Instead, he kept talking to me.

—Yeah, yeah, yeah…but I think in that written diary there may be the clue I need to know why my old man turned against her…maybe even killed her.

—Killed her!

I shouted and actually clapped both hands over my mouth. Val cringed and looked toward the closed curtain. But there was no noise from Julio and Perdita below.

Nor did Val turn his back to me. Not yet. His whisper now was a fast, hot hiss, devoid of any joint-assisted relaxation.

—Leonard, you've asked me about a thousand times why I hate my old man. The answer might be in that encrypted diary text. It's the main reason I've kept the goddamn phone all these years.

—Val, you don't *hate* your father…, *I began.*

—I do, goddammit. I hate the cocksucker's guts and if we somehow manage to get to Denver alive, I'm going to track him down to whatever flashback cave he's rotting away in and kick him awake and put a bullet in his guts…

I had no idea what to say to this madness so I said nothing. It turned out to be the only way I could have kept the agitated boy talking.

—He found out that Mom was doing something, Leonard, and I think he killed her. Or had her killed. I really do.

I started to say something like—"But your mother died in an auto accident, Val"—but I knew at once that I would lose him with that. The conversation would end as suddenly as it had begun. I cleared my throat.

—What kind of things was she doing that would so anger your father?

Val seemed to fold in on himself until he was a mass of defensive knees, elbows, curved back as sharp as those elbows, and lowered head.

—I don't *know*. But she was gone a lot in those last weeks—hell, *months*—before she was killed in that convenient auto *accident.* She was sneaking out a lot. When the Old Man was putting in double shifts down at the precinct, gone whole weekends—sometimes four or five days at a time—so was Mom. She used to have me stay with my friend Samuel's weird, smelly old grandmother—Sheila—down the street when she was going to be away overnight. Sometimes for several nights in a row. And the Old Man never knew. Mom swore me to *secrecy,* Leonard. Imagine a parent swearing her ten-year-old kid to secrecy.

I thought about it. It didn't sound like the way Dara, my daughter, the light of my life, had ever behaved before. Or would behave.

—What do you think she was doing, Val? Having an... affair?

I couldn't believe that I was asking my sixteen-year-old grandson this question. But suddenly I wanted to know the truth as much as this tormented boy had for the past six years.

Val shrugged. He suddenly looked very sleepy.

—Yeah, I suppose. Probably with that fat slob of an assistant district attorney she worked for, Harvey Cohen. That whole last year, he was always picking Mom up at weird hours when the Old Man was away at work. And the Old Man was *always* away at work.

My mouth was very dry and my chest hurt now not from emotion but from the more alarming pain of an old man's thrice-treacherous heart.

—So, Val, you think that Dara was having an affair with her employer, Harvey whoever, and your father found out and killed her? Or arranged for her to be killed in that automobile accident that also killed an old couple and a truck driver? Does that make sense, Val?

He glared at me now and I knew that he was sorry he'd said anything about the old cell phone. The pot and the closeness between us were wearing off.

—Yeah. And if you want to tell me that the Old Man *wouldn't* hurt her, save your breath. You don't know the Old Man. You don't know cops.

*I merely nodded at that. It was true. I'd never spent much time
around police officers—or wanted to—and for all my visits when
Val was a baby and I still lived in the area after Carol, my third
wife, died, I really had never been comfortable talking to Detective
Nick Bottom. So instead of defending a man I didn't know, I said…*

—Could I see the encrypted text?

*I could feel Val's reluctance to show the files to me, mixed with
his anger at himself and me for saying as much as he had about something he'd kept secret for six years, but without letting go of the phone,
he activated it, thumbed through icons, and held the screen up so I
could see it in the Nevada darkness.*

*I looked for a long moment, only asking Val to thumb forward
through the pages of text. He did so—gracelessly. Then he turned the
phone off and thrust it away in his pocket. He rolled away from me,
pulling the thin blanket high up on his bony shoulders, but I wasn't
quite finished with our conversation yet.*

—It's a word- or book-cipher, Val. Based on a five-letter
key word.

The boy snorted.

—Tell me something I don't know, old man.

*I let the rudeness pass. Something like excitement was stirring in
me. Those encrypted pages might include a message to me. Dara and
I had loved sending coded messages to each other when she was little.
It irritated Carol, but Dara and I continued doing so, even after
Carol got sick.*

—Perhaps I could help with…

*But I'd let my enthusiasm show through. Val pulled the blanket
higher and edged farther away on his cot, showing me his back again.*

—I know the kind of words that Mom would've used for
such a cipher. None of them work. And it doesn't matter anyway, old man. We're probably going to get killed in the canyon
tomorrow anyway. It don't matter. Nothing matters.

*The sudden bad grammar was a parody of his father's police-
speak, although Nick Bottom didn't speak that way either. I was
tempted to say aloud the "Bullshit, you tiresome little twerp" I was
thinking but stayed silent until I said softly…*

—"Carol." It could be "Carol." Her mother's name.

Val did sound almost asleep as he answered groggily one last time.

—Nope. Tried it. I told you... I tried *all* the fucking five-letter words that would've meant something to her. It's just gonna... stay... encrypted. Go... to sleep, Leonard. We gotta get up early to get shot at tomorrow. Let *me* sleep, for Chrissakes.

I let him sleep.

After about an hour of lying there looking up at the cold desert stars, I sat up silently. My eyes had adapted to the darkness and I could see the phone protruding from his pocket as Val lay there snoring rather more loudly than I'd heard before.

I knew the five-letter word. I was sure of it.

I started to reach for the phone but stopped. If possible, I wanted Val to give me permission to try the word and for us to watch the encrypted pages of Dara's diary decrypt into readable text in front of us.

If possible. If it wasn't possible, I'd take the phone away from him soon and read those pages for myself. For some reason I was sure that Dara's last, secret message to the world was more important than the feelings of a surly sixteen-year-old.

I've written this in my own hand-written journal—hiding it away so Val won't find it—and will go to sleep thinking of my daughter and of why she would have chosen the five-letter word that I am certain is the key to her final message to the world.

1.11

North of Las Vegas, New Mexico—
Wednesday, Sept. 15

THE TANK SHELL that hit Nick and Sato's Oshkosh–Land
Cruiser was a lucky shot that exploded partially through
the osmotic panel of the weapons dome atop the truck,
beheaded the gunner Joe in a shaped-charge surge of fiery
plasma, incinerated the rest of the ninja mercenary's body in a
microsecond, and instantly flowed down into the vehicle like a
supersonic wave of hot lava that vaporized everything inside
the truck that it did not set aflame.

Until that second, two and a half hours of the trip had been
eventless to the point of boredom.

For the first ten miles down and away from Raton Pass, the
two vehicles were technically under the protection of Major
Malcolm's hilltop artillery, but driving at forty-five m.p.h., they
soon passed out of that zone.

Nick didn't notice because he was too busy half paying
attention to Sato going through all the evacuation, PEAP,
comm, fire, and other details about the truck. Also because he
was too busy trying to find a comfortable position. Not only did
his oxygen mask, comm earbuds and microphones, all of his
personal body armor and helmet, as well as the seat-sarcophagus

itself, get in his way, but he'd shoved the big duffel bag holding his personal weapons in the space under his legs and now it was also getting in his way.

When Sato was done with his flight-attendant spiel and Nick paused in his squirming—using the relief tube *did* help—he paid a little attention to the large monitors that took the place of the broad windshield. Back when travel was easier and New Mexico and Texas were still states, Nick and Dara had come this way over Raton Pass to points south, and it had been one of their favorite state borders. New Mexico had *looked* different once they'd driven across the state line up on the pass and descended: the high prairie here looked different than its counterpart in southern Colorado, the foothills of the Sangre de Cristo mountain range to the west had looked different, and especially the buttes and mesas and extinct volcanoes visible to the southeast said "American Southwest!" more clearly than any landscape in their home state of Colorado.

It all still did, although now there were distinct smoke plumes rising to the south and southwest that gave the sense that not all those cones of former volcanoes ahead of them were quiescent. But Nick could see from the smaller look-down displays that it was burning tanks, vehicles, and abandoned towns or fortifications causing the smoke, not volcanoes.

"If Major Malcolm and the U.S. Army—or the Texas Republic and *reconquistas*, for that matter—can't keep a recon drone in the sky down here," said Nick, "how do *you* do it? Most of these are drone images, not sat, right?"

"*Hai*," grunted the red-armored samurai mass that was Sato. "Our miniature unmanned aerial vehicles are much more . . . miniature . . . than any available to Major Malcolm."

"Like the tiny drones that were hovering around videoing me before I got up the hill to Mr. Nakamura's house," said Nick, still angry at how they'd recorded him nodding to a ten-minute flashback fix.

Sato said nothing.

Nick watched the landscape passing by on 3DHD monitors so clear that he forgot they weren't windshields and windows, wriggled to get comfortable, and found himself wondering if the relief tube valve might have leaked down his leg a little. The trip to Santa Fe was projected to take about eight hours—mostly because of the poor state of the highways and occasional missing bridges and overpasses—and Nick couldn't wait to be there and out of all this stupid armor and restraints.

About forty miles from Raton, at exit 419, they passed a former gas station on their left. The closest tiny town, Springer, was still miles ahead and this gas station used to stand alone here, its light a beacon for night travelers. Nick remembered the place from his vacations with Dara: it had showers and bootlegged DVDs for truckers, a fancy soda fountain, and a display of classic cars from the 1950s and '60s. The wind used to blow hard here, coming down cold from the distant Sangre de Cristos, and it still did, but now the gas station was a burned-out husk, even the asphalt and concrete blasted apart where the storage tanks had erupted.

A few miles farther, between the empty houses of Springer and the equally abandoned little town of Wagon Mound, they came across the twelve-truck convoy that Major Malcolm had talked about.

Sato radioed to the truck behind them—Willy driving, Toby riding shotgun, and Bill in the top-gunner's position—and drove slowly off the highway and through the tumbled fence to bypass the smoking mess on the pavement.

Still warned not to touch anything, Nick did zoom his side-camera view to get a better look at the ambushed caravan of fifteen vehicles—the twelve trucks and three armed escort SUVs—as they passed.

It was pretty bad. Nick winced at the burned-out vehicles with the crispy-critter remains visible through the windows—more bodies reduced to ash and miniature carbon-armature versions of human beings, many of the arms raised in the "boxing" position common to burn victims when ligaments and tendons charred. The trucks not burned to the ground had been looted. There seemed to be a lot of skulls lying around, white in the midday New Mexico September sun. There was no sign of any survivors.

Heavy tread tracks—armored vehicles for sure, some

probably full-fledged battle tanks—came from the west, went past or through the burned-out convoy and shell-shattered fighting SUVs which never had a chance, then moved on toward the eastern horizon.

"Texan?" asked Nick. "Or *reconquista?*"

Sato tried to shrug in his thick, red samurai armor. "Impossible to tell. The bandits here—Mexican or Russian mafia or both—also have armored vehicles. But they probably would have taken hostages."

Nick looked at the still-smoking wreckage disappearing behind them and thought that he'd rather be almost anything than a trucker.

Wagon Mound, the little town consisting of sixty or seventy charred ex-homes and a flattened old downtown that had been half a block long, was named after the saggy-centered butte or hill that rose immediately east of the former water stop along the former train lines. Nick thought that it did sort of look like an old Conestoga wagon.

"How do you feel about it?" Sato asked suddenly.

Nick, who'd been thinking about the scorched bodies and vehicles back at the ambushed convoy site, was actively startled by the question. It wasn't the kind of open-ended question the security chief was likely to ask.

"How do I feel about what?" asked Nick. The Oshkosh M-ATV's air system had filtered out all the stench from the burned bodies and melted tires of the convoy, but Nick had mentally smelled it all. It was just *odd* that Sato should be asking about feelings.

"How do you feel about all of this?" came Sato's voice through Nick's earphones. *Arr of this.* "About your nation coming apart like this."

What the fuck? was Nick's immediate thought. Was Sato writing up a psych report for Nakamura?

"I'm not sure what you mean," Nick said cautiously.

"Bottom-san," said Sato, "you are old enough to remember when the United States of America was rich, strong, powerful, complete. Fifty states strong. Now it has...how many?"

You know how many, ass-wipe, thought Nick.

"Forty-four and a half," said Nick.

"Ah, yes," grunted Sato. "That 'half' would be California, I presume."

Nick didn't have to answer that, so he didn't.

"I was curious if it bothered you, Bottom-san. This step down from being a great world power to being an impoverished nation, in debt to yourselves and to everyone else. This breaking-apart of the nation you knew as a child and grown man."

Is he trying to provoke me? wondered Nick. If he was, it was a good time for it. Nick was so armored and strapped in and otherwise restrained that he couldn't even get to the duffel bag of guns under his legs without going through half a dozen emergency escape procedures that Sato had lectured him on twice.

"We're not the only country that's had everything hit the fan in the past decade or two," Nick said at last.

"Ahh, true. True." Sato's voice was all satisfied growl. "But surely no others have fallen so far so fast."

Nick tried to shrug. "When I was a kid, my old man had a friend—I don't know where they met, police academy, maybe—who'd been born in the Soviet Union and who watched that country implode and disappear in a few months. New flag. New anthem. Captured republics all escaped. Lenin's embalmed corpse still in the tomb or mausoleum or whatever you call it in Red Square, but communism itself as dead and useless as Lenin's waxy nuts."

"Lenin's waxy nuts," repeated Sato as if in admiration of the phrase.

"So if the Russians could get through it without major trauma, why can't we?" finished Nick.

"The Russians staged a . . . what do you call it, Bottom-san? A comeback. Of sorts."

"Yeah, sure," said Nick. "With new dictators like Putin running things, they were bound to try that energy blackmail of Western Europe and the military moved back into Georgia or wherever it was. But demographics were against them in the long run. Birthrate down. Alcoholism rampant. Their economy totally dependent on oil and gas."

"But they *had* much oil and gas," said Sato.

"So what?" said Nick. "They couldn't beat the numbers... in the end. Just like we couldn't beat the numbers here."

"You are talking about the economy, Bottom-san? The entitlement programs that destroyed the dollar? Or immigration numbers? Or personal habits of no thrift?"

What the fuck is this, a seminar? wondered Nick. He also wondered if there was a recording device in this overpriced truck. But why would Mr. Nakamura be interested in the opinion of one of his hired hands? It'd be like recording the opinions of one of the *gai-jin* gardeners Nakamura hired to do the mowing at his estate. (He'd never allow Americans to work on his private gardens.)

Finally Nick said tiredly, "All the numbers. You have to understand, Sato, that I was born into a nation and society that had only known greater wealth, greater prosperity, and all sorts of what we thought of as progress in the life of every citizen except the oldest farts who remembered the first Great Depression. My old man's generation couldn't even *imagine* things getting worse. So when they—and we—had the money, we spent it. And after we didn't have the money any longer, we still spent it."

"Do you speak of individuals, Bottom-san? Or your government?"

"Yeah," said Nick. "Both. Remember, I was just coming of age when we had the first sort of financial meltdown and unemployment mini-quakes—we thought it was the Big One, having no clue that the problems were just early tremors of something much worse—and the president we elected right then made it all worse... no, we *all* did... by passing those staggering entitlement programs that he knew, we all knew in our guts, that we couldn't begin to pay for."

"But Europe had such entitlement programs for generations," said Sato. *Entirermehn.* Except for the pronunciation, Nick thought, the massive security chief was beginning to sound like a college prof trying to keep a dull conversation going with even duller students.

Nick laughed. "Yeah, and look where *that* got them!"

"Do you think much of European countries, Bottom-san?"

"Every goddamn hour and minute of my life, Hideki-san," Nick said emphatically.

After a few minutes of silence, perhaps feeling sorry for the obviousness of his sarcasm, Nick added, "No. I don't think hardly any of us Americans think about the Germans or French or those other poor fucks these days. They invited the tens of millions of Muslims into their house. They made the laws and *sharia* exceptions to their laws that ended up with them turning their cultures over to the Global Caliphate. Fuck 'em. Our attitude—*my* attitude—is the old saying, *You buttered your bread, now sleep in it.*"

"Buttered...your bread...," Sato began hesitantly. Nick looked at the cabin monitor and could see the security chief's large dark eyes shifting his way like beetles within the eye openings of the red samurai mask.

"Sorry," said Nick. "Old joke that my wife and I used to make. It's a dumb take on the saying *You've made your bed, now sleep in it.*"

"Ahhh," said Sato but the syllable did not suggest real enlightenment.

Finally... "But how do you *feel* about all this change, Bottom-san?"

Nick sighed. For whatever reason—and perhaps it was Mr. Nakamura's curiosity—Sato really wanted to know his fucking feelings. If he hadn't been strapped and clamped and armored in place, Nick might have left the room then, but the room was moving at forty-eight miles per hour at the moment. Their next town, he saw by the GPS display, would be Las Vegas...Las Vegas, New Mexico, not the Nevada gambling town.

"I feel like almost the full second half of my life has been a goddamned nightmare," said Nick. "I expect to wake up any day and find out it has all been a fucking nightmare...that Hawaii didn't secede and you Japs didn't take it over after them being a monarchy again for six lousy years. That Dara and I could honeymoon there again if we wanted to. That Santa Fe was just a quaint town in a neighboring state with good food and some good art, rather than being a place run by bandits where someone stuck a six-inch blade in my bowels.

"I expect to wake up and see that I live in a country that projects power in the world for good reasons—to find justice there—rather than watch us send our children, my kid next year, Sato, to battlefields we can't pronounce where they die fighting battles for you Japs...and not even for your goddamned country, but for your *zaibatsu* or *keiretsu* or whatever you call those damned teams of corporations that really run Japan these days.

"I expect to wake up and be able to walk down the street of my own city in my own country without being afraid that some goddamned jihadist kid is going to explode a suicide vest on me for no sane reason and where I can go to a Rockies game on a summer evening without worrying about bombers and snipers. I expect to wake up and find that the money I saved could actually buy something—like a plane trip somewhere, or a driving vacation—and that my wife is still alive to go with me.

"But the nightmare's real. The bad dream is the reality, and everything good that we dreamed about—Dara and me, my whole fucking country—that's gone, history, a fading dream."

Nick was breathing hard when he finally fell silent. His cheeks were wet with what he hoped to Christ was sweat.

"This is why you take flashback, Bottom-san?" Sato said softly.

"You bet your ass it's why I take flashback, Hideki-san," answered Nick. "And it's why half the cops I used to know have swallowed their guns."

"Swallowed their...ahh, yes," said Sato.

Nick shook his head as much as he could within his helmet and armor mask. Sato asks him three or four obvious, stupid questions and has former homicide detective Nick Bottom blubbering—or at least sweating—like a little girl. It was pathetic. It made Nick realize—or at least be reminded of— what a wreck he was. All he wanted to do right now was to get back to his cubie in the corner of the old Baby Gap, lock his door, and settle into several hours of flash.

He said to Sato, "But Japan has changed, too, hasn't it?"

"Ah, yes, Bottom-san," said Sato. "In the past years of upheaval everywhere, Nippon has shrugged off this shell of culture and government forced on it by MacArthur and the occupying Americans after the lost war and has returned to its natural form of hierarchy and government."

"Which is what?" asked Nick. "Rule by the family and strongman who wins the constant battle between the *zaibatsu* or *keiretsu* teams of companies we were talking about?"

"*Hai*," grunted Sato. "Yes, Bottom-san. More or less. In that sense, Nippon has thrown off the uncomfortable pretense of democracy forced upon us—a cultural form that never fit us—and returned to something like the *bakufu* or tent-office or *Shogunate*, the *seii taishōgun* form of strong military-industrial leader that ruled Nippon for so many generations."

"During your Middle Ages," said Nick, not completely hiding the sneer in his tone.

"Yes, Bottom-san. Our Middle Ages which continued until you Americans forced our island and culture to open to the world, almost to the twentieth century. But be cautious in your contempt, Bottom-san. *Seii taishōgun* means 'great general who subdues eastern barbarians.'"

"That's us," said Nick. "The *gai-jin*. The foreign devils."

"*Hai*. Foreign but not devils. That is the way the Chinese think and speak. They, the Chinese, are the greatest racists in the world. Not the Nipponese. *Gai-jin* may translate best simply to 'the outside persons.'"

"Meanwhile, your boss, Mr. Nakamura, wants to be a modern *Shogun*."

"Of course. As do the heads of the Munetaka, Morikune, Toyoda, Omura, Yoritsugo, Yamahsita, and Yoshiake *keiretsu*."

"There's an Omura as Advisor in California and a Yoritsugo Advisor in the Midwest somewhere—Indiana and Illinois?"

"*Hai*, Bottom-san. And Ohio."

"So being a Federal Advisor here in the States is a big step toward seizing the *Shogunate* in Japan?"

"It can be, yes. Depending upon whether the Advisor and

head of the *keiretsu* clan succeeds or fails here. Whether he gains honor or loses it. For you see, this is another thing that has returned in recent decades—the ancient and long-forgotten but deeply embedded centrality of honor and courage and sacrifice. The *bushido*, the way of the warrior that demands honor unto death, reigns once again in the thoughts and actions of many Nipponese."

"Including whaddyoucallit, *seppuku*—ritual suicide—if you fail."

"Oh, yes."

"But what's the point?" said Nick.

"The point, Bottom-san?"

"I'm talking about your Japan being a victim of the same demographics that killed Greece and Italy and Holland and Russia and those other countries we were talking about—declining birthrate. Greeks have all but disappeared. Half the European countries have seen their native populations mostly replaced by Muslim immigrants..."

"Yes, Bottom-san, but Nippon does not allow such immigration, Muslim or Korean or any other sort."

"Yeah, but that's not my point, Sato-san. Your birthrate is still declining. Your population was what—around a hundred and twenty-seven million or something when I was about twenty. Now, just twenty-some years later, it's...what?...ninety million or something?"

"Closer to eighty-seven million, yes," said Sato.

"And declining rapidly," said Nick. "Almost forty percent of your population is sixty-five or older. That's old, man. No more little Nipponese running around on the *tatami* mats to fill your jobs, man your factories, and enlist in your armies. What will it profit Nakamura—or any of the other *keiretsu* billionaire big shots—to become *Shogun* in a country where no one's left but a fcw old farts?"

"Exactly," said Sato. *Ezacry.* Nick was beginning to understand the fat sonofabitch without straining to. "This is why we must conquer China, Bottom-san."

"*Conquer* China?" repeated Nick, his jaw sagging as far as

it could in the helmet with its tight chin-strap. "I thought our guys were being paid to fight there for you as part of your contribution to the UN effort to help stop the Chinese civil wars."

Sato said nothing.

"Your plan is to *conquer* China?" Nick repeated stupidly. "Eighty-seven million of you elderly Japs trying to *conquer* a country with a population of...what?...one-point-six *billion* people?"

"Exactly," Sato said again and it didn't sound quite so funny to Nick this time. "But China is a country of one-point-six billion people that has imploded far worse than your United States, Bottom-san. Economic disaster. Cultural chaos. Inflation. Stagnation. Riots. Revolt of the military. Total breakdown of their outmoded Communist political system. Warlords. Civil war."

"So Japan is just trying to conquer a chunk of it."

"*Hai*, Bottom-san. Merely a chunk. Perhaps a third of it—but the most productive third. Including Shanghai, Beijing, and Hong Kong. India—another UN 'peacekeeper' there—can have much of the rest. Negotiations with India are ongoing."

Nick thought, *India with its one-point-eight billion people or whatever it is now. Holy shit, Japan and India and Indonesia and the Islamic Caliphate are carving up the world while we freebase flashback and blow ourselves up.*

Restraining the urge to weep again, or laugh, or bark at the moon just visible on the monitors rising above the smoke-hazy eastern horizon, Nick said, "And little Keigo Nakamura was going to be the heir apparent of this possible *Shogun* who may be ruling over a new empire of three-quarters of a billion people."

"Probable *Shogun*," said Sato. "And yes. Although a shogun is not exactly a king and although power does not always descend through the oldest—or only—son, if Hiroshi Nakamura becomes the first *Shogun* in one hundred and sixty-four years, Keigo Nakamura would have been the *daimyo* most eligible for ascension to the *Shogunate* upon his father's death...if the other *daimyo*s, *keiretsu* warlords, would have agreed."

"All that going on," murmured Nick, but the bead-microphone was clearly transmitting his murmurs, "and the stupid little twerp was over here in the States shooting a video documentary about flashback."

"Yes," said Sato.

"And you let someone kill him," said Nick.

"Yes," said Sato.

"Well, if that screwup didn't earn you an order to commit *seppuku* from Old Man Nakamura, I can't imagine what would," said Nick.

"Yes," said Sato.

"Boxcar One, this is Boxcar Two," came ninja Willy's voice over the truck-to-truck comm net. Willy was driving the second vehicle. "Do you see that boy on a horse, Sato-san? Over."

Boy on a horse? Nick looked from display to display. The ride had been so uneventful, except for this truly weird conversation, that he'd forgotten all about where he was and what was going on outside the sealed vehicle.

"Roger, Boxcar Two," replied Sato on comm. "I've been watching him for some time now, Willy. Over."

Nick finally found the screen showing the boy on a horse. The mini-drone sending the images seemed to be only forty or fifty feet above the kid. The boy seemed to be about Val's age—thirteen or fourteen at the most.

No, Nick corrected himself, *Val's older. He just turned sixteen a few weeks ago. And I forgot to call him to wish him happy birthday.*

This boy was spanic, shirtless, shoeless, and wearing only dirty, raggedy shorts that looked to have been cut down from a man's pair of chinos, and he was mounted on a nag so old and swaybacked that the boy's bare toes almost touched the dusty earth. The boy and old horse were scrawny enough that ribs showed through scabbed brown flesh on both of them.

"I don't see a phone," said Bill from his position in the top gun bubble turret of the other vehicle.

"Me either," said Joe from their own gun bubble.

"Boxcar Two, Boxcar One," broke in Toby from where he

rode shotgun in the front of the second Oshkosh M-ATV. "It could be in his pocket, voice activated. The kid could be sending coordinates to artillery right now."

"Roger that, Toby," Sato said calmly. "Has anyone heard anything?"

Nick realized that the drone was sending audio as well as the video feed, but when he managed to match frequencies with it, all he could hear was the wind through the dry grass around the kid and the occasional lazy swish of the swaybacked horse's tail.

"Negative that, Boxcar One," replied four voices.

"Boxcar One and Two," continued Sato. "Has anyone seen his lips moving?"

Again, four negatives came back over comm. Nick felt like an idiot. A left-out idiot.

"Boxcar One, I have the fifty-caliber mounted," said Bill from the bubble of the second truck. "He's about a hundred and thirty meters east of us. I can reach him easily." *Easiry.* They were obviously all speaking in English for Nick Bottom's benefit.

"Roger that, Boxcar Two," said Sato. "Please keep tracking him until we are out of sight about a kilometer ahead. Joe, do you have him?"

"Yes, Sato-san."

"Allow Bill to keep his eye on the child and the horse. You keep pivoting and report anything else."

"Roger that, Sato-san."

"Boxcar Two...Bill?"

"*Hai,* Boxcar One?"

"I am watching the monitor but driving, so please be sure to tell me the second the boy moves...especially if he turns his horse around. Please tell me which way his horse's head is pointing. Watch the drone monitor when we pass out of visual."

"*Hai, j-shi,*" came Bill's fast, sharp response.

Tell me which way his horse's head is pointing? thought Nick.

When they'd passed over the little rise and started descending into a broad valley toward a bridge over a dry riverbed, Nick asked, "What was all the questioning and talk about my feelings and Japan and China all about? I don't believe it was random."

"It is about Don Khozh-Ahmed Noukhaev and your meeting with him tomorrow morning, Bottom-san."

"Don Khozh-Ahmed Noukhaev? And what do you mean *my* meeting with the guy? You'll be there, too, won't you?"

"Negative, Bottom-san. Don Khozh-Ahmed Noukhaev contacted *us*, Mr. Nakamura himself, to arrange this meeting, and Khozh-Ahmed Noukhaev stipulated that it must be just with you. No one else."

Nick tried to shake his head. "I don't get it. And even if he does want to talk just with me, what's that have to do with all the talk of countries coming part, Japan, China, the whole nine yards?"

"You must understand what Don Khozh-Ahmed Noukhaev *is*," said Sato over their private comm link. "What he represents."

"He *is* a drugrunner," said Nick. "What he represents is a giant shitload of money."

"Yes, Bottom-san, but there is much more. Don Khozh-Ahmed Noukhaev's parents also went through this loss of a nation's culture and integrity when the Soviet Union imploded."

"Well, boo-hoo for them," said Nick. "Besides, isn't Khozh-Ahmed Noukhaev *Chechen?* He and his parents should have been cheering when the old USS of R went belly up."

"His father was Chechen, Bottom-san. Don Khozh-Ahmed Noukhaev's mother was Russian and he was raised in Moscow…"

"I still don't see…" They were approaching the bridge. Ahead of them, I-25 cut a long shallow ramp through the opposing valley wall. The somewhat greener, somewhat grassier bottomlands here were interrupted by ancient cottonwood trees, both standing and fallen.

"Don Khozh-Ahmed Noukhaev represents not only Russia's waning interest in the parts of the United States currently occupied by the forces and colonists of Nuevo Mexico, Bottom-san, but also the Global Caliphate's very active interest."

"You saying the drugrunner is a shill for the Muslims?

That they want control of what used to be Arizona, Southern California, New Mexico, parts of…"

"I am saying that it is very unusual and interesting that Don Khozh-Ahmed Noukhaev contacted Mr. Nakamura and agreed to an interview with you, Bottom-san. *Insisted* upon an interview with you. Have you had any dealings with him in the past that we do not know about? If so, it is very important that we know of them, Bottom-san."

"No, nothing," Nick said truthfully. The DPD had tried to arrange interview times with the man after Keigo Nakamura's murder, since the late video-documentarian's people had said that Keigo had interviewed him just days before he died, but Don Khozh-Ahmed Noukhaev had been a ghost. They couldn't even contact his *people*. The local Santa Fe cops and New Mexico highway patrol people—all of them on someone's payroll, of course—hadn't even tried to help. The FBI, Nick knew, had also struck out with the Russian-Chechen-Mexican-Muslim drug- and gunrunner.

"I still don't see…," began Nick.

"Boxcar One, Boxcar One," came Bill's voice from the turret of Boxcar Two, "the boy is turning his horse around…looks like a hundred and eighty degrees. Yes, he's stopped."

"Very well, Boxcar One," Sato said calmly. The security chief was throwing switches on his panel. "Stand by to…"

At that instant the 120mm HEAT high-explosive antitank round struck the transparent Kevlar bubble atop the first Oshkosh, beheaded Joe in a microsecond, and poured the hypersonic lava of its shaped charge down over Joe's immolated corpse and into the small space where Sato and Nick sat.

1.12

North of Las Vegas, New Mexico— Wednesday, Sept. 15

FOR NICK THERE WAS ONLY an instantaneous sensation of great heat, then a terrible pressure as a solid wall of darkness surrounded him and pressed in on him, and then nothing.

In the second Oshkosh–Land Cruiser M-ATV thirty meters behind them, the driver Willy—whose real name was Mutsumi Ōta—saw Sato's vehicle get hit. The gun bubble on top shot two hundred feet into the air with a pillar of flame seemingly supporting it. Sato's Oshkosh flipped, hit the left edge of the bridge it was crossing, and dropped down into the empty riverbed, trailing guard rail and concrete rebar behind it and rolling a dozen or so times. Pieces of flaming metal had flown off the leading Oshkosh upon impact of the tank or artillery shell and now the large back hatch sliced the air toward Ōta's vehicle like a 300-pound piece of shrapnel, missing by ten inches. In the riverbed below, more geysers of flame erupted from every sprung hatch, air vent, and the entire rear of Sato and Nick's burning, tumbling truck.

Ōta jerked his Oshkosh off the highway to the right so hard that the huge vehicle actually teetered on its right wheels for a few seconds before crashing all wheels back to the earth. The patch of Interstate thirty meters behind where he'd been an instant before exploded upward and outward as a second HEAT round slammed into the pavement. A third exploded just to the left of Ōta's Oshkosh where it had been tilting seconds earlier.

There were at least two tanks firing.

Toby shouted in Japanese from the right seat, "I saw the flashes! Two tanks, hull down, just at the base of the hill about one klick ahead."

Ōta reached the steep bank of the riverbed and drove straight off, all 25,000 pounds of the Oshkosh seeming to hang in air for an eternity before it fell below the level of the riverbanks, all the wheels compacting fully on the TAK-7 independent suspensions.

The north bank of the riverbed exploded behind them.

"Three tanks!" shouted Bill in Japanese from the gun bubble. "Saw the third flash."

Ōta's M-ATV crashed through willows and fallen cottonwoods before skidding to a teetering stop in the sand near the south bank. They should be out of direct-fire view and range of the tanks, Ōta knew, although mortars or artillery could get them easily through indirect fire.

"Infantry!" shouted Bill from above. Bill's real name was Daigorou Okada. "Saw them just before we dropped. Several hundred, I think. Carrying small arms and RPGs and TOWs."

"Where?" asked Mutsumi Ōta in his slow, calm voice. He'd have to find out if his boss, Sato, was alive, but that could wait a minute until they understood the tactical situation and could find a way to get into the fight.

"Coming out of holes due south about halfway to the tanks," said Okada, his own voice more calm and professional now.

Toby, whose real name was Shinta Ishii, had been busy on the vehicle-to-vehicle comm lines, trying to raise Sato or Joe, real name Tai Okamoto, or the *gai-jin* with them. There was no answer.

"How did the drones and sats miss the tanks?" asked

Shinta Ishii in Japanese when he broke off trying to raise Sato's truck.

"Probably good cryocamo blankets covering the buried hull-down tanks and people in their holes," said Ōta. "Keeping the temperature exactly that of the soil. Someone's going to have to go out there to give us a look at what's coming."

"*Hai!*" said Shinta Ishii from the right seat. He disconnected his comm and other umbilicals, slapped the restraint release, pulled a PEAP temporary air-supply and comm system from the dash and clipped it in place on his helmet, took a video camera and 9mm pistol from the glove compartment, opened the passenger door, and rolled out.

A second later the image flowed to the Oshkosh's monitors from Ishii's camera as it was tentatively shoved above the edge of the south bank. Ishii did not raise his head.

About a hundred infantry in light armor were crossing the half kilometer or so between them and the riverbed. Behind them came three tanks.

———

NICK BOTTOM RETURNED TO consciousness with the sound of gunshots popping all around him. It got his attention.

No, it wasn't gunshots, he realized as his eyes began to focus. The front part of the truck's cabin had filled almost instantly with solid foam. Now that foam was evaporating or deliquescing or whatever it was doing, one loud pop at a time.

Nick hit the big release button at the center of his harnesses and they snapped back even as his sarcophagus of a crash-couch hissed and pulled back. Nick fell headfirst onto the ceiling and almost broke his neck as his helmet met hot steel with a loud bang.

The Oshkosh was upside down at an angle. The driver's side seemed to be buried in the dirt. Some sort of metal fire panel had slammed down behind his and Sato's seats and now that panel was glowing cherry red with bright white spots. The heat threatened to make Nick swoon. The fire behind that panel, Nick knew, must be terrible. Unless Joe the top-gunner had gotten out another way, he was dead.

Remembering Sato's advice, Nick unclipped his suit's O-two and comm channels, removed the PEAP—Personal Egress Air Pack—bundle from the console, took two tries to clip it into place on his helmet and oxygen mask, and plugged the mobile PEAP comm links in.

"Sato?"

No response.

Heaps of loose items and metal debris had tumbled onto the truck's ceiling where Nick now crouched, sliding down under Sato's hanging body, but when he leaned over to look up at Sato in the driver's seat he still couldn't be sure if the security chief was alive or dead.

Sato's eyes were closed; he looked dead. His body hung from the straps. The blast from behind had ripped most of the red samurai armor off Sato's right arm and Nick could see with a single glance that the arm was broken. Some of Sato's blood had spattered the dark windshield panels and other video monitors and more blood was now dripping from the arm onto the ceiling-turned-floor.

Nick tried to remember the names of the men in the second truck.

"Willy?" he called on comm. "Toby? Bill?"

No response. Not even static. Maybe the PEAP comm unit wasn't working. Or maybe the second truck had also been hit and destroyed.

After making sure that his 9mm Glock was still clipped on the belt on his armored hip, Nick crawled across the seat, grabbed his heavy duffel bag from where it had dropped onto the ceiling, and kicked the passenger-side door open.

He threw the weapons-duffel out first and then followed. The right side of the Oshkosh was raised about four feet above sandy soil, a trickle of river, and a line of burning willow bushes. Nick wedged himself over the edge and dropped the four feet, grunting with pain when he hit. He didn't think anything was broken, but his entire body felt bruised as if after a good beating. Sweat dripped out of the eye sockets of his mask.

He took a deep breath to get some fresh air, but he was still on the thirty-minute PEAP air supply. He left it in place.

Nick grabbed the duffel bag before the flames got to it and dragged it and himself twenty feet away from the burning Oshkosh along the steep, sandy riverbank. He saw now that the huge M-ATV had done a corkscrew off the bridge above, tumbled flaming across the floor of the riverbed, and dug its heavy snout and right side into the heaps of soft sand just short of the riverbank on this side. Whether "this side" was the north or south bank of the river, Nick had no idea.

Nick pulled the Glock from his hip, unzipped the duffel, and looked at the weapons he'd brought. They seemed all right. He looked back at the burning Oshkosh.

The rear of the big truck was totally engulfed in flames and those flames were working their way forward along the shattered outside of the vehicle. The steel tires were melting. Ammunition from somewhere, probably next to the absent top gun bubble, was cooking off at random and rounds were impacting in every direction.

"Well, fuck," breathed Nick.

He staggered back to the truck.

This side was too damned high to get up onto while he was in armor so he scrambled as high as he could on the twelve- or fifteen-foot-high riverbank, clambered up onto a shattered, steaming wheel, and crawled along the passenger side of the truck. The door was open but he still had a clumsy time of it as he wedged himself into the black, smoking hole and let himself drop until his feet were on the center console.

"Sato!!"

No answer. He called for the others in the second truck: no response. Maybe he just didn't know how to reset the comm frequency.

Sato still hung upside down from the straps, his body leaning a little toward the driver's-side door. The heat in the front part of the cabin was much worse than it had been just a minute earlier and Nick could see white parts of the fire bulkhead beginning to melt.

He pulled himself under Sato's hanging body, tried to keep the naked and broken arm to one side, braced himself and his shoulders and upper body under Sato like a crouching if underweight sumo-wrestler, and hit Sato's harness release with his Kevlared fist.

The big man's body fell on him, the dead weight of Sato's three hundred pounds crushing Nick against the ceiling, breaking at least one of Nick's ribs, and driving the air out of him.

"Oh…Jesus…fuck," breathed Nick. "You…fat…"

He didn't finish the thought. If Sato was as dead as he felt, limp as a slaughtered heifer, he didn't want to speak ill of the dead. "Fat…fuck," he breathed out despite himself.

Then he was shoving with his boots, grabbing with his gloves, putting all his energy into moving Sato's huge, inert, unhelpful form up and toward the open door. Smoke had filled the cockpit. Sato's body quit moving and Nick noticed various leads and wires running from the man's blood-red samurai helmet back to the crash chair.

"Oh, PEAP, shit," gasped Nick.

He had to brace Sato's body in place while he crouched again and found the red-symboled section of the dashboard console in front of the driver's seat. He hit the right spot and the PEAP unit came out. It took Nick forty-five seconds of cursing and struggling and uselessly trying to wipe sweat and blood out of his eyes to get the PEAP unit in place and sending oxygen to Sato's almost certainly dead brain. It took even longer to get the old comm leads unplugged and the new ones attached.

"Sato? Sato?"

No answer.

And no time to wait for one. Flames were licking through the partially melted blast shield and igniting the backs of both couches. Nick could smell something cooking and realized it was Sato's bare and broken right arm.

"Ugghh!" screamed Nick and deadlifted the three hundred pounds and more of red-armored Jap. He felt like he was holding the whole armored mass over his head as he shoved Sato up through the smoke-obscured open door and left him balancing precariously on the edge of the Oshkosh.

Nick clambered up next to the body, gasping and blinking away sweat. If he hadn't put his own PEAP on, he knew, he'd be unconscious from smoke inhalation and burning up below.

"Sorry." Nick used both boots to push the red mass of Sato over the edge of the overturned truck. Sato fell the four feet and landed on his broken forearm without a word or sound through the earphones.

A round whizzed by Nick's left earphone. The ammo on the lockers was cooking off now and it sounded like a firefight with automatic weapons. Nick knew that there were TOW missiles and other serious ordnance down there, waiting to go.

Nick jumped down, grabbed Sato by the armor handclasp set between his shoulders, and began dragging the body facedown through the sand and gravel and burning willows. When he got to the duffel, Nick lifted the heavy bag with his left hand and kept dragging Sato with his right. *Adrenaline,* he thought. *Breakfast of champions.*

Another hundred and fifty feet or so along the riverbank and he thought they might be safe when the truck exploded. They had come around a slight bend in the riverbank—more of a little alcove here—out of direct sight and range of the burning vehicle and igniting ammunition. Nick had no idea if the "radioactive-element-powered" fuel cells that drove the seven-hundred-horsepower Oshkosh turbines would explode when burned enough, but he assumed they would. Most things that powered big trucks would and did when set afire.

The thought of those "radioactive elements" beneath them in the breached and battered truck made Nick wonder if he'd already received a fatal or sterilizing dose of radiation. Or if he would as the truck kept burning or when it exploded.

"Fuck it," he breathed.

Grunting like a pig, he rolled Sato over onto his back.

What would be the best plan here? To get Sato's red helmet and other armor off? Check for a pulse and see what other wounds the big man had? If Sato was dead, it would mean a lot less work for...

Suddenly Nick realized that the sand and gravel around where he crouched over the big man were leaping up in the air as if there were giant sand fleas there.

Or like someone's shooting at me.

Nick peeked around the bank at the burning truck and then looked in the opposite direction, toward the riverbank on their right.

Someone in light body armor, not one of Sato's four ninjas, was firing an automatic weapon at Nick and Sato from about thirty-five feet away. The person was holding the weapon out at arm's length and spraying back and forth, the way Nick had seen in videos of the *hajji*s in Yemen or Somalia or Afghanistan. The Old Man had once said that this was the way untrained assholes fired their weapons. But sooner or later this mook might get lucky.

The soil on the bank a foot above Nick erupted, throwing sand over his helmet.

He removed the 9mm Glock from his hip, went to one knee while using his left arm and hand as a brace, and shot the guy three times center mass.

The shooter dropped the assault rifle and fell rolling down the riverbank. But the 9mm rounds hadn't penetrated his cheap chest armor. The guy staggered to his own knees and started to rise, reaching for his rifle.

Standing now and walking slowly closer, Nick shot the figure again in the chest, once, this time from about twenty feet away.

The shooter went down, rolled, and got to his knees again, gauntleted hands flailing sand while trying to reach his weapon.

Every time the guy tried to get closer to his gun, Nick shot him in the chest again, slapping him rearwards onto his ass or back. The shooter's last attempt had his gloves missing the stock of the rifle by just a few inches. Nick had been shot in such simple Kevlar-3 armor before and knew it felt like getting hit with a baseball bat. But the shooter staggered to his knees again, arms reaching for his dropped rifle. The little fuck was tough.

But he wasn't wearing a combat helmet, Nick saw now, only a sort of Kevlar motorcycle helmet with a regular Plexiglas visor.

Counting his shots — he'd fired six and had nine left in this magazine — Nick braced himself and put a bullet through that visor from seven feet away. Blood and broken plastic and the shooter went down, face-first this time.

Nick rolled the dead shooter over with his boot, saw through the sharded Plexiglas face shield that it was a woman, and, adrenaline surging, fought the daemon-urge to put another round into the bloodied face.

Nick felt the adrenaline peaking and knew he'd have the shakes in a few minutes. Before it hit, he clambered up the riverbank to get a look over the edge. The shooter, through her rolling and grabbing as she fell, had made a sort of rough stairway in the dirt for Nick. He gingerly poked his head above the roots and grass and weedy edge of the bank.

There were twenty or thirty more shooters — light infantry, maybe, but very irregular — just forty or fifty feet behind this first one he'd killed. In a long line behind them, scores more, all carrying weapons of some sort. Several started firing at Nick in the instant before he dropped down out of sight, allowing himself to slide until he came up against the young woman's body.

Tanks. He'd seen at least two fucking tanks behind the skirmish line of fighters. Big fucking tanks with big fucking tank guns swiveling, hunting for a target. Hunting for him.

This isn't right, thought Nick as he sprinted back toward Sato and his duffel bag of weapons. *I am — was — a goddamned homicide detective, not some mercenary or soldier. I am — or was — a private detective, a flatfoot, a dick. I'm in my forties, for Chrissake! I'm too old for this shit. And I'm in the wrong movie!!*

Nick stopped running and stood there vibrating in shock. Sato was alive and on his hands and knees, favoring his broken arm and crouching like a three-legged dog. His helmet visor was up and the big man was vomiting silently into the sand.

"No time for that," said Nick, shoving his own visor up so Sato could hear him. "Infantry closing in. And tanks, Sato. Tanks!!"

"You're welcome, Bottom-san," said Hideki Sato and retched again.

Nick stared. Did this man have the stupidest sense of humor of anyone alive, or was he only semiconscious and a little bit nuts from the shelling?

It didn't matter.

Four figures with guns appeared on the riverbank above the woman's body and began firing at them. They were also members of the spray-'n-hope school of marksmanship. But with that many rounds hitting the bank and riverbed above them, below them, and next to them, one of the idiots *was* going to get lucky soon.

Nick crouched and fired, hitting two of them in the visors. He whirled before their bodies fell, threw his heavy duffel bag over his shoulder, and grabbed Sato with his free hand, dragging the big man back around the bend in the riverbank and out of direct line of sight of the two attackers behind them.

There were twenty or thirty more figures with guns between them and the burning vehicles, most watching the flames. But some noticed Nick and the red-armored giant—it was hard to miss seeing Sato in the early-afternoon sunlight—and that dozen or so turned and started firing.

Sato used his left hand to reach across his big belly, pull the heavy Browning Hi-Power MK IV semiautomatic pistol from his clip, and then crouched as he began firing. Nick shot three of the distant figures through their visors and dropped them before the others started throwing themselves down and scattering, still returning heavy fire. Left-handed, Sato dropped three who were slow in finding cover.

"Got any...?" gasped Nick. He turned and looked around the corner of the bank and immediately jerked his head back as automatic-weapons fire churned up the dirt and roots there. There were at least twenty-five hostiles with them in the river-bed now, approaching cautiously.

Nick threw himself on his belly, swung his head and both arms around the corner, and shot four of them. The others dropped to prone position or scattered, but most kept firing at him.

"...ideas?" finished Nick.

"Hai," grunted Sato. The security chief's face was blood-covered, although it seemed to be due to cuts from his head banging around in his helmet during the initial explosion.

That's it? thought Nick. *Hai?* The dry riverbed was about a hundred feet across to the north side from which they'd come. There was no real cover out there except for one dead cotton-wood trunk, washed downriver long ago, possibly in the spring when there'd been enough water here to wash things down-river. But it was a small-diameter tree trunk, rotten at its core, and Nick knew that slugs from the attackers' assault rifles would go right through it.

Still, it would be harder to be flanked out there. Nick pointed to the fallen tree, grabbed the heavy duffel, and crouched in preparation for the sprint. Odds were excellent that he'd be hit before he got to the trunk.

"No," grunted Sato. "Stay here, Bottom-san. Fight."

"That's the fucking plan?" demanded Nick. He'd meant to put a little irony in the statement—devil-may-care irony if possible, *Beau Geste* irony—but it came out as a pathetic combi-nation of squeak and whine and squeal.

More infantry were dropping down in front of them, ignor-ing the last of the ammo cooking off from the burning Oshkosh. The attackers were aiming more carefully now, their slugs kick-ing up dirt all around Sato and Nick. For some reason, Nick found himself more worried about the guys behind him around the corner of the riverbank. Nick realized that it had always been the *unseen* that scared him most, not the obvious threat.

Nick handed an egg crate of grenades to Sato and then tugged the bulky Negev-Galil flechette sweeper from the duf-fel bag. It felt to Nick like it took him forever to rummage around in the bottom of the bag before he came up with the nylon strip holding the five heavy flechette mags. He tugged the first one out, slapped it in, and stood, leaning around the edge of the bank.

There were about two dozen armored men—or men and women—less than sixty feet from him with more unfriendlies milling on the bank above. All of them started shooting at him at once. One of the taller forms shot Nick square in the chest, but not before Nick triggered the ugly Negev-Galil.

About thirty thousand mini-flechettes swept the area clear, turning the walking figures into bloody rags, tatters, and shreds of armor and shattered visor. One pair of legs stood alone and separate, no longer connected to groin or hip. One of those legs fell over but the other remained standing.

Nick fell back against the bank. He couldn't breathe.

"Are you all right, Bottom-san?" asked Sato. The chief had thrown the grenades Nick had handed him and was now firing—clumsily—the old M4A1, its archaic grenade launcher working hotly. When that was out, he dropped it into the dirt and lifted his Browning MK IV pistol and fired it left-handed. Running figures went down and most did not get back up.

"Urrrr," gasped Nick. The round hadn't penetrated his armor but he was pretty sure that he had a second broken rib somewhere around his breastbone. He slapped in the second flechette box, extended the ugly weapon around the edge of the bank *hajji*-style, and fired off another cloud of flechettes, moving the blocky muzzle even as he fired. It was like swinging a fire hose.

With his visor open now, he could hear the diesel throb and tread clank of an approaching tank. It struck Nick with something less than high humor that the tank was probably irrelevant—more infantry were dropping into the riverbed and firing down from the banks every second. Four of them ran for the very cottonwood trunk that Nick had lusted after. By the time the tank got here, Nick guessed, it'd all be over.

Sato shot two of the troopers but the other two made the cover and began returning fire. Two slugs hit Sato's armor and knocked him back against the sandy bank where Nick had slapped in another magazine for his 9mm Glock and was firing it at someone peeking down at them from above. One of the bodies, shot under the chin up through the too-loose helmet, fell next to Sato.

With a sinking feeling, Nick realized that Sato was praying, his lips moving rapidly. Nick vaguely wondered if it was a Buddhist prayer. No, wait, Nakamura, Sato's boss, was a rare Catholic, so maybe Sato'd had to convert to...

Who gives a damn? thought Nick as two brave figures came hurtling around the curve in the bank, assault rifles barking at their hips.

Nick shot both through the visor and then again when they'd gone down, but not before at least one slug caught him in the upper shoulder and spun him around and propelled him face-first into the sandy bank. That shoulder and part of his chest felt numb. Had the round penetrated?

"Lie down, Bottom-san!" shouted Sato.

"What!?"

Sato dropped his weapon, reached out as quickly as a cobra-strike with his working left hand, grabbed Nick by the loose ridge of armor above his numb chest, and dragged the taller man prone onto the riverbed. Dozens of the enemy infantry were rushing them from the east and Nick could hear footsteps and shouts coming from just around the bend in the bank.

Boxcar Two, the second Oshkosh, roared under the highway bridge and around the bend. Nick heard what sounded like a chainsaw working at high speed and knew it to be a mini-gun mounted in the top turret bubble. The line of impacting slugs was about three feet high and it literally cut openings through the infantry rushing at them from the east, raised and knocked down more of the enemy from atop the riverbank.

The two troopers who'd run for the cottonwood popped up and began firing at the Oshkosh. The turret whirred, the mini-gun chain-rattled, and both the fallen tree trunk and the standing troopers exploded into random chunks.

The Oshkosh roared past them, the turret whirred back, and Sato's ninja called Bill began pouring volumes of fire into the troopers who'd bunched up in the sand cove. Nick peeked around the corner in time to see the survivors scrambling and clawing up and over the riverbank, running back toward the south.

Sato set his helmet against Nick's. "The man you know as Bill is really Daigorou Okada, the man you know as Willy's real name is Mutsumi Ōta, Toby's real name is..."

"Introductions later!" shouted Nick. He grabbed the bulky duffel with one hand and Sato with the other, and the two men began staggering and limping toward the stopped Oshkosh. The big rear hatch opened and Toby stood there pouring out streams of flechettes from a Japanese-built assault sweeper as Nick threw the bag in first, then shoved Sato in, and then started clambering in himself.

A round caught him between the shoulder blades, driving him face-first into the piles of spent cartridges littering the metal floor of the Oshkosh.

Toby slammed the hatch shut and the rounds banging and pounding against it sounded like a hailstorm.

Sato was on his knees, inspecting Nick's back. "Didn't penetrate!" he shouted over the whine-howl of the M-ATV's turbines. Nick caught a glimpse of the front monitors and realized that they were heading back the way the Oshkosh had come, east under the highway bridge and then a bend to the northeast.

"You weren't praying," Nick gasped to Sato. "You were calling in Boxcar Two."

Sato stared at him without expression.

One of the video feeds was obviously from a camera set up on the south bank and others were from the mini-drones buzzing around. The three tanks were clearly visible and not more than a hundred meters from the south bank.

Nick followed Sato and staggered forward past gunner Daigorou Okada's legs in the swiveling top mount. It was a dangerous place to linger with thousands of red-hot mini-gun cartridges flying out and down, not all of them landing in the asbestos spent-sack.

Nick leaned against the back of Toby's passenger-side crash-couch.

"Shinta Ishii," said Sato, completing introductions of the living.

Nick nodded recognition and thanks. Mutsumi Ōta behind the wheel—it was actually a console-mounted omni-controller of the kind found in hydrogen-powered Lexuses—was turning them toward the south riverbank, toward which, the monitors showed, were advancing two or three hundred infantry and the three tanks.

"Can this Oshkosh take those tanks?" Nick asked no one in particular. With broken ribs and impact bruises fore and aft, he had to gasp out each word as he exhaled painfully.

"No," said Shinta Ishii from where he was busy tapping at a foldout dashboard keyboard that Nick hadn't even noticed when he was in the right-hand seat. "Not even one of those."

"TOW?" queried Nick. It sounded and felt like a prayer.

Sato shook his head. "This kind of battle tank"—he jerked his left thumb toward the monitor showing a tank from an aerial drone's point of view—"has antimissile countermeasures. We have no chance against any of them."

"Air cover?" asked Nick. "Some sort of armed drone or a jet from Colorado or…" *Or any sort of* deus ex machina? thought Nick. He'd learned that literary term from Dara. *A god from a machine.* Being lowered, often in a basket, to rescues the heroes and heroines from a situation they couldn't get themselves out of. Bad form in fiction and theater, Dara had taught him. But Nick thought it was definitely time for a *deus ex machina.* Maybe two or three.

"No air support, Bottom-san," said Mutsumi Ōta as he drove the Oshkosh back toward the southern riverbank. *Back toward the enemy troops and tanks.*

"Surrender?" gasped Nick. It wasn't so much a question as it was a very, very strong suggestion.

"Leave the one mini-drone in place and use all three of its lasers to light up the tanks," Sato said softly to the man sitting in the crash chair that Nick was leaning against so he wouldn't fall down. "Bring the others back out of range."

"*Hai*, Sato-san," said Shinta Ishii. He was rapidly typing commands on the keyboard.

Nick peeked at the screen, but all the words were in *kanji* or *hiragana* or whatever they called their script.

"Super lasers?" asked Nick, his voice sounding pathetic even to himself. "Weapons lasers on your mini-drones?"

"Oh, no, Bottom-san," said Mutsumi Ōta as he brought the Oshkosh to a stop against the steep south bank and parked it there. "Just regular lasers. Would not hurt a fly."

"Final coordinates in?" asked Sato.

"*Hai,*" barked Shinta Ishii. "*Do no kid ga kanry moe te i masu. J kid wo nokoshi kuma.*"

Nick, who'd taken twelve weeks of instruction in conversational Japanese with Dara during his push for detective first grade nine years ago, didn't understand a word of what he'd just heard.

"Gee-bear *t chaku jikan?*" barked Sato.

Gee-bear? thought Nick.

"Thirty-eight seconds," said Shinta Ishii, obviously using English for Nick's benefit.

Above them, the turret whirred and Daigorou Okada's mini-gun opened up again and hot, spent cartridges started raining down on the steel floor. Nick could see through four of the monitors that the line of infantry was almost to the south riverbank, the tanks less than a hundred meters behind. The tanks were also accompanied by infantry. The figures in the front were visibly firing on the single mini-drone video feed and now Nick could hear the bullets pinging against the Oshkosh's outer skin. Slugs hitting the turret above had a slightly more resonant sound.

"Shouldn't we at least go out and...I don't know...," said Nick. "Fight?"

Sato put his strong left hand on Nick's wrist and said nothing. The pinging on the outer hull became a solid roar. Nick thought of a time when he was a kid and he and his father had run to a farmer's tin-roofed shed during a violent downpour. This was louder.

The mini-gun above them fell silent. "Out of ammunition, Sato-san," announced Daigorou Okada.

"Ten seconds," Shinta Ishii said softly from in front of Nick. The man sat back deeper in his crash chair and tugged at the already tight five-point harnesses holding him in. Okada dropped down from his perch and Nick heard and saw a metal panel sealing off the top gun bubble. Okada pulled down a jump seat and harnessed himself into it.

Are we going somewhere? wondered Nick with a child's sense of hope. He watched on the single working monitor as six or eight of the infantry jumped from the riverbank to the top of the Oshkosh, weapons firing as they sought out any aperture. Fifty more were rushing to join them. The enemy tanks rumbled closer.

Suddenly Sato moved up behind Nick as if to hug him, despite the shattered arm hanging limp at his side, and the big man shoved his huge and armored body tight, pressing Nick against the crash-couch ahead of him.

Later, Nick swore that he'd caught a glimpse of them via the single drone monitor and the last working Oshkosh external cam. Six slim shapes—about the size and configuration of tele-phone poles—hurtling down from orbit at eight times the speed of sound.

The mini-drone turning on a widening gyre a thousand feet above them that was painting the three tanks with its laser beams was vaporized in the first seconds of the blast, but the more distant drones opened their channels and sent images—recorded for later study—of the three mushroom clouds rising and converging into one great mushroom cloud that folded and unfolded and then refolded itself toward the stratosphere.

The tanks were vaporized in an instant. The hundreds of infantrymen and -women, anyone standing within a radius of two kilometers of the three targeted and simultaneously struck tanks, were caught up in the shockwave and blast front of dis-turbed air and thrown a hundred meters or more through the dust-filled sky. None appeared to have survived.

The riverbank collapsed in on and completely buried the Oshkosh.

"On one hundred percent internal air," came a computer voice that Nick hadn't heard before.

The vibrations and tremors were very strong. If it hadn't been for Sato pressing him against the crash-couch, it was quite possible that he would have rattled around the inside of the truck like a BB in a shaken steel can.

"Holy shit," whispered Nick when the up-and-down oscillations had stopped and Mutsumi Ōta had fired up the Oshkosh's big twin turbines and driven them out of the landslide.

Ōta guided them up the rough ramp onto the scorched area atop the bank and stopped, engines idling. Daigorou Okada had opened the top turret and clambered back up, carrying heavy magazines for the mini-gun, but there was no firing.

Nick stared at the monitors as more of the mini-drones moved back within range. The scorched area was an almost perfect circle extending across the riverbed and another mile or so to the north and up the river valley cliffs almost two miles to the south.

The doors opened and the driver, Mutsumi Ōta, and Shinta Ishii had attached their PEAPs and climbed out, heading back down the bank toward the still-burning first Oshkosh.

"Please to lower visor and activate PEAP," Sato said softly. "The air is very full of particles. We must retrieve Joe's body from our vehicle. His real name was Genshirou Itō and though there will not be much left after the fire, we must find what we can. We shall send others back for a more complete job before sending Itō-san's ashes back to Nippon for a hero's burial. We honor our dead."

Nick nodded and closed his visor with a shaking hand. His hands were too unsteady to activate the PEAP comm, so Sato helped. Then the security chief pushed a button and the big rear door swung out and clanged down. Nick followed Sato down the ramp onto earth so fried that it snapped and crackled under their boots. Not even a blade of grass had survived the flames.

"Nukes?" managed Nick.

"Ahh, no," said Sato over their personal comm. "A purely hyperkinetic weapon. From orbit, you see. Many hundreds waiting for the call. Six used here. No warheads. No radioactivity, of course. Merely speed turned into energy. Much energy."

"I didn't know such things existed," whispered Nick. They were walking toward the first Oshkosh now. Ōta and Ishii were using large foam fire extinguishers from the surviving Oshkosh to fight the flames. Behind Sato and Nick, the bubble turret whirred as Daigorou Okada covered them.

"No," agreed Sato, using his good arm to pull another fire extinguisher from an outside locker and handing it one-handed to Nick before he took another for himself.

"That arm's in terrible shape," said Nick. "You'll need to get airlifted to a surgeon. Soon."

Sato smiled and shook his head. "Okada-san is a very good medic, as was Genshirou Itō. There are adequate painkillers and medical materials aboard this Oshkosh for Okada-san to set the worst of the break and to allow me to travel the last three or four hours to Santa Fe in relative comfort."

Before they went down the bank into the riverbed, Nick looked south and then all around again at the miles of devastation. Ten thousand small fires still burned. It seemed as if the ground were on fire.

"What do you call this weapon?" he asked.

Sato smiled. "The man who came up with the idea for such an enhanced, self-guided kinetic kill weapon—especially designed to penetrate deep bunkers—called them OWL."

"Owl?" repeated Nick.

"Orbital Warhead Lancet. Very simple. Very useful for such small-unit fighting when regular air support is not available. It is used occasionally in China, not often. It is very expensive."

"And these six OWLs came from Mr. Nakamura's private stock."

"*Hai.*" Sato grinned, although Nick was certain that the man must be in terrible pain. "We do not call these kinetic weapons OWLs, you see. But, rather, gee-bears."

Nick remembered hearing the odd word. "'Gee' as in gravity, high-boost, acceleration, that sort of thing?"

"Yes," nodded Sato, as if enjoying some private joke. "But also 'Gee' as in the first letter of the first name of the American

skiffy writer who came up with the idea for this particular technology. We like to honor creators when we can."

"Skiffy writer," repeated Nick. S-c-i-hyphen-f-i.

Sato quit smiling. "It was important, Bottom-san, that we
get you to your interview tomorrow with Don Khozh-Ahmed
Noukhaev. I promised Mr. Nakamura that you would be there."

As they began walking down the crumbled riverbank
toward the burning Oshkosh, Nick was wondering how they
were going to get the pieces of Joe's charred and crumbling
body out of that mess. Or if they'd find his head.

"This Don Khozh-Ahmed Noukhaev had better be worth
it," he muttered.

"Yes," Sato agreed grimly. "He had better be worth it."

2.03

I-70 West of Denver — Friday, Sept. 24

VAL FELT THAT he was being held high on some invisible cable, dangling between Heaven and Hell. Sometimes he rose until he could see light. More often, he dropped precipitously until the loose cable snagged on something and brought him up just short of black crags, sulfurous pits. But, dangled there in darkness, he never reached either place. Val had come to welcome either destination just so long as he could *arrive*. This Friday night, he was near Heaven.

The irony, of course, amusing only to himself, was that Val Bottom didn't believe in either Heaven or Hell and never had.

Utah was a sort of Heaven. It was one of the few states left in what was laughably still called the Union that actually repaired and policed its highways, even the Interstates that had once been under federal control and maintenance. Once the twenty-nine-mile gauntlet of the Virgin River Diagonal was successfully run — bandits had fired on them from the cliffs for two-thirds of the way, but their security SUVs had returned fire until the convoy could pass with no real casualties — the drive north in Utah on I-15 and then east on I-70 toward Colorado was more like an easy, high-speed excursion from the days of the Old Man's childhood than anything Val had ever experienced.

Eastern Utah from the tiny town of Richfield not far past the junction of I-15 and I-70 for the two hundred miles or so to the Colorado state line was the most magnificently empty upthrust of ancient mountains, sandstone ridges, and high plateaus that Val had ever seen. He'd never even imagined such a place.

For the last two days, Val had spent most of his days and nights riding in the cabs with two of the solo drivers — the black man Gauge Devereaux and the Navajo Henry Big Horse Begay.

The previous night, driving down from the Utah high country, Devereaux had seen the bulge in Val's jacket where he kept the Beretta tucked in his belt behind his back and had asked to see the gun. Discombobulated, Val had finally pulled the weapon from his belt, slid the magazine out, and handed the semiautomatic to the driver.

"You left one in the spout," said Devereaux. Taking his left hand from the steering wheel for a moment, the big man ratcheted the slide, caught the cartridge in midair, and handed it to the boy. Val thumbed it into the magazine.

Devereaux sniffed the muzzle and breach. Val knew that even after several days, the stink of cordite was in the weapon.

"Been shooting somebody?" said the driver.

Val remembered Billy grunting "Ugh" and the blotching red circle expanding above Vladimir Putin's face on the T-shirt. He remembered the sound of Coyne's front teeth hitting the concrete after the second, killing shot, and flinched despite himself.

"Target practice," he said.

Devereaux nodded. "Nice gun. You need to keep it clean."

They rode in silence for a while. I-Seventy had been dropping out of the mountains since sunset back near Richfield an hour or two earlier, and as they approached the exit to the abandoned city of Green River, starlight and moonlight now painted more high desert than the tortured sandstone and granite they'd been descending through.

Val tried not to think of Billy Coyne. It had been with him constantly, mostly at night, when it kept him awake, and much of the emotion had been encysted in the single thought—*I've killed a human being.* The thought and images made him almost sick at times, especially toward dawn, but there was also something darkly exciting—almost ecstatic—in the memories of those minutes in the tunnel. Part of Val wished he could go back and live it again just to feel the sense of power and release that had flowed through him when he'd put those two bullets into Billy Coyne's chest and throat.

But so far, Val hadn't used one of his vials of flashback to relive it. Doing that seemed...dirty...for some reason.

He was watching the convoy lights and highway stripes ahead of them and drifting into sleep when Devereaux's voice startled him awake.

"You really thinking of trying to be an independent trucker?"

"Yeah," said Val. "I mean, I don't know. Maybe."

"Yeah, that's the way I was when I was thinking about it. But it's doable, if you decide to try. About one fucking kid in a thousand who *says* he can be an independent driver actually makes it. But it'll take some money up front."

Here it comes, thought Val. Somehow Devereaux was going to offer him some lameshit path to trucking, *if* he handed x amount of cash over to Gauge Devereaux. *The world's bullshit just keeps on coming.*

But no, the driver was talking about something else.

"I'm not talking about the fortune it takes to buy your own rig. That comes years later."

"How'd you get the money for this cab?" asked Val.

"Luck," said Devereaux, shifting the toothpick that he was always chewing on from one side of his mouth to the other. "And with the way the price of rigs is going up, you'll need even more luck...and balls...than I had. But I'm just talking about getting started. You know, riding shotgun as relief driver for a good solo long-distance guy those first few years. That's possible...*if*..."

Here it comes, thought Val.

"If what?" he said.

"If you got a decent fake National Identity and Credit Card with a passable name and background and a decent fake Teamsters Union holo in it," said Devereaux. The black man shot a glance sideways at Val. "My guess is that you wouldn't want to use your own card for personal reasons...right?"

Val hesitated, then nodded.

"So you'll need the best sort of fake card...the kind that can get you through all the various highway patrol and weigh station and militia roadblocks. But it'll cost you about two hundred bucks...*old* bucks."

"Let me guess," Val said tiredly. "You can get one for me."

Devereaux took his eyes off the road for a long moment as he glared at Val. "Fuck you, kid. I'm not saying I can get you shit and it's not like you have two hundred old bucks. You or that loony professor of a granddad you got riding back there with Perdita and Julio. I'm not offering nothing but advice, and it was going to be for free. But fuck you."

"I'm sorry," said Val. And he meant it. "I'm...tired. Sorta worn out. I haven't been sleeping and...I mean, yeah, I'd love to get a new NICC. But how? Where?"

Devereaux drove in silence for several minutes. Finally, shifting down to get up a rare rising grade in the long descent to flatness, he growled, "There's a guy in Denver. A lot of new solos use him to get their Teamsters NICC. The last I heard, he charged two hundred old bucks. It's probably gone up."

"You're right," said Val. "I don't have the money. Neither docs Leonard."

Devereaux shrugged. "Then it doesn't matter, does it?"

"But I'd still like his name," said Val, sitting up straight and rubbing his face to wake up more. "If I got a Teamsters NICC, could I ride shotgun with you?"

"I'm a real solo," grunted Devereaux. "I don't haul no snot-nosed apprentices with me. But there's a lot of guys who do."

"Like who?"

"Like Henry Big Horse Begay. He's got a kid riding and learning from him about half the time. Doesn't charge them much, either." Devereaux shot Val another glance. "Henry's not queer, either. He likes teenage girls and younger, but none of them seem to want to be solo long-distance truckers. So old Begay takes punks like you under his wing."

"How much of a charge would 'not much' be?" asked Val.

Devereaux shrugged again. "Beer money for the old fart. But in terms of learning trucking, riding a few months or a year with Henry Big Horse Begay is like going to Harvard or Princeton or one of those schools for...you know...someone like a young version of your granddad."

Val licked his chapped, broken lips. "Do you think he'd let me hook up with him east out of Denver?"

The driver shook his head. "This convoy is getting into Denver tomorrow and laying over there about twelve hours, kid. Long enough to deliver our Denver shit, get a new trailer filled with shit headed east, get some sleep, and then we'll be rolling toward Kansas City on I-Seventy by two a.m. Sunday. That wouldn't give you enough time to *find* this fucking guy who does the NICCs. And it takes a while for those cards to get made up — usually about two weeks. That's assuming you got the cash to pay this guy with up front."

Fuck, thought Val.

"But I'll give you the guy's name and the last address in Denver I had for him," said Devereaux. "There's a piss stop coming up in about ten miles. Go ride with Henry for the rest of the night and talk to him about this apprentice shit. He'll explain to you why it ain't easy — why so few punks like you actually learn how to become long-distance drivers — but at least you'll keep the old redskin awake during our drive through the Colorado Rockies 'til dawn."

"Thanks" was all that Val could manage. His chest hurt for some reason.

Devereaux said nothing for the rest of the ride.

———

THE FORMER INTERSTATE REST stop was on a high ridge overlooking a desert valley ten or twelve miles across. Beyond that point I-70 rose into low, rocky mountains again, but Devereaux had shown Val on the truck's GPS altimeter that it was essentially all downhill into Colorado after this final climb.

Below in the starlit and moonlit valley, a dirt road ran twenty or so miles from the south, passed under the Interstate overpass built just for it, and ended at a scorched area that had once been an Indian-run general store, gas station, and a few huddled houses and trailers. Those were gone now, even the windbreak of trees north of the absent structures burned away.

Also gone were the restroom facilities at this high ridgetop turnout. Someone had blown them up more than a decade ago, although why someone would come way out here in the middle of nowhere and waste ammunition or C4 or dynamite on blowing up a restroom, Val had no idea. That's just the way things were everywhere. Once vandalism turns into wholesale destruction, his grandfather was always pointing out—a society tearing itself apart from the inside, as it were—it was hard to stop the dynamic. There were now trucker-dug slit trenches in the shrubs where the men could shit, slit trenches in the higher junipers on the south side of the turnout for women, and rocks overhanging the cliff face where the men pissed.

Val found his grandfather standing back from the edge, shifting from foot to foot in the chilly pre-winter night wind. Val knew that Leonard wouldn't join the drivers and other men in pissing over the edge. Leonard was shy that way. Val knew that the old man would hold it in all the way to Denver if he had to.

"I'll be riding with Henry Big Horse Begay the rest of the night and into Denver," he told Leonard.

His grandfather hesitated as if deciding whether to permit it, realized that Val hadn't asked for permission, and nodded. With his skinny silhouette, his hands tucked in the pockets of the inadequate windbreaker, and his long white hair blowing in the cold wind, Leonard looked *old* to Val—really old, aged during this trip, King Lear old.

Val, who'd already pissed alongside Gauge Devereaux and the other men—enjoying watching his stream of urine joining the others arcing out in the moonlight, brighter ribbons against the dark, desert-varnished cliff face beneath them — spent another minute standing alongside his visibly tired, cold, and unhappy grandfather.

"Val, have you been watching satellite-TV news coverage of the fighting in Los Angeles?" his grandfather asked, voice dropping as if the topic were toxic.

"No. Devereaux doesn't even have a TV in his cab. Still bad?"

"Worse. The city seems to be coming apart for good."

Good, thought Val. He'd hated L.A. every day of the five years and eleven days he'd spent in it. His hope had been that a new Big One would swallow it completely, but this scorched-earth fighting would suffice.

"The governor has declared martial law and is asking Washington for help," continued his grandfather. "But there just aren't any resources to commit to the fight."

Good, Val thought again. He said, "So your pal, Emilio whatshisname, and the *reconquistas* aren't taking over like they thought they would, huh?"

"Evidently not," said Leonard, glancing at the clumps of drivers smoking and talking and showing no eagerness to get back into their heated cabs. "It's a good thing we both got out when we did, Val."

Tell me something new, Leonard. Val nodded and zipped up his old leather jacket. Julio had given him an old indie-trucker ball cap and he wore that now constantly, even when he slept, pulled low. "Have you given any more thought to what Mom's password might've been, Grandpa?"

He saw Leonard hesitate and wasn't sure what it meant. He'd told the old man about the encrypted material deliberately, of course, figuring that Leonard — who was great at cross-word puzzles and basic cryptography in the first place — might have a clue as to some word that would have been important to his daughter. But it wasn't *necessary* for Val to have that huge clump of text, or text and images, or video, or whatever the hell it was, decrypted.

Val already had enough proof that his father had somehow conspired to murder his mother and must pay the penalty for that.

He reached back and felt the Beretta snug in his belt against his back.

"I have given it some thought," said Leonard. "I may have some suggestions when we're together next. This is our last night before we reach Denver—if all goes well in the Colorado mountains—so are you sure you want to ride with this Mr. Begay?"

"Yeah," said Val. Then, almost without volition, he asked, "Grandpa, do we have two hundred bucks left?"

"Yes...yes, we have more...wait, Val, do you mean new dollars or old dollars?"

"Old dollars."

Leonard looked shocked. "No, of course not. I spent almost everything I had—that we had—to get us on this convoy, Val. You know that. For what, may I ask, do you need two hundred old dollars, almost three hundred thousand new bucks?"

Val almost smiled at the old man's determination not to let a preposition dangle. Or was that a participle that dangled? *Fuck it.*

"Something really important," he said. "Something that might let me be a trucker."

"Well, that might be a laudable goal someday, Val. Although I'd hoped that, with your intelligence and general acumen, college might be..."

"I don't want it *someday*, Leonard," he said, letting his disgust at the old man's slowness be heard. "I want to leave Denver with *this* convoy on Sunday. But I'd need two hundred old bucks to make it happen. Maybe a little more." *Never mind that Devereaux said that it'd take weeks or a month to get the fake Teamster-approved NICC anyway. It's the principle of the thing with Leonard that's important.*

His grandfather merely shook his head. "I don't have it, Val. Not close. Not nearly close. We barely have enough to get by for a day or two once we get to Denver. I only hope your father is there and reachable."

"Why wouldn't he be?" said Val, thrusting his own balled-up fists deep in the pockets of his leather jacket. "He's a fucking flash addict. He'll be there, all right. He just won't be awake or able to talk or remember who the fuck *we* are. Oh, yeah, it's gonna be a great reunion. Just don't have your hopes up that Nick Bottom's gonna feed us and give us shelter and pay our way, Leonard. He's a flash-junkie fuck-up and has been for years."

Realizing that part of his anger came from flashback withdrawal that was hitting him as well—he was sure he had a one-hour vial left, but the empty vial suggested that someone else must have found and used it, so Val hadn't flashed for almost forty-eight hours now—Val turned his back on his grandfather and walked toward the huddle of truckdrivers, hunting for the tall, old Indian.

———

THEY CROSSED THE COLORADO state line around midnight.

Bandits were not a problem in Colorado for a convoy this large and security-protected and the *reconquista* armies only conducted nuisance raids this far north, but all but fifty or so miles of I-70 across half the broad state before Denver were through serious mountains, and lack of federal and state maintenance had turned the highway into its own obstacle. Twenty-five years earlier, Begay told him, a convoy of heavy trucks would have covered the 243 miles between Grand Junction in the west of the state to Denver in four hours—less if there were no Smokies waiting to pounce.

Now the trip took twelve hours. On a good day or night.

This was a good night, Begay grunted. The weather was holding. Pretty soon snowstorms would close Loveland Pass for the winter, and that was the end of the relatively easy I-70 access from Utah to Denver. After Loveland Pass closed, said Begay, truckers would have to take the northern route to Salt Lake City and then take I-80 across Wyoming to Cheyenne and then south to Denver, adding hundreds of miles to the trip.

"Can't they keep the pass plowed?" asked Val. "Just keep it open during the winter?"

Begay barked his Navajo laugh. "Who's to pay for the plows and workers, kid? The state of Colorado? It's been bankrupt longer than the federal government of the United Fucking States of Fucking America. Besides—there are other passes between here and there, including Vail Pass, that'll be closed for good after the first couple of serious snowfalls."

"Wasn't there a tunnel?" asked Val, remembering something his old man or grandfather had said.

Begay nodded, his face all sharp, chiseled edges and points in the amber light from the dash instruments. He usually wore a black cowboy hat, but tonight it was just a band to hold his long hair back. "Yeah, the Eisenhower Tunnel at about eleven thousand feet. It went under the Continental Divide about sixty miles west of Denver. Two tunnels—one eastbound, one westbound. They were about a mile and a half long but they saved that last miserable fucking climb up Highway Six over Loveland Pass. I think the summit of the pass we'll go over tonight is... I don't know, around twelve thousand feet."

"What happened to the tunnels?" asked Val and immediately wished he hadn't. The lack of sleep and flashback withdrawal were making him stupid.

Begay just laughed. "One of the first things the motherfuckers blew up when things got weird after the Day It All Hit The Fan. Took the state and feds a year and a half to repair just one of the tunnels, get traffic flowing across the nation again in winter... three weeks later, they blew it up again. Pretty soon, like everything else in this fucking country gone down the drain, they just quit trying."

Val nodded, trying to stay awake. "If the pass is just a thousand feet higher," he said, voice thick with fatigue, "it shouldn't make that much difference. Should it?"

Begay barked his laugh again. "You'll see, kid. You'll see."

The highway was all but empty except for their convoy and a rare convoy headed westward. The quarter-moon and stars seemed very bright against the permanent snowfields that soon showed up on the peaks to either side.

Begay didn't have a TV in the cab either but he kept his

pirate radio blaring through the night. Val was used to the officially sanctioned sat radio stations—NPR, CNR, MSBR, VOA—but what Begay called his pirate radio pulled in a lot of unlicensed, fuzzy AM and FM pirate stations that blasted away through the night.

Most of them were right-wing talk radio, outlawed for years, and old Begay seemed to drink the crap up.

Val half dozed to the singsong revival-preacher-sounding right-wing polemics being shouted out by the all-night talk-jockeys, interrupted only by weird call-in programs where the people calling in were crazier and more right-wing than the radio announcers.

"The radio stations and announcers and engineers and shit have to keep moving," Begay said at one point. "Stay one step ahead of DHS and the other feds."

Val woke up for a few minutes at that but then started dozing to the rhythms of the radio gabble again.

"...no, we weren't always like this, friends. Thirty years ago... twenty-five years ago, even...we were still a great nation. A united nation. Fifty full states, fifty stars on the flag. We chose decline, my friends. We chose national bankruptcy and the bankruptcy of forty-seven states to keep the government's entitlement programs going... seventy-three percent of the population pays no taxes at all, my friends, but still expects cradle-to-grave health care, cradle-to-grave guaranteed employment with a minimum wage of four hundred and eighty dollars an hour, thirty-hour workweeks—when anyone chooses to work in this great, lost, botched, ruined nation of ours...and retirement at age fifty-eight with full Social Security benefits, even though there are now eighteen nonworking retirees in this country—including the eleven million illegal immigrants who've just received the most recent amnesty and citizenship—yes, eighteen nonworking retirees for every working American in this country that's forgotten what hard work really is..."

The voices droned on. Val half slept.

Just a few hours beyond Grand Junction, they ran into one of the reasons that it took twelve hours rather than four to get from Grand Junction to Denver.

Just past an abandoned husk of a mountain town called Glenwood Springs — with food distribution all but broken down except for major cities, little towns across the nation had just dried up, but especially impossible-to-get-to-in-winter *mountain* towns — there was a twelve-mile stretch of canyon, Begay said, that had been one of the most spectacular dozen or so miles in the entire continental U.S.'s grid of Interstate highways.

No more.

What had been double ribbons of elevated two-lane highways, the westbound lanes rising forty feet above the eastbound lanes for miles and miles, punctuated with lighted and well-ventilated tunnels through stubborn outcroppings of the sheer cliffs that rose more than a thousand feet on either side, slicing the sky into a thin sliver of stars, was now a narrow two-lane gravel road, filled with potholes and hard curves around fallen boulders and tumbled sections of the Interstate itself, where the convoy crept and bounced and jounced along in low gear beside the churning, dam-broke, no-longer-harnessed Colorado River.

But after ninety minutes or so to get through those twelve miles, they were back on battered but serviceable concrete and asphalt again and Begay was shifting up through the gears.

"God, I'd love to learn how to do that," said Val.

Henry Big Horse Begay looked at him and then back at the road and taillights ahead of them. "What? Shift gears? There's sixteen forward gears on this lovely baby. Four back. That's what you want to learn? How to shift and split gears on a big rig?"

"Just how to drive a truck," said Val. The fatigue and withdrawal were working on him like sodium pentothal. Or just turning him into a baby again, he thought.

Begay nodded. "Yeah, Gauge said that you was going to ask me that. The answer's yes... maybe. I'll give you a week or two's tryout, riding shotgun. Learning the gears. You can pay me as we go. Providing you got the NICC, of course."

"I don't," said Val. He was very close to tears. If he started blubbering like a baby here, he thought he might throw himself out the door toward the white-watered Colorado churning by to their right. "I won't have one," he managed. "No fucking money to buy one with. And no fucking time."

"Time?" said Begay.

"Devereaux says it takes weeks…sometimes a month… to get the NIC Card, even when you can pay for it. You guys are leaving…when? Sunday morning in the middle of the night sometime?"

"For Chrissakes, kid. I wasn't talking about this weekend. I'm coming back through Denver in late October, right before Halloween. You got the NICC then, I'll give you a week or two probation. No promises, though. You fuck up the way I think you probably will, I'll leave you by the side of the goddamned road. That's a damn promise."

Val could only stare and keep himself from bawling after all.

Begay turned the radio up.

"…*that president pursued a policy that flattered and encouraged our enemies, alienated our allies, and abandoned Israel to be destroyed by a country that had nuclear weapons that* we could have prevented, my friends! *The United States could have prevented the Islamic Republic of Iran…the heart of the current Global Caliphate…from ever having those weapons! Now that country… and that Caliphate…have thousands of atom bombs and this country, after our big deal with the Russians five years before that country went belly up, has, by the final START treaty, twenty-six bombs.* Twenty-six! *And no way to deliver 'em and no* will *to deliver 'em and…*"

Val dozed off.

THEY CAME OUT OF the mountains above Denver at about ten o'clock in the morning. The roar of gears and engine had wakened Val during the climb over Loveland Pass and it would always remain one of the most terrifying things he'd ever experienced.

The long 6 percent and steeper grade of the last dozen miles or so out of the mountains toward Denver, the high-rises gleaming in the midmorning light ahead, was all lower-gear, high-revving engines braking by compression, and the stink of overheated brakes. Two of the trucks in the convoy had to use runaway truck ramps.

And then they were down. Val could see other cars on I-70 and the adjoining roads and highways. It was the first real traffic they'd seen for hours. It made him dizzy.

"One thing I gotta ask you before we seal this maybe deal," said Henry Big Horse Begay, switching off the radio. This close to a major city, it was NPR and the other official stations.

"What's that?" asked Val. He was terrified that the Indian was going to renege on his offer. With a month to get the $200 old bucks—maybe steal it from the Old Man before shooting the bastard, although Val doubted that the old flashback addict would have that much anywhere—and then to get the NICC, he might just be ready for Begay.

"That piece you had in your belt in the back and been shiftin' around, furtive-like, all night so it wouldn't dig into your back or side or gut. You ever shoot it?"

Val hesitated. Finally, not knowing what the right answer was, he said, "Yeah."

"Not at a goddamned target or rabbit or some such, I mean," said Begay, taking his full attention off the road ahead and laying it on Val. "I mean at a living person. A man."

"Yeah," breathed Val.

"Hit him?"

"Yeah."

"Kill him?" Begay's eyes were flinty lie detectors.

Val tried to swallow. Couldn't.

"Yeah."

They were approaching the interchange with I-25, but the old one had been blown up. There was a temporary gravel ramp. The convoy was shifting down, bouncing down the grade in unison.

"Did he deserve it?" asked Henry Big Horse Begay.

Val started to answer with the same syllable he'd been using and then stopped. This question had been most of what had kept him awake at night the last week. He cleared his throat.

"I don't know," said Val. "Probably not. But I think it was either him or me. I chose me."

Begay drove south on I-25 in silence for several minutes.

"All right," he said at last. "I'm gonna be coming back through here—Ăttsé Hashké permitting—around October twenty-seven. Supposed to be at the big loading docks at the South Broadway GOVCO Center all that afternoon. I'll look for you. Schedule now says the convoy leaves at eight p.m. You ain't there, I won't ever look for you again."

"I'll be there," said Val.

1.13

Santa Fe, Nuevo Mexico— Thursday, Sept. 16

THE REST OF THE VOYAGE to Santa Fe had gone without incident with paramilitary "technicals"—pickups with large-caliber machine guns mounted in the back—escorting them the last seventy miles or so from Las Vegas, NM, to Santa Fe.

The three mercenaries, Sato, and Nick stayed at the Japanese consulate in Santa Fe, formerly the old La Fonda Hotel right on the plaza. Joe's remains were taken into the basement of the complex for cremation.

Upon arrival, Sato had led Nick and the others to the consul's medical clinic—better equipped and more modern and clean than any medical facility left in Denver, Nick was sure; while Nick and the others had a quick checkup, Sato had his burns and cuts treated and his serious fracture was set into one of those expensive new polymorphic sports casts—a smart-cast, they called it, too expensive for any Americans other than the top athletes, or rather, those athlete templates for their digital avatars— that allowed full use of the arm even as the bones healed.

Nick's interview with Don Khozh-Ahmed Noukhaev at his hacienda compound outside of town was scheduled for 10 a.m. The invitation had gone to Mr. Nakamura and the specifics were clear—neither the Oshkosh vehicle nor Hideki Sato was to come within ten miles of the don's home. Nick had been told to be at the St. Francis Cathedral—formally, he knew, the Cathedral Basilica of St. Francis of Assisi (and, Dara had told him when they'd come to Santa Fe on vacation early in their marriage, the cathedral which the archbishop spent his life seeing constructed in Willa Cather's *Death Comes for the Archbishop*)—at 9:30 a.m. Alone.

The half-block walk from the consulate to the cathedral took Nick about one minute. And that only because he dawdled to study the 145-year-old church from a distance before crossing the street to stand on its stairs. Nick remembered Dara telling him that the French Romanesque cathedral with its twin towers was begun by French-born archbishop John Baptiste Lamy around 1869 and discontinued and dedicated in 1887 without the spires because they'd run out of funds.

It had always looked odd—doubly truncated—to Nick Bottom.

It was a warm, sunny day and Santa Fe smelled as it always had to Nick in the autumn: a mixture of the sweet aroma of burning piñon pine logs, dried leaves from the tall, ancient cottonwoods that lined many of the streets in the old section, and sage. Dara had once said that there wasn't a better-smelling city in all of the United States.

Back when Santa Fe was *in* the United States.

Now, Nick knew, the wealthy city wasn't part of any nation. Nuevo Mexico claimed titular control of the town, but Santa Fe had enough money to hire its own small army to maintain its independence. Besides still being a second-home capital for movie stars, famous writers, and Wall Street types, Santa Fe had received heavy Japanese investment in recent years and the Japanese didn't choose to live in a Mexican village.

So Santa Fe had become a modern small-town version of World War II's Lisbon, with spies, double agents, retired soldiers of fortune, and international ne'er-do-wells like Don Khozh-Ahmed Noukhaev making the lovely little adobe-cottage mountain town, nestled in its fragrant valley at the foot of the

Sangre de Cristos, one of their homes and their center of operations.

The black Mercedes S550—all-electric or super-expensive hydrogen drive—whispered to a stop at the curb. There were three men in the car, all dressed identically in white Havana shirts; their race might be hard to pin down, Nick thought, but their profession was easy to see. They were hard men. Hard beyond the everyday hardness of mere mercenaries. These were fifth-generation killers from another continent.

The man in the backseat opened the curb-side door and beckoned Nick inside.

Nick didn't speak and neither did any of the three men in guayabera Cuban shirts—the kind of formal, perforated white shirts a Cuban might wear to a funeral—as they drove north out of the city on Bishops Lodge Road.

Nick knew this bumpy old backroad ran for about six miles to the little crossroads village of Tesuque, once the address of more than a few aging movie stars and starlets. This was a good place to hide large homes in the hills above the narrow, heavily forested valley, and Nick assumed that Don Khozh-Ahmed Noukhaev's hacienda would be one of those compounds between Santa Fe and the Tesuque crossroads.

It was.

About four miles out, the Mercedes turned to the right, followed a narrow gravel road up a runoff gully, and came out onto a wider, asphalt-paved driveway that switchbacked up to the top of the hill, moving from a cottonwood forest to brown-grass meadow and then back into pine forest again. Nick noticed camouflaged bunkers set back along the switchbacks; assuming that this driveway was the main way in, this would be an eminently defensible position against vehicles or ground forces.

It turned out that the don's hacienda had more security levels than Mr. Nakamura's mountaintop mansion. There were three walls with gates—the half-mile spaces between the walls and fences true killing zones, covered by visible towers and inevitable hidden gun positions—and two CMRIs for the car and three for Nick and his minders on foot.

Once they reached what he presumed was the main build-ing, Nick was sent on into a blastproofed windowless room where more men in guayaberas fluoroscoped him, frisked him, and cavity-searched him. He was in a truly foul mood by the time the last guayabera'd guard silently led him into a huge room with tall windows and told him to take a seat. Because of the bookcases and gigantic leather-topped desk, Nick assumed that this was Don Khozh-Ahmed Noukhaev's study.

The first thing I have to do when he comes in, thought Nick, *is ask him what I can call him. That Don Khozh-Ahmed Noukhaev business gets old fast.*

Nick had taken a seat but rose when the door opened and someone entered, but it wasn't the don. Four more guards came in, the tallest, oldest man coming straight at Nick and signify-ing silently that Nick should raise his arms again.

"You've got to be kidding," said Nick. "The other guys have already..."

He didn't see the guard behind him or the knockout taser. But he felt it.

His last thought, falling, before his neurons became as totally and painfully scrambled as his nerve endings, was... *Fuc...*

Then he was gone.

———

NICK CAME TO IN slow stages, as one always does after being tasered. The first stage was confusion followed by a slow and muddled focus on trying not to urinate down your own pant leg. The second stage was pain and twitching and a little less confusion. The third stage for Nick now was trying to breathe.

He was trussed up, ankles and wrists—hands in front of him, which had allowed for some circulation—and blindfolded and gagged and there was some sort of cloth over the top half of his body. It took him a minute or two to realize that he hadn't gone deaf; there were sound-deadening earphones over his ears.

But he could still tell that he was in a moving vehicle. Vibration and the body's sense of balance as the vehicle took turns and jounced over rough parts told him that. So he was either in the trunk or backseat of a truck or car, being driven… *somewhere.*

More security or am I a hostage? wondered Nick when he could put together a full thought. Neither made much sense—why invite him to the hacienda and then shanghai him to another meeting place? Hell of a way to treat a guest. But what value did he have as a hostage? Did Don Khozh-Ahmed Noukhaev possibly think that Nakamura would pay to get him back?

Or did the Chechen don believe that Nick might know something important? If that was the answer, Nick knew that there was probably a short future ahead of him and one that might include torture as well as execution.

Do I know anything that could be important to this Russian gunrunner, drug dealer, and would-be empire maker? If he did, Nick sure couldn't think of what it might be.

As a former cop, Nick knew that the knockout tasers usually kept their targets unconscious for about fifteen minutes (if, as was more common than civilians knew, they didn't cause a heart attack or stroke or leave you a drooling vegetable or just kill you outright). If he could time his heartbeats, he might be able to figure out how long the drive would be from the hacienda to wherever he was going to end up.

As if knowing that's going to help you, dipshit, Nick told himself. *Sato and his boys won't be coming in like the cavalry with guns blazing. The don's men made damn sure there were no tracking beepers on or in me and even if Sato was watching the hacienda by satellite or drone, they almost surely drove a dozen trucks out at the same time, all going different directions. Sato'd have no way of knowing which vehicle I was in.*

It didn't matter anyway, Nick realized. His heart was pounding so hard and fast that it was useless as a timekeeper. A lot of hostages, he knew, died when gagged and restrained—again through heart attacks or suffocation brought on by asthma or even a head cold, often through gagging on their own vomit. He tried not to think about any of those things and to slow his heart rate. He might need the adrenaline later; he didn't need it now.

They're taking me to a landfill.

That was probable, he realized, but why? Then Nick wondered how many millions or billions of men throughout history had died with that one syllable as their last living thought—*Why?*

Don't get philosophical on me now, shithead. Plan your next move.

The vibration stopped. A moment later, strong hands grabbed him, pulled him up and out of something, and set him on his feet. He felt someone cut or release the binders around his ankles.

Nick saw no reason to pretend that he was still unconscious. He stood there blind and deaf and swaying. With hands around both his arms, gripping hard through the heavy bag fabric, he was half lifted, and propelled across what felt like gravel, then perhaps inside a structure and onto a hard surface—Nick's lower body was outside the bag and he could feel a difference in the quality of air around him, more still, *interior*—and then down a corridor with a tiled floor, then down steps, then down another corridor.

They stopped and pressed him to sit.

The bag was removed, the earphones, the gag and blindfold, and finally the wrist binders.

Nick did the usual blinking against the light and yawning to get more air. He did resist rubbing his chafed wrists.

The men who released him—wearing guayaberas like all of Don Khozh-Ahmed Noukhaev's other chattel—left by one of the two doors.

It was a small room, windowless, bare walls, with an old metal desk in front of Nick and a few battered metal filing cabinets against one of the walls. Nick was sitting on a light metal-frame chair and there was a second one behind the desk. Both were too flimsy to be of much use to him. He thought that the place might be the basement office of a high school gym coach, save for the absence of trophies.

I'm the trophy, thought Nick.

There was nothing on the desk or atop the filing cabinets

that he could use as a weapon. Nick had just struggled to his feet—still swaying—in preparation for going through the desk drawers and cabinets to find something, anything, that he could use when the second door opened and Don Khozh-Ahmed Noukhaev came through, striding quickly to his place behind the desk.

"Sit down, my friend. Sit down," said the don, waving Nick back into his seat.

Nick stayed standing and continued swaying. "I'm not your friend, asshole. And after that ride you can put me down as one of your enemies."

Noukhaev laughed, showing strong, nicotine-stained teeth. "I would apologize, Nick Bottom, but you are man enough and smart enough not to accept my apologies for such indignities. You are right. It was barbarous of me and unfair to you. But warranted. Sit, sit, please."

The older man sat but Nick remained standing. "Why was it warranted?"

Don Khozh-Ahmed Noukhaev was quite a bit older than the photos which Sato had shown him would have indicated. Nick wondered how many years it had been since Nakamura's people or any law-enforcement or intelligence agency had managed to get a photo of this man.

"A good question," said the deeply suntanned and wrinkled don, folding his hands on the metal desktop. "I would answer sincerely that nothing could warrant such treatment of a guest, Nick Bottom, but you are, of course, something more than a mere guest. Your employer, Mr. Hiroshi Nakamura, has reasons—good reasons, both political and strategic—for wishing that I no longer existed. He also has, under his control, certain orbital hyperkinetic weapons that the Japanese whimsically refer to, I believe, as gee-bears. Have you heard this term?"

"Yes," said Nick, suspecting that Noukhaev knew all about Sato's use of the things against the tanks the day before.

"So you see," said the don, "it was tempting fate to give Mr. Nakamura *absolute* knowledge of my presence at the hacienda at any specific moment on any specific day." He grinned.

"Yes, you are thinking, Nick Bottom—*This man is paranoid*—and I would agree with you. I ask myself only, *Am I paranoid enough?* Please sit down before you fall."

Nick sat before he fell.

Don Khozh-Ahmed Noukhaev was reminding him of someone. He got it almost at once—Anthony Quinn, that twentieth-century movie actor that he and Val had liked—not so much because Noukhaev *looked* like Quinn, but because the voice and slight accent were similar, the quirk of the mouth into an arrogantly amused smile was similar, and because Noukhaev was hard to place ethnically, the same way that Anthony Quinn had played Mexicans, Indians, Arabs, and Greeks. The don also had a powerful body resembling the late actor's—compact but broad-chested, massive forearms, a man's strong hands.

Nick said, "So where are we now?"

Noukhaev laughed as if Nick had made a joke. "Somewhere safe. Somewhere that I believe even your omnipotent Mr. Nakamura does not know of."

"He's not *my* omnipotent Mr. Nakamura," Nick said sourly. "And if he *were* omnipotent, he sure as hell wouldn't have had to hire me to help find out who killed his kid."

"Exactly!" cried Don Khozh-Ahmed Noukhaev, holding up one brown finger. "Why did he hire you, Nick Bottom?"

"I have a hunch *you* want to enlighten me on why Naka-mura hired me," said Nick.

"You must know, Nick Bottom," said the don. "And if you do not know, you must suspect."

"I suspect everyone and no one," said Nick. He'd wanted to say that line since he was nine years old. Nick guessed that it was probably the oxygen deprivation while he was gagged and bound that prompted him to say it now.

Don Khozh-Ahmed Noukhaev squinted at him for a silent moment. Then the older man threw his head back and laughed uproariously.

Shit, he is nuts, thought Nick.

Noukhaev opened a lower desk drawer, removed a box, offered the box to Nick. Cigars. Nick shook his head and the don chose one for himself, went through the usual stupid ritual of biting, spitting (Nick had learned through movies that more sophisticated types cut the ends of the cigar off, or had their butlers do it), and lighting the expensive stogie with a lighter he produced from his khakis' pockets.

Nick still thought the room was in a basement or deep underground, but the ventilation was very good. He got only a slight whiff of the cigar smoke.

"Why would one of the most powerful men on the planet hire you, Nick Bottom?" Noukhaev said rhetorically. Nick hated it when speakers got rhetorical. It insulted your intelligence.

"Nakamura has already carried out multiple investigations of his son's murder," continued the don, sitting back in his chair and exhaling blue-white smoke. "The Denver police—both before and after you—the CBI, the FBI, Homeland Security, his own security people, the Keisatsu-chō…"

If the Japanese National Police Agency had investigated Keigo Nakamura's murder, it was news to Nick. For most of its history the Keisatsu-chō had just overseen and regulated local Japanese police departments—mostly setting standards, a bureaucracy with none of the powers of the FBI, not even agents or officers of its own—but in the last few decades since It All Hit The Fan and Japan had ended up on top (or at least *near* the top), the National Police Agency had grown real teeth, both with its new secret-police security agency, the Keibi-kyoku, and its overseas intelligence agency, the Gaiji Jōhō-bu. Beyond knowing their names and hearing and reading that the agency's subdepartments were lethal, Nick knew nothing about them.

"…and then Mr. Nakamura hires you, Nick Bottom," Noukhaev was concluding. He seemed to be enjoying the cigar. "Why do you think he did that?"

Full circle, thought Nick. He said, "Obviously not to solve his son's murder, Don Khozh-Ahmed Noukhaev. That leaves… what? To set you up as a target in this meeting at your hacienda so Mr. Nakamura could gee-bear you to dust and ashes? But there's a problem with that, isn't there?"

"What is that, Nick Bottom?"

"It was *you* who called Nakamura's people and suggested this meeting," said Nick. "At least that's what Hideki Sato told me. So Nakamura couldn't have known when he hired me that you'd be inviting me down here."

Noukhaev nodded and exhaled more smoke. "Very true. But, Nick Bottom... 'Know thy self, know thy enemy. A thousand battles, a thousand victories.' Do you know who said that?"

"It would have to be Sun Tzu, Don Noukhaev."

"Ahh, you know Sun Tzu, Nick Bottom?"

"Not in the least," said Nick. "But I've met a hundred arrogant, condescending bastards playing the big, tough, intellectual generals who go around quoting him as if it meant something important."

Don Khozh-Ahmed Noukhaev froze, cigar halfway to his mouth, and Nick thought—*Shit, I went too far.*

He didn't care.

Noukhaev threw his head back and laughed again. It sounded sincere.

"You are right, Nick Bottom," growled the don after finishing his laugh and inhaling his smoke. "I was patronizing you. You were right to call me on it. But Sun Tzu *did* say that, and it *does* apply to our...ah...situation here. Hiroshi Nakamura *is* a general and he *does* know his Sun Tzu. He might well have hired you simply because he knows that I would be tempted to talk to such an underling...no offense intended, Nick Bottom."

"None taken," said Nick. "So is that why Nakamura hired me? If so, I guess my job's at an end. And I failed, since if Sato and his boss watched the various trucks or Mercedeses or whatever leaving the hacienda at the same time, they'd probably know you were taking me somewhere else and call off the gee-bear strike."

"There were eleven vans that left the hacienda at the same moment thirty-nine minutes ago, Nick Bottom," said the don. "Hiroshi Nakamura has the resources to hit a hundred targets with his kinetic missiles. Allowing time for you to be brought into the place and for me to enter, the orbital weapons should be arriving about...*now.*"

Nick glanced at the ceiling. He couldn't resist the impulse. Nor could he stop his testicles from trying to climb back up into his body. He'd seen what six gee-bears could do.

"Do you play chess, Nick Bottom?" The don's eyes looked serious.

"Sort of. I guess I could be called a chess-duffer."

Noukhaev nodded, although whether that was a confirmation that there was such a stupid term, Nick had no idea. The don said softly, "As a chess player, Nick Bottom, even a beginner, how would you improve the odds that Nakamura *not* use his weapons on the eleven possible targets?"

"I'd have each of them go to some important, public, crowded, and—if possible—historic spot," Nick said at once. "And unload the trucks out of sight. At the St. Francis Cathedral, say, or the Loretto Chapel or the Inn of the Governors... places like that. Nakamura might still do it—what do American historical sites and American casualties mean to him or Sato?—but it might give him pause."

Don Khozh-Ahmed Noukhaev smiled slowly and it was a different sort of smile than any he'd shown Nick before. "You are not as stupid as you look, Nick Bottom," said the don.

"Neither are you, Don Khozh-Ahmed Noukhaev."

There was no hesitation this time before Noukhaev's laugh, but Nick decided to quit pressing his luck.

"No, I do not believe that Hiroshi Nakamura hired you just so that he could locate and kill me, as much as he wishes and thinks he needs to do that. No, Nakamura hired you, Nick Bottom, because he knows that you may be the only man alive who can actually solve the crime of the murder of his son, Keigo."

What's this? thought Nick. *Heavy-handed flattery?* Nick didn't think so. Noukhaev was too smart for that and—more important—he already knew that Nick was as well. What, then?

"You need to tell me why I'm the only man who can solve Keigo's murder," said Nick. "Because I don't have a fucking clue—either to who did it or to why I'd be the one to know."

"'The one who figures on victory at headquarters before

even doing battle is the one who has the most strategic factors on his side,'" said the don and this time there was no game-playing about the provenance of the quotation.

Nick shook his head. He wanted to tell Noukhaev just how much he'd always hated people who spoke in riddles — it was one reason he wasn't a Christian — but he resisted that impulse. He was tired and he hurt.

"Hiroshi Nakamura knew when he hired you that you probably could solve the crime that none of the American or Japanese agencies — nor his own top people — could solve," said the old don. "How could that be, Nick Bottom?"

Nick hesitated only a second. "It has to be something about me," he said at last. "About my past, I mean. Something I know. Something I encountered when I was a cop...something."

"Yes. Something about you. But not necessarily something you learned when you were a detective, Nick Bottom." The don had pulled what looked to be a mayonnaise lid from the desk drawer and continued to flick his cigar ashes into it. It was almost full.

I could have used a real ashtray as a weapon, Nick thought stupidly.

"Something in my past, then," said Nick. He shook his head. "That doesn't make sense."

"Because of whom you do suspect as being behind the murder," said Don Khozh-Ahmed Noukhaev.

"Yeah."

"And who is that?"

"Killers from one of the Japanese...whatyacallthem? *Daimyo*s. The other corporate lords in Japan who want to be *Shogun*."

"Do you know the leading *keiretsu* warlord clans?" asked Noukhaev.

"Yeah," Nick said again. "I know their *names*." He'd known them before Sato had recited them to him during the drive down. Why *had* Sato recited them to him? What was *that* bastard up to?

Nick said, "The seven *daimyo* families and *keiretsu* clans running modern Japan are the Munetaka, Morikune, Omura, Toyoda, Yoritsugo, Yamahsita, and Yoshiake *keiretsu*."

"No," Noukhaev said flatly, no joking or feigned friendship in his voice.

"No?" said Nick. This stuff was common knowledge. It had been true even back when he was a working homicide detective with his whole department looking into the Keigo Nakamura murder. Sato may have lied to him, but...

"The *keiretsu* have become *zaibatsu*," said the don. "Not just interrelated, clan-owned industrial conglomerates, as in the late-twentieth-century *keiretsu*, but *zaibatsu* again—clan-owned corporate conglomerates that help win the war and guide the government, just as in the first empire of Japan a hundred years ago. And there are eight leading *zaibatsu*-clan *daimyo*s running Japan. Not seven, Nick Bottom, but eight. Eight powerful men who want to be *Shogun* in their lifetimes."

"Nakamura," said Nick, naming the eighth super-*daimyo*. Was the don just being a wise-ass, or did this correction mean something?

"Both the Denver PD and the FBI thought that the key to Keigo Nakamura's murder had nothing to do with local suspects—the mooks I've been reinterviewing—but with internal Japanese politics and rivalries," said Nick. "We just didn't know enough about those politics or deadly rivalries to make any sort of educated guess, and interviews with Mr. Nakamura and others didn't help. Those *keiretsu*... or what you're now calling *zaibatsu* again... are essentially above the law in modern-day Japan, or maybe I should say modern-day *feudal* Japan, so the Japanese police authorities weren't of any help either."

Don Khozh-Ahmed Noukhaev gave that toothy, not-really-amused smile again and flicked cigar ashes into the mayonnaise lid. "You don't even really know who Hideki Sato *is*, do you, Nick Bottom?"

"He's Mr. Nakamura's chief security guy," said Nick, willing to play the stooge to get more information from this egoist.

Noukhaev laughed softly. "He's a professional assassin and the head of his own *daimyo* family—one of the top forty *daimyo*s in Nippon today and not necessarily out of the line of becoming *Shogun* on his own. Have you heard of Taisha No Shi?"

"No," said Nick.

"It means 'Colonel Death,'" Noukhaev said. "Do you remember Soong Jin?"

"Not really. Wait...that Chinese actress-turned-warlord about eight years ago?"

"Yes," said Noukhaev, drawing deeply on his shortening cigar. "Soong—that's her family name—was China's last, best hope for reuniting. After she left the movies, she had an army of more than six million fanatics, plus the support of four or five hundred million more Chinese. She also had about six hundred bodyguards, including sixty or so of the best security people in China."

"And she died in...I can't remember. Some sort of boating accident," said Nick.

Noukhaev's smile looked sincere for a change. "She died when Taisha No Shi—the man you know as Sato—went to China and killed her," said the don. "Whether on Nakamura's orders, we do not know."

"Colonel Death," repeated Nick, drawing out the syllables. "Sounds cheesy to me. But if you're suggesting that Sato works without Nakamura's permission and direction, I find that hard to believe."

Noukhaev nodded slowly. "Still, Nick Bottom, you need to appreciate that one of the foremost assassins in the world has been assigned to stay with you during your...ah...investigation. Were I in your position, I would treat that fact with sobriety and ponder its implications."

"Whatever you say," said Nick. He was tiring of this asshole's sense of self-importance. "Do you want to tell me something I can use about Keigo Nakamura's murder?"

Noukhaev smiled thinly. "I just did, Nick Bottom. 'If ignorant both of your enemy and yourself, you are certain to be in peril.'"

More fucking Sun Tzu, thought Nick. He was beginning to realize that it was Don Khozh-Ahmed Noukhaev who was acting like a second-rate Bond villain. They always tried talking the hero to death rather than just pulling the trigger when they had a chance.

"Can you tell me any questions that Keigo asked that seemed unusual?" asked Nick to change the subject. "Odd? Out of the ordinary?"

Don Noukhaev smiled. "He did ask me if I would distribute F-two the way I've distributed flashback. His tone suggested that the fantasy drug was a reality...or would soon be one."

F-two again, thought Nick and something in him leaped with the hope that Keigo Nakamura had known something no one else did about the fantasy-directed superdrug. With F-two, Nick's imagination could structure a whole new life with Dara and even with Val, not the surly sixteen-year-old Val but a cute little five-year-old. As Nick understood the promise of the drug, with Flashback-two, there would be no bad memories, only happy fantasies that *felt* as real as real life. On all levels. And the F-two believers always insisted that unlike being under the flash—where you were always a little separate from the experience, floating *above* your original self even as you reexperienced things—F-two would be totally immersive.

"What did you tell him?" asked Nick.

Noukhaev laughed. "I told him that I'd sell and distribute any drug that people wanted, if it were real...which F-two isn't. We've all heard the rumors of it forever. It's an impossible drug. Take heroin or cocaine if you want fantasies, I told him."

"And what did Keigo Nakamura say to that?" asked Nick. Part of him was crestfallen that the rumors of F-two were still just fantasy rumors. *But Keigo asked the poet Danny Oz if he would use F-two. What the hell was Keigo Nakamura up to?*

"Keigo changed the subject," said Noukhaev. "Which I am going to do as well. Are you aware, Nick Bottom, of who wants all this land that used to be New Mexico, Arizona, and southern California?"

"I would take a wild guess and say Mexico...or Nuevo Mexico or whatever the hell the *reconquistas* call themselves hereabouts," said Nick. "Given that it's their goddamned troops, tanks, and millions of colonists squatting on most of it and fighting for the rest."

Noukhaev blew blue smoke and shook his head. The lined, rugged face looked mildly disappointed — an aging tutor discouraged by his pupil's thickheadedness. "You've truly been away, haven't you, Nick Bottom? Lost in your flashback dreams and your incessant self-pity? The first man ever to lose a wife."

Nick felt his face flush and his anger grow, but he held it down, attempting to ignore the adrenaline surge that made him want to smash in Don Khozh-Ahmed Noukhaev's head with...

With what? The chair he was sitting on was the only loose thing in the room that he could use as a weapon, and it was just too damned light to be of any real use. And Nick had no doubt whatsoever that Noukhaev had a pistol in his belt under that loose white shirt he wore outside his trousers.

But Nick didn't have to answer the rhetorical insult and decided to change the subject.

"All right," said Nick. "If not Mexico, who? Japan?"

"What would Japan do with all this space — mostly desert — with *their* declining birthrate?" asked Noukhaev, obviously enjoying his little performance as schoolteacher. "I know that foreign events isn't your forte, Detective First Grade Nick Bottom, but put your addled shoulder to the wheel... think! What aggressive and thriving political entity needs *Lebensraum* and more *Lebensraum?* And is *used* to deserts?"

"The Caliphate?" said Nick at last. It was not a statement, just some dumbfounded syllables. He heard himself repeat the idea. "The Global Caliphate? Here in the Southwest? That's... absurd. Absolutely ridiculous."

Don Khozh-Ahmed Noukhaev clasped both hands behind his head and leaned back in his chair, the cigar firmly clamped between his strong teeth. He said nothing.

"Worse than absurd," said Nick, waving his hand as if batting away a fly. "Impossible."

But... was it?

The world's Muslim population, according to CNN or Al

Jazeera–USA or wherever the hell Nick had heard it, had just reached 2.2 billion people. Of those, according to polls the network had quoted, more than 90 percent claimed membership in the Islamic Global Caliphate, even if they were in nations that weren't yet technically part of the expansive regime with its tripartite capitals in Tehran, Damascus, and Mecca.

That meant, especially after almost a decade of the full civil war in China and India's aggressive moves toward achieving a huge middle-class population (largely through restricting population much as the Chinese had three generations earlier), that the Islamic Global Caliphate was the most populous political entity on earth. And the birthrate of Muslims, someone had once told Nick—perhaps it had been his pedantic father-in-law—could now be charted in terms of what he'd called an asymptotic curve. The most common birth name in Europe had been Mohammed for more than twenty-five years now, which meant that it had been so even before the Caliphate was officially established there.

Hell, thought Nick, feeling his brain cells still reeling from the tasering, *the most common baby name in fucking* Canada *is Mohammed.*

That didn't mean anything. Did it?

"The Caliphate moving into southern California and Arizona and New Mexico? Sending…what?…*colonists* here? Immigrants?" Nick said dumbly, his tongue thick. "The United States would never stand for it."

"Oh?" said Don Khozh-Ahmed Noukhaev. "And what could the United States do about it?"

Nick opened his mouth angrily…thought a moment… and then shut his mouth. America had a standing army of draftees of a little more than six hundred thousand kids like his son, but poorly armed, poorly trained, and poorly led, mercenaries all as they fought for Japan or India in China, Indonesia, parts of Southeast Asia, and South America. The dregs of the regular Army and the National Guard were overextended just guarding the southern border with Nuevo Mexico from the Colorado–Oklahoma state line to the Pacific Ocean near Los Angeles.

Could a U.S. president break the all-important mercenary contracts with Japan and the other hiring nations and bring that leased-out army home to fight a million or so immigrant jihadists? *Would* she?

Nick felt very dizzy. "Mexico wouldn't stand for it," he said flatly. "The *reconquistas* fought too hard to retake these states, to undo the eighteen forty-eight American land grabs."

Noukhaev laughed and stubbed out what was left of his cigar. "Trust me, my friend Nick Bottom, this Nuevo Mexico you speak of does not exist. You are talking to someone who has traded with it, worked with it, and moved within its confused borders for more than twenty years. Nuevo Mexico is a marriage of convenience—a *fictional* marriage of convenience—between leaders of murderous drug cartels, fleeing land barons from Old Mexico, younger speculators, and spanic warlords as loyal only to themselves as are the Chinese warlords. *There is no Nuevo Mexico.*"

"It has a flag," Nick heard himself say. Even the tone of his voice sounded pathetic.

Noukhaev grinned. "Yes, Nick Bottom, and a national anthem. But the fiction that is Nuevo Mexico is as corrupt and rotten from the inside as Old Mexico was before its fall. The 'colonists' here cannot feed themselves, much less replace the large American ranches, farms, high-tech corporations, science centers, and civilian populations that they have occupied and overrun. They would starve in a month without food supplies from the cartels. They survive by sucking at the tit of cartel money—cocaine money, heroin money, flashback money. If that tit is denied them, eighteen million former Mexican 'immigrants' will be on the move again."

"But...the Caliphate," said Nick. "They don't have the... the...language, the culture, the infrastructure..." He heard what he was saying and shut up again. He shook his head. "Who would *sell* the Southwest to the Caliphate?"

Noukhaev lowered his chin to his white-shirted chest and smiled in a way that could only be called diabolical.

"Me," he said. "Among others."

Nick blinked and really looked at the man across the desk from him. Don Khozh-Ahmed Noukhaev wasn't joking. Was he insane? A megalomaniac, yes...Nick had known that from the earliest parts of this crazy conversation...but fully insane?

Maybe not, thought Nick.

"Who would do the selling?" repeated Nick, speaking more to himself now than to the don. "Not Nuevo Mexico, although their military forces and new colonists here will be in the way."

"No, not really," said Noukhaev. "No more in the way than, say, the native populations and so-called armies of Belgium, Norway, Denmark, and European Russia. The new Islamic owners of all those former nations have gained much experience in efficient expansion in the past three decades."

"But still...," muttered Nick, his nerve ends twitching and misfiring from the tasering. "Who would do the real selling? Who would get the billions of old dollars involved in such a..."

Nick looked up and met Noukhaev's dark-eyed gaze. "Japan," he said softly.

Don Khozh-Ahmed Noukhaev opened his callused palms.

"Not the country of Japan," Nick said. "But the *keiretsu* and the *daimyo* who has most control here in the States when the time comes to make the deal with the mullahs in Tehran and Mecca. The new *Shogun*."

Noukhaev was no longer smiling, merely staring. The gaze burned into Nick. He could feel it like a finger of fire against his face.

"A sort of second Louisiana Purchase," murmured Nick. "But millions of Islamic colonists in former U.S. states? America would...never stand for it."

Nick's voice had been dropping from lack of conviction even before he finished the sentence. America had stood for *a lot* in recent decades. More to the point—what could it do to stop an organized and Caliphate-backed colonization of these desert states? America hadn't been able to keep the territory out of the hands of the Mexican cartels in the first place.

Will they bring their own camels? wondered Nick. He rubbed his eyes with the heels of his hands. He suddenly had one hell of a headache.

"I have been a poor host," said Noukhaev. "Are you thirsty, Nick Bottom? Shall I call for some wine?"

"Not wine," said Nick. "Just some water."

Don Khozh-Ahmed Noukhaev seemed to be talking to the desktop when he spoke in low, conversational tones. "Please bring some water for my guest and myself."

A minute later, the side door opened and a guayabera-wearing man came in carrying a silver tray upon which were a crystal carafe of water, so filled with ice that it fogged the crystal with its cold, and two crystal glasses.

Noukhaev poured for both of them.

"Please," said the don, gesturing. Nick waited, holding the cold glass. He couldn't remember a time when he'd been this thirsty or when his head had hurt quite this much. Both, he imagined, were byproducts of the tasering.

But he didn't drink.

Don Khozh-Ahmed Noukhaev laughed easily and drained his entire glass of ice water. He poured more for himself.

Nick sipped. No taste, chemical or otherwise. It was water.

"Can I ask some questions now?" asked Nick. "That was supposed to be the purpose of this meeting."

"By all means, Nick Bottom. *You*, after all, are the investigator. This is what Mr. Hiroshi Nakamura has said, and Mr. Hiroshi Nakamura is seldom wrong. Please, please, ask your questions."

Noukhaev extracted a second cigar, prepared it, lit it, and sat back in his chair smoking it.

"Do you know who killed Keigo Nakamura?" asked Nick, his voice flat and hard. But the effort of speaking drove white-hot spikes of pain into his aching head.

"I believe I do," said Don Khozh-Ahmed Noukhaev.

"Will you tell me?"

"I would prefer not to," said Noukhaev with a small smile.

Bartleby, thought Nick. Dara had introduced him to the

wicked and memorable Melville story with that sad and memorable repeated line. He thought that the full title had been *Bartleby, the Scrivener: A Story of Wall-Street.* Either way, right now Nick envied the little scrivener who could just roll over on his cot and turn his face to the wall of his prison. *And die,* remembered Nick.

"Why not?" he asked, voice still hard. "Just tell me what you know or what you think you know. It'd make everyone's life a hell of a lot easier. Especially mine."

"Yes, but *you* are the investigator, Nick Bottom," the don said again, this time through the haze of blue smoke. "In the first place, I might be wrong. In the second place, I would never deny you the triumph of identifying the murderer or murderers yourself."

Nick shook his head to clear it. "We know that Keigo Nakamura came down with his little video documentary team five days before he was murdered. His assistants said Keigo interviewed you on camera. Is that true?"

"Yes."

Why would you allow such a thing? Nick thought, squinting at the older man. Why would a gunrunner, drugrunner, information seller, and international expediter of all things illegal allow himself to be interviewed, on camera, by the son of one of his greatest enemies — perhaps a deadly enemy — for a stupid documentary on Americans and their flashback addiction?

Nick struggled to put the question into a few clear words and then gave it up. His head hurt too much for such efficiency. Instead, he said, "Did Keigo say something — or ask you something — while he was here that made you want to kill him? That *required* he die?"

"No to your first question, Nick Bottom. A sad but total yes to the second question."

Nick rubbed his brow as he worked that out. "So Keigo said something here that caused *someone* to have to kill him. That's what you're saying?"

Noukhaev inhaled cigar smoke, enjoyed it, expelled it. He said nothing.

"That something was on the memory chip of his camera?" Nick asked.

"Oh, yes," said the don. "But that is not why Keigo Nakamura had to die the way he did, when he did."

"What *is* the reason, Don Noukhaev?"

The don smiled, shook his head sadly, and flicked ashes into the makeshift ashtray.

"Someday," Noukhaev said at last, "you must look into the kind of documentary the young Nakamura was really making. Why would the scion of a modern *zaibatsu* clan almost sure to produce the next *Shogun* come to America to waste his time documenting useless flashback addicts...no insult intended, Nick Bottom."

"None taken," said Nick. "You tell me what Keigo was doing with his little documentary, if it wasn't to document American flashback use. I've seen hours and hours of the unedited rough footage. It's all about how people use flashback."

"*All* about that?" said the don.

"That and how the dealers get it...how the drug itself is transported into the country and sold. That sort of stuff. But all related to flashback and Americans using it. Are you suggesting that there's a *hidden* film in his footage...a movie within the movie or something? Something telling us to expect this F-two you mentioned? Are you suggesting something like that?"

"I suggest nothing," said Noukhaev. "Except that, regrettably, our time together is growing short."

Nick sighed.

"But you think the one who gave the order to kill Keigo is one of the seven family *daimyo*s competing with Nakamura for the *Shogunate?*"

"I did not say that." Noukhaev turned his cigar around and blew the ash into flame.

"If I guess and give my reasons, will you confirm or deny the names?"

Noukhaev laughed his broad, aggravating laugh. Nick had had just about enough of it.

"Investigators do not *guess*, Nick Bottom. They deduce. They eliminate the impossible and improbable until only the inevitable remains."

"Bullshit," said Nick.

"Yes," grinned the large-knuckled don.

"But *you* invited *me* to this meeting," said Nick, more thinking aloud than communicating now. "If you're not going to help me with the investigation, then you must have brought me here—and put yourself in some danger from Nakamura's gee-bears—because you want to send him, Nakamura, a message."

Noukhaev smoked his cigar.

Nick sipped more water. "Or maybe a message to Sato," he said at last. "Were you serious about Sato being his own important *daimyo* in Japan? Colonel Death and all that? Ten thousand ninjas or samurai or whatever at his command?"

Nick hadn't expected an answer but the don said, "Yes."

"So, you're saying, Sato's *also* a player in all this. That he might have his own motives and not just be a mindless Nakamura vassal...someone who will commit *seppuku* at Mr. Nakamura's order."

"Oh, Hideki Sato will commit *seppuku* at once upon his liege lord's command," said Noukhaev. No smile. "*He has already done worse than that.*"

Nick wondered what could possibly be worse than being ordered to disembowel oneself. Much later, he realized that if he'd asked that question of Noukhaev then, the entire mystery would have been solved. Instead, he said, "And Sato's really an assassin?"

"Oh, yes."

"Why would Nakamura assign one of the world's top assassins to spend so much time with me? To risk such a valuable man's life by sending him down here through enemy-held territory, with me, so that I could see you, Don Khozh-Ahmed Noukhaev? Sato was almost killed when we were attacked, you know."

Again, Nick was sure that there would be no answer to this ill-shaped, amorphous question, so he was deeply surprised when the don replied so earnestly.

"When you solve this murder, Nick Bottom—*if* you solve this murder—for the short period of time they will allow you to remain alive, perhaps just hours, more probably mere minutes, you will be the most dangerous man on earth."

Nick set down his water glass. "Dangerous to *whom*, Don Noukhaev? To just the murderer and his *keiretsu?* Or *zaibatsu* or whatever the hell it's called today?"

"Much more dangerous than that," Noukhaev said softly. "And to many more people. To millions of people. Which is why they cannot allow you to live once you solve this crime."

Me, dangerous to millions of people? That made no sense, no matter which way Nick turned it. He was totally at sea. Nothing explained anything to him and everything he heard made his head hurt more and his insides feel more queasy.

"Then I'd better not solve the fucking crime," Nick said at last. His voice came out slightly slurred, as if he'd been drinking vodka rather than water.

"But you *must* solve this crime, Nick Bottom." The don didn't seem to be bantering or waxing sarcastic. His voice was as low and as serious as Nick had heard it.

"*Why* must I solve this crime?" Nick had gone for a sarcastic tone, but it had come out merely tired-slurred.

"Because she would have wanted you to," said Noukhaev.

Nick sat up straight in his uncomfortable metal chair. *She* would have wanted him to?

"Who's 'she,' Noukhaev?"

"Your wife, Nick Bottom," said the don, flicking ashes with a relaxed move of his hairy wrist. "The lovely lady named Dara."

Nick was on his feet, his hands balled into his fists. On his feet but swaying slightly. "How do you know my wife's name?" Stupid thing to say, Nick realized at once. Noukhaev must have multiple dossiers on him, compiled as soon as Nakamura had hired him. He shook his head and tried again.

"What's my wife got to do with anything? Why bring her into this?" Nick put a fist onto the desktop to help steady himself. The don had remained seated.

"Your wife, Dara Fox Bottom, was a beautiful woman," Noukhaev said in low tones. "She sat right there...in the same chair that you just vacated..."

Nick swiveled awkwardly to look down at his empty chair. When he turned back to Noukhaev, he had to set both fists, knuckles first, onto the don's desk to keep from falling.

"Dara here? Why? When?"

"The day after Keigo Nakamura interviewed me," said Noukhaev. "Four days before the young Mr. Nakamura was murdered in Denver. He and his retinue had already flown home by the time your wife met with me."

"Met with you...why?" managed Nick.

The room was spinning now. *The water*, thought Nick. No, not the water. Noukhaev had drunk the water. Something in the glass that interacted with the water. Something slower-acting than the fucking taser, but just as sure.

"The man she came to Santa Fe with and stayed with at the Inn of the Anasazi while they were here," Noukhaev was saying from a thousand miles away, his voice rattling and echoing down the quickly closing tunnel. "That assistant district attorney Harvey Cohen. He was a man of little or no imagination. But your lovely wife, Nick Bottom...your lovely wife, Dara, *she* was..."

Whatever his lovely wife Dara was, had been, Nick never heard it from Don Khozh-Ahmed Noukhaev.

Nick had already begun the long slide down the dark tunnel into blackness.

1.14

Denver and Las Vegas, Nevada: Friday, Sept. 17 — Sunday, Sept. 19

DENVER WAS STILL STANDING when Nick got back on Friday evening. Most of Denver, at least. Some group had blown up the Denver branch of the U.S. Mint on West Colfax, near Civic Center Park.

Why the U.S. still *had* a mint, Nick had no idea. No one used coins any longer. So the destruction of that particular ancient landmark had been of interest only to the terrorists who built the bombs and to the five bored guards who'd been blown apart in the middle-of-the-night blasts. It was the sort of information that Nick and a million other Denverites had learned to file under *Ignore and Forget*.

What did get Nick's attention immediately upon stepping naked out of the shower was a ten-minute-old text message from Detective First Grade, Lieutenant K. T. Lincoln: "Nick — Everything checked out okay. No worries. No need to see each other. *Mami*."

The *"Mami"* was their old cop-partner code for "Must Arrange Meeting *Immediately!*" and also signified that all preceding sentences in the message meant the opposite of what they said. It was an I'm-under-some-duress code.

Something was very wrong.

Nick phoned her cell and got her message voice telling callers that she was on duty, so leave a message and she'd get back to them.

"Just back in town and checking in," Nick said, working on the closest he could get to a bored tone of voice. "Glad everything's okay. Call me when you get a chance. Oh, I broke my old phone and have a new number." He gave her the number of the onetime phone he'd dug out of a duffel hidden behind the wallboards. After her return call, he'd pitch the thing.

Fifteen minutes later, K.T. phoned. "I'm supervising a stakeout and ESU thing over here on East Colfax. But it's gotta be over before eleven-thirty because the ESU guys have to get their van back. I'll meet you at midnight at that place where that guy did that thing that time." She broke the connection. Nick was sure that she'd used a onetime as well.

Getting dressed, Nick checked the clock on his cubie's TV. Just after 9 p.m. He had almost three hours to kill. He'd use some of that time speculating about just what the hell K.T. could have turned up that would call for such an urgent get-together.

NICK HAD BEEN CONSCIOUS by the time Don Khozh-Ahmed Noukhaev's people had dropped him off in front of the cathedral. Legs shaky, his insides quaking with anger, Nick had walked the short block to the Japanese consulate.

He'd assumed that Sato and the other Japs at the consulate would be so eager to hear what the don had said to him that the interrogation would go on all that afternoon and night, moving to sodium pentothal and other so-called truth drugs if Nick didn't give them everything they wanted. But there was no interrogation.

Sato, his right arm looking slick-wet in the active sling, had come to Nick's room, knocked, walked in, and said, "Did you learn anything important from Don Khozh-Ahmed Noukhaev? Anything that could help our investigation?"

Biting the inside of his cheek, Nick had looked up at Sato

349

and said, "I don't think so." That was a lie, but *how much* of a lie wasn't quite clear yet.

Sato had just nodded and said, "It was worth a try."

A few hours later, when Nick awoke from his nap but was still feeling drained and stupid, Sato invited him to dinner at Geronimo, a famous upscale restaurant that he and Dara had loved (and saved up to enjoy during their annual visits to Santa Fe). Without pondering why Hideki Sato would take him out to dinner at such an expensive spot, Nick accepted. He was hungry.

Geronimo was as Nick had remembered it — a small adobe building that had been a private home in 1750, its entrance area dominated by a large central fireplace with a mantel topped by both a huge floral display and a giant pair of moose antlers — but the restaurant itself was small. Since it was cool and raining out that evening and the porch dining area closed, the small interior seemed crowded. Luckily, given Sato's girth, they were seated in a corner banquette all to themselves. The two men said little. Nick was finished with his first course — Fujisaki Asian pear salad with sweet cashews and cider honey vinaigrette — and was halfway through his main course of filet mignon "frites," the hand-cut russet potato fries alone worth killing for, when the memory of his last time here with Dara struck him.

He felt his chest ache and his throat tighten and, like a fool, he had to set down his fork and sip water — Sato had ordered a bottle of Lokoya '25 Mount Veeder Cabernet Sauvignon for the two of them at a price just slightly less than Nick's last full year's salary as a police detective — and pretend he'd bitten into something too spicy to hide his tears and flushed face. Nick's strongest wish at that moment was that he could immediately go back to his room at the consulate and use one of the last one-hour vials of flashback he'd brought along to call back his dinner at this restaurant with Dara nine years ago. The ache and need was more than mere flashback withdrawal, it was an existential matter: he didn't belong *here* and *now*, eating this fine food with this huge hulk of a Japanese assassin, he needed to be *there*, *then*, with his wife, sharing a wonderful meal with *her* while both of them looked forward to going back to their room at La Posada.

Nick sipped water and looked away until he'd blinked away the idiotic tears.

"Bottom-san," Sato had said when both were eating again, "have you considered going to Texas?"

Nick could only stare at the big man. What the hell was *this* about?

"Texas doesn't accept flashback addicts," he said softly. The tables were very close together and Geronimo's was a very quiet restaurant.

"Nor do they execute them as do my country, the Caliphate, and some others," Sato said. "They only deport them if they refuse or are unable to drop their addiction. And the Republic of Texas does accept *rehabilitated* drug and flashback addicts."

Nick set down his wineglass. "They say that getting into Texas is harder than getting into Harvard."

Sato grunted that male grunt of his. What it signified still escaped Nick. "True, but Harvard University has little use for important life skills. The Republic of Texas *does*. You were an able law-enforcement officer, Bottom-san."

It was Nick's turn to grunt. "*Was* is the proper tense of that verb." He squinted at the big security man—or Colonel Death assassin and *daimyo*, if he were to believe Noukhaev. "Why the hell do *you* care, Sato-san? Why would you—or Mr. Nakamura—want me in Texas?"

Sato sipped his wine and said nothing. Gesturing toward the emptied plates, he said, "I will be wanting dessert. You also, Bottom-san?"

"Me also," said Nick. "I'm going to try some of that white chocolate mascarpone cheesecake."

Sato grunted again, but the grunt sounded like approval to Nick's wine-sotted ears.

THE RETURN TRIP TO Denver had been totally uneventful, thanks mostly—Nick felt sure—to the two black Mercedeses that

Don Khozh-Ahmed Noukhaev had sent along as "escort." Why Sato would trust them to serve that function, Nick had no idea, but with one black limousine eighty meters in front of them and the other eighty meters behind on the Interstate, no one bothered them, even though they'd seen dust clouds suggesting tracked vehicles both to the east and west of their highway.

Sato had ridden in the front passenger seat while "Willy" Mutsumi Ōta drove, "Bill" Daigorou Okada handled the topside gun, and "Toby" Shinta Ishii sat in the back in a fold-down chair opposite Nick. For the first hundred miles or so, Nick could not put the image of the back of the first M-ATV Oshkosh—all flames, the metal and plastic interior walls melting, with "Joe" Genshirou Itō's headless body turning to ash and burned bone in seconds—out of his mind. But when they passed the ambush site north of Las Vegas, NM, he relaxed. Soon he'd taken off his helmet and set his sweaty head back against the webbing and closed his eyes.

What had Noukhaev been trying to tell him?

The last night at the Japanese consulate, Nick had spent six of the eight hours of his sleep period using the last of his flashback. Most of the time he'd spent with the now-familiar hours with Dara—the dialogues just after Keigo was murdered where she *seemed* to be trying to tell Nick something (and where Nick, absorbed in his own job and the murder case, and in himself, had paid no attention to her attempts).

But to tell him what?

That she'd been having an affair with Harvey Cohen? That seemed the most likely. But what could have brought Harvey and her to Santa Fe four days before Keigo's murder? Obviously it had something to do with Keigo Nakamura and his little movie, but what? And what interest could District Attorney Mannie Ortega have had in Keigo? What could be so important that they'd send an ADA and his research assistant all the way to Santa Fe?

Nick would just have to ask Ortega—now Mayor Ortega—when he got back.

As for all that crap about selling New Mexico, Arizona, and southern California to the Global Caliphate...

Nick opened his eyes and, using the Oshkosh's comm uplink, used his phone to log on to the Internet. Shinta Ishii was paying no attention to him. Nick slipped his earbuds in place, shifted the screen to display inside his sunglasses, and surfed.

He had argued to Don Noukhaev that the Islamists wouldn't come to North America because these desert states overrun by the *reconquistas* lacked infrastructure.

But looking at the data, Nick realized that if the Islamic Global Caliphate had shown anything in its last quarter century of expansion, it was that it had no respect or use for local languages, cultures, laws, or—other than milking the European or Canadian welfare states dry—infrastructure. They brought language, culture, laws, and their religious infrastructure with them. And much of that infrastructure was from the Middle Ages: tribes, clans, honor killings, and a murderous religious literalism and intolerance that neither Christianity nor Judaism had practiced for six hundred years or more.

And the core of the expanding Islamic infrastructure, Nick was reminded as he flicked from page to page, was *sharia* for those people who lived within its confines, for both Muslim human beings and the only partially human (under *sharia* law) infidel Dhimmis alike, and outside of that, the House of War stood aimed like a poised and poisoned spear at all those unbelieving nations and cultures around it.

Nick went to the proper archives page and saw that the Caliphate now boasted more than 10,000 nuclear weapons, easily surpassing Japan's 5,500.

It took him thirty seconds of searching to see that the United States, after its proud unilateral disarmament (in START agreements with Russia, but in competition only with itself) in the second decade of this century, now was reported to have 26 nuclear warheads on aircraft or missiles and another 124 in storage—none of them less than fifty years old, all unreliable and untested and largely undeliverable.

Nick surfed and saw the image so often shown on TV of the sickle—"crescent moon" was the way proud Global

Caliphate leaders always described it—of Muslim cultural and overt political dominance that spread from the Mideast through Eurasia and Eastern and Western Europe to the north, down and east through Africa in the south. The other crescents swept from Indonesia through much of the Pacific regions— coexisting with great tension alongside Nippon's New Southeast Asia Co-Prosperity Sphere. The larger European crescent swept through what had been the United Kingdom and across the polar regions, the tip of the scythe now deeply embedded in Canada. The Canadians had been willing—almost eager— to "share the wealth" of their northern part of the continent. Their religious creed of state-enforced multiculturalism and diversity—long having replaced Christianity in Canada—had, in less than two generations, produced a single minority-driven theocratic culture which eliminated all diversity in its realms.

From what Nick was reading, the remnants of the white Canadian culture up there, despite still being numerically in the majority, more or less got by in isolated cantons—almost reservations. Even though Muslims constituted slightly less than 40 percent of the total population, *sharia* was now the primary law of Canada, and most of the whites there—both English- and French-speaking—had meekly accepted their roles as Dhimmis. They'd built the 3,800-mile border fence between Canada and the U.S.—erected to keep fleeing Americans out—in less than eighteen months.

Wherever the Caliphate rule had come in contact with the formerly pampered "First Nations"—the Indians and Eskimos treated with such extravagant political correctness in the late-twentieth and early-twenty-first centuries by the English- and French-speaking white Canadian majorities—those native peoples who wouldn't convert had been eradicated by their new Muslim rulers, mostly through starvation via the simple act by their new provincial masters of shutting off food supplies.

The so-called First Nations had lost their skill of feeding themselves through hunting and fishing.

After die-ought-if, after the Day It All Hit The Fan, when the U.S. ceased to be a serious trading partner and world power, and especially after the surprise attack that Tehran had called Al-Qiyamah (the Resurrection, Day of Judgment, and Final Reckoning, three days that removed Israel from all maps) and then by the global Islamic triumphalism that swept across all of Western Europe in less than a decade, Canada had turned to the Caliphate for trade and military protection. It had no other choice. Just as it had no choice now about the heavy Islamic immigration that had already changed Canadian laws and culture forever.

And now Nuevo Mexico would have no choice but to sell its *reconquista* lands back to...to whom?

Nick slaved his phone to the outside monitor views.

North-central New Mexico was sliding by on either side of the M-ATV—overgrazed fields with no cattle left, empty ranches, abandoned small towns, abandoned rail lines, empty highways. Except for the damage done to the high-prairie environment by more than a hundred years of cattle overgrazing and the minor tread-tracks vandalism of modern mechanized armies on the move, this area was almost as pristine as it had been to the first white explorers more than two centuries earlier.

Why shouldn't the Global Caliphate want this southern part of North America, even if they had to pay for it in a priced-to-sell second Louisiana Purchase? wondered Nick. It was the perfect place for a former desert people to colonize. And with the upper tip of the Islamic scimitar-crescent pressing down against the Canada–U.S. border to the north and now the lower tip thrusting up from Mexico against and into the cash-strapped and militarily impotent western states like Colorado, how long would it be until the two horns of the *sharia* crescent came together?

Nick had to ask himself the central questions—*Do I care? Do I give the slightest shit if this part of the country goes to the* jihadis? *It isn't even part of America any longer. Is there any reason in the world that I should give a damn if the Caliphate towelheads replace the Nuevo Mexico beaners as America's nasty new neighbors to the south? Or even as our new masters in Colorado, for that matter, replacing the fucking Japanese looking down on us from their fucking mountaintops? The Mexicans are all about drugs and corruption, the*

Japanese all about . . . well, all about Japan. Why should I care if it's a hajji *bureaucrat rather than a Jap bureaucrat running things? They'd be more efficient than the Mexicans and more honest than the Japanese. Word on EuroTel, Sky Vision, Al Jazeera, and the CBC is that the life of Dhimmis in old Europe and Canada is pretty damned easy.*

As long as the hajjis *leave me alone to spend my days and nights with Dara,* thought Nick, *is there any reason I should care if their stupid crescent-moon-and-scimitar flag flies over Denver's rotting gold-domed capitol?*

Nick had taken off his sunglasses, removed his earbuds, shut down his phone, and set his head back in the webbing so that he could sleep the rest of the way home.

————

THE PLACE WHERE THAT guy did that thing that time was all that was left of the old Tattered Cover bookstore out in the 2500 block of East Colfax Avenue. Colfax, which ran from the prairie to the east of Denver all the way through the rottenest parts of the city to the foothills of the Rockies in the west, was once called by *Playboy* — one of the early stroke magazines, now out of print for decades — as "the longest, wickedest street in America." It was true that it was one of the longest main streets in the country, but cops knew that it was mostly East Colfax that was the wickedest, if one judged liquor stores, run-down taverns, prostitutes, pimps, and really bad poets as proof of wickedness.

The Tattered Cover had been a huge independent bookstore in its day, before print-and-paper books just got too expensive to publish and the general population just too illiterate to read books. The old store had been across the street from Nick's Cherry Creek Mall Condominiums, but sometime in the first decade of this century, the bookstore had moved to this East Colfax location, where it quoted Longfellow in offering "sequestered nooks, and all the serenity of books."

The sequestered nooks were still there, but the serenity of books had been missing for decades now. The newer TC, across Colfax Avenue from the huge flophouse for the homeless that had been the once-proud East High School, was now a combination of flashcave and all-night beer joint. Oddly enough, many of the flashback addicts who inhabited the sequestered nooks of the lower levels of the cluttered old bookstore had come there to read: after they'd lost or sold their old books, they used flashback to relive the experience of reading *Moby-Dick* or *Lolita* or *Robin Hood* or whatever the hell it was for the first time again, somewhere on a cot here in the rotting confines of the once-great independent bookstore. "It's like that old zombie movie where the walking dead go back to the shopping malls," Dara had once said. "Their rotting brains associate the malls with a sense of well-being... like these flashers gravitating back to a bookstore."

"They're paying a fortune to flash on reading entire books" had been Nick's surly response. "How much of that expensive time do you think is spent reliving sitting on the can? For that amount of money, they could download quite a library."

"They don't want to download books and suck on yet another glass teat, as you would say, Nick, to read them," Dara had said. That was about as vulgar as she ever got, but she was emotional about books. "They want to *hold* them and *read* them. And nobody publishes the holding-and-touching kind of books anymore."

At any rate, TC was the place. Nick and K. T. Lincoln had been patrol officers when they'd responded to a call of a man with a gun. The Tattered Cover was still trying to keep itself going then by selling and trading moldy old used books, but some crazy-ass heroin addict had shown up waving a semiautomatic pistol and demanding that the store sell him a *new* book by some writer named Westlake who'd died more than a dozen years earlier. It seemed like a joke until the addict shot and killed the manager of the coffee shop and threatened to kill a hostage every half hour until the *new and original and never-before-read* Westlake novel was delivered to him.

It had been K.T. who'd gone in dressed as a FedEx delivery person carrying the new book in its parcel. In the end, she'd had to shoot and kill the addict, who'd been trying to unwrap the parcel with one hand while holding his pistol in the other.

Nick parked his gelding in the old parking structure next to the store, taking great care not to run over the scores of bundled, sleeping men and women on the slanted floors of the big garage—Kipling's "sheeted dead." Nick had put fifteen slugs into the hood, windshield, and tires of the old Government Motors wreck, but while he was traveling, Nakamura's people had replaced the tires, windshield, and central drive battery and the thing was running as well as it ever had. The gasoline engine had been shot to shit, but it had been mostly dismantled for parts many years ago. Nick sort of liked it that Nakamura's mechanics hadn't patched the many bullet holes. Usually when parking in an inhabited parking garage, Nick set the blue bubble on the roof to warn looters that there'd be a problem if they tried to strip this particular car, but now he just let the bullet holes in the hood send that message.

The TC was its usual badly lit, smelly labyrinth. Nick bought a beer in what had been the old bookstore's coffee shop and carried the bottle down a long twisting ramp to the lowest level, where there were tables and lights. Below that area were the flashcave cots and sleepers.

K.T. was waiting for him at their usual table. There was no one else—or at least no one conscious—in this part of the maze of old shelves, rotted carpets, and twenty-watt bulbs. Lieutenant Lincoln had set her battered briefcase on the chair next to her and there was a stack of folders in front of her.

When Nick sat down with a tired sigh, she said, "Are you packing, Nick?"

He almost laughed but then saw her eyes. "Of course I'm packing," he said.

"Put it here on the table," said K.T. "Just use the thumb and little finger of your left hand. *Now.*" She raised her right hand from beneath the table and let Nick see the 9mm Glock. It was aimed at his midsection.

Nick didn't protest or ask questions. He wore his holster on his left side under his leather jacket, butt of the Glock forward for a cross-body draw, and K.T. knew that. He lifted the pistol out gingerly, just as she'd directed, and put it on the table in front of her. She whisked it out of sight, setting it on the chair next to her big briefcase, and hissed, "Scoot back."

Nick scooted back.

"Get up real slow. Lift your jacket and do a full turn. Then show me your ankles."

He did what she'd said, pulling each trouser leg up to show her that he'd brought no ankle gun.

"Sit down," said K.T. "Stay scooted back there. Keep your hands spread open on your thighs where I can see them."

He sat and spread his fingers as she'd directed. Somewhere in the dark flashcave down the ramp behind him, a man screamed in flashback terror or ecstasy.

"All right," said K.T. "I'm going to be giving you three pieces of news. You may know all of it already. You may not. But you're not going to do a damn thing when you hear each piece but sit there with your hands still on your thighs like that. Understand?"

"I understand," said Nick. The Westlake-lover years ago had his pistol more or less aimed at K.T. when she'd pulled her piece from under her short FedEx delivery jacket and shot him five times before he could react. She might be a little slower now what with age and a desk job, but Nick wasn't going to bet his life on it.

Still holding her Glock low with her right hand, K.T. extended her phone with her left hand. "Least bad piece of news first," she said.

The faces of seven boys—each obviously dead, each obviously *shot* to death—flicked across the screen. The eighth boy's face was Val's.

Nick grunted and was halfway up out of his chair but the rising muzzle of K.T.'s Glock froze him in place. She silently gestured him back in his seat. Nick complied because of the gun, but more because of the photo of Val. It wasn't a crime-scene shot of a dead boy like the others, but clearly something scanned from a high school virtual yearbook. Val wasn't smiling in the photo, hadn't dressed well for it, and his hair needed cutting, but the picture, unlike the others, wasn't of a shooting victim. It kept Nick in his seat.

"What?" he managed after half a minute. "Tell me."

"Word came in about two hours ago," whispered K.T. "A flashgang of young punks tried to assassinate Daichi Omura in Los Angeles earlier this evening…"

"Omura the California Advisor?" Nick said stupidly. He felt as if his jaw and lips had been injected with Novocain.

"Yeah. The kids ambushed Advisor Omura and his retinue at some opening or the other in downtown L.A., the flashgang shooters firing from a storm sewer near the Disney Center." K.T. paused to take a breath. The muzzle of her Glock never wavered. "The flashgang was carrying a lot of firepower—almost all of it illegal…"

Them, thought Nick. The giant ants and the army Jeeps and trucks trying to find the queen ant's nest in the L.A. storm sewers. He and Val had loved that old movie.

"Advisor Omura wasn't seriously hurt and some of his detail whisked him away in a limo while his security people and some L.A. cops returned fire and killed six of the flash-gangers right there where the storm sewer opened onto the street," said K.T. "The seventh kid was found dead a few hundred meters away in the tunnels, shot three times. Do you know him?" She flicked through the photos again and stopped on the death photo of a teenage boy, eyelids half lowered with only the whites showing, mouth open, front teeth broken off, two visible entrance wounds in his chest—some sort of interactive face on the blood-soaked T-shirt—and a terrible wound that had torn his throat open.

"No," managed Nick. "I've never seen him before. You showed Val…"

K.T. waved away the question. "The L.A. juvenile-crime units say that Val ran with these boys…especially with this guy, Billy Coyne. Did Val ever mention him?"

"Coyne?" repeated Nick. He could taste vomit low in his throat. "Billy Coyne? No…wait, maybe. Yes, it's possible. I'm not sure. Val never talked much about his friends out there. Is Val OK?"

"There's an APB out on Val Fox, as he's known at his school," said K.T. "The LAPD haven't been able to trace his phone. Neither he nor your father-in-law is at Leonard Fox's address. We know he hasn't tried to call you today or tonight on *your* phone, but have you been in touch with him some other way, Nick?"

Nick was thinking, absurdly, and with pain—*I hate it that Val's not using my last name.*

"What? No!" he said, shaking his head. "Val hasn't called and I've been meaning to phone him but…I mean, I missed his birthday the other week and…no, I haven't been in touch with him. Is there any evidence that Val was in on this attack on Omura, or is it just a juvie-division hunch?"

"There must be some evidence," said K.T. "Homeland Security has a national watch for Val. Right now they're treating him as a material witness, but they and the FBI are serious about apprehending him."

"Jesus," whispered Nick. He looked K.T. in the eye. "You say this is the *least* bad news you have for me?"

K.T.'s brown eyes never seemed to blink. She was staring at Nick the way he'd seen her stare at perps they had to take down one way or the other. "What are you going to do, Nick?"

"What do you mean? Are you asking me to drop a dime on my son?"

"No," said K.T. "I think you need to bring him in if he shows up in person. You still have cuffs, don't you?"

It would have been wrong for Nick to have his DPD handcuffs, but he did indeed have some that had been part of his junior private detective kit when Nick had considered making money as a bounty hunter tracking down skippers who'd violated their bonds. He tried to envision slapping those cuffs on his son. He couldn't. But Nick realized that he was visualizing Val as he'd been when he'd last seen him, not quite eleven years old, his face still rounded by baby fat. Even this recent high school photo showed a different person.

Nick said nothing.

"DHS and the FBI and local departments won't mess around with him, Nick," K.T. was saying. "It says on the APB that he's armed and dangerous."

"Who says he's armed?"

"Galina Kschessinska," said K.T.

"And who the fuck is Galina Kschessinska?"

"Formerly Mrs. Galina Coyne. The dead Billy Coyne's mother. She once worked in an office that helped coordinate Advisor Omura's travel and security in L.A."

"So it was an inside job," said Nick. "Why would Ms. Galina Kschessinska know if Val was armed or not?"

"She told the LAPD that her son had told her that he'd given a nine-millimeter Beretta to Val. The pistol had fifteen rounds in the magazine."

And what's teenager Billy Coyne doing handing out 9-mil Berettas and why hadn't Ms. Kschessinska mentioned this to the cops before the massacre at the Disney Center? thought Nick. But he said nothing. If what the bitch said was true, then the "armed" part of the APB was appropriate. But the "dangerous"? Nick thought of how his son used to take his fielder's mitt to bed with him, like a stuffed animal.

"They're doing analysis on the two slugs taken out of Billy Coyne and the third one pried out of the tunnel wall behind him," said K.T., her voice a monotone. "But CHP Assistant Chief Ambrose, who I spoke to tonight, said the one he'd seen that came out of the wall was nine millimeter."

"CHP Assistant Chief Ambrose?" Nick repeated stupidly. "*Dale* Ambrose?"

"Yeah." K.T. had lowered the Glock to the tabletop and covered it with a newspaper, but Nick knew that it was still aimed in his general direction. "You know him?"

"Yeah. No. I mean—the Old Man helped train Ambrose here in the Colorado State Patrol. I think they had sort of a mentor-*sensei* thing going. I know the Old Man thought that Ambrose was going to be a good trooper. Then, a few years before my father was killed, Ambrose moved out to California. Remember when I went out to L.A. about nine years ago to transport that child rapist-killer back? I spent some time with Ambrose then and he and I have called each other for some help on things. Last time I heard, he was an assistant chief in the CHP."

362

"Maybe you should talk to him, then," said K.T.

"Yeah."

"Part of his job as assistant chief is to head up the CHP protection details for both the governor and the Advisor. It was Ambrose's guys, along with Omura's own Japanese security people, who exchanged fire with the kids."

"But not with Val," said Nick. "There's no evidence yet that *he* was there." His voice was hard-edged but hopeful.

K.T. shrugged. The APB on Val suggested that there was plenty of evidence to assume that Val had been in on the thing with his fellow flashgang members. With the state of DNA analysis these days, if Val had been in that tunnel and done so much as breathed, they'd have the evidence soon. Nick knew what K.T.'s shrug meant—*The night is young.*

Just the idea—fact—of Val being in an L.A. flashgang made Nick crazy. Denver's flashgangs, committing crimes of violence just so they could relive them again under the flash, were made up of some of the sickest fucks Nick and K.T. had ever dealt with. And the L.A. flashgangs were said to be much worse than Denver's.

Nick felt dizzy, almost as if he'd been tasered again.

"What else?" said Nick.

"You up to hearing the rest, partner?" asked K.T.

Nick blinked at the "partner." Either Lieutenant Lincoln was being viciously sarcastic or she'd seen how hard the news about Val had hit him. Maybe it was a bit of both.

"Yeah. Tell me."

K.T. slid a short stack of colored files toward him.

"You can read them without leaning or sliding closer," she said softly. She'd covered her right hand and the Glock with some sort of open catalogue or brochure. "Use just your left hand to turn the pages. Don't lift the whole file."

"Jesus, K.T.," Nick said disgustedly.

She didn't respond.

Nick read, slowly turning pages with his left hand. When he was done he said nothing.

They were copied pages of a report stating that Dara Fox

Bottom and Assistant District Attorney Harvey Cohen had shared motel and hotel rooms at least ten times in the five weeks previous to Keigo Nakamura's murder six years ago. Along with the bald statements were copies of Harvey's business credit-card statements and payment vouchers from the district attorney's office.

"This is bullshit," Nick said. He pushed the files back toward K.T.

"Keep them," she said. "How do you know they're bullshit?"

"This one voucher shows that Harvey and Dara shared a room at the Inn of the Anasazi in Santa Fe," he said, tapping the green folder. "I happen to know that they didn't. They had adjoining rooms there."

Now K.T. blinked. "Dara told you this?"

"No, but I've been using flash recently to see times when she tried to tell me that something was going on — not between her and Harvey, I don't think, but some special project that had them running around after Keigo Nakamura. Even down to Santa Fe."

"The invoices say that they shared a room."

"The invoices are bullshit," repeated Nick. "I know. I talked to someone at the Inn of the Anasazi yesterday. A maid who's been there about forty years and who remembers Dara being there six years ago. She liked Dara."

K.T. shook her head. "I don't get it. What were you doing in Santa Fe and how long have you known that there was a suspicion of Harvey and Dara sharing rooms together?"

Nick answered only the second question. "About thirty-six hours ago, Don Khozh-Ahmed Noukhaev told me that Dara had stayed at the Inn of the Anasazi with Harvey six years ago, one day after Keigo Nakamura had interviewed him, just four days before Keigo was whacked. I was in the city, so I dropped by the hotel and asked around. The dipshit at the desk wouldn't give me any information, despite me flashing my fake shield, but I found two old spanic maids who remembered Dara being there. The one old gal even remembered their room numbers — Harvey's and Dara's. Adjoining, but not the same room. Not even the same suite."

"Why would a hotel maid remember someone's room number after six years?" asked K.T. "Someone she only met once?"

"I told you," said Nick. "The maid, whose name was Maria Consuela Zanetta Herrera, *liked* Dara. They chatted and discovered, Ms. Herrera told me, that they both had boys named Val…although Maria's son's name was short for Valentín. And her son was twenty-nine while she remembered Dara saying that her boy was only ten."

"Sorry I doubted you," said K.T. She didn't sound sorry, only tired. "But, Nick, why would all these other hotel vouchers also be faked?"

"You haven't told me where this crap came from," he reminded her. "It almost looks like the kind of report you see submitted to or from a grand jury."

"It *is* part of a grand jury report," said his ex-partner. "Submitted to a grand jury but gathered during an internal investigation by the office of the district attorney in March, five and a half years ago. While Mannie Ortega was still DA."

"An internal investigation?" muttered Nick. He'd rarely been so confused. "Two months after Dara and Harvey were killed in the accident on I-Twenty-five? An interdepartmental investigation *and* grand jury looking into whether one of the assistant DAs was having an affair with my wife? That makes no fucking sense. None at all."

K.T. shook her head, as if in agreement. "The joint investigation wasn't looking into whether Harvey and Dara were screwing behind your back, Nick. It was looking into who killed Harvey and Dara."

"Who *killed* them?" whispered Nick. He was glad he was sitting down. As it was, he had to grab the sides of the old wooden chair to hold himself steady.

"I told you it got worse," whispered K.T. "Can you take this last part? I'm serious."

"Show me," growled Nick. "*Now.*" His tone told her how serious *he* was.

She slid the rest of the colored dossiers across the table toward him.

Nick scooted his chair closer and hunched over the table, flipping photocopied pages and reading. If K.T. wanted to shoot him, let her shoot him. Instead, she pulled the Glock out from under the concealing catalogue and holstered it. Four white-stubbled men wandered by, talking about books and heading for the flashcave cots in the darkened room at the base of the ramp.

Nick was looking at more than two hundred pages of grand jury paperwork. The secret grand jury had been seated by then district attorney Manuel Ortega in late February of the year Dara had died—seated less than a full month after her death—and the thrust of the investigation seemed to be that ADA Harvey Cohen and his assistant Dara Fox Bottom, while working on a DA department project that was still classified, had begun a clandestine love affair.

That DPD Detective First Grade Nick Bottom had learned about the affair and arranged to have his wife and her lover killed.

Nick sat back, his mouth open. He felt like screaming or moaning but knew that neither would help. Lieutenant K. T. Lincoln was watching him very carefully.

"K.T.... For more than five years I've tried to convince myself that Dara and Harvey died in a car accident. The facts stay the same. The old couple braked suddenly in front of them...the driver of the eighteen-wheeler behind them tried to stop, couldn't...the driver died in the fire. And nobody knew anybody else, nobody was connected to anybody. *That's what all the reports said*, remember?"

K.T. tapped the photo of the truck driver, her short fingernail making a sharp, ugly sound. "Do you recognize him, Nick?"

"Yeah, of course. Phillip James Johnson. I looked into it myself. He'd been a trucker for twelve years, no serious accidents, no safety violations. He just couldn't..."

"The name and most of his paperwork history were bullshit," said K.T. She slid another photo out of the heap. "Phillip Johnson was actually *this* man. Recognize him?"

It took the better part of a minute for Nick to do so. Even then he couldn't believe it was the same man as the truck driver. He set the photos next to each other. The second photo was of a man sixty or seventy pounds lighter than Phillip James Johnson—different facial structure, even allowing for the fat, different nose, different chin, different hair color…hell, even the eye color was different.

"The DNA showed conclusively that Phillip James Johnson was actually your old CI, Ricardo 'Swak' Moretti."

Nick kept looking. He'd used Moretti as a confidential informant when he'd still been a patrolman and a few times after he made detective. The petty crook's nickname of Swak came from his involvement in insurance scams—especially highway and street swoop-and-squats where the mob enlisted the "victims" just as they did for slip-and-fall claims. Moretti had never become a made man, just the kind of scumbag always found bottom-feeding near the real mob, always running errands for punks and hit men, always dreaming of a real score. But as a confidential informant, Moretti had been unreliable in most instances—not even worth keeping on a small dole that came out of the patrolman's or detective's own pocket. Nick hadn't talked to Swak Moretti in ten years. Longer.

He studied the photos again. Yes…it was possible. Something similar about the eye sockets and teeth—they hadn't fixed the teeth—but…

"This guy's undergone major plastic surgery," Nick said aloud, rubbing his cheeks and hearing the stubble scrape. "Why? The mob would never pay for such a thing. Swak Moretti was a nobody. And if you're paying a fortune in old bucks for cosmetic surgery, why make yourself fatter, with an uglier nose and bigger, dumber-looking ears? It doesn't make sense. Plus, I read the original DNA identification, K.T. It showed the dead driver was Phillip James Johnson."

"All good cover story," said K.T. "Including the plastic surgery. Somebody was setting your old pal Swak up as a hit man, weren't they?"

"It doesn't make any…," began Nick.

K.T. slid another stack of photocopies toward him. "We have phone records of you calling Moretti four times—twice in November of the year Keigo was killed, once in late December, a final time three days before the...accident...that killed Dara and Harvey."

Nick's head snapped back. "It didn't happen. I never phoned him."

K.T. touched the photo of the old couple who died when their Buick gelding had been struck first by Dara and Harvey's car, then by the truck that had burst into flames. "Javier and Dulcinea Gutiérrez," she said. "Their names were real. Only their citizenship status on their NICCs and local background histories were fake. They were brought in from Ciudad Juárez three weeks before the so-called accident. We have Swak Moretti's phone records arranging that as well."

"I never phoned Moretti," repeated Nick.

K.T. gave him the same look that he'd given to so many cornered and lying-through-their-teeth perps.

"Look, Nick," she said softly. "You're the one, just this week, who begged me to look into this stuff. I said it was an accident. I said 'Who volunteers for a swoop-and-squat where you're going to die?' You said...You owe me this favor, K.T. Look into it. So I did. Here it is."

Nick rubbed his cheek and chin again. "It doesn't make any sense. Even if Moretti was some sort of deep-cover hit man for the mob—and trust me, K.T., the asshole wasn't smart enough to be a hit man for anyone. Even the Denver branch of the Mafia, as decrepit and decadent as it is, wouldn't think of hiring him...much less pay for all those weird plastic surgeries to hide his identity. And why would they hide his identity anyway? Mob hits are two twenty-two-caliber slugs to the skull so they rattle around in there, drop the gun, walk away."

"Unless someone *really* didn't want this to be considered a hit, Nick."

"Yeah, but the mob doesn't work that way."

"I agree," said the lieutenant. "But *you* could have."

Nick didn't answer. He pawed through the dossiers. "This

grand jury stuff is nuts. They have enough evidence here—fake though most of it is—to indict anyone. But there was no indictment. The grand jury was dissolved in April, five and a half years ago, K.T., and this stuff has been sitting around gathering dust since then. How'd you get all this?"

"I called in every favor I ever had and made some promises I hope I never have to deliver on," she said tiredly. "You *asked* me to, Nick." She shoved the entire stack of colored folders closer to him. "But you keep it. If you ever say I know anything about any of this, I'll call you a motherfucking liar."

"What am I going to do with this?" asked Nick, stacking the folders. They made a pile almost eight inches high.

"Who gives a shit, partner?"

Nick slammed his fist on the stack. "If Ortega had a grand jury seated and all this evidence piled up through his own department investigators and someone in Internal Affairs in our department, why didn't he use it? Obviously there was no indictment. Not even a leak to the press. How can you gather so much evidence that one of your Major Crimes Unit's top detectives is a rogue killer—murdering his own wife and an assistant district attorney—and then just sit on it? That's obstruction of justice right there."

"You'll have to ask Ortega."

"I will," said Nick. "Tomorrow morning. In his office."

K.T. shook her head. "The mayor's in Washington with the governor and Senator Grimes. Something about more immigration reform or some such. Advisor Nakamura's supposed to be meeting them there on Monday for testimony for some subcommittee."

"I'll go to Washington," said Nick. He rubbed his tired eyes. What was he thinking? As always, he was forgetting about his son.

How many years had he put his son down the priority list? Lower than his flashback addiction. Before that, lower than his grieving for Dara. Before that, lower than his fucking job as a detective. Before that, lower than his love of his wife. Before that... had he *ever* put his son at or near the top of his priorities?

Nick had a rush of absolute certainty, as physical as a wave of nausea, that Val would tell him he, Val Bottom, had *never* been his father's top priority.

"No," said Nick. "I'm going to L.A. To get Val. To find my son and bring him back here. I'll deal with Ortega later."

K. T. Lincoln stood. "Whatever you do, whomever you do it to, don't call me again, Nick. I never dug out those grand jury files. I didn't meet you here tonight. The only time I've seen you in the last three years was at the Denver Diner last Tuesday—too many people saw me there for me to deny that, plus I had to give the diner's number to Dispatch—but that's also the *last* place I'll ever see you. If anyone asks, I'll say you wanted some money—I said no—and then we chewed the fat for a few minutes about old times, and I decided that our old times together hadn't been all that hot. Good-bye, Nick."

"Good-bye," Nick said absently. He'd opened the accident investigation dossier and was looking at the diagrams and photos from the fire that had killed all five people, including his wife. "K.T....what kind of undercover hit man volunteers to die horribly in a truck fire of his own making? How does that..."

But K. T. Lincoln was gone and Nick was talking to himself in the dirty, poorly lighted space.

———

SUNDAY MORNING AND THE gray *Sasayaki-tonbo* whisper-dragonfly 'copter touched down on the flat roof of Nick's Cherry Creek Mall Condominiums building. Or, rather, *a Sasayaki-tonbo* whisper-dragonfly 'copter landed there. This one was larger and fancier than the one Nick had flown in down to Raton Pass.

Hideki Sato jumped out and frisked Nick carefully. The ex-detective was carrying no weapon. Sato went through the small gym bag—no weapons there, either, although there were six extra magazines of 9mm ammo—and then removed the unsealed padded mailing envelope. Nick's Glock 9 was in there, no clip, no round in the spout, and broken down.

"Just like you specified," said Nick.

Sato sealed the envelope and said nothing. Taking the gym bag, he gestured for Nick to enter the helicopter. Above, the broad, strangely tufted rotors were idling.

There was an airlock-sized room, evidently a CMRI security screen so necessary in the decades since dedicated *jihadi*s had discovered that they could pack their body cavities full of plastic explosive, and then another door to go through. Nick and Sato stepped into a small luxurious room—luxurious in a spare, *shoji-* and *tatami-* and flower-decorated sense—that might have been in Nakamura's mansion up in Evergreen had it not been for the view out the broad, multilayered windows. Nakamura was sitting in a swiveling leather chair behind a lacquered desk by two of those windows.

Nick hadn't seen the billionaire since he was interviewed and hired nine days earlier—it seemed much longer ago to him—and Hiroshi Nakamura seemed exactly the same, down to the carefully parted gray hair, the manicured nails, and the black suit and narrow black tie. There were other comfortable-looking chairs and a couch in the small space, but Nakamura didn't ask Nick to sit. Sato also remained standing, far enough to one side to seem subordinate but close enough to act as a bodyguard if Nick were to lunge toward Nakamura. Sato's polymorphic smart-cast was thin enough and flexible enough to fit under the right sleeve of his dark suit jacket.

"It is a pleasure to see you again, Mr. Bottom," said Nakamura. "Mr. Sato has explained to me that you have a request. I am traveling to Washington, D.C., today and my private jet is scheduled to leave from Denver International Airport in fifteen minutes. I give you one and a half minutes to make your request."

"My son's in serious trouble in Los Angeles," said Nick. "His life is in danger. I need to get to L.A. and don't have the money for an airline ticket. No cars are getting through, and the truck convoys aren't even allowing passengers going west. I don't have enough money for that either."

Mr. Nakamura cocked his head ever so slightly to one side. "I have not heard a request yet, Mr. Bottom."

Nick took a breath. He had less than a minute left.

"Mr. Nakamura, you offered me fifteen thousand dollars—old dollars—if I solved your son's murder. I'm close to solving it. I think I could name the killer right now, but I need a bit more confirmation. I was going to ask you for the price of an air ticket to L.A.—seven hundred old bucks now—in exchange for that fifteen thousand. But they've shut down all commercial, freight, and civil-aviation flights into and out of L.A."

Nakamura waited. He did not glance at his Rolex, but there was a black-face clock with a second hand right there on the cabin's bulkhead.

"Nakamura Enterprises have regular flights to Las Vegas," said Nick. He felt sweat trickle down his ribs. "I checked. From Las Vegas I'd be able to book some sort of transport—private plane, Jeep, whatever—into Los Angeles to look for my son. So get me room on any of your cargo or courier flights, today if possible, and advance me, say, three hundred bucks—old dollars—so I can pay someone for that last leg of the trip, and I swear that I'll tell you who murdered your son when I get back. You can keep the rest of the fifteen thousand."

"Very generous of you, Mr. Bottom," said Nakamura with only the slightest hint of a smile. "Why don't you tell me right now who murdered my son, collect the full fifteen thousand, and thus pay your way to Los Angeles—perhaps in your own private aircraft?"

"I can't *prove* it now," said Nick. "I guarantee that when I show you who killed your son, you'll demand your proof."

"But instead of concluding the investigation," said Nakamura, "you are asking to take time off—how long? A week? Two weeks? In order to aid your son in his flight from justice. I understand he is wanted for murder."

"No, sir. The LAPD and Homeland Security just have a warrant out for Val as a possible material witness. Look, I'm going to get to L.A. one way or the other to search for my boy, Mr. Nakamura. You'd do the same if your son were still alive and needed your help. If you help me get there today, I'll be back sooner and able to wrap up the investigation. I know *what* evidence I need to find, if my hunch about your son's killer is correct...and I think it is. Help me save my son so I can close the investigation on your son's murder."

Nakamura looked at Sato, but the security man's expression did not change. The billionaire's wristwatch chimed softly. Nakamura steepled his fingers and looked at Nick.

"Mr. Bottom, do you know where John Wayne Airport is?"

"Yeah, it's in Santa Ana or Irvine—near there—about forty miles south of L.A."

"We have no cargo aircraft going there presently," said Nakamura, "but next Friday, September twenty-fourth, a flight from Tokyo will be refueling there between five-thirty and seven p.m., Pacific Daylight Savings Time. You will be on that flight, with or without your son. Is this understood?"

Nick wasn't sure he did understand. "You're giving me a way home to Denver if I find Val? Next Friday?"

"Yes," said the billionaire. "There is a Nakamura Enterprises cargo flight leaving Denver International Airport freight terminal at eleven a.m. today bound for Las Vegas, Nevada. I shall make a call. They will find room for you on the flight. It will not be comfortable but it will be a quick flight. This will give you until the Friday fueling stop at John Wayne Airport to find your son. If you find him earlier, or must...ah...leave the Los Angeles area, go to the freight terminal at John Wayne Airport at any time before Friday and you will receive food and shelter there until the Friday-evening flight. At that time— Friday—you must return and tell me what you know about my son's death. Or even what you *think* you know."

"Yes, sir. Thank you, sir," said Nick. He was trying not to weep but the effort made his throat and chest hurt. "About the money, Mr. Nakamura...the bribe money I'll need to..."

"Mr. Sato has the contract ready, Mr. Bottom. Only your thumbprint and signature are necessary. We will advance you five hundred dollars today, old American dollars, in exchange for your waiving the fifteen-thousand-dollar payment if you solve my son's murder. The five hundred dollars is not a gift. If you do not solve my son's murder within the next two weeks, there will be...penalties."

"Yes, sir," said Nick, not giving a fig for any penalties.

Sato held out an AllPad with the contract on the screen. Nick ignored the words, thumbprinted it, and used the pad stylus to sign. Sato gestured. Nick fumbled out his NICC, which the security chief ran through the same AllPad.

When Nick got the card back, he saw that he had a new balance of $750,000 new bucks—$500 in old, real dollars.

"This has taken longer than you promised," snapped Nakamura. "You may ride with us to Denver International Airport, Mr. Bottom. If you are ready."

"I'm ready."

"Not in here, Mr. Bottom. You may ride up front with the pilots. Mr. Sato will show you the way and hand you your luggage."

The door—hatch was more like it—was only just large enough to allow Sato to squeeze through. The *Sasayaki-tonbo* dragonfly was airborne before Nick got strapped into his jump seat behind the pilots.

———

NICK FOUND A PILOT willing to fly him into L.A. within an hour of his landing in Las Vegas. Actually, the flight would be to the untowered civil-aviation field at Flabob in Rubidoux, out near Riverside just south of the Pomona Freeway east of the I-15.

That was close enough for Nick. He'd find his own way into the city, to Leonard's apartment near Echo Park. He'd have a little more than $300,000 in new bucks left—plus his Glock 9.

But the pilot wouldn't fly until after dark—actually, until almost midnight—since all flights into the city were illegal, so Nick had too many hours to kill in Las Vegas. The delay drove him crazy, but all the bootleg pilots flew only after dark, so he had no choice but to wait.

After dinner, toward sunset, Nick made his way to the high wall that surrounded modern Las Vegas. He decided to walk the six miles around the south end of the city along the top of the wall, then the other mile back to the airport. It would help him get rid of some of his nervous energy.

Just after sunset, Nick paused to look out at the hundreds, possibly thousands, of trucks and the tent city that had grown up in the desert beyond the southern edge of the city. He could hear motorcycles roar, gunshots, and shouts. Countless vehicle lights illuminated the hardpan out there and torches and bonfires roared in the tent cities that catered to the hard-assed independent truckers.

Nick knew that convoys headed west to L.A. had been shut down, but some convoys were still coming east from the city. Looking out at the lights and listening to the distant roars, he realized that if Leonard and Val had somehow bought their way onto one of those final convoys, they could be out there in the desert right now, part of that light and noise, less than a mile away.

Is Professor Leonard Fox savvy enough — connected enough — to get Val and himself out of town that way? thought Nick. And even if Leonard were that smart and connected, Nick would have no idea where to look for them.

No, getting into the battlefield hellhole that was Los Angeles was Nick's best shot. Nick had no idea what the odds were of him getting *out* of L.A. alive — much less of actually finding Val and getting them both out, Leonard too if he wanted to leave — but he'd worry about that later.

Nick tore himself away from the sight of the torches and bonfires and truck lights. His loaded Glock holstered on his hip and his small duffel bag in hand, he continued walking east along the southern wall around Las Vegas, planning to get back to McCarran International Airport with at least two hours to kill before his pilot tried to get him and the little Cessna into Battlefield Los Angeles.

3.03

I-25 and Denver: Friday, Sept. 24— Saturday, Sept. 25

PROFESSOR EMERITUS GEORGE Leonard Fox was seventy-four years old and knew that he might not see many more years of life, if any. If this adventure he and Val were on didn't kill him soon, there were the cough and pain in his chest that his doctor had been worried about. The X-rays had been inconclusive, so the doctor had ordered a CT scan and an MRI to determine if it was cancer and, of course, with the National Health Service Initiative, neither test would cost Leonard a cent. But since the waiting time for both of those NHSI-covered procedures now ran to nineteen months and longer, Leonard suspected that he'd be dead from whatever was causing the pain and cough before he got the test. This was the way it had been for seniors without private wealth for many years now.

It was no one's fault—Leonard had been an enthusiastic supporter of the original health reform bill that had guaranteed eventual government control of all health decisions—but sometimes the irony of it all, and the reminder of what his college mentor, Dr. Bert Stern, had called the Iron Law of Unintended Consequences, made Leonard smile a bit ruefully.

But however long he had to live, Leonard knew that he would never forget this last night of the truck convoy through Colorado.

Leonard had paid little attention to the Rocky Mountains during the years he'd lived and taught in Boulder, so this long night of crossing the mountainous part of Colorado held surprises for him.

He wished, of course, that Val weren't riding separately all that day and night, first with the solo trucker Gauge Devereaux and then with Henry Big Horse Begay. Leonard was extremely anxious about what his grandson might do when they were reunited with Nick Bottom the next day in Denver and hoped he could allay the boy's suspicions. And Leonard also needed to talk to Val about the password for the encrypted part of the text on his late daughter Dara's phone. What Leonard wanted was to try the password he felt might be the correct one and read the encrypted file by himself—just in case it did contain something damning that would make his grandson even more intent on attacking Nick Bottom—but Val kept the battered old phone with him wherever he went.

After hours of this fruitless anxiety, Leonard tried to relax and talk to the driver, Julio Romano. Julio's wife, Perdita, was asleep in the lower-rear sleeping compartment and her high-decibel but not unfeminine snoring came through the curtains as they moved closer to the Continental Divide.

Julio had wanted to talk politics and recent history and—after ascertaining that the driver seemed to be one of those rare fellows who could discuss such topics without losing their temper, even with amusement—Leonard had complied.

"Good," said Julio earlier that night. "It's not often that I get a tame professor of literature and classics in my cab. Do you prefer to be called Doctor or Professor?"

"Leonard, actually."

"Well, good, Lenny. That'll make things easier. But I won't forget that you're a professor emeritus."

Normally, Leonard would have been irritated at anyone calling him Lenny—no one ever had—but coming from Julio, after Leonard had ascertained that the middle-aged driver wasn't using the name as an insult, it sounded all right.

As the climb over Loveland Pass approached, Julio was leading a discussion on the decline of nations. Leonard was continually surprised at how well informed and literate the truck driver was.

"But I don't think the United Kingdom *chose* decline," Leonard was saying, trying hard not to slip into his lecturing-prof tone of voice. "After World War Two, it was just an inevitable outcome of Britain having bankrupted itself fighting the war...that and the people's innate refusal to return to the pre-war class system after five years of sharing hardships and scarcity."

"So they fired Winston Churchill without so much as a thank-you-sir and chose socialism," said Julio, shifting down several gears as the huge truck followed the convoy off I-70 before the blocked Eisenhower Tunnel and up the narrower, twisting Highway 6 rising toward the night sky.

"Well, yes," said Leonard. He was a little anxious at the prospect of a discussion of "socialism" with a working man. All those working fellows he'd known, the *few* he'd known, found the word and concept toxic, sometimes reacting to it in violent ways.

"But the British Empire would have been finished no matter who they'd kept as prime minister or what system they'd adopted," said Leonard, raising his voice slightly so he would be heard over the rising roar of the truck's engine. "The scarcities would have been as real after the war, socialism or not."

"Maybe," said Julio Romano with a smile. "But remember what Churchill said."

"What's that?" asked Leonard. The first sharp turns were approaching and he grasped the padded armrest to his right more firmly.

"'Socialism is a philosophy of failure, the creed of ignorance, and the gospel of envy; its inherent virtue is the equal sharing of misery,'" cited Julio. "I agree with old Winnie that once a society has declared that the sharing of misery is a virtue, then there's going to be a lot of scarcity and misery in that culture's future to share. Certainly you and I have lived through that change of outlook, Lenny."

"Yes," said Leonard. The red taillights of the trucks ahead of them kept swerving and disappearing with the sharp curves of Loveland Pass, as if the trucks were hurtling over the edge and out of sight down into the abyss. Leonard could see by their own truck's headlights that the road was patched and broken and the guardrails to the side were largely missing or collapsed. There was nothing but Julio's attention to his driving to keep them from hurtling through the gaps to a fiery death below. "Yes," he said again, trying to regain the thread of the conversation, "but choosing a more…ah…communitarian approach to the rationing of scarcity and the social amelioration of misery does not necessarily mean that a culture has *chosen* decline."

"But have you ever known a modern culture that chose socialism — the enforced redistribution of wealth of the sort we saw about twenty-five years ago, Lenny — that *didn't* inevitably have to embrace decline? Decline as a world power? Decline in its people's productivity and morale?" said Julio, shifting down three more gears and grappling the wheel hard right and then hard left again as the narrow road rose sharply and twisted even more sharply.

"Perhaps not," said Leonard. He was eager not to force an argument on this section of highway, no matter how jovial and relaxed Julio sounded.

With his free hand, Leonard grasped the hard dashboard. Amazingly, snowfields were appearing in the starlight and moonlight on either side of the narrow highway. It was only September! Leonard had forgotten how early snow could come to the high country of Colorado.

"Lenny, you're the professor. Wasn't it Tocqueville who said—'Democracy and socialism have nothing in common but one word—equality. But notice the difference: while democracy seeks equality in liberty, socialism seeks equality in restraint and servitude'? I think it was de Tocqueville. I still read him on long hauls when Perdita's driving and I can't sleep."

"Yes, I think it *was* Tocqueville," managed Leonard. They were approaching the summit. Their convoy was taking up every inch of the damaged, pavement-heaving, narrow road. If a vehicle came the other way, headed west, Leonard could imagine all twenty-three trucks of their convoy hurtling over the edge. Above them, something looking like a row of giant white posts or skinny headstones ran north and south along the Continental Divide. It took a minute for Leonard to realize that these were the mostly abandoned wind turbines from the short-lived "Green" era. It was a spectral sight in the night.

"Lenny, I'm sure you can remember the year—maybe the exact day, perhaps—when the majority of American citizens were no longer paying taxes on April fifteenth but were still voting in entitlements for themselves. The tipping point, as it were."

"I can't say I do remember, Julio," said Leonard.

"The election year of two thousand eight we were almost there. The election year of twenty-twelve we were there. And in twenty-sixteen we were beyond that tipping point and have never gone back," said Julio as the truck growled in its lowest gear to reach the summit of the pass.

"Does this relate to something?" asked Leonard. He'd met a few men like Julio Romano—autodidacts who thought of themselves as intellectuals. The type always had an amazing memory and had read their translations of Plato, Thucydides, Dante, Machiavelli, and Nietzsche. What they didn't know was that their counterparts in academia—the *real* intellectuals— had read these authors in the original Greek, Latin, Italian, and German. Leonard's opinion of autodidacts was that most of the poor devils had a fool for a student and a poseur for a teacher.

They were passing between the Continental Divide wind turbines now, all inactive, and Leonard realized that the things were taller than he'd thought—each easily four hundred feet high. The scarred white pillars sliced the starry sky into cold sections.

"You know, Julio," he said to change the topic, "there's an

odd thing about your and Perdita's first names. And your last name as well. Julio Romano was..."

"A sculptor from Shakespeare's *The Winter's Tale*," said the driver, his broad grin glowing whitely in the dash lights. "The only artist of his day that Shakespeare ever cited by name. I know. Act Five, a celebratory dinner is supposed to be held in the presence of a lifelike statue of Hermione, Leontes' dead wife—*'a piece many years in doing and now newly perform'd by that rare Italian master, Julio Romano, who, had he himself eternity and could put breath into his work, would beguile Nature of her custom, so perfectly is he her ape.'* Weird, huh, Lenny?"

"But an anachronism in Shakespeare's day," Leonard couldn't stop himself from pointing out. The old academic could allow one anachronism to pass without challenge, but not two in one night. "The Julio Romano was a reference to Giulio Romano, an Italian artist from the early and midsixteenth century. But why Shakespeare would have cited Romano as a great artist—and a sculptor—is a mystery. I don't believe he was even a sculptor."

They were crossing the broad, snow-covered plateau of the summit. The headlights of trucks ahead of them illuminated a battered but still-standing sign—*SUMMIT, 3,655 m., 11,190 ft.* Julio shifted gears as the truck prepared for an even more tortuous descent on the eastern side of the Continental Divide. Behind them, the idle wind turbines receded like so many white columns holding up the dome of the brilliant night sky.

"Actually, Lenny," said Julio, "that Giulio Romano *was* a sculptor, so the early Shakespeare scholars were wrong about that. In Vasari's *Lives of Seventy of the Most Eminent Painters, Sculptors and Architects*, not translated until eighteen-fifty, there were two Latin epitaphs for Romano that showed he was an architect and rather famous sculptor as well as a painter. Shakespeare *would* have heard of him as a sculptor, it turns out."

"I stand corrected," said Leonard. The descent, he now knew, was going to be many times more terrifying than the climb to the summit.

"I only know because I share the name," said Julio. "My father was a professor of art history at Princeton."

"*Really?*" said Leonard and immediately wished that he hadn't put so much amazement in his voice.

"Yeah, really," said Julio with another grin as he down-shifted rapidly and wrestled the wheel hard left. Beyond the emptiness where the missing guardrail should be only inches to their right, there was only more emptiness for a mile or more to rocks below. "But I know what you were thinking...how odd it is that I married a woman named Perdita, since Perdita is King Leontes' long-lost daughter with whom he's also reunited, before the statue of his wife, Hermione, comes to life. I mean, what are the odds that Julio Romano from *The Winter's Tale* would marry a Perdita named after a character in the same play?"

"Was she?" managed Leonard, hanging on to armrest and dashboard as if his life depended on his grip. "Named after Shakespeare's Perdita, I mean?"

"Oh, yeah, absolutely." Julio grinned at the highway ahead. "Her parents were both Shakespeare scholars. Her father, R. D. Bradley, met Perdita's mother, Gail Kern-Preston, at a confer-ence in Zurich that accepted papers exclusively on *The Winter's Tale.*"

"*The* R. D. Bradley and Gail Kern-Preston?" gasped Leon-ard. For a moment he was too astonished to be terrified.

"Yeah." Julio turned the bright grin toward Leonard. "Per-dita's mommy kept publishing under her maiden name after she got married. I guess scholars are like movie stars in that way...they build up too much equity under the original names to change them for a stupid little thing like marriage."

Leonard had to smile at that. Two of his wives—his first, Sonja Ryte-Jónsdóttir, and his fourth and last one, Nubia Weusi—had felt that way. Leonard had certainly understood at the time, especially since both were better known in their respective fields and specialties than he was.

"So did you and Perdita meet at some sort of academic conference?" asked Leonard.

Julio chuckled. "Sort of. We met at a We're-*Free*-Truckers,

You-Fuckers Peterbilt Convention in Lubbock, Texas. I heard that there was this woman at the tattoo stall getting an image of Cerberus tattooed on her ass—two dog's heads on her left cheek, one on her right—and I *had* to see that. It was Perdita, of course, twenty-three years old, been an independent trucker her own self for four years already, and was looking for fun or a fight that weekend. I took her out for a shot with a beer back afterwards, to help dull the pain, I said. We got the name thing with each other right away, both realized that the other's parents had been into the *Winter's Tale* scholar thing, and we both sort of figured that we were destined either to be enemies or mates. After a week or so on the road, during which I got to admire her Cerberus, we chose mates."

"*O seclum insipiens et inficetum,*" muttered Leonard, not realizing that he'd spoken aloud. *O stupid and tasteless age.*

"Yeah, exactly," laughed Julio. "True in his day and true in ours. I love Catullus. Especially when he said they make a desert and call it peace. We've seen that in our lifetimes too, haven't we, Lenny?"

The "make a desert and call it peace" line was by Tacitus, but Leonard did not choose to correct his new friend. "Yes. Well, Julio, I'm getting a bit sleepy…" Leonard shifted in the deeply upholstered seat, setting his hands on his shoulder harness and the heavy center clasp. The trucks ahead of them seemed to be diving ever more steeply into the darkness of the broad canyon on this side of the Divide.

"Yes, absolutely, Lenny, you need to get some sleep. We'll be pulling into Denver midmorning or so—before noon, certainly. But can I ask you just one more question before you head up to the bunk?" The driver laughed, a bit ruefully, Leonard thought. "Who knows when I'll have another professor-emeritus intellectual in my cab."

"Certainly," said Leonard, taking his hands off the seat belt. "One question. I've enjoyed tonight's conversation. But you'll have to pardon me if my answer is short. I'm feeling my years these days…also feeling all the sleep I've missed this week."

"Of course," said Julio Romano. His right hand and left leg seemed to move without thought when he performed the complex actions needed to shift down several gears. The big rig moaned its response to him. Brake lights winked in the convoy ahead and Leonard could already smell the overheated brakes on some of the other trucks ahead or behind.

"Lenny, are you a Jew?"

Leonard felt as if he'd been slapped in the face. Not necessarily an insulting or aggressive slap, but the kind a doctor might give to bring someone to full consciousness. In all his life—seventy-four long years—no one had ever asked him that question. The only one of his four wives he'd told was Carol, his third wife. For a second Leonard was sure that this truck driver was no lonely, earnest autodidact—no highway semi-intellectual in the making as he'd generously thought a few minutes earlier—but, rather, just another redneck asshole.

Julio hadn't even worded it politely, as in "Are you Jewish?" He'd used the casual anti-Semite's "Are you a Jew?" Leonard suddenly felt fully awake. Not angry or alarmed yet, just very, very alert.

"Yes," he said tightly. "I'm a Jew. Or at least from a long line of Jews. I've never practiced the religion. My grandfather changed his name when he came to the United States after World War One."

"What was it originally?"

"Fuchs. Evidently it was a German variant of the English name Fox. Reportedly, red hair ran in the family and the men on my grandfather's side of the family were supposedly very cunning. Because Fuchs sounds too much like the f-word in English, some Jews added a suffix—Fuchsman or some such— but German-sounding names also weren't that popular right after the Great War, so my grandfather just used the cognate form Fox when he arrived." Leonard realized that he was talking too much and fell quiet.

Julio was nodding—not as if a suspicion had been confirmed, but the way someone does when an almost unnecessary preliminary was out of the way.

"So was that the question?" asked Leonard. He didn't succeed in keeping the edge out of his voice and he didn't really care.

"No," said Julio, who showed no sign of hearing any irritation. "You see, Lenny, you're a Jew *and* a university left-wing intellectual, so it's really important for me to get your take on one issue."

"What's that?" Now Leonard's voice had no edge. It just sounded unutterably tired, even to himself.

"A lot of people think that Israel was destroyed because it had let the flashback drug they'd invented escape from the secret Havat MaShash lab hidden in the southern desert there in Israel," said Julio.

Leonard had also heard this "fact" since the destruction of Israel, but it wasn't a question and he had no comment on it.

"What I need to know, Lenny," said the driver, sounding a bit breathless, "is what you think."

"What I think? About what?"

"About the destruction of Israel. What you think as a Jew, I mean. A Jew as well as a liberal and intellectual."

"I've been in synagogues exactly four times in my life, Julio," Leonard said softly. "Three times it was for some friend's son's bar mitzvah. Once it was for a memorial service for another friend who died. None of these friends and acquaintances had any idea I was Jewish, especially the first ones, who had to show me how to wear the kippah or yarmulke—the skullcap. I'm the wrong Jew to ask."

"But you have an opinion," persisted the truck driver. Leonard could see that Julio was also very tired. The pouches under the pudgy driver's eyes were almost as blue-black as the dark dropoffs on either side of the descending highway.

"Yes, like almost everyone else, I have an opinion about the destruction of Israel," said Leonard. "As someone said even before that day—and I apologize, I forget who said it, my memory is that of an old man's and is not as sharp as yours, Julio—'The day that Israel is destroyed is the day that the world's true holocaust shall begin.'"

"That's not biblical?" asked Julio. "It sounds biblical."

"I am sure it's not. It may have been said by one of Israel's last leaders. I really can't recall. Is that all, Julio?"

"But, Lenny…" The man was struggling toward something, with something. "One last question. How did you feel about the American president…presidents, really…and Congresses who turned against Israel…abandoned it long before the attack?"

Professor George Leonard Fox took a breath. He was the man who—even when he was a boy—was incapable of striking another person. He'd studied pacifism as a philosophy for more than six decades, and while he knew it could not be an answer to the world's problems, he still admired it beyond most other efforts at human sanity.

"Julio," he said quietly, "I wish those presidents and senators and representatives had been hanged from lampposts all over Washington. And I wish to the God of Abraham that the state of Israel had responded the way it had said it would and turned Iran, Syria, and the other embryonic Caliphate states into a vast wasteland of nuclear glass, instead of dying passively the way it did. I'm tired, Julio. Tonight's talk has been interesting—I'll remember it—but I'm going to bed now."

"Good night, Professor Fox."

"Good night."

Leonard climbed up the short ladder to his topside bunk. Perdita's soft snores came through the curtain below but when Leonard drew his own curtain, they were all but inaudible.

He wished that Val had spent this last night in the truck so they could talk about tomorrow. Leonard was terrified that the boy was going to kill his father.

The curse of Cain killing his brother and Abraham being willing to kill his son, he thought tiredly. *And I gave it to him.*

Leonard got out of his clothes and struggled into the flannel pajamas he'd brought with him. The world was ending, the police and Homeland Security and FBI and who knows what other agencies were chasing Val—and thus Val's grandfather—

and he was careful to bring along his flannel pajamas and slippers and to brush his teeth every night and morning.

Life goes on. It was something every Jew knew in his DNA.

Leonard was very tired, but he was also more lonely than he had been in many years.

Feeling guilty, the old man switched on a small flashlight, unzipped Val's duffel, and pawed through the few contents. Dara's phone was gone, of course, along with the Beretta pistol, but Leonard already knew that. In a zippered side compartment that he hadn't noticed earlier, Leonard found five flashback inhaler vials. Four were empty. Only a single one-hour vial remained.

Feeling even more guilty—it must be a cardinal crime among addicts and criminals, he was sure, to rifle another man's stash—Leonard crawled under the covers, concentrated on the hour he wanted to relive, broke the seal, and inhaled the aerosol drug.

Leonard knew that it was a quickly learned skill, this focusing on a specific memory to target the flashback so that specific times could be relived. He imagined that Val and other common users had it down to a science; they must be able to relive an experience starting on almost the exact moment or precise second. It had been a long time since Professor Emeritus George Leonard Fox had tried to use the drug. He was nervous. All he wanted this long, dark, lonely night was to spend one hour with his darling third wife—and only true wife, he always secretly thought—Carol.

He wasn't sure as he tried to focus his memory whether to spend one of her birthday nights with her—she always loved to celebrate her birthday with him—or perhaps an hour from just after they were married, or perhaps even before they married, when they took those long walks together. He panicked even as he tried to focus in the second he had to inhale.

For the next hour, Leonard had to relive a painful root canal from his late fifties. The dentist had been brusque, rough, and unsympathetic. The anesthesia hadn't seemed to work well. Leonard's lifelong fear of choking had added to the pain and anxiety. His pain and fear then added to his pain and fear now reliving the hour. But there was no turning back with flashback, he knew. Once started, the vial amount of a relived experience would not be changed, escaped, or denied.

It serves me right, he thought as the hour of horror moved slowly, glacially, through the night. *It's my own fault. I deserve this punishment for stealing the boy's flashback and for trying to escape reality by communing with my dead. We should respect our dead through memory, not through pharmaceuticals. I deserve this.*

Yes, thought Leonard with a wincing smile, he felt very much the Jew this night.

———

DROPPED OFF A LITTLE before 11 a.m. near Union Station just off I-25 in the LoDo section of Denver, Val and Leonard began walking. They had spent only eight days with the caravan, but it had felt like much longer to Leonard and it felt strange to him now *not* to be continuing on with the truckers. He felt somewhat abandoned and he imagined Val did as well.

Both of them were tired and grumpy but his grandson's usual surliness seemed to be tempered by excitement. Before the boy remembered that he didn't communicate important things to his grandfather, he'd blurted out Henry Big Horse Begay's promise to take Val with him if the boy had acquired a counterfeit NICC by the time Begay was scheduled to return on October 27. Val showed Leonard the slip of paper with the Denver card counterfeiter's name, address, and phone number. There was a second man's name and number and a street address scrawled beneath the first one.

"That's the best NICC guy that Begay knows, period, supposedly does cards that no one can tell from the real things, but he's not even in the country. He lives in Austin or someplace like that in Texas, so I don't know why he gave me that name. I need to find two hundred old bucks and see this guy on South Broadway here in Denver." Val hurried to take the folded card back.

Leonard didn't have to point out that the old-dollar equivalent of $300,000 in new bucks was as far away as the pale scythe of moon that still hung above the mountains in the blue sky.

The day was warm for late September, almost summer-like, and the blue sky was cloudless. The leaves on the few trees along the streets in this old section of town looked as tired and dusty as the two pedestrians, but hadn't yet begun to change color. Leonard remembered autumn days like this when he'd lived in nearby Boulder, the aspen leaves getting brittle enough to rattle in the breezes, the blue skies darkening toward that unmatchable blue of a Colorado October, and the thin air free from even the slightest hint of the humidity that so often hung over Los Angeles.

The two plodded to Blake Street and then turned right and walked three short blocks to Speer Boulevard. They argued about what to do next. Val wanted to see his old house and neighborhood near Cheesman Park, but that was miles east of here and certainly a dead end. Nick had sold that house and moved out just after he'd sent Val to Los Angeles more than five years ago. Even the neighbors Val had known as a boy were probably gone...either gone, Leonard pointed out, or already alerted by the FBI or Homeland Security to be on the lookout for Val.

"We should walk to the Cherry Creek Mall Condos, where your father lives," said Leonard as they turned left onto the so-called Cherry Creek Trail.

"The FBI will be watching there too," said Val.

"Yes," said Leonard. "But with luck your father will shelter us from them."

The old man and boy walked southeast a couple of blocks to a point just beyond Larimer Street where the pedestrian walkway ducked under North Speer Boulevard and ran along the banks of Cherry Creek to a point at which the river meandered between the lanes of the busy divided boulevard.

It was about four miles to his son-in-law's condominium complex and after the first mile or so, Leonard wasn't sure he was going to make it. He collapsed onto a bench by the walkway and Val fidgeted nearby.

389

When Leonard had lived in Colorado a couple of decades earlier, the area along Cherry Creek had been known for its homeless—at least one bearded man per intersection holding up a cardboard sign—and the less visible homeless sleeping under the many overpasses along the sunken pedestrian walkway. Now, he realized, there were thousands of homeless—entire families—permanently living along the banks of this small river. They didn't seem threatening because the walkways on both sides of the river were a constant stream of bicycle traffic heading toward and away from Denver's downtown. Businessmen and -women in expensive suits pedaled by, their briefcases in baskets attached to the handlebars.

But now that they'd stopped for a moment, the homeless men along the banks and in the shadows of the overpass they'd just walked under began taking notice of them.

"We'd better get going," whispered Val.

Leonard nodded but didn't rise immediately. He was very tired. And all during their walk so far, he'd kept raising his hands to feel his teeth through his cheeks, as if his flashback root-canal torture the night before had been real. "My bag is heavy," he said at last, hating the hint of a whine he heard.

"Leave it," said Val, tugging at his grandfather's arm. Four men were ambling over from the shadows.

"I can't leave it," said Professor Emeritus George Leonard Fox, sounding shocked. "My pajamas are in it."

Val got his grandfather to his feet and moving again and the four homeless men lost interest and went back to their bedrolls in the shade. Val said, "One of the motherfuckers in the convoy broke into my bag sometime last night and stole one of my last vials of flash. Can you believe it, Grandpa?"

"That's terrible," said Leonard.

They continued south along the river walk. The homeless men in the shadows under the overpasses backed away from Val in a way that made Leonard realize that his grandson was becoming a man.

"If we had a usable phone," said Leonard, "we could call your father. He could come pick us up."

"We don't have a phone," said Val.

"If there were still public phones, we have enough on my NICC to make a local call."

"There aren't any public phones, Grandpa. And you have to remember that we can't use our cards."

"I'm just saying that if they had phones and if those phones took change—if we still used coins—then we could phone and save ourselves this walk."

"If we had some ham, we could have a ham and cheese sandwich," said Val. "If we had some cheese."

Leonard blinked. It was the first sign of humor, however sarcastic, that he'd heard from his grandson in a long time. He realized that something Begay had promised the boy—a chance, however remote, of joining the free truckers' convoy—had brought Val out of the darkness. At least partway.

"If buses still ran, we could take a bus," said Leonard. "Four miles is a perfect distance for a city bus."

Val said nothing to that. Suicide bombers loved American buses in the same way that Palestinian terrorists had loved buses in Tel Aviv and other Israeli cities decades ago. Subways and elevated trains still ran in major American cities because people and packages could be screened—with a fair degree of efficiency, even given the bad news of one or more explosions a month around the country—but buses were not defensible. Leonard thought that it had been a major retreat from civilization when American cities had given up on their bus systems.

Val's small duffel bag had a strap on it and the boy put the strap over his shoulder, turned around, and took the heavier duffel from his grandfather. He didn't say a word. They walked on with Val just a step ahead, but Leonard noticed that the boy kept his right hand free. The pistol was in his belt on the left side under his jacket.

Leonard found himself wishing that he'd fled his home and Los Angeles while wearing his sneakers rather than these dress shoes. His feet were already swollen to the point that it hurt to walk. Leonard had thought that his half-mile walk to Echo Park every day had kept him in shape, but obviously not.

The last news about Los Angeles he'd heard in Julio and Perdita's truck that morning had said that the worst of the fighting in the city and suburbs was over and that the *reconquista* military forces were falling back along I-5 toward San Diego. The California National Guard and various anglo paramilitary groups had reestablished control of I-5 and the coastal corridor all the way from Long Beach to Encinitas. It was being announced as a major defeat for Nuevo Mexico expansion.

Leonard had mixed feelings about all this. As an amateur historian as well as classicist, he knew the injustice of southwestern states being taken from Mexico in the 1840s. But he was also one of the few people he knew who were old enough to remember the 1992 L.A. riots after the police who'd beaten a man named Rodney King were acquitted. In less than a week of rioting, thousands of fires were set—many of the burned-out areas still had not been rebuilt, forty years later—and more than fifty people had died with a couple of thousand injured.

Leonard had thought of those riots that morning when he'd heard details of how an entire company of *reconquista* infantry in armored personnel carriers had been pulled from their vehicles and beaten and killed by a mob at the same place in South Central L.A.—the intersection of Florence and South Normandie avenues—where truck drivers and other innocents had been pulled from their vehicles and attacked in 1992. In this case, according to NPR, more than two hundred *reconquista* fighters were dead and the black rioters had moved into East L.A., burning everything they came across in the wake of the Nuevo Mexican forces' retreat.

This upset Leonard. He wondered how his friend Emilio Gabriel Fernández y Figueroa and Emilio's son Eduardo were. He wished them well. There was no doubt in George Leonard Fox's mind that even though he'd demanded payment, Emilio had saved Val's life—and perhaps Leonard's as well—by getting them out of Los Angeles nine days ago.

Leonard noticed that Val had led them up a flight of steps out of the sunken Cherry Creek walkway and onto the street-level sidewalk that ran alongside Speer Boulevard. There were fewer bicyclists on the pathway below, Leonard saw, and many more homeless filling the path and riverside banks.

He'd just been thinking about the Alamo—he'd once proofread a friend's essay about Texas's Alamo and the fighting of February–March 1836, where Travis, Crockett, Bowie, and the others had died at the hands of General Santa Anna, the essay focusing on the failure in leadership of Sam Houston, Austin, and the other self-named Texians—so he was surprised to see the greensward of Denver's Alamo Placita Park across the street to the north. On the south side of the boulevard was the smaller Hungarian Freedom Park.

There were hundreds of hovels and tattered tents in both parks, but especially in the Hungarian Freedom Park just to their right, and many more hundreds of the homeless, mostly men, milling around.

Val dropped back next to Leonard. "Stay close to me, Grandpa."

A group of the lean, angry-looking men, perhaps twenty-five or so, crossed the busy street to the median sidewalk and began following them.

Speer Boulevard turned into East First Avenue here and ran due east and west. To their right now was a high fence shutting off access to what had once been the Denver Country Club with its extensive grounds. Cherry Creek disappeared into that forbidden area.

Across the street to the north was one of the oldest wealthy areas of Denver with shaded streets and what had once been multimillion-old-dollar homes, small estates, really, set back on deep lawns. Now those houses were in ruins, many burned down, others occupied by street people or turned into low-quality flashcaves.

The group of men behind them rushed to cross South Downing Street and catch up to them.

Val dropped Leonard's duffel bag, turned around, and removed the Beretta pistol from his belt.

The group of men stopped about thirty feet away. They launched curses and one threw a small rock from the street, but—still cursing and flashing obscene gestures—they turned around and headed back toward the Hungarian Freedom Park.

Leonard found that he was having some trouble breathing as Val tucked the pistol back into his belt, picked up his grandfather's duffel bag, and, gripping Leonard's elbow firmly, moved him more quickly down the sidewalk outside the country club barriers.

"I'm surprised they didn't have guns themselves," managed Leonard when he could talk. He kept glancing back over his shoulder.

"If they had guns," said Val, "they wouldn't be homeless. And we'd be dead. Let's keep moving."

Passing the entrance to the country club, Leonard's heart pounding from the exertion and adrenaline in his system, he looked into the grounds and saw blue tents pitched everywhere on what had been the tennis courts and an eighteen-hole golf course behind the large main buildings. In the few clear areas, those large swivel-wing planes the military called VTOLs or... what was it?...Ospreys were lined up, their engines and propellers aimed skyward.

"I wonder what...," he began.

"Keep walking, Grandpa. We're almost there."

———

LEONARD'S SON-IN-LAW'S SHOPPING-MALL-TURNED-CUBIES TOOK up a very long and wide city block, with the river at its backside. High fences and razor wire between the former mall's parking garage and the river kept squatters from taking up residence along the banks. Across Cherry Creek to the south, Leonard and Val could see more expensive condominium complexes guarded by more razor wire, gun positions, gates, and private security guards. This side of the river was more problematic.

Leonard remembered Cherry Creek as one of the most upscale shopping districts in Colorado. Now the two- to four-story buildings across First Avenue from Nick Bottom's mall-condo complex were a maze of stall shops and burned-out structures left over from old rioting or turf wars. None of the high-end shops had made it through the last decade.

So much depends upon maintenance, Leonard was thinking. Decades ago, before the Day It All Hit The Fan, there'd been a book and TV series about what the world would be like if human beings suddenly disappeared; not died off, just... disappeared. It had fascinated Leonard, who'd still been teaching his Shakespeare and Chaucer then.

What he hadn't really understood until that TV program— he never did read the book it was based on—was that the physical web of modern life was so dependent upon almost constant maintenance. Leonard had always imagined, in the few apocalyptic visions he'd had, that cities would stay pretty much the way they were for years, decades, a century perhaps, until weeds, grass, trees, and wild animals began to intrude upon the urban landscape. But no, that turned out not to be the case. The program had shown how service tunnels, subways, and the rest of the subterranean parts of a major city like New York would be underwater within a day without human intervention and maintenance. The flooding alone would soon result in high-pressure explosions of pipelines, basements of tall buildings submerged, foundations undercut, and an amazingly rapid dissolution of the urban grid.

Humans weren't gone in the United States—far from it— but the national sense of having given up, linked to the ubiquitous use of flashback to the point that very few people were actually doing their jobs at any given moment, had created a similar breakdown of infrastructure.

Leonard's son-in-law's cubic was in a huge fortified, windowless concrete mass. It was on the wrong side of the tracks— or in this case, the wrong side of the river—and it hulked there like a sightless Fort Apache deep in Indian territory. During the day, Leonard saw, people lived and shopped for basic items and moved through the ruined blocks of what had been the North Cherry Creek shopping area across the broad street, but at night it must be a nightmare for unarmed civilians.

On the river side of the building, the gaps in the once-open parking garage had been covered with electrified fencing. The

fenced-off, grassless, muddy riverbanks were under video surveillance from the condo complex. The west end of the building was bordered by the private drive to the parking garage.
Any car approaching that parking garage had to pass through
automated gates, a bang box—a concrete structure designed to
search automobiles and contain the explosions if they were
rigged with bombs—and then through another inner gate and
only then up the ramp into the garage.

The north-facing front of the Cherry Creek Mall Condominiums had main doors of windowless steel. Surveillance
video-cam bubbles looked down from above those impenetrable doors.

Leonard and Val had crossed First Avenue and paced back
and forth for the two blocks facing the mass of the mall.

"If we could just phone," Leonard said. He had to sit down.

"Be quiet, Grandpa," snapped Val. They'd been staying in
the shadows, hiding their faces from the higher-surveillance
video-camera bubbles hung like cheap jewelry along the front
of the mall. "You're going to have to go in and see if the Old
Man is home."

"Me?" said Leonard. "Alone? Aren't you coming?"

"The Denver cops are looking for me. We heard on the
truck radio all the names of the guys I hung around with, so
there has to be some sort of bulletin out on me. Probably FBI
and DHS looking for me too. They figure the first place I'd
come is here…and here I am. But they might not be looking
for you, Leonard."

He'd never liked it when Val called him by his first name.
"They might be looking for me as well."

Val shrugged. "But Nick Bottom's still our best chance.
He's a stinking flash addict, but he may still have some contacts
with the Denver PD. Or at least know how to get us out of town.
Building security probably won't let you past the lobby or security airlock or whatever they have in there, but if they don't
detain you and call the cops right away, they'll probably let you
phone up to the Old Man's cubie in there. If they do grab you,
just tell them that you got out of L.A. but haven't seen me."

"They'd never believe that I left Los Angeles without you," said Leonard.

Val shrugged. The silence stretched.

"And you assume your father will be home in the middle of the day?" Leonard finally said. His voice was not completely steady.

"The Old Man's a flashback addict," snapped Val. "Flashers are almost always home—unless they're in a flashcave somewhere."

"If he is there, and if they *don't* detain me and call the police, what do you want me to tell your father?"

"Tell him I'm here and that he should come out to talk to me. Tell him to bring two hundred bucks in cash—old bucks. If he doesn't have that much in cash, we can go to an ATM together. There are still a few of those things left."

Leonard didn't know whether hearing this made him want to laugh or weep. "That's what this is about? Getting money from your father? So you can get that forged Teamsters NICC and be a trucker?"

"Yeah."

"What about your anger at him, Val?"

"Well, fuck that. It doesn't matter anymore. I don't know what went down between him and Mom and I don't really care anymore. If he's there—if he hasn't spent every last cent he has on flashback—have him come out to meet me and bring the two hundred old bucks in cash. You can tell him that I'll never bother him again after I get the money. I figure that after sending me into exile for five fucking years, he owes me at least that much."

Leonard shook his head. He paused, then said: "I may have the password to the encrypted text on your mother's phone, Val. I've thought of several possibilities."

The boy's head snapped up. "Does that matter now?"

"It might." Leonard didn't know if it mattered or not. And even though he'd known his darling daughter well when they'd lived together, odds were against him actually guessing the password she'd chosen. Dara had been extremely intelligent:

she'd have known that a near-random mixture of letters and numerals would have been the most secure password she could have chosen. Leonard was almost certainly being sentimental and foolish when he thought he might have guessed the five-letter word.

"I'm not thinking anymore that the Old Man actually had her killed," muttered the boy. "I just hated it when he didn't cry when she died. He didn't cry at the funeral or when we cleaned out her stuff. The sonofabitch never showed the slightest bit of emotion. Then he shipped me off and . . . well, I guess I was a little nuts for a while. I just want whatever money he'll give me and then I'll go somewhere where I never have to see him again as long as I live."

Leonard began to speak but bit his lip instead. "Will you give me my daughter's phone then? *I* want to read her text diary."

"If you get the Old Man out here and he brings money so I can find the card guy, you can have the goddamned phone, Grandpa. Now go on."

———

THE CONDOMINIUM LOBBY WHERE Leonard's son-in-law lived was a bulletproof, blastproof vault. Surveillance cameras watched. Inner doors were metal and multilayered. One was supposed to speak to a microphone and video camera next to a screen that showed a 3DHD video loop of flowered meadows, grazing deer, and eagles floating in a blue sky, all these images laid over inspirational music that would kill a diabetic.

A man's voice came from the grill: "Welcome to the Cherry Creek Mall Condominiums. Can we help you?"

Leonard said that he wanted to talk to Mr. Nick Bottom.

There was a hesitation and the voice said, "Please stay where you are. Someone will be right down."

Leonard panicked. They were calling the cops. They'd called building security and someone was coming to grab him until the police arrived.

Leonard moved quickly to the heavy outer doors and tried

one. It opened. He knew the people watching him on video could lock it from their control center, so they weren't holding him prisoner, which they certainly would have done if the goal was to arrest him. Looking out the door, he couldn't see Val across the street but traffic moved up and down First Avenue.

Leonard closed the door and waited, his old heart pounding and the constant flower of pain in his chest unfolding to something the size of a fist. It wasn't his heart, he knew. It was something growing—and becoming more painful—in his left lung. George Leonard Fox felt mortality press down on his shoulders like a lead collar.

The inner door opened and a stolid, heavily muscled older man in a simple black security uniform came through. He carried a radio and other paraphernalia on his belt, but no gun.

"You're Dr. Fox?" said the man, offering his hand. "I'm Gunny G., the head of security for Cherry Creek Mall Condominiums."

Leonard shook the offered hand. The man's fingers were short, blunt, and wide, but shaking the man's broad callused palm was like grasping a relatively smooth-barked tree.

"Mr. Bottom asked me to watch for you and your grandson," said Gunny G.

We're under arrest, thought Leonard.

"...and to escort you both to his quarters and make sure you're comfortable," finished the security man. Leonard noticed that this Gunny G. person's face was a lunar-terrain map of subtle white scars under the permanent tan.

"When did my son-in-law talk to you about us?"

"This morning, sir. Before he left."

"So he's out right now?" Leonard said stupidly. If one of his students had responded this way, he would have put a tiny "n"—for "nullwit"—next to the student's name in his attendance book, just to save time when the grading period came around.

Gunny G. nodded. "But Mr. Bottom said that he'd be back this afternoon or early evening and asked me personally to make sure you and your grandson were comfortable."

"How did you recognize me?" asked Leonard, his voice not quite feeble but certainly sounding lost.

"Mr. Bottom showed me photos, sir," said the security chief with a smile. "Do you have luggage? I'll be happy to carry it as we head upstairs."

Upstairs to the holding cell, thought Leonard. He was so frightened that it was almost funny.

"My grandson has our luggage," he murmured, almost as if the real world still existed. "Perhaps we'll come back later."

Could they outrun the authorities? Leonard knew that he couldn't. He couldn't even outhobble them.

Gunny G. — what kind of name was that? — reached into his shirt pocket, removed a slip of paper, and said, "I'm sorry, Dr. Fox. I forgot that Mr. Bottom asked me to give you this."

The note read — *"Leonard and Val — I'm glad you're safe. Please trust this man. He'll let you into my cubie. I'll be home later today — Saturday. It's imperative that I see you. I've left cafeteria chits on the table in my room if you're hungry or thirsty. See you soon. — Nick."*

There was a hastily scribbled postscript: *"Gunny G. will phone to inform me that you've arrived."*

Leonard had no idea if it was his son-in-law's handwriting since he'd never seen Nick's handwriting. He put the note in his pocket, more confused than ever.

"I'll go get my grandson and the luggage," he said at last. His words echoed in the blastproof tomb of an entry box.

"Very good, Dr. Fox," said the square-faced security chief. "I'll wait here for you."

Val wasn't waiting for him across the street where he'd left him, but at the west end of the condo building. Leonard told him the situation.

The boy frowned at the huge structure. "It sounds fishy to me, Grandpa."

"Yes," agreed Leonard. "But they let me leave to get you."

"They want *me*, Grandpa. Maybe there's a reward for me. Omura might have offered one."

"Yes, but..." Leonard showed him the note again. "Is this your father's handwriting, Val?"

The boy frowned. "I think so. I'm not sure. It's been so long since..." He squinted up at the afternoon sun, crumpled the note, and tossed it away. "They'll want to take my gun away."

"Yes, I'm sure building security will demand that," said Leonard. "There was a notice next to the TV screen that..."

"They can't have my gun," said Val.

"I'm sure they will return it when we leave."

Val smiled. "Come with me, Grandpa."

To the west of the huge mall building and beyond the private drive that paralleled the parking garage, an old paved bicycle path ran down to the river, where a small bridge had once crossed Cherry Creek. The bike and pedestrian path resumed on the south side of the river, but someone had blown up the narrow span. Val led his grandfather to the west side of the ruined bridge where they were out of sight of the condo's many cameras. The creek was too high under this bridge to allow for the homeless to huddle or camp there.

Leonard watched as Val took two rocks, using one as a hammer and one as a sort of chisel, and pounded at the rusted cap on an old pipe extruding from the riverbank. The cap popped off with a screech of rusted metal. Whatever had once flowed through the small pipe flowed no more. The inside was dirt and cobwebs. Val reached into his duffel, pulled out one of his T-shirts, removed the Beretta pistol from his belt, and wrapped it and several magazines of ammunition with it. After stuffing the bundle wrist deep into the pipe, he used the two stones to pound the pipe lid back into place.

"Let's go," he said.

LEONARD WAS AMAZED AT how tiny Nick Bottom's cubie was and how loud the neighbors in the former storefront were. There was room only for the bed, a tiny desk and cheap chair, a small bathroom with toilet and shower, and an even smaller closet.

Leonard lay back on the bed, breathing shallowly, while Val paced like a predator in an undersized cage.

"The chits are there," said Leonard. "We could go back to that cafeteria the Gunner person showed us and have some lunch. It's been a long time since that breakfast with the convoy."

Val said nothing as he looked through his father's small desk. The single drawer was empty except for a remote and flexible generic keyboard mat for the TV. Normally, Leonard knew, the resident's phone would operate the TV and its computer functions.

Val then looked through the closet, going through his father's hanging shirts, trousers, and sport coats. He pulled a mass of rope and webbing out of the corner. "What the hell's this stuff?"

"Your father must have taken up climbing as a sport," said Leonard, noting the metal-clip carabiners and ascender-handgrips that had been called jumars back in the last century.

"Like hell," said Val. "I'll bet you anything that this is the Old Man's way off the roof if something goes bad in here. See this?" He held up a small rectangular bundle of orange-and-black nylon.

"What is it, Val?"

"Some sort of flotation device," said his grandson. "Maybe a belly boat like fishermen use. The Old Man rappels down off the roof into that grassy area, inflates this thing, and paddles his ass across the river."

"It's wise to take precautions in case of fire...," began Leonard.

Val barked a laugh and started going through the built-in wall drawers.

"Your father won't like it that you're invading his privacy," said Leonard.

"My...father...can kiss my serene ass on my couch of many colors," said the boy. "If I find the money, I'm out of here." He tossed some flashback vials onto the bed from where they'd been tucked under clean underwear.

"You wouldn't even wait to say hello to your father?"

"No."

Val looked under the bed, behind the big flatscreen, in the toilet tank and shower. He came back into the room, looked at the cubie's rifled-through drawers, and muttered, "Wait. I remember when they used to try to hide stuff from me in the house..."

Val pulled out the drawers and dumped their contents on the floor. He flipped the upside-down drawers onto the bed, waving Leonard aside. There were stacks of colored folders attached by duct tape to the underside of each drawer.

"Hey," said the boy.

"It doesn't look like money," said Leonard. "And your father will be furious when he comes home and finds..."

Val had torn away the tape and was stacking the many dossiers on the nearby desk. First he flipped through the pages—obviously hunting for cash—but then sorted through the files, arranged them in some order, and began reading.

"Jesus Christ," breathed the boy.

"What is it?"

Without speaking, Val tossed the folder he'd just read through to his grandfather. He did not look up from reading the second one. "Jesus Christ," he said again.

Leonard began reading with perhaps the worst sinking feeling he'd ever had outside of the day his wife Carol had come home to tell him she had ovarian cancer.

These were photocopies of some sort of grand jury report. All the evidence, photostats, phone records, and other information led to one conclusion—that five and a half years ago, Major Crimes Unit Detective First Grade Nick Bottom had learned that his wife was having an affair with a Denver assistant district attorney named Harvey Cohen and had arranged to have them both killed in what would appear to be a highway accident.

"Jesus Christ," whispered Dr. George Leonard Fox.

Val finished speed-reading through the last dossier, stood up, pulled the coiled climbing rope from his father's closet, and dumped it on the floor. He opened his own duffel bag and started pulling things out even while he emptied the pockets of his own jacket.

Leonard realized that the boy was stuffing his pockets with magazines for the pistol and with handfuls of bullets.

Then Val threw the coils of climbing rope and carabiners over his shoulder, walked out the door, and disappeared into the warren of cubies in the former Baby Gap.

"Val!" Leonard ran to the outer door of the store and shouted after the boy, but his grandson was out of sight, probably down the frozen escalator or around the bend in the mall mezzanine.

Leonard pivoted in helpless circles. What could he do? He could phone the Gunny G. security person and tell him to stop Val from leaving, but of course there was no phone in Nick Bottom's mess of a cubie. Leonard's chest hurt from his short run from the cubie; he could never catch Val in time.

The old man went to the railing and looked down to the first level of what had once been a bright and upscale shopping mall. Garbage bags were stacked outside of all the grimy-windowed and grubby-tiled former storefronts, and the place stank. If it hadn't been for the little light coming through dirt-crusted skylights—a few of them propped open above—the mall would have been dark and airless.

"My God, my God," whispered Leonard. He felt almost certain that Val had gone out to retrieve his pistol and that his grandson would be stalking around outside, waiting for his father to return. Whether on foot or in a car, Nick Bottom would be a target.

Leonard was almost back to the cubie when he heard thuds and the sound of breaking glass. *Oh my God, they've hurt Val!* He ran back out onto the mezzanine, but there was still no one in sight and everything looked normal. Leonard would have stayed there until someone came out to explain what the noise had been, but his chest simply hurt too much.

Gasping for air, Leonard returned to Nick Bottom's cubie, shoved aside the empty drawers, and sat on the bed. His chest hurt so much that he thought he might faint.

He forced himself up and walked to the desk, looking down at the heap of dossiers.

Val had emptied his pockets of everyday things—penknife, a notebook, other detritus—to make room for the pistol magazines and loose ammunition he'd taken with him. There on the desk was Leonard's daughter Dara's cell phone, set down and forgotten by Val in his hurry. With shaking hands, he sat on the bed and activated the few functions that still worked on the phone, clicking to the private text and massive video files.

The demand for the five-letter-digit password came up.

Remembering his lovely, elfin daughter telling her Shakespeare-scholar father why she'd fallen in love with a man with the absurd name of Nick Bottom, Leonard thumbed in the letters—*d-r-e-a-m*.

The encryption fell away. Leonard opened the video files first but this wasn't a video diary by his daughter: people whom Leonard could not identify were staring into a camera, obviously a much higher-quality camera than the one on Dara's phone, and talking about their use of flashback. The video files were huge, but skipping around in them just showed more men and women speaking into the camera. There was no sight of Dara, and Leonard couldn't imagine why this stuff was on her phone.

One hand massaging his aching chest, Leonard closed the video files and opened the encrypted text files. This was by his daughter—a private diary kept by Dara between the late spring and early autumn of her last full year of life. It was password-protected but Leonard guessed *Kildare*—the name of Dara's parakeet when she was eight years old—and the file opened. He read quickly, keying the daily entries faster and faster until he reached the last one, recorded just one day before her death.

"My God, my God," Leonard said again, his voice filled with infinitely more terror and astonishment.

This changed everything. It made the hundreds of pages of the grand jury indictment information in the dossiers accusing Nick of murder nothing more than a sad joke. It changed *everything.*

He *had* to get to a phone and call Nick no matter what the consequences of the police tracing the call. He *had* to find and stop Val. He had to...

Leonard felt the sudden pain in his chest expand, a pain much more intense than the mere flower-fist of discomfort he was used to, until the pain became a widening cloak of darkness that first fluttered about him like a black bat and then settled tight around him, cutting off his vision and breathing.

I have to stay conscious, thought Leonard. *I have to tell Nick. I have to tell Val. I have to tell everyone...*

He did not feel himself fall.

1.15

Santa Ana and Airborne—Fri., Sept. 24

JOHN WAYNE AIRPORT was outside the area of the battle that had raged around Los Angeles for six or seven days, but the heavy amount of National Guard and other military traffic rumbling by on the 405 San Diego Freeway crossing the airport grounds just beyond the northeast end of Runway 1L/19R had been constant for days. No military air traffic was using John Wayne, only the usual commercial freight and occasional passenger traffic that regularly used the small field in unincorporated Orange County. Noise-abatement restrictions that had once made large aircraft takeoff from Runway 19R somewhat problematic for passengers with the required steep climbs and hard banks over Newport Beach had been eliminated in recent years.

Even though no Nakamura-owned commercial or private aircraft were allowed to land in Los Angeles–area airports, John Wayne Airport had for years been a negotiated exception. This Friday evening a modified FedEx A310/360 Nakamura courier-freight flight from Tokyo, with a stopover in Hawaii, had landed, refueled, and was awaiting a scheduled 7 p.m. takeoff, bound for Denver.

At five minutes before seven, the captain of the Nakamura

aircraft requested a change in their flight plan to accommodate an 8 p.m. takeoff time. Tower personnel at John Wayne Airport forwarded the request to both the civilian Los Angeles Air Route Traffic Control Center in Palmdale and the temporary Los Angeles Military Region Air Traffic Control located at the former Bob Hope Airport in Burbank, which was currently being operated as regional control center by the California Air National Guard for the duration of the military emergency. Both centers agreed to the one-hour delay. Along with that permission came the notice that military air traffic over the combat area currently centered on Lake Elsinore some fifty miles east of John Wayne Airport was so intense—and the evening military traffic out of LAX so busy—that all westbound commercial traffic from John Wayne was required to fly west out over the Pacific, northwest along the coast to a designated turning point near Morro Bay, and only then turn east by northeast, resuming their usual flight lanes to Denver at a point north and east of Las Vegas. All pilots were notified to refigure their fuel requirements accordingly.

The crew of the Nakamura aircraft was also notified that there would be no further delays granted this Friday night since, under local wartime regulations, John Wayne Airport would be shutting down for the night at 8:15 p.m. PDST.

At three minutes before 8 p.m., the Nakamura A310/360 started its engines and began taxiing to its takeoff position on Runway 19R. It had tested both engines and had requested final permission for takeoff when suddenly a California Highway Patrol cruiser pulled out onto the runway ahead of it, all of the police cruiser's bubble lights flashing.

The A310/360 received permission to taxi onto the apron, although it was informed that it would have to be airborne in less than fifteen minutes or spend the night at John Wayne. It did not shut down its engines. Ground crews arrived in an old Ford electric pickup with Wollard Truck Model TLPH252 passenger stairs mounted on it and the aircraft opened its left front door. The CHP cruiser approached and stopped, its lights quit flashing, and Nick Bottom got out and came around to the driver's side to talk to the newly appointed chief Ambrose at the wheel.

"Thanks, Chief," said Nick, shaking the heavyset trooper's hand.

"I'll always be Dale to you, Nick," said Ambrose. "I hope you find your boy." The CHP vehicle drove off the tarmac as Nick climbed the steps to the aircraft. He favored his right side because of the injured ribs there.

———

THREE HOURS EARLIER, ADVISOR Daichi Omura had said to him, "If you go back to Denver, Bottom-san, you *will* die."

"I have to go back, Omura-sama."

"Hideki Sato will be waiting for you on the aircraft at John Wayne Airport, Bottom-san. You will never be out of his custody again for the short remnant of your life...*if* you try to go back."

Nick had shaken his head and sipped the very fine single-malt Scotch Omura had provided. "I don't think so, Omura-sama. Sato's in Washington with Mr. Nakamura. They weren't scheduled to get back to Denver until Saturday...tomorrow sometime. Plus, this flight's coming from Tokyo via Hawaii. Mr. Nakamura himself told me that they didn't have any flights going west from Denver to Los Angeles–area airports."

"Sato will have to be there," grunted the old man.

"Why is that, Omura-sama?"

"Because if you do not show up at John Wayne Airport tonight, Security Chief Sato's job—Colonel Sato's job—will be to enter the firestorm that is Los Angeles—*my* domain, Bottom-san—and find you, dead or alive. I understand Hiroshi Nakamura well enough to know this for a certainty. He will not let you escape if he can help it. Not now."

Nick had shaken his head at that, but the words chilled him.

———

A CREW MEMBER BUTTONED up the hatch behind him as Nick stepped into a luxuriously appointed cabin just aft of the flight deck. The swiveling leather seats at the windows, deep-cushioned couches, and 3DHD flatscreens on the bulkheads would have been at home in a billionaire's executive jet, but this space was larger.

Sato was seated and buckled in at one of the starboard leather seats that had a low table in front of it. He did not rise as Nick entered but gestured to the chair opposite him.

Nick settled gingerly into the full-grain leather seat and buckled his seat belt. Cabin lights dimmed as the A310/360 returned to the head of the runway and tested its engines again at full throttle. The pilot said something over the intercom in Japanese and the big aircraft hurtled down the runway, lifted off into the night, and banked steeply to the left, coming around to a west-by-northwest course out over the ocean.

Nick looked at his watch. It was 8:14 p.m. PDST.

THE FIRST TWENTY-FOUR HOURS — just getting into the city from the untowered landing field out east of the I-15 — had been the most dangerous. But after surviving the slums and exodus of half a million panicked spanics and the gangs behind them, Nick was finally shot on a quiet side street in San Marino near Pasadena, in one of the most upper-class suburbs L.A. could offer.

It was more than fifty miles by car from this hillbilly Fla-bob Airport to his father-in-law's neighborhood near Echo Park just northwest of the huge Homeland Security holding pen at Dodger Stadium. Using surface streets and alleys to keep out of the way of the fighting and massive evacuation, it was — Nick saw on the GPS mapping function of his phone — more than sixty miles with most of the route winding up through Ontario, Claremont, or Pomona, and down through south Pasadena. If he had to do it on foot, Nick thought, he might as well have started walking from Las Vegas. So the first thing he did was to steal an electric moped from a spanic kid who was just trying to flee the chaos behind his family, packed into an overloaded gelding SUV. Nick would have stolen the SUV, but the father — seeing the man with a gun emerge from the darkness — floored the rattling wreck of a vehicle, getting every dying amp he could from it while leaving his teenage son on the moped to a gunman's mercy.

Nick used the Glock to wave the weeping kid off the moped, untied and tossed the bundled luggage to the now-howling teenager, and drove away without feeling the slightest hint of guilt. The father and family would return for the kid, even if they had to lash him to the roof rack with the rest of their belongings.

Probably.

The primitive display showed that the moped had been recently charged and had a range of two hundred miles. Nick told his phone to plot a bicycle-friendly trip to Echo Park and was informed that it would take him five and a half hours, but Nick knew that if he had to dodge fighters and fleeing civilians all the way, the trip would take at least twice as long.

Nick didn't have the time for this shit. He knew now that he should have pulled his Glock on the pilot as they approached L.A. and demanded that the coward land them at some civil-aviation field much closer to his destination—or even some-place like the Brookside Golf Course in Pasadena.

Cursing his own stupidity, Nick squatted on the under-sized moped and goosed the little machine to its full speed of thirty miles per hour. Somehow the fact that the moped gave forth only a low electrical hum made it seem to go even slower.

To the west, northwest, and southwest, as Nick left the empty, dark airport grounds, all of Los Angeles looked as if it were on fire. Scores of helicopter gunships and TV news chop-pers flitted in front of the orange glow like bats fleeing a burn-ing belfry. Ancient California Air National Guard A10 jet ground-support bombers were making runs on targets some-where in Chino. The sound of the distant explosions arrived long after the tiny flashes.

For the first three hours of his circuitous route west toward the city, no one shot at him. He'd brought a ball cap that he tugged low so his ethnicity wasn't obvious in the dark, and there was something about a grown man on a kid's battery-powered

moped—perhaps it was the knees higher than the handlebars—
that made him a nonthreatening figure.

Even though it was after midnight, the freeways and surface
streets were filled with fleeing civilians. Nick realized that he
was seeing the tail end of several days of evacuation from L.A.—
mostly from East L.A.—of hundreds of thousands of spanics,
both residents who'd been there for many decades and hordes of
the new immigrants who'd come north on the wave of *reconquista*
victories. Nick caught only a few glimpses of the remnants of
that Nuevo Mexican military force—clusters of battered Hum-
mers forcing their way through the mobs of civilians in the night
and the occasional N.M. helicopter roaring low above the freeways in an attempt to escape that was every bit as panicked and
purposeless as the east and southeast surge of civilians.

Nick kept his phone GPS—he'd long ago named her
Betty—constantly updating his route to keep him out of the
path of these refugees, and Betty's sexy voice whispered through
his earbud to lead him down alleys across Claremont and Glen-
dora, along empty bikepaths through Monrovia and Arcadia—
most of the explosions and fighting seemed to be going on
south of his route—and across the empty campus and soccer
fields of Citrus College. The moped was happier on sidewalks
than it was on streets.

Except for the military aircraft, there was no sign yet of the
anglo military as the stars began to disappear behind him to the
brightening east and the birds began to make their usual pre-
sunrise clatter. Back in Glen Aven and southern Ontario, Nick
had caught just enough glimpses of the shooting going on in the
valley to the south to be sure that it was Aryan Brotherhood
paramilitary, motorcycle gangs, Vietnamese and Chinese gangs
from farther west and north, Mulholland mercenaries in armored
Jeeps, and thousands of rioters from South Central L.A. whose
parents and grandparents might have taken part in the Florence and Normandie fun forty years earlier. Leonard had
described the ancient history of those riots to his daughter, and
Dara, once calling the outbursts "the beginning of the modern
era," had passed on his account to Nick.

The gangs were looting and terrorizing the last of the refu-gees, but Nick saw enough to know that their primary goal was to burn down everything south of the Ventura Freeway and north of the Santa Ana Freeway. They appeared to be succeeding.

Nick had brought two water bottles and as many food bars as he'd been able to stuff in his jacket pockets and he sipped and munched as he drove west. The mobs of refugees were gone by the time he approached San Marino, the occasional police or anglo military presence visible only on primary roads and the entrance to freeways. As Nick headed west paralleling California Boulevard just north of the Huntington Botanical Gardens—the upscale neighborhoods were absolutely dark, their power obviously cut, as he wound along Betty's chosen bikepaths and side streets—he congratulated himself on get-ting past the worst of it and essentially being home free.

Several shots hammered the pre-dawn grayness. Nick felt a bullet bite the back of his left calf muscle even as a second slug killed the moped's battery-driven motor.

Nick dumped the little bike on its side and rolled toward the gutter and a line of Dumpsters there as half a dozen more shots rang out. He scrabbled on all fours into a darker alley, ran half a block knowing that he was leaving a blood trail, and then crouched behind another Dumpster to check the damage.

The bullet had taken a lot of skin and some solid flesh but no real muscle. But it hurt like hell. Nick hiked up his pant leg and tied the wound off with a clean white handkerchief. He waited in the dark, Glock in hand, hoping that it was a random shot—or that, if they wanted the moped for some reason, his assailants would call it a morning when they saw they'd destroyed the little machine.

No such luck. They stalked him for the next half hour.

There were three of them—the big, stupid-sounding guy whom Nick thought of as the Linebacker, an older, skinny guy with the rifle whom he thought of as the Quarterback since he seemed to be literally calling the shots, and a greasy-haired teenager whom he thought of as Billy because he reminded

Nick of the character Billy Clanton played by the young Dennis Hopper in the 1957 *Gunfight at the O.K. Corral.*

Nick hobbled south through front yards, dodging from tree to tree and wall to wall, with his three shooters following on foot. All three of them fired at him as he dodged and weaved across Orlando Road, hurtling a low fence and crashing his way into the 120 or so acres of the botanical gardens. The hunters each carried a backpack full of ammunition and seemed intent on firing it all off.

Nick had no idea what these idiots wanted of him... other than to make him dead. His best guess was that they had been playing cowboy for the duration of the Los Angeles fighting, raiding East L.A. neighborhoods at night just for the fun of killing someone. And they'd obviously gotten addicted to the killing. He had no other explanation for why they'd fired at him in quiet San Marino.

Nick had Betty bring up a map of the botanical gardens, but he'd been here about five years ago with his father-in-law, who'd had some academic business at the research library here. It was the week that Nick had brought Val out to live with Leonard. He could find his way to the library, but the historic structure was near the center of this large urban mix of forests, flower gardens, formal Japanese gardens, and meadows, and although there might be security guards at the library, Nick didn't want to get them involved.

The shooting trio had RadioShack walkie-talkies but kept shouting back and forth to one another. This was great sport to them and they'd obviously been drinking or using drugs. It became clear that they weren't comfortable stalking someone in these manicured woods and meadows—they'd probably spent a good part of the last week shooting people in urban settings—but then, Nick wasn't comfortable being stalked in the woods either. He would have preferred an alley.

He soon realized that they were making noise and firing at random in order to herd him to their left, toward Oxford Road bordering the gardens to the east. Nick didn't want to go back east. He had business to the west and south.

It was starting to get light in earnest now. He had to get this over with.

He'd come into an area where a Doric-columned circular mausoleum stood in the middle of a clearing. Nick hobbled as quickly as he could across the clearing but his trackers still had time to get off two shots. One tugged at his jacket and then he was in the trees and panting to catch his breath. He'd seen the muzzle flashes and knew that the hunters were directly across the clearing from him. He shouted, "What do you want from me?"

"Everything you got, pal," shouted one of the men. The other two giggled.

"Let's meet in the middle and settle this," shouted Nick. He ducked low and began running as quickly as he could through the thick undergrowth, no longer heading away from the shooters, circling the clearing back to the west, in their direction. There was a park road only a few meters to the north and he knew they'd also want to use the maximum amount of cover as they attempted to flank him.

Nearing the west end of the circular clearing, Nick stopped, knelt, and slipped in a fresh magazine of ammo. He crouched low and chambered the first round as silently as he could.

All three men came out into the clearing, crouching and silent. They were moving too quickly for Nick to get a clean shot at all of them at once. Counting on the fact that they were amateurs—no matter how many men and women they'd killed in recent days—Nick shouted, "Hey!"

Soldiers, mercenaries, or professional killers would have kept moving, throwing themselves in different directions. These three amateurs froze, turned, and opened fire. Even the Quarterback had a pistol in his right hand—while he carried the rifle in his left—and was joining in the shooting.

Two slugs caught Nick in his lower right side, not penetrating the Kevlar-3 he wore under his shirt, but cracking some ribs, knocking the wind out of him, and spinning him around. He knelt in a combat firing crouch, ignored the fusillade of bullets ripping branches just over his head, and fired eight times.

All three men went down hard. After a minute, seeing

everyone's hands empty in the increasing light of dawn, Nick crabwalked toward them, gun raised and steady in both hands.

He'd somehow managed to miss the great bulk of the Linebacker except for one high center-mass shot, but that had pulped the big man's heart. Blood had exploded from the man's mouth, ears, and eyes. He'd been dead before he hit the ground.

The Quarterback had taken two of Nick's slugs center mass but it had been the third shot—a round, bloodless hole in the precise center of the ferret-faced man's upper lip—that had done the job.

Billy Clanton had also absorbed three slugs but was still alive, writhing and curling in pain.

Nick kicked all the visible weapons into the bushes and crouched over the teenager.

"Help me, mister, please, help me, I hurt…oh, Jesus God, Jesus, it hurts…help me, please, for the love of Christ, mister, please…"

Nick studied the wounds. None was fatal in and of itself, but the boy would bleed out soon enough if he didn't get medical attention. Nick was sure there'd be a medical station at the California Institute of Technology just a few blocks to the northwest.

"Where's your car?" asked Nick, bending low so that he was hissing almost into the boy's ear. "Where are the keys to your car?"

The mantra of pain and entreaty paused long enough for the boy to squint up at him. Like most young Americans, this one had never felt real pain for more than a few minutes at a time. He wanted a pill or shot or IV for this pain…and *right now*.

"You'll…help me? I didn't wanna come along, you know. It was all Dean's idea. I didn't wanna…"

"Where's the car?" whispered Nick. "Where are the keys? Medical help's only a few minutes away by car. I can't carry you."

The boy nodded and then belched blood. This terrified him and he started babbling through his groans and weeping.

Dean's blue Nissan Menlo Park was parked on Landor Lane, just half a block from where they'd shot at Nick. They all lived up in Altadena and were just regular guys, you know, and were coming home from having some night fun down in East L.A.—everybody was doing it this week—when they'd seen the moped and Dean'd said, one more for a nightcap, but…

"Keys?" hissed Nick.

"Dean…Dean's pocket…Dean…front pocket, I think… help, for the love of Christ, mister, it hurts *so* much."

Nick guessed that Dean was the Quarterback and found the keys in the dead man's front pocket. The key ring was labeled NISSAN. Nick also checked both the dead Linebacker's pockets and the moaning, writhing boy's, as well as all three backpacks, but found only some extra ammunition, billfolds, cards, and some cash. He kept the cash and Dean's NICC.

Nick opened his shirt and checked the Kevlar-3 undershirt on the right side. It had stopped both pistol slugs but there was definitely some damage to his ribs on that side. Trying to take deep, slow breaths, he buttoned his shirt back up. The bullet crease on his left calf had finally stopped bleeding, but not before soaking through the handkerchief and his pant leg. It would be a bitch to pull the solidly caked material free later.

"Please…mister…you promised…you promised…it hurts so much…you promised."

Nick knelt over the wounded boy and decided that he really didn't look much like the young Dennis Hopper. He didn't look *anything* like Val.

"You *promised*…"

He could get Dean's van, drive back here, load the kid in, and try to find some medical help before the boy bled out. Or he could point his would-be killer in the direction of the Huntington Library and tell him to crawl, although odds were low that he'd get there before he bled to death.

Either way, he'd be leaving someone behind who could describe him and the Nissan to the cops—if the cops were still a factor in this L.A. suburb—and raise Nick's chances of being detained somewhere, thus lowering his chances of finding Val.

You try to kill a stranger for fun, thought Nick, *you need to be ready to face the consequences.* He wasn't absolutely sure at that second whether he was thinking of the young man moaning beneath him or of Val's alleged involvement in the attack on Advisor Omura. The difference was that Val, whether he ran from his father's last name or not, carried Nick's own blood and DNA.

Nick used his left hand to shield his face and eyes from backspatter as he set the muzzle of the Glock within three inches of the boy's pale forehead and white, widening eyes and squeezed the trigger.

The Menlo was parked right where the kid had said it would be. Betty whispered to him that there were less than twelve miles to go even if he avoided the Pasadena Freeway by taking Monterey Road to North Figueroa Street and the Nissan's own nav system confirmed it. There might be roadblocks ahead, Nick knew, but one way or the other, he'd be at Leonard's address in half an hour or so.

———

AS THE PLANE FINALLY banked back toward the east an attractive female flight attendant wearing a kimono entered the cabin from aft and Sato said, "Are you hungry or thirsty, Bottom-san?"

Nick shook his head. The flight attendant took Sato's order of *tako su*, pepper tuna, and *sunomono*—the big man specified that he wanted it sauced with ponzu and wasabi mayonnaise—and barbecued squid in soy ginger sauce. He also ordered a bowl of *nabeyaki udon* without the poached egg. And *sake*.

When the flight attendant turned to Nick and bowed, obviously inquiring as to whether he'd changed his mind and would like something after all, Nick said, "Yes, I'd also like some *sake*."

When the woman was gone, Sato asked, "Do you need medical attention, Bottom-san? One of the crew has military medical training and the proper equipment and drugs."

Nick shook his head again. "Just some scratches and dinged-in ribs. I had them taped."

They flew in silence for a few minutes. The A310/360's two engines were so quiet that almost no sound from them entered the cabin; Nick knew they were on only because of the faint vibration underfoot and in the arms of his leather chair. He was close to dozing off when Sato spoke.

"You did not find your son, then, Bottom-san?"

"No. I didn't."

"Nor any clue as to his current whereabouts?"

Nick shrugged. "What are you doing here, Sato? You were supposed to be with Mr. Nakamura in Washington until tomorrow."

The security chief—or was it assassin?—grunted. "Nakamura-sama is returning to Denver tomorrow, but a company flight to John Wayne Airport opened up today and he suggested I come out to make sure you made this flight."

"If I hadn't?" said Nick. He was very aware that no one had frisked him and that he still had the fully loaded Glock 9 on his left hip.

Sato made his clumsy version of a shrug. "I would have contacted authorities to inquire as to your fate, Bottom-san. Beginning with your assistant chief Ambrose, whom you mentioned in Denver. Or is it, as you said on the tarmac, 'Chief' Ambrose?"

"Promotion," said Nick. Even talking sent pain through his tightly taped but still-aching ribs. "The regular CHP chief had a fatal heart attack on the third day of the rioting and fighting in L.A. and Dale received a temporary field promotion."

"But your friend in the California Highway Patrol was not able to help you find your son?"

Nick shook his head again. The food came in, carried by three beautiful female attendants, and looked delicious. Nick wasn't sure why he hadn't ordered something: he hadn't eaten in more than ten hours and it would be after midnight, Denver time, when they landed at DIA. Even his mall condos' late-night cafeteria would be shut down by the time he got there.

Nick found himself salivating from just looking at Sato's dinner laid out on the table, but it was the smell of the *nabeyaki udon* broth that really made his stomach rumble.

He gulped some *sake*, rose painfully, and said, "Where's the lavatory?"

There were two doors on the aft bulkhead. The flight attendants had come in through the one on the right. Sato pointed to the door on the left.

A few minutes later, Nick stood in front of the wide mirror. This aircraft lavatory was three times the size of the bathroom in his cubie and had an actual bath as well as shower. The face and figure staring back at him looked out of place in the lemon-soap luxury of the executive-jet lavatory: Nick's shirt was torn and bloodied, his tan jacket and chinos filthy—the left pant leg ripped and blood-soaked with white bandages showing through—and Nick had scrapes and new scars on his cheek-bone and right temple. He'd received nine stitches along that cheekbone at the CHP barracks and the effect was moderately Frankenstein-like. They'd scrubbed off the worst of the grime there, but Nick still washed his hands and face vigorously in the plane lav, handling the thick hand towel gingerly, as if he didn't want his dirt and blood to contaminate it.

Nick removed the Glock from the crossdraw holster, made sure the safety was off and that there was a round in the cham-ber, and set the heavy pistol back in place. If Omura-sama was correct—and Nick had believed him—then Sato was escort-ing him home to a death sentence. And one that would be car-ried out soon, probably tomorrow afternoon or evening when Nakamura arrived home to his mountaintop above Denver.

But Nick had his pistol now. An oversight? A test?

Either way, the 9mm Glock was real and his to use. But use how? Come out shooting, kill Sato first, then move from one hanging oxygen mask to the next until he could get onto the flight deck and demand that the pilot fly him...

Where? There was no nation in this hemisphere now that did not have extradition treaties with the New Nippon.

And what if Val had made it to Denver and was waiting for him?

But all this was academic, since Nick knew the door to access the flight deck could probably take repeated RPG rounds without opening or giving way. And that the crew was almost certainly armed, but wouldn't even need that. All they'd have to do was keep the plane at altitude—assuming that some of his rounds either made it all the way through Sato or missed and depressurized the aircraft—and shut off the oxygen to his compartment. They could do that, of course, even if a stray round hadn't depressurized the compartment. Nick shook his head and stared at the much thinner, almost gaunt by his standards of the last five years or so, and visibly beaten-up figure in the mirror. He was too tired. Too many nights with too little sleep. It was hard to think.

When he came out, there was a cluster of little plates and a bowl and a replenished glass of *sake* on his side of the small table as well.

"This meal was so good that I took the liberty, Bottom-san," grunted Sato. "I personally do not enjoy the poached egg with the noodles in *nabeyaki udon,* but most people do. I had them serve it to you on the side. The slices of cooked octopus in the *tako su* are garnished with sticks of pale green cucumber, bathed in ponzu sauce and topped with sesame seeds, sliced scallion, and a drizzle of wasabi mayonnaise. I believe you will find that the sauce has an engagingly smoky, citrus taste that complements the octopus. Why are you smiling, Bottom-san?"

"No reason," said Nick, although he'd come close to laughing at Sato's impersonation of an eager maître d'. "I guess I'm more hungry than I knew, Sato-san. Thank you."

Sato nodded abruptly. "The pepper tuna and *sunomono* are similarly sauced with ponzu and wasabi mayonnaise," he said. "The black pepper–crusted tuna, seared on the outside but still raw, then sliced thin, is a favorite of mine. I hope you enjoy it, Bottom-san."

"I am certain I will, Sato-san," said Nick. He was still standing and he realized that he was bowing his thanks, and bowing low.

Sato grunted and Nick settled into his chair, giving out his own involuntary grunt from the pain in his ribs. The smell from the bowl of broth and other food brought tears to his eyes.

———

GALINA KSCHESSINSKA, AKA GALINA Sue Coyne, was of a kind that Nick had interviewed many times, sometimes as eager witness, although more often as perp or accomplice. In any of the roles, the clinical description of the Galina Kschessinska type remained the same: malignant narcissist.

"I haven't had anyone come to talk to me for several days," said the middle-aged woman. Her eyes looked like small, pale oysters that had been swallowed by successive layers of makeup. Nick thought that her plastic surgeon should be arrested and tortured for crimes against humanity. "I was beginning to think," she continued, inhaling smoke from her No-C stick at the end of a pearl cigarette holder, "that the police had lost interest in the case."

Why would that be, just because the world is burning down here? thought Nick. He shook his head. Vigorously. "Oh, no, Ms. Kschessinska, the case is still very much open and we're very interested in finding the culprit or culprits who shot your son...and for his death, let me say again, I'm very, very sorry."

The woman lowered her eyes and gave herself a half-moment of dramatic silence. "Yesss," she said finally, sending the pitiful purr-hiss out through projected pain. "Poor William." Whatever her relationship with her son Billy had been, thought Nick, her mourning period for the kid hadn't quite lasted the past week. And she'd obviously enjoyed the attention she'd received from the media and cops and wanted more of it. Today she seemed either drugged or drunk or a bit of both. Between her mild accent and the more-than-mild slurring, Nick had to concentrate to understand what she was saying.

Nick had flashed his Rent-a-Detective badge with his name on it, so if she'd known Val's real last name, Nick's cover—such as it was—was blown. But Ms. Kschessinska hadn't paid close attention. Nick had the feeling that she hadn't paid very close attention to many things—including her recently deceased son—for some years now.

"You mentioned that your son William gave this missing

boy, Val Fox—the one we're looking for—a gun shortly before the...ah...incident at the Disney Center?" said Nick. He had a small notebook out and pen poised, but so far all he'd scribbled in it in his tiny cop script was *She smells bad.*

"Oh, yes, Detective...uh...Botham, William did tell me that not long ago. Yes."

And you didn't call the cops to tell them that your kid was dealing guns? thought Nick. He didn't correct her on his name and was phrasing his follow-up question carefully when Ms. Kschessinska forged ahead.

"You understand, Detective, my William was always concerned about my safety, about his little friends' safety, about everyone's...why, this is a very dangerous city in which to live, Detective! Just look out the windows!"

"Yes, ma'am," said Nick. "Do you remember what kind of gun it was that your son gave to the Fox boy?"

"Oh, the other policemen mentioned it. Just talk to them. It started with a 'B,' I seem to remember."

"Browning?" said Nick. "Bauer, Bren, Beretta..."

"That's it," said Ms. Kschessinska, "that last one. Beretta. Pretty name. Would you like a little drinkie, Detective? I always allow myself a little one in the afternoon, especially in these terrible days since William was...was..." She threatened to dissolve into tears.

"No, thank you," Nick said hurriedly. "But you have one, please. I know this is hard for you." He didn't point out that it was not quite ten o'clock in the morning.

She mixed and poured and stirred with a serious drinker's full attention. "You sure you won't join me, Detective? There's plenty to..."

"Did you happen to see the Beretta, Ms. Kschessinska?"

"What? Oh, no! Of course not." She returned to her favorite chair with a tall glass. "But William told me about it. He used to share everything with me. He told me that this friend of his, Hal..."

"Val," said Nick.

"Whatever. He told me that this friend of his was part of

their little club, their little boys' club, but that this Hal, Val, whatever it was, wasn't really a team player."

"How's that?" Nick asked quietly.

"Oh, just little things...like the fact that this other boy wouldn't take part when the boys were doing their little experiments."

"Experiments?"

"Oh, their little experiments into sex and such. All boys do it, you know."

"You're talking about experiments with sex with girls, Ms. Kschessinska?"

"Of course I mean with girls!" shouted the heavy woman with the painted face of melting clay. She was truly angry. "William would never...could never..."

"So you're saying that this Val Fox boy didn't take part when the ga...when William's boys' club had sex with one or more girls?"

"Yes, exactly," Ms. Kschessinska said primly, still not mollified.

Nick wrote *Gang rape* on his notebook page. Even six years ago when he'd still been with the Denver force, male flashgangs almost always began with gang rape. They'd relive the violation of some girl, frequently a minor, over and over under the flash. Then the gangs usually moved up to physical violence: tormenting and brutalizing younger kids or winos or other flashback addicts found helpless under the flash. Then—most frequently—murder. Or murder after a brutal rape. The ultimate event to flash on. Two for the price of one.

"Did this Val boy not participate in their flashback use of these...experiments?" asked Nick.

"That is precisely correct," said Ms. Kschessinska, taking great care not to slur. "William told me that this person wasn't enough of a man to join in the experiment and wasn't enough of a friend to join the others when they relived the event as part of their...rite of passage, as it were."

"What did William say this boy did when they were experimenting?"

"Oh, various excuses," she slurred, waving her hands as she tried to light a real cigarette, plucking the No-C stick out and flinging it away angrily. "Standing guard. William said the boy always lost his nerve and stood apart, saying he was going to stand guard for the others. That sort of nonsense. The boy was not a true friend of William's, no matter everything my dear boy tried to do for him. No matter what wonderful gifts William gave him."

She looked up and Nick thought of shell-less oysters again as the mottled, mucusy gray eyes within their pools of makeup tried to focus on him. "But if he did indeed murder my son, I guess it ghosts... goes, that is... goes without saying that he was no real friend. This Hal Fox was probably always planning to betray and murder William." She inhaled deeply, held it, and then exhaled smoke through her nose.

"No idea, then, where this boy might be?" asked Nick.

"Nothing more than what I've already told your colleagues, Detective... was it Detective Betham? Nick Betham?"

"Yes, ma'am," said Nick. He'd already checked out the various overpasses and other flashgang hangouts that Ms. Kschessinska had told the LAPD and CHP about. It hadn't been easy going to those places either, since Leonard's apartment and the entire neighborhood near Echo Park had been first reduced to rubble and then burned down in the fighting. Aryan B gangs numbering in the hundreds had blown the walls at the Dodger Stadium Homeland Security Detention Center, flooding that entire neighborhood with more terrorists, killers, and self-proclaimed jihadists. The area around Chávez Ravine was not a safe place to spend time this week.

Checking out the storm sewer system, including the area still a crime scene under the Disney Center, had also had its nasty surprises. But none that had given Nick a clue about Val's current whereabouts.

He'd left Galina Kschessinska Coyne smoking, drinking, sobbing, and hiccupping. With the investigation into the attack on Advisor Omura being called off—due not only to the press of current events but to Omura's own request that it be discontinued—it was doubtful that any authorities would come to visit Ms. Kschessinska again. Or at least, Nick thought as he let himself out, until some patrol officers, responding to complaints of a terrible smell, someday entered the apartment to find her corpse.

———

"**DO YOU WISH ANY** more pepper tuna or *sunomono* or *nabeyaki udon* or *tako su*, Bottom-san?" asked Sato. "Or *sake?*"

"No, no, no thank you," said Nick. "Especially no thank you on the *sake*. I've had too much already."

He was a little drunk. That would be fine if he were just going straight home to his cubie and bed after they landed in Denver in the next hour or so, but Nick wasn't sure what Sato might have in mind.

"Sato-san," he said, "tell me again when I'm going to see Mr. Nakamura?"

"You remember me saying, Bottom-san, that Nakamura-sama is scheduled to return to Denver tomorrow night. You are invited to come speak to Nakamura-sama as soon as he arrives home in the evening. He is most eager to hear what you have to say."

To name Keigo Nakamura's murderer, thought Nick. *If I don't know by then, I'm expendable. If I do have the murder figured out, I'll be even more expendable.*

"I brought these," said Sato and set a nylon bag on the side of Nick's table where it had just been cleared by the kimonoed flight attendants.

Suspicious, Nick unzipped the top. Ten vials of flashback cradled in foam, four of the vials obviously multihour flashes.

"Thanks," said Nick, closing the bag and dropping it on the carpet next to his feet. It had been seven long days and nights since he'd last gone under the flash, but he found that the sight of the vials hadn't excited him the way they had for the last half-dozen years. In fact, the thought of inhaling the stuff and going under its influence made him feel slightly nauseated.

"Sato," he said softly, "I keep hearing from people who

Keigo interviewed that the boy kept asking them about F-two...
Flashback-two, that old legend. Is there something going on
there?"

"Going on there, Bottom-san?"

"Is there something happening with F-two that I don't
know about?"

The big man shook his head in that Sato-way that involved
his shoulders and entire upper body more than his massive
neck. "There are rumors, Bottom-san, that this F-two has been
sold on the streets of New York City and Atlanta, Georgia, in
the last months, but as far as I can tell, they are only rumors.
There are always rumors of the fantasy drug being available
somewhere."

"Yeah." If any of the rumors had turned out to be real,
Nick knew for a certainty, F-two would have been available
everywhere in what was left of the country within a week. A
nation addicted to its own past via flashback was ripe for the
fantasy version of the drug. Since it hadn't popped up everywhere, Flashback-two was still a myth. Part of Nick was sorry.
Part of Nick was just...confused.

And very weary. He shouldn't have drunk the *sake*.

Nick looked out the aircraft window. They'd passed beyond
a region of clouds and the starlight and moonlight illuminated a
convoluted western topography five miles below. When Nick
had traveled by air as a young man, there had been more constellations of lights from small towns dotting even these barren
stretches of the country at night, but those constellations had
all but disappeared as the small towns in the west and elsewhere in what remained of the United States had fallen victim
to the economy and other new realities. One's instinct was to
think of small towns as a better survival-center come catastro-
phe, but it had turned out that they were more brittle and less
resilient than the big cities. Staring now at the solid darkness
below, Nick imagined the millions who'd fled those now dark
and silent towns over the past decade and a half—millions of
the newly homeless who'd embraced at least a *chance* of survival
in the battered big cities.

He dozed off while watching the tousled-gray bedspread of the western canyons, mountains, and deserts roll on darkly beneath them.

———

"**WHY DO YOU HAVE** him in custody?" Nick had asked Chief Ambrose as his father's old friend and former student led Nick back through overcrowded holding cells to an isolated cell now holding only one man.

"His father and grandfather were both assassinated shortly after the fighting began," said Ambrose, unlocking a door that led to the isolated cell. He paused to finish saying what he had to say before opening the door to the room. "Evidently they weren't killed in the general fighting, but were assassinated... or so Roberto believes. His own *reconquista* unit had been cut off in the Culver City fighting and Roberto was sure that if he surrendered to the National Guard or state authorities or to any of the mercenary armies down from Mulholland, Beverly Hills, and the rest, they'd execute him as well. So he and the few surviving members of his unit found some CHP patrolmen to surrender to and we brought him to the Southern Division barracks' lockup here in Glendale."

Nick's stolen Menlo was parked in the walled and razor-wire-protected visitors' parking lot outside this North Central Avenue CHP headquarters. He just hoped that no trooper decided to run the plate numbers.

"Do you think he'll talk to me?" asked Nick.

"Let's find out," said Dale Ambrose and swung open the door. The metal cell in the center of the larger room looked strange to Nick. Ambrose nodded and left.

Nick and the young man—in his late twenties, Nick thought—were alone in the room, except for the very obvious video camera near the ceiling in the far corner, and sat opposite each other on bunk beds in the oversized cell.

"I am Roberto Emilio Fernández y Figueroa," said the young man in a strong voice. "Someone assassinated my grandfather Don Emilio Gabriel Fernández y Figueroa and my father,

Eduardo Dante Fernández y Figueroa, last week, and those assassins will reach me soon, Mr. Bottom. Ask me what you wish to know and if I am able to help you without dishonoring my name or informing upon my family or comrades, I will do so."

"I'm only hunting for my son," said Nick. "But are you sure your grandfather and father were assassinated? It's been a pretty crazy week."

Roberto smiled ever so slightly. He was a handsome man and had been even more handsome before someone had broken his nose and beaten the right side of his face into a swollen red mass. "I am certain, Mr. Bottom. My grandfather knew of one assassination attempt scheduled for the very morning the fighting began—a Great White predator drone missile attack on one of our family compounds—and avoided that. But in the end, he and my father were killed by two separate assassins, people from within our own organization, who had obviously been suborned by the state of California or by Advisor Omura's people. It was the loss of my father's and *his* father's leadership that turned the tide against us so soon in the fighting."

Nick had nothing to say to that. He showed Roberto photos of Val and then of Leonard. "My father-in-law reportedly knew your grandfather," he said softly.

"Yes. I have heard of their Saturday chess games in Echo Park," said Roberto. The thin smile returned despite the massive bruising around his mouth.

"I'm trying to find out if my boy's alive, Señor Fernández y Figueroa," said Nick. "I was thinking that their only chance— my son's and his grandfather's—might have been if Leonard had come to see your grandfather to ask for help. It would have been immediately before the fighting. I'm hoping you might know whether my son and father-in-law left on one of your Friday convoys."

Roberto nodded slowly. "I have met neither your son nor his grandfather, Mr. Bottom. But my father did mention that Grandfather Emilio's 'old chess partner' had visited not long before the fighting began. It would make sense that your son and his grandfather might have been seeking escape on one of the truck convoys or railway services to which my family extended its protection and patronage."

"Do you know if that's what happened on Friday, September seventeenth?" asked Nick. "Do you know if my boy and his grandfather actually got on to some train or truck convoy?"

"I do not," said Roberto, shaking his head sadly. Even that amount of movement must have pained the man, thought Nick. "I fear that events were too violent and too confused that Friday…my father never got around to telling me what the nature of Grandfather Emilio's visit from your father-in-law was about. *Lo siento mucho*, Señor Bottom."

They both stood painfully, two men moving slowly with bruises and aching ribs as well as two men with death sentences hanging over them. They shook hands.

"I wish you luck, Señor Roberto Emilio Fernández y Figueroa. And I sincerely hope that things turn out better for you than you fear."

Roberto shook his head wryly but said, "And I wish you luck, Señor Bottom. And I will say a prayer asking that, if it is possible, your son and father-in-law are well and that you will all soon be reunited. At the very least, we must believe that we will be reunited with our family members in the *next* life."

Nick had felt some strange emotions as he finished talking to Chief Dale Ambrose, left the South Division CHP lockup, and got that Nissan Menlo Park the hell out of there.

———

HE TWITCHED AWAKE. SATO was snoring loudly, sitting in the chair across the table from him and sleeping with his massive arms crossed over his chest, the polymorphic smart-cast barely visible under his right shirtsleeve. Nick knew that if he made any noise at all, the security chief would be fully awake in a microsecond.

Nick checked his watch without moving his arm or body. If they were still on the schedule Sato had interpreted from the pilot's earlier announcement, they should be landing in Denver in about thirty minutes. Nick leaned toward the window just enough to look down into the darkness. Starlight gleamed on high snowfields while a few headlights moved along dark canyon roads. I-Seventy? It didn't matter. But the mere presence of vehicles on the highways meant that they were approaching the Front Range of Colorado.

Nick silently folded his own arms and closed his eyes.

———

HE'D PHONED K. T. Lincoln a little after 2 a.m. Los Angeles time, after 3 a.m. in Denver. He'd bought the use-once disposable phone that afternoon at a street market on an elevated and abandoned slab of the I-5. There were a lot of guns for sale there. And a lot of Arabs selling them.

"Lincoln," came the sleepy voice. And then, more angrily as she saw it wasn't the department calling and that the caller was shielding his name, "Who the hell is this?"

"It's me, K.T., Nick. *Don't hang up!*"

Nick knew that if they...always the invisible, hovering, omnipotent and terrifying *they*...had tapped K.T.'s cell phone, he was really and irrevocably fucked. But, as he already knew but would confirm beyond any doubt a few hours later in his interview with Advisor Omura, the addicted entity known as Nick Bottom was *already* really and irrevocably fucked.

"What do you want, Nick?" The tone of anger was far worse now, cold and deadly.

"I want to stay alive and to have any chance at all of that, I need your help, K.T."

"Feeling a little melodramatic tonight, are we, Nicholas?" She'd always known that her using "Nicholas" had amused him when they were partners. But could mere teasing be a good sign?

"I'm feeling surrounded and closed in on tonight, K.T., but that isn't the point. I need your help if Val and I are going to get out of this alive."

"Have you found Val?" At least her tone sounded interested.

But how much of that, Nick wondered, was a cop's interest in capturing a material witness and probable felon with an APB out on him?

"Not yet, but I think I will." Nick took a deep breath. He was on a fire escape outside a flophouse-cum-flashback-cave in downtown L.A. He'd spent $10,000 new bucks on a cot and blanket that were crawling with lice and bedbugs. Nick had dozed some on the floor, his jacket balled up under his head for a pillow and the Glock in his hand, until it was time to make this call. It helped a little to think of all the winos, flash addicts, and street people snoring around him as the geese a Roman legion would spread around their bivouac area; at least they might make some noise if the stocky guys in black Kevlar and laser rangefinders came crashing in on rappel ropes after Nick.

"I need you to do things for me if Val and I are going to have any chance at all," said Nick.

"Now it's *two* things," K.T. said sarcastically. *But she's still on the line.* Given the grand jury dossiers she'd seen and photocopied, just the act of her continuing to listen was a miracle.

"First," hurried Nick, "I need you to get a meeting set with me and Mayor Ortega for as early Saturday morning as you can make it. He's supposed to be back from the junket tomorrow. I don't know what strings you can pull to get a Saturday meeting set but..."

"Nick..."

"...but it's essential that I get in to see him early Saturday," Nick galloped on. "Or to make it safer for him, we can arrange to meet somewhere other than his office. In City Park, maybe, near the..."

"Nick!"

"What?"

"I don't know where you are or why you've been out of the news loop, but Mannie Ortega's dead."

"Dead," Nick repeated stupidly. He was glad he was already sitting down. Digging his heels in between the grating bars, Nick shoved backwards hard against the ancient steel of the fire escape, feeling each rusty bar of the balusters pressing deep into his back. "How?"

"Today...yesterday, I mean," said K.T. "Thursday. In Washington. A suicide bomber in a Georgetown restaurant. One of the waiters with a vest. Some other mayors bought it, too—mayor of Minneapolis, mayor of Birmingham, mayor of..."

"All right," interrupted Nick. "I should have known that they'd have to silence Ortega before I got back. Stupid of me to think they wouldn't."

There was a sort of snorting noise from K. T. Lincoln's end of the connection. "They blew up Ortega and six other mayors because of *you*, Nick? That's more than mere melodrama. Feeling a little *paranoid* tonight, are we?"

"Yeah, but am I paranoid *enough*," said Nick, finishing their tired old joke. "They made a mistake in preparing that grand jury frame-up, K.T. *You* saw how elaborate the frame-up was... phone records altered, hotel credit-card invoices faked. Mannie Ortega couldn't have done that on the city level even if he'd wanted to. Hell, the governor couldn't have faked all that 'evidence' that they set up for the grand jury. It takes a lot more juice than that...juice on the Jap Advisor level. So they made a mistake in preparing that frame-up, a second mistake in keeping it in the records and not using it, and a third mistake in keeping it where you could...K.T., are you there?"

Silence.

Nick feared that he might have gone too far, sounding too much like the paranoid wife-killer that K.T. probably thought he might be, and that she might have hung up during his rant.

"K.T.?"

More silence. His last chance and he'd blown it due to his goddamned inability to keep his mouth shut when...

"I'm here, Nick." The voice was flat, cold, giving him nothing but its existence.

"Thank Christ," breathed Nick. "OK, forget the first favor. That just leaves one, K.T., but it's a huge one."

"What?"

Nick paused and looked out at the empty but not quite silent downtown Los Angeles streets. Flashes and tiny explosion sounds still came from far to the east. Small-arms fire sounded much closer.

"I need you to find something close to Max's Pursuit Special out of impound...," began Nick.

"Max's...what the fuck are you talking about, Bottom?"

Nick gave her a minute to let the allusion sink in.

"Pursuit Special," she said at last. "Are you drunk, Nick?"

"I wish I were, but I'm not. Remember how we used to check out the impound lot, trying to find the closest match to Max's Pursuit Special?"

Silence on the other end again.

K.T. had come to the house to watch a double feature of the two Australian *Mad Max* movies starring a very young Mel Gibson, but *really* starring the black-on-black supercharger-modified GT351 version of the Australian 1973 Ford XB Falcon hardtop that Mad Max drove past, through, and around bad guys. Dara had absented herself from those movies—which they'd watched more than once when K.T. came over—but Officer Lincoln and Val and Nick had loved them. Occasionally Nick or K.T. would see some drug dealer's car that vaguely resembled the erroneously labeled Last of the V-8 Interceptors from the ancient movies and drag the other over to the impound lot to admire it.

"You want the nitrous oxide tank, too?" asked K.T.

"I think that was Humungus's vehicle," said Nick. "But if you find one, I'll take it."

"You *are* nuts," said K.T., and there followed a more ominous silence than the earlier ones.

"K.T.?"

"You realize what you're asking me to do, Nick? Steal a car from impound for you? Have you been an ex-cop so long that you've forgotten that we tend to keep track of little things like that? Impounded cars and such?"

"All the heroin from the real French Connection was sto...," began Nick.

"Oh, *fuck* the heroin from the French Connection case!" shouted K.T. "You're talking about *me* getting thrown off the force here, Bottom. About *me* going to jail."

"You're too smart to..."

"Oh, shut the fuck up," said K.T. "If you...you and Val... were running away from these Vast Invisible Powers that you say framed you, where would you *go* that they couldn't reach you?"

It was Nick's turn to be silent.

"Oh, shit," said K.T. after a moment. "The good ol' Republic of Texas doesn't take in addicts and felons, Nick. It's almost impossible to get into that crazy country. You have to be a combination of James Bond and Albert Schweitzer just to get considered. *You* know that! How many perps have we chased who headed for Texas only to be turned back at the Texhoma border portal and nabbed by the Oklahoma cops?"

"Yeah." Suddenly Nick was impossibly weary. He just wanted to crawl back into the lice- and bedbug-infested flophouse/flashcave and go to sleep on the filthy floor.

"Call me sometime next week, Nick. Maybe we could figure something else out and..."

"I need the car tomorrow, K.T. By noon, if possible. After tomorrow is too late. Tomorrow *night* will be too late."

Detective Lieutenant K. T. Lincoln said nothing.

After a minute, Nick said, "Good night, K.T. Sorry for waking you," and broke the connection.

NICK OPENED HIS EYES. Twenty minutes until they were scheduled to land. Sato still sat with his eyes closed and arms crossed, but was no longer snoring. Nick had no idea whether he was awake or not.

He studied Sato's face as the sound of the Airbus 310/360's twin engines dropped in pitch and the plane began jolting in its rough descent into the never-forgiving thermals and downdrafts of Colorado's Front Range.

—————

NICK HAD BEEN MOST worried about getting to see Advisor Daichi Omura before he had to leave, but in the end, Omura set up the interview and demanded to see *him*.

This time, after Nick had surrendered his Glock and suffered the various indignities of high-tech and no-tech searches, he realized that there was no special reason that Omura should let him go if he didn't want to. This might be the permanent last stop on his five-day Los Angeles tour.

Except for the fact that both this former Getty Center and Nakamura's beautiful Japanese home were on mountaintops, the setting with Omura couldn't have been more different than it was with Nakamura.

A smiling young man, no bodyguard, politely led Nick to a vast but strangely cozy room—the sense of coziness probably created by the intimate lighting and clusters of modern furniture set tastefully around the large space. Exquisite paintings decorated the walls (it had been the Getty Art Museum, after all), and the amazing Richard Meier modernist buildings situated on the double ridgetop, the 24 acres of campus, and the more than 600 acres of carefully planted trees and shrubs surrounding the campus were all promised to be returned to the people of Los Angeles once the current national emergency was over.

There was no sign of that emergency ending soon, and in the meantime, Advisor Omura and his delegation determined the future of not only California but of Oregon and Washington from these rooms.

While he waited for Omura to arrive, Nick allowed himself to be stunned by the view through the 30-foot-wide south window. This main building was 900 feet above the I-405 that cut past its feet and dropped down into Los Angeles to the south and to the San Fernando Valley to the north, but it seemed to be perched miles above Los Angeles. Toward the eastern horizon, Nick could see smoke rising from the looted wasteland that had been East Los Angeles. He could only imagine this view at night with the solid carpet of city lights close in and the complex constellations farther out.

Daichi Omura entered alone and Nick got to his feet, forcing himself not to wince from either his damaged ribs or the surprisingly painful gouge through the back of his left calf. A CHP medic at Dale Ambrose's Glendale barracks had put an elastic corset-plus-tape thing on Nick for the cracked ribs, told him that the corset really wouldn't help all that much, congratulated him on just cracking and not fully breaking the ribs, and then dressed the leg wound. Now Nick hurt more than before the medical treatment.

Omura was wearing a black gym suit and running shoes. Where Hiroshi Nakamura had been tall for a Japanese man, Daichi Omura couldn't have been an inch over five feet. Where Advisor Nakamura had been vital in his mid or late sixties, Omura seemed far more lively and animated in his early eighties. Omura had no hair; his head was not only as bald as an egg, but gave the sense of ovoid perfection that only an egg and a very, very few human beings' skulls could project. That perfect, tanned egg had neither eyebrows nor eyelashes.

Where Nick had once noted to himself, in his cop's way, that Hiroshi Nakamura smiled the way a politician smiled—profoundly, whitely, perfectly, and totally superficially—a few minutes with Daichi Omura gave Nick the sense that this man could swap stories after a few drinks and laugh sincerely at his own jokes as well as at others'.

Advisor Nakamura had struck Nick as someone who had studied the subtleties of how to project wealth, power and destiny; Advisor Omura impressed Nick the way he'd always imagined Franklin Delano Roosevelt affecting people around him—as someone born to wealth and power, who wore them as comfortably as he wore patched old tweed jackets and dirty running shoes, as a man who laughed at the very idea of destiny even as he accepted his own as he would any other duty. But—Nick suspected—he accepted all of that duty and destiny joyously, even the tragic parts.

Nick knew this was a hell of a lot of impressions to file

away in thirty seconds of looking at a short old man; maybe a function of fatigue and flashback withdrawal. He was trying to replace addiction with half-assed profundity, but he didn't think it was going to work.

"Would you like a drink, Mr. Bottom?" asked Omura. "I would. I drank some water after my pathetic little two-mile run, but I could use a real drink now. It's only four p.m., but we could pretend we're in New York."

"Whatever you're having, sir."

"You don't have to say 'sir' to me, Mr. Bottom. May I call you Nick?"

"Yes, Omura-sama."

The old man had walked over to a small assortment of liquor bottles on a marble counter near the north wall of books, but now he paused. "You've learned the honorific we Japanese use toward people we respect. Especially our elders. I appreciate that, Nick." He began pouring Scotch in two glasses, not asking Nick if he wanted ice and not providing any from the small ice bucket. "Did you refer to your employer as Nakamura-sama?"

"No, I never have," Nick said truthfully.

"Good," said Omura and handed Nick his glass and took his seat on a sofa opposite. He waved Nick to his seat on the facing sofa.

"We have several important things we need to discuss, Nick," said Omura. "Where do you think we should start?"

"I presume you'll want to discuss the charges of my son's involvement in the attack on you at the Disney Center on seventeen September, Omura-sama."

The old man shook his head. "It's not one of the truly important things we need to discuss today, Nick, but I certainly understand why you'd want to get it out of the way. Do you think your son, Val, was involved in that attempt to murder me a week ago today?"

Nick had sipped the single-malt Scotch. He noticed only distantly that it was strong and infinitely subtle, obviously twenty-five years old or older and of a quality he'd never encountered before. None of that mattered as he used the few seconds of subterfuge in tasting the Scotch to mask his wild mental scrambling to find the best response to Omura's question. Something told Nick—based on no empirical evidence yet whatsoever—that this old man probably possessed the most earthquake-proof bullshit detector of any man or woman Nick had ever met.

"I've become convinced that my son ran with that particular flashgang that attacked you, Omura-sama," Nick said slowly, carefully. "But from things said by people—and from everything I know about my son's character—I don't believe Val was involved in the actual firing at you that night. My best guess is that he ran from it… that he never had any intention of harming you."

"My forensics people are all but certain that a bullet from your son's weapon killed the Coyne boy, in the tunnels but some distance from their ambush site. No… what's the English words… no slugs from that weapon were found among all the other bullets and flechettes recovered at the site of the ambush itself. You're a detective. What is your opinion of that, Nick?"

"I have no… no solid evidence, Omura-sama, but that looks to be the case—that my son didn't shoot during the ambush, but did shoot William Coyne some distance away down the tunnel. Val had been given a nine-millimeter Beretta semiautomatic pistol and my best guess is that he shot the Coyne boy three times with it."

"So your son, Val, is a killer," Omura said quietly, his voice as flat and featureless as a leveled blade.

Nick couldn't respond to that other than to nod. He gulped more Scotch and didn't taste it at all.

"Nick, do you think he was attempting to protect *me* by shooting the Coyne boy?"

Nick looked at the old man's tanned, smooth, hairless face. Other than a slight residual impression of pleasantness, there was no expression there at all. None. Yet somehow Nick knew that everything teetered in the balance depending upon how he answered this question.

"No, sir," Nick said firmly. "There's no sign that Val shot

439

DAN SIMMONS

the other boy to protect you or anyone else. Coyne was shot too far from the drain opening, for one thing."

"Why, then?" asked Omura.

Nick shrugged. "Something between the two of them is my hunch. What I want to believe is that Billy Coyne, who had quite a history of violence—including the rape of children—came after Val for some reason, perhaps because Val had run from the ambush scene, and my son had to shoot to protect himself. But that's only a father's wish, sir."

Omura nodded. "Then the issue is closed. I've already directed my security people and the Los Angeles Police Department to cease their search for your son. And right now there are much more important things for you and me to discuss."

Nick could only blink. *More important things?* He blurted out, "Do you have any idea where my son is, Omura-sama?"

The Advisor set down his glass and opened his palms as if to show he had nothing to hide. "I do not know his whereabouts, nor do I have any clue, Nick. If I did, I would tell you. If my security people had tracked your son down and...executed him...I would tell you the truth even about that."

And you'd die here and now, by my bare hands, thought Nick. And as he looked at Daichi Omura, he knew that the old man was aware of that fact. No security guard could break into the room and kill Nick before Nick had snapped Omura's neck.

"Shall we speak of the more important matters?" said Omura. He picked up his glass of Scotch again.

"Sure," said Nick, his throat still tight. "What are they?"

"First, your involvement in this struggle between me and Hiroshi Nakamura and Don Khozh-Ahmed Noukhaev and many others. Are you beginning to feel like a pawn on a chess board, Nick?"

Nick laughed. It was probably the easiest, most relaxed laugh that had escaped him in weeks. "I feel more like a piece of lint that's blown onto a chess board, Omura-sama."

"So you feel powerless," said the old man, studying him. "And as if you have no moves left."

"A few moves, maybe," admitted Nick. "But they don't get

440

me anywhere. It's like when the king's under check and can only shuffle back and forth in the same squares."

"That results in a stalemate," said Omura.

"Well, I don't see how to force anything as grand and bold as a stalemate," said Nick.

Omura smiled. "A minute ago you were a piece of lint blown onto the chess board by mistake. Now you are a king under check. Which metaphor is it, Nick?"

"I was always piss-poor at metaphors, Omura-sama. And, as must be obvious, I know dick-all about chess."

It was Omura's turn to laugh.

"One thing," said Nick. "In Santa Fe, Don Noukhaev was blathering something about me—for a short time before I died, at least—being in the position to affect the lives of millions of people. I assumed it was just more Noukhaev bullshit. But is there any sense or truth to what he was saying?"

"Yes, Nick, there is," Omura said softly. He did not explain further. After a minute he said, "By tomorrow evening, my spies tell me, Hiroshi Nakamura will have returned to his aerie above Denver and will demand that you tell him exactly who murdered his son. Are you able to do that, Nick?"

Nick paused again, this time not to consider dissembling but just to sort out the truth of what he thought. "Not yet, Omura-sama," said Nick. "But perhaps by this time tomorrow night."

The elderly Advisor smiled again. "And perhaps the horse will learn to talk, eh, Nick?"

Nick, who'd heard the folktale from Dara, also had to smile. "Yeah, something like that."

This is where Omura said, "If you go back to Denver, Bottom-san, you *will* die," and had warned Nick that "Colonel" Sato would be waiting that night at the John Wayne Airport. It made Nick physically shiver.

"If I admit that I haven't really figured out who Keigo Nakamura's killer was, Advisor Nakamura will have me killed," said Nick.

"Yes." The syllable ended in a sort of hiss from Omura.

"If I do find the final evidence I need to finger the killer by tomorrow night, Nakamura will *still* order me killed," said Nick.

"Yes."

"Why?" said Nick. "Why kill me if I've done what he hired me to do? Why not just pay me—or don't pay me? I guess I screwed the pay-me option when I took a tiny advance against that payment to get my ass out here to L.A., but why not just let me go back to my little flashback-riddled life?"

Omura looked at him in silence for a long moment. "I believe you know the answer to that already, Nick."

Nick did, and knowing it brought him nothing but nausea. "I know *too much*," he said at last. "I'll be a danger to Nakamura and his plans to become *Shogun*."

"*Hai*," agreed the old man.

"What can I do?" asked Nick and immediately despised the desperate whiny undertone in his own voice. He'd always hated perps, witnesses, or even victims who whined like that. The pathetic squeak of a rat in a trap.

"You can stay in Los Angeles," said Omura, still watching him carefully. "Under my protection."

"Nakamura would send assassins—like Sato—until I was finally killed."

"Yes," said Omura. "You could flee—New or Old Mexico. South America. Canada."

"Someone like Sato would find me within months. Weeks."

"Yes."

"And I can't leave Val and his grandfather behind... to the mercy of... whomever."

"But you have no assurance your son and father-in-law are even alive, Nick."

"No, but... still...," said Nick. Everything he said sounded pathetic to him.

Both men had finished their Scotch. Advisor Omura did not offer to refill the glasses. Outside the amazing window wall, the sun moved lower toward the Pacific Ocean and a late-September sunset.

Nick felt no rush to leave since Dale Ambrose had promised to get him to the John Wayne Airport in time. Nick had already dumped the Nissan Menlo Park, leaving it at the curb in South Central L.A. with the keys in the ignition. It had been a racist move and the best one. The interview with the California–Oregon–Washington Advisor must be over, Nick knew, but between the Scotch and his exhaustion—and the comfortable room with its beautiful view—Nick decided he'd get up only when Omura reminded him that the interview was over.

"Did you know, Nick," said Omura at last, "that Hideki Sato had, for years, an American-born mistress...no, *mistress* is not the right word. *Consort* or *concubine* is closer to the meaning of our word *sobame*."

"Oh?" said Nick. *Why is the old man telling me this?*

"By all accounts he loved her very much. His own wife of many years, Sato sees only twice a year upon formal family occasions."

"Yes?"

Omura said nothing else. Nick felt the way he had in junior high school when he'd attempted a conversation with a pretty girl and simply ran out of things to say.

"You said Sato had a concubine...a relationship with her... for many years, Omura-sama. *Had*, past tense. It's over?" Nick tried to imagine Sato feeling and showing love for anyone or anything. He failed.

"*Hai*," Omura said with Japanese harshness on the syllable, slashing it like a blade. "She died some years ago."

"Died...violently?" asked Nick, trying to find a handle on this line of discussion.

"Oh, no. Of leukemia. It was said that Sato-san was devastated. His own two sons, by his wife, both died in battle in the last decade, died as military advisors early in the Chinese civil war. It is said that Sato mourned his boys, but that his mourning for his...concubine...was deeper, darker, and continues to this day."

"What was her name, Omura-sama?"

The Advisor looked at him. "I forget her name, Nick."
The old man seemed to be saying *I'm lying* with his gaze and
tone...but why?

"They had a child together," continued Omura. "A daughter. She was, by all reports, quite beautiful. And almost completely Western-looking, with only the slightest hint of the
Japanese race in her appearance."

Nick was totally lost. He found it hard to believe that Sato
could love anyone, but especially not a child that didn't look
Japanese. Was this some sort of riddle he was supposed to
solve?

"You used the past tense again, Omura-sama," Nick said
softly. "Is the daughter born to Sato's late concubine also
dead?"

"*Hai.*"

"Also from natural causes?" Nick heard his old detective
voice working: stomp all around the missing piece with a thousand stupid questions until all the vegetation is flattened and
what you're looking for stands out.

Or doesn't.

Omura leaned forward. He didn't answer the question, at
least not directly. "Hideki Sato, as you know, Nick, is a *daimyo*
in his own right, with vassals and soldiers and *keiretsu* interests
of his own. But Hiroshi Nakamura is *his* liege lord. Sato is *Nakamura's* vassal."

"Yes?"

"So when *daimyo* Hideki Sato's own powers and influence
became too great for Nakamura's comfort, he demanded—in
the best feudal Nipponese tradition from our own Middle Ages,
you understand—that Colonel Sato hand over his beloved
daughter to be held as a sort of captive, a hostage to Sato's continued loyalty and service, as it were."

"Jesus," whispered Nick.

Omura nodded. "I believe this sort of taking your vassals'
or enemies' most beloved children was a common thing in
Western feudal times as well."

"But this is the twenty-first century...," began Nick in

self-righteous tones but quickly shut up. Most of the thirty-plus years of this century had been one giant leap backward toward barbarism and clans and czars and theocracies and warlords and a more violent but also more stable feudal system everywhere in the world, the United States not excluded.

"She died in Nakamura's captivity?" said Nick. There was something important here, if he could only find it and dig it out.

"Let us say that she arranged to take her own life," said Omura. Even his eyes looked sad. "Out of shame."

"Shame for being a hostage?" asked Nick. "For being... what? Sato's child? For doing something wrong? I don't get it."

Omura said nothing.

"I would think that the Sato I know would've gone nuts," said Nick at last. "Gone nuts and tried to kill Nakamura and everyone else even remotely involved in his daughter's death."

Omura shook his head. "You do not understand us, Nick. In twenty years, we have largely returned to *bushido* and our earlier form of feudal life and thinking. It will be what helps us survive as a culture...as a people. If a man is ready to give or even *take* his own life for his liege lord, he must also be willing to sacrifice his entire family if that is his lord and master's will."

"Jesus," Nick said again. "So Sato did nothing about his daughter's death?"

"I did not say that," murmured Omura. "I merely said that he sought no revenge. There is one other thing we must discuss before you leave, Nick."

Nick glanced at his watch. It was getting late. Ambrose would have to push it to get him to the John Wayne Airport in time. "Yes, sir?"

"Do you understand why Nippon is engaged in the war in China, Nick?"

"I think I do, Omura-sama. Japan had all but underbred itself out of existence by the beginning of this century...at least it was on the path toward doing so. By pretending to be UN peacekeepers when China tore itself apart in this civil war and general collapse—and by hiring American troops to play that role—Japan's sort of reinvigorating itself with almost a

billion young Chinese to do their work. New ports. New products. New workforce. But in a two-tier sort of Greater Japan,
with you Japanese nationals always in the upper tier."

"But not in thinking of the Chinese and others as slaves as
before," Omura said quickly. "Not this time. This Daitoa
Senso—this Greater East Asia War—will not include a Rape
of Nanking. Nor will it end with a second attempt by the Japanese to become *shido minzoku*—'the world's foremost people.'"

Nick shrugged. He didn't really care that much what or
how the Japanese people thought of themselves.

"But all that is mere preparation," said Omura.

"Preparation for what?"

"For the real war, Nick."

"The real war with…China? India? What's left of Russia?
Nuevo Mexico? Not America, certainly." Nick was confused.

Omura shook his head and got easily to his feet. The little
man seemed to balance on the balls of his sneakered feet like a
boxer or athlete. Nick stood up, but in stages, and painfully.

"The coming war—and it will come in the next five years,
Nick—will be a total war, an existential war, a nuclear war,"
Daichi Omura said as he took Nick by the elbow and began
leading him toward the door. "That culture or ours will inherit
the earth. Only one culture will survive this war and determine
humanity's future, Nick. *And it cannot be theirs*. It is why we
need to settle the issue of who will be *Shogun* soon."

"Holy shit," said Nick and stopped in his tracks. Omura
gently moved him along. Outside, the sun was setting and the
L.A. basin and its surviving tall buildings glowed gold. Sunlight
glinted back from windshields on the remaining freeways.
"*Nuclear* war, Omura-sama? With who? And why? For God's
sake, why? And what does this have to do with…"

Omura silenced him with a gentle hand on Nick's back.
"Bottom-san, if you do see Colonel Sato, would you please give
my greetings to him in the following way? Say to him, as one
old chess opponent to another, *In this world there is a tree without
any roots;/Its yellow leaves send back the wind.* Can you remember that, Bottom-san?"

Nick said, "In this world there is a tree without any roots; / Its yellow leaves send back the wind."

Omura opened the door and saw his guest through it. "You are a smart man, Nick Bottom. This is one reason—although not the important reason—that Hiroshi Nakamura hired you to solve the murder of his son. Certainly you are up to the challenge of solving the larger mysteries as well, especially since they are all one. Good luck, Nick."

Nick shook the old man's hand—a firm, dry, affectionate handshake—and then the door was closed in his face.

———

"WE ARE LANDING, GENTLEMEN," said the child-faced flight attendant. Her kimono made small rustling sounds as she cleared the last of their glasses and glided into the aft cabin.

Sato was awake and had been looking at Nick as *he'd* slept. Nick rubbed his eyes and face, feeling the stubble on his cheeks and chin.

The A310/360 landed gently at Denver International Airport and taxied to the Nakamura private hangar.

Nick grabbed what few things he'd brought aboard. He left the nylon bag of flashback vials on the floor.

Sato raised one eyebrow as he waved Nick to go down the stairway first. "I have a vehicle waiting. Can I drop you at your condominium, Bottom-san?"

"I'll phone a cab."

"Very good. I shall notify the hangar manager that you can wait inside until your cab arrives," said Sato. A long, black, hydrogen-powered Lexus hummed to a stop on the tarmac and two of Sato's men stepped out. One held the rear door for Sato while the other watched the perimeter with a professional bodyguard's quick flicks of glances. Another samurai, whom Nick also recognized from the trip to Santa Fe, was at the wheel of the Lexus.

"Oh," said Nick, "Omura-sama sends you his greetings, Sato-san. He told me to say to you, as one old chess opponent says to the other, *In this world there is a tree without any roots; / Its yellow leaves send back the wind.* I think that's the phrase."

Nick had expected something from Sato—surprise, irritation—at hearing that he'd met with the California Advisor, but the big man showed no reaction whatsoever. "Good night, Bottom-san," said the security chief. "We shall see you tomorrow."

"See you tomorrow," said Nick.

2.04

Denver — Saturday, Sept. 25

STUPID SHITHEAD.

Val was furious at himself.

He should have just walked out the front door of the condominium building. But he hadn't been sure that the big man with marine tats who'd shown them in would *allow* him to leave. The last thing on earth that Val wanted right now was to be sitting in detention somewhere in that building, waiting for the Old Man to arrive home.

So he'd stalked back and forth on the mezzanine with the mass of climbing rope thrown over his shoulder until he found a side corridor and a door that *had* to open to a stairway to the roof, but of course it was locked with a numeric access pad. So much for that.

He went back to the mezzanine and continued pacing, knowing that there had to be some way *out* of the goddamned building, but also knowing that Gunny and the other security people would be on his ass soon if he didn't find that exit.

Then he saw the dried-up fountain below and the steel cables dangling from a ceiling seventy feet above the marble floors and patches of dirt with their crude gardens. There were skylights up there and someone had opened two of them a foot or so to allow a little fresh air in. From the mezzanine, it was only thirty or forty feet up to those skylights. One of the cables was secured by the weight of a bronze goose hanging fifteen or twenty feet below, a goose that once must have appeared to be landing on water back when the fountain had *held* water.

Making sure that the climbing rope and carabiners were secure over his shoulder, not giving himself time to think about it, Val took a run at the railing, jumped high to catch the railing as a jumping-off step under his right boot, and threw himself far out into empty air forty feet above the fountain and floor. He caught the cable in both hands, swung wide, almost let go, and then got his legs and ankles around the steel rope.

He'd given no thought as to whether the cable would hold his added weight—the Old Man had taught him that engineers always built in a wide safety factor for such things—but this cable and its bolts above were old, so Val was surprised when the whole setup creaked and sagged at least a few inches. The cable swung with his weight and the heavy bronze goose below flew back and forth in a six- or seven-foot arc, seemed to bank left, and then began spinning.

The leap hadn't created much noise and no one stepped out of their cubie. Val grinned despite the surge of terror that suddenly gripped him and then he began to climb, the coils of Perlon-3 and dangling steel 'biners over his shoulder weighing him down.

At the top he was still six feet below and to one side of the open skylights with no way of getting up to them. *I guess I didn't really think this out*, thought Val as he hung there seventy feet above the hard floor, his forearms beginning to shake with the tension of holding himself on the cable. *Nothing new there.*

Holding on with his upper arm, legs, and ankles, Val freed his hands long enough to pull the end of the climbing rope free and to attach one of the carabiners to the end. When he was done, he had about an eight- or nine-foot free bit of rope with the steel clip on the end.

Val tossed twice before getting the 'biner and a wad of rope up and over the metal frame separating the two glass skylights. But the first time he made it over, the carabiner went too far and landed on the outside of the glass with a dull thump. Val pulled it back—the weight almost pulled him off his perch—and then tossed again. And again. And again.

Finally four or five feet of rope with the carabiner at its end was hanging free. Since he still held the rope, he was able to get it swinging until he caught the carabiner free end with one hand.

He was tiring now, his ankles and legs slipping down a foot or so on the steel cable. Val knew that he'd be out of the strength he needed to dangle here in another minute or less. He clipped the carabiner on the main strand of climbing rope and let the mass of it fall from his shoulders.

Getting rid of the weight helped. The rope reached the dirt in the old fountain with a coil left over. Val pulled the noose tight on the steel frame above and transferred his hands to the dangling rope.

The Perlon-3 was a lot more slippery than the steel cable and his ankles weren't getting much of a grip. He had to run a loop of the bright blue rope around his right hand and wrist to gain a few seconds where he could rest. Then, with a loud grunt, he began climbing.

It was only six feet or so. *Only.*

When he got to the point where he could reach up and grab the rusted steel horizontal frame on which the glass skylights closed, Val thought—not for the first time—*Now what?*

The damned skylights were only open a foot or so. The gaps weren't wide enough for him to get his body up through there even if he somehow pulled himself up that far.

Now what, you dumb shit?

Now it was just like climbing around on the girders under the overpass on the I-10, was what. Val swung his legs high, managing to get his ankles crossed just above the metal.

Still hanging from the rope, he freed his right leg and

began kicking at the skylight on that side, trying to concentrate his blows just on specific sections of the angled steel frame that held six large panes of glass in it.

It was too heavy. Its cranking mechanism up there on the roof was too rusted. It wouldn't budge.

Val crossed his ankles again and hung there panting. He didn't have much strength left. His only chance in a few seconds would be to swing back to the climbing rope and slide down it the sixty or seventy feet to the marble below. Did he have enough strength to hang on during that descent? He didn't think so.

Emitting a noise somewhere between a huge grunt and a low scream, Val freed *both* legs and swung both boots up at the metal frame. One way or the other, this was his last try.

His boot soles missed the metal frame but fractured the grimy pane of glass. A large segment of that glass fell out of the frame and tumbled end over end to shatter with an impossibly loud noise below.

Val's right foot was through the empty space of the missing pane and up and over the metal pane-frame.

"Fuck it," he gasped, sweat pouring off his face into empty space. Using just the leverage of his ankle on that thin strand of metal, he swung his body out, his left leg up and over the right side of the steel strut above, and he grabbed at the far side of that strut with his left hand. Val dangled there for a second, his body contorted and broken glass cutting into his right ankle, and then—with a final violent grunt—he pulled himself onto the six-inch-wide steel strut, lying there on his back, teetering, almost falling, and then releasing the rope below to grab the skylight frame just above him.

It creaked upward.

A few seconds later, Val was off the girder and out onto the graveled roof and pulling up the climbing rope. His arms were shaking wildly and he barely had enough strength to pull up and coil the line.

This is where Gunny G. and his security guys just come up the stairs and arrest me, thought Val.

But they didn't.

His legs as shaky as his arms, Val walked to the southwest corner of the building where the fence began below, found a pipe that looked like it might bear his weight, maybe, clipped his carabiner-noose around it, and dropped the coiled mass to the definitely unyielding pavement way down there. Val closed his eyes and tried to stop shaking.

He knew he should wait until he got some arm strength back, but he didn't know if he had the time to wait. So Val sat on the edge of the building—here on this side it was probably less than fifty feet to the concrete below—wrapped a coil of the rope around his wrist, and swung out until he could get his shaky legs and bleeding ankles around the rope again. *Pretend you're in gym class* was his last thought before rolling off.

He slid down—too fast, it took skin off his palms—and when he got to the bottom his legs were too wobbly to hold him upright. Val collapsed on the cement there, his back to the building, and panted loudly for a moment. The panting sounded a little like sobs but—he decided—that wasn't his fault.

HE RETRIEVED HIS BERETTA from the pipe and just stood by the rubble of the broken pedestrian bridge for a while.

What next?

It had been the only question for a long time now and it seemed that Val Fox never had the answer.

I kill the Old Man and get out of here.

The thought seemed obscene to him, despite its familiarity. Always before it was a black-souled fantasy, something rising more out of the secrets that young Val had known—the fact of his mother lying to his father about her whereabouts that last year, the fact of his father's maddening denseness when Val's mother said she'd spent the long weekend at Laura McGilvrey's when ten-year-old Val had known that she'd been with Mr. Cohen, the fact of his father's total lack of tears in the long month after Val's mother had died in that crash—all facts woven into the fantasy of his father having discovered the affair and having acted on the knowledge.

453

But Val had never believed his own black-souled fantasy. Not really. The dark dream that his father had also hurt Val's mother had been nothing more than a focus for his rage at the reality of his father exiling him, a substitute fury at his father for sending Val away when he wanted and needed to be near the Old Man, a fantasy revenge aimed at his father for not weeping when Val's ten-year-old heart had been torn to shreds.

But now, this absolutely damning grand jury evidence...

Val arched backwards over the railing of the broken bridge and screamed into the blue Colorado afternoon sky.

So what next?

Kill the Old Man and get out of Colorado.

No, wait, that was the wrong sequence...

First, get the $200 in old dollars from the Old Man, and find the guy here in Denver who'd get him the new NICC with the faked Teamster membership and...

Well, that's fucked.

Killing his father in cold blood—a cop, ex-cop to be sure, but still part of that fucking fraternity that tended to take the killing of its own real seriously—and *then* hang around Denver two weeks or more to get his fake ID? Didn't quite parse, did it, Valerino?

He fumbled in his pockets until he found the slip of paper with the NIC Card counterfeiter's name scribbled on it. There were two names there, the other being that guy in Austin, Texas, who did the *best* work that Begay had ever seen...

But getting into the Republic of Texas would be harder than staying in Denver for two weeks without being caught after committing a public murder.

No plan of action made any sense at all.

Val had been watching a few cars pull off the street and drive into the security boxes on their way up into the parking garage. All the vehicles had tinted windows. Val couldn't have made out the faces of the drivers from here if he'd had a pair of binoculars, which he didn't. He could stand right next to the approach driveway in hopes of seeing the Old Man's face as he drove up, but this was a sure way to get the cops called on his ass.

The cops were probably on their way anyway. That stunt with the climbing rope and breaking the skylight glass hadn't brought an immediate mob—those who stayed home all day hidden in their condo cubies weren't exactly the types who responded quickly to scary noises, especially since most of them were almost certainly under the flash and hadn't heard a damned thing—but Val was sure that that scary Gunny G. and his security pals would be responding soon enough. Probably the only thing right now keeping that Gunny from calling the cops was that he seemed to be on the arm to the Old Man. He might phone Val's father first before siccing the cops on anyone.

And thus warn the Old Man that I'm out here somewhere waiting for him, thought Val.

Time to get out of there.

Val had hobbled half a dozen steps west along the old river path before he realized that he could barely walk. His right ankle was cut worse than he'd noticed. There was a pool of blood where he'd been standing by the bridge and he was leaving red pools as he walked.

Fuck.

He sat down and rolled up his torn pant leg. It was a pretty deep slash—the kind you needed stitches for. The kind you went to the emergency room for.

Fuck! Fuck! Fuck! Fuck!

Val shucked off his jacket and flannel shirt, tugged his T-shirt over his head, and tore it into rags. He tied the cleanest strip as tightly around the wound as he could and then got dressed again.

He was filthy, his right pant leg was torn to shit and bloody from the cuff halfway to the knee, and his boots were so sodden with blood that he made squishy noises as he walked.

I'll deal with it later.

Hobbling as fast as he could, trying not to let the pain and nausea make him puke, he turned left on South University

Boulevard at the light since he didn't want to head west past the Denver Country Club on First Avenue the way he and Leonard had come. Six or eight painful blocks south, he turned right—heading west—on East Exposition Avenue. He could see a park up ahead. Where there was a park, there'd be homeless people—and with the homeless, there'd be what he needed to steal in order to do what he had to do.

1.16

Denver — Saturday, Sept. 25

K.T. HAS OUTDONE herself.

Nick, with Val riding shotgun beside him and Leonard in the backseat, is barreling due south on Highway 287-385 through the empty Comanche Grasslands at 130 miles per hour in the 2015 Chevy Camaro supercharged SS that K. T. Lincoln provided from the impound lot.

Endless grasslands unspool on either side of the white automobile roaring down the empty two-lane highway. They've long since outrun the puny Denver PD and Colorado Highway Patrol interceptors, and Nakamura's hydrogen-powered skateboards never had a chance to catch up once they turned south from I-70. Val has been cheering and pumping his fist for forty miles now.

The almost-twenty-year-old Camaro is pouring out its Vortech-supercharged 603 horsepower and 518 pound-feet of torque. No plug-in electric motors here, just the raging 6.2-liter L99 V-8 engine gulping down gallons of rare high-octane gasoline.

The windshield and windows on the Camaro Vortech SS are just glassed-over gunslits and Val has already had the

457

DAN SIMMONS

opportunity to use his as such. The hood of the highway patrol cruiser in pursuit had exploded upward from the shotgun blast and the car had spun into its own dust cloud. That had been the last of the pursuit before they passed through Springfield, Colorado, just north of the grasslands. Leonard is busy in the backseat double-checking unfolded paper maps, even though both Betty and the Camaro's nav system are providing minute-by-minute information.

"When we get to the town of Campo ten miles ahead," calls Leonard over the engine howl and roar of the Nitto Extreme Drag NT55R rear tires, "it'll be about ninety-eight miles to the border station at Texhoma."

"How many people in Campo?" shouts Nick. He finds it hard to believe that there's a town out here in the endlessly undulating grasslands.

"A hundred and fifty," shouts Leonard.

"One hundred thirty-eight," answers Betty.

"One...hundred...forty...one," says the Camaro's mildly retarded nav system.

"Dad!" cries Val. "There's some sort of helicopter coming in behind us. But I don't hear it, just see it."

"That's a *Sasayaki-tonbo*," says Nick, proud to share his knowledge of such things. He has had to concentrate hard on the driving the past hour and more. At more than 130 m.p.h., a chuckhole or jackrabbit could mean disaster. "It means 'dragonfly' in Japanese."

"What do you want me to do?" shouts Val as he opens the sunroof, shucks off his shoulder harness, and stands, holding the RPG that Nick's brought in his duffel of weapons.

"Just a warning shot across the bow," shouts Nick over the roar of air that's joined the engine and tire noise. "Sato might be in it. I don't want to kill him."

"Roger that," shouts Val and takes aim and launches a rocket. The dark back-exhaust of the rocket scorches the white hood of the Camaro.

The rocket misses the nose of the dragonfly 'copter as planned, but it does catch the tip of one of the huge, intricately

458

warped rotors. The big but elegant machine corkscrews to the right, out of sight over a grassy hill.

"Did you see it hit?" calls Nick as Val sets the spent RPG in back, closes the sunroof, and straps himself back in. They're approaching Campo at 140 miles per hour.

"It's all right," says Leonard from the back. "It autorotated down and just landed hard in a big cloud of dust. No one hurt."

Val high-fives his father, who quickly returns his hand to the steering wheel.

"Turn right onto Main Street and the highway marked four-twelve, two-eighty-seven, sixty-four, three, fifty-six in front of the town hall in Boise City," says Leonard, leaning forward between the father and son.

"Why does one highway have so many numbers in Oklahoma?" laughs Val.

"What they lack in actual number of roads, they make up for in numbers for them," says Nick and is surprised when both his son and father-in-law laugh.

Then they are in Texhoma, Oklahoma, population 909 according to Leonard, 896 according to Betty, not-enough-data according to the Camaro's nav, 364 miles and less than three and a half hours' Camaro SS driving time from Denver.

And then they are approaching the Republic of Texas border station.

"Jeez," says Val, "they're on *horses*."

Nick turns right at the flagpole with the flag showing a single white star on the triangular field of blue. The red and white stripes look familiar. The Texas cavalry is escorting them through the opened gates that cut through the two high fences and intervening minefields.

Nick's amazed to see a familiar building just beyond the open border gates. "I thought the Alamo was much farther south," he says softly. The Camaro's big V-8 is just rumbling softly now.

"A lot of people make that mistake," says Leonard, who is leaning forward to shake Nick's hand. When Nick offers his hand to Val, the boy hugs him instead.

NICK CAME AWAKE GASPING and with tears running down his cheeks.

Flashback addicts rarely dreamed at all. Now that real dreams, as opposed to flashback trips, were coming back to him, he was astonished at how *powerful* they were. Why would anyone trade such things for chemically induced reruns of fragments of a life? Why had *he?*

He was up and showered and shaved and planned to be dressed, armed, and out of the condo complex by 6:30 a.m. His ribs hurt worse today under the tape-corset, but he didn't care. Looking in the mirror after he'd shaved, Nick saw that something was *different*.

He'd managed to lose quite a bit of weight for two weeks on a case, and his cheekbones were sharper, his features more gaunt, but that wasn't the primary change. His eyes. His eyes were different. More clear. For almost six years now, he'd stared at himself and at everything else out of the cave-stare of either wanting and needing flashback more than anything else in the world or staring at the world through the glaze of a heavy flashback hangover. His eyes were different now.

Can they stay that way? Nick shivered and finished getting dressed.

At weapons-check, he signed out his 9mm Glock for the clip-on crossdraw holster at his belt and a tiny .32-caliber pocket gun for his rarely worn ankle holster. The .32 had been his throw-down for all the years he'd been a patrolman and homicide detective—numbers filed off, grip taped, no traceable history on it—but he'd never fired his service weapon in anger, much less come close to having to use a throw-down for himself or his partner. He trusted the short-barreled .32 to be accurate at distances of five feet or less.

Before leaving for the day, Nick took security chief Gunny G. aside, showed him the photos of Val and Leonard, and paid the ex-marine $50 in old bucks—more than a third of what Nick had left after paying the pilot to get him to Los Angeles and a fortune by anyone's standards — with more promised if Gunny were to take care of the two until Nick got back. Or if he *didn't* get back.

"The FBI and Homeland Security were here last week asking about the boy, Mr. B.," said Gunny G.

"I know," said Nick, handing the fortune in hard cash to the white-scarred ex-marine. "But I swear to you that it's only because they wanted to question my son as a material witness to something he wasn't involved in. And even that's been dropped. You won't get in trouble helping them, I promise you that, Gunny. And there's another twenty-five in it for you after you do help them get settled 'til I get back — and keep anyone from bothering them."

"I'd do that for you no matter what, Mr. B.," said the security man as he pocketed the cash.

Nick scribbled a hasty note — he had little hope that Val and his grandfather would show up today, but the remnants of the dream he'd had made him a little more optimistic than usual — and then he was out the parking garage door and into his vibrating, wheezing gelding. It was hard to drive that voltbucket after the dream-memory of real V-8 power and freedom. The charge indicator's happy face showed that he had a range of thirty-one miles today, if a major part of it was downhill.

"K.T.!"

The police lieutenant spun, crouched, and had almost cleared the Glock from its holster before she froze.

"Nick Bottom. What the fuck do *you* want?"

"And a good morning to you, too, Lieutenant Lincoln."

K.T. lived on Capitol Hill in one of the big old nineteenth-century homes in that once-prestigious neighborhood that had been converted to a dozen or more cubie rentals late in the last century or early in this one. It had been a high-crime neighborhood for more than six decades now, but this only gave the cops who wanted to live there a better deal. The residents of K.T.'s building who could afford cars kept them in an oversized detached garage down this long driveway and that's where he'd planned to intercept his old partner.

"What are you doing in your uniform, Detective?" asked Nick. Seeing K.T. in her patrol blacks, gunbelt, visible shield, baton and all, reminded him of their early years together.

"There's been a little unpleasantness in Los Angeles this past week," said K.T., straightening. "Or perhaps you've been too busy playing Philip Marlowe to notice."

"I've heard rumors," said Nick. "So?"

"So the *reconquista* armies and militias out there got their collective asses kicked, there are more than a million and a half spanic residents of East L.A. running south for their lives, and word is that the Nuevo Mexican forces haven't been able to draw the line at San Diego but are falling back to the old border."

"So?" repeated Nick.

"So there are about half a million yahoos in Denver who are getting big ideas of kicking spanic ass here in our own back-yard," said K.T. "The whole force is on duty today—full riot gear—and drawing a protective line in Five Points, north Den-ver, West Colfax area, the old Manual High School feeder neighborhoods, and all of southwest Denver beyond Santa Fe Drive."

"You don't have enough people, K.T."

"Fucking tell me about it," said the lieutenant. "What the hell do you want, Nick? I gotta get to work."

"Any progress on getting me that impound V-eight I asked for?"

K.T. squinted at him. "You were serious?"

"As a heart attack, partner."

"Don't call me 'partner,' you flashcave dweller. Why on earth would I risk my entire career and pension by stealing you a car from impound, Nick Bottom?"

"Because they'll kill me if I don't have real wheels to get out of here."

"Who's 'they'?" demanded K.T. "The black helicopters coming for you?"

Nick smiled at that. She was closer to the truth than she could know.

"You read the grand jury notes," said Nick.

"Another reason not even to talk to you, mister. Much less commit a felony for you."

Nick nodded. "Assuming they were a frame-up—assume that for just a minute—ask yourself who'd have the juice to change phone records, suborn testimony, do all the things that grand jury near-indictment required to be done. The late mayor and former DA Mannie Ortega?"

K.T. snorted a laugh.

"Who, then?" pressed Nick. "The governor? Who?"

"It'd have to be someone on the level of Advisor Nakamura's group," said K.T., glancing at her watch and glowering. "But why would Nakamura spend all that time almost six years ago framing you—at great effort and expense—and then hire you now to find the killer of his sweet widdle boy?"

"I'm working on that," said Nick.

"But that's assuming that all that grand jury work was a frame-up," snapped K.T. "Which has to be bullshit." She turned to walk away.

Knowing how much K. T. Lincoln hated to be touched—he'd watched her scowl a supervisor into retreat for doing so, not to mention baton the teeth out of a begging perp—he grabbed her by the upper arm and turned her around.

"That grand jury information meant that I *killed* my wife. You knew us for years, K.T. Can you imagine me hurting Dara?" He shook her with both hands. "God *damn* it, can you?"

She removed his hands and glared at him, but then looked down. "No, Nick. You couldn't hurt Dara. Not ever."

"So one way or the other—whether I find Keigo Nakamura's killer or not, and I only have until this evening to report on that—Advisor Nakamura's going to have me whacked. I'm certain of it. But with a fast car..."

"You're nuts," said K.T. But her voice was softer now. "Why did you say in your call yesterday morning—I never got back to sleep, by the way—that you were trying to save Val *and* you? Is Val back from L.A.?"

"I was out there looking for him from Monday until last night," said Nick. "I think odds are decent that he and his grandfather got out of the city before the shit hit the fan."

"And he'd come here…to you? Why, Nick?"

He may want to kill me, thought Nick. Instead of saying that, he shrugged. "All I know is that if he arrives today, I need a fast way out of town. A car with balls."

"How far do you have to get to be…away…out of town?" asked K.T.

"Three hundred sixty-four miles would about do it," said Nick.

"Three hundred sixty…Nick, no car goes that far these days without an overnight charge or a hydrogen top-off. What on earth is three hundred and sixty-one miles from here that you'd need to…" She paused and her eyes widened. "*Texas?* Are you shitting me?"

"I shit thee not, Lieutenant Lincoln."

"The Republic of Texas doesn't take felons on the run, Nick. Nor do they take flashback addicts. Nor do they…" She paused again.

Nick said nothing.

K.T. took a step closer. "You look…different. Your eyes… Are you off the flashback shit?"

"I think so," Nick said softly. "The last nine days or so have been too busy for me to think about the drug."

"Nine whole *days,*" said K.T. There was some sarcasm in her tone—there always was—but Nick could also hear the serious question beneath the derision.

"It's a beginning, partner," said Nick. He remembered when he'd helped her go off both painkillers and cigarettes in the months after a minor shooting—the nicotine being harder to kick than the narcotics. Dara had understood when he'd sat up nights with his partner, listening to her moan and bitch. He knew that K.T. also remembered it.

"Maybe," she grunted. "But this car thing is a nonstarter,

Nick. For one thing, the city just held their annual auction of impounded vehicles a few weeks ago. The lots are mostly empty."

"You'll find something for me, K.T."

"God *damn* it," she snarled, balling her hands into fists. "Quit doing that to me, you asshole. I don't owe you *anything.*"

Nick nodded assent but K.T. looked down, almost panting in her anger, and said to the ground, "Except my life, Nick. Except my life." She raised her head. "If I find a car—which I don't think I can—where do you want me to deliver it? Your cubie mall?"

"No," said Nick and thought fast. It had to be someplace public but also fairly safe from thieves. Someplace with security nearby but a non-noisy security. "The Six Flags Over the Jews parking lot," he said. "As far on the south side as you can park it. They don't check the vehicles until the end of the visiting hours about nine p.m., but the guards at the main gate sort of keep an eye out on the cars in the lot. Just park it as far south as you can but not so off by itself that it'll be noticeable."

"How will you know which car it is?" muttered K.T., checking her watch again.

"Text me. And park it, you know, the opposite direction of other cars in the row."

"Where do I put the key fob for this car I won't be able to get for you?" she asked. "Over the visor?"

Nick produced the small metal box he'd got from Gunny G. that morning. "This is magnetic. Set it inside the left rear wheel well...like in the *Mad Max* movies."

"Right, like in the *Mad Max* movies." She took the little box, clicked it open and shut, and rolled her eyes at the nonsense.

"Never mind," said Nick. "Just don't get the box anywhere near your phone or other computer stuff...that powerful magnet will wipe the memories clean."

K.T. started to hand it back to him as if the box had the plague.

Nick held his palms out and shook his head. "I was joking.

It's barely strong enough to stick to the car. Left rear wheel well."

"All right," she said and turned again to leave. "But I'm not promising anything…"

Nick touched her shoulder again but gently this time. "K.T.?"

She glared back at him, but not with the real fury he'd seen before. *"What?"*

"Whether you find a car for us or not, if today doesn't turn out well for me…and I have a hunch…" He shook his head and started over. "If something happens to me, and Val and his grandfather show up, can you look out for them for me? Find a safe place for them until…"

She stared at him and there was real pain in her dark eyes. She said nothing. Nor did she walk away.

"You've met Leonard," Nick hurried on. "He's a good man but he's…you know…been an academic his whole life. If he got Val out of L.A. safely, he's probably already exceeded his real-world survival capabilities and Leonard is already almost seventy-five years old…" He shut up. He couldn't find the right words.

"You're asking me to watch over Val if Nakamura or some-one kills you today," said K.T.

Nick nodded stupidly, his eyes full and his throat tight.

"Oh, Nick, Nick…," K.T. said sadly and turned on her heel and walked away from him toward the distant wall of garage doors.

Nick knew that this was a yes. Or at least he took it as one.

———

HE PULLED THE GELDING into a thirty-minute parking area near the capitol at the top of the hill and looked down from south of the flaking gold capitol dome toward the valley where the Coors Field prison and Mile High DHS Detention Center straddled the junction of Cherry Creek and the Platte River. He lowered his driver's-side window and shut the batteries off.

What next? For the first time in the two weeks since Naka-

mura hired him, he had a few hours to and for himself. In twelve
hours or less—probably less, maybe a lot less—he'd be sum-
moned to appear in front of that billionaire again to either
announce he was sure who'd killed Keigo Nakamura or admit
that he'd failed. Either way, he thought, Nakamura's response
wasn't going to be gentle.

Nick Bottom hated puzzles. He'd hated them since he was
a kid. But he had always been eerily good at figuring them out.
It had been the ratiocination part of police work that had
boosted him through the uniformed ranks to first grade so
quickly and got him up into the rarefied air of Major Crimes
detective work in his youthful midthirties.

But now...

Now what? He was sure that he had all the facts he needed
to come up with a solution to this crime, but even the goddamn
facts kept shifting and blurring. Nick felt like a blind artist trying to sculpt with a heap of marbles. For the most part he was
where he and his investigative team had been six winters ago
when they'd decided that while it *could* have been one of the
witnesses who snuffed Keigo and, perhaps as an afterthought,
Keigo's girlfriend Keli Bracque—the poet Danny Oz, who had
the logically weak but strong-enough-for-murder-in-the-real-
world motive of his general smoldering anger and incipient
insanity; the thief and drug dealer Delroy Nigger Brown,
maybe because of something he said while he was high and
being interviewed by Keigo which he didn't want shown in the
finished documentary; the addict and dealer Derek Dean, who
was currently rotting in full-time flash immersion up at the People's Republic of Boulder's Naropa Institute, possibly killing
Keigo just for the flashback fun of it; or Don Khozh-Ahmed
Noukhaev for a dozen reasons, half of which he'd teased Nick
about when they'd met in Santa Fe—the best chance was that
it had been a hit team from Japan, ninja assassins from one of
the eight *keiretsu* or *zaibatsu* (actually seven *kereitsu* and *zaibatsu* not counting Nakamura's) and seven *daimyo*s who headed
those clan-company confederations. Seven deadly *daimyo*s, including kindly old bald-as-an-egg Daichi Omura, whom Nick, in his

fatigue and posttraumatic stress after his fun five days in L.A., had honored every way short of kissing the Jap runt's ass...seven deadly *daimyo*s, each of whom was egomaniacally sure that his nation's and the entire world's survival depended upon him, *that one man*, becoming *Shogun*. Seven deadly *daimyo*s each willing to kill a thousand Keigo Nakamuras and Keigo-ish sex-slave girl-friends to see that his *Shogunate* dreams of power came true.

This is where Nick and K. T. Lincoln had ended up in their investigation six winters ago, and this is where most tracks, new and old, seemed to lead again.

Almost, thought Nick. *Not quite.*

Denver from the capitol hill didn't look like a city about to explode in racial and ethnic violence. Some of the leaves in the tree-filled park below the capitol were beginning to change color. The temperature was perfect—low seventies—and the sunlight had that clear, pure, crystalline, late-September quality that made residents of Colorado want to live there forever. (Or at least until the arrival of shitty springs with no spring weather, offering up winter until June's heat.)

Nick tried to clear his mind of any thoughts about the case as he stared at the city buildings below. It used to help when he just let his subconscious weave threads together without any deliberate herding of facts.

Nestled in the little patches of park below was the city library, thrown up by some hotshot postmodern architect in the 1990s. The cuteness of the tower that looked sort of like a pencil—or maybe a crayon—had worn off before the last century was over. Beyond the library was the main part of the art museum, made to look "modern" but more than sixty years old now, Nick thought, which still looked like some tiled and para-peted castle huddling against its neighbors. Its windows were tiny, oddly shaped, and scattered almost at random around the building.

Nick remembered his mother, who'd loved art, taking him to the museum when he was a little kid and pointing to the windows and telling him, "The man who designed this building in the early nineteen-seventies, Nicky, made these windows in the shape they are—and put them *where* they are—to frame beautiful views of the mountains and foothills as if *they* were paintings on the walls, too. Clever, don't you think? But what the architect didn't take time to think out was that newer, taller buildings would pop up all around and hide those views… making these windows-as-frames silly."

Leonard had once talked to Nick, after a few drinks, about some scholarly mentor of his who'd called such inevitabilities the Iron Law of Unintended Consequences. As if a college professor had to explain to a cop and a son of a cop anything about the tyranny of unintended consequences.

Across the street from the old modernist art museum where his mother used to take him was the newer *post*modernist annex to the art museum. Nick actually remembered the name of that architect—Daniel Libeskind. The titanium-and-glass structure was all shards and points and angles, looking like a smashed chandelier or shattered Christmas-tree star. That building had gone up in the first decade of this century and Nick remembered all the self-congratulatory whoop-de-do about the structure—how it put Denver back on America's architectural map (as if that would matter at all in the dark decades after the Day It All Hit The Fan)—but the leaping up and down in joy had abated somewhat when the city had discovered that a) the inside of a broken Christmas decoration was a lousy place to try to show art and b) every angle and surface that *could* leak *did* leak and always would.

Wait, some of this bullshit I was remembering could help. What was it?

He ran his little Molly Bloom batch of free associations backwards like an old reel-to-reel tape, the way he'd taught himself to do, and found it.

The picture-frame windows on the old windows were useless because of the new buildings that had grown up to block the views.

He was still trying to solve this case using the old frames

that were out of date. Something he'd stumbled over in the past week—some new thing that had grown up to block the old view—held the answer. It was there. He just couldn't see it yet.

Nick turned on the fine four-wheeled G.M. appliance, checked the smiley-face and leaf-sprouting interfaces to make sure the gelding had actually started, noted that even though he'd hardly driven the thing it now had only nineteen miles left in its daily charge, and let the piece-a-shit glide down the hill toward the west.

———

THERE WERE ONLY A dozen or so cars in the Six Flags Over the Jews parking lot. Nick knew that it was ridiculous to check for his Camaro SS escape vehicle—K.T. would have needed the *Star Trek* transporter teleportation doohickey to beam one here from the impound lot in this short of a time—but he looked anyway. No vehicles parked the wrong way or by themselves to the south.

He found Danny Oz smoking a cigarette—regular, not cannabis—and drinking coffee in a mostly empty mess tent under the rusting Tower of Doom. Oz didn't seem surprised by the early-morning repeat visit.

"Coffee, Mr. Bottom?" asked Oz, gesturing toward the big urn on a counter. "It's terrible but strong."

"No, thanks."

"You've thought of more questions." Oz had been writing with a pencil in a small book of blank pages, but he set that aside.

"Not really," said Nick. "At least not officially in terms of the investigation. That's over."

"Oh, did you find Keigo Nakamura's killer?"

"I'm not sure," said Nick, knowing how absurd that sounded. No matter. It was true. "I just had some free time and I wondered, Mr. Oz…"

"Danny."

"I wondered, Danny, how you might describe Keigo's demeanor and attitude when he interviewed you."

Oz was silent for a minute and Nick was sure that he hadn't understood the question—Nick wasn't sure that *he* understood what he'd been asking. He was about to rephrase it when the Israeli poet spoke.

"That's interesting, Mr. Bottom. I did notice something about Mr. Keigo's demeanor and mood that day."

"What?" said Nick. "Depressed? Worried? Apprehensive?"

"Triumphant," said Oz.

Nick had been ready to write in his little notebook but now he lowered his pencil. "Triumphant?"

Danny Oz frowned and sipped his coffee. "That's not quite the correct word, Mr. Bottom. I'm thinking of the Hebrew word *menatzeiach*, which probably most closely translates as 'victorious.' For no good reason other than my years of observing human beings as a poet, I had the distinct impression that Keigo Nakamura thought that he was on the brink of some triumph...some victory. A victory of epic...one might say 'biblical' proportions."

"He was close to finishing his documentary on us Americans and flashback," said Nick. "Is that the kind of triumph you might have detected?"

"Perhaps." Oz was silent a long moment. "But I felt it was more a sense of having been victorious in some great struggle."

"What kind of struggle? Personal? Bigger than personal? Something on his *father's* scale of success or failure?"

"I have no idea," said Oz and shrugged. "We're in the area of totally subjective impressions here, Mr. Bottom. But I'd take a wild guess and say the young man felt victorious in some battle that had been both personal *and* larger than the mere personal to him. Corporate, perhaps, or political. But definitely something larger than himself."

Nick sighed. "All right. Speaking of totally subjective impressions, I have two questions for you that don't really relate to the investigation at all."

"About your wife?" Oz asked softly. He rubbed his neck as if still feeling Nick's forearm there. There was still a red spot on the poet's left temple where the muzzle of Nick's Glock had broken the skin.

"No, not about Dara," managed Nick. He opened his mouth to apologize and then shut it without speaking. "Just a question. If you could have saved Israel from destruction by killing a single person—one human being—would you have done it?"

Danny Oz blinked several times. The pained expression on his face showed that the question was not only unfair but impossible to answer. Still, he answered.

"Mr. Bottom, the Talmud taught us—and I'm sure I've bollixed up this verse since I haven't studied the Sanhedrin part of the Talmud since I was a boy, but I'll try to quote—*'For this reason was man created alone, to teach thee that whosoever destroys a single soul…scripture imputes…* I think the word is 'guilt'*…to him as though he had destroyed a complete world; and whosoever preserves a single soul, scripture ascribes merit to him…* or maybe the passage said 'righteousness,' I'm not sure*…as though he had preserved a complete world.'*"

"So you wouldn't have killed someone to save Israel?" said Nick.

Danny Oz looked Nick in the eye and the former thousand-yard stare was completely absent from his gaze. And from Nick's.

"I don't know, Mr. Bottom. God forgive me, I simply don't know."

"One last question," said Nick. "If you had the chance to return to Israel now, would you do it?"

Oz snorted derisively. He drank the last of his cold coffee and lit a new cigarette. "There is no Israel, Mr. Bottom. Only a radioactive wasteland inhabited by Arabs."

"It's not all radioactive," said Nick. "And what if someone removed the new Arab settlers who came in after the bombings?"

Oz laughed again. It was a hollow, sad sound. "Remove them? Sure. Who would do that, Mr. Bottom? The United Nations?"

The UN, always a dependable ally of the Arab bloc and of Palestinians at the end of the twentieth century, was now—

except for its Japanese-run "peacekeeper" operation in China—
a full-fledged subsidiary of the Islamic Global Caliphate. The
irony, as Nick saw it, was that even after six million Jews had
been murdered and the state of Israel destroyed, the so-called
Palestinians were denied their nation-in-radioactive-rubble by
Shi'ite Iran and the competing and ever-wary and ever-jealous
Sunni Arab states.

"No," said Nick. "Cleared out by someone else. Would
you go?"

"I have prostate cancer and other radiation-induced can-
cers," said Oz. "I'm dying."

"We're all dying," said Nick. "Would you go back to Israel
if other Jews joined you there?"

Danny Oz looked Nick in the eye again and—once more—
there was the new clarity to his gaze. "I'd go in a minute, Mr.
Bottom. In a minute."

Nick came out to the parking lot knowing that he'd learned
almost nothing that could help him when he would have to
stand before Mr. Nakamura in a few hours and be commanded
to tell the billionaire who'd killed his son.

But I learned something important, thought Nick. He just
wasn't sure what it was.

The three Oshkosh M-ATVs roared in and blocked his
vehicle before he got the doors to his car unlocked.

Mutsumi Ōta, Daigorou Okada, and Shinta Ishii—Nick's
fellow survivors from the Santa Fe trip—jumped out of the
lead vehicle. Each was dressed for urban combat but not for
war: SWAT Kevlar and black boots, even their black ball caps
made of ballistic cloth. And each held an automatic weapon at
port arms.

Nick didn't move a muscle.

Sato moved his mass out the rear hatch of the M-ATV,
nodded at his three ninjas, and said, "Bottom-san, will you come
with us, please?"

Oh shit, thought Nick. *Too soon. Too early. I'm not ready.* He
wondered once again how many billions of men and women
had died with equally unworthy final thoughts.

He licked his lips. "Mr. Nakamura's back?"

"Not yet," rumbled Sato. "But Mr. Nakamura did direct us to show you some things before your meeting with him later today. Please come with us."

"Do I have a choice?" said Nick.

"Please come with us, Bottom-san," said Sato. "We shall return you to your vehicle here in an hour or less."

Keeping his hands away from his Glock, making no sudden movements, Nick went up the rear ramp into the idling M-ATV.

———

THE RIDE WAS SHORT, less than two miles, and ended at a grassy sward of what had once been a long park on the east bank of the Platte River in front of a series of high-rise condos that had gone up around the turn of the century. Sato, Sato's three ninjas, and Nick exited the lead M-ATV and moved to one of Nakamura's dragonfly 'copters—the less luxurious one that Nick had flown in down to Raton Pass a week earlier. A dozen more of Sato's people from the other M-ATVs, all in ballistic black and Kevlar, had set up a perimeter around the machine. Mutsumi Ōta—whom Nick had once thought of as Willy— gestured and Nick clambered into the open door of the dragonfly. Sato put on a headset with microphone, waited until everyone else was belted or clipped in, spoke a few unheard Japanese syllables into the mike, and the *Sasayaki-tonbo* fluttered silently, hovered, pitched to one side, and flew east above Denver's downtown.

They'd left the side doors open and Nick looked out at his own reflection in the gold-tinted glass of the fifty-one-story former Wells Fargo building, the modest skyscraper that Denver residents had called the cash register building for decades because of its distinctive shape at the top. Buildings continued to flash beneath them and then, suddenly, they were beyond Denver and flying southeast over farms and high prairie.

This had been the reality of Denver for many decades now, Nick knew. To the north and south and west, suburbs extended the city beyond the horizon. But to the east there had always been this startling line — city and then a few farms where irrigation worked and high prairie beyond that stretching toward Kansas. Nick didn't ask where they were headed and his only guess was a very dark one.

He smelled their destination before he saw it and in smelling it, Nick knew his guess had been correct.

The dragonfly landed, everyone unbelted, and the ninja guards hopped down, gesturing politely for Nick to join them. Nick lifted his shirt front and put it over his mouth and nose. It was that or throw up.

"Do you know where you are, Bottom-san?" asked Sato, stepping close to Nick and close to the edge of a reeking chasm.

Nick nodded. He didn't want to talk because he didn't want the staggering stench to get into his mouth.

They were at Denver Municipal Landfill Number Nine.

"Have you been here before, Bottom-san?"

Nick shook his head. He didn't know how Sato could stand speaking and breathing in more of this air. Nick had seen many forensic photos and videos taken from this spot, but he'd never had to come out here in person before.

Originally, the landfill had been a deep ravine that ran north to south for about a mile. Bulldozers had deepened parts, built low tabletop mesas and hills along its edge, and leveled some crude roads from the nearest county road to the fill. On the west side, the tons of garbage dumped there were of the usual twentieth-century urban sort — countless rotting garbage bags, ruined furniture, heaps of rotting cloth and organic materials. Here on the northwest side, there was plenty of that, but from the rim of the chasm to the bottom there were also rotting human corpses — many hundreds of them. Some were wrapped in cloth or plastic shrouds, but most lay open and exposed to the hot September sun. Clouds of seagulls and crows had risen from their feeding sites at the appearance of the dragonfly 'copter and now returned to their dining. One area was reserved for the turkey vultures that circled on thermals above, like aircraft in an approach pattern at DIA, awaiting their turn on the exposed corpses. Many of the corpses at the base of the ravine were mere skeletons, sexlessly clean, gleaming white, with only a few shreds and tatters of flesh left on the exposed ribs or pelvises or leg bones. But the majority of bodies were still flesh-filled, bloated beyond recognition as human, crawling with maggots, and with only obscene glimpses of white bone poking through their fermenting masses.

Nick noticed that many of the medium-old corpses seemed to be moving and twitching on the hillside: a trick of the light due to the movement of the millions of maggots on their surfaces and below. Even the gulls weren't dining on those bodies.

Every American city had a landfill such as this near its borders now, a third of the way through this glorious twenty-first century. All those *reconquista* fighters, Cinco de Mayo militia, Aryan Brotherhood gangs, jihadists, neighborhood protection groups, motorcycle gangs, and sometimes the authorities themselves needed such a disposal place if proper urban hygiene was to be observed.

Sato touched Nick's left arm and urged him closer to the edge.

They hadn't disarmed him and Nick's right hand was already raised. If Okada, Ishii, or Ōta were to raise one of his weapons behind him, Nick was going to throw himself in front of Sato, grab the bigger man while emptying the full clip of his Glock into the security chief's belly, chest, and face, then roll down into the heaps of corpses, using Sato's body as a shield while he fired the Glock and then going for the useless little .32 pocket pistol at his ankle to take down the three body-armored ninjas carrying full-auto M4 carbines.

His body was ready to do that. But what Nick was thinking was—*Val and Leonard and K.T. will never know what happened to me.*

Well, K.T. might. The DPD checked Denver Municipal Landfill Number Nine about once a month for corpses of interest. And she might tell his son and father-in-law, if those two didn't soon join him here.

Which Nick didn't think was very likely.

Sato put his hand on Nick's left shoulder and Nick put his hand on the butt of the Glock under his light jacket. The three ninjas shifted close behind him.

"Mukatsuku yō na-sō desu ka?" said Sato.

Nick had no idea what the words meant. A good-bye, maybe. An ultimatum, maybe. He really didn't care. His index finger slipped under the Glock's trigger guard. Everything from this point on would happen in fractions of a second.

"Zehi, Bottom-san. *Iko u."* Sato dropped the heavy hand from Nick's shoulder, wheeled, and led the way back to the dragonfly. Before climbing in after the four Japanese, Nick noticed that the pilot and copilot had put on their oxygen masks to avoid the physically debilitating stench.

————

WHEREVER THEY WERE HEADED next, they weren't taking him back to the Six Flags parking lot. Not yet.

Whatever it is, thought Nick, *it can't be as bad as Denver Municipal Landfill Number Nine.*

As it would turn out, he was wrong.

The dragonfly hurtled west at somewhere above 150 m.p.h., never climbing higher than two or three thousand feet above the unscrolling terrain. They flew over the northern Denver suburbs and followed Highway 36, the Boulder Turnpike, toward the gleaming slabs of the Flatirons.

They were headed to the People's Republic of Boulder.

Nick felt his phone vibrate. Moving slowly so as not to spook Sato or his ninjas, Nick withdrew the phone from his jacket pocket. It was a text message:—*Mr. B—Your two visitors are here and I've shown them to your quarters and will watch over them. Chits for the food court and everything. Gunny G.*

Nick tried not to show any emotion as he slipped the phone back in his pocket.

The dragonfly passed over Boulder, flying low over the buildings on the CU campus, and then climbed above the foothills and hovered. Nick leaned over and looked down. They were landing in what had been the parking lot at NCAR.

Nick remembered the Anthropogenic Global Warming furor. He was already in his twenties when that hysteria hit its apogee. Now it was just a cautionary tale from the early-century Dark Age of long-range computer modeling. Nick, for one, had looked forward to longer summers, easier winters, and palm trees in Colorado, but the weather the last few decades had been colder and snowier than average and the science of Anthropogenic Global Warming had joined that of Herr Becher's phlogiston and Soviet Lamarckism evolutionary theory.

One of the first victims of the public's disgust at the AGW false alarm, combined with disappearing federal budgets, was the group for which the beautiful building growing larger beneath them had been built: NCAR, the National Center for Atmospheric Research. The architect I. M. Pei had designed this Mesa Lab NCAR center out of sandstone and glass and meant for its stone to age with and blend in with the giant sandstone Flatirons just above the building while the glass reflected the turbulent Colorado skies. It had done so beautifully for almost seventy-five years now, but the atmospheric research people had long since sold the structure—the *only* structure allowed to be built in the miles of greenbelt separating urban Boulder from the Flatirons and foothills—to some private company.

They landed gently. NCAR—NAKAMURA CENTER FOR ADVANCED RESEARCH said the small sign to the right of the entry walkway.

"Mr. Nakamura kept the old initials," Sato said redundantly as he opened the door.

Damned white of him, thought Nick.

The outer sections of the old laboratory, in the towers and where the broad windows looked out on sky, stone, and brown grasslands, were still offices. But the basement and former courtyard core of the building had been converted into… something else.

They donned green cloth surgical booties and little cloth surgical shower caps in a sort of airlock outside the long, wide underground room. But Nick had already caught a glimpse of what was inside.

The three ninjas stayed in the airlock as Sato escorted Nick into the space. Two medicos or technicians, both wearing full surgical robes and masks as well as the caps and booties, hurried up to say something, but Sato waved a single finger that silenced them. One of them bowed low to Sato.

They walked past tall tanks of Plexiglas or some stronger, clear plastic-glass material. Each tank was filled with a greenish liquid. A score of pipes and tubes snaked into each tank, and half of the tubes connected to the human beings—mostly men, but a few women—who floated in each vat. They were naked except for a sort of diaper from which more tubes came and went. Tubes ran into the men's and women's nostrils, and broader tubes were forced down their throats. Other IV drips connected to wrists and arms. Sensors on the figures' chests and bellies and shaven heads fed data to control boards on the exteriors of the tanks.

"The tubes are for nutrients and other functions, Bottom-san," Sato said softly, almost whispering, as if they were in a church or shrine. "They receive no oxygen in gaseous form. You see, their lungs are actually filled with the liquid. The fluid is a highly oxygenated mixture. The initial immersion is difficult for the subject, if conscious, but the human body—once the lungs are completely filled—soon learns to use the oxygen in the fluid as easily as if he or she were breathing air."

They moved from tank to tank, walking in single file between the tall containers. Each of the hundreds of tanks was illuminated from the inside and the overall effect in this subterranean chamber was that hushed, almost solemn sense of being in some fantastic aquarium. The only sound came from the quiet machines or the occasional rustle of soft-soled slippers on the tile floor. The laboratory space did have a churchlike hush and reverential feel to it.

"Except for a few cases, in which the subject is being punished," whispered Sato, "we remove the eardrums, eyeballs, and optic nerves. There is no need for them, you see. They could only be a distraction."

Nick thought, *They're being punished by* not *having their eardrums, eyeballs, and optic nerves removed?* He feared that this would make sense in a moment.

"What is this?" demanded Nick. "Some sort of sci-fi experiment for long-distance space travel? Are these clones or something? Adapting the human body to live under the oceans? What the fuck is this nightmare?"

They stopped by a tank where a man who looked to be in his early sixties floated amid his Medusa-hair tangle of tubes and microtubes. His eyelids were sutured shut and sunken. He had no external ears and the ear openings had been covered over by grafts of flesh and skin.

"These are the first test subjects," said Sato. "A few hundred here at NCAR from thousands finishing their testing nationwide. These are the final quality-control check before Flashback-two is distributed in America and elsewhere."

"F-two?" Nick repeated stupidly.

"Precisely," said Sato. He set his strong hand on the glass inches from the floating man's face. Nick noticed that this man's skin—the skin covering the faces and scalps and bodies of all the figures in all the tanks—was fishbelly-white and as wrinkled as an albino prune.

"They will spend the rest of their lives in flashback happiness," continued Sato. "Less than two miles from here, people are spending millions of dollars to relive their entire lives under supervised flashback medication at the Naropa Institute. But regular flashback demands that the subject be awakened for several hours out of each twenty-four—to exercise, to eat, to avoid bedsores and other ailments of the permanently immobilized. Their relived lives are constantly being interrupted, the flashback illusion interrupted and violated. But here..."

Sato gestured around.

"Here Mr. Nakamura's science department has provided full lifetimes' worth of only the happiest moments, not merely relived as with flashback, but *restructured* as one's imagination and fantasies would have them. People here are spending happy futures with loved ones they've lost to death. Cripples in real life walk and run here and will for the rest of their F-two lives.

Failures in life find success in these tanks, with this drug, and no one is harmed. There is no failure or loss under this kind of flash, Bottom-san. There is no pain under Flashback-two. None at all."

"It's real," mumbled Nick. He meant the drug. After all these years of rumor and myth about F-2, it was here. And real.

"Oh, yes. To these men and women, everything they are dreaming is *totally* real," said Sato, misunderstanding Nick's comment. "The only difference separating life under Flashback-two and what we call 'real life' is the wonderful absence of physical pain and painful experiences or memories or emotions for this privileged group."

"How long do they... *live?*" asked Nick. His clothes still carried the stink of Denver Municipal Landfill Number Nine. He wished he were back there.

"Our best projections, based on a decade of research, suggest a normal span of seventy or eighty years," said Sato. "Sometimes longer. A full, rich, *happy* life."

Nick covered his mouth with his hand. After a moment he removed it and grated, "The penalty in Japan or anywhere else for Nipponese nationals using flashback is death."

"As it shall remain, Bottom-san," said Sato. "And that law will continue to be strictly enforced, just as it is in the Global Caliphate."

Nick shook his head. "You'll sell this stuff, this F-two..." He broke off when he realized he didn't know how to end that sentence.

"At a lower price than the original flashback," Sato said proudly. "F-two will be street priced at a new dollar for forty or fifty hours. Even the homeless will be able to afford it."

"You can't give three hundred and forty–some million people each a fish tank to float in," snarled Nick. "And who's going to feed the flashing millions? It's hard enough to do that now."

"Of course there will be no tanks, Bottom-san. The customer will have to find his or her own flashcave or comfortable, private place in which to go under Flash-two. The tank really is the best option. We imagine that providing such places—perhaps some not so different than NCAR—will be a growth industry in the next few years. We imagine that other nations, ones that do not allow either form of flashback within their own borders, might be helpful in manufacturing such total-immersion tanks for Americans."

Nick counted cartridges. He had fifteen rounds in the magazine already in the Glock and one more magazine in his jacket pocket. Thirty rounds total. It might take several 9mm rounds to crack one of these tanks, if they *were* breakable by small-arms fire. The .32 didn't count since it almost certainly couldn't smash this type of super-Plexiglas. It might be transparent Kevlar-3, in which case even the Glock would be useless here. He later realized that this probability was the only thing that stopped him.

The two men stood in green-shadowed silence for a long moment: Hideki Sato contemplative, Nick Bottom seething in murderous frustration.

"Why are you showing me this?" asked Nick, staring Sato in the face.

The big security chief smiled slightly. "We have to leave now, Bottom-san, if I am to return you to your vehicle before the hour is up as I promised. Later today, when you speak to Mr. Nakamura, do not forget the possibility of NCAR."

"I'll never forget NCAR," said Nick.

1.17

Denver—Saturday, Sept. 25

WHERE ARE THEY?"

Nick was in the weapons-check airlock and Gunny G. was the only one behind the counter.

"Your son's gone, Mr. B. And your father-in-law has had some sort of stroke or heart attack," said the ex-Marine.

"Gone?" shouted Nick. "What do you mean Val's *gone?* Where to?"

"We don't know, Mr. B. He went up and out the skylight and down a rope. I'll show you."

"Is Leonard—my father-in-law—alive?"

"Yeah. I brought him to Dr. Tak."

"Let me in, Gunny. Buzz the door open."

"I can't, Mr. B. Not 'til you surrender the two guns you checked out this morning. You know the rules."

"I know the rules," said Nick. He came back to the counter and slipped a $50 old-bucks bill across. He was nearing the last of his "advance" from Nakamura.

Gunny G. buzzed the heavy door open.

DR. TAK'S REAL NAME was Sudaret Jatisripitak but everyone in the mall called him Dr. Tak. He'd fled from Thailand during their last *"Thai Rak Thai*—Thais Love Thais" revolution that had killed a fifth of the nation's population and found that he could make a decent living, without ever being medically certified in the United States, simply by giving black-market medical care to the few thousand residents of the Cherry Creek Mall Condominiums. Accordingly, Dr. Tak's cubie was one of the largest in the mall, half of the upstairs part of the former Macy's department store, and Nick found Leonard asleep in one of the ER cubicles near the entrance to Dr. Tak's lair.

Nick's heart leaped in terror when he saw the IV drip and other tubes going into his father-in-law. No, he wouldn't be forgetting NCAR any time soon.

Tak, a small man in his seventies but still with short jet-black hair, came into the cubicle, shook hands with Nick, and said, "He will live. Mr. Gunny G. found your father-in-law unconscious in your cubie and I directed he be brought here. I've done various diagnostic tests. Professor Fox regained consciousness briefly but he is currently sleeping."

"What's wrong with him?" asked Nick. Leonard looked much older to him than the old professor had five years earlier when he'd dropped Val off in L.A. in his care.

"I believe it was an attack of angina brought on by aortic stenosis," said the old Thai doctor. "The syncopic episode was a result of the pain and lack of oxygen to the heart."

"What does 'syncopic episode' mean, Doc?"

"Fainting. His loss of consciousness."

"I think I know what angina is, but what's the . . . aortic stenosis?"

"Correct, Mr. Bottom. Aortic stenosis is an abnormal narrowing of the aortic valve. At certain times—say, times of great exertion or tension—this narrowing can shut off blood from the left ventricle of the heart. His symptoms were the sudden onset of angina and the fainting."

"Is it fixable?" Nick asked softly, staring at the sleeping old man's face. Dara had loved her father. "Will he survive it?"

"Two quite different questions," said Dr. Tak with a smile. "About four percent of the time, the initial symptom of aortic stenosis is sudden death. Your father-in-law was lucky that his symptoms were limited to angina and loss of consciousness. From my initial tests—and I have good diagnostic equipment here, Mr. Bottom—my first guess is that this was a form of the heart problem called senile calcific aortic stenosis…"

"Senile!" said Nick, shocked.

"Used only in the sense that it occurs naturally in people over sixty-five years of age," said Dr. Tak. "As one ages, protein collagen of the valve leaflets is destroyed and calcium is deposited on the leaflets. Turbulence then increases, causing thickening and stenosis of the valve, even while mobility is reduced by calcification. Why this progresses to the point of causing aortic stenosis in some patients but not in others is not known. It has in Professor Fox's case."

"What about fixing it?" said Nick.

Dr. Tak turned away from his patient and spoke very softly. "Once the symptoms of shortage of breath, angina, or fainting occur, there's little that can be done for a patient of Dr. Fox's age short of the surgical procedure called aortic valve replacement."

"Is that expensive?" asked Nick. "Can he get it on government coverage?"

Dr. Tak smiled grimly. "I am not a surgeon. Since the health care meltdown in your country, Mr. Bottom, the waiting time for the National Health Service Initiative–covered aortic valve replacement is a little over two years. Bioprosthetic valves taken from horses or cows are used in the procedure and that harvesting itself takes a long time and must be prioritized for patients. Also, all surgical recipients of mechanical prosthetic valves require immune-system drugs, including lifelong anticoagulation treatment with blood thinners such as warfarin—also known as Coumadin—to prevent clot formation on the valve surfaces. This is a very expensive drug and not covered under Medicare Two."

"And, don't tell me, let me guess," grated Nick through his teeth, "most people suffering this…aortic stenosis…don't live long enough to get to the government-subsidized surgery. And if they do, they can't afford the blood thinner they'll need."

"That is correct," said Dr. Tak. "Years ago, when I was a young physician in Bangkok, we all expected breakthroughs in genetic research to produce cloned human heart valves which would make such valve transplants *not* require immune-system and anticoagulant medications—since even the rare transplant of valves from human cadavers in this procedure had avoided the autoimmune problems—but, of course, with the crash of the great pharmaceutical companies in North America after your so-called health care reform, and in the absence of government-funded research in America and the post–EU countries, those hopes have disappeared."

"So there's nothing you can do for Leonard, Dr. Tak? Nothing *we* can do for him? Nothing *I* can do?"

"I will give him painkillers for when the angina returns," said the old Thai. "And he must avoid all strenuous exercise. And, of course, any great excitement or tension."

Nick couldn't keep himself from laughing at that. When Dr. Tak frowned at him as only a doctor can frown, Nick said, "Leonard just escaped from Los Angeles and got my son out of that war zone, Doc. I don't know how he did it, but I'll be grateful to him for the rest of my life for saving my son. If I could give him my entire heart now in a transplant, I'd do it."

"I accept," came Professor Emeritus George Leonard Fox's reedy voice from behind them. "Dr. Tak, please prep my son-in-law for an immediate heart transplant to me. And while you're at it, take his kidneys and prostate. Mine keep me awake all night."

Nick and the doctor turned, but only Nick blushed. He went to one knee by the bed. "How long have you been awake, Leonard?"

"Long enough to hear all the bad news," said the old man. "Did I miss any *good* news about this condition?"

"Well," said Nick, "four percent of those who have it show a first symptom of sudden death. You didn't."

Leonard smiled. "I've always enjoyed being in the bland majority. Actually, I feel sort of good for a doomed old fart who's just had a near-death experience. Mellow. Did you give me something in this IV, Dr. Tak?"

"A mild tranquilizer."

"Please give me a few hundred of those pills in a doggie bag when I leave," said Leonard. He squeezed Nick's hand. "And we will be leaving soon, won't we?"

"I think we have to," said Nick.

"Did Val return?" asked Leonard and his grip intensified.

Nick shook his head. "I have trouble believing he got *out* of the building."

As if just remembering something, Leonard whispered, "The phone," and released Nick's hand, beckoning him to lean closer.

Nick put his ear almost to the old man's mouth.

"Dara's phone, Nick. It's in your cubie. It's double-password-protected. The first password is 'dream'—*d...r...e...a...m*. The second-level password is 'Kildare,' the name of her pet parakeet. I just figured out that second-level password. 'Kildare.' That opens text files from the months before she died, Nick. The text I understand. It's important. *Very* important. More important than finding Val. You need to go read it...see the videos. Her diary...or notes she made for you, I think...it changes everything."

Nick blinked in response. *More important than finding Val?* What could be more important than that to Val's grandfather? Or to Nick?

"Go now," whispered Leonard. "Go look at the phone *now*." More loudly, he said, "Dr. Tak will help me get dressed and ready to travel, won't you, sir?"

Tak frowned again. "You should not travel for some time, Professor Fox. You need to *rest*. Days of rest."

"Yes, yes," said Leonard. "But you'll help me get dressed,

won't you? While Nick goes to tend to some things? Not being part of the Really Surprised Four Percent, I need to get on with what's left of my life."

Dr. Tak continued frowning but nodded.

"I'll be back for you in a few minutes, Leonard," said Nick. He took Dr. Tak aside and squeezed all the remaining big bills he had from the Nakamura old-bucks advance into the old Thai doctor's gnarled hand. It left him with about thirty bucks in small bills with none left on his NICC card, but that didn't matter.

"This is too much money," said Dr. Tak.

Nick shook his head. "You've helped me before when I couldn't pay enough. And you can put it toward whatever pills Leonard needs for the immediate future. Anyway, if I keep this cash, I'll just blow it on wine, women, and song." He again squeezed the old medic's hands shut around the little wad of bills.

"Thank you, Dr. Tak."

———

GUNNY G. WAS WAITING in the hall and eager to show Nick Val's escape route. Since it appeared to be on the way to his cubie, more or less, Nick followed along as the stocky ex-marine sprinted up the unmoving escalator like a boot at Parris Island. Nick followed more stiffly, favoring his tightly taped ribs.

"My kid did that?" said Nick as he stood on the mezzanine and looked out at the cable—beyond his own reach or jumping ability, he was sure—and then up at the shattered skylight glass forty feet above.

"He did," said Gunny G., not hiding his own admiration. "With about twenty pounds of climbing rope, pitons, and carabiners hitched over his shoulder. When I showed him and the old man into the place earlier, I sorta thought that the boy was a bit of a runt for the sixteen-year-old described on the DHS all-points-bulletin."

Nick was going to let that pass but heard himself saying, "Not a bad jump and climb for a runt."

Gunny G. keyed in the access code and they went up the

stairs to the roof. Once at the skylight, Nick paused for a second to look down through the missing glass pane at the long drop to the glass-shard-littered soil of the dirt-filled fountain far below. Then he followed spatters of blood to the southwest corner of the roof.

"I pulled the rope up and coiled it," said Gunny, "but left it anchored here."

Nick was disturbed by the amount of blood. It was obvious that his son had slashed himself pretty badly during the climb.

Gunny was pointing down the south wall of the parking garage. "The video cam down there caught just a blur when your son shinnied down past it, then picked him up when he walked over to the bridge there."

"What did he do there?"

The security man shrugged. "My guess is that he had a weapon hidden there, but he was wearing a jacket so it was hard to say for sure. Your boy stayed over there on the other side of the bridge for a while and then walked off—limped off, really—to the west. I was busy getting your father-in-law to Dr. Tak, but when I had time later I went out and checked the bridge and saw where the kid had bled quite a bit."

"Bad?" said Nick. He heard the concerned edge in his own voice. *A little late to play the concerned daddy, isn't it, asshole?* demanded a more honest voice in his head.

"It'll probably need some stitches and tending," said Gunny. "But he's not going to bleed out or anything. I've had Lennie and Dorrie watch the external cams extra close this afternoon, but there's been no sign of Val watching from across the street or coming back to the bridge."

"Okay," said Nick. "Thanks." He headed back to the stairway, trying not to stare at the blood trail. It was true that he'd seen much worse.

Suddenly there flowed in the unbidden memory of his youngest attacker, wounded and begging for his life in the pre-dawn dimness of the Huntington Botanical Gardens the previous Monday. That young man had been three or four years older than Val, at least, and had almost certainly spent his night with his older pals shooting at unarmed civilians as if they were deer in the woods—it was just his bad luck that Nick hadn't been unarmed—but who was going to be the merciless older man aiming the muzzle of his Glock at Val's forehead and shielding his face from spatter if this crap kept up?

Knock it off, shithead. It doesn't help.

"Whaddya wanta do with the climbing rope, Mr. B.?" called Gunny from the corner of the roof.

"I'll get it later," lied Nick.

———

HIS CUBIE WAS A total mess. Not only had it been tossed, clothes strewn everywhere, the contents of his dresser drawers dumped out and then the drawers themselves thrown around, but there was the usual paramedic mess of discarded plastic and paper wrappings from where Dr. Tak had done his initial work on Leonard.

Nick ignored the mess. All he could focus on was the scatter of colored dossiers.

Did Val read the grand jury stuff?

Of course he had.

Nick brushed the pile of folders off his desk with a furious sweep of his forearm. *Would Val believe that I tried to kill his mother?*

Of course he would. Nick was, after all, the same man who'd dumped his son with an elderly grandfather in Los Angeles and never come to visit him...who never found enough money to fly the son home to Denver for a visit...who only phoned a few times a year and who totally forgot that son's sixteenth birthday. Why wouldn't a so-called father like *that* conspire to kill a wife who'd been unfaithful to him?

Nick sat on the chair with his elbows on his knees, his hands gripping the sweaty sides of his head, and concentrated on trying to breathe.

For 4 percent of people with this problem, the first noticeable symptom is sudden death.

Yeah, and ain't that a great practical joke on the 4 percent? Nick's father had been careless to get himself killed when Nick was pretty young, but at least he'd paid attention to Nick when he was still alive and had the time. With no shade of melodrama whatsoever, Nick realized that he would never be able to make things up to Val, no matter how much time the two might have in the rest of their lives.

Almost certainly less than eight hours for me, thought Nick.

This flood of certainty washed over Nick again as a mere fact, no melodrama. If he couldn't escape with Val and Leonard, if he couldn't live in real life that lovely dream he'd had that morning just before waking, he was certain that the meeting with Mr. Nakamura would not end well for a certain ex-cop named Nick Bottom. It was as if he could already smell the decomposing stench of his own death...

"Shit," said Nick. Slamming his cubie door shut, he stripped naked, throwing everything he'd been wearing, down to his boxer shorts, into the far corner of the room. Then he went into the bathroom and showered fast but hard, scrubbing until his skin almost bled. Even then, Nick could still detect the death stench of Denver Municipal Landfill Number Nine.

The remembered NCAR smell was more subtle—a faint hint of chlorine and other chemicals, as when lying near a well-tended swimming pool—but just as terrifying.

Nick dressed quickly and carelessly—clean underwear, clean socks, a blue-plaid flannel shirt washed so many times that it was almost obscenely soft, clean chinos that weren't as tight on him as they'd been two weeks earlier. He clipped the holster and Glock on his belt on the left side and velcroed the little holster with its tiny .32 on his right ankle.

Then he looked for Dara's phone. It wasn't there on the desk or bed.

Someone's stolen it. The neighbors or some other residents came in and took it while Gunny G. and Dr. Tak were parading back and forth, the place unlocked and unwatched. Or maybe Val had taken it with him or come back to get it...

Nick forced himself to calm down. He'd have to borrow some of Dr. Tak's tranquilizers from Leonard's doggie bag if he kept flirting with hysteria this way.

Getting down on his hands and knees, Nick looked under the bed and under the desk, pawing through the mess. He found the old phone between the faux wood and the wall base-board where someone had knocked it off the back of his desk.

Please God, tell me it's not broken.

As usual, God did not deign to tell Nick Bottom anything.

The phone's scratched screen lit up, but only to inform him that the long-term battery was too weak to run the old phone.

Nick again looked through all the junk removed from his room's various drawers until he found the charger-adapter for his own phone. Nick and Dara had bought their phones at the same time; the charger fit both.

The files had closed and reencrypted at the power-down so Nick had to reenter the *dream* password.

Eight-to-five odds that the password won't work for me.

But it did.

Nick went to the massive video files, hoping to see Dara. Even though he'd visited her for hours every night and day of his life for the past five and a half years—this past week excepted—his heart pounded wildly at the thought of seeing new video of her.

She wasn't there.

But Danny Oz was. And Delroy Nigger Brown. And Derek Dean. And Don Khozh-Ahmed Noukhaev. And two dozen other talking heads, all familiar to Nick Bottom through the homicide investigation of Keigo Nakamura's messy murder.

The missing last hours of Keigo's documentary.

Nick didn't even ask himself—yet—how Dara could have gotten a copy. *Unless she was the murderer.* He shut that problem out for now and flicked through the video-recorded interviews, too impatient to listen to them in their entirety, but jumping from interview subject to interview subject.

It was there. *Something* incredible was there.

Don Khozh-Ahmed Noukhaev talking about the laborato-ries in Nara in Japan where flashback had *really* been invented and the larger, newer laboratories outside Wuhan and Shantou and Nanjing in China that would be producing the Flashback-two. Noukhaev smiling and talking about distribution networks flowing from Japan and reaching everywhere—just as they had for fifteen years now.

Nick jumped from person to person, hearing Keigo's distant voice asking the questions—only the answers were to be in his documentary—and while most of the questions and answers were like the billionaire's son's earlier recorded footage, there were new parts—hints—clues—which began to come together for Nick, even hearing only fragments and unrelated snippets.

This footage alone might help him understand what Keigo Nakamura had been *doing* with his goddamned documentary—if not who murdered him for it—before Nick's meeting with Nakamura later this afternoon or evening.

Of course, Nick realized, if he was still here when it came time for that meeting, he probably would have lost everything anyway. The trick was not to solve Keigo Nakamura's murder after six years of both it and Nick being lost in the cold file, the idea was to get his son and father-in-law and *to get away*.

Even if, unlike in his dream that morning, there was no place to get away *to*. The Republic of Texas didn't take in wanted felons—and he would be such by the time he got to any border—much less wanted felons and their sons and fathers-in-law.

Nick closed out the video and used the second password—*Kildare*—to open the text files.

The first ones, made about two months before Keigo's murder, made Nick stop breathing.

It was not a long or thick text file, despite the fact that it covered the last seven months of his wife's life. She'd made only a few notes for him (or for herself?) in the weeks before and after Keigo's death, and then almost none through the winter months until just the days before her own death.

Nick didn't skip through these files as he had through the videos. He read them straight through...

…participation of Homeland Security and the FBI, but Mannie Ortega is keeping it within his department…

…Harvey doesn't want to lose the time with his family, but he sees it as a once-in-a-lifetime career opportunity…

…if I could only tell Nick, but I've sworn to both my boss and my boss's boss, in writing, that this will stay quiet until…

…speculating on her motives won't help, Harvey keeps saying, but those motives still seem important to me since we're all taking such risks with…

…the DA thinks another week before we bring the witness home, or rather the Feebies or Homeland Security or the CIA does, but Harvey's afraid that if they wait too long, even with all the video and audio recordings we have, it might be…

…Love? A sense of betrayal? How can someone who loves someone—two someones—so very much do such a thing to them? Ortega and Harvey aren't interested, but the question consumes me. If I only could talk to Nick about…

…to love two men so much in such different ways is possible, but to be pulled between them the way she's been is terrible…

…the murders would seem to me to change everything, but Ortega insists, and I think Harvey agrees, that they change nothing. It hurts me inside to watch Nick working so hard, not knowing what Harvey and I have been up to right under his nose…

*…sometimes I just want to leave Nick a note—*real name Kumiko Catherine Catton*—and see what happens. But I can't…*

…just reading her transcripts makes me miss and love my own father more, as weird as he is. I have to give him a call tonight, wish him Happy New Year at least…

…what Ortega says just isn't acceptable to me. Harvey's going to go along with it. He tells me that all this sneaking around has almost cost him his marriage already and that his kids don't recognize him when he does *come home, but down deep I think he agrees with me that we can't end it like this. Not like this. I'm supposed to sneak away to spend time with Harvey tomorrow at the Denver motel where we keep the stuff and he insists it's the last time for us there, but I won't accept that. I've told him I won't. I told him that I'd*

go to Nick with the whole sad, sick story unless we found a way to carry on...

Nick wiped tears from his eyes and read it through. To the last fragmented, incomplete entry, made by a woman who didn't know she was going to die the next day.

How many of us do? wondered Nick. Know we're going to die the next day.

Or this evening?

When his phone rang, Nick almost jumped out of his skin. He'd been watching the videos and reading Dara's notes for forty-five minutes. Poor Leonard must think that he'd been forgotten down there at Dr. Tak's.

"Nick Bottom," he answered but there was no one there and the caller ID was blocked in that way that prepaid phones worked.

Well, realized Nick, setting his phone back in his jacket pocket, Leonard *had* been forgotten. This data on Dara's old phone changed *everything*, all right. Nick felt the old gears begin to work the way they'd used to for him, in Major Crimes Unit and before...the pieces coming together, the full picture of the puzzle being assembled.

It was all there. He wiped away more tears and cursed himself for a blind fool.

It had always been there. All of it. Dara had tried to tell him without telling him. And he'd been too full of his own ambition and self-centered game of playing cop twenty-four hours a day to really listen to her, to really look at her.

The first thing he had to do, even before fetching Leonard, was to e-mail the full contents of Dara's text notes and the video to all the people he trusted in this world.

After two minutes of thinking in the silence, he came up with five names. Then, after more hard thinking, two more, including CHP Chief Dale Ambrose. K.T. was on the list...but it also had to go to people with better connections, people beyond the reach of those who'd reached Nakamura and Harvey Cohen and Dara Fox Bottom and probably Delroy Nigger Brown by now.

The eighth name, incredibly, was that of West Coast Advisor Daichi Omura.

Do you let the murderer know, however indirectly, that you know he or she is the murderer? Nick had played that game before, for various reasons, and it had worked.

Sometimes.

But he wasn't sure here if he'd be getting the word to...

His phone rang and vibrated again and Nick jumped again.

"Nick Bottom."

There was a silence on the line but the connection was there. Again, no caller ID.

"Hello?"

"Come pick me up," came a voice that it took Nick's buzzing mind ten seconds to identify as his son's.

"Val?"

"Come pick me up, as soon as you can."

"Val, where are you? Are you all right? Val, your grandfather... Leonard's had a sort of heart attack. He's going to make it for now, but he needs to be taken care of. Do you need medical attention? Val?"

"Come *pick me up*." There was something more than stress or pain in his son's strangely aged and altered voice. Rage? Something beyond rage?

"I will," said Nick. "Where are you?"

"You know Washington Park?"

"Sure, it's only a few minutes from here."

"Drive on Marion Parkway on the west side of the lake... the big lake, Smith Lake, I think it's called... past the tent and shack village there."

"All right," said Nick. "Where will you be..."

"What will you be driving?"

"A rusty-looking G.M. gelding with bullet holes in it."

"Can you be here in fifteen minutes?"

"Are you hurt badly, Val? Or in trouble with someone there? Just say 'yeah' if you can't speak freely."

"How soon can you be here?"

Nick took a breath. His phone and cubie Internet hookups

might be tapped. Probably were. He'd use Gunny G.'s fancy encrypted computer set up in the security shack to e-mail the video and text diaries out to his eight people. That might take a few minutes to do right. Then he'd have to get Leonard into the car with whatever clothes, IV tubes, or other medical things he needed.

He could go to the Six Flags Over the Jews parking lot to get the getaway car before picking up Val, so they could head straight for I-70 and out of town, but it might be better to pick the boy up sooner rather than later. Val sounded weird.

"Give me an hour, Val. I'll look on the west side of Smith Lake in Washington Park and we'll…"

The line went dead. Val had broken the connection.

2.05

Denver — Saturday, Sept. 25

VAL'S PLAN WAS to use his gun to make someone in Washington Park give him their phone so that he could call the Old Man and set up the meeting—the plan was to *steal* some homeless person's phone—but as it turned out, the people he met in the park were happy to loan their phone to him. *After* they'd made him a good, hot lunch and given him a blanket and pillow and let him sleep a few hours.

There were various homeless in the park but the two Val ran into first were an older black couple who he soon learned were named Harold and Dottie Davison. They were older than the Old Man but younger than Leonard, somewhere in that hard-to-estimate age for Val, in their midsixties, maybe. Harold's short, curly hair and long sideburns had a tinge of gray. Thinking that they'd be easy to intimidate, Val approached them with his hand in his jacket and fingers on the butt of the 9mm Beretta.

They immediately welcomed him and introduced themselves. Dottie made a huge fuss out of the cut on Val's ankle and made him sit down on the stump outside their little tent while she bustled around in a makeshift medical kit, finding iodine and other antiseptic, folding back the leg of his jeans and cleaning his wound, saying that it *should* have stitches, and then cleaning it and wrapping it in clean, white, tight bandages.

When that was done, Val was on the verge of demanding their phone when Dottie said, "You must be hungry, boy. Look at you, I bet you haven't eaten since breakfast or before. Lucky for you, we have some bean with bacon soup going on this very campfire and a clean bowl and spoon waiting for you."

Val loved bean with bacon soup. His mother used to make it for him on weekends and days he was home from school. Just the out-of-the-can Campbell's kind, but it was salty and tasty of bacon and he'd loved it. He'd never had it in all the years he was living with Leonard.

Dottie Davison had also made fresh, hot biscuits, which Val couldn't seem to get enough of.

The couple ate some soup with him—Val had the sense that they'd already eaten but were keeping him company to be polite—and asked him some questions. Trying to keep the answers vague, Val told them about how he'd come into town on a truck convoy with his grandfather.

"Where is your grandfather now, Val?" asked Harold.

Kicking himself for giving out so much information—at least he hadn't told them he'd come from L.A.—Val said, "Oh, visiting some relatives. I'm supposed to hook up with him later. That's why I needed to borrow a phone. To let him know where I am." Wanting to change the subject, Val looked around between mouthfuls of soup and biscuits and said, "This tent village is full of families. It looks a lot friendlier than the Hungarian Freedom Park and others Leonard—my grandfather— and I walked by today."

He told the couple about the men who'd followed them, obviously intent on robbing them. But Val didn't mention that he'd chased them away by showing a gun.

Dottie waved her hand. "Oh, those parks along Speer Boulevard are terrible places. Terrible. They're all just single men— the New Bonus Army, they call themselves—and I doubt if one of them is above theft or rape. The city of Denver pays them a weekly stipend so that they *don't* create a riot. It's black-mail and it's not right."

Val grunted and ate.

As if to shift to a happier topic, Dottie Davison said, "Did you walk past the old Denver Country Club and see all those blue tents?"

"Yeah, I think I did notice that," said Val, helping himself to another fresh biscuit.

"Very strange," said the woman. "There have been thousands of Japanese soldiers camping there for two months now. They never come out. No one knows why Japanese soldiers would be here in Denver...while our own boys not much older than you are over in China fighting for *them*."

"Japanese?" said Val. "Are you sure?"

"Oh, yes," said Dottie. "We have a Japanese lady here with her children and grandchildren—she'd married a nice American marine on Okinawa and came back with him years ago, but he died—and she tells us that she heard those soldiers talking, the sergeants or officers or whoever they are shouting at the troops, and they were all speaking Japanese."

"Weird," said Val.

"Oh, they have tanks in there and other sort of armored... things...and those airplanes with the wings that fold up and down and that fly like helicopters."

"Ospreys," said Harold. "They're called Ospreys."

"Weird," Val said again.

When he was finished, Val sat there feeling full and sleepy and a little stupid, sure of what he had to do, but not sure of *how* to do it. He needed to tell the Old Man to bring as much money as he could—Val needed that $200 old bucks for the fake NICC—and then he needed a private place to *do* it.

To shoot my father, came the phrase from the more honest part of Val's exhausted and overloaded mind.

His first plan had been to steal a phone, tell the Old Man to meet him with the money, take the money, and just shoot him here in the park. Nobody need know he'd ever been here.

Except...when Harold and Dottie had asked his name, he'd given it to them. He'd even mentioned Leonard by name. He'd done everything but give them his goddamned fingerprints.

So it would have to happen somewhere else.

"You look worn out, son," said Harold. "These are both clean. Why don't you lie down a spell there in the shade of the vestibule awning? It's getting hot out here in the sun."

The older man gave Val a pillow with a clean pillowcase — how could they keep things clean and ironed-looking living homeless out here in the park? Val wondered — and a thin, gray blanket.

"No, I'm good," mumbled Val, but the shaded area in the grassy vestibule area just outside their oversized tent did look cool. He lay down for just a minute so he could think through what he had to do and what sequence he had to do it in. The breeze came up and he folded the blanket over himself.

VAL AWOKE HOURS LATER — he had no watch but it seemed to be almost dusk — and cursed himself. He was such a fuck-up.

"I guess you were tired after all," said Dottie, who had something heating up on the grill over their campfire. Whatever it was, it smelled good.

Val threw off the blanket. For a second upon awakening, he'd forgotten the pages of indictment in the colored folders he'd found hidden in his old man's cubie — forgotten the fact that his father *had* conspired to have his mother killed. Any thought of hunger disappeared as that obscene revelation came back to him like black goo flowing out of a backed-up sewer pipe.

"Can I borrow your phone to make a call?" he asked the woman. "It's a local call. I don't have the money right now, but I'll pay you back later."

"Phooey on paying back," laughed Dottie. "We all get a chance to pay back in different ways, to different folks. Here's the phone, Val."

He carried it fifty feet away until he could speak privately. For some reason he didn't expect the Old Man to answer and was mentally preparing the message he was going to leave, so when he heard his father pick up and say his own name, Val panicked and clicked the phone shut.

He took a minute to regain his composure. Val realized how screwed up he was these days. The first thing he'd been tempted to shout when he heard the Old Man's voice was, "You didn't call me on my birthday!"

Stay frosty, Val my man, he told himself. Oddly, he heard the words being spoken in Billy Coyne's mocking voice.

Val hit redial. But when he heard his father's voice again, he began shouting and babbling—just telling the Old Man to come to this side of the park to pick him up—and it was only after he'd broken the connection that Val realized that he'd forgotten to tell Nick Bottom to bring at least $200 old bucks in cash.

All right . . . all right. You can't do it here at the park anyway, so you get in the car and make him drive to an ATM and do it after he gets the cash out.

But do it where?

An hour. The Old Man had told him it would take him a fucking hour to come a few blocks to get him. Here he was, hurt and bleeding—or at least he would be if it hadn't been for Harold and Dottie's bandages and antiseptic and aspirin and hot meal—and the fucking Old Man couldn't even bother to come to get him right away.

Maybe he knows it's a trap. He must've seen all the grand jury stuff thrown around his cubie and Leonard's probably told him how pissed I am.

And what was that the Old Man had said about Leonard having a heart attack? That didn't make any sense. His grandfather had been fine when Val had left him a few hours earlier. The Old Man must be lying . . . but why that lie?

And if Leonard *had* suffered a heart attack—Val was pretty sure that the Old Man had said *a sort of heart attack,* whatever the fuck that meant—Val didn't know what he could do about it. It was too bad, but Leonard was *old*. And Val had known for a while now that his grandfather had been hurting, some kind of chest pains, no matter how hard old Leonard had tried to hide it from him. Nobody lives forever.

Nothing I can do about it, thought Val. But he realized at once that if he killed his father, there'd be no one left to take care of Leonard. That Gunny G. character would almost certainly throw a dying old man out of that shitty mall-turned-cubies fortress, whether Leonard was dying or not.

Not my fucking problem, thought Val. That had been the shout-mantra of his—Billy Coyne's, really—flashgang. *Not... my...fucking...problem.*

Dottie Davison wanted to feed him another meal, but Val gave the overly friendly old couple their phone back, thanked them awkwardly for the use of the pillow and blanket, and said he had to be going. He said his grandfather was going to pick him up down the street a ways.

Harold still tried to talk him into staying a while but Val shook his head, turned his back, and walked around the lake toward the trees and larger tent village of the homeless on the other side until he was out of sight of the old couple. He kept his hand on the butt of the Beretta in his belt.

———

HE FINALLY SAW THE rusty old G.M. gelding the Old Man had described. There'd been several beaters come driving through this west side of the park, but Val could tell by how slowly this one was going, and by the weird bullet holes in the hood—even with the low sunlight reflecting and making it impossible for Val to see through the windshield—that it had to be the Old Man. Hunting for him. Not knowing what was really waiting for him.

At the last minute, Val ducked behind some pine trees and let the car go slowly past.

Chickenshit!

But it wasn't just fear, Val knew as he crouched behind the

trees and waited for his Old Man to make another slow circuit of the park loop back to him.

He just wasn't sure that he could get *in* the car and show the gun and force his father to take him to an ATM and all that crap and *then* do what he had to do. He hadn't been able to talk to the Old Man on the phone, he hated him so much…how could he sit in a car with him for ten minutes?

Plus, the Old Man was a cop. Or had been before he became a hopeless flash addict. He used to be fast. The Old Man had seen people—punks—brandishing guns at him before and had handled the situation. The front seat of that piece-a-shit car would be a cramped space. A cop might know how to get a gun away from someone in the passenger seat without getting shot himself.

Val realized that he was losing his nerve.

Just shoot him. Just walk up to the car and shoot him. And fuck the money.

He realized that the whole thing about becoming a free trucker was bullshit. He didn't even know how to drive a car. He'd never learn how to drive a truck with all its gears—just backing one of those rigs up with the trailer attached was a nightmare. And he'd never get $300,000 in new bucks to pay for that fake NICC. It was all bullshit.

Just shoot him. He murdered Mom. Walk up to the car when he comes back around and shoot him.

The old G.M. gelding rattled around the parkway loop north of the lake again and headed south toward Val and the homeless tent village.

Val pulled the Beretta from his belt, worked the slide to chamber a round, and held the weapon behind his back. He took five steps out of the pine trees to stand next to the road.

He could see the Old Man's face this time and saw the jerk of his head as his father saw him. The car brake-screeched to a stop.

Val realized that he was on the wrong side of the road. To get a clean shot, he should have been on the east side, the driver's side. The Old Man would know something was weird if Val walked around the front or back of the car to get closer to the driver's-side window.

As if understanding Val's problem, the Old Man touched a button and the passenger-side window clunked down.

Val walked right up to the car and—holding the suddenly heavy Beretta in both hands—aimed the muzzle at the Old Man's blandly staring face. Stiff-armed, not shaking, Val extended the pistol inside the window until it was less than three feet from its target.

Doitnow doitnow doitnow don'twait doitnow . . .

Nick Bottom didn't seem to be surprised. He said softly, "I'm wearing Kevlar-three under my shirt, Val. You'll have to aim for my head . . . the face."

Val blinked. The Old Man was trying to mess with his head.

Squeeze the trigger!! Doitnow . . . doitnow . . . don'twait . . . doitnow . . .

Val's finger was off the trigger guard and on the trigger, exerting pressure.

"The safety's still on, kid," said the Old Man in the same tone he'd used to help Val learn how to balance his bicycle.

Val didn't believe his father but looked anyway. It was true. The safety lever was down, the red dot covered. *Fuck!!* Fumbling with both hands, he got the safety lever up until the red dot was visible.

The Old Man could have floored the gelding and gotten away in those seconds, but he hadn't done a thing. His left arm over the steering wheel, his right hand empty and visible on the beat-up old console between the seats, the Old Man just looked at Val.

He knows he deserves to die for killing Mom, thought Val. *He came here knowing what I had to do. He's guilty as hell.*

Val's finger was on the trigger again when he saw movement in the backseat. His arms still extended stiffly, the pistol aimed at the middle of the Old Man's forehead, Val flicked a glance left.

Leonard was lying across the backseat nestled in a clumsy

DAN SIMMONS

nest of pillows. The old man's mouth was open and his eyes were closed. A bottle with some sort of clear liquid in it had been wired to the hook above the left-side car door where dry cleaning was usually hung and an IV line ran to Leonard's bare and bruised left arm.

"What the fuck?" said Val.

The Old Man turned his head to look back at Leonard. "He's all right. Or rather, he's a mess from that attack I told you about. It's called aortic stenosis and means that one of the valves of his heart is pretty messed up. Unless he gets a surgical valve replacement, your grandfather's future looks pretty dim. But he's okay right now. Dr. Tak gave him a sedative so he'd sleep awhile."

Val didn't ask who Dr. Tak was. He shook his head, although he wasn't sure what he was denying. The Old Man's attempt to distract him, maybe. Val peered down the iron sights at his father's face.

Now!

Val knew he could do it. He remembered the muffled blast and kick of the Beretta as he'd fired it through the ski mask in his hand. He remembered Coyne saying "Ugh!" and dropping the flashlight. He remembered the round hole in the T-shirt just above Vladimir Putin's pale face blobbing out into a red butterfly and continuing to grow and Coyne smirking at Val and saying "You shot me."

Val remembered shooting the other boy in the throat and remembered the sound of Billy's teeth snapping off as Coyne's open mouth hit the cement floor of the tunnel. He remembered killing the animated T-shirt Putin AI by putting a third bullet between the Russian's two beady little eyes.

That's what he had to do now.

Squeeze the trigger, don't pull!

Val realized that he was panting and weeping at the same time. His arms were shaking.

The Old Man leaned forward, but not to grab the gun. He opened the passenger-side door.

Val pulled the pistol back from the window as the door

506

opened. The muzzle was aimed up under his own chin now and his finger was still on the trigger with the safety off.

"Get in," said Nick. "Be careful with that thing." He did reach for the pistol now, but only to push the safety lever back down. He didn't take the gun away from Val as the boy collapsed into the passenger seat.

NICK PULLED OUT OF the park onto South Downing Street and drove north.

"I know what you read in my cubie," he said, "but I didn't kill your mother, Val. I could never have hurt your mother. I think that down deep, you know that."

Val was shaking and concentrating on not throwing up in the car. The air from the open window helped a little bit.

"*You're* the one I hurt," continued Nick. "I've spent the last five and a half years with Dara under flashback and I completely fucked up every responsibility I had toward you. Sorry doesn't come close to covering it, but I am sorry, Val."

Val felt the hatred surge up into his chest again. He *could* have shot his father in the head at that moment—the rage would have allowed it—but his arms were totally without strength. He couldn't lift the heavy Beretta if his life depended on it.

Approaching Speer Boulevard, there was a tremendous roar and both Val and the Old Man looked up as a massive Osprey III VTOL roared overhead, its wings and turboprops shifting into level flight. Canvas covering the high Denver Country Club fence that ran hundreds of meters along the street there vibrated and tried to tear free of the wire.

"What the fuck?" said Nick.

"Japs," muttered Val. "Dottie and Harold Davison said that there are thousands of Jap soldiers in the old country club here."

Nick didn't ask who Dottie and Harold Davison were. Watching the Osprey fly off to the west, he said softly, "It's illegal for the Japanese to bring troops into this country."

Val shrugged. "Can we go to the old neighborhood?" he asked. Maybe, he thought, if he could just see the old house, the memory of his mother standing on the porch waiting for him the way she did every day he walked home from school would help him lift this pistol, aim it, and squeeze the trigger.

"We don't have enough charge," said Nick, turning west onto Speer Boulevard. "I have about nine miles left on this piece of crap and it's four miles to Six Flags Over the Jews."

"Six Flags…," repeated Val, looking at the Old Man. Had his father gone completely nuts?

"K.T.'s left us a car there…a real car," said Nick. "At least I hope to God she has. You remember K. T. Lincoln? My old partner?"

Val remembered her…a dangerous lady, from a young kid's perspective. But his mother had liked K.T. for reasons young Val hadn't understood.

"Anyway," said Nick, "the same people who worked so hard to create that grand jury frame-up you read about are out to get me right now. They might hurt you and Leonard if you don't get out of town. This gelding'll be lucky to get up the street to Six Flags where the car's waiting, but once we get there, you take the car K.T.'s parked there and get Leonard the hell out of town."

"I don't know how to drive," said Val.

Nick barked a bitter laugh. "Leonard told me before he got his sedative that you wanted to get an NIC Teamsters Card so you could drive big rigs."

"It was all bullshit," muttered Val. "Everything is bullshit."

"I won't argue there," said Nick. "Leonard said you had some NICC counterfeiter guy's name and address. Show it to me."

Feeling as drugged as his grandfather, Val poked through his jacket pockets—filled with extra magazines and loose rounds for the useless Beretta—and found the card. He handed it to Nick.

"Yeah, I know this guy," said Nick. "K.T. and I sent him

up for five years when you were a baby. He lives deep in *recon-quista* turf now. You'd have a hard time getting there today."

"I don't have the money anyway," said Val. They were passing the Hungarian Freedom Park with its Bonus Army of single homeless guys. There were police cars and vans parked along the curb and a lot of uniformed cops in riot gear. It all seemed a million miles away to Val. "I'd need two hundred bucks for the new card...*old* bucks."

"I'm sorry I don't have it to give to you," said Nick. "A few days ago I did. But I blew it on bribes and on paying a pilot to fly me from Las Vegas to L.A."

Val stared. "L.A.? Why did you go there?"

"To find you."

"Bullshit," barked Val.

"All right, it's bullshit," said Nick. "I blew it all on gambling in Las Vegas. I don't care what you think. But I couldn't give you the two hundred now even if I had it."

"Why not?"

"I'd use it as a down payment in getting Leonard this valve replacement surgery. He needs it to live and Medicare won't get around to paying for it until he's been dead for a decade or two."

As if hearing his name, Leonard stirred and groaned in the backseat.

Val looked at his grandfather and his own chest hurt.

"In a dream I had last night," said Nick, "the three of us were hightailing it to Texhoma, Oklahoma, in an old Chevy Camaro SS with a supercharged V-8."

"What the fuck is in Texhoma, Oklahoma?"

"A border-station crossing into the Republic of Texas."

"They'd pay for Leonard's surgery in Texas?"

Nick shot a glance at the boy. "No, but they'd have it available if *we* could pay for it. And I'd find a way to."

"I hear that Texas doesn't let in useless people," said Val. "Especially useless people who are flashback addicts."

Nick didn't respond to that.

After a moment, Val said, "So the car that your friend…
K.T.…is leaving for us at Six Flags is an old gas-burning V-8
Camaro?"

"Probably not," said Nick. "I just wanted the fastest car in
the DPD impound lot. Remember Mad Max's Last of the V-8
Interceptors?"

"I don't know what the fuck you're talking about," lied Val.

Nick shrugged. They were approaching the overpass crossing I-25 and he turned left toward the abandoned towers and
roller-coaster steel of the old Elitch Gardens. The gelding told
him that it had 3½ miles of charge left in it.

There was one vehicle parked away from the others, facing
the wrong way, in the parking lot. Nick stopped near it and
whispered, "Ah, Jesus Christ, no."

He checked on Leonard and got out of the gelding. A
moment later, Val did the same, still carrying his pistol.

Nick pulled a little box from the left rear wheel well.
Folded around the ignition key fob was a note in K.T.'s
handwriting—"The impound lot's almost empty and I could
never get anything out of it today. This is my personal vehicle.
Good luck."

Nick and Val stood looking at the blue Menlo Park all-
battery mini-van. On a good day, these things had a range of
around 100 miles.

"At least it's a lighter blue," muttered Nick. Val had no idea
what the Old Man was talking about.

Nick had just offered the keys to Val and was about to say
something when four desert-camouflage tan M-ATVs roared
across the parking lot and screeched to a stop around them. A
dozen Japanese men in black ballistic cloth SWAT armor, all
carrying automatic weapons, boiled out of the big vehicles and
aimed their weapons at Val and Nick.

Val started to bring his Beretta up and the Old Man
grabbed his wrist, squeezing hard until he dropped the gun.
Nick himself made no motion toward a weapon.

A bulky Jap also in ballistic black came down the rear ramp
of the closest Oshkosh M-ATV and looked silently as one of the

younger men frisked Nick and took a 9mm Glock from his belt and a .32-caliber pistol from an ankle holster. Another ninja, who'd picked up the Beretta, now frisked Val and relieved him of all the pistol magazines and loose rounds. Two other men in black were easily lifting Leonard—still sleeping—out of the back of the gelding. A third man held the IV bottle.

The two ninjas who'd frisked Val and Nick nodded to the big man as other men with automatic weapons began herding the father and son into the back of the big M-ATV.

"Bottom-san," said the man in black, "it is time."

1.18

Denver — Saturday, Sept. 25

NICK HAD DONE everything possible to avoid this final meeting with Hiroshi Nakamura, but he'd always known it would have to happen.

In his mental rehearsals of this final encounter, the meeting was always set in Mr. Nakamura's office in his mountaintop compound up in Evergreen where Nick had first met the billionaire. However, when Nick and Val were led out of the back of the Oshkosh M-ATV — both blinking in the low but bright early-evening light — Nick saw that they were in LoDo, on Wazee Street, in front of Keigo Nakamura's bachelor-pad building. The murder scene.

Now this street in Lower Downtown reminded Nick of scenes from the countless urban-war videos on the TV each night showing American troops in some city in Pakistan or in Brazil or in China, with several big M-ATVs parked front to rear across the street at both ends of the city block being used as roadblocks, two helicopters landed in the middle of the street, and soldiers on the street and rooftops of evacuated buildings.

But this was an American city and these soldiers weren't tired American troops in their bulky body armor and scuffed kneepads, but scores of Nakamura's — or perhaps Sato's (did it make any difference? wondered Nick) — ninjas in jump boots and ballistic black and carrying automatic weapons, all wearing identical tactical sunglasses and tiny bead earphones and microphones beneath their black ball caps.

Nick and Val had both been flex-cuffed, but with their wrists tied *in front of their bodies*. This gave Nick the slightest flicker of hope. Every cop and prisoner-taking grunt in the world knew you flex-cuffed dangerous prisoners — and anyone worthy of being taken prisoner should be considered dangerous — *behind* their backs. Arms, wrists, and fists tied in front could be, far too easily, used as weapons.

Either they weren't in serious captivity (which Nick didn't believe for an instant) or Sato's men did not consider Nick and his son to be serious threats. Or, more likely, Sato's people considered Nick and the boy dangerous but were certain that their numbers and firepower eliminated any real threat in the few minutes their prisoners would be allowed to live.

Given the number of ninjas illegally deployed along Wazee Street here in Lower Downtown Denver and the number that came with them as they entered Keigo's building, Nick tended to agree with this last assessment.

"Careful there!" shouted Nick as three ninjas carried the still-unconscious Dr. George Leonard Fox down the ramp of the M-ATV, two using their arms as a sort of upright litter, the third man carrying the attached IV bottle.

The ninjas ignored him as the stream of men entered the building and made straight for the stairway. Nick remembered that Keigo's old converted warehouse had no elevator. More work for the two men carrying Leonard, although Nick's father-in-law looked as disturbingly thin and light as a professorially dressed scarecrow.

Sato led the way up to the third floor and, once there, did not turn right into the private quarters and bedroom where the murder took place, but left from the foyer to the fancy library where Nick had first seen the video recording of Dara standing down the darkened street. Today, for the first time in the two weeks since he'd stood shocked into silence by that image, Nick Bottom knew exactly why she'd been out there that night of Keigo's party and Keigo's murder.

He'd suspected ever since that night that Sato had *known* that Nick would see Dara on that video recording, had brought him down here to the murder scene precisely so that Nick *would* see Dara outside the building that night. But Nick hadn't been able to figure out why his wife would have been there or why Sato would want him to know.

And now he had figured it out. And the solution to both those mysteries made Nick want to weep.

Hiroshi Nakamura had stood throughout their previous meeting, but now the billionaire was seated behind the big mahogany desk in front of the north-facing windows. There were four black-garbed ninjas with guns already standing on either side of that desk. The men carrying Leonard set him carefully on the leather couch by the bookshelves on the wall behind Nick, and Val was pushed down to sit next to his grandfather.

Sato stepped to one side of the room and nodded. One of his men closed the twin library doors. Counting the four who had already been there with Nakamura, there were now ten armed ninjas — not counting Sato — in the room, but the library was so large that the space didn't seem crowded. No one had offered Nick a chair so he stood there on the Persian carpet in front of the desk, squinting slightly so he could make out Nakamura's features against the evening light coming in through the wooden blinds behind him.

Nakamura looked as perfectly calm as he had at their first meeting.

"Mr. Bottom," said Nakamura, "I had hoped that we would meet under more fortuitous circumstances. But that was not to be."

"Let my son and father-in-law go, Nakamura," said Nick. His words struck him as bad dialogue from a thousand TV dramas. It didn't matter. He had to go on. "They're civilians. They're not part of this. Let them go and you and I will talk."

"You and I will talk at any rate," said Nakamura. "Your son should see what kind of man you are."

The few electric lights in the room dimmed and a flatscreen rose from an elaborately carved bureau on the south side of the room. As soon as the screen was fully visible, the video began playing. There was no sound to accompany the images.

Nick saw himself from a viewpoint about twenty-five feet above the ground, looking almost straight down. The color tones seemed very strange until one realized that the lens on the miniature unmanned aerial vehicle was compensating for very low light.

Nick watched himself pawing through the pockets of three men on the ground, two obviously dead, the third and youngest man pleading for his life.

Suddenly there *was* sound and everyone in the library could hear the young man's moans and words—"Please...mister...you promised...you promised...it hurts so much...you *promised*."

Nick watched along with his son and the other men in the room—only Leonard had his eyes closed—as his image on the screen set the pistol to within inches of the young man's shocked, pleading face and blew his brains out.

The flatscreen went black and hummed itself back down into the bureau.

"We know that you met with Advisor Omura in that gentleman's aerie above Los Angeles yesterday, Mr. Bottom," said Hiroshi Nakamura. "We have no recording of *that* conversation, but we can imagine how it went."

"Let my people go, Nakamura."

The billionaire ignored him. "Since everything that Omura told you is almost certainly either distorted or totally untrue, I will explain the real stakes of the struggle you have become involved in."

"I don't give a shit what the stakes are for...," began Nick.

"SILENCE!!!" roared Sato.

Everyone in the room except for Nakamura and Leonard seemed to jump at the explosion of sound. Nick would not have thought that the human voice, without electronic amplification, could produce so many raw decibels. He imagined the

black-garbed ninjas up and down Wazee Street and on the rooftops jumping in their tracks.

"Very correct," said Nakamura. "If you interrupt me again,
you and the other two will be gagged. And, given your
father-in-law's unfortunate condition, that might not be the
best for him."

Nick stood there. Swaying with anger.

"More than twenty years ago," said Nakamura, "a group of
my fellow Nipponese businessmen and myself watched as your
new young president gave a speech from Cairo that flattered
the Islamic world—a bloc of Islamic nations that had not yet
coalesced into today's Global Caliphate—and praised them
with obvious historical distortions of their own imagined gran-
deur. This president began the process of totally rewriting both
history and contemporary reality with an eye toward praising
radical Islam into loving him and your country.

"The name for this form of foreign policy, whenever it is
used with forces of fascism, Mr. Bottom, is appeasement."

Nick said nothing.

"This president and your country soon followed this self-
mockery of a foreign policy with ever more blatant and useless
appeasement, attempts at becoming a social democracy when
European social democracies were beginning to collapse from
debt and the burden of their entitlement programs, unilateral
disarmament, withdrawal from the world stage, a betrayal of old
allies, a rapid and deliberate surrendering of America's position as
a superpower, and a total retreat from international responsibilities that the United States of America had long taken seriously."

Nick looked over his shoulder at Val. The boy's mouth was
opened slightly and his face was parchment white. He looked
physically ill and Nick knew that Val didn't want to throw up on
the obscenely expensive Persian carpet in front of all these men.

"Mr. Bottom?" Nakamura said sharply. "You are listening?"

Nick looked back at the megalomaniac billionaire, who
leaned forward, folded his hands on the gleaming desktop, and
continued with his speech.

"The economic crises which resulted in the death of the

European Union and the collapse of China—as well as the violent and unnecessary deaths of more than six million Jews in Israel, and another million non-Jewish Israeli citizens, *all* abandoned by your country, Mr. Bottom—were merely further steps in this decline—at first deliberate and then merely inevitable—of the United States of America."

There was a long pause and Nick spoke into it, risking the gags. "What's this history lecture got to do with anything, Mr. Nakamura? Especially with the reason you hired me to solve your son's murder?"

Nakamura closed his eyes as if seeking patience. Then he smiled thinly.

"As I said, Mr. Bottom, these are the stakes of the game you have entered. We industrialists in Japan almost a quarter of a century ago knew that our nation would someday have to step in to fill the void left by America's self-willed decline. It was not a duty we welcomed…the memories of what we called Daitoa Senso, the Greater East Asian War, and which your historians called World War Two…were still too painful.

"We were reluctant, Mr. Bottom, once again to acknowledge ourselves, the citizens of Nippon, as *shido minzoku*—'the world's foremost people'—even though we understood that we would have to fill that role.

"That first war, started in China almost a century ago, was a function of our hubris—militarism combined with hopes of an empire combined with self-inflicted distortions of our religion and the samurai code of *bushido*. But this coming war, Mr. Bottom, a war much wider and more terrible for the enemy than Daitoa Senso, will not be the *kurai tanima* 'dark valley' of that last war. It will be a global war of liberation."

"War with whom?" said Nick. He had to hear it all said out loud before he could say what they would demand that he say.

Nakamura shook his head sadly. "With militant Islam, Mr. Bottom," said the billionaire, his voice soft. "With the hydra called the Global Caliphate. Islam was always, despite America's absolute resistance in acknowledging it, a violent and barbarous religion, Mr. Bottom, its prophet a military man no less cruel than our field marshal Hajime Sugiyama or your Army Air Force general Curtis Le May. The twentieth- and twenty-first-century fundamentalist terrorist-driven forms of expansionist Islam are vile obscenities. The citizens serving the Imperial Son of Heaven of Dai Nippon, descended from the Sun Goddess herself in the Land of the Rising Sun, where all eight corners of the universe have been brought together under one divine roof, will not be pulled back to the seventh century by a barbarous desert religion intent on ruling the earth and treating its conquered people as less-than-human slaves!

"But *it will not happen! We shall not let it happen!!*"

Now it was Hiroshi Nakamura who was shouting, and while his voice had none of the rock-concert amplification of Sato's blast, it was loud enough and sincere enough and fanatical enough to cause Nick to take half a step back.

When the billionaire continued and concluded, his voice was much softer.

"Thus we Nipponese business leaders turned our *keiretsu* back into wartime *zaibatsu*, our family-run business interests no longer merely serving Japan's leadership, but deciding it. Thus we returned to the honor of the samurai and the true code of *bushido*. Thus we will soon need a single, all-powerful *Shogun* to advise the emperor in this time of total war."

Nick cleared his throat. "Of total *nuclear* war," he said thickly.

"Of course," Nakamura said dismissively, almost contemptuously. "All *daimyo*s, even your weak friend Omura, agree that this final struggle for the future of our world will be nuclear—and thermonuclear. The enemy has shown its ruthless resolve in the murder of Israel. We shall show no less in the eradication of an infectious mental disease that is two billion persons strong across the planet."

"Omura-sama believes that Texas will be an ally," said Nick.

Nakamura shook his head. "Advisor Omura is weak and sentimental when it comes to the last vestige of your once-strong nation, Mr. Bottom. He will not be considered when it comes time for us *daimyo*s to select our first *Shogun* in a hundred and sixty years. The weak remnants of America are currently serving their role in preparation for the coming struggle."

Nick nodded. "With two hundred thousand of our drafted kids fighting the war for you in China," he said.

Nakamura said nothing for a long moment.

Nick could hear a regular helicopter, not one of the whisper-dragonflies, flying low over the building. Somewhere nearby a police or ambulance siren sounded in the unoccupied part of Denver. Nick thought he could hear distant gunshots.

Had the city come apart at the seams today as K.T. and the DPD had feared? Did Nick give the slightest shit if it had?

Nakamura said, "So now you understand what is at stake, Nick Bottom. It is time for you to deliver your report on the investigation you were hired to carry out."

Nick held his flex-cuffed wrists out. "Untie me."

Nakamura and Sato ignored the demand.

Nick knew that he could leap at Nakamura, try to get his cuffed wrists around the billionaire's slender neck, but he also knew that Sato or the four guards on that side would kill him the second he tried.

Nick sighed, looked back over his shoulder at Val and the apparently unconscious Leonard, and began to speak.

———

"I FINALLY KNOW WHY you hired me. It all came together just today, and mostly by accident. You hired me to do this investigation because you weren't certain of what I knew. You didn't know what my wife, Dara, had told me or what notes she might have left behind for me to find. You'd searched and never found her phone, so you just weren't sure.

"In the end, you needed someone to make something public..."

Nick paused and looked up into the high corners of the library until he spotted the red lights on the video cameras.

"You needed someone other than yourselves to make something public—as this video recording will do after my son, father-in-law, and I are dead—so you hired me.

"I was your perfect fool. So eager to get some money to buy flashback that I'd go anywhere, do anything, betray anyone to get the information you needed to be let out into the world.

"And so I have."

Nick paced a few steps. Sato and the other guards tensed, but there was no need. Nick was organizing his thoughts, not preparing a futile leap at Nakamura.

"Flashback was a drug developed in Japan," he said at last. "There never was any biowar lab at Havat MaShash Experimental Agricultural Farm in the Israeli desert. It was just another blood libel the Jews had to suffer after they were murdered en masse—again. You Japs designed and developed flashback—at a lab in Nara, if my sources are correct—and it's you who transported it to the United States and elsewhere, sold it way below its production price, and have continued to have your dealers, from the heights of Don Khozh-Ahmed Noukhaev to the street depths of poor Delroy Nigger Brown and Derek Dean, deliver it to the growing number of addicts in the States."

"Why would Japan do that?" interrupted Nakamura. His voice was soft to the point of exuding oil.

Nick laughed.

"You got what you wanted from what was left of us after the Day It All Hit The Fan," said Nick. "After we screwed our country into near-oblivion through debt and cowardice. You wanted our soldiers and you have them. You wanted the rest of us tranquilized, and we paid one new-buck dollar a flashback minute to accommodate you. Our leaders turned away from the future decades ago—abandoning faith in the free market system, abandoning our worldwide responsibilities, hell, even abandoning our manned spaceflight program—and the rest of us turned the rest of the way from the future when we decided to go back to the past by using flashback. Three hundred and forty million American addicts, including me until this past week, all living—*re*living—our little masturbatory fantasies because we couldn't face the real world."

Sato spoke.

"Bottom-san, how did you discover that it was Nippon who developed and delivered flashback to America?"

Nick laughed again, with even more bitterness than before.

"I didn't. My wife did. And she was murdered for it."

He looked from Sato to Nakamura and then around at the other men with weapons in the room. Finally he looked at his unconscious father-in-law—had Leonard once told him that he spoke some Japanese?—and then at his son. He knew that he would not get the chance to say again to Val how sorry he was.

"The woman murdered in the bedroom not thirty steps from here was known to us Denver cops as a sex-pleasure woman from Japan named Keli Bracque. She was represented to us as Keigo Nakamura's favorite sex toy, nothing more. We knew her as Keli Bracque because that was her name in the totally fabricated dossier that the various Japanese police services sent to us. Advisor Nakamura's offices confirmed that fact."

Nick paused. He was getting so angry that his arms were shaking, his hands were balled into fists, and his legs felt weak.

Sato snapped something in Japanese and one of the ninjas carried over a chair for Nick. He didn't sit in it, but he grabbed the back to help hold himself up.

"Keli Bracque was supposed to be the daughter of American missionaries in Japan," continued Nick, his voice thick with phlegm and fury. "That was a lie. It was all a lie. Keli Bracque's real name was Kumiko Catherine Catton and she was the daughter of Sakura Catton, an American-born woman who'd spent her entire adult life in Japan. A woman who was a courtesan of a famous Japanese *daimyo*. What's the Japanese word for 'girlfriend' or 'mistress' or 'courtesan' or 'second wife,' as you used to say? *Keisi* or *gosai* or *aijin* or *sembo* ... you Jap guys have a lot of words for your out-of-marriage lady friends. The American Mafia bosses just called them *goomahs*."

The very air in the library seemed to have stopped stirring.

Nick glanced out of the corners of his eyes and saw that no one was looking at anyone, even the ever-vigilant ninjas staring only at their own feet. Nakamura had assumed the kind of inward-looking thousand-yard stare that Tokyo residents had perfected for traveling in their overcrowded subways.

"Here's the complicated part of this whole scenario," Nick said into the thickened silence. He pointed at Hiroshi Nakamura. "It wasn't enough for your family and the families of Munetaka, Morikune, Omura, Toyoda, Yoritsugo, Yamahsita, and Yoshiake just to take all of modern Japan back to feudal days to prepare yourselves for this holy war with Islam. You couldn't just draw the line at rebuilding the old feudal system from Japan's own Middle Ages—turning *keiretsu* into clan-run, government-ruling *zaibatsu* and industrialists into *daimyo*s—it wasn't enough just to bring back the feudal realities of *Shogun* and samurai and *ronin* and a resurgence of the code of *bushido*—no, you super-*daimyo* heads of the über-*zaibatsu*, you had to bring back feudal ways of assuring the allegiance of your vassals, including your vassal-*daimyo*s."

Nick paused and looked up at the still-glowing red eye of the video camera, then back at Nakamura.

"Hiroshi Nakamura had a problem with one of his vassal-*daimyo*s becoming too popular with the people and with Nakamura's own soldiers as a warrior-prince in China. Your *daimyo*'s loyalty was never in question, Mr. Nakamura—you knew he'd die for you or commit *seppuku* if you demanded it—but such popularity in an underling is a dangerous thing all by itself. So you—and Yoritsugo, Yamahsita, Yoshiake, Morikune, Omura, Munetaka, and Toyoda—began doing the same thing Japanese liege lords and their liege-lord counterparts in Europe's Middle Ages did as insurance for such loyalty...

"You took the popular warrior-*daimyo*'s child as a sort of hostage. Not the two grown sons of this popular *daimyo* by his real wife—one of those sons had already died in battle in China and another soon would—but, rather, this *daimyo*'s beloved daughter by his American-born courtesan.

"Thus Kumiko Catherine Catton—who we were told was

a sex worker named Keli Bracque—entered your household. She was not treated as a prisoner, Mr. Nakamura. Just as in feudal Europe during the Middle Ages, you raised Kumiko as if she were an honored member of your own family.

"But the unthinkable happened. Kumiko Catherine Catton fell in love with your only son. When Keigo came to the United States to shoot his documentary, fourteen months before you were appointed Advisor by your emperor—before you *arranged* to be appointed as a Federal Advisor in Colorado—Kumiko, aka Keli Bracque, came with him. She wasn't Keigo's sex toy. They were passionately in love."

Nick paused.

Nakamura cleared his throat and said softly, "May I ask how you came by this information, Mr. Bottom?"

"You hired me to find it," said Nick. "But I didn't. I never would have followed up on Ms. Keli Bracque's background. I was too stupid.

"But Keli—Kumiko—became alarmed for her beloved Keigo Nakamura's safety. Your wastrel son was pretty bright after all, wasn't he, Mr. Nakamura? Thrown out of Tokyo University, but not because he was stupid...because he was a born rebel. In the States, we have the expression *The squeaky wheel gets the grease.* In Japan, you say *The nail that stands up gets hammered down.*

"Well, Mr. Nakamura, I don't have to tell you that Keigo was the nail that stood up. He was a rebel in a society devoted as never before to blind obedience. The video documentary he was shooting wasn't about how pathetic Americans were for getting hooked on the drug flashback...it was about *where flashback had come from,* Japan. And it was about the damage that the deliberate and premeditated introduction of this addictive drug had done to human beings here who used it—from pathetic Israeli survivors of the Second Holocaust to hopeless inner-city blacks to suburban housewives."

"Prove it, Mr. Bottom," said Nakamura.

Nick did not smile. "I don't have to. I've seen several hours of his footage, Mr. Nakamura. And pretty soon, so will millions of other Americans. Keigo Nakamura will show the damage you and the other Japanese warlords have done to this nation."

Nakamura said nothing.

"Kumiko Catherine Catton didn't give a damn about any of the politics of the issue," said Nick. "She just was afraid that someone would whack her beloved Keigo. Like her mother, Kumiko had grown up in Japan—had seen the changes there in the past twenty years. She knew that the *daimyo*s weren't going to allow Keigo to show and distribute his quixotic documentary. She knew that someone would stop Keigo...and stop him hard.

"So in Kumiko's naïveté—she was still more used to the way things worked in Japan than in her mother's birthplace of the United States—she went to local officials for help. Her thinking was that if the shocking information behind Keigo's little movie went public first, there'd be no reason for the *daimyo*s to harm the boy.

"Kumiko went to Denver's district attorney—an ambitious but moronic political appointee named Mannie Ortega. Not even understanding what the girl was offering to give him, Ortega handed it off to a mere assistant district attorney—a poor, hardworking but unlucky sonofabitch named Harvey Cohen—who, with his assistant, my wife, Dara, began interviewing Keli Bracque, aka Kumiko Catherine Catton, and just what they learned about the origins of flashback was astounding.

"Ortega was an idiot, but Harvey and Dara knew what they were dealing with. They insisted, over Mannie Ortega's insistence that it was no big deal, that the FBI and Department of Homeland Security be brought in.

"Both the FBI and DHS *were* brought in. They carried out their own 'complete investigations.' Then they assured District Attorney Ortega, Assistant District Attorney Cohen, and Cohen's research assistant, Dara Fox Bottom, that Keli Bracque was a stone liar, that the girl was indeed an ambitious sex worker and a drug addict—heroin—and that there was no such person as Kumiko Catherine Catton.

"The FBI and Homeland Security told Mannie, Harvey, and Dara that this kind of hysteria could hurt American-

Japanese relations at a time when we depended on Japan and would personally insult the soon-to-be Federal Advisor to Colorado and the southwestern states, Hiroshi Nakamura. These federal agencies recommended—strongly recommended—that the investigation into this crazy woman's allegations be shut down immediately and that all interviews and records be destroyed.

"So Ortega immediately terminated the investigation, burned and wiped all the files he had, and ordered Harvey and Dara to do the same.

"But my wife and her hapless boss were stubborn. They continued meeting secretly with Kumiko Catherine Catton—and began discussions with Keigo Nakamura himself, foolishly promising him safety in the Witness Protection Program—right up to the time of Keigo's and Kumiko's murder in October six years ago.

"Even after those murders, Harvey and Dara kept hard-copy and computer files in a room they rented, using Harvey's own personal credit card—and he couldn't afford it—at a motel here in Denver. Their plan was to turn the information over to the Attorney General of the United States, with duplicate copies to all the AGs in forty-four states.

"Right up to the day of their deaths—their *murders*—more than three months after the execution of Keigo and Kumiko, Harvey and Dara didn't understand what they had. Dara tried to tell me—tried to lead me toward the real killers in my own investigation—but she knew that if she revealed the secrets she and Harvey had been sitting on, I'd lose my job. A job I loved. And the truth is—she never really did figure out who'd killed her friend Kumiko and the billionaire's son, Keigo."

Nick paused. He hadn't spoken this much for this long in more than six years. His throat was sore.

"She and her boss Harvey never understood how big the whole thing was," he rasped at last. "They thought it was just a revelation about who invented and distributed flashback. They didn't see that it was really about the future of who controlled this country. That it was really about *power*."

He stopped.

Hiroshi Nakamura sat far back in the plush leather chair behind the big desk. He steepled his fingers, looked at Hideki Sato, looked back at Nick, and smiled. His voice was purr-soft.

"You still haven't told us who the murder or murderers *were*, Detective Bottom."

Exhausted, Nick leaned on the back of the chair they'd given him. He looked Nakamura in the eye.

"The fuck I haven't," he said flatly, coldly. "You haven't been listening. *You* ordered your son and his girlfriend to be killed, Hiroshi Nakamura."

He would have pointed at the billionaire, but it seemed melodramatic to do so and he was too tired to lift his arm.

"You did it to show the other *daimyo*s—not just the top boys, Yoritsugo, Yamahsita, Yoshiake, Morikune, Omura, Munetaka, and Toyoda, but the scores of other important *daimyo*s back in old Nippon—that you could be ruthless when it came to protecting the Motherland's secrets. Or is it the Fatherland's?

"At any rate, you called back your top assassin and most loyal *daimyo*, Hideki Sato—Colonel Death himself—from China to do the job. A bullet in the brain was enough for the girl, you told him, but Keigo had to be...massacred. To show what happens to those who reveal a future *Shogun*'s secrets."

Nick turned wearily toward Sato.

"And you were never Keigo's bodyguard here. It was always that other guy, Satoh. But you'd known Keigo Nakamura all his short life. He trusted you. When he went up to the roof to meet you—when you stepped out of that whisper-dragonfly 'copter or rappelled down a rope from it or whatever the hell you did—he never would have believed that you were the assassin his father would send.

"Especially, Sato-san, since you were Kumiko Catherine Catton's father."

There was no buzz in the room. No one made a sound. But Nick could feel a buzz as all eyes, even the ninja guards', shifted in the direction of Sato.

The huge security chief stared at Nick with no expression whatsoever.

"You did your job," Nick said, his voice rough and devoid of energy. "Three months later, when it was decided that poor Harvey and my Dara were still a threat, you arranged for their 'accidental deaths' on I-Twenty-five here in town. Two days ago I'm sure you either personally whacked that stupid mutt Mannie Ortega in Washington or had your boys do it."

Nick looked away from Nakamura and up at the red-glowing video camera.

"Is that enough? You can edit this down later to the good stuff. But this should show you other *daimyo*s that Hiroshi Nakamura will be a *Shogun* who means business and that Colonel Hideki Sato will do whatever he has to do to serve his liege lord and boss. Is this enough? Because all I have left to say is that perhaps—just perhaps—you *daimyo*s won't be the only ones to be seeing examples of Nakamura's and Sato's cruelty."

Nick walked around the chair and sat down. It was either sit or fall.

And he needed to conserve his energy. Whether they offered him a chance now or not—and he was sure they would not—he was determined to take one. Just saying Dara's name aloud several times had made that a certainty.

Nick hadn't expected a round of applause for his Inspector Clouseau performance and he didn't receive one. The silence was absolute. But what he heard next was something he *really* hadn't expected.

Nakamura stood and looked around the room. He was smiling. "Our guest's last comment—the last vague threat—was due to the fact that earlier today, Mr. Bottom e-mailed copies of his wife's diary and my son's video to eight people. Unfortunately for our detective friend, Colonel Sato's people have been monitoring all Internet access from that sad condominium and intercepted all eight e-mails sent from a certain Gunny G.'s computer."

Nick felt as if he'd been hit in the solar plexus. Spots

danced in his vision. The end of even the most cynical twentieth-century movies he loved had the hero turning over the evidence of government or CIA conspiracies to the *New York Times* or *Washington Post* or some other crusading newspaper. Now those newspapers were gone forever and so was any hope of Nick's getting Dara's notes and Keigo's videos out to the world.

"Which leaves," continued Nakamura, "the detail of Ms. Dara Fox Bottom's actual telephone with its…ah…compromising files. Colonel Sato?"

Sato walked close to the desk and produced the old phone that they'd confiscated from Nick. The security man held the phone over Nakamura's wastebasket and squeezed until plastic ruptured and microchips crumbled. When he opened his hand, the shards and shattered filaments fell in a silvery waterfall into the wastebasket.

Nick was too defeated to look over his shoulder at Val.

Still standing, Nakamura fired a rapid-fire salvo of Japanese at Sato.

Sato barked back, "*Hai*, Nakamura-sama," and gestured for the guards in the room to take Nick, Val, and the still-unconscious Leonard out.

Nick was concentrating on the few seconds when they were in the open air before they'd be loaded on the sealed M-ATVs again, but Sato led the way upstairs rather than down.

They all came out onto the roof—a small army of black-clad guards, the boy, the exhausted ex-cop, and the sleeping old man being carried again—and the *Sasayaki-tonbo* whisper-dragonfly 'copter was hovering there, three feet above the building's roof, just as it must have been the night it had brought Sato there to murder his young friend Keigo and his daughter, Kumiko.

The ninja were very, very good. They never crossed into each other's field of fire. They never got close enough for Nick to grab and grapple. At least three of them always kept their automatic weapons aimed at Nick's, Val's, and even Leonard's heads while the others did what they had to do.

Nick's old friends from the Santa Fe trip—ninjas Shinta

Ishii, Mutsumi Ōta, and Daigorou Okada—jumped into the hovering dragonfly along with two men he didn't know, and all five turned to cover Nick, Val, and the sleeping Leonard as they first loaded Leonard aboard, then pulled Val up, then beckoned Nick forward. The three prisoners were made to sit against the forward bulkhead—Leonard still out and his IV bottle suspended on a bracket above him—while Sato jumped aboard.

Their 'copter moved away and hovered a hundred feet above Wazee Street while a second dragonfly loaded a dozen of Sato's men, then a third.

Even in the closer confines of the helicopter, Ishii, Ōta, and Okada kept the muzzles of their low-velocity automatic weapons aimed steadily at all three of the Americans' heads, but there was a second or two—just a second or two—where Sato's attention was distracted as he was putting on and plugging in his dragonfly-intercom earphones and microphone.

The few seconds were not enough for Nick to act, but he leaned against Leonard as if checking on his unconscious father-in-law and had time to whisper—"Did you understand what Nakamura said in Japanese?"

The seemingly unconscious old man nodded.

"What did he say?" whispered Nick.

"Something about taking us all to Landfill Number Nine," whispered Leonard without moving his lips.

Ōta shouted something in Japanese and Shinta Ishii repeated the shout in English, "No talking! No talking!"

"Sit back against the bulkhead, Bottom-san," said Hideki Sato. He had his pistol out and it was aimed at Nick's head. He gestured gently with it.

Nick sat back, setting his cuffed wrists on his knee, and glanced once toward Val. His son's eyes were bright, but he did not seem to be afraid. This astonished Nick. Val nodded once as if Nick had sent him a telepathic message.

The line of three whisper-dragonflies banked hard to the right and flew fast and silently east over Denver as the last of the evening light bled out of the Colorado sky.

1.19

Airborne—Saturday, Sept. 25

THE ONLY SOUND was the air rushing over the dragonfly's airframe and into the open doors. Nick was not seated close enough to the open door to see when they'd flown over the eastern edge of Denver, but his view of the horizon suggested that they were out over open country.

The flight to Denver Municipal Landfill Number Nine would take only a few minutes. Ninjas Ishii, Ōta, and Okada as well as one other black-clad guard, whom Nick didn't know, all kept their low-velocity automatic weapons aimed. All of them had tasers hooked on their belts or combat utility vests. The fifth guard, who might have been a medic, had gone over to check on Leonard's IV after the apparently unconscious man had lolled to his left and pulled out the IV needle.

Nick only wished that he could go back to those few seconds in the parking lot at Six Flags where both he and Val could have reached for their weapons and gone down fighting. It had all happened so *quickly*, but that was no excuse. Cops were trained to react quickly. And cops were also trained *never* to surrender their weapons. Not ever. In the movies and TV there were a thousand scenes where the bad guy has some hostage—

530

sometimes the hapless cop's even more hapless partner—and the hero or heroine cop puts down the gun—"Look, I'm putting it down!" Nick remembered when he was a little kid sprawled on the couch watching such a cop melodrama on pre-3D TV and the Old Man, passing through the room, said, "Never gonna happen."

Had it been the presence of Val and Leonard this afternoon that had kept Nick from fighting—that had made him grab his son's wrist to force the Beretta out of his hand? Probably. Nick had more or less come to terms with dying over the past couple of weeks, but he hadn't been prepared to watch his son die.

Still—you surrender your weapon, you surrender all hopes of ever regaining control of a situation. Cops knew that and at one time Nick's country had understood that. And then they'd shown the way to peace through one-sided nuclear disarmament, annual budget cuts to the military in order to feed the exponentially growing entitlements...

The most sickening thing about Hiroshi Nakamura's little history speech was that Nick had agreed with much of it.

Now Nick shoved all such thoughts out of his mind, concentrating on being *aware*. If the ninjas and Sato gave him a single instant of inattention, Nick was going to take the chance.

And if they didn't give him a chance, he knew he was going to take it anyway. Sato was standing by the open door, one arm casually hooked through a strap from the aft bulkhead. Nick knew exactly what he was going to try.

FOR SOME REASON, ONE of the ninjas was still attending to his captives' wounds and injuries. Why? It was crazy to fuss over medical stuff with your prisoners when you were going to execute them in a few minutes anyway. Nick assumed that it had something to do with the Japs' medieval samurai code of *bushido*. Maybe it wasn't *honorable*—that all-purpose Nipponese concept that seemed to cover all sorts of self-imposed insanity—to allow your doomed prisoners to die from their wounds on the way to their executions.

But it didn't matter why the ninja playing medic was doing so; the only thing that mattered was that it gave Nick an opening.

The fifth ninja had removed the tape from Leonard's wrist and was preparing to reinsert the IV needle—the bottle hanging from a bulkhead bracket was almost empty—when Leonard kicked the man between the legs, under the armor there, and when the guard doubled over, Leonard was shouting to Val and Nick and on his feet, physically lifting the shorter Jap off his feet and thrusting the ninja and himself forward, blocking all lines of fire.

Another guard jumped at Leonard, clubbing at him and reaching for his taser. Val leaped past his grandfather and began wrestling with a ninja for his submachine gun. Nick propelled himself straight at Sato.

There was confusion and shouting. The weapon Val was struggling for discharged and insulation flew from the forward bulkhead where Nick's head had been an instant earlier. Perhaps it penetrated the forward compartment and hit one of the pilots, for the dragonfly suddenly listed to the left.

Nick had leaped *onto* Hideki Sato and was head-butting the big man and pummeling his face with both flex-cuffed fists. Sato lurched backward, shielded his face with his injured right forearm that still had the polymorphic smart-cast on it, and caught a swing-arm girder that was used for hydraulic cable lifts of people and things from below. Sato had his pistol in his left hand and was clubbing at the back of Nick's head, but Nick was hunched over and the heavy blows fell on his back and shoulders.

A ninja had gone down and Val was straddling him, still trying to wrest a long gun from a second guard. Leonard's medic was down, writhing, but the larger man he was wrestling with zapped Leonard with a taser. Nick saw his father-in-law drop like a bag of bricks and just had time to wonder if the taser had killed him.

Sato shoved him back, trying to clear a space between them, and for a few perfect seconds, Nick's back was against his son's back as he and Val swung and clubbed and butted away opponents and for those few seconds he was so close to his boy that their combined fury and determination to survive became a single force, almost a form of love.

Then there were numerous taser zaps behind him and Val fell away.

Sato squared himself off to finish with Nick but Nick leaped in the air, landing on the broad man's upper body, head-butting him fiercely again, and shoving both of them out the open door of the wildly banking helicopter.

Sato had grabbed the winch-frame girder again but it had swung out on its heavy hinges over nothing, Sato's huge weight dangling from it by one hand and Nick clinging and grabbing and hanging on to Sato. He was screaming and clawing, determined to pull the Jap from his perch and make him fall *with* him.

The dragonfly banked steeply back to its right and Sato's and Nick's legs flew high, almost touching the whirling rotors. Sato did a complete three-hundred-sixty-degree swing *over* the horizontal winch bar — like an Olympic athlete doing his routine on the high bar — and the metal frame was bending and tearing out of its hinge sockets from their combined weight. Nick had no idea how Sato still had so much strength in an arm that had been broken so recently. Maybe the polymorphic smart-cast *added* strength.

Ninjas crouched in the madly tipping open doorway, aiming their weapons at Nick and screaming in Japanese.

Nick realized that he was snarling, clawing at Sato's eyes with his nails, and biting at the big man's huge neck like a wild animal. The two men spun back and forth under the groaning and swinging winch bar, connected to the dragonfly 'copter only by Sato's right hand.

Nick began chewing Sato's right upper arm above the cast, biting for muscle, willing to chew to the bone to get the sonofabitch to release his grip. It was more than a thousand feet to the tilting ground below. Nick thought he could already smell the stench of Landfill Number Nine.

All right, I'll go there, but we'll go together, you motherfucker, thought Nick through his snarls and chewing and clawing. *Terminal velocity, two hundred miles an hour, the both of us.*

Sato threw away the pistol he still held in his free hand and clubbed Nick on the side of the head with a giant fist. Nick saw flashing lights and he lost his cuffed grip on Sato's bleeding neck and head.

He was loose and falling. *By himself.* Sato still hung on.

Nick screamed his defiance even as he fell away. But the dragonfly banked hard left, the tilted rotors slashing air inches above Nick's tumbling head, and then he felt Sato's lunging left hand—impossibly strong—close around his cuffed wrists.

Then, even more impossibly, Sato hung on to the screeching and bending winch girder with his right hand while he swung Nick up and around and threw him—contemptuously, it seemed—back into the open door of the helicopter.

Val and Leonard were sprawled out, either dead or unconscious. Nick smashed against a bulkhead and felt something tear in his leg but leaped up against the dark shapes coming toward him. He could see Sato swinging back into the chopper behind the ninjas. Nick's teeth were bloody with Sato's blood and he had flesh in his mouth and he wanted more...

Nick heard the zaps of at least three tasers at once and then he heard nothing at all.

1.20

Texline, Republic of Texas— Saturday, Sept. 25

IT WAS THE pain that finally made Nick open his eyes.

He was astounded that he *could* open his eyes. Had Sato waited until he regained consciousness to carry out the executions? Had that been part of Nakamura's orders? Was Nick supposed to watch his son and father-in-law be shot before he received the merciful bullet to the brain?

His head hurt so much when he opened his eyes that he felt as if he'd already been shot in the head. He tried squinting through the headache and through a strange pain from his left leg.

The first thing he noticed was that he wasn't lying among the rotting corpses at the edge of Denver Municipal Landfill Number Nine. It was dark outside and he was in a lighted, open-sided tent. Lying on a cot with clean sheets under him. There was something on his face...a clear oxygen mask. Nick clawed it off with his free hand.

His free hand. He wasn't flex-cuffed anymore. His left leg was in a cast and he wasn't wearing his chinos.

Nick tried turning his head to the side to see what was

535

around him, but the motion made lights flash behind his eyes again and made him too dizzy. He closed his eyes.

"You're awake," said a woman's voice.

Nick managed to squint again without inducing the vertigo. He tried to sit up. A woman wearing some sort of gray-shirted uniform with a round shoulder badge and a red-cross armband pushed him back into the pillows. "Try not to move too much, Mr. Bottom. You have a concussion as well as a broken leg and a lot of bruises and contusions. Captain McReady will be right in to talk to you."

Nick could turn his head to his left as long as he kept his eyes shut while he moved it. There were some empty cots to his left and outside the first-aid tent he could see it was full-dark night. Overhead electric lights illuminated some old Humvees parked along a wire fence, some new armored personnel carriers with the single white star and thirteen red-and-white stripes of the Republic of Texas flag on them, and beyond the vehicles—in an open area lit with searchlights and within a circle of green and red landing lights that pulsed in syncopation with the pounding of his headache—sat Nakamura's three whisper-dragonfly 'copters, rotors still. Men in various uniforms stood around talking. Nick didn't see any of the black-garbed ninjas.

He closed his eyes and turned his head all the way to the right.

Next to him was an empty cot and beyond that a cot with Leonard lying unconscious under a blanket. There were two IVs going into the old man now, but Nick could see that he was breathing. Snoring softly, actually.

He looked for Val, but the other cots in the first-aid tent were empty. *Where's my son?*

"Mr. Bottom?"

Nick found that if he opened his left eye wider than his right, he could focus on things without total vertigo. The man standing over him looked to be in his sixties, had a rich white mustache, wore the same gray uniform as the female nurse or medic with the same shoulder badge with a white star in a blue-

and-white circle, carried a long-barreled sidearm in an old-fashioned holster, and was wearing a big Stetson.

"I'm Captain McReady, Mr. Bottom," said the man, removing the big hat. There was a line in his gray hair, the kind of line that Nick imagined only a Stetson could carve over decades of wear. "Greg B. McReady, the 'B' standing for nothing at all, captain in Company C of the Texas Ranger Division, Department of Public Safety. This here is the Texas Army border station at Texline, along the New Mexico border just southwest of the Oklahoma Panhandle. We're glad you made it here, Mr. Bottom."

"My son...," croaked Nick. He tried to push himself up on one elbow.

"Val's okay," said Captain McReady. "A bunch of bruises, but he was the first to get over the taser shock. He was waiting here, watching over you and his grandpa for quite a while, but we convinced him to go get some chow. He's in the mess tent next door but should be back soon."

"My father-in-law," managed Nick. He raised his right hand and gestured. "Going... to live?"

"Oh, yes," said the white-mustached Ranger. "Professor Fox is just sleeping. He was awake for a while. We know of his medical condition—the aortic stenosis—from Colonel Sato, and we'll be discussing surgical options with the good professor over the next day or two."

"Sato," hissed Nick. He still had the taste of the assassin's flesh in his mouth and he wanted more. He wanted his heart.

McReady set a wrinkled, liver-spotted, but very strong hand on Nick's shoulder. "Easy, son. We know what happened. It should have been handled better, but there wasn't enough time for finesse. Colonel Sato wanted to be here to talk to you when you woke, but we were afraid that you'd kill him before he could explain."

"Kill him," repeated Nick. It wasn't a question. He remembered the killer crushing Dara's phone and thought of how he must have planned Dara's and Harvey's deaths.

Yes, he would kill Sato if he could. In fact, nothing on earth could stop him.

"What's wrong with my leg?" he said stupidly.

"You broke one of the lower bones there in the scuffle on the dragonfly," said Captain McReady. "Clean break. We set it while you were out. It should heal quickly enough."

"*When*...is it?" asked Nick.

"Same night, son," said the Ranger. "A little before midnight on the twenty-fifth of September. A Saturday. A busy one for you, from the looks of it."

Sato and Val walked into the tent together. Sato had a bandage on his neck and stitches on his cheek and forehead. Nick risked the vertigo to look around to see if there was anything sharp—a scalpel, a dinner knife, a bottle he could break, anything. There wasn't. His eyes went to the big pistol in Captain McReady's holster.

"Take it easy, friend," said the old Ranger. He pushed Nick back into his pillow, stood, and stepped back.

"Bottom-san," said Sato. He sat on the empty cot to Nick's right and the cot frame groaned under his weight.

"Whoa, Dad, did you see Grandpa knee that ninja's *cojones* up into his mouth?" cried Val. The boy was still chewing on the remains of a sandwich. "I mean, who knew old Leonard had it in him?"

Dad? thought Nick. That was a word he was sure he'd never hear again, even if—somehow, impossibly—both he and his son survived. Off to Nick's right, Leonard continued to snore softly, either oblivious to the praise or faking unconsciousness again so he could listen without commenting.

"We need to talk, Bottom-san." Sato's voice was very soft.

Nick noticed more stitches and bandages on Sato. Two of the fingers on his left hand were in a splint. The big man's black shirt was partially open and it looked as if his ribs had been taped as well.

"Fuck you," breathed Nick. He was only sorry that he'd been so groggy that he'd stupidly *looked* at Ranger Captain McReady's horse pistol before grabbing it.

"No, Dad, it's okay. Colonel Sato...," began Val.

"Killed your mother," said Nick, his tone low and lethal. "Stay out of this, Val."

The boy blinked in surprise and took two steps back.

"No, Bottom-san," said Sato. The big man shook his head back and forth in that weird way he had that involved his whole upper body. "I did not kill or arrange to kill your wife and Assistant District Attorney Cohen. This I swear to you on my honor."

"Your honor!" laughed Nick. The laugh hurt his head so much that he almost blacked out. "Your honor," he repeated. "The honor of a man who killed his own daughter in cold blood. Shot her between the eyes with a twenty-two-caliber slug so the bullet would bounce around in her skull and do the most damage."

"*Hai*," grunted Sato. "I admitted that I killed my beloved Kumiko. She—as her mother before her—was the light of my life. And I extinguished that light by my own hand. You see, it was a form of *jigai*—a woman samurai's form of ritual *seppuku* that does not involve disembowelment—and my darling Kumiko was indeed a samurai."

"Your daughter didn't commit suicide, Sato," snapped Nick. "You killed her. You shot and murdered her, along with Keigo, a boy who trusted you completely."

"*Hai*," Sato said again, bowing his head slightly. "This would have happened at Nakamura-sama's order at any rate. There was no escape for either my darling or her lover. Kumiko knew this would be the fate of both of them when she decided to go to your local Denver authorities—your beloved wife's boss's boss—to reveal the true origins of flashback. It was her *jigai* and I gave them both a quick and painless death."

"You tore the boy apart," said Nick.

Sato's bowed head moved slowly from side to side. "Only the body. He died instantaneously."

Nick had been holding himself up on one elbow but now collapsed on his side, still staring at Sato. Captain McReady, Val, and other people who'd come into the tent were just distant silhouettes to him. For Nick, it was just Hideki Sato and himself there in the night.

"I don't understand," said Nick.

"I needed Hiroshi Nakamura's total trust if I were to do

what I had to do," said Sato. "Both my darling Kumiko and young Keigo had chosen their fates...Keigo's attempt to tell the world about Nippon's use of flashback to complete the collapse of America was daring and bold, as the young man himself was. As you said, Bottom-san, a true rebel in a culture with very few rebels in its history. By carrying out the executions myself, I passed Nakamura's test for me."

"To what end?" asked Nick.

"Your message to me from Omura-sama...*In this world there is a tree without any roots;/Its yellow leaves send back the wind*...a poem composed by Omura-sama's and my own beloved teacher Sozan in the moments before he died...was the last coded message I needed to receive to know that tonight was the night to proceed."

"Proceed with what?" asked Nick, his words dripping with audible suspicion. There was no need to believe a single word this man said...this man who had shot his own daughter in the face.

Sato was looking at him as if reading his thoughts. He nodded and looked at his wristwatch. "It is midnight here and four p.m. Sunday in Tokyo. Currently, hostile takeover offers are being made against eight of Hiroshi Nakamura's eleven major companies which constitute the heart of his *zaibatsu*. Tomorrow, when the markets open in Japan, at least five of these eight takeover attempts, perhaps more, will succeed. The Nakamura dynasty will crumble."

"He's still a Federal Advisor here," said Nick. "He controls the Colorado National Guard and a dozen other armed groups."

"Nakamura and his people are being arrested as we speak, Bottom-san," said Sato. "It is his punishment for never coming down off his Colorado mountain...and for believing too much in the reports of his spies, my people. For seven weeks now I have brought several thousand Japanese commandos—my own *Taigāsu* Tiger Troops—from China."

"We saw them at the old Denver Country Club this afternoon, Dad," said Val, stepping forward and sitting on the far end of the cot that Sato was on. "The Ospreys were just deploying."

Nick forgot everything else for a moment as he extended his right hand and grasped Val's hand in a grip that was more than a handshake.

Captain McReady and the other men had also moved closer. "It's true, Mr. Bottom. Colonel Sato, Advisor Omura, and others have been in touch with us for weeks now. Colonel Sato informed us of your record with the Denver PD. We need good investigative people in the Texas Rangers. Our role is going to be greatly expanded in the coming months and years."

"Expanded?" repeated Nick, looking from Sato to the broad-mustached old Ranger. "Texas is Omura's ally? Japan's ally? In this big fight with the Caliphate that's coming up?"

"Damned right we are," said Captain McReady. "First we take back our own country, then we begin settling some old scores with others. We hope you'll join us, Detective Bottom."

"You don't even allow flashback addicts to live in Texas," said Nick. "You drive them to the nearest border and boot them out."

"Are you a flashback addict, son?" asked the old Ranger.

"No," said Nick after only the slightest hesitation. "No, sir."

Sato stood and it pleased Nick to see that the standing hurt him somewhere.

"I must get back to Denver. There will be much to organize in the next few days. Many things to coordinate with Omura-sama and with certain *daimyo*s back home who have long awaited Hiroshi Nakamura's downfall. Sometimes, Bottom-san, even under the code of *bushido*, the best *Shogun* will not be the harshest or cruelest or most ruthless one of the candidates. Nakamura forgot that in his hunger for power."

Nick said, "But you showed how ruthless you could be, Sato-san. Just in case anyone in Nippon had any doubts."

"Yes," said Sato. "I will not offer to shake your hand this day, Bottom-san, for I respect your anger." He touched the thick bandages on his neck and smiled the broadest that Nick had ever seen him smile. "I thought, for a moment on the dragonfly, that you were going to eat me."

Nick returned the smile and made sure he showed his canines.

"But perhaps we will shake hands and be allies again at some future date," said Sato. "After your nine-eleven, many people—however briefly—spoke of the Long War that was coming. They were right about the Long War. They were just wrong about the two world-historical opponents who would be fighting to the death."

Sato started to leave and then turned back.

"I thought you might want these, Bottom-san," he said and handed across Nick's phone and a stamp-sized flashdrive. The phone display showed Dara's text files and Keigo Nakamura's documentary video files.

"The drive has the video recording of your recent inquisition by Nakamura in the library," said Sato. "Use all of these as you see fit."

The big man clasped Val on the shoulder and walked out.

The nurse came back to check Nick's blood pressure and to urge him to use the oxygen mask.

He shook his head. "Help prop me up, would you?"

In the end, Val and the young woman both worked to help him sit almost upright.

The pain in his head was less and the ground had quit tilting every time he turned his head. Captain McReady and three other Texas Rangers were still standing there. The old captain's Stetson was back on his head.

"What do you say to joining the Rangers, son?" asked McReady.

"Let me get a night's sleep and I'll give you my answer," said Nick. He nodded toward the sleeping Leonard. "You people do surgeries like valve replacements for money without a long wait, right?"

"Yeah," said the younger Ranger to the right of McReady. "We're old-fashioned that way. Down here we let you keep most of what you earn and let you pay for what you need."

McReady turned to Val.

"How 'bout you, son? You going to talk to me tomorrow about joining the Texas Rangers?"

Val smiled and the sight of that smile made Nick's heart lurch.

"No, thank you, sir," said his son. "I want to see a man in Austin about something and then I may have some plans of my own."

McReady nodded, touched his hat, and led the men out of the tent. Outside, the three dragonflies were lifting off silently in a rush of hot night wind.

Val sprawled on the empty cot next to Nick's, bunching the pillow under his head. "The top doctor said we should spend the night here—sleep in these cots—and I think I'll take them up on it. Talk to Leonard in the morning."

"Good," said Nick. In a few minutes, he was going to ask the way to the closest latrine and make his way to it. No bedpan for him. Not in this open-sided tent. Not for any reason.

"Wow, Dad, Grandpa really kneed that ninja's gonads right out through the top of his head, didn't he?"

"Yeah, he did," said Nick, getting ready to swing his cast over the edge of the cot to the floor. He could use some help hobbling and he wasn't going to wait for the Texas Ranger nurse. Might as well put Val to some use while he was still close by. "He really did."

0.00

NICK FLOATED in green weightlessness.

Nick floated in no-space, no-time. He was coming up from the smell of canvas walls and grass floor of the tent in Texas, away from his son and father-in-law, up into the real world of no-world.

Nick's eyelids were sutured, but not quite shut. His eardrums were punctured, but not quite without hearing.

Nick floated with his lungs full of oxygen-rich liquid. They had drowned him into this death-life. They had not removed his eyes. They had not removed his optic nerves. It was punishment.

White-coated shapes, distorted in shape and size, moved in the nonliquid spaces outside his tank. Occasionally a green-tinted and lens-distorted semihuman face would peer in at him in the intervals when he was up and out of his dreams.

NCAR.

NCAR.

The basement of the floating dead in NCAR.

Nakamura Center for Advanced Research.

And Nick Bottom's punishment was to have his eyes, to

have his shattered eardrums, to be brought up from the Flashback-two dreams from time to time.

Dara was dead. Val was dead, murdered on that Saturday in September. Leonard was dead. Nick wanted to be dead but they would not let him die. This was Nakamura's punishment, Sato's punishment, for opposing their *Shogunate* will.

Nick's world was dead.

Except for this dream-fantasy happy-ending world into which they submerged and resubmerged him like a kitten being drowned again and again.

Nick floated like a white, bloated dead thing. But he dreamt on. And between the dreams... this...

He felt the feeding tubes and catheters boring into his body like barb-burrowing eels. He felt his muscles gone flaccid and rotting away like white mushrooms in the thick fluid. He stared out through sutures at a green world.

He had dreamt he was a man. The dream, Bottom's dream, had brought them together briefly. But she was gone. And he was not allowed to follow.

I have had a most rare vision. I have had a dream, past the wit of man to say what dream it was. Man is but an ass if he go about to expound this dream. Methought I was—there is no man can tell what. Methought I was—and methought I had—but man is but a patched fool if he will offer to say what methought I had. The eye of man hath not heard, the ear of man hath not seen, man's hand is not able to taste, his tongue to conceive, or his heart to report, what my dream was.... I shall sing it at her death.

Nick Bottom floated in the NCAR green tank of thick liquid and the drug entered his body and carried him back to his dream.

1.21

San Antonio, Republic of Texas—
Saturday, Feb. 26

NICK AWOKE GASPING and sweating from his nightmare.
It was the old nightmare. The recurring nightmare.
The NCAR nightmare.

He got out of his barracks bed, peeled off his sweat-soaked
T-shirt, and flung it across the bedroom. He went into the tiny
bathroom wearing only his boxer shorts, splashed water on his
face and neck, and toweled himself off.

He walked into his kitchen and looked out the window as
the sun was rising. Nick was on the tenth floor of the Texas
Rangers barracks in San Antonio, formerly the Menger Hotel
on East Crockett Street, and he didn't like it that the Alamo
was right across the street in the plaza named after it, the resurrected old mission visible in all its stony reality. He didn't like it
because he'd dreamt about it once—the Camaro dream—and
Nick Bottom no longer trusted dreams.

He watched the sun touch the curved-bedstead gray-stone
top of the Alamo.

His T-shirt off, Nick looked down at his body. It carried its
scars: the wounds in his belly from the knifing in Santa Fe years
ago; the scars on his leg from when they'd set the broken bone

there five months ago in Texline; the lesser scars on his face and hands and back.

But it was the tiny spiderweb of scars on his deeply tanned left forearm that drew Nick's attention now.

He went back to the bedroom and came back into the kitchen with the switchblade knife that was part of his Ranger kit. Many of the men carried huge knives—some actual Bowie knives—but Nick carried only this city switchblade, as sharp as a scalpel. He'd brought iodine and rubbing alcohol from the bathroom.

The phone-computer screen was on and winking. There was a new message from Val. Nick set the iodine and alcohol bottles and knife on the counter and tapped open the message.

It was as brief as all Val's e-mails were. He was coming back from Boston with a southwest-bound convoy in March and would like to see the Old Man if he was still going to be at the San Antonio Rangers Company D barracks. If not, next time through. How was Leonard doing?

Leonard was doing pretty damned good, thought Nick, thanks to an aortic valve surgery that would cost Nick almost thirty thousand dollars. Texas dollars. He was paying the bill a little each month out of his lieutenant-detective Ranger salary. There were a few years of installments still ahead.

It was worth it.

An e-mail from the poet Danny Oz was waiting. Oz was going back to Israel—that radioactive wasteland that used to be Israel—in the Big Push in May. The Japanese and Republic of Texas forces were bringing 1,100,000 Jews—some expatriates, many from America and other countries—back to the Mideast this summer.

The beachhead had been cleared by American and Japanese conventional forces, but the returning Jews would have to hold it. And expand it. Oz wrote that his cancer was in remission and even if it were not, he'd be returning with the Big Push and let cancer and the Caliphate do their worst.

Nick was sure the Caliphate would.

But their worst might not be as bad as it would have been a

few months earlier. The new *Shogun* of Nippon had warned the core Islamic states of the Caliphate that any use of nuclear weapons on the Caliphate's part would be met by an instantaneous gee-bear and nuclear retaliation, but not, at least initially, on their crowded cities. The *Shogun* had specified that the seven holiest Islamic shrines would be destroyed—each after twenty-four hours' evacuation warning—should the jihadist forces ever use weapons of mass destruction against anyone again. To show his new allies' earnestness in this promise, the *Shogun* had given twenty-four hours' warning and used fifty gee-bears to vaporize a minor Shi'ite shrine in Basra as an example.

If Al Jazeera coverage was to be believed, more than a billion citizens of the Caliphate literally went into convulsions and foamed at the mouth at this sacrilege. More than fifty thousand people died in urban riots.

But no weapons of mass destruction had been used by the Global Caliphate against the beachhead near where Haifa used to be.

Next year in Jerusalem! Oz had written at the end of his note. Nick knew that it was a serious invitation.

Well, why not? Professor Emeritus Dr. George Leonard Fox was going. The old man with his new cloned heart valve—friskier than ever, in his own words—would be there on the beachhead with 1,099,999 other Jews.

Dara had never told him that her father was a Jew. It must have slipped her mind.

Nick wouldn't be going to the New Israel any time soon. Starting today, his Ranger division—12,000 men and women strong—was moving across the border into New Mexico with more than 200,000 men and women in the Republic of Texas Sam Houston Army.

The armored forces were tasked with clearing out the last of the "foreign presence" in the once and future states of New Mexico, Arizona, and southern California. Then the armored divisions would sweep south, at least as far as Monterrey and Torreón and Culiacán. They would decide about Ciudad de México later.

To those who cried "Imperialism!"—and there were many of those kind left in what were now being called the Timid States of America—the answer was "If you can't stand the heat, get out of your neighbor's kitchen."

The last e-mail was from Dr. Linda Alvarez, a woman Nick had met at a Christmas party on the Riverwalk and with whom he'd spent quite a lot of time since New Year's. He would open that e-mail later.

I'll tell you more about her later, Dara.

When he'd been using flashback, Nick had never sent mental e-mails to Dara. He hadn't really *thought* about her much in those days. He hadn't needed to, since he was reliving hours and days with her constantly. But those were frozen memories. Now, without flashback, his thoughts turned to Dara often— even as the immediacy of her touch and look faded for him— and he sent her a daily mental e-mail. They were brief, but not as brief as Val's two-sentence notes.

We have to learn to accept our losses. It was not a pseudo-profound thought that Nick was generating, but something Major Trevors had said in the Company D briefing the day before. The losses for the Texas Rangers should not be too dear—they were following the army as a civilian infrastructure and police force.

But one never knew.

In three weeks, Omura's troops—Sato's commandos plus the California and Washington State National Guards—would be going into Canada to face the Caliphate militias assembled there. *That* might be fierce fighting with many losses to face. Nick rather wished he'd be part of it...but not all that much. Not when he was spending time with Dr. Linda Alvarez. Or when reading a good book. Or watching one of his old movies. Or waiting for one of Val's rare overnight layovers.

We have to learn to accept our losses.

Nick was ready. He'd already learned the hard part, he thought.

He set a towel on the counter. Then he flicked the scalpel-sharp switchblade open and dipped the slender blade in alcohol. He leaned on the kitchen counter, the city coming alive with morning light outside his window, the Alamo glowing—today was some sort of anniversary for it, he'd heard—and then Nick drew the blade across his forearm until blood welled up and flowed in rivulets down his forearm and soaked in red butterflies into the towel.

Nick dug the knife blade in deeper, clenching his teeth as he moved the blade *into* his flesh. He'd cut to the bone if he had to.

But no, this pain was enough. It was a sharp, real, undeniable pain. It was precisely the sort of pain that Flashback-two would never allow in its dreams. *Never.*

Nick withdrew the blade, treated the wound, then quickly bandaged it. There would be a scar there but it would soon join the dozens of others in the small spiderweb of scars.

For this Nick Bottom had learned from his Dream—from his years of drugged dreaming—*Being alive means suffering pain*. Being *willing* to suffer pain.

Nick finished tidying up, cleaned and put away the knife, tossed the towel in the tub to soak, and put water and coffee into the coffeemaker. What the hell—he was going to make a big breakfast today: eggs, bacon, toast, the whole nine yards. Muster wasn't until 0900, but it was going to be a long day and he didn't know when he'd eat again.

You can't have life without pain, Nick now understood. You can't have a future without pain. Being alive means having the strength to face pain and loss and to find something real through it and beyond it.

Anything less is just flashback.

Acknowledgments

The author would like to thank his agent, Richard Curtis; his editor, Reagan Arthur; and his publisher, Michael Pietsch, for understanding what the novel *Flashback* was really about and for helping him shepherd it to publication. The author acknowledges the unique and important contributions of all three of these good people.

The author would also like to thank Dr. Dan Peterson both for the gift of the Wisdom ballcap—from a bar in Wisdom, Montana, it turns out—which almost certainly added wisdom to the author's efforts, and for the gift of the various homemade jazz-mix CDs which the author played all during the writing of *Flashback*. Unbeknownst to most readers, almost every novel has its own secret soundtrack that the author will always associate with the many months of work on a particular book. Dr. Peterson knows the beautiful *Flashback* soundtrack well because he created it. The author thanks him for that and doffs his Wisdom cap in Dr. Dan's direction.

The author would like to thank Deborah Jacobs both for her outstanding level of effort, professional expertise, and insight in copyediting the manuscript of *Flashback* and for suggesting the Proust epigraph that was perfect for this book. The author and Marcel P. both bow to her in sincere gratitude.

Finally, the author needs to acknowledge and thank his

wife, Karen, who was always there with the calm insight, important suggestions, and quiet confidence that have helped steer this author through twenty-eight published books. The author also wishes to acknowledge his daughter, Jane, whose energy and joy during the hard writing period for *Flashback* helped make the seemingly impossible more than possible. The author thanks his wife and daughter for being the fixed stars for him to steer by in a rich and beautiful and otherwise ever-changing Hawaiian night sky.